Philip Boast was born in 1952 in London and educated at Mill Hill. Finding writing incompatible with academic education, he left school at sixteen and sailed to the Galapagos Islands to study wildlife. Back home in London, he wrote at least two books a year and paid his way by selling origami paper and artists' materials, keeping chickens, working as a sanitary estimator, moulding asbestos sheet, and finally as a chauffeur. In 1976 his book *The Assassinators*, which he wrote when he was twenty, was published. Two years later he met his wife under very romantic circumstances in a well known south coast library, but his second love is London.

Also by Philip Boast

The Assassinators

good reading Pt.

London's Child

Philip Boast

HEADLINE

Copyright © Philip Boast 1987

First published in Great Britain in 1987
by Century Hutchinson Ltd

First published in paperback in 1989
by HEADLINE BOOK PUBLISHING PLC

10 9 8

All characters in this publication are fictitious
and any resemblance to real persons, living or dead,
is purely coincidental.

ISBN 0 7472 3186 9

Printed and bound in Great Britain by
HarperCollins Manufacturing, Glasgow

HEADLINE BOOK PUBLISHING
A division of Hodder Headline PLC
338 Euston Road
London NW1 3BH

For my father

London's Child

Part I

THE FALLEN WOMAN

Chapter One

1

'Help me!'

Where do you go, when no one will help you, and you have nowhere to go to?

Just keep on walking . . .

2

THE WORLD ENDS AT MIDNIGHT TONIGHT.

It was midday in London and the low winter sun struck brilliantly up Old Bond Street from Piccadilly, illuminating a stalled mass of vehicles ahead. Bert Simmonds dragged on the brake handle and the heavy dray shuddered to a halt. He cursed under his breath and looked quickly behind him, meaning to turn around out of it if he could, but his big Great Central Railway dray was already boxed in by the many-coloured fronts of vehicles, drays, hackney carriages, carts, gleaming in reflection of the sun, and horses' heads tossing like waves on the sea at Brighton. This was a big one, he realized: he could be here for hours.

The church bells had started chiming: he recognized the fast tolling of St James's church down by Fortnum and Mason, St Martin-in-the-Fields slower and more distant. With a phlegmatic shrug he wound the reins around the brake handle and settled back on the wooden bench seat as

3

comfortably as he could. He put his hands on his knees and looked about him with a show of indifference.

'Here we go again!' someone cried, and Bert grinned, recognizing the authentic tone of a fellow professional.

It was the same old London story – another traffic jam. Nothing he could do about it. Probably he'd never even know the cause of it. He suspected that most probably it was due to a horse-tram in one way or another, it usually was. Either they fell off their rails, or were the helpless target of a runaway, or sometimes it was just that so many of the bloody useless things got bunched up, because they couldn't get past one another, that they blocked up the whole intricate system for miles back, just from one thrown shoe at the front.

Old Bond Street was completely locked solid now. People were getting angry. That was the way it went at first. Bert yawned. He'd seen it all before.

He was a small man, small enough for it never to be completely off his mind, wearing a large leather apron and the corduroys and gaiters that signified his trade. But his arms were heavily muscled and covered only with shirt sleeves despite the frosty weather. On his head he wore the hard bowler hat called a billy-cock, not for reasons of safety or because it kept his head warm, but because it added to his stature and his dignity in the eyes of other men. Although he smiled a lot, his smile had a challenging air, and he had a bitter temper.

He had been his own man for twenty years, but now he was a Company man since the recession, and instead of earning his own money he was paid a handsome wage by the Great Central Railway, and lived in a subsidized railway flat at the Wharncliffe Gardens Settlement, on the fourth floor, with all his children. Gloria, his eldest, worked at the railway shop; Annie's fourteenth birthday fell on Christmas Day, which saved on her present. Then there were the two boys Albert and William, who wanted to work their way up to being engine drivers – and the railway would probably encourage them, if they showed they had level heads on their shoulders. Last and least of all his

4

children was little Jack, who was a mistake, Mrs Simmonds was still nursing William and he shouldn't have happened. Although he was now seven years old he cried and bawled loudly enough to make the neighbours complain through the thin walls on each side.

Bert watched the traffic jam develop according to the usual rules. At first, red-faced drivers stared angrily straight past one another, not even acknowledging anyone else's right to exist. Then, as he had known they would, they started to relax. This was obviously going to last a while. They caught one another's eye, shrugging. All in the same boat together, what? Someone mentioned the weather – the traffic might be bloody, but at least the weather was sunny, it could have been worse . . .

Like Bert, who was finishing up the parcels run before the holiday tomorrow, many of them had cunningly short-cut down here to avoid Regent Street and the certainty of the crush there – and so they'd all caught it in the neck here in Old Bond Street instead. He gave a digusted spit over the wheel and took the whip out of the whip-holder and put it back again, wishing he'd brought a newspaper, but he didn't move from his vehicle. Some less experienced drivers than he were getting down and peering ahead, then strutting up and down with their chests thrust out and their hands on their hips, making a fuss. Omnibuses with stairs curling up the back towered over dog-carts. Pony-carts and donkey-shays pushed forward within an inch of locking their wheels or tangling the harness. Wiser spirits rested their hands on their horses to keep warm.

Bert rested his chin on his hand, watching. About time for the next stage, he reckoned: the shop storemen, who'd be low on stock after the Christmas rush, and would have the morning-suited managers breathing down their necks, would decide to make the best of it any minute now. And it happened. Shivering urchins in shorts and ragged shirts were called out from the invisible places behind the posh, glittering façades of the exclusive shops that lined the street, and started unloading the tradesmen's carts

5

wherever they were in the road. Right beside Bert's horses a couple of lads were heaving trays of New Year capons from a crimson four-wheeler painted *Geo. Stevens, Son & Nephew, High Class Poulterers* with an impressive gold coat of arms, and setting them on their heads.

He watched them carry the trays down out of sight somewhere ahead through the jostling crowd, to Leibig's probably . . . Bert remembered Hawk, who would be bound to be there.

A mongrel came sniffing the ghosts of capons around the open back of the four-wheeler, and Bert watched its efforts with interest. The lads came back wiping their noses, pulled out the last trays, the glistening breasts making tempting white curves in the sunlight, and the mongrel followed them away hopefully. Meanwhile the hot-chestnut man took up his brazier-barrow and wheeled it between the vehicles. 'Nice 'n' hot, piping hot, who'll buy my nice hot chestnuts?' Bert saw him take fivepence inside a minute, and reckoned the old boy had got a good racket going – and he wouldn't be forced to take a day off without pay tomorrow (except for a shilling to come in to the Lodge Road stables in Lisson Grove to feed and water the horses). Bert's temper started to fray and he felt his face flush hot. He spat again and leaned out, rubbing his arms, looking back. Everything was piled up as far back as Oxford Street by the look of it. The sandwich board man he had overtaken earlier was much closer now, the tall message he bore above his head shining in the sun above the hats of the crowd: THE WORLD ENDS AT MIDNIGHT TONIGHT.

Bert reckoned that in his opinion the end of the world would be a mercy. People said that by 2000 AD the streets of London would be twenty feet deep in horseshit, and no way round it. Trains went shooting here, there and everywhere at over a hundred miles an hour, so that people couldn't work at their own pace. Balloonists flew six miles high above the earth, damaging a layer in the atmosphere, so that nowadays the Thames often froze over, and people went ice-skating from London Bridge up the river Lea for twenty or thirty miles, to villages deep in the country, like

6

Broxbourne, and had to catch the train back. You couldn't help feeling that things were going bad. Our own Cornish boxer, little Bob Fitzsimmons, first middleweight champion of the world and then the lightest heavyweight champion ever, had just got knocked out after eleven rounds of spirited slugging by some great bear of an American: that was what modern fighting with gloves did to you. It upset the natural order, and you didn't know where you were. They never used to fight with gloves in Grandad's day.

Grandad had talked – try and stop him – of the old-fashioned, glorious, romantic days before the empire when the air was clean and there were no big railway companies and no one lived layer on layer in the vast modern blocks of the Railway Settlements, because they didn't exist; St John's Wood really was a wood, not a jerry-built pre-fabricated suburb, and you could afford the price of vegetables. Everyone knew their place, there was no cheap sensationalism in those days, no gutter press. Those were the days.

Mind you, the Great Dictator was massing his armies in France, building fleets of barges. Invasion seemed certain and so canals were dug and defensive earthworks thrown up all over southern England (you could still see them), the Government was getting out of London – but he never came. And the big yellow and black ships of the line were museum-pieces now, Bert thought. Nowadays, it was bloody great bellowing steaming ironclads with guns that could fire over the horizon, and a great sod of an empire that, although you had to admit it was quite nice to have, cost an arm and a leg in taxes.

And there were the traffic jams. Jesus Christ, it made you wonder if it was all worth it. At this rate he wouldn't get home to bloody Wharncliffe Gardens in time for tea. He'd go straight to the pub and Mrs Simmonds could find him there.

He stood up on the seat with his hands balled into fists and pushed into his pockets, staring angrily over the roofs ahead. The flat afternoon sun struck painfully into his eyes.

His side of the street, the left, was almost blinding with sun; the other side was black with shadows that he'd have to shade his eyes to see into. The driver of an omnibus glanced at him, then back to his newspaper. Bert wanted to say: 'Hey, mate, any idea how long it's going to take to clear?' but he was afraid of being rebuffed. London & General horse-omnibus drivers could be a snooty lot. Some of them still wore the old top hats.

He could just see the traffic starting to inch along Piccadilly.

'It's moving, it's clearing,' he said to no one in particular.

THE WORLD . . .

The top of the sign wobbled along beside the cargo piled high on the dray, then for a moment it blocked the sun as the sandwich board man turned to squeeze past the bus. Because he was momentarily in shadow himself, Bert could see into the shadows. It was like looking into another world. Where there had been only blackness were doorways, shop windows, mouths of alleyways, the shapes of people slowly walking.

And he saw the girl.

3

Hawk saw her next. He did not like what he saw. He believed in rules, and she did not look like she obeyed them. This worried him immediately.

The church bells were ringing in the mid-afternoon. This side of the street had been in shadow for hours and Hawk felt like a pillar of ice, but of course he did not betray any sign of discomfort at all. Twenty feet in front of him the motionless traffic glared like a river of garish colours frozen in mid-motion under the midwinter sun. Some of the drivers had wrapped themselves in blankets and fallen asleep, others walked down onto Piccadilly to watch the workmen repairing the leaking gas main that was the cause of the trouble. He snorted. Bloody Irish navvies.

Hawk stood in the entrance to Leibig's Emporium. He

almost blocked the imposing mahogany, brass and glass-paned doorway. The windows on each side of him were filled with bottles of champagne and claret, oranges and baskets of nuts, dried Arleens plums and packets of oatmeal military biscuits, a bottle of Camp coffee with the drawing of the faithful Hindoo wallah, Dewar's Highland Whisky, tins of Nestlé's Swiss milk, the familiar logotype of Bovril beef extract, cheeses, German sausage, cured meats of every colour from pale speckled grey to deep maroon, and a row of whole hams, all beautifully displayed and brilliantly gaslit against the shadows of approaching night.

He was an exceptionally good Head Doorman, and he knew it very, very well. Visitors from abroad doing the Grand Tour of European capitals had him on their list of sights to see. Hawk glared at them with such intensity that they never dared enter the shop. One woman, probably an American, had gone so far as to exclaim, in his hearing, that he looked 'Gorgeous'; he had been outraged of course, but also secretly flattered. There was an element in Hawk's personality, never admitted, which had always wanted to be an actor. His aunts would never have permitted that. But it was there, nevertheless.

He had been appointed Head Doorman of Leibig's Emporium, Suppliers of Fine Foodstuffs to the Gentry, thirteen years ago, when Leibig's had been just a glorified grocer. Now the flagstone on which he stood had been sanded by the soles of his platform shoes to a fine gloss. He stood as the British Army had taught him to stand, at attention, chest out, elbows in, an intimidating and almost inhumanly motionless (the secret of keeping the blood flowing was to flex the toes) pillar of Leibig's impressive house livery, a uniform of immaculate purple with plenty of gold braid, and a peaked cap which shadowed his eyes but that did not shield unruly passersby or window shoppers from his disdainful stare. He made those who entered Leibig's feel special. Hawk detested the general public. It was his duty to protect Leibig's Emporium from those undesirable elements.

The girl had stopped just off his patch, the oasis of

scrubbed pavement that comprised his territory. She dropped her cheap cardboard suitcase outside Larsen the shoemaker's, and stood swaying slightly.

Hawk's long, hooked nose twitched. It was his job to sense trouble coming and to prevent it before it had a chance to happen. His nostrils bristled with clipped but sensitive hairs, and now they itched. He wished the girl would go away.

It was an invariable rule of the profession that doormen fell into two types: doorman, and doormat. It was a fact of human nature that people would wipe their feet on your back if you let them, and make you whistle for a cab without feeling they had to tip you, unless you commanded their respect. Every inch of Hawk's six foot three inches – which was six feet five inches in the special shoes – was an inch of Head Doorman. A Head Doorman dominated his environment from the start. That was his job. It was not his job to open the door. They had plenty of boys to do that.

Most people put his age at about fifty. That was what he wanted. Extra years brought a man extra respect. Thirty-nine years ago, in Putney, Hawk had been born Peter Aloysius Lucan Hawkins. His mother had died in childbirth and his father was at sea, so his aunts named him after his father and grandfather. Lucan was an invention of their own, after the commander-in-chief of the Crimean war, who they admired as a man of sensitivity. The lonely boy grew up waiting for his father to return, never quite giving up hope. He still had not, now. His aunts expected him to take up the sea as a career, but for some reason the idea of this repelled him. In the Army, they called him Hawk, because of his hooked nose and penetrating eyes, which gave him a naturally impressive demeanour to live up to. Hawk liked that, and as he gained confidence, he began to rise through the ranks. He worked hard, although giving orders and taking responsibility for them did not come naturally to him; and he had just made the big jump, the really important step up in the non-commissioned hierarchy, and been confirmed Lance-Corporal, when the battalion soup tureen dropped off the fire and the iron lip sliced deep into his hand, although he avoided a bad scalding from the gallons of boiling liquid. With the ink on his medical discharge still wet, Hawk got his job with Mr Leibig and entered his natural element.

He guessed that the girl, who was pretty in a strong way, if you liked pretty girls – which Hawk was not disposed to do – couldn't have been more than sixteen or eighteen years old. The shoemaker's had no doorman, so she was still there beside that suitcase. Hawk examined her, moving his eyes without moving his head. That poor suitcase was a bad sign, a very bad sign, yet the long cape she was wearing was of excellent quality and looked brand new. It was black or very dark navy blue. Its hem was only lightly speckled with mud and horse manure. Hawk decided not to leave his post to deal with her, yet. A glance at his own shoes and trousers confirmed that they were splashed to the knee with exclamation marks of mud. Although the pavement in front of Leibig's was kept so spotless, washed and scrubbed by chars every morning, beyond the kerb was a heaving pit.

In London you couldn't help getting dirty; that was why there were bootblack boys on every corner.

Each morning, just before nine o'clock, even the gutter in front of Leibig's Emporium was rinsed. Old Mr Leibig arrived at 9 a.m. precisely, with Germanic precision. Rumour supposed that Leibig, once a mere pork butcher, had killed a man in one of the regular state upheavals before the Iron Chancellor, Bismarck, imposed order there. (Hawk had always thought that Bismarck sounded like a natural Head Doorman; perhaps that was why he and Leibig got on so well.) Leibig had arrived in London with only the clothes he stood up in but nowadays he arrived in a self-important, rather un-British gig, although he lived not far away. He was a real tartar. He was well into his sixties but he hadn't relinquished his control over the business one little bit. Each morning, grey as iron, dressed in the stiffest of stiff collars and an English bowler hat that didn't suit him, Leibig descended fastidiously, peered at his shop front through pince-nez spectacles, and missed nothing, whether an unsymmetrical arrangement between the tonic cordials and the captain's biscuits . . . or a bloom on an orange. Young Mr George Leibig, who everyone had nicknamed Georgy in a relief reaction against old Leibig's teutonic stiffness, stood red-faced, choleric, impatient and bored in the shadow of his father's shoulder, having to enter every little criticism into a special book . . . Old Leibig then marched stiffly into his domain while Hawk held open the door and saluted simultaneously.

Sometimes Mr Georgy brought his little daughter, Vanity, with him, just old enough to be learning to speak, a sweet darling always dressed in precious white frills. Hawk adored her. They played a game whenever old Mr Leibig wasn't watching. Hawk picked her up and said:

'Hallo, Vane!'

She'd regard him seriously, hanging like a little white doll in his arms. She'd shake her head and say in her baby voice, 'Me not Vane.'

'Yes you are!' She was the only person in the world he had a smile for.

She would look round to her father for reassurance and Georgy would say shyly, 'Come with me into the shop, Vanity.'

And Hawk would hold open the door and salute simultaneously.

Now Hawk eyed this girl.

Then a client – Leibig's customers were always called clients – pushed out of the crowd. This was a man Hawk knew, a retired major, a pleasant old duffer. Leibig's clientele was drawn far more from the military than from the gentry, unfortunately. Hawk saluted briefly. He put his hand out towards the door but let the boy actually open it.

'Good afternoon, sir.'

'Hallo, Hawk. Can't move on the streets today.'

'Everyone's getting ready for the celebrations tonight, sir.' Hawk's voice was as rich and deep as melted chocolate. He still dropped his aitches, because it was expected of him. It was death to be thought to be competing with anyone from a higher station in life.

'Celebrations! Headaches in the morning.' The major

pointed at a sandwich board throwing its message above the heads of the crowd. 'I say, end of the world.'

'We won't have headaches in the morning, then,' Hawk joked. The major didn't smile. For a moment he looked like a man who feels things slipping away from him, just a little bit. The great British garrisons in South Africa were starving and surrounded, cut off by a few thousand Boer farmers. It broke the rules.

The old man shivered. 'How are your children, Hawk?'

'Fine, sir.' He didn't have any, but a lot of them asked. It was another of the rules.

'Very well. Carry on.' Hawk saluted briefly again and the major went in.

He flexed himself up on his toes slightly. That girl was still there.

Hawk did not salute women. He did not like them. He got the impression that they shopped for fun. Sometimes they came in groups, with poodles. The only ones he liked were those who were not intimidated by him.

Who was this girl?

Was she going to make trouble in front of Leibig's?

Hawk kept looking at the girl warningly from time to time without moving his head, but she hadn't entered his patch yet. She was still standing by her rotten suitcase outside Larsen's. She was definitely swaying, either from weakness or pain. This was bad. Hawk wondered if she'd come up to him and ask for a glass of water. They did that sometimes, to get attention – or fainted.

Hawk knew himself to be a man brimming with natural sympathy, but that was not the point. He had no private income: he couldn't afford messes at work, or anything that might compromise the clean, high-class face that, through him, Leibig's Emporium presented to the world. Hawk would kick a dog if it came too close, he couldn't stand the thought of their piss. It was his duty. When a passing workman had an epileptic fit – a shameful disease, symptom of chronic self-abuse – right in the middle of Hawk's spotless patch, Hawk dragged him screaming round to the side alley and looked after him while he had

13

his fit there, enabling important clients to enter the shop undistracted.

Horrible things happened in the world, Hawk knew, but while he was alive none of them would be permitted to happen near Leibig's.

Now Hawk turned his head towards the girl and cleared his throat in a deliberate warning.

The sandwich board man trudged round an omnibus and stopped at the kerb. Lice crawled in his shoulder-length hair. He was dressed in rags that swung from his shoulders and elbows, a waistcoat out of a newspaper, and one of his wooden clogs had split from toe to instep, looking like the open mouth of a clothes peg.

THE WORLD ENDS AT MIDNIGHT TONIGHT.

'What are you doing here, Billy?' deigned Hawk at last. It was his custom to call them all Billy.

'Wotcher, Hawk.'

'Bit of a funny sign you're carrying,' Hawk said. 'It's too exact.'

'What's that, Hawk?'

'Saying it's going to end at midnight. It might not, Billy. Suppose the world did not end?'

'I don't read them, see, Hawk, I just carry them.'

'You could disappoint a lot of people, Billy. I mean,' Hawk said, joking heavily, 'suppose it *didn't* end at midnight. Suppose it ended at eleven-thirty. You'd get a lot of complaints, wouldn't you, Billy?'

'It's the Society of Theosophical Christians,' Billy said, obviously reciting a spiel from memory, pointing at one of his blurry handbills with a finger that looked to Hawk strangely sleek and bald until he realized that it had no nail. 'They get messages from the Other Side. Horse's mouth, dead serious. Midnight tonight, see – New Year – end of the Sinful Century. The end of everything.'

'I don't believe it,' Hawk said. 'Bugger off now, there's a good little fellow.'

Hawk turned his head back towards the girl. He inhaled through his nose and flexed himself up on the balls of his feet, then again cleared his throat. This was the last polite warning he was going to give her.

'I followed her all the way down from the New Road,' Billy said, with a confidential air. 'She came out of a posh place on Regent's Park. I seen her go in the front, Hawk, but they sent her out sharpish, from the side – with her suitcase coming arsy-varsy down the steps after her. Listen, Hawk. She was wearing a motheaten old coat then. But guess what?'

'Get on with it,' Hawk said. Motheaten old coat. He didn't like the sound of that. Where had she got the lovely cape from? Stolen it?

'She went straight into a shop and bought that cape out of the window,' Billy said. 'Didn't care whether it even fitted, just chucked the money, gold, down on the counter as if she hated it, and it was pounds and pounds, Hawk, and she could hardly wait to get rid of it.'

'They gave her the money in the house,' said Hawk thoughtfully.

'And she could hardly wait to get rid of it!'

'Why?' wondered Hawk. 'Why did they pay her? And why did she buy something she didn't need? She already had a coat.' Suddenly it made sense. She was a big girl; if she was a shop-thief, there was plenty of room beneath that cape to hide stolen goods. But she didn't *look* like a shop-thief.

'She's just a pintle-bit, Hawk,' Billy said, wondering how he could turn this information to his advantage. 'She's been shot in the giblets. You can see it when—'

'She isn't having it on my doorstep!' Hawk said, galvanized. He turned the full force of his gaze on her. 'You!' he bellowed. People looked round. 'Go away, madam! Move on there!'

Her eyes slowly opened, bright blue under firm, straight brows. She looked confused, as though she was waking from a faraway dream, and her lips moved as if she was asking a question. She shook her head, then stooped, one hand fumbling for the handle of her suitcase. Hawk snorted. Valise, she probably called it, and she'd have a mouthful of teeth like Billy's. Hawk saw women like this a

15

thousand times a year. 'Yes, you, move on!' he roared. 'Chop chop, madam!'

Billy made his move. 'Hawk, I could let you have a lovely song for Mrs Hawkins to play you on the piano, imagine your little children singing it, only a halfpenny a sheet.'

'Not now.'

'But, Hawk—'

Hawk looked through him.

'Push off, young man. Take your cock songs with you.'

Billy cut his losses. 'Cheerio, Hawk, see you Wednesday.'

'Bye-bye, Billy.'

Hawk turned his attention back to her.

She was staring at him.

The girl lifted her suitcase, which didn't look very heavy, and now she walked onto Hawk's gleaming pavement. She broke all the rules. She actually stopped right in front of Hawk. She was quite tall, though not nearly as tall as him. Her strong features were stamped with determination. Her teeth were white and even. She stood so close to him that he feared assault, a public scene, public humiliation from a mere slip of a girl. He glared at her but she did not look down, and he was appalled at the expression he saw in her hot blue eyes. He felt as though he was being struck a blow.

She said: 'Help me.'

If she had looked like an angel he would have helped her; of course he would. But she was too striking to fit into any category he put people into; and not submissive enough to her condition. A devil with those hot blue eyes. *Help me.* He spread his hands ingenuously.

'Who, me?' he said. She stared at him with contempt. Then she turned away.

He saluted, staring blindly across the street, his missing finger a magnificent demonstration of his war wound, and watched her thread through the traffic into the sunlight then turn left along Piccadilly. The stone corner of Burlington Arcade obscured her from his view. He knew that the doormen wouldn't let her in there, London's smartest, most exclusive shopping arcade. In fact, nowhere would let her in. It was difficult to imagine anywhere she could go. She was beyond the pale. And serve her right, too.

He resumed his righteous stance in front of Leibig's, on his little patch of polished flag, chest out, elbows in.

In a minute or two a dray liveried in Great Central Railway green rumbled past. The shirt-sleeved driver looked at Hawk and touched his whip-handle to the brim of his billy-cock hat in greeting. Hawk recognized Simmonds, and since they were related, through cousins of their mothers' families, Hawk gave Bert a short nod in acknowledgement of the vast hidden network of aunts, nephews, brothers and cousins that connected them. Hawk hardly thought of London as a place: London was an intricate map of relationships. Hawk couldn't imagine what it would be like to live in a city without them. He had already forgotten the girl.

4

What do you do, when you haven't got a single friend left in the world?

How long can you keep walking?

5

Bert Simmonds turned his green Great Central dray into the traffic proceeding up Piccadilly, and gave the horses a taste of the whip. They clopped forward at a stately pace.

She was nowhere in sight.

He tried to relax. That was the knack to driving in London, Bert knew, and he told anyone who listened. London was a giant machine, and you had to work at the machine's pace – *had* to for your health's sake. Some drivers got so tensed up with the stress of driving in London they wore themselves out before their time. What with the queues and delays, the road works – the railway companies putting in Undergrounds at millions of pounds per mile, the rivers being roofed over, sewers being dug, the roads being resurfaced with hardwood Denver blocks to make the traffic run quieter – with all that going on, it was easy for a

17

driver to fret himself into heart failure and an early grave.

The knack was to keep your mind interested. Not to be involved. You had to develop your powers of observation.

He told himself that was why he was interested in her.

He wondered about her. He wondered who she was, and he wondered where she was going.

It didn't quite make sense.

He wondered if he would recognize her again if he did see her.

He knew he would, even though she had been walking in the shadows and his eyes had been adjusted to the sun. There had been the anonymous but, for a lady, slightly indiscreet, flash of her shapely ankles beneath the hem of her long cape. Curls of hair had escaped from beneath her hat and were trailing down her back, and she was carrying a suitcase in her ungloved right hand – it could have been purest pigskin Vuitton or the cheapest cardboard, he was unclear on that. It was her other hand that had caught his attention.

Her left hand was clenched into a fist at her side. The knuckles stuck out like white knobs. Just looking at her, there in the shadows, he could feel her tension, her anger.

Her fear.

And he had glimpsed her face.

She was striking. Her features were too strong to be beautiful: level eyebrows, a straight nose, eyes that were either royal blue or navy blue with a direct gaze that either made people quickly look away or else respond with an equally open stare. Then she looked suddenly down. As if hurt, hurt so easily.

He grinned. She was so strong, but so vulnerable, that he was fascinated in her. He had a manly desire to see himself reflected in those angry blue eyes. He imagined himself feeling that clenched fist slowly melting against him. Mrs Simmonds was very good really, God bless her, she was a good mother and a good cook, he wasn't being unfaithful. Not at all. Although he knew a woman would never understand. It was just that he imagined that mouth . . . those voluptuous lips, longing to be parted . . .

18

Then she had gone.

Piccadilly stretched in front of him, full of rumbling vehicles, steaming horses, brassy sunlight, pedestrians dodging everywhere, though it seemed to him empty without her.

He told himself that he was just keeping up his powers of observation. What was a lady in Old Bond Street, one of the richest shopping streets in London, dressed in a fine cape, doing carrying her own suitcase? That was all he was interested in. The Sherlock Holmes stories they did in the *Strand Magazine* and now brought out in library books always started with beautiful girls, mysterious errands, helpless requests, followed by Sherlock's deductions, penetrating deductions. *Why was she carrying a suitcase?*

'Yaa!' he shouted. He cracked the whip over the horses' backsides. 'Giddyup! Giddyup there!'

A man in a broad-brimmed hat was selling baked potatoes to a lady. His donkey-cart was set up with an iron oven and a tall, smoking chimney. He juggled the potatoes, grimacing to show how hot they were. Was that her standing there? Bert stared, but the woman who searched for a coin to buy one wore a tatty hat and was no lady. Bert was well aware that a lady would rather have been seen dead than eating in the street. He ignored her.

He thought he saw her beneath a big ornamental lampstandard in the middle of the road, waiting for a break in the traffic coming the other way to cross to the far side. But then she turned towards him, and it was just a tired-faced girl with dull eyes and lacquered lips.

He looked away. The traffic was very heavy ahead. He'd missed her.

His horses slowed up and joined the slow crawl of traffic around Piccadilly Circus. The statue of Eros balanced above the crowd there, aiming sooty arrows from his Cupid's bow. The buildings were a mass of advertising hoardings, except for the long and forbidding outer wall of Devonshire House, the Duke's crest across its massive gates. Ahead there was a to-do; a lady walking alone had been accosted by a streetwalker, but the policeman who was called seemed merely amused. What did she expect, walking by herself in Piccadilly or Regent Street, with evening approaching? The prostitutes had long ago seized one side of Regent Street, across Piccadilly, down the Haymarket to the Strand, as their exclusive property. Bert sat back. She'd eluded him somewhere. He wouldn't see his girl with the suitcase here.

He saw no sign of her.

Bert left the horses to it – they knew the way as well as he did – and got out the sheaf of way-bills. He was going to be very late. He reckoned he'd probably missed his connection with the Brighton train. That was all right; he wasn't his own man now, where being late would lose his customer's goodwill and affect his cash in hand, he was a Company employee. The Great Central wouldn't even fine him for being late, as they would if he'd been early. The Company schedule regarded lateness as an Act of God, but arriving early as proof of reckless driving.

Now it was getting really cold, and he pulled on his coat and half-gloves. He was at the Circus. It was like bedlam. He yawned. Flower-girls hawked hothouse roses, already drooping, from the steps beneath the statue. A boy begged pennies by feeding rats he had caught in the sewers to the owl tethered to his wrist. Two gentlemen hailed the same cab and played the game of 'After you, Claude' with traditional courtesy. A prostitute staggered against Bert's wheel and leered up at him, done-over drunk. He looked away from her with disgust and dreamed about his girl. Two lads sold homemade fireworks. The traffic moved on.

He shook himself, licked his fingertips out of his half-gloves and flicked through the papers on his knee. Roundels of Leicestershire cheese for the Grand Hotel, Brighton, and a crate of live Aylesbury ducks for the Metropole. Machine parts. Bales of cloth. Samples of Nottingham tinware stamped *A Souvenir of Brighton* for an antique shop in the Lanes; brass models of the Daddy Long-legs sea-going railway (he smiled: the same one that he'd taken Albert and William on one Sunday day-trip during last summer, that ran from Volks Railway to Rottingdean). Lastly, a case of special Darjeeling for a grocer in Southampton . . . The Railway would organize something, for the ducks at least. The rest of it would be left piled on the platform under the eagle eye of a passenger guard.

A blind girl begged him to buy one of her fledgling birds.

He followed the traffic down the Haymarket.

Here the pavements, and even the middle of the road, were swarming with people hurrying home to get spruced up for the shindy. The capital would be one big street party tonight, he knew. Everyone had been stocking up for weeks. Christmas had been almost a sober affair compared with normal years, but now even the children's money pigs had been ransacked, and the real booze would be shifted tonight. Fireworks everywhere, and all the church bells ringing, and special services, and everyone was going to get stony drunk, even the railwaymen, because they wouldn't have to work tomorrow. Everyone would have the time of their lives celebrating the twentieth century. After all, it only happened once in a lifetime.

He put away the papers, yawning.

She turned out of a side road ahead of him, to his right. He could not have been more startled. She hadn't even gone as far as the Circus, she'd cut the corner through the back streets! That was taking an amazing risk, the Haymarket was a notorious cunny-warren of hovels, with garish gin-shops and dens where unspeakable but not unimaginable offences against morality took place. The alleyways were open brothels. Everyone knew that, from the lowest crossing sweeper to the greatest gentleman. You didn't go in there innocently unless . . . unless . . .

Sweet Jesus, he thought, *she doesn't know London.*

The traffic stopped. She was getting far ahead of him into Trafalgar Square. He stared after her.

She's just walking, he realized. *She isn't a lady, she's only a girl. She's just walking anywhere, she doesn't know where she's going. She doesn't even know where she is now. She's just – going. Going to nowhere, carrying a five-bob suitcase.*

This was terrible. He was witnessing a minor tragedy. He imagined how heavy the case must be, because she was walking so awkwardly. *Why doesn't she call a cab?* he wondered.

Then he thought: *And where would she tell the driver to take her to, anyway?*

She must have come from the provinces, where life for girls in service or the factory was just a dreary routine of work, work, stitch, stitch, church-and-chapel-going, according to the popular *Saturday Review*, to which he subscribed. He visualized her life: her parents had died or didn't care, she had no family, nothing to keep her where she was, no one who loved her. Like thousands of others she had come to London to the pavements of gold, seeking her fortune, a new life, free of drudgery and perhaps with hopes of marriage, and she had found instead that London was a vast and heartless place to those who did not belong. If she had no family, where could she go? Nowhere. If she had no family, who could look after her? No one. She was alone. One person wandering alone counted for very little amongst five million, in the largest city in the world.

The traffic moved and he almost caught up with her in Trafalgar Square; she had stopped against a lamp-post in the plaza, standing in her own shadow, too far for him to call her. He stared. In the buildings, around the hoardings, above their heads, gas lamps burned with hard white stars of flame, but seemed to cast little light. Pigeons swirled in free patterns across the pale blue sky, and Nelson's Column made a tall black cylinder, but the lions guarding around the base were like lumps of soot.

The traffic had to go around the square, but she cut across the centre. He had to give way to a horse tram and stood up in the seat, shielding his eyes from the sky, following her progress through each low pool of light. She crossed the road somewhere ahead of him while he was stuck behind an omnibus, and he thought he'd lost her, but then he saw her hesitating on the corner of the Strand. Which way would she go?

The brightest lights were up the Strand.

'Get out of the bleeding way!' someone shouted behind him. The omnibus had moved on and he was by an abrupt reversal now not the victim but the instigator of a traffic jam. He had to decide one way or the other. Girls usually stuck to the bright lights; it was safer. He chose the Strand.

She didn't. He cursed as she crossed away behind him. Peering over his shoulder, he saw her go into the relative darkness of Northumberland Avenue. He had chosen wrong. 'God damn!'

He stared back. That way led down to the river. On her left was the Charing Cross slum area, with one of the worst reputations in London. Why in hell's name did she want to go down to the river? She was hopelessly lost! He dragged on the right-hand rein, turning the horses across the crown of the road. They broke rhythm, confused, knowing as well as he that their usual way was up the Strand and a right turn across Waterloo Bridge. He forced them round, then cracked his whip.

Hauling on the left-hand rein, he turned down the centre of Northumberland Avenue.

There she was.

She was walking slowly. He caught her up then reined in, pacing the girl in the cape from just a little bit behind. Finally he licked his lips and called across.

'Where are you going, love?'

She walked across the entrance to a side street, glanced up it, then carried on. Probably she assumed, in the habit of someone who lives alone, that he was talking to someone else. The iron wheels of the dray rumbled softly.

'Nice evening,' Bert said. 'Nice weather for it. Going somewhere, are you?'

Her shadow crept up behind her as she passed beneath a street lamp, then swung around in front of her. Now he could see the curls of shining hair trailing down her back, swaying as she walked, and her white knuckles, and her white, ringless fingers.

They were halfway down the street. Lights flicked regularly across the end, traffic proceeding along the Embankment. Beyond it a boat's lantern and a single red light drifted soberly down river through the swarming reflections of the lights of Waterloo Station on the far side.

23

Christ, he thought, she's going to the station, and she'll cross the river on the Hungerford railway footbridge, where I can't follow.

'Yes, you, darling,' he said loudly, 'I'm talking to you!' He clicked his tongue and pulled in in front of her. She stopped too. She flinched, then stood with her head down. The case dropped from her hand.

'I won't hurt you, darling,' he said. 'Come from far, have you?'

Her hat moved; she was shaking her head. No. That was a lie. Obviously she had. A mill town, a provincial factory, domestic service somewhere.

He asked: 'Where are you going to?'

She shrugged, still with her head down.

'Got friends, have you?'

Another headshake.

He said: 'Who's expecting you, darling? Who are you staying with?'

She didn't move. That meant no one. He'd got her sorted out in his mind now. He licked his lips with anticipation, then called out:

'Is it worth a bob to you?'

She showed no sign of understanding. They were alone under the street light. He leant forward, trying to see under the brim of her hat.

'Well?'

Her shoulders were shaking. She must be crying. He looked up and down the street, then wiped his lips with the back of his hand. She mumbled something.

He had to crane down to her, and when she lifted her head they were suddenly close.

'Help me.'

She was so young! The casual thoughts he'd entertained about going into an alley with her and having her for a shilling were suddenly obscene: she was hardly older than his two eldest girls. He passed his hand across his face, shivering at the thought of what he'd nearly done, ashamed of himself. He had nearly behaved like a seducer, not father, and she was an innocent child. He imagined his own

24

daughters out, and how he would want a stranger to behave.

He looked paternally down at her, wanting to protect her. The young girl's eyes, which were the most beautiful part of her, or would be when of course she came of age, regarded him steadily through glittering moisture.

He asked gently: 'What can I do for you, love? Are you lost? Where's your father?'

He sat with his forearms resting on his knees, the reins trailing limply between his hands. Perhaps it was only his kind tone of voice, but her left fist slowly unclenched. A little of the tension drained out of her face. She looked less striking and very tired. He realized how lonely she was.

Yet the wary vitality did not leave her eyes. She learned quickly.

He tipped his hat back with his finger. 'You don't know London, do you? From up north somewhere are you?' No answer. 'Look, love, don't just stare. Yorkshire, is it?' A lot of the railwaymen came from up north, and her words had the same flat sound theirs did. 'Aren't you going to talk to me? You can trust me, we can be friends. Look, I'm sorry – about just now. It was my mistake. I was joking. How old are you?'

A locomotive clanked across the railway bridge, sending up sparks. The carriages followed, bright squares of light flashing through the girders. She held her cape closed against the cold, smelly wind gusting off the river.

'What's your name then? You remind me of my two girls,' he smiled. 'Gloria, that's my number one. You haven't been walking all day, have you?' She looked as though she had; that close to exhaustion. 'Here,' he said, concerned, 'Haven't you had anything to eat?'

No answer.

He asked impatiently: 'Haven't you got anywhere to go?'

She shook her head, very slowly, not taking her eyes off his face, just staring at him. She didn't trust him at all, not one inch. He felt baffled and then angry. He felt suddenly out of his depth.

'Look!' he shouted angrily. 'You'd better start being a bit

more bloody co-operative.' He was holding the whip. His temper was up.

She spoke.

'You wouldn't do anything,' she said. 'You bloody men. You don't care. *You bloody men.*'

'Don't you swear at me!' he blustered. He wouldn't really have used the whip on her. Many would have. He said bitterly: 'Who do you think you are?'

'What's your name?'

He looked up the street. Then he looked down towards the river. He blew out his cheeks. He couldn't decide what to do. Who did she think she was talking to? His own daughters would not have dared to speak to him like this in a thousand years.

'Albert Simmonds,' he said gruffly.

'Mr Simmonds, I'm very frightened,' she said softly. 'I need your help. I don't know what to do. Please help me.'

He laughed, having decided to take whatever she said lightly. She was only a child. 'Bert Simmonds, always ready to oblige a damsel in distress. Dragons killed.' He had already thought of taking her in on a lodger basis. They had the room and she could pay it back when she got a job. Gloria could help her . . .

'Men are good at killing things,' the girl said.

It was like a squirt of cold water. He realized: she *does* hate me. Why? What have I done?

The wind blew open her cape. She let it blow wide. He thought: *Oh no.* It was worse than anything he had imagined. Her skinny body was swollen with child; that strange, swaying walk had not been from the weight of the suitcase, but from the baby – a bastard baby, for he could see by her naked fingers that she was unmarried.

'Oh my God,' he said. 'You're a prostitute.'

He felt a heavy gob of anger and disgust form in his stomach.

At home his family would be waiting for him to return, grouped around his kitchen table. By the time he arrived the fire would be blazing up and his tub filled ready, everyone quiet while he sweated out the tension of the working day, and afterwards his supper would be slipped in front of him piping hot. He knew it would taste sour in his mouth tonight. He wondered if he would be able to believe anything his children said. Everything that he stood for, that society stood for, that elevated them above the level of shit and the animals, had been betrayed by this guilty figure below him. Everything.

And he had thought she was like Gloria.

His father would have horsewhipped her; he merely felt betrayed. She did not weep, she did not beg his forgiveness, she did not even have the decency to be ashamed of herself — she looked at him as bravely as though *he* were the guilty one. '*You bloody men,*' she had said, a fallen woman, yet not cast down.

'Listen, girl, go and throw yourself in the river,' he told her. 'That's all you're good for.'

He clicked his teeth to get the horses going. She didn't try to run alongside. She didn't beg or plead. She wouldn't do it. She stood where she was, and let him drive away down to the river. He knew she didn't take her eyes off his back. It was a relief when he turned out of her sight, and felt the breeze off the stinking water blowing on his face and over his bare head.

6

Lisa stood alone.

She thought: I don't know what I'm going to do. I'm desperate.

I know what I'm *expected* to do. They've made that as crystal clear as the water that comes tumbling down Blane Ghyll into the artificial leet which takes it arrow-straight beneath Clawfell into the holding ponds at Home Farm. I'm trapped as a trout, that I am.

She wrapped the cape back around her and huddled herself into its soft warmth. It was the most beautiful garment that she had ever owned. All her other clothes, for almost as long as she could remember, had been hand-me-downs in one way or another, down the chain of consumption that started with the Lockhart family and continued, thanks to the organizing genius of Miss Bell, through the above-stairs senior servants eventually down to the kitchen staff and those outside. She hugged the pure wool around her – the cape was lined with navy-blue satin, the collar lightly trimmed with fur. It was that beautiful.

She imagined herself, slim and fine as she used to be, running into the great kitchen at Clawfell Grange, crying, 'Mrs Parkinson, look what I bought me, with my own money too!' But the plump cook behaved no more kindly in her daydream than she had in real life, saying, 'What's a young girl like thee doing wearing lovely clothes for? Thee's just a maid of all hands, getting ideas above thy station, indeed. Quick, take it off before Mr Crane sees it—' Lisa clapped her hands over her ears.

She tried to see herself standing wild and free by the perished stones of the old Roman fortlet on Clere Mount, at the very peak of Clawfell, the sky all around her washed-out blue, cleansed by the Yorkshire gales, the green patchwork of dale fields spread out pin-sharp far below. She gasped. The illusion was too painful. She opened her eyes. London. She had come to London to die, brought here by the man who loved her. The city surrounded her with dark geometrical planes of dirt and stone, and from time to time, with people. They didn't care about her. Charles, pressing the ten coins into her hand; the sandwich board man; the Head Doorman; Mr Albert Simmonds, all upright Victorians pushing her into something she didn't want to do. *I won't do anything they want*, she thought. *I won't cry, and I won't die.*

And . . and I won't commit murder.

Then she thought, with rising panic: *But what other choice do I have?*

He had been in such a hurry to get away that his hat had blown off. She watched it lying in the road, upside-down, still wobbling. She picked up her suitcase and gave that hat the best kick she could. It rolled into the gutter.

Lisa had told him the truth exactly. *I'm very frightened. I need your help. I don't know what to do.* And for a moment, she had thought he *would* help her. God knows, she needed someone's help. Her heart had lifted.

No. She was a fallen woman. She had sinned and to help her was the same as encouraging sin, that was the way their minds worked. An outcast, beneath contempt, and beyond help, only worth praying for, because of what she carried inside her like a blazon of guilt. She had seen the change come over his face.

'*Go and throw yourself in the river. That's all you're good for.*' Suicide.

Pay for a sin with another sin, because two wrongs make a right.

It hadn't been a sin, it had been pure joy. And a part of her had *known*, even as that flood of pure joy was rushing through her, the coarse moorland grass prickly beneath her back, the sun hot on her thighs, bosom, cheeks, blazing too bright for her eyes so that her closed eyelids were swirling patterns of red, it was the moment of conception.

She had denied it then.

She could not deny it now.

She realized that she would have to wee again, although she had drunk nothing all day. Since her eviction at 8 a.m. prompt that morning by Mrs Grinling, she had had to go (from nerves, probably) behind a bush in Regent's Park before her last, pleading visit to Lockhart House at eleven; then her anger had kept her going until the Haymarket, when again she had been overcome by desperate need and she had found a quiet back street to relieve herself. Whether such frequency was a signal of her baby's imminent arrival, or just a normal symptom of her condition, she did not know. The physical swelling had been unmistakable, unavoidable, for about the last three months, but she had not been regular since that day in spring. She had no idea how long you kept the baby inside you.

She turned into the maze of Charing Cross, found a narrow street, and relieved herself in the drainage ditch down the middle. Rats squeaked, candlelight leaked around boarded-up windows and Lisa sensed the weight, the heat, behind them of families living fifteen to a room, cooking, eating, dying, multiplying. A young girl with bowed legs and deformed hips crouched watching her, picking her nose, her feet wrapped in rags tied around her ankles, but the old whores in the doorways were too busy shivering and mumbling amongst themselves, and eyeing the suitcase, even to call out obscenities. Lisa moved on before they could decide to smash her up for her suitcase, cutting back down an alley to Northumberland Avenue. She was getting enough in the know about London to be confident that they wouldn't follow her out of their little patch of territory.

She had arrived at the broad thoroughfare that Mr Simmonds had disappeared into on his dray. Hackney-cabs clip-clopped to and fro, and she noticed how well-fed and sprucely harnessed the horses were. Gentlemen with tall silk hats, brushed moustaches and wigga-wagga sticks walked briskly to their Clubs. She pushed through them and crossed to the far side of the road. She paused by a long trough in beautifully worked stone:

**METROPOLITAN DRINKING FOUNTAIN AND CATTLE TROUGH
ASSOCIATION
THE EMBANKMENT**

So, thought Lisa, this is the Embankment.

Lisa had heard of the Embankment. This was the place you came to lose your baby – your life, too, if you wanted. The man she loved – and still loved – had said the name of this place to her at eleven o'clock this morning. The Embankment. And he had given her ten pounds, in gold: ten gold sovereigns pressed into the palm of her left hand.

It was the place she would have given anything to avoid. Here she was anyway, she sighed.

She walked slowly across the spacious promenade towards the river. Her feet ached as though she walked on the naked bones, and her suitcase, though it contained so little, seemed to weigh a ton. It was all she had.

Lisa stared over the top of the retaining wall at the black water lapping the stones below. She guessed that once there had been nothing here but marshes and slums. The impressive thoroughfare of the Embankment would have been built both to shore up the river bank from the marshes and to protect the noses and fine sensitivities of well-to-do commuters from seeing the slums and slum life. The good people, like Charles, could just drive straight past it. Out of sight was out of mind, behind a crust of smart façades.

Lisa thought: I wish the Embankment would crumble back into the river, and let the water in again.

How do you have your baby?

Farther out, the lights wavered prettily on the Thames. Closer in, things that were unidentifiable rolled in the wavelets and there was a strong smell of bleach, like cleaning fluid, reminding her of Clawfell, that other world.

She thought: Shall I do what is *expected* of me, throw myself in here and drown romantically, paying for my love with my death? Drowning is very romantic, just paying for all and going to sleep. They sell it in shop windows and magazines, and lovely paintings like I saw in Bond Street this morning, and stared at so long that the assistant looked at me hopefully. *Found Drowned*, a drowned woman sleeping on a mudbank, her hair beautiful, under a single star.

Why do men deceive us? What makes them lie, what possible reason, do they think they're protecting us? I'm no fool, drowning is a terrible death, I've seen the bodies of drowned sheep dragged out of the Blane Ghyll pools, and their eyes had burst and their tongues stuck out blue. If they say that's beautiful, they're probably lying about everything else. Aye, they call this river Father Thames, and it's awash with sewage.

Turn beauty round, and here's the beast.

If I close my eyes I see you in my eyelids. I taste orange sweetly on my lips. Charles, it was beautiful between us, not sinful. I don't understand you; I don't understand what changed you; I love you, and you hate me. You give me life inside me, and you cause my death.

The lights in the water were very pretty, that they were. But everything else was darkness.

31

Chapter Two

1

Lisa remembered.

It was dark. She knew it had stopped snowing because the flames burned quietly now; no more snowflakes came whirling down the narrow grit chimney, hissing. She was being a good, quiet girl, like she'd been told by Miss Bell. It was a treat to be allowed up so late, sitting in front of the kitchen fire with Mr Benjamin the one-eyed teddy bear cuddled warm in her lap, his yellow fur a bit threadbare in places, because she loved him to death. Miss Bell, who visited when Mam went through a bad patch with her lungs, had been unusually quiet this evening, and hadn't even told her to *stop wriggling*. On the other side of the fire was Dad's rocking chair, but it was empty, and no one sat there since Dad had gone to heaven to be with the angels. Miss Bell, Mam's teacher friend – they had been awarded the official certificates together (Miss Bell had been the York family's oldest friend for years and years, before little Lisa was even thought of, Mam had said) – now opened the bedroom door, which had been closed all night, and came out. She was a thin woman with a square, prim face and hair dragged back into a severe knot. She looked at Lisa, then back into the room, shaking her head, and speaking in a low voice that she thought Lisa couldn't hear.

'No, doctor. She's wide awake,' she said. She looked at

Lisa again. She had a stern way of looking at a little girl that made Lisa's knees turn to jelly, and a thin straight mouth. Lisa had learned that she had a heart of gold beneath that grim outside. But she never disobeyed her.

The doctor came out, taller than Miss Bell but so stooped that his head was lower than hers. She trembled, clinging tight to Mr Benjamin; that had been her father's name, and it comforted her.

'I'm not sleepy,' she cried. 'I want to say good night to me Mam.' She went in every night because Mam couldn't sleep without her good night kiss, and now it was extra important because it was so late.

The adults glanced at one another. 'I think it would be for the best. Since she lost her father too—' Miss Bell left the rest unsaid. She took Lisa's hand and led her into the empty bedroom.

Lisa was confused. She did not see her mother, but there was no other door for her to have escaped through. The window was closed. There was the bed, as always, where Mam had been for months, but now the coverlet was stretched fully over it. Then Lisa realized that she was hiding beneath the cover – she could see the peaks Mam's feet made, her body, her head. Her face was underneath, too.

'But she can't breathe!' Lisa cried. The grownups did not move. Lisa tried to tug free so that she could save her Mam, pull the heavy suffocating cover from her face, but the terrifying doctor loomed forward and gripped her shoulders.

'Lisa! Thy Mam doesn't need to breathe now, see, lass.'

'She does, she can't breathe!' Lisa wailed. 'Help me!' How could they have made such a silly mistake?

'She's happy now,' he explained. 'She's at peace, lass.'

No she wasn't, she couldn't be, not under there. Lisa twisted forward and felt the coverlet under her hands. She clenched her fists and pulled, and Mam's face came sliding out. One glassy eye was half open, the other was closed as if she was asleep. Her mouth yawned with rigid black lips in an airless gasp for breath. There was nothing there inside her mouth, no teeth, no air, no spit, no tongue. Lisa could just see the tip of her tongue lying in the back of her throat. She stared.

'Come away, lass!'

'Let her see,' came Miss Bell's voice distantly. 'I told you she had a mind of her own – just like Eliza,' she said fondly, then Lisa felt her hand close around her own little fist. Someone put the cover back.

Lisa asked earnestly: 'Do people's tongues always disappear when they die?'

'Aye.' The doctor's breath smelt of liquorice. 'It always happens when they're lying back like that.'

Lisa wiggled her tongue inside her mouth. The feeling meant she was alive. Then grief washed over her. She felt so lost, so alone.

'Who's going to give me my breakfast in the morning?'

'We'll see,' Miss Bell said. 'Would you like to go back to Mr Benjamin now?'

'Where's Mr Benjamin?' Lisa asked, forgetting her tears.

Miss Bell turned her firmly towards the door. 'Let's go and find him, shall we, Lisa?'

'I've got another death tonight,' the doctor murmured, picking up his Gladstone bag. 'Altogether that's six and eightpence.' Lisa heard the chink of coins. She cuddled Mr Benjamin. Mam had sewn his name into the collar around his neck in red letters when she was alive.

'Thee's right, she's a wilful lass,' the doctor said from the door. 'She'll have it knocked out of her at the Workhouse school before many days have passed, I'm sure.'

'I'll not have her in that place!' Miss Bell sounded very defiant. She added: 'I'm taking her with me to Clawfell Grange.'

The doctor laughed. He said something about them having room enough.

In the still before dawn, in the greyness, Lisa's feet crunched across the smooth snow. Miss Bell was tall and walked with a long, rangy stride that covered ground with easy speed. Lisa was jumping along behind her, trying to tread in her deep footsteps but having to do two to her one.

They climbed steadily. The moor was like a white wave breaking above them. Then as the brow of the snowfield dropped away Lisa saw an ugly jagged stain ahead with lights burning in the turrets, and smoke rising from its chimneys even this early. 'At Clawfell the servants have many more duties than they can fit into the hours of daylight God gives,' said Miss Bell grimly. 'The Lockhart family are not forgiving employers.'

And so Lisa came to Clawfell Grange.

Arriving on that winter's day years ago, too young to do the work of an adult, Lisa had been grudgingly granted board in lieu of wages, and Miss Bell fitted her out from her own pocket. From age thirteen, gawky but now strong, she was paid board wages of one and ninepence a week all found, except her parlourmaid's blue serge uniform, apron, and starched white cap, which she had to find for herself.

Because she was young master Roland's governess, Miss Bell was a person of power in the establishment, though surely her tart tongue would get her into trouble one day. She was a trained teacher and she had no one to love; by firelight she spread what she knew wider than just master Roland upstairs.

Lisa listened. She learned.

Grange means farm, Miss Bell had told her, but now that Clawfell was a great house that work was done at the Home Farm, on the far side of the medieval fishponds. There had been a dwelling here on the windward edge of the moor from time immemorial, meaning in England law from before 1189, but the Lockhart family didn't arrive until much later.

Robbie Lockhart was the first.

Of lowland Scottish stock, handsome (according to the account of Thomas Osborne – his portrait was destroyed in 1644) Robert Lockhart was a favourite of James VI, who, according to Osborne, 'shower'd kisses on him' in public. Lockhart followed his monarch south when he was crowned James I of England. Robert the courtier must have had a silver tongue in his forgotten, handsome face, because he kept the King's favour even after his retirement from Court; and must have had rich friends to call on when the King indulged him to buy the Crown lands at Clere Mount, Blane and Clawfell.

'Flattery, immorality, and borrowed money. The usual basis of a proud dynasty.' Such wit was intolerable; the truth of it unforgivable, if ever it were repeated to the Lockhart family.

In the library Miss Bell had discovered the family's curious love–hate relationship between north and south, one generation moving to London, the next rediscovering the plainer northern appeal of Clawfell, the next (by now Eton or Rugby educated) forsaking the great house to return to London. This division was fixed in the blood, said Miss Bell, passed down the generations. Few of the Lockhart daughters married, another family trait that in any one generation would have been put down to individual will or chance, if it was noticed at all. Brains forgot, but the blood remembered. The history of most families is unrecorded, so the living cannot know themselves fully; what blood shapes them, what forces move them.

But the Lockharts knew. The eldest son always married, he had no choice. It was his absolute duty. Nothing was as important as making an effective marriage and producing a male heir, and the family had achieved that successfully for hundreds of years, whether in London or Clawfell, prisoners of the blood. They lived without love, as remorselessly as the dinosaurs, and as solidly successful.

The family was 'old money'. Their fortune had been founded on wool revenues and the capital inheritances passed down from father to son were substantial. They would never have dreamed of soiling themselves with buying and selling, they employed agents and managers to deal with sordid business. They were gentlemen. They stared down on Lisa out of a long row of dark portraits around the grand staircase.

While she dusted Lisa imagined Clawfell growing from the simple farm with a sandstone tile roof into a Jacobean country house, burned by the Roundheads in the Civil War after the battle of Marston Moor, where Stewart Lockhart was killed. Young Robert rebuilt it in Restoration style, with Dutch gables copied from his years in exile: she could see it painted in the background of his picture. She pulled back: looking so close to the musty surface had made her nose tickle. The frames were dusted once a week in summer, each day in winter because of the fires, and the dust got up her nose but she didn't dare sneeze.

James extended Clawfell, his son Charles hated the place. John, who was painted by Gainsborough and his horses painted by Stubbs, added a portico and classical wings; miserly William, who preferred London, let it fall into decay. But his son, of course, was opposite in character.

George hated London, loved the moors, and loved spending some of the enormous fortune he inherited. The architect Wyatt extended the modest classical mansion to make Clawfell into a rambling Gothic castle, complete with a barbican, battlements and jutting towers in the most fashionable and extravagant style of the day – at the awesome cost of £115,000. The towers cunningly concealed water tanks, and the rooms were lit by plate glass windows – three hundred and sixty-five of them, one for every day of the year – and illuminated at night by gleaming flares of colza oil. George gave brilliant entertainments, but he was also deeply religious: prominently in the porte-cochère entranceway was carved, 'Except the Lord buildeth the house they labour in vain that build it.'

Not that Lisa was ever allowed in that way. In fact the coachmen and outside workers never went inside the house at all, ever. They lived in quarters by the stables and their food was taken to them through a tunnel from the kitchens, so that no servant should be seen crossing the yard. The servants were kept apart from the family and from each other, the laundry staff from the kitchen staff, the scullery maids from the parlourmaids, and the sexes were never allowed to work together except under strict supervision. Lisa only saw the lads from a distance, which was a pity, because they seemed to be rather fun. They were strange and mysterious, and sometimes she saw them looking at her as curiously as she looked at them, across the courtyard, or from opposite ends of the kitchen.

She sighed and picked up her duster again.

When George died, the blood worked its way. His son Edward was as parsimonious as his grandfather, keeping the place going only out of loyalty to tradition and his sisters, who preferred to live there, and in fact his son Henry was born there.

Now an old man, his lordship loved the place where he had been born and spent his life, caring not for pomp and circumstance but only for horses and bloodstock, and the wild fells.

The Old Man loved Clawfell. He was a hard man and it was a hard love, as indifferent to lesser beings as the moorlands are. Even the family whispered when he was around, for his temper was like a whip. His face was cracked and broken with the intractable lines of a shattering grief – for his firstborn son, Lisa wondered, dead these long years? – and he had eyes as cold as grey millstone grits, even for Charles, his second son, hating him because he was not the son he had loved.

Yet one day Charles Lockhart's picture would hang there.

Lisa grew up alone. Because of her closeness to Miss Bell, she had few friends among the servants. She was not allowed to see the family in the gentry part of the house, for it was her duty to avoid them by using the back stairs and the maze of back corridors. She learned to open doors with her hands full, to close them as quietly as a mouse; to dust, polish, sweep, brush, in silence; to blacklead grates, to clean glass without leaving smears; to be neither seen nor heard – to be neither happy nor unhappy, in fact hardly to exist.

She did not realize that her work was so terribly hard, or her life so terribly empty, because she had no one else her own age to tell her so. Scrubbing and scouring with bleacher and buckets of sand and tangles of wire wool up and down those back stairs, fourteen hours a day, her slim adolescent body always hungry and her hands always

38

chafed red, she thought that everyone of her class lived like this, and that her life was normal. And it was. Until one day, another winter's day, when everything changed.

Much of the house was shut up by this time, and the roaring fires never did keep the rest of it warm. Even here, in the library, was cold. She looked up from her polishing for a moment, and shivered. Miss Bell had all sorts of classical works and history books in her room, but nothing like these magnificent rows of morocco bindings, Jane Austen, the romances of Harriet Martineau and Sir Walter Scott – Lisa looked longingly out of a window, and wondered what the world outside was like.

'Lisa, isn't it?'

She whirled round with her heart in her mouth. He had entered so silently he could have been watching her for any length of time while she was woolgathering in her dream world beyond the window – she was in terrible trouble.

'Cat got your tongue?' young Charles Lockhart smiled, closing the door behind him.

'Cat, sir?' she quavered. There were no cats at Clawfell, the Old Man didn't like them. She remembered to curtsey – what was wrong with her today? – getting flustered, tripping on her ankle. She knew that she was going to get a stripping from Mr Crane about this, all right. And deserve it.

She stood with her eyes cast respectfully down, trying to hold back her fingers with their cracked and broken nails from fiddling with the frill around her apron.

'You've been with us several years, have you not?'

'Yes, sir,' she answered. She felt tears prickle the backs of her eyes. Now she would be Let Go.

'Are you frightened of me, Lisa?' He laughed.

The Honourable Charles Lockhart was dressed in a stylish black suit with a small soft collar, of a type that she had never seen before; it must be London fashion. She did not care for it very much, although it made him look even taller than he was, and ever so elegant. He spoke with a southern accent that she supposed must be London, very precise yet somehow the words were so drawn out that it was difficult for her to follow their meaning, they sounded so different. He had a wide forehead, as pale as a gentleman's should be, and his eyes above his black moustache were the colour of ice, the deep blue-green ice over the Blane Ghyll pools towards spring, with the melted depths moving below. She felt immediately that he was interested in her, not in any wrong or low way because of course for him that was impossible, but as a human alive in her own right, even though she was only a parlourmaid.

'No, sir, I'm not frightened.' Though it was in his power to make her be.

'Of course not. No reason to be, is there? Do you like working here?' he remarked conversationally. She noticed that his necktie was crooked; his valet had let him down.

They heard footsteps approaching in the next room. Charles Lockhart closed his lips into a slim line, then for some reason went to the opposite door, not the one he had come in through. 'I'll see you again.' He opened the door over there and went out, closing it after him.

She did not see him, in fact, for some time. But she imagined him constantly.

Lisa thought: But books don't warn you about life. When it actually happens to you, it's all new to you. It seemed to her that what was happening between the two of them must have been as new to Charles as it was to her.

Charles Lockhart was the Old Man's only surviving son. She felt so sorry for him. He was a prisoner as much as she was, although no one would think it to look at him, a gentleman and all, a good school, and a handsome wife with money behind her, and the certainty of inheriting Clawfell Grange when the Old Man passed on.

But Charles, she knew, hated the Grange, the moors, the dour country people, and longed for the brittle lights of London. All the female staff felt that. He was the generation that did. It was in his blood. And they knew that the Old Man would never let Charles leave, except for an obligatory week or two at the London house in the Season. He was too afraid that the son he despised wouldn't come back.

40

Charles brought Lisa a blue silk headscarf back from London. She held the soft folds of his secret gift against her heart: it meant that he had been thinking of her while he was away.

Charles needed people. All the women peeling sprouts around the kitchen table were agreed on that. For all that he was a gentleman he was just as trapped as them, and in Lisa's opinion he was the unhappiest man in the world at Clawfell. Missing no detail of him, she had even noticed that he pronounced it deliberately like a southerner, down his nose, Claawfell, not the local short *a* used by the Old Man and the rest of them: Clafell.

Lisa imagined how it must be to live like Charles, having everything, but not freedom, not even the freedom to marry the woman he loved. She told herself that she alone understood the feelings wrangling in his heart: he needed someone – he never wanted to marry his wife, never loved Lady Henrietta Rownslee, it was just the Old Man forcing poor Charles into it because of her fortune, and after the difficulty she had when young Master Roland was born, she would not allow anything further to happen between them: they slept in separate rooms, she would not do her duty. She hated him.

Lisa thought: *He needs me. No one else even notices me. He does love me . . .*

'What does thee call that?' shouted Mrs Parkinson. She slammed a bowl of sprouts on the table. Lisa jerked back so suddenly that her knife cut against her thumb. The chatter around the table stopped. Mrs Parkinson seized a miserable green thing that Lisa had thoughtlessly peeled down to the size of a nut from her hand, and held it up between her plump fingers so that everyone could see it.

'*What does thee call that?*'

'It's a Brussels sprout, ma'am,' Lisa whispered.

The women laughed.

Lisa stared at the table. It was oak, washed and scrubbed over so many years that the softer, paler wood between the lines of harder grain had been worn into a pattern of smooth grooves between the ridges, like your fingertips looked if you peered very close, as if girls too were made of unfeeling wood. Blood dripped from her thumb. She hid it.

'That thing is what thee calls a Brussels sprout?' Mrs Parkinson flicked the nugget contemptuously into the bowl and thrust her great round face close. Lisa could see the hairs on her chin. 'Thee's supposed to peel two or three leaves off the outside, *at most*, and cut a score across the bottom so it cooks soft. Not peel the thing down to a stupid pellet. What's that good for?'

'Nothing, Cook.' Lisa heard the other girls, who were all so ugly, giggle.

Her head rang as Mrs Parkinson's hand came round. 'I'm fed up with thee young girls, thee's all dumb as sucking ducks. I'm nithered half to death or I wouldn't have thee in my kitchen. I don't know what gets into thee.' Lisa wept. She wouldn't tell her. It was her secret. Mrs Parkinson's hands, as red as raw meat, boxed her ears from side to side.

'Two or three leaves off the outside at most,' Lisa cried obediently. 'Cut a score across the bottom so that it cooks proper. Put it in the water. Peel two or three leaves off the outside at most. Cut a score across the bottom.' Her eyes dripped tears down her cheeks.

In the autumn she had been cleaning the gallery windows; they faced the sun so the slightest mark showed. She was concentrating hard on polishing the vinegar well into the corners, so that the grime which had collected there didn't come off in greasy streaks across the clean glass, when suddenly she realized Charles was in the gravel court outside. He was dressed in a white open-necked shirt with very pale brown trousers, and slim riding boots. Something had frightened the temperamental black Arab hunter he was leading, and it was playing up. She knew little about horses, but she felt that the cause of its fright could have been her shape moving in the window, and kept still. The horse kicked so wildly that she feared Charles would be killed at any moment. But Charles quieted the horse just by stroking it. He had long fingers. The beast shivered, then shook its mane and stood still. He smiled up. Lisa's heart pounded. It was as though they shared a secret.

For months, with the headscarf spread open beneath her pillow, she dreamed of what that secret was. It was that he was falling in love with her too.

Yet he was married to that Rownslee woman, Lady Henrietta. None of the servants liked her. She was new to her class and she'd studied how to behave as though it was a set of rules, just a set of rules instead of proper feelings and values, Lisa thought. Lady Henrietta wasn't a born lady, she had no feelings, no emotion. She wasn't of the gentry, she was middle class, from a mill family, new money. She treated her servants like machines, when she deigned to notice them at all. She'd stare straight into your eyes completely blankly when she gave her orders, Lisa remembered, as though you were a piece of equipment she bossed about. It took honest Mrs Parkinson, who had to discuss the menu with her every day, to put her finger on it: Lady Henrietta was frightened of her servants. That they were human. Cold efficiency was all she was interested in. Efficient cleaning. Efficient dressing. No room for error, for being out of control.

Lisa understood. Lady Henrietta's own body had let her down. Apparently she'd nearly died birthing Master Roland. She never dared to be a wife again, because something had gone wrong with the machinery inside her, so that left her free to put whatever feelings she had solidly into hatred. Lisa could imagine it plain as day. She hated life. Lady Henrietta hated Charles for fathering Roland, and Roland for nearly killing her. The boy was nearly ten by this time, delicate, with long eyelashes, a lovely little boy; completely unforgiven. No play, no love, no books, except Latin and mathematics, which she called the two pure disciplines. Miss Bell did her best to widen his horizons, to slip him different books as she did to Lisa too, but after one or two terrible run-ins with Lady H. she was finally dismissed. No notice, not even a thank you. Just – out. Miss Bell looked ten years older, and her face was covered with wrinkles. Lisa cried. It was snowing, too, like when they had arrived together, when Miss Bell had to leave alone.

Lisa thought with horror: *I have nobody now – nobody in the world.*

The long winter passed. The snow slowly melted. Endless days of haar and mist trailed away into brightening spring. The sun shone warm again. Sunday was Lisa's afternoon off, so she borrowed Jane in the scullery's overcoat and stout shoes, them taking the same size in everything, and took out an old book. It felt wonderful to walk in the outside, and it could be beautiful. Beyond the battlements of the house and the ornamental gardens rose Clawfell, great and grey, with the green fingers of sheltered valleys reaching up towards the bleak skyline by growing along the grooves and clefts cut by the ghylls, but never reaching the wild rim. Up there on top it was like the moon, scoured by gales – Clawfell faced north, and took the brunt. Sometimes she'd sit up there and read under the shelter of a drystone wall for hours, or beside the water spraying down into one of the Blane Ghyll pools, until the sun went down. She had a favourite place to go to, a little knoll of grass that she felt was her own. She knew a lot about the world, but she hadn't experienced any of it. She loved Charles Lockhart; he loved her.

He was there when she arrived, standing dressed in smart tweeds on the grass by the pool, a paintbrush in his hand, dabbing at an easel with a view over the Dales. His horse, the Arab, was hobbled and cropping peacefully.

'Hallo, Lisa.'

She had been startled to see him, because she'd thought that this was her private place, known only to her, but here he was, making free as he pleased and not too surprised to see her, she thought.

'I'm sorry, sir, I didn't know you was here.' She curtseyed and turned away.

'No, don't go.' He pushed back his cap with the tip of his paintbrush, revealing his pale forehead and sensitive features out of the shadow. He had grown his moustache a little wider than she remembered, but it was just as carefully razor-trimmed. 'Lisa, tell me what you think of my poor effort, if you would.' He beckoned her to the easel.

44

'Sir, I don't know about paintings, sir.'

'But I would value your opinion.'

She crept forward, feeling ashamed of the shabby overcoat and its faint smell of camphor mothballs. He took her shoulder. She gasped. The painting was truly good, deeper than the view. He had changed the light, marking the river Aire in the far distance with a silver flash to point it out, which wasn't there at the moment but which she realized would be when the sun was low over that way, which it was at dawn; and he had added numerous touches, she noticed, grey or purple added to the clouds, which came together to suggest early morning. It *was* early morning, in the picture. She didn't know what to say. It was ever so clever. She was overwhelmed.

'It looks just like the early morning, sir.'

'I have been here since the early morning.' He was looking at her look at the picture. 'From before dawn, to be exact.'

'It was worth getting up so early, sir.'

'Now that you are here.' His hand on her shoulder turned her towards him. 'I did not know what time you commenced your hours of leisure, morning or afternoon.' And of course he could not ask. His valet had tied his necktie correctly this time. She glanced up at his eyes. He was staring over her shoulder, looking almost bored. Then he smiled, looking down. He had fine white teeth. 'I've had my eye on you for some time, Lisa.'

'Thank you, sir.'

'You have an interesting face. I thought I should like to paint you.'

Her feelings jumped in two directions, one up, one down. She clapped her hands to her cheeks. 'Oh, sir, I should be too embarrassed!' At least he had noticed her face; but then he must also have noticed the smell of mothballs in this coat. She knew his feelings and the secret that was in his heart as well as she knew the secret that was in her own; they talked of love without mentioning it.

'Nevertheless, I wish to paint you,' he said directly. 'Be so good as to remove that coat.'

She did as she was commanded. The air was cool but the spring sun was hot enough. The splashing waters flashed light in her eyes. Charles's shadow fell across her and she felt the coat removed from her fingers. He threw it across a mossy rock with the casualness of someone who does not need to care about such things. There was still that gap between them. She put out her hand, but he was not there.

'You are beautiful,' came the voice. 'Stay there. You have the sunlit Dales behind you.' She shaded her eyes. He was looking at her from the point of view of his easel. He came back. 'Please sit.' *Please.* He could have ordered her. She lowered herself a little unsteadily, grasping his hand tightly when he steadied her. The grass was dry. Her feet rested beside the rippling water. A beetle toiled between the stalks of grass and disappeared under a pebble. She sat with her arms wrapped around her knees, feeling the sun hot on her exposed ankles, her neck and her upturned face. Would he sit beside her?

'You're so thin,' he said in a voice that sounded sad. 'Don't we feed you enough?'

They were always tired, they were always hungry. Didn't he know? He must know, she decided. He was no stranger to unhappiness, to a loveless life. Still they skirted around the subject that had brought them here, she sitting on the grass, not looking at him, her face towards the sun with her eyes closed, but knowing that he knelt beside her now.

'I brought you a gift.' He held out an orange – a real one, not wax, a big round fresh orange. She smelled its scent, saw the moisture sparkling in the pores across its vivid skin.

'Oh Charles!' She felt tears start. An orange wasn't special to him, he could eat an orange any time he wished, but he had thought to bring her one knowing how special it would be to her. Or had it just been in his pocket anyway? That was impossible. He'd said, *'I've brought you a gift,'* those exact words, and it didn't matter anyway. It was the thought that counted. The orange: the love. She felt a warm thrill spread through her. *He thinks about me, he loves me, and I am allowed to call him by his name.*

'Shall I eat it now?'

'I insist.' His face looked suddenly eager, reflecting the slow growth of emotion that must have been showing on her own face, flushed cheeks, a sheen of perspiration, but almost instant in his case. The speed frightened her. Perhaps men's emotions expressed themselves differently. He was kneeling near her and she could see a pulse beating in his neck. He watched her bite into the rind. A cloud of fine moisture puffed out. She gave a squeak of surprise, then laughed, wiping the condensation from her cheeks.

'Let me kiss the zest from your lips,' he said seriously. She did not know how to say yes or no. He still did not say he loved her. She did not know what zest was. He kissed her. She tasted the sweet flavour of the orange. She asked him: 'Do you love me?' He kissed her again. He murmured something. On her shoulders she felt his hands wandering over the sun-heated material of her blue dress. This was not proper. She felt his hot caresses on her chest. She could not stop him. The air was lifeless, she was panting for breath, she was all in a rage of tempestuous feeling and could not make him stop. She clung on to his head. 'Do you love me?' The sun burned her shoulders, the air was cold. She felt her clothes moving over her body, his face in her bosom, his hands on her knees. She gasped for breath. 'No, please.' The pressure of his face increased, she fell back. His fingers wriggled between her thighs, tickling, and she could not help giggling they tickled so. She felt all in a frenzy and a terror of embarrassment at what he would find, and did find, but he just said, 'Oh,' almost reverently, as if it was marvellous and to be desired. He knelt between her thighs, pulling at his trousers, while she lay inert, with her head on one side and a forest of grass in front of her right eye. She said:

'Do you love me?'

She felt an endless thrust of unbearable pain and tears trickled from the corners of her eyes. He laughed, mistaking them for tears of joy, making her feel a little of that emotion too; then, as he continued to move his hips against her, a little more. She hugged her arms around his shoulders. She felt the coarse moorland grass prickling her bare flesh. The sun burned hot on her thighs, bosom, cheeks, and into her closed eyes so that her eyelids were swirling patterns of red – and she cried: 'Do you love me?'

'Yes!' he shouted, his handsome face above her, 'Yes, yes, yes!'

She remembered: *We were lovers. I loved him. He loved me. I now know that the heads of men and women hardly know one another at all, and all is lies and only love is true.*

They were infatuated. He could not see her without caressing her. They met everywhere, whenever there wasn't a risk, and even when there was. The library, the gallery, his study, the conservatory, all places where anyone could come in, anytime, and sometimes where she had no excuse to be. She was not mad; she simply trusted him. Later, it seemed so obvious that he was just using her, but at the time it wasn't that complicated. She could feel that his need was as genuine as hers was. And really, he had little more experience of the world than she did. His love for her was genuine. London destroyed that love – buried it deep beneath a façade of worldliness, drink and much new company – but it still existed, she told herself. Still exists. Charles loved to be loved, and London for him was an irresistible pot full of sweets where before there had been only one in his life – herself.

The Old Man had died on midsummer's day, of a seizure, at the bloodstock market in Leeds. His had been a heavy hand, but when he was laid to rest in the chapel there were that many glum faces in mourning among the staff as if he'd been much loved. For now, they knew, Charles was free to leave Clawfell. 'But you will come with me to London, Lisa,' he whispered, caressing her hair, which always excited him to lust.

Clawfell Grange was to be shut up, perhaps forever. Only a caretaker and a gardener would remain. Everyone else was dismissed, even Mrs Parkinson, although after a lifetime of service they had nowhere else to go; only Mr Crane the butler was sent ahead down to London to prepare Lockhart House.

During the excitement of the last days at Clawfell, Charles could hardly bear her out of his sight. She could not refuse him, but she feared that their secret was almost common knowledge. Jane would not speak to her, Mrs Parkinson turned her broad back on her. 'Some of us won't even have bread to put in our mouths, but one of us will have a nice warm bed to go to – for a week or two.' Lisa dropped her head. *For a week or two.* She wished she could have explained that it was not lust between them, but love. But somehow, she could not.

Lady Henrietta knew. Her eyes . . . lingered on Lisa. But there was no hatred in them, or even envy at a parlour-maid's place in her husband's affections. Lady Henrietta saw a young girl so ignorant of the ways of the world that she dreamed of marriage, but Lady Henrietta knew her position was safe. She knew what would happen. The expression in her cruel eyes was not even pity. It was enjoyment.

All Lisa saw of London was what she could see from the train as they arrived, rattling over points for mile after mile, seeing ranks of chimneys pouring smoke though it was high summer, past stinking tanneries and knackers' yards, church spires and endless dirt, and endless houses. The third-class guard laughed in Lisa's astonished face. 'Nawce, innit! Cheese an' crust, dun spec the trine ter tyke yer dahn the Mall all la-di-da, do yer?' Lisa shook her head. She didn't understand a word.

And so she came to London.

Lockhart House was a tall dwelling that together with lots of others looked over a place called Regent's Park in north London. Lisa worked in the basement and slept in the attic. She had to buy a new uniform. Apart from that she did not go out. Her work took her little into the public rooms and never outside. London remained unknown to her, a huge, foreign, intimidating world as far beyond her understanding as the canyons of the moon, shining, swarming, stinking, frighteningly full of life.

From her window she saw gentlemen bowing to one another with elaborate manners in a street of sheer chaos:

cabs, carts, drays, dogs, traction engines, workmen with shining muscles and bloody blisters digging holes, shouting filthy jokes, gulping water or beer from stone pots they swung up on their elbows. It was all so different. She felt like a living person watching the pounding machinery of heaven and hell.

Curates preached morality in reedy voices, but beyond the railings she was horrified to see men and women openly lusting. Ladies strolled between them with parasols and little dogs. Stern nannies marched behind big black perambulators. Children played, but not on the grass, which was forbidden.

Prostitutes touted for business on the pavement. Lisa lay awake at night listening to their drunken screams. She kept the casements tightly closed. Yet the gentlemen, both their neighbours and passers-by, seemed not to notice anything. She could not understand why not, for it was common knowledge that this country was the most moral in the world; everyone said so.

She saw little of Charles. He was rarely at home, arriving back very late from his Club, but her tummy swelled nevertheless. She ignored it; she didn't think about it; she wore a tighter corset, but finally she had to face the fact. After the house was quiet she went down into the cold hall – it was almost the end of October – and waited for him to return. A grandfather clock tocked as slowly as a heartbeat. Even the traffic died away. A dozen times she nearly ran away. At last she heard the key and Charles stood there, tall, black cloak, tails, white tie, detached collar, eyes staring.

'Lisa.'

'Sir, I am with child!' She wept; she could not stop. She had rehearsed what she meant to say and it had gone, she could not remember it. She could only tell him the truth. 'I am carrying your child.'

He closed the door and walked across the marble hall to his study. He turned on the electric light and beckoned her. She went past him and stood in front of the overstuffed sofa that faced his desk. He swung the door closed and walked around behind the sofa to his desk. He sat, opened a drawer, uncorked a bottle of whisky or brandy, and poured a glass.

'Now, Lisa, what is this silliness?'

'Sir, it is not silliness—'

'So, you have got yourself *enceinte*,' he stated coldly.

Her belly. She nodded. He drank. He did not ask her to sit.

He said: 'Why are you bothering to tell me this?'

Lisa was horrified. 'It is your own child, sir!'

'Rubbish,' he said instantly. 'That is a slanderous, scurrilous accusation.'

She thought she would faint. She felt behind her for the sofa. She heard him say, 'Sit down before you fall down.' She sat on the hard leather. He had made her feel dirty. Beautiful paintings personally selected by him hung along the walls, each with its own electric light. 'You aren't the first maid to get in the family way and blame it on your master,' he said distantly in the difficult-to-follow southern accent.

'It was that day on the moor.'

'What day?'

She *knew*. She put her hands over her ears but could not shut out his dreadful words denying it. He spoke as though this most singular and precious event of her life was so regular and casual in occurrence that the Master had to be protected by the Law of England.

'You cannot sue me, the master of the household . . . you have no redress . . . even if I were to admit paternity, which I certainly do not, my liability would be limited to a payment of eighteen pence a week.'

Two loaves of bread!

'Charles, I love you.' Perhaps saying it would bring him round.

'Oh, Lisa, really.' Men were proof against that.

'You said you loved me too. And you did,' she added defiantly, 'I know you did.'

He finished his drink, then stroked his moustache with his long fingers. He laughed. 'Let's forget all that, Lisa. Put

51

it all behind us, what? You're a good girl. Have a drink.'

'No, sir.'

'Shall I tell you what to do?'

'Tell me the truth, sir.'

'Take a bottle of gin from that cabinet, Lisa, and go and have a nice hot bath.'

What did he mean?

'Get rid of it,' he smiled. 'The problem disappears.'

She felt as though he had stabbed her with a long curved knife. She loved him. She had hoped that she had got through to his kindness, but there was nothing there. He carried nothing inside him.

She tried to stand up, shaking her head. 'No, Charles, I won't do it.'

'You'll do as I say.' He raised his eyebrows.

'No.'

'Don't be so pigheaded, Lisa. Oh really – I've had enough of this—'

She shouted: 'You loved me and I said, "Do you love me, do you love me," and you said yes! Yes, yes, yes! And our child at that exact moment came into my tummy. I felt it!'

'You are overwrought.' He looked bored. She had seen that look before.

'I felt it,' she wept. 'I *know*.'

'I can't trust you,' he said sadly. 'I shall have to ask you to leave. Come on, Lisa, don't take it so badly.'

'How can you be so cold to me, Charles?'

'There are reasons.' She thought: He's going to blame it on Lady Henrietta. *She hates you, Lisa, and this is the price I had to pay. Have you seen the expression in her eyes? Enjoyment.* But he merely said: 'You are dismissed. You know what my advice is, Lisa. It won't hurt. I shall tell Crane to pay you two months' wages in advance, on condition that I don't see you again.'

She turned back. 'You loved me once,' she said. He had no answer to that.

On the last day of October, she acted as decisively as she could. She went to a pawnbroker's and bought, for 7s. 6d., an unredeemed suitcase, without which she understood it would be impossible to obtain a lodging anywhere. She wore her Sunday-best dress and topcoat with her tightest corset beneath. There were many boarding-houses, streets of them, each with whited steps up to the front door and identical styles of gloomy curtain hanging heavily in the parlour window, and the same smell of stale food. None of them would take her. Finally she grew desperate. She lied. She wore her mother's wedding ring and said her husband was away, an officer in the army fighting for the *uitlanders'* right to vote in South Africa – she had studied a copy of *The Times*. Every officer was a hero.

Mrs Grinling's gaze softened. Lisa said that she had been nursing her grandmother, but that now she had died after a long illness. Her shame was taken for grief.

'My dear, how terrible for you.'

Lisa sensed that still something more was needed.

'I can pay you two months' rent in advance,' she said.

And so Lisa came to that oasis of ostentatious respectability on the edge of a wilderness of poverty and decay, Mrs Grinling's boarding-house, Lisson Grove, Marylebone. She felt like a criminal already. A corner of a kitchen cupboard was given over to her food, but she could hardly bring herself to eat. She heard that one of the lodgers was a retired military man, and she was terrified that he would start to question her. Mrs Grinling ran a tight house: no more than three inches of water in the tub, lights out at ten, and the wearing of shawls was not permitted.

During the day Lisa sat in a chair by her attic window, looking out over the terrible views of Lisson Grove. It was a wasteland of crooked roof-lines. It crawled with people. When the Railway built Marylebone Station they evicted the people who had lived on that land and they had nowhere to go. They went to Lisson Grove. They were outcasts – like her.

During the night she lay under the coverlet of her bed holding her tongue between her teeth, sometimes fully clothed, not sleeping but living in a nightmare. One day her secret would be found out and she would live in Lisson Grove. There was nothing she could do to avoid it.

And her baby grew, and grew, and grew. She knew Mrs Grinling was going to find out sooner or later. Lisa felt as big as a ship. She didn't walk, she waddled. It seemed that Mrs Grinling must notice, but she did not. She didn't even notice Lisson Grove, which was hidden behind lace curtains in all the downstairs rooms. Lisa realized that she had been successful in her lie. Mrs Grinling classed her as a respectable person, and during the Black Week in the middle of December she almost overwhelmed Lisa with sympathy. The Afrikaners had smashed the British army with three major defeats within a week, at Stormberg, Magersfontein and Colenso, killing more than three thousand.

Lisa's lie started to run out of control. Had her husband fought in the battles? She did not know. Mrs Grinling knew, of course, that there had been no letters. She took this very sadly and tried to embrace Lisa in her soft flabby arms, which of course Lisa dared not allow. 'No!' Mrs Grinling understood the reason for her grief. She prayed for his safe return from South Africa.

'I pray for you also, my dear. You're looking peaky, ever so. Now you mustn't worry . . .'

Such kindness. Lisa came close to breaking down.

And her baby grew. It felt that the other lodgers' eyes must be fixed on her enormous tummy, that they couldn't miss it, it felt as big as a Christmas turkey carried in front of her . . .

She wanted her baby. Yet each morning she woke up hoping that he would somehow have disappeared, evaporated. She was so afraid.

At Christmas one of the guests was a sharp young traveller, Mr McAllister, who could not get home to his mother in Scotland because of the weather there. He noticed Lisa's condition: she saw it in his eyes. He said nothing then.

However the next morning, when she went into the parlour, the old major did not return her greeting. He turned his back on her. She pretended to stay for a little while, looking at a newspaper, then fled and stood on the stairs with the back of her hand to her mouth. She felt the narrow walls closing in. She climbed slowly to her little slanted room at the top of the house with its dark view of Lisson Grove, and waited, sitting on the edge of a hard chair. She did not have long to wait. Soon she heard Mrs Grinling's ponderous footsteps on the stairs, and then her wheezing breath. She never knocked, just opened the door and came in. If one objected, why? What did one have to hide? This time Lisa opened the door before she could.

'My dear. I wish to speak to you on a serious matter, ever so.'

'Yes, Mrs Grinling.'

She stood aside. Mrs Grinling bowed her head beneath the lintel and came into the attic. From the way she looked around her, with her eyes gleaming in the flabby face, Lisa felt immediately that she was regaining possession, mentally checking the inventory, and with each measuring glance Lisa's heart sank further, until she felt that her little room was no longer her own. One water jug with pink flowers, one porcelain washing bowl with a blue rim, one chest of drawers with a chenille cloth . . . Lisa tried to hide her trembling hands. Mrs Grinling said:

'How long have you been *enceinte*?'

That word again. Lisa wanted only the truth, no more lies.

'Mrs Grinling, I am pregnant.'

The landlady looked away. One wardrobe with six wooden hangers, a mirror screwed on the inside of the left door. One, two, three, four, five . . . six.

'How long have you been in this condition?'

'Eight months and a few days,' Lisa said honestly.

'So you knew when you arrived.' One bed with bolsters, underblanket, sheets, two plain Witney blankets, a coverlet. Lisa pushed herself between Mrs Grinling and the bed. It was still *her* bed while she was here, and for a moment they locked eyes. Mrs Grinling added insult to injury. 'When did you say your dear husband left for the war?'

She's right, Lisa thought, *I deserve it*. 'I have no husband. I am unmarried.'

'You deceived us.'

'I'm sorry. I had to.' Mrs Grinling looked shocked. 'You would not have taken me in otherwise.'

'I would not!' The landlady stared from the window, seeing nothing. 'You are shameless, miss.'

Lisa threw herself on Mrs Grinling's mercy. 'I am desperate.'

'Deservedly so.' Mrs Grinling shrugged off the appeal. 'You cannot remain, of course. This is a respectable establishment.'

'Mrs Grinling—'

'You will have departed by eight o'clock tomorrow morning.'

Lisa felt an agonizing movement in her tummy.

'But I have nowhere to go!'

Mrs Grinling's eyes lit up with sweet victory. 'You should have thought of that . . . first.'

Lisa pushed her out of the door and gave herself up to the dreadful pain. She pulled herself to the bed. When it ebbed she lay chilled to the bone, staring into the dark. Her mind ran in frightened circles. Blind panic. She could see nothing that was a way out. But there must be.

She sat on the bench in Regent's Park for hours, getting her nerve up. Lockhart House had been repainted in cream, with white window-frames, and shone prettily in the sun. Smoke slanted from the chimneys. Sometimes she walked to keep warm, then came back to the bench, watching through the railings. A dray delivered milk to the tradesmen's entrance at the side. A housemaid, who could have been Lisa a few months ago, came out and swept the steps, then polished the front door and the brass knocker, returning inside without having looked away from her work once. The postman, who had delivered soon after Lisa arrived, brought the second post as the church bells struck eleven. Charles had not come out.

She picked up her suitcase and came out of Regent's Park clutching her old coat around her. The roadway was busy. She had to push past a hurdy-gurdy man with a bright little monkey shivering on his shoulder, a sandwich-board man prophesying the end of the world and a couple of drunken girls with their heads slumped together. Then she slowly mounted the steps.

She knocked on the door with the freshly cleaned brass lion's head. Crane opened it. His blade face hadn't changed – then she remembered that it had only been a couple of months. He remembered her.

'You!' he said.

She stepped inside. 'I've come to see him.'

'You can't come in here. Orders.'

But it was too late. The same old marble hall; the seat where she had waited, the same grandfather clock, its tocking quieter than she recalled. But this was day, and the traffic was very heavy.

'Who is it, Crane?' called Charles's voice from the study. She walked across the hall. Trembling, she said:

'It is I.'

'Lisa? It is Lisa, isn't it? My God. I didn't recognize you for a moment. Hell.'

He wore an Eton blazer. His moustache had been shaved off, which made him look younger and less mature. He stood in front of the fire swirling a concoction of dark liquid around a glass. He noticed her looking at it. 'Hair of the dog that bit me,' he explained. He hesitated, then put it down without drinking it. She felt hatred stab through her body like an electric current and she wanted to throw his glass in the fire and break it. On the other hand she wanted to gently remove a curl of cotton fluff she saw on his lapel, and see him smile. Her fingers were no longer chafed red, the nails cracked and dry: after two months her nails were beautifully long, and her fingers were whiter and finer than his.

He said: 'I thought I wasn't going to see you again, what?'

'Sir, I'm so frightened.'

He said lightly: 'Have you done nothing about it?'

By *it* he meant her baby. Their baby. He gave her a look as though he was accusing her of laziness.

'I think he's going to be born, sir.'

57

'*He*? You've decided on the brat's sex already, have you, Lisa?'

'Men don't know what women know, sir.' Her voice trembled.

'Oh, really.'

She wanted to shout at him. Instead she repeated in a very low voice: 'I think he is going to be born, sir.' *Help me!*

'It's nothing to do with me.'

That made her really angry. She hissed: 'You seduced me.'

He looked angry too. '*You* seduced *me*. Seductress.' She could not have been more surprised if the floor had opened under her feet.

'No, sir!'

'That's exactly what you did to me, don't deny it!' he cried furiously. Obviously he couldn't believe what he said; he was trying to put her on the defensive. Or was he serious? She closed her eyes for a moment and felt herself swaying.

'At least you admit that what happened between us did happen.'

'Don't be so damned insolent,' he shot back quickly. 'I don't admit anything, certainly not to you.'

'Charles—'

'Don't call me that!'

They both fell silent and after a moment he picked up his glass and drank from it. Then he looked back at the fire as he spoke to her, glancing at her for an instant at the end of each sentence.

'Lisa. There are certain facts of life. I believe that . . . they say that . . . the place for you to go is the Embankment. There's no danger, Lisa, it's very simple.'

'What are you talking of, sir?'

He coughed. 'It's a thing like a knitting needle . . . a long spoon.'

She bit her fingers. 'But he's alive. Sometimes I can feel him kicking.'

'Don't be disgusting. Oh, damn it, Lisa, don't look at me like that! Why are you making a mountain out of a molehill?

Is it some sort of perverse female pride? Why do you keep coming back?'

'I know I need help.'

'Then, Lisa, have it induced. You just drink some sort of bitter cordial, like soda-pop, and that's the end of it, they chuck it in the river.' Brutal, but he spoke the truth.

She began to weep. She could not help it. His feelings were so different from hers.

'What do you think everybody else does?' he said in a high voice. 'The world is full of poor unfortunates in your condition.' He added: 'Lisa. Stop it.'

She was a woman. She was not supposed to have feelings. She wiped the tears from her eyes. 'I cannot believe that you are speaking to me like this.'

He poured himself a brandy and tossed it back. He turned towards her with a smile. 'I see, it comes down to a commercial transaction.'

She thought: *We are so far apart. He did love me, and perhaps still does – he would not have talked to me at all otherwise. When he speaks, I hate him. What I really want, I suppose, is for him to agree that he is the father. That he will not do. I have nothing and I cannot make him understand. We're trapped: he is what he is; I am a housemaid standing before him. If only I could touch him.* But Charles was already moving, reaching smoothly into an inside pocket, bringing out a slim leather money-purse, which he opened.

He selected ten coins, counting them for her benefit, as though she could not. He took two quick steps and pressed them into her hand. They felt very heavy. Very tempting. *We can end your trouble*, they said.

'I give you that sum out of charity, without prejudice. Is that clear?'

She stared at the gold coins. Money for the abortionist.

'Crane!' Charles called. She heard him pouring himself another brandy. She heard the door open. She heard his voice: 'She's leaving.'

'This way, miss.' She found herself following Crane's back, not to the front door, she suddenly realized, but to the side. A cold draught blew in as he opened it. Then she was holding her coat around her with her free, cold hand as she descended the steep concrete steps. 'Thee forgot this, lass,' Crane called, not in his butler's professional accent but in his own native voice, the warm, comforting tones of home. Her suitcase came tumbling down past her, dislodged by his foot. Had it been full, it would have been deliberately burst open . . .

She didn't know where she walked. She was not walking *to*, she was walking *from*. Her mind was blurred with anger. She was enraged. She had been treated like an object. *We can end your trouble*. Yes. She wandered blindly. Did she walk towards the Embankment? Or away from it? She did not know where the Embankment was. It could be around any corner. The coins seemed to sweat in her hand. Ten pounds. Blood-money. But she could find herself on the Embankment. She might say yes! She could end her trouble. *Yes!*

She leaned against the window of a high-class ladies' outfitter. She felt very thirsty and weak; she might weaken. In the window was a mannequin dressed in a cape, a beautiful cape. She found herself inside. 'How much is the cape in your window?'

'Madam will look exquisite in it—'

Lisa bit her lips. '*Please*, how much?'

The assistant raised one eyebrow. 'It is nine pounds nineteen shillings and sixpence.'

Enough. Her baby was safe from Charles. She threw down the coins he had given her onto the counter and wiped her trembling hands. A pain had started in her tummy and she felt dizzy.

'Madam wishes to wear the cape now?' The assistant came back from the window.

'Yes.'

'And sixpence change.'

'No!' Lisa cried.

He did not understand. 'Madam is too kind.' He bowed as he opened the door.

She snatched up her suitcase and got out into the street. Light, colour and men's voices dizzily assaulted her. She thought she would be sick, but no one seemed to notice her, or to care. '*Here we go again!*' someone jeered. The stink of horses and manure and smoke was sickening. She found herself staring at a drowned woman, until the salesman looked at her hopefully.

'*Nice 'n' hot, piping hot, who'll buy my nice hot chestnuts?*'

Men swarmed around her, unloading cargoes from vehicles all over the road. They jostled her aside, and one man shouted:

'*Go away, madam! Move on there!*'

She thought: *You bloody men. Leave me alone. Help me. Look what you've done to me.*

The pain released her a little, and she walked. The town went on and on. It got dark, and still she was not in the countryside. All she wanted was a quiet place. A man followed her, she was trapped. He said: ' *Is it worth a bob to you?*'

Lisa wept. She had thought that she was past weeping, but she couldn't help it. She remembered Charles's voice shouting: '*You* seduced *me*! Seductress!'

Mr Simmonds said almost the same thing: he called her a prostitute. They were all the same.

'*Go and throw yourself in the river. That's all you're good for.*'

Charles wanted her to kill her baby. Mr Simmonds wanted her to kill herself. She was determined that the last place in London she would go would be the Embankment or the river.

She crossed the road and found herself standing by a long trough in beautifully worked stone:

METROPOLITAN DRINKING FOUNTAIN AND CATTLE TROUGH
ASSOCIATION

THE EMBANKMENT

So this was the Embankment. And this was Father Thames, fittingly awash with sewage. Paying for the cape with every penny she possessed had not bought her freedom; and dreaming of the free winds of Clawfell only brought her through the sequence of events that led her here. However hard she tried she could not break free. There was no escape.

She crouched and opened her suitcase. She left her old coat in there, and a second-best dress; took out her mother's wedding ring, worn very thin, shamed by her but not hers to give away, not even to Father Thames, so she slipped it on her finger.

And a blue headscarf. The blue headscarf that Charles had given her, that she had held against her heart. Now she hardened her heart and left it where it was.

From the very bottom of the suitcase she pulled out a little teddy bear. Even now, just looking at him brought a smile to her face. He was very battered, with only one eye, and stuffing leaking out of his ear, but still he had the red felt collar around his neck with his name so patiently sewn into it by her grandmother for Dad when he was a little boy, all those years ago: Mr Benjamin. Her mother's ring; her father's name. These were the only things that mattered.

She closed the suitcase and drew a deep breath. She swung it in her hand, then threw it out as hard as she could over the river. A moment later she heard the splash.

'There!' she cried. 'There's your sacrifice, Father Thames.'

She had won; she had thrown away not her life, but her old life.

Lisa walked away from the Embankment.

2

She thought: Now I have no choice. Somehow, my baby will be born.

And what will I do then?

She did not know where she walked. It was all new. The names were meaningless to her: a place called Aldwych with road works everywhere, frozen in the dark, and looming signboards showing where a great new road, Queensway, was to be driven from somewhere to somewhere else through the houses; Fleet Street, then an iron railway bridge echoing above her with her footsteps; from a big building with a dome came the sound of people singing hymns; then the City, vast Greek buildings with pillars, all silent, all in black, and no lights showing.

She walked along a broad highway called Whitechapel Road, E., with a swarm of black side streets off that made her gasp with the stench. Later there were men with black beards, in long coats, and the smell of strange foods cooking. She kept on the main road, which was almost empty of people now, a few horse-trams and buses, a last dog-cart going home, then none at all, just shut-up shop fronts shrinking away through pools of yellow light towards the country.

In the country, amongst the trees and bushes, she would be safe.

The pain returned. It was much worse than before.

She thought: It's starting to happen. I'm going to have my baby. Here.

Here in this great, broad street.

She wrapped her arms around herself until the pain passed.

On the other side of the road she saw a gap in the buildings. She crossed over and went down a turning of small, neat houses. It wasn't a slum. There were people everywhere here. They all seemed to know each other, calling to one another, joking and singing. A group of men staggering in the middle of the road laughed, their arms around each other's shoulders, then looked at her, saying nothing. She was a stranger. She walked past them close to the wall, with her eyes cast down.

The pain came in long slow waves, an irresistible tide.

I'm going to have my baby with these men standing around me, looking at me.

There was nowhere to go, just more houses, more people wishing each other Happy New Year. She staggered as some men she had not noticed shouldered past her into a pub.

Then she saw that beyond the glaring windows of the pub the buildings ended. There were no more houses, just a line of railings with darkness behind them. She walked towards them, but must have been unable to hide her distress because she saw that she was attracting the attention of a man in the pub doorway. She turned away, but too late. He came over, swaying slightly, and laid a solicitous hand on her shoulder.

'You all right, love? Where's your husband?'

'She's drunk,' came another voice. 'Go home, you bloody drunk.'

You bloody men, she thought, *you did this to me, can't you see, can't you understand? Help me!*

Someone slurred, 'Glad you aren't my mother, you bloody drunk cow. Ought to be ashamed of yourself.'

'Come on,' said the other voice, 'we all know it's your treat at the pub.'

'They're starting the fireworks,' said the swaying man. 'Look!'

The waves of pain ebbed a little. She clung to the railings to hold herself up. Distant fireworks starred the sky with patterns of silent light.

The men had gone away.

She guessed that she had another few minutes, though perhaps very few. It was less each time. That irresistible need to push, push, *push* was growing stronger.

She had the terrifying feeling that next time something inside her was going to break.

She leaned against the railings. It seemed that every house door gaped open, and the roadway was full of people cheering and singing. They danced under the gaslights, wild with joy. To her it seemed so menacing: their black shadows, their cries, and the glare of fireworks coming closer, growing so bright that she turned away. Above her head, illuminated in the glow, she saw the Board of Charges advertising Tower Hamlets cemetery.

She crept along the railings, one by one, feeling the rust flakes scour her fingertips. On the far side of the street was a horse and cart. She saw a firework flower in the horse's eye, silent petals of colour mirroring the fire in the sky.

And the pain came again, brutally, overwhelmingly. She half-fell against the gate latch, the bars swung aside, she stumbled in. The gate clanged shut behind her, drowned by the detonation of fireworks. The pain rose and rose inside her until she screamed. But silently. She had bitten down on her hand.

Her feet crunched on the frozen grass between the rows of cold, mouldy headstones. A firework flared and briefly revealed a tremendous dark horizon, the spires of London stretching around her under a fall of manmade stars from the vast, empty sky.

What do you do when no one in the world will help you? *You help yourself.*

'I'll do it by myself,' she hissed. She forced herself to be calm, not to give up to blind panic. She forced herself to be quiet, although she wanted to scream. She summoned all her strength. She fought the pain. Her fingers trembled. She felt blood trickling from her lips. 'I can do it,' she whispered, 'I can do it without you, by myself.'

Cold evergreen leaves rustled against her face. She pushed into the laurel bushes. The place was full of them, quiet and dark beneath. She was surrounded by tortuous shapes of gnarled bark. She lay down, her head on a root, then raised her knees and tunnelled through her petticoats.

At the centre, her fingers found that her petticoats were soaking wet, and she felt a fresh flush of terror in her agony, but it was water, not blood. Her body was opening in rhythmic waves, and she was forced apart by blows of terrible pain until she feared that she would die.

I won't die.

Oh, you bloody men, she thought.

'I can do it,' she hissed, 'I can do.'

She pressed down against her belly with her hands, then stuffed them into her mouth to stop her scream, then pressed again.

Everywhere was quiet now, only her stifled screams muffled inside her skull, her blood hissing in her ears.

'I can do,' she panted. '*I can do.*'

Suddenly the mass of contractions paused and she lay inert, listening to herself gasping like a steam engine. There was dead silence everywhere, broken only by her gasping breaths. Yet the city was not asleep – London never slept.

A contraction seized her that was so intense that her body arched then bent round like a prawn. Her toes curled down until her nails jammed into the soles of her shoes. She opened her mouth in a helpless, endless scream but she had no air, her lungs were sucked thin and dry, her windpipe was a vacuum, and in that intolerable moment she felt the magic: smooth and round, the head of her baby sliding into her palms.

'Oh God,' she cried, 'oh God, help me.'

She held her baby's head. She was nearly exhausted. Colours raced across the sky. Bells were chiming in her ears. She writhed weakly, feeling her insides still pushing, her hands gently pulling the baby's shoulders – no, she saw by the flare of a firework, *his* shoulders – then his little legs and his tiny, perfect feet followed in a rush, and she lay with him.

She lay with her son listening to him cough and mewl while Bow Bells clanged to welcome the twentieth century. The cord that still connected them bothered her instinctively until she nibbled it through and tied it off close to him with a sewing knot that her fingers remembered flawlessly; she wrapped him in petticoats to keep him warm. She did not allow her mind to dwell on the horror that must soon come.

Can you look after him?

No, no, no.

Do you love him enough that you can let him go?

She could not keep him.

She was exhausted to the marrow of her bones, drained of her strength, so tired that she was desperate to sleep the clock round, but she stayed awake, cradling her son and not allowing the future any existence. She had this night with him, this one night, and she wanted to live it so that she would never forget one single moment of him.

'Please,' she prayed, 'let them love him as much as I do.'

A few slants of gaslight came through the leaves. His face was pink and screwed-up, and the blemish under his right ear was almost hidden by his quite impressive amount of fine, curly hair. She touched his fingers and toes, counted them: they were all exquisitely there, yet so tiny, so miraculous, so helpless.

'I love you,' she whispered. 'Never forget, I love you.'

She had given him the gift of life; now she gave him the only other gift it was in her power to give, the teddy bear, Mr Benjamin, which her own mother and father had given to her. Now she gave it to her son, who had no father, or a mother that he would ever know.

The city had been growing quiet a long time now. A few cabs sounded from the main road, toffs going home. Once she heard drunken shouting, breaking glass, then laughter. Later a man came round dousing the lamps, and she realized that the air was filling with a soft grey light. Soon she could see the railings beyond the grey grass, the grey buildings sleeping, with only a yellow glow here and there, under a dull whitewashed sort of sky.

She felt tired out of her mind, but she knew what she must do. First, she kissed him.

Then she cuddled him tight, kissing him again.

Finally she gathered her aching bones and stood, swaddling him carefully in her petticoats, wrapping him in the cape for an outer layer, and settled him gently into the crook of her arm. She followed the path back to the gate. It opened with a piercing metallic squeal – and she gasped as his eyes opened for a moment, flew wide and seemed to stare directly into her own, piercingly blue. It hit her like a jolt of recognition. Why, she thought, he *is* me, really a part of me, my son.

Then he was asleep again.

Shivering, for she was dressed now only in her dark Sunday-best dress, she walked towards the main road.

The Mile End Road was wide and deserted; a single cat fled across the glittering frost between the pavements; then nothing moved except the woman in the dark dress. She moved very slowly, as though reluctant to reach her destination. In the shadows her dress made her almost invisible, and the shadows beneath London Hospital were very deep. The frost on the ten steps caked them up like layer

67

after layer of grey icing sugar towards the porter's office. She saw no fresh footsteps, but the shift must surely change soon.

She kissed him for the last time. He had gone very pale on the cheeks, almost a blue colour. Was that normal? He did not open his eyes again.

She laid him down where he would be safe, above the top step, and walked slowly away backwards. She watched from behind a corner.

Nothing happened.

What about that blue colour? Was that a very bad sign? Perhaps he was cold. Perhaps he was hungry.

She waited.

Perhaps he was dying? She came half round the corner. She'd take him back, she'd look after him herself somehow, anything was better than letting him go – then she heard footsteps tapping closer along the road, and slowly drew back.

A plump middle-aged nurse arrived to start work. She walked in the roadway, presumably to avoid the slippery pavements. She had a round, kindly face with cheeks as pink as plums. She was dressed in a long blue coat with several buttons dangling, obviously forgotten. She carried a battered brolly in one hand and a sensible brown bag in the other.

She stepped gingerly onto the pavement, and seemed to gain confidence when she didn't slip. She took the steps two at a time, then saw the baby. She stopped, then went slowly over to it.

'Goodness gracious.'

She looked around her carefully, examining the shadows, the corners and doorways, but obviously saw nothing. She bent down to the baby.

'Oh my goodness gracious me.'

Then she looked around again, saw nothing again, and carried him inside, out of sight, and the morning was empty.

Part II

THE FOUNDLING

Chapter Three

1

But surely I can remember him?

Nothing, only the ringing of her alarm clock.

Edith Rumney realized grimly: *It's the start of another day.*

She reached sleeplessly out into the dark, patting her big hand across the bedside table, fumbling for the button that silenced the clattering bell. Her heart softened. Dear Benjamin's clock, one of the last of his effects that had been left to her, roughly tied up in brown paper by the Fever Hospital porter all those years ago and handed to her together with a few other remnants of his life, of a whole life they had not had.

The note of the bell changed to a harsh death-rattle as her hand came down. She had hardly slept. She was not one for celebrations, she had no one to celebrate with; it would not have been proper for Mr Pungle to have visited her here at home. The fireworks had kept her awake, and then the dead silence had not let her sleep.

Today was the twentieth century.

No dreams; no Benjamin. How distant he seemed. *My love died in the last century, and I never loved another man, and I never will.*

Why can't I remember him?

She swung her legs out of bed and lit the candle, looked at the clock. It was now a very old clock, she realized – ancient history, tarnished brass, the glass face cracked. Five o'clock; the day hardly born. She shivered, and stood.

Her bedroom was very cold. Ice streaked the inside of the window glass and she could see her breath. Crossing resolutely to the chest of drawers, she turned the photograph there chastely to face the wall and poured icy water from the pretty rose-coloured pitcher into her cracked green washing basin. She'd broken the rose-coloured basin years ago and never been able to find one of the same lovely hue. But had she tried? There had always been so much work to do. A nurse had no time for pretty things for herself, no time for anything but working to help other people.

And then one day it was the twentieth century, and your time had passed away.

'Don't be silly,' she said aloud, shivering at the horrid caress of the icy water on her body.

She dressed in her uniform – except her white apron and starched cap, which were in her brown bag. Her greying hair hung loose. She snatched a brush and hairpin and quickly knotted it back into a severe bun. She stared at herself in the mirror.

I'm forty-seven years old.

Edith thought: I'm starting to look like an old nurse, too. Like the others. Look how easily I frown. I used to have lovely deep brown eyes – Benjamin said – now they look hard and grudging, as if the world was a tiresome patient always whining for another glass of water. Look at the lines around my mouth – so proper, so severe. But I'm not like that!

I'm still a young person inside.

She reached across the dresser and turned Benjamin's photograph to face her. Time had not aged him; he was forever young, never changing, a fixed point for her to cling to. He had been dead for twenty-two years. But there had not been a day that he had not been with her.

I remember—

No. Suddenly she noticed how faded his photograph had become. His eyes were almost white, his moustache a pale blur.

She could not see his eyes, and his face had no expression. Glancing over her shoulder, troubled, she went down the narrow stairs and hesitated in the tiny hall. She was thirsty. The kitchen range was cold, and she would need time for church. But of course Peter Pungle would be happy to make her tea at the Hospital – he always was. Dear Peter. She wondered what he saw in her.

Outside, the gaslamps looked dim, and the sky was as smooth and dull as old whitewash. She crossed the frosty street.

Lichfield Road was a 'good' turning. Most of the houses belonged to Lord Tredegar. Edith, who had been a gentlewoman of private means before she *went off the rails over that man*, as her parents long ago put it, was rare in owning number 35 outright. Edith looked back. Most of the long flat-roofed terrace had brightly coloured doors with the steps whitestoned daily. Women who didn't whitestone, like Mrs Kent next door, soon got the message from their neighbours; the whole street of two or three hundred people knew each other by name. But Mrs Kent didn't fit in; Edith didn't understand why people tolerated her. Mrs Kent primped herself to the nines in fine clothes, and she had fancy ways, but she wasn't houseproud, and her husband Harry was a poor sort. Edith looked up at her window. The curtain showed holes where she had allowed the moth in.

About half-way down the street was the Lord Tredegar pub, dark and cold now, with a few empty bottles and used fireworks littering the stones outside. The red-brick bulk of the Coopers' Company Grammar School facing the pub was also quiet and dark. Edith hesitated at the gates of the Holy Trinity Church, staring through the cast-iron rails at the frozen fountain and the huge black church. This morning she felt reluctant to enter. Holy Trinity seated over a thousand in its vast draughty interior, but never did, and this morning Edith couldn't face being in there so alone.

'Hallo, Miss Rumney.' She felt a small, warm hand slipped into hers.

Edith was not surprised to be called by her formal name. Everyone in the turning did; she was a person of standing in their community. She smiled and looked down at the young girl holding her hand.

'Hallo, Mo. How did you know it was me?'

'You were talking to yourself.'

'First sign of old age.'

'No,' said the blind girl, squeezing her hand, 'you've got a young voice. Can I walk with you to the corner?'

'Come on then.' As they walked Edith looked down into Mo's white, unconcerned eyes. The child's face was bruised down one side again. Her mother drank. Often the babies of drunkards were born blind, as were the babies of those with the social disease, though in fact Mo had been blinded during birth by the midwife's forceps. Midwives were supposed to wear an official uniform now but the girls hated them and stuck with the old five-bob midwife they knew in any turning, or best of all with Mum.

'Are you at the Hospital even today, Miss Rumney?'

Edith nodded, then said: 'Yes.'

'I'm working the Mile End Road today.'

Edith felt that there was so much grief in the world this day that she was determined not to ask Mo what she meant. She prayed it was not selling . . . herself. Edith preferred to ignore such a horrid idea. Let it be begging. Mo's Mum had a terrific hold over her, naturally; even gin was not as cheap as it was. Edith could not bear to hand over the sixpence in her pocket, fearing what it would buy.

'Promise me you'll have some food for lunch,' she insisted in a strict voice as they parted. Perhaps it would do good.

'Yes,' lied Mo.

Edith came out of the turning and walked past the now miraculously silent Grove Road tramway depot down to Mile End. As she turned along the broad, deserted thoroughfare a single cat fled across the glittering frost. No cabs waited at the Burdett Road rank, the shelter was empty, and from the doorway of the subterranean urinal below it came the hiss of untended burst pipes. The young trees lining the road, protected by iron palings, reached up stiff and white; the protruding, tin-roofed shop fronts dwindled into the distance looking ramshackle and dead. The paving slabs seemed so treacherous with frost that Edith crossed out and followed the tram-lines down the centre of the road, a rare luxury. But still she was not happy.

'Don't be silly,' she told herself firmly, and made herself swing her brolly happily as she walked, listening to the lonely, hollow echo of her footsteps.

Are you happy?

Yes, I'm happy!

She thought helplessly: Benjamin is dead. Why can't I accept it? I thought I was past all this at my time of life but nothing changes. What is wrong with me? I gave up everything, love, children, a family, for the work I had to do, and I should be happy, but it isn't enough. I still love him after twenty-two years and I don't know why. He hasn't even got a face. God help me, I've forgotten what he looks like . . .

Older than me. Well into his fifties now. White whiskers, white hair . . . no, I'm remembering my father, all white, red face, but for him a black cassock, ascending his pulpit in West Dereham parish church to admonish us, his family, his flock in a reedy voice . . . Benjamin would be as old as my father was. But not the reedy voice, surely. One can imagine him with his baritone admonishing his patients though, browbeating them for their own good on the virtues of sanitation, however, rather than the perils of sin . . .

But what did he look like?

I remember . . . very long hair by today's standards, and black curls to his shoulders, and at the front a stiff winged collar jutting up under his chin. A long black coat. Well, terribly old-fashioned really. Of course, he didn't seem so at the time. A god.

I was nothing, he was everything to me. His profession was mysterious – a doctor, way down in London – his parents opposed it apparently, saying the Devil lived there, but he was so strong-willed and determined – and I, I had hardly been out of my parents' home, let alone travelled beyond the county of Norfolk! We met, of course, through the adjacent ministries of our parents. He was convalescing at home, for his constitution was weaker than his spirit. He talked at me most learnedly; he probably found me very silly. Yet he must have found something about me or my plain, unworldly ways pleasing. Everyone said that I amused him, and he was generally considered rather serious by nature. He assured me seriously that the Devil did not live in London. I loved him. I adored him. I worshipped him. He was everything; I sensed a whole world opening within me.

But then he was called back to the Fever Hospital – an outbreak, though fortunately limited, of the cholera. He had to stay to tend the dying; in those days we didn't even know the difference between typhus and typhoid. We corresponded by letter. We never wrote *I love you*.

Now we never can. Those words would have lasted me a lifetime.

At last he travelled up to Norfolk to ask my father's permission for my hand in marriage. I knew; all of a-flutter, I was pretending to tend the roses in the vicarage garden. I could see their heads nodding through the study window as they agreed terms. Then Benjamin came out and – I remember his smile. I remember his blue eyes lighting up. He bowed seriously and his voice trembled, I remember his baritone voice trembling as he asked me to marry him. Did I utter my breathless affirmative? Yes, yes, for he kissed my cheek. Oh. I remember. . . I remember . . .

He died, quite slowly, over the next three or four days. It may have been five. Yes, yes . . . and five nights. Is it possible for a girl in love not to sleep for five days, for five nights, for her to keep the man she loves alive by the constant strength of her will alone? Yes, I kept him alive by the power of love. I nursed him without sleeping for five days and nights, willing him to live. Then I slept, and when I awoke he was dead. The deadly typhoid infection had been circulating in his bloodstream even as he had proposed marriage to me. Even at the moment I said *Yes*! I had not the strength or the constancy to save the man I loved from the death multiplying inside him.

I did not weep. I was no longer a girl. The dead are dead, but I could keep his memory alive. I would not spare myself again.

I gave up my life of ease. I travelled to London and was inducted as a lady nurse, with no qualifications, simply by answering an advertisement. The London Hospital needed me desperately; I gave up my life to doing Benjamin's work, to his memory. I was a woman. I had the strength.

Are you happy?

Yes, I'm happy!

Then why couldn't she see his face?

Why couldn't she even remember what he looked like?

Edith crossed the Regent's Canal. A mass of barges were tied up below the lock gates, the tarpaulins that covered them stiff with frost. Smoke came from the cranked iron chimneys, and she caught a whiff of frying bacon. Her mouth watered involuntarily.

Next to the People's Palace was St Benet's Church, soot-blackened bricks rising to a square brick tower with a spire. She entered through the arches and sat in the cold gloom. The Reverend Cryer was not there this early, only a sexton she did not know, standing with his arms wrapped around his black shoulders, puffing white breath. He watched her for a while, then went out.

Edith sat alone in the empty church.

The pew was hard.

She sat very upright with her feet flat on the floor, and her brolly propped against her thigh. Then she sat with just the toes of her shoes resting on the flagstones and her forehead in her hand. Slowly the brolly slid, then before she could reach out, clattered to the floor. The echoes died away. Finally there was silence. There was no one here; no one at all.

She had to face up to that.

She got up and looked inside her coat at her watch – a nurse was now allowed to wear a timepiece with a second hand on the top slope of her chest, just below the shoulder, instead of concealed in a clumsy pocket somewhere. 'Goodness!' She was still more than half a mile from the London Hospital and she wouldn't have time for the comforting ritual of her morning cuppa in Peter Pungle's little office if she didn't get a move on . . .

Outside, the sky was piercingly blue now and the light hurt her eyes.

In his office, Peter Pungle didn't feel guilty at all. You couldn't imagine English women posing like this, not like these saucy little French tarts who looked like they enjoyed doing it.

He dreamed of unlocking Edith's hard heart, of having her love him.

Of course he knew these pictures were posed, he wasn't born yesterday. It wasn't real love. They knew the camera was there all right. Girls in their corsets; you could see their legs, even down to the dimples on their thighs. These keyhole photographs were genuine imports. Peter's brother-in-law Joe worked in the Spitalfields market and they came in from abroad with the winter vegetables. Expensive, but you could get things cheap if you had the pull. He had the pull. You bet. Down at the Market they still talked of Pete Pungle's fists with bated breath. Young Joe had said as much. 'Yes, they still talk about that fight, Pete. When you laid old Ben Flanagan out.'

No, it had been old Finnegan.

'Come on!' Joe said. 'It's a dodger for the French art. Ten bob. Ta.'

Peter called after him: 'But his name was Finnegan.'

'They still talk about it,' waved Joe carelessly.

Now Peter smiled. The one with her breasts hanging out of her dress as she combed her hair made him go hot inside. He leaned back in his creaky hoop-back chair. You could actually *see* them. The whole things. He tightened his fists. Abruptly the kettle began to scream.

With a grin of frustration Peter took his feet off the table and crossed to the stove. His back gave a twinge – he must have been sitting wrong. It was catching him out more often lately, even though he was an official person now and his responsibilities required less physical work.

Carefully he took the lid off the huge brown fire-clay teapot that he had left to warm on the edge of the stove, opened the spout of the kettle, and chuckled. It drove Edith round the bend when she saw him doing this, just pouring the boiling water straight in. She said you had to use a dash of water to warm the pot first. That was just being a bloody female in Peter's opinion, just doing it that way because they'd always done it that way. Peter preferred to use his manly intelligence and think of a better way. Let's face it, putting a drop of boiling water in the pot to warm it first is downright tedious, and half an ounce of water doesn't do a thing to a couple of pounds of fire-clay. But unless the water in the pot's blazing hot for quite a while, the tea won't brew properly. The really clever idea was *to warm the pot on the side of the stove while the kettle heated*. Brilliant idea. By the time the kettle was ready the pot was thoroughly warmed! Would women do it? Not a chance. Even Edith, who was an enlightened woman, an educated woman, who most mornings tried to arrive early so that she had time to come in here for a cuppa, couldn't get used to it. 'It just is not the done thing, Mr Pungle – that's all.' This had been a couple of years ago.

'Look, if you're going to slag my ideas,' Peter had grinned stiffly, 'you can at least sound friendly about it and call me Peter.'

A couple of years at least; maybe three, or four. Even then he'd wanted to be more than friendly with her. He kept grinning at her, frightened of losing her, and she always smiled back, not understanding.

He wriggled the lid off the teapot and peered inside. Today's brew would have to be a re-hash of yesterday's. He'd spent all his money at Christmas and run plumb out of the old rosie lea. He looked up.

He thought he saw a deeper shadow move in the shadows beyond the bright reflections of himself in his window. For a moment it frightened him, then he realized that it was outside, on the Hospital steps. Edith already? Couldn't be, tea wasn't ready. He decided that if it was some lazy good-for-nothing bugger dumping rubbish on his steps he'd give them an earful.

But now he saw no one.

*

Outside the church the pavement was horribly slippery. Circling the Vine Tavern, which stuck its weatherboarded front almost to the gutter, Edith Rumney nearly fell and decided to take to the road again. The pavements were a solid mass of shabby signboards stretching out into the distance. Frederick Harding's Eel & Pie House. The Blind Beggar. Then the offices of the *Jewish Times*. The Whitechapel Working Men's Temperance Club, the Joe Lyons café, Abraham Schapiroff M.D., Physician & Surgeon. All were shut up and dark, all so lifeless today, so anonymous, as if the world had ended. She walked past the varnish-maker, the boot-maker, the trouser-maker, the synagogue, the corset-maker, the hat manufacturer and the London Hospital Tavern. The London Hospital appeared ahead of her.

Staring, Peter swilled the tea around in the pot. He was a manly looking man, not the sort another man would tangle with lightly, short ringlets of grey hair, thin eyes, high cheekbones that caught the sun in summer, a long mouth and a very heavy jaw. He'd had a Roman nose when he was younger but now it was pulped. He had a bulging cauliflower ear from his days as a fighting man. Very wide shoulders, plenty of muscle there, no fat. They stuck out like corded bands, still iron-hard, more or less. He braced them and said: 'Watch out, Flanagan.'

When he was a boy he'd been in bother with the police enough. Finally the bridewell sergeant looked from the bruised constable to Peter, still panting, and said: 'Lad, you can go one way or the other. You don't have to be on the steep and slippery slope down like this. You got the speed and you got the muscle. But have you got the sense?'

'For what?' demanded Peter, tightening his fists.

The sergeant, who also had the sort of face a man respected, the face of a prize-fighter, said, 'To pull yourself up by your bootlaces.'

Peter thought about it. 'You can't do that.'

The sergeant said: 'Lad, you got to.'

Right there in that mucky bridewell Peter said the

cleverest thing he ever did say. 'You tell me how,' he said, 'and I'll do it.' The sergeant wrote out the address of Premierland, the rendezvous of all East End boxing enthusiasts. 'You're a bright lad,' he said. 'You tell Bob I sent you.'

Peter was bright; and he found there was more money in prize-fighting than in organized boxing, and more respect in the street, because you didn't wear the cissy gloves, only bandages strapped over your knuckles to stop them splitting. The bouts were illegal, like cock-fighting or badger-baiting, and sometimes they went on for thirty punishing rounds. Only a knockout could end them, or throwing in the towel, cowardice which finished a man's career more brutally than broken bones.

Winning was not knowing where you were and hating, hating and smashing at the face in front of you and not feeling the horrible injuries to your own face, and smashing at his bruises and blood as the other man staggered away from you, and smashing into his nose and lips and teeth and tongue with your fists until he went down. Winning, winning was everything. The next day, nothing was said, but everyone knew you were a hero. You'd got to the top.

During a contest in Limehouse or somewhere Peter's opponent leapt forward between rounds and punched him in the back. The pain was excruciating. Peter carried on. But then in the next round he was getting so smashed up that it felt like little bits of his brain were exploding. He did the sensible thing, the terrible thing, he threw in the towel.

He was finished. He lost his friends, and he was the sort of man who liked to feel he had friends around him. Wouldn't even talk to him.

He was a coward. He'd lost his nerve.

He had to get a job. Getting a job was impossible. He got desperate, got hungry, used his intelligence. He was bright, very bright. He went to Spitalfields Market, weaving through the narrow alleys of piled-up crates and porters groaning under their loads until he saw one of the foremen, recognizing him by the official-looking bowler hat.

'I need a job, sir.'

'No jobs today.' The brown-coated foreman turned busily back to his clipboard.

'I'm a better man than any of the men you've got here, sir,' Peter said. He had already marked his prey, a heavy-drinking Irishman, big but sodden.

'You mean Ben?' The foremen glanced at Peter's hands, then his shoulders. 'I wouldn't let him hear you talk like that, chum.'

'He's a ball of fat,' Peter said in a loud voice. A crowd gathered. 'I'll fight him for his job, sir. If I win, it's mine.'

The foreman said: 'What do you say, Ben?'

'I'll tear him in half,' rumbled the big man. 'Ben Flanagan never backed away from a fight yet.' He slowly stripped off his shirt and before he could bunch his clumsy fists Peter hit him beneath the heart, following up with a roundhouse left and they all clearly heard the *click* of cartilage as the jaw dislocated out of its shallow socket, an old prize-fighter's trick which led to almost paralysing muscular pain. Ben staggered, howling. Peter landed a straight right and that sent the big man windmilling back over a crate.

'You've got the job,' the foreman said calmly. 'But I'll keep Ben on and get rid of one of the little ones,' he shrugged, pointing. Peter remembered that someone said:

'But Jim's got six kids.'

'I'm not a bleeding charity!' the foreman shouted. 'Peter, shake hands with Ben Flanagan and get to work.'

Or was it Finnegan?

He found a spoon and mashed the tea-leaves around in the pot. Of course, your strength didn't last forever, but he'd seen that coming and made his plans accordingly. He was as bright as ever though his head buzzed sometimes and he got confused, but all in all he was in the clover here at the London Hospital. A Head Porter didn't have to carry much to fulfil the responsibilities of his position. He had to have the right official attitude. He had to be obeyed by the men under his charge. But it was lonely and he had few friends apart from Bill Madeley – some people still remembered that Limehouse bout. He looked forward to Edith's visits.

She was the only one he could talk to, she had class. She didn't have to work here. Everyone else who worked here was East End born and bred, and they worked because they had to. Most of the nurses didn't like him much, and he despised them, dirty ugly cows, pauper nurses. Edith was different. She was hard, and bright, like him. And she talked to him here in his room without looking down on him. One day more would happen. Grinning, he wondered what she looked like without her clothes on.

He put the teapot on the edge of the stove to keep warm while he rinsed a couple of mugs in the Belfast sink. It was a good room, better than the lodge, which was icy in the winter. He didn't have a proper place to live. Here he had the stove and the sink, a table with drawers in, and two chairs . . .

Someone knocked on the door, much louder than Edith's knock. Frantic. Peter scratched his face with his fingers. That couldn't be Edith – she was always as cool as a cucumber. 'All right, all right! You'll have to wait a minute,' he called. He wasn't a man who liked to be rushed. He looked for the tea towel to dry the mugs on. Edith would come soon, and he liked to try and be friendly by showing her he cared about details.

He found the tea towel and started rubbing the mugs. The door rattled again. Yet the notice outside said plain as punch, Knock Once And Wait.

'Wait!' he shouted.

Edith's footsteps had begun to echo as she came under the shadow of the huge, soot-yellow façade of the London Hospital. The glass collecting boxes were full of used tram tickets. The clock pointed out the time with frosty hands. The steps rose towards the shadowed arches. She stepped gingerly onto the pavement, but it wasn't as slippery as it looked. Swinging her brolly, she took the steps two at a time, and entered between the pillars into the deep shadows beneath the arches, stepping by a bag of rubbish someone had thoughtlessly left there.

And stopped.

She stared.

The bag of rubbish moved slowly, like something struggling to be born. Edith shivered. There was something frightening about those tiny movements: the sense of something using all its strength, yet achieving almost nothing. Yet trying.

She stepped slowly over, one step at a time. It was a cape, a beautiful cape, black or a very deep navy blue, lined with satin. A month of nurse's wages could not have afforded that cape. Yet the inside was padded with cheap white material. She thought it was petticoats. And swaddled deep within the petticoats was a baby.

Edith Rumney said: 'Goodness gracious.'

A dead baby; its face was blue.

Who had left the poor thing here? She looked around her carefully, but there was no one. The fiend had deserted her baby, left it here to die and run away.

Or left it here to live?

Edith bent down. It was still alive. Again the cape gave those weak wriggles that were so frightening. 'Oh my goodness gracious me.' The baby struggled to live. There was not a moment to lose. She could not let it die. But where was the mother? The foundling had no mother. Edith looked desperately around her, saw nothing, no one. She could not wait. It was now or never.

She picked the baby up, held it against her, and went inside.

She heard the door swinging to and fro behind her until it closed.

She stood stock-still on the red linoleum of the lobby. Corridors painted a dull institutional brown branched away from her in every direction except back the way she had come. Every other way took her down, down deeper into the hospital. Somewhere a man was screaming. From another direction she could hear the rattle of tin trays and bedpans. From somewhere else she heard voices approaching, calm professional voices, reasonable voices, coming rapidly closer.

The baby was dying.

But what if it had been left here to live?

What if the baby *lived*?

She hesitated for one more second.

She ran to one side, to the brown-painted door set in the wall. She tried the handle but it was locked. She knocked with the knuckles of her free hand, staring over her shoulder, then back at the door. It remained closed. She knocked again.

There was a sign screwed on the door by the handle, neatly painted and official-looking.

MR PUNGLE
Head Porter
Knock Once And Wait

She bunched her hand into a fist and beat on the door panel.

From the other side came a muffled voice saying, 'All right. All right!'

She gave the bottom of the door a kick for good measure. The voice shouted: '*Wait!*' But then she heard his footsteps, and the jangling of his keys.

'All right,' Peter called. People never learnt. He knew who this was. This was some bloody person who'd been in an accident and was in a gibbering panic for the Outpatients' Department. The signs were perfectly clear but they didn't bother to read them. He wished he got a penny every time he told someone the directions. People. The doctors made them wait for hours when they did get there. The door rattled violently in its frame. 'All right!' he bellowed. He pulled on his blue serge jacket and official cap, went to the door and unlocked it angrily.

'Can't you read the bloody notice?' Peter shouted. Then: 'Edith!'

He was so startled that he just stood there, gaping, blocking the doorway. She looked over her shoulder again. The lobby was still empty but a shadow was looming in one of the corridors. The warm bundle she held to her bosom writhed weakly. 'Please,' she whispered, 'I must come in.'

85

His big ugly face just stared at her, as if his brain had turned off.

Perhaps he wouldn't let her in. Perhaps he'd see the baby and say: *That mustn't come in here.* Where else could she go? The Outpatients' Department, built like a factory warehouse with its roof of criss-crossed girders four storeys high, its ranks of long wooden benches, and no heat? She shuddered. Or Maternity, bare board floors, iron cots, and classical pictures on the walls, cheap landscapes by Claude? And someone would tell Matron, and Miss Lückes would come, Nightingale School, with roars of rage, and they'd take the baby away . . .

'What – but –' Peter sounded wholly confused.

Then he said, ' 'Course you can, Edie, come in, no need to ask.'

2

He'd never dared call her that before, although he'd often thought about it. *Edie.* Now it had just slipped out. He let her push past him. 'What's the matter?'

She went to the table. 'Please, shut the door.'

He shut it without taking his eyes off her.

She laid a bundle of something on the table. She normally had a brolly and a brown bag. Something terrible had happened. She'd been attacked. If he found out who the bastards were he'd kill them. She was panting and her face was flushed, her eyes were sparkling. What a lovely deep brown they were.

He said: 'Has something happened?'

'Yes,' she said.

He said: 'Oh Christ, Edie, I'll kill them.'

'I think something wonderful has happened. I think something wonderful may have happened to me, Peter.'

He crossed to the stove. 'I've made the tea. Sit down, calm down. I wish I'd made better tea for you. I don't know what happened to me over Christmas.'

'Peter, do you believe in miracles?'

'No,' Peter said. 'I think you only get what you work for.

86

And you've got to be lucky to get work. Why?'

Her voice began to shake with emotion. 'I think what I prayed for all my life without knowing it may have happened to me.'

'What's that?' He was pouring the tea. He had to calm her down.

'I think— Look what I— My—' Her voice was breaking up. She was almost in tears. He could hardly hear a word. She put her hands to her eyes and began to turn. He put down the tea quickly, just in time. She flung her arms around him and burst into tears on his shoulder. He didn't know what to think when women did this. He didn't know what to say. It had never happened to him before. She was soft. Her cheek was hot and damp against his neck as she shook with sobs. He could feel her breasts moving against him. 'There there,' he said. 'Edie, Edie.'

She pulled away from him and squeezed her eyes shut. She clapped her heels of her hands to her cheeks. 'I mustn't do this. I must think. I must think.'

He stood there feeling alone, then reached out and tried to take one of her hands. She snatched her fingers away. He shrugged and finished pouring the tea. If she didn't need him, he didn't need her.

Edith picked up the bundle. 'I've got a baby.'

'Oh my God,' Peter said. He felt warm tea flooding down his trouser leg. He was holding the pot crooked.

Her voice changed again. Soft. Yet he sensed a hard edge in there that hadn't been there before. He'd heard a bit of it in other women in the hospital sometimes, down in Maternity. Victory. They'd fight anyone to keep what they had gained, too. Their mucky, mewling little lumps of flesh.

'Look,' Edith said.

Peter looked cautiously. A dead baby. Pale as death.

'Where'd you find it?'

She sat in front of the stove, cuddling the bundle to her. 'Outside,' she said.

'I didn't see it.'

'You weren't looking.'

He put his head on one side, then crouched beside her. He said, very gently, looking into her face: 'Edie, what are you doing?'

She stroked the dying baby's face. Her finger was longer than its face.

Peter said: 'Edie, you can't do this! You know that.'

'I was looking. I found him,' she said defiantly. Victoriously.

'You don't even know it is a him. It's just a baby.'

'I know.'

'His mother was probably a scarlet woman.'

'I don't care.'

'She must have been an inhuman bitch. And the baby's got the same blood. He won't be that size forever, Edie. Think what he'll grow up like. Give it up.' He realized she wasn't listening.

'Get me some milk,' she said. He obeyed automatically, picking up the jug on the table, then put it down.

'I'll get Dr Hutchinson from Outpatients,' he said. He went to the door.

'No!' she said. 'He doesn't need a doctor.'

'Edie, that baby is blue!'

'*My* baby.'

'It's dying, Edie.'

'He's cold, that's all. All he needs is love, and tenderness, and care. Where's that milk? Put it on the edge of the stove to warm, please.'

'Edie, you're only a nurse. He needs a doctor. A man who knows what he's doing. Professional attention. He should have those things stripped off for a start and then the doctor will plunge him in a hot bath—'

'That's the last thing he needs!' she flared. 'He doesn't need any of that – the shock of hot water – or to be rubbed with olive oil to make him look clean and neat – or bound up in tight bandages to stop him moving – he doesn't need an iron cot or a tag on his toe!'

'Then what does he need?' shouted Peter.

'Love,' she whispered fiercely.

'Just holding him to you?'

'Yes.'

'Just rubbing his fingers and toes like that, is that all?'

'Yes.'

'And you're not even going to take him out of those filthy indecent clothes?'

'Look at this cape. It's natural wool. It's kept him alive so far. Why add to the trauma?'

'He's mucky,' Peter said. He sounded revolted by the idea of birth; at least, out of his depth. 'He's still got blood and things on him.'

But of course, she realized, the poor man *was* out of his depth. He had no idea what she felt. How could he? It was a whole area of human experience denied to them. So much of it was instinctive. His brain didn't even contain the machinery to imagine her feelings with. And she felt so much! Now he was saying, 'All right, if you won't have Hutchinson there's a doctor coming over from St Thomas's this morning. Maugham, a surgeon. He'll help you.'

She said: 'Is the milk warm yet?'

He jerked. He'd forgotten it. It was still on the table. He picked the jug up. As he went to the stove he felt he had to say something, because she was saying nothing, just caressing the baby's tiny hands to warm them. It was as if she'd forgotten him, and he suddenly felt alone, excluded. He wanted her to give him some of her attention.

'I hear there's going to be another Public Health Act this year,' he remarked. 'The hospitals are going to be forced to open without charge to all Londoners who need them. Free. We're going to be crowded out. There'll be no end to them now. Sick people. We got enough sick people already if you ask me. People take anything they can get, don't they? Oh, Edie! You got everything, Edie,' he begged, 'don't throw it away.'

She dipped her finger in the milk, making sure it was warming properly.

All she seemed to care about was that bundle in her lap. At least its face was pink now. Yes, he thought, a pink face for a son of a scarlet woman. Why had the bloody cow dumped it here? On his doorstep? Why not somewhere else? These street women might be stupid and corrupt and hateful, but they knew the ropes. They could have their baby in the Workhouse, but of course very few did, because then it was on record, and also the Whitechapel Workhouse had a deliberately frightful reputation – not like good old Bill Madeley's place down in Poplar, a Workhouse which was always being had up by ratepayers' associations with accusations of extravagance to the inmates. Which were not true. Extravagant as hell. A hell on earth. Why, that was the idea of the Workhouses, wasn't it? Only fair and right, saving the taxpayers from the poor.

He nodded.

Or if the woman just wanted to get rid of an unwanted mouth quickly for some reason – probably so she could tell a husband desperate to fill the mouths they already had that she'd simply had a miscarriage – she could throw it in the river. Peter frowned. Here was the mystery: Did the mother mean she wanted it to live? Yes. In that case, why not leave the baby on the straw the Magdalen Homes or the Foundling Hospitals put outside their doors? Or in one of the unofficially recognized places – the Salvation Army had a policy of looking under tarpaulins that had not been tied down. All this was well known. Yet . . . He shook his head. No. There was no explanation. The woman must have been exceptionally stupid.

He watched Edith dripping warm milk from her clean white handkerchief into the baby's mouth. The baby sucked noisily, their faces very close together. Edith made little noises to encourage the baby. Peter stood in front of Edith and drank his tea noisily.

'You can't keep him,' he said.

She looked at him and smiled. But somehow he knew she was not really looking at him. She only had eyes for the baby.

The baby gurgled. Peter coughed. He was an outsider in his own room.

'You're throwing away your career.'

She didn't answer.

'You can't bring him up alone. Think about it.'

She was smiling secretly. 'What?' he demanded.

' "Him",' she said victoriously.

'He, she, it, I don't care, you can't keep him, it. Edie, you can't. Your career. Your life. Your neighbours.' He wouldn't see her again. His job took up twelve hours a day.

'Peter,' she said, 'I'm forty-seven years old.'

'I'm sorry,' he blushed, 'I didn't mean—'

'It's my last chance.'

'There are plenty of foundling charities. There's a Barnardo Home just off Albert Square—'

She stared at him. He saw something changing within her. It was frightening to watch. He knew that she'd made up her mind now. He knew that if he said a word she'd storm out of his room. She'd just pick up the baby and go, and nothing would stop her. Peter felt dwarfed. He held up his enormous, misshapen hands in defeat, almost obscuring her from his view.

'He's mine,' came her voice.

He dropped his hands. He didn't say anything. He tried to think of something soothing to say. He thought: She doesn't know what she's letting herself in for.

'He's mine,' she repeated. He realized that she did know. She held up the cape. He saw the baby's face in the dense folds of dark material, very pink and healthy-looking now. She pulled the folds away. The cape unfurled and slipped down to the floor, leaving the baby swaddled in loose swirls of white chambry, and something yellow, Peter caught it as it slipped out, a teddy bear, very old, very battered, with a name embroidered into his red collar.

'Mr Benjamin,' he said.

She stared at him. She had gone absolutely pale at the name Benjamin. Then her face flushed.

'I shall call him Benjamin!' she said. 'Yes! *Yes*!'

What a long name for a very little baby, Peter thought, but then he saw the utter, ruthless determination, and an expression of . . . *love* – was that what love looked like? was it really so absolute, so terrifying? – stamped into Edith's features. It frightened him. Peter Pungle decided to swim with the tide. He stretched his mouth into a grin.

'Lovely,' he grinned, stroking the baby's head, thinking: *I'll call him Ben, like Ben Flanagan who I knocked out.*

'Don't touch him!' Edith snapped, and Peter snatched his hand away, startled, submissive, feeling awed and intoxicated by being so close to her love, and wanting to share in it.

As she held up the baby the rest of the swaddling fell away and there it was, the innocent penis, still stained with the marks of birth.

'He's mine now,' Edith said. 'I've got him. I'll never let him go.'

Peter grinned at her, then he grinned at the baby. His heart was racing, wondering how he could turn this to his advantage; played for time.

'What else are you going to call him?'

She said contemptuously: 'Where are we?'

He didn't get her meaning. He grinned helplessly.

'London!' she said. 'I shall call him Benjamin London. It's everything we know about him. Everything he is.'

3

Edith Rumney sat at home in the dark with him. Only the firelight moved. She felt intensely peaceful. Ben London was sleeping with the drowsy light playing in slow patterns on his face, with one small, incredible fist curled against his mouth. Together their shadows swayed on the ceiling of her hot, small front room, a giant woman cuddling her tiny baby gently to the pillows of her breasts. Tomorrow the wet-nurse, Annie Saltings from Tredegar Square, a woman who had lost her own baby, would come again. *If only I had milk to give him*, thought Edith now, imagining how his puckered mouth would feel gulping at her nipple. *It would give me almost unbearably intense pleasure*. She closed her eyes. *If only*. She could not give him milk, but she could give him love. He would have love; she would drain her life dry to give it to him, wring it out, every last drop; he would have everything. She would give him such love that he would grow up glowing with her love like an invisible aura, he would never forget. He was hers. He was loved. He had everything. He would never want for anything. Edith was determined that he would have the happiest childhood a child ever had.

She remembered how Peter grinned that morning, when she told him.

'What's the matter, Peter, have I said something funny?'

'Well, you make 35 Lichfield Road sound like the Garden of Eden,' he had said, still grinning.

'Yes,' she had told him eagerly. 'I can do it.' Heaven; heaven on earth, she and her child together.

Ben London would grow up in her little home and he would think of her as his mother (although she would *insist* that he called her Aunty, because that was only proper) and he would come innocently running to her when he grazed his knee, sometimes running to her when there was a word he couldn't understand in a book, or running to help her carry back the coal.

But all that was in the future. For the moment she had tonight with him, her first night, sitting in the dark in the red firelight with him, in her comfortable old armchair, at peace. In love. Cuddling her baby, her own baby, learning him, knowing him, loving him. She was so happy that her throat hurt, and sometimes her sight blurred and she felt tears on her cheeks.

Tomorrow she must worry about so many things. This morning Peter had gone on and on about how much there would be for her to do: a cot for baby, a perambulator so that she didn't have to leave him here while she walked to a shop, which she would have to do often now, clothes – a baby needed quantities of clothing, most of which she wouldn't have time to knit herself – and there would be the food, and the medical bills, and the shoes, and the house had to be kept warm with plenty of coal, and . . .

It came down to making ends meet.

And she had no job. You couldn't have a job and a baby.

'You'll have to take in a lodger,' Peter had told her confidently, leaning his hips against the Belfast sink in his office and crossing his arms. 'You could get five bob a week for that back bedroom, easy. Double that, with half board.'

'A lodger!' Edith had said, horrified. But it had to be faced. She thought of advertising in *Bradshaw's Railway Guide*.

'Careful,' Peter had warned her. 'You need someone reliable. Someone who could be useful about the place. Help out with the odd job. And there's the coal to be brought in. It'll all have to be done for the baby, won't it?'

'Yes!' How right Peter was. Now she kissed her baby's cheek. Tomorrow she'd have to think about all that . . . But not now. Tonight she had the firelight, and her home, and her baby, all warm and alone together.

'You're so lucky to have your own house,' Peter had said. 'I know. I haven't got a place. Still, you're going to have to mortgage it, aren't you? You need your money now, you can't have it all tied up like that. Locked up in bricks and mortar.'

'But I don't like the idea of my house not being my own home,' she had murmured.

Peter had shrugged. He had forgotten about it because at that moment someone had knocked on the door of his office.

Now, sitting dreaming in the firelight, she thought: No, no, I won't think about money now, I will write to my brother Marcus tomorrow. I'm sure he owes me tons of interest due under the terms of father's will. I've never pursued the matter before. I will. I must remember. Tomorrow.

The person who had been knocking on the door of Peter's office introduced himself as Mr Maugham, a surgeon from St Thomas's hospital. He had come to see a Caesarian section performed – a rare operation that no longer meant certain death for the mother, although it was condemned by many members of the public as unnatural and in defiance of the Will of God. While he listened to Peter's directions to the ward, Maugham's eyes fell on the baby. He had a sensitive yet cruel face, with the eyes set in it very far apart. They had flickered, taking in the cape on the table, the sprawl of petticoats, and the baby that Edith, then still in her nurse's uniform, was holding.

'Another one for Dr Barnardo's!' he had said cuttingly. He had a high, unattractive voice and a speech defect that stammered some words. He smiled tightly. She thought: *He can't know what it is to suffer, to love and have no one to love.* She clasped the baby to her. *Ben London is mine.*

Peter had interrupted tolerantly, 'You see, she wants to keep him, Mr Maugham!' A patronizing wink: some sort of man-to-man communication.

'Close the door,' Edith said furiously, 'you're letting in the draught.'

'I'm sorry, sir,' Peter said to Maugham, with another tolerant gesture man-to-man.

But Maugham's voice changed. He ordered sharply: 'You heard the nurse. Shut the door!' The young surgeon enunciated his words very clearly, as if he thought he was speaking to a punch-drunk imbecile; or perhaps he spoke in that sharp way to avoid the humiliation of his stammer. Peter looked startled, then obediently closed the door.

Maugham took off his gloves. Edith looked at him measuringly and realized: he *does* know what it is to suffer. The cruel look in his face is because of the cruelty that has been done *to* him – it is his defence against the cruel loneliness of this life.

Edith said: 'Would you look at him, please?'

Maugham put down his gloves and examined the baby. 'He has a small haemangioma – a red birthmark – under his right ear. Otherwise he seems free from defects, I sh–should say.' He smiled kindly at Edith.

Peter said, 'But she wants to give up her job and look after him.'

Maugham half-turned. 'Why do you object to that?' he demanded irritably.

Peter shrugged and said nothing.

Maugham sat across the table from Edith. His gaze softened. He got out his pen. 'The birth has to be recorded. Merely a formality, but a useful one. I recommend the sh–short certificate. Then we won't have to make any mention of the names of the parents, and he need not grow up unnaturally stigmatized by his illegitimacy.'

95

In other words, Edith knew, he would not be called a bastard.

'Thank you,' she had said gratefully. 'Thank you!'

When the surgeon had flourished his signature, *W. Somerset Maugham*, pulled on his threadbare gloves and left, Edith noticed Peter's attitude towards her change. He had obviously become convinced that she really would keep the baby, and he didn't try to oppose her any more. Instead of patronizing her, he tried to help her by anticipating the problems she would face. 'Who's going to carry the coal up? Who's going to repair that window, and the roof . . .?' As he reeled off a long list she began to realize fully what a great burden bringing up the baby was going to be for her, a woman alone. She saw how much freedom she had lost, and how difficult life was going to be for her from now on.

'I'll have to advertise for a lodger in *Bradshaw's Railway Guide*,' she said fretfully. Peter was nodding, so she saw that there was no way round it. But all types of people read *Bradshaw's*, she fretted. A monster might come to her house.

'Hold it a minute,' he said, 'I've got an idea.'

'What is it?'

'No, it wouldn't work,' Peter said sadly. He poured out a mug of tea. 'No, I shouldn't have said anything, Edie. Me and my big mouth, always speaking out of turn.'

'Go on, tell me,' she said eagerly. She knew that he was leading her on; and, knowing it, trusted him.

'You wouldn't like it.' His eyes flickered at her as soulfully as a dog's out of that wonderfully ugly face of his, and he was so obviously acting that she burst out with laughter.

'Peter, what is it! Don't keep me in suspense.'

'It's just that . . . I'm paying four-and-six a week where I am now, I couldn't afford any more than that . . . otherwise I could be your lodger, Edie,' Peter said in a rush.

She didn't like to mention that she had been counting on at least ten shillings a week.

'I could do the odd jobs,' he grinned. He was always grinning.

'Peter, that's sweet of you, but . . .'

'That sash window, the roof, carrying the coal,' he went

on quickly. 'I could have the back bedroom. I know it must be noisy what with the trains, Edie, but don't mind me. You have the nipper with you in the front room.' He uncrossed his arms, extended his big knobbly fingers, and caressed the baby's cheek gently, smiling.

She still hesitated. 'I'm not sure . . .'

'What's the matter,' he asked directly, 'don't you like me?'

'Of course I like you!'

'You've been coming to my office for years,' Peter said stiffly, 'drinking my tea, and I wouldn't like to think you hadn't wanted to, all those years.'

'Of course not—'

'I wasn't forcing you.'

'I know—'

Peter was still smiling and caressing the baby's cheek. Yet his manner was not paternal; he never took his eyes off her. She decided that Peter Pungle would be no competition for the love of her baby. Finally she nodded. 'I'll move my stuff over on Friday,' he said instantly. 'You won't regret it, Edie.'

And so she had walked home with her baby.

The flickering firelight had died away to a smooth, hot glow of embers now. Edith's giant shadow and Benjamin's little one no longer flickered on the ceiling. Edith slumped comfortably down in the armchair with him cuddled to her bosom, wrapped in her big soft arms. She was wider awake than she had ever been in her life. Her mind and body were a tumult of emotions. Benjamin was dead. Benjamin London would live forever. She watched over him while he slept.

This time, she promised, she would have the strength: she would have the constancy. She would not sleep, so that he could sleep. She could save him from the horror, the terror, the hate, the loss, the dreadful emptiness, and everything dirty in life, so that he would never suffer. Though only called his aunt, she would be much more than a real mother to him – his real mother had deserted him, betrayed him, callously left him to die. Edith's mouth set into a hard line. She would be *better* than a real mother. With her strength, with her constancy, she would save him and give him everything.

The long night faded into day. From somewhere upstairs came the familiar note of an alarm clock with a cracked glass face, ringing. It was the voice of the past. No one's hand fumbled in the dark to silence it. No one's fingers tried to muffle the bell. Gradually the mechanism ran down until it was silent.

The wet-nurse rapped loudly on the door. A new day had begun.

Chapter Four

1

He was such hard work! She had never imagined all the work! Edith swept back her greying hair as she bubbled his boiled egg on the black range. At least he didn't need to wear nappies now, although she did make him wear them, just in case of accidents. You couldn't be too careful.

She turned and looked at Benjamin lovingly. She wished Peter didn't call him *Ben*, which was not right, and he had a coarse way of saying it. Benjamin sat, not struggling any more, in the high chair. She had pushed the chair up close to the kitchen table to make doubly sure that he could not escape. She fondled his long hair. Being at the back of the house, her tiny kitchen faced north, so that it received no direct sunlight and was cold and dark, but now a train pulled out of the Coburn Road station with the sunlit windows flashing reflections brilliantly across the dingy room. She wondered fretfully when Peter would paint it, as she had made him promise faithfully that he would. She would have to have a firm word with that Peter again about his duties and responsibilities around the house.

Suddenly Ben – she called him that herself, when she was weak or felt depressed – bashed at his empty egg-cup with the teaspoon she had incautiously left out. Edith started guiltily. How could she have done! What other mistakes had she made? She tried to prize it from his tiny fingers. He looked up at her innocently.

'Ma . . .' he said. He was learning to talk.

'*No*.' she said at once, as always. Not mother. She had to

control him; yet it was a constant battle of wills. A grown woman against a baby: it should have been no contest. He seemed to know her weak spots instinctively, to sense where she was vulnerable. If only she really was his mother! If only he was really *her* Benjamin! She pulled the spoon firmly from his hand.

'Mama . . .' he said wilfully.

She ignored him.

Now he achieved the word: 'Mummy.'

Still she ignored him.

'Mummy!' he shouted joyously. At last she was goaded into a reply.

'No. Say, Aunt.'

'Mummy, Mummy.'

'Aunt Edith. Say, *Aunt Edith.*'

'Mummy!' Was it defiance, or just his playful boyishness? She let him have his spoon back.

Where did he learn that word? she wondered. *I have never lied to him. I have never pretended to him that I was his mother. Did Peter teach it to him while I was out?* She checked the clock. She believed in proper five-minute boiled eggs. Ben followed her eyes. He said:

'Eggy!'

She put it carefully into the egg-cup. 'Yes, Benjamin, here is your egg.' Then she held it back. 'What do you say?' It was never too young to learn manners.

'Eggy. Give eggy.'

'We say please, don't we.' She wasn't going to let him grow up like the other children in the street, who had no manners. She waited patiently: she would bring him up properly if it killed her.

'Please give me my egg, Aunty.'

She'd won. 'Good boy! Here is your egg. See the egg? Benjamin's egg. No, we don't hold our spoon in our fist. Let Aunty help.'

But Ben said, looking up her with those innocent blue eyes: 'Mummy.'

Edith was upset. *I have brown eyes. His look such a piercing blue, no one could mistake him for my son. No one in the whole street*

100

calls me his mother. Where did he learn the word?

'Mummy.' That terrible word. Edith hid her feelings. He was not really hers, and never would be. He had no mother!

Is it in his blood? she wondered uneasily. Does something in him somehow remember his shameful past? *No*, she reassured herself: doctors are certain that a baby is totally ignorant, a blank sheet of paper, knowing nothing, only what we teach him. So perfect parents bring up a perfect child! I speak properly so that he will speak properly, not learn the lazy dialect of the other children in this road. I behave properly so that he will learn the proper standards of behaviour for a young gentleman.

He knows nothing, remembers nothing.

'Mummy.'

Yet he says this word. He must . . . *feel*. He feels more than he should.

'Have you finished your egg now?' she demanded. 'It's time for your rest.'

He held out his arms. 'Give Mr Benjamin.'

'I'll give you Mr Benjamin when you're tightly wrapped up in your cot.'

'Mummy give Mr Benjamin.'

Edith told herself: it's just coincidence. He doesn't know anything. He doesn't know that he did have a real mother, and that she did give him that dirty old bear. He's just a baby. I mustn't let what I feel show in my face or it would upset him. Any more than I showed my feelings when Marcus's dreadful letter, admitting that he had spent every last penny my father left us, arrived in the post this morning. Lost, squandered, gambled, wasted. Although Ben must have sensed something, because he did begin to cry, though Heaven knows I honestly betrayed nothing. No, it was just coincidence.

'Mummy give bear!'

Edith gave in. 'Here you are, then.' She hoped he would grow up out of his love for that disreputable animal soon. Otherwise it would have to disappear.

He cuddled the bear tenderly. 'Mr Benjamin,' he whispered softly.

Watching him, Edith could not hide her true feelings any longer, hard though she always tried: 'I love you,' she said.

He looked up at her and she was struck by the feeling in his lovely blue eyes. *Love.*

'Oh, I do love you, baby!' she cried.

Love.

Edith held Marcus's letter. She was now poor. She accepted that; our Christ had not needed money or to own clothes and houses, only to have the use of them.

But the punishment was hard, with a little baby to look after.

Marcus was a man of ideas. Edith was proud of that in other people; he was weak, but she did not hate him. He had fallen in with a German called Ullwig who wanted money to build a factory to make ammonia – a revolutionary process for an endless supply of artificial nitrates that would transform farmland everywhere and make even poor land green. How nice, thought Edith. Marcus always had these grand, marvellous schemes. He had been a brilliant graduate of Cambridge and Rothamstead. As a practical farmer, he was a sad failure. Father had been wrong to force him into it; and now, it seemed, he was locked into it by tumbling land prices.

Edith sighed. She felt so sorry for Marcus.

She allowed herself a brief moment of hatred for Ullwig, who had stolen Marcus's money, then nothing, because to hate someone was un-Christian. She didn't blame Marcus at all for losing the money, because you couldn't blame a man for being what he was. She had been disloyal enough to think him weak, so it was her own fault that he had proved her right.

Very well, she decided, crumpling the letter. So it had come to this: to save Ben she would use her house as security for a loan. It was only a small sacrifice, and she would do *anything* for her baby. All she had to do was give Mr Brodie that scrap of paper called a Deed in return for hundreds of pounds, which she would use to bring up Ben properly; they would still be able to live here

102

cheaply. There was no need for Peter even to know.

She busied herself with the washing-up.

After Ben had finished his nap she put on her brown shoes and, despite the heat, the heavy brown coat and brown tight-brimmed hat that proclaimed her status – since she no longer wore a uniform – as a respectable person.

She dressed Ben in a miniature sailor-suit with sharp navy-blue creases and put him carefully into the big black pram Peter had brought back, for a price that was not quite as low as she had hoped, from his nephew who ran a stall in Petticoat Lane.

She felt as proud as a mother hen wheeling him down through the dusty turnings to the Mile End Road. Going into the branch of the London & South Western Bank, she spoke with the manager, Mr Brodie. Of course, no difficulty. It would be a pleasure to loan her two hundred pounds with her house as security. She gave them the scrap of paper; they deposited the money in her account. It was so easy! Mr Brodie could not have been more charming. She came out smiling, then went and basked with her baby in the sun on the grass beside the Regent's Canal lock, thinking no more about it. God was in His heaven and the sun swung along its ordered path in the sky, and she had secured the future of her baby.

Nothing could go wrong.

And nothing did. It had been such a little sacrifice that with the passing years she almost forgot about it.

2

Ben remembered.

The Queen was dead. He could dimly see, deep down in his brain, a memory-picture of the black flags hanging motionlessly from the gaslamps lining the Mile End Road. He remembered Edith's voice booming: 'Don't cry! We have a King now. Long live the King!'

The King made the red uniforms come home from Africa. Ben remembered Edith hurrying him past the old soldiers standing begging with tattered pride on the street corners of Whitechapel – she always did if there was something nasty. But often the men smiled back at him.

Ben wondered. Sometimes he ran away and watched them – but this must have been years later, because the gaslamps along the Mile End Road had been replaced with rows of ornate electric lights. 'Poor old douser's thrown out of a job,' Uncle Peter said. That was the sort of thing he always said, and Ben always looked quickly at Edith, because he knew she would be frowning to hear it.

It made her frown, too, when he called her Mummy, but it was so cruel when she made him say Aunt, because all the other children in the turning were looked after by their mothers. Ben knew Edith wasn't cruel. She simply didn't understand about Mummy any more than she understood about the soldiers, and that made him love her more. He called her as she wanted to be called, each time showing how much he loved her.

Aunt Edith approved articles from the *Times* for Ben to read to her, following his finger earnestly through each word: only four years (though to him that was nearly a lifetime) after the ending of the Boer war, the rebel leaders were being fêted as heroes in London. *Fêted* was a difficult word. Edith looked up smiling from the sampler she was embroidering, and said that it was a French word. Ben remembered Uncle Peter talking about the French. He wondered whether to tell Aunt Edith.

'We Brits always admire the people we beat,' a very old porter told Peter in the London Hospital Tavern. 'Except the French,' he added, and blew the froth off his beer.

'I like the French,' Peter said.

'I heard about them pictures,' winked the old man. 'Give us a look.'

'Not at your age,' Peter bragged. 'You'd have a heart attack.'

Ben asked: 'What's a heart attack?'

Peter nearly jumped out of his skin. 'What the – what are you doing here?' He clambered down from the great height of the stool and confronted Ben by bending right down with his hands on his knees. His breath stank of beer.

Ben knew how to get at Uncle Peter. 'Aunt Edith sent me.'

'She never did,' Peter said. Edith hated pubs; he always sucked a mint before returning home. 'You're a little liar – aren't you?' he added uncertainly.

'No I'm not.'

'Yes you are.'

'If she did know,' Ben said, 'she would have wanted you to come home.'

Someone said: 'Out of the mouths of babes and little children, Peter . . .'

Peter looked angry for a moment, then turned his face to the other old man and bragged: 'She's ready and waiting, see. She just can't wait for me to get back to her.' Ben ran: there was something horrible about the way the two men laughed together.

Later Uncle Peter bought him a sweet honeycomb and Ben forgot to tell Aunt Edith; she wouldn't have understood anyway.

Edith said that the King, who was in his sixties, had nearly died before he was even crowned, but a revolutionary new operation removed his appendix and saved his life. Queensway, the huge new road driven through slums in the West End, was renamed Kingsway in his honour. King Edward, who ruled a glittering court but who had little real power, but much influence, was said to dislike his cousin the German Kaiser intensely, and to prefer the French government. So an Entente Cordiale – nothing more than an agreement to be friendly – was signed between the two countries. There had been violence enough in the last century; being friends couldn't hurt anyone, Edith smiled.

Yes, that made sense. But then everything that Aunt Edith said made sense. Ben nodded. He understood. *Being friends is good*. Edith's smile broadened, and he glowed. A smile from her meant as much as the warm hugs that the other mothers in the road gave their children. No hugs; but of course, Aunt Edith was not his mother.

She educated him herself. Ben patiently followed his

finger: Kaiser Bill, now terrified of being surrounded, renewed Germany's Triple Alliance with Austria and Italy until 1914, and signed an agreement with the Turkish Empire for a strategic railway to join Berlin with Baghdad. Tirpitz persuaded the Reichstag to pass an Act doubling the size of the German Navy by 1920.

It was very boring.

Ben played truant with the noisy, dirty boys in the street. He was sure that Edith must really know that he slipped out when he was supposed to be studying. While the girls played hopscotch the boys started a game of cricket across the middle of the street using a broomstick for a bat, a rolled-up rag for a ball, and the water standpipe as a wicket. Later Maria Saltings smiled shyly at him, and as they sat on the kerb she showed him how to play jacks and how to make a drab old piece of string into a magical cat's cradle. Then the girls were called in and he lost his penny pocket-money to the bookie's runner on the filly Sceptre to win the Derby. It was wonderful! He had such a wonderful time that he ran home gasping with excitement, his jacket torn, his shoes scuffed, to tell Aunt Edith all about it.

She was furious that he had gone out behind her back – she really hadn't known – and sent him up to bed without any supper. 'I've been worried out of my mind about where you were!'

'But I was playing.'

'Go to bed!'

He lay with Mr Benjamin clasped in his sweaty hands to his chest. Darkness fell and the sound of children playing faded from the street. He whispered rebelliously: *I'd do it again.*

He meant it and he did do it again. The next time she caught him, Edith punished him as she would any other normal boy. She locked him in the wardrobe in her bedroom, or rather she just shut the door and it had no handle on the inside. She was sorry to do it, but it was for his own good, and it was better than letting him run wild like the other mothers did in Lichfield Road.

Because she was not his mother. Ben was not an accident

of birth. She had chosen him, she loved him, and he would be perfect.

It was as dark as Hell is in the wardrobe. There was no sound of Aunt Edith or from the street, nothing living . . . except the occasional scuffling of a mouse. At least he hoped it was only a mouse. Ben gulped, terrified. He knew from the *Just So Stories* that there were animals that lived in the dark who had big teeth to eat you up with. And he knew all about Hell from Sunday School. Cramped in the camphor-smelling dark of the wardrobe, he was frightened, and he needed to go out to the privy – the other boys were allowed to call the toilet the airey, but he never was.

Ben buried his head between his knees and sobbed quietly in the dark – quietly, so as not to lose face. He must take his punishment like a man. He wondered if men were ever locked in wardrobes. Uncle Peter was too big to punish like that.

Obedience. That was the key. If you were obedient, Ben realized, nothing happened to you.

It was unbearably hot and dark in the wardrobe, and the reek of mothballs made his head spin. Aunt Edith had called that she was punishing him because she loved him. Ben understood this. Aunt Edith was not his mother so she had no other way of showing her love. Each punishment was a privilege, showing that she loved him more; that she loved him enough to forgive him. Aunt Edith's goodness was like an unassailable beacon, and he understood it clearly.

But he did not understand Uncle Peter, who sometimes smiled at Aunt Edith with all his teeth like the *Just So* crocodile, and could cry crocodile tears too. He could manipulate his feelings, which Aunt Edith could never do.

Ben understood one thing.

Uncle Peter did not like him.

There was no reason for Uncle Peter not to like him, but sometimes, when Uncle Peter played teaching him boxing in the front room when Edith was out (Edith hated boxing), laying his great fists against the side of Ben's head, he started hitting him a little harder until sometimes Ben's

107

ears rang. Yet it wasn't a punishment. To Uncle Peter it was – *fun*.

Aunt Edith's footsteps approached. The door swung open and light flooded in, framing her smiling face.

'Have you learned your lesson?'

'No,' Ben said defiantly.

Edith knew how to deal with childish tantrums. She plucked him up in her arms and wiped his tears away, then carried him downstairs to supper. She made him eat his spinach down to the last mouthful, watching him, with love shining through her eyes.

Uncle Peter would enjoy the fun: chuckling with excitement, Ben half-filled the small saucepan with water from the pitcher, his eyes bright with the anticipation of how funny the joke would be. Maria's cousin Tim had given him the idea – promise not to tell, cross your heart and hope to die – and Ben had nodded, delighted, and promised. Tim whispered. He'd actually done it – got his Ma with the water – well, nearly. That was April Fool's day. Ben couldn't wait to get home.

Aunt Edith was out.

Uncle Peter would be back from work any minute.

Ben stood teetering on the kitchen chair. Like this he was just tall enough to reach the top of the door. He opened it a few inches and balanced the half-full saucepan of water between it and the wall, very carefully.

Chuckling, his face vivid with pleasure, he jumped down, stepped back, then remembered to put the chair back in its place at the table. He waited, staring at the saucepan so wonderfully balanced.

He imagined Uncle Peter opening the door, and the saucepan bouncing down off his head, and the water pouring all over down his blue uniform. And when Aunt Edith came back and saw, she'd have to laugh. She'd punish him later, but that was fair enough. Ben imagined himself standing beside her and both of them laughing at Uncle Peter looking so funny.

Down the hall, the front door opened.

Ben was horrified – he hadn't thought of it – *suppose it was Aunt Edith*? Uncle Peter was one thing. Aunt Edith was different. He opened his mouth to gasp an excuse, a warning. The door opened.

It was Uncle Peter.

The saucepan fell.

It caught Uncle Peter's shoulder, splashed him a little. His face went rigid with shock, then the saucepan dropped away and sluiced a dark stain of water across the floor. Uncle Peter stared at it. If only he would laugh – but he didn't. He wiped the droplets slowly from his craggy face. He said deliberately:

'You little damned bastard.'

Ben knew that word. He had heard it from the older boys in the street, and he had heard it between the adults he saw staggering out of the pub late at night. He began to tremble.

'You've taken all I've got away from me,' Peter shouted. Ben didn't understand. He backed away behind the table at the words Peter flung at him. 'We'd be damned happy together but you come between us, you keep us apart, it's all you, you, you!'

Ben was afraid to cry in front of Uncle Peter. Damned, that was a new terrible word. He pressed himself back into the corner, but he didn't take his eyes off Peter's face, which stared – not at him – over his head, almost blind with rage, and jealousy, and frustration. Peter's boxer's fists folded and unfolded helplessly.

Ben began to realize that Uncle Peter, for all his size and strength, was somehow a failure even though he was a grown-up. He felt sorry for Uncle Peter, but he still didn't trust him. Now sadness filled Peter's eyes, too late.

'Get out of here,' said Peter bitterly.

Ben sat in the dark. This time no tears flowed from his eyes. He felt lonely. He *was* a bastard. His fists clenched until his nails bit into his hands. He lay back and drummed at the door with his bare feet.

'If I'm a bastard, I'm going to be a good one,' he screamed defiantly. He used Peter's terrible word. 'I'll be a damned good one!'

There was no reply from below. Probably Uncle Peter had gone off to get drunk. Probably by morning he would have forgotten everything that had happened.

Ben curled up. He yawned.

He slept, and remembered nothing, except in his dreams, where everyone remembers everything.

3

About five years ago they had replaced the gaslamps lining the Mile End Road with electric lights. Peter looked up at them as he walked home from the hospital to Lichfield Road. *Remember*, he thought. On Fridays he always remembered to go into Kemsley's the confectioner to buy a penny lump of honeycomb for the boy.

Nowadays the London sky was criss-crossed with a mass of ugly electric wires looping between the buildings, cables for the new electric trams, telephone lines, telegraph wires, private electricity supplies. Often they came down, dropping across the road like black snakes spitting blue sparks, and naturally people went to pick them up and turn them off, poor fools. Electricity wasn't like water, it was a dangerous world. Policemen were trained to trap broken cables between the wooden legs of a chair and drop a carpet over them. The new electrically illuminated signboards presented a bright face to attract the well-heeled commuters travelling from the wealthy suburbs to the City. Peter shook his head. The new web of cables overhead made the sky look lower somehow. And the electric trams made a racket like Bedlam. The City wouldn't even allow them in, apparently. Disturbed the quiet chink of all that money.

The poor old Mile End Road looked quite rich though, but only because rich people drove along it. On each side of the road behind the bright shop fronts, just the thickness of a brick wall behind them, he knew, lay the stinking maze of the Jewish ghetto, a spider's web of alleys and courts where he had wandered once in search of a woman. Yet these immigrants from Poland and Russia had the morals of Puritans, and he found no one. The men, who wore long coats and black caps, shouted at him in foreign lingo, calling him a *Schnorrer*, and other words he did not understand. It was brave of them to defy him, with his pugilist's face and corded muscles, and his loose, dangerous walk.

South of the ghetto sprawled dockland, enormous inland seas of enclosed water jostling with ships: the forests of masts and cranes were buried under great plumes of smoke and steam. The docks were built like fortresses, surrounded by brick walls twenty feet high topped with iron spikes and glass. Most of the dockers were casual labourers; at dawn each day, or when a ship came in, a great lump of them formed at the dock gates and waited for the lucky few to be chosen. Those who were not chosen did not eat that day, and neither did their families. Last winter had been very bad. They couldn't unload the ships for day after day, then week after week, then over a month, then into the next month. You started to see casuals roaming as far north as Mile End here, almost foreign territory to them, whole families of them, emaciated men with frost on their beards towing their wives and children in rags after them, desperate for work. Police patrols had been doubled, and people started locking their doors, if they had locks. Then spring had come and the intruders had returned their few miles south back to Wapping, Poplar and the Isle of Dogs as the ships came in.

Peter was widely travelled for a Londoner because of his fighting days. Dropping a couple of miles down to Poplar wasn't strange to him, though many never went that far in their lives. Sometimes he went down to the Workhouse for a pint or three with his old friend Bill Madeley, who was Master there. Bill was quite a success story. They relaxed together in his room, complete with chandeliers, bragging about the women they'd had. Bill's wife was a mousey creature. Peter told him about the ghetto, and the plump beauties to be had there. He saw Bill making a mental note and knew he'd go. He'd get a flea in his ear and think: Christ, Pete Pungle must've got the magic, if he did all right there, and Peter's stock would go up accordingly. Peter hugged this thought to him. He loved to be looked up to.

111

Only once he'd gone down deep into the Isle of Dogs, the heart of dockland. This was a couple of years ago. It had been a windy day. The violent river, grey-brown and rushing with tide, made a stinking loop around three sides of the island. It took him hours to walk down to the end. They'd just dug a footpath underneath the Thames there. You could walk across to Greenwich beneath fifty feet of water. Had he? Now he remembered. He remembered how he'd taken the lift down and walked it, all the way across and back again, just to show Edith his independence. She had been nagging him to paint the kitchen wall, which was a serviceable shade of green, nagging on about how un-hygienic it was. He tried to remember if he'd repainted it eventually. He'd forgotten. Women noticed these things; not him. He was a real man. Patting his blue serge pockets – the long evening was quite warm, but he liked to wear his thick official uniform – he turned off the racketing, roaring Mile End Road into the side streets.

About half a mile from Lichfield Road, he started seeing people he knew by sight. Each turning was a separate compartment, a miniature world inside London's world. Each had its own group of women in aprons and slippers, nattering and laughing around the water standpipe. Each had its own four or five shops; ironmonger, butcher, baker, eel and pie shop, grocer, pub. Each had its own specialist experts: whore, midwife, washerwoman, bookie's runner, and a jack-of-all-trades who could repair your bicycle or replace your gas mantle. Each had its own feuds, Peter knew, people who would walk past each other with eyes averted, whole families that did not speak to each other, and an intricate system of alliances. Nearly always, a boy would marry a girl from the same turning or just round the corner. Tiny communities, one after the other. At Whitman Road they ignored him. At Clinton Road one or two people glanced at him and acknowledged him with a fractional nod of the head. Crossing Grove Road someone said: 'Hallo.' In Aberavon Road they said: 'Good evening, Mr Pungle.'

In Lichfield Road several men called, 'How's it doing, Pete?'

Not that Lichfield Road was as good as some. It was a touch classy, and he felt that some of the people were stand-offish about him. They weren't as warm as he was used to. Perhaps the street felt less like a home because it was mostly on one side of the road, strung out with the railway embankment, a ropewalk and sawmills directly behind the houses, and at the front most of them faced nothing but the huge intimidating church and the Coopers' school. It made you feel unbalanced. He liked to be really close to people: here they preferred to stand back a bit. No, he was making it up. It was the best place he'd ever lived, and it was his fault he was lonely. His back had been hurting lately and he'd been grouchy. He'd been grouchy with Edith too, and that was why she'd been cold to him and they hadn't talked in the evenings, and gone to their separate bedrooms at different times.

But it was her fault too. She was so besotted with the kid. He'd been nearly going out to work at that age. She was training the kid not to like him, too. No swearing, Peter, don't set a bad example. Leave your boots by the door. Please, Peter, cover your mouth when you cough. She was turning into an old maid. That kid was her life, and he wasn't even her own. Ben this, Ben that, Ben everything. He got all of her attention. What did he do for it? He didn't work for it, but he ate enough! Last Sunday, when they had a small joint of roast lamb, it was Ben she carved the best bits off for. *He* got the best. Peter thought: I'm paying four and sixpence that I've sweated to earn, and they don't appreciate it. Or me. They don't look up to me, they just take me for granted.

She doesn't even feel she has to give me the best cuts any more.

She doesn't treat me with respect.

How can she be so cold?

He wanted to see Edith smile at *him*, not at the kid. To see her eyes go that lovely warm brown, to hear her laugh. They used to laugh in the old days over a cuppa. Those mornings in his office. He'd touched her hand once or twice, warm flesh. He'd dreamed of her simply getting up

113

and taking her nurse's coat off, standing by the table, looking at him, then pulling her dress off over her head and standing there before him in whatever she wore underneath, something frilly, her lovely dimpled thighs rising into black lace, red satin, French, all that . . . and letting her hair fall down so that it flowed down around her breasts. Then nodding, slowly. Yes.

Incredibly, it hadn't happened. Not even at Lichfield Road. He'd touched her hand; she hadn't noticed. Sex was a constant need with him, a constant probe in the base of his brain; he couldn't look at a woman without sizing her up – who could? Edith had a different obsession. Her boy. She hadn't even had to go through sex to get him. No wonder she was so hard on him, reading, writing, 'rithmatic, rules. Her body must be screaming. And she didn't even know how to interpret it. Didn't know about sex, only love. The only way she could give herself was by giving Ben the best cuts of meat.

He was just the odd-job man to her. Maybe he wasn't forward enough. Maybe, besotted as she was, she hadn't noticed him trying to worm his way into her bed. Nothing – not even after he'd so cleverly got into her nest. Just when he was congratulating himself on getting to her through the baby, as it was then, he found himself excluded. He was actually inside her nest, but found that the baby was Edith's world – all of it. He was an outsider looking in. He couldn't penetrate it. He just paid his four-and-sixpence a week and repaired the sash window and the leak in the roof, carried the coal, repainted the kitchen. But as far as anything more was concerned, he was locked out.

She needed him, but she wouldn't admit it. She needed to give herself and get something back for once. She needed to let her hair down. He imagined her without her clothes on in her front bedroom. She stood by the bed, looking at him, startled, then thoughtful. He imagined taking his clothes off too, slowly at first, and her just looking at him. He imagined her getting excited at the sight of his corded muscle and the hairs that bristled over his iron-hard chest. Her body trembling. All these years she'd had to wait for him to make

114

the first move. A woman couldn't just give herself – *she had to be taken*.

Peter stopped in the middle of the street.

Christ, he thought, I've been a fool.

'Good evening, Uncle.'

Peter looked down. He hadn't noticed the kid standing there. 'Hallo, nipper,' he said vaguely.

'Have you had a good day at the office, Uncle?' asked Ben politely.

Peter looked at him suspiciously. *Doesn't he like me?* The kid didn't speak like other East Enders. He spoke more like Edith, sort of precisely, saying every letter in a word. He obviously wanted you to understand exactly what he was saying. You heard what he said, but you were suspicious about what he meant. He didn't mean anything, it was just Edith's manners, but it made you feel awkward with him, as though you ought to say an answer in the same sort of accent. *Or does he really not trust me – good old Uncle Pete?*

'It's been all right,' he said gruffly. 'How about you?'

'Yes.'

They walked slowly. It must be about eight in the evening. The church cast a long shadow. A train rumbled by behind the houses and suddenly the street smelt of smoke mingling with the hot dusty smell of the day. Children were playing by the standpipe, yelling, and he saw a silver splash of water. A dog bounced around them, barking. Some older children were playing cricket with a broom handle and a ball of rags. Ben ignored them.

'Why don't you go and play?' Peter asked.

'No, thank you.' He didn't say he wasn't allowed to, or that he didn't want to, or that he wanted his supper instead. *No, thank you*. What did it mean? Peter frowned. Ben's face was scrubbed, his cheeks red with health, his hair slicked, his grey clothes carefully brushed, his shoes shining. He was a mother's dream. The other kids hadn't beaten him up or torn his suit, chucked him in the gutter, not even scuffed his shoes. Some boys were never bullied. They had something about them. Ben was one of those. He needed you, but you had to go to him. Peter didn't like it. It was a bit like the reserve that Edith had. Another of her teachings. He scratched his trousers. Ben wasn't even holding his hand, like most kids would've. If you gave the little bastard your hand you felt he'd politely shake it and step back, instead of happily skipping along beside you holding on.

Then he remembered.

'Hey,' Peter said, 'I haven't given you your honeycomb!'

He saw a flicker of intense joy in those polite, piercing eyes, quickly suppressed.

'Lord, you should have said.' Peter searched through his pockets for the penny lump he always brought back from Kemsley's on a Friday. 'Today's Friday, isn't it?'

'Yes, Uncle,' Ben said.

' 'Course it is. It must be here somewhere. I remember clear as day. I went in and George was behind the counter and he said, "Would you believe this rain we've been having all day?" '

Ben said gently: 'It's been sunny today, Uncle.'

' 'Course it has. Don't be clever with me, lad,' waffled Peter. 'That was last week. I was just—'

'You were just testing me.'

'I was just testing you. Watch it! Now, what did George say today.' He stopped, scratching his head. He couldn't remember.

Ben said politely: 'Would you believe all this *sunshine* we've been having today?'

'Cheeky bugger!' Peter rapped his knuckles against the boy's ear. 'Any more of that and I'll box your ears for you, right?'

'Yes, Uncle.' Obediently.

'I forgot your damned honeycomb, if that's what you want to know.'

'It's all right.'

'I don't know how I forgot. I just did.'

'It doesn't matter.'

It *did* matter. Why did the boy hate him? Peter flared: 'Well what do you want me to say? Oh, I am so bloody sorry that I forgot?'

'Come on,' Ben said. They walked on up the road with

116

the sun in their eyes. Peter tried to think of a way to get rid of the boy. Obviously he had to get Edith on her own. At first she would say *no no no*, she had to, it was expected, just as it was expected of him to break the shell of that feminine reserve. At first she would pretend to be horrified, no woman wanted to be seduced, she couldn't give herself, she had to be taken. But then she would soften, then she would melt. Her struggles would become easy, almost helpful. And when the dam burst . . .

From the dark, nearby doorway of number 37, a woman's voice came.

'Mr Pungle.'

He stopped, squinting.

'Mrs Kent,' he said uncertainly.

Edith loathed her neighbour, but Mrs Kent did not return that unreasonable hatred. She was a widow in her forties, slim but well-moulded. Her husband had died about a year ago, but he must have left her well provided for, because she hadn't remarried or moved away. She leaned in the shadow of her doorway wearing a long colourful dress tied with a sash around her waist, rather daringly, Peter thought, but impressively: she had enough character to get away with it.

'Isn't it warm?' she murmured. He had to lean forward to catch her words.

'Yes, it is.'

'I'd love to take off my clothes and splash about in the water with those children,' she said. The naked children jumping around in public by the standpipe. He tried to see if she was smiling. He didn't know if she had any children of her own.

'It's very hot.' His words sounded awkward and out of place. Peter longed to take off his necktie, but he was wearing his uniform.

She folded her arms, watching him. She had very red lips, and large, slow eyes. He looked from side to side. She didn't take her eyes off you, he realized. Her eyes moved from your eyes to your mouth, then from your eyes to your necktie, but always her eyes came slowly back to your eyes.

117

'It must have been very hot for you working today,' she said.

'I'm Head Porter at the hospital. I'm responsible for over seven hundred beds.' He was eager to impress her; her personality was so powerful. He realized that he hadn't quite replied to her question. 'Yes, it was very hot,' he added.

'Really?' Her eyes swayed indifferently to Ben, then moved back to Peter's eyes, becoming warm and interested again. 'And will your son follow in your footsteps?'

'He isn't my son.' Suddenly Peter understood what she was getting at; what he had told her. He felt humiliated. In real life Edith was so cold to him that it had never occurred to him that everyone would naturally assume that he was in her bed. It explained so much. He must be the talk of the street. Doing it was disgusting out of wedlock, but fascinating. That explained why everyone in the street was so interested in him, yet isolated him. Now Mrs Kent had wormed it out of him: the actual admission that he wasn't in Edith's bed. He had lost face; he wasn't a man in the place that counted. Peter cast trapped glances to the left and the right.

'Goodbye!' he said. She looked startled, Ben thought, at such a sudden departure.

'Good night, Mr Pungle.' She watched him go.

'Good night, Mrs Kent,' Ben said.

She glanced at him. 'Ta-ta, kid.'

She turned inside her house and disappeared.

Ben caught Peter up at the steps to their house. Suddenly Peter held his shoulder with hard fingers to stop him going in. 'Er, look, do me a favour, lad. I'm parched. Pop down to the jug and bottle counter of the Lord Tredegar and bring me back some beer, will you?'

'Aunt Edith says I'm not to go near the public house.'

'Do as I tell you, boy. You like ginger beer, don't you?'

Ben caught on quickly. 'But there's a lot of people waiting. I can't be quick. She'll wonder where I am.'

'I'll square it with her,' Peter said confidently. 'Here's thruppence. Now, you know what to do with it.'

'A penny for beer, tuppence for ginger beer.'

Peter thought about it. 'Very funny. That tongue of yours is so sharp you're going to cut yourself on it one day. Tuppence for beer, penny for ginger beer, it's that way round. And remember to wipe the froth off your lips. Not that you're going to be quick back, right?'

He watched the boy go off, then mounted the steps. He did not notice Ben stop and look back with that sensitive, learning, almost feminine intuitive light in his child's eyes that Peter always mistook for cleverness and hit him for. Ben did not know he showed it. His Aunt and Uncle did not allow themselves to show their feelings, it was simply not done, so he was not allowed them either. He accepted that. His behaviour was always proper, because there were rules and orders from above and they had to be obeyed, or else one was punished because one was loved. But he couldn't help wondering.

What was Uncle Peter doing? Was it a game?

He pocketed the money and looked back at the door as it closed.

Inside, Peter closed the door quietly behind him and looked up the dark, narrow hallway towards the kitchen.

'I've sent the boy out to play, Edith,' he said. 'He won't disturb us.'

4

Edith was happy. So much of her life had been spent in mourning. I was living in a purgatory of my own making, she thought, working in that hospital, an angel in those dreadful wards full of death. She remembered the stink of the beds on hot days like this, the smell of rotting, and how cheerful she had looked, keeping her face wreathed in a smile while she was crying out inside. Then Ben London came.

Now she could guiltlessly remember her fiancé's face, if she wished, distant but clear. Suffering was ended, and this was happiness. Taking the sausages out of the frying pan she thought: I'm happy.

She stopped for a moment. Yes, this was what happiness was: God's gift of her home around her; her dear child doubtless reading a book in her front room as she had not heard him go out, and of course he would not dare to go out without telling her; the feeling of fulfilment, of contentment, that she got from even the little things in life. Happiness was these things. Simple pleasures, and the absence of guilt. Her family needing her. Happiness was even peeling these potatoes, because she could make sure that not the smallest blackeye or smear of soil remained to blemish the peeled white surface. She could not afford the best cuts of meat or the finest quality potatoes, but her meals were always filling and nutritious, and she never fed her family anything that had the slightest imperfection remaining on it. They always ate every scrap, showing respect, showing love. She scratched away at the potatoes with the little grooved knife, up to her elbows in the sink. They were a happy family.

The front door slammed.

Was that Ben going out? He always ran out to meet Peter on a Friday evening, goodness knows why.

She glanced at the clock that Peter had hung on the wall. It was later than she had thought.

'Peter, is that you?' She hoped he had remembered to take his boots off. He was turning into a bit of a crotchety old bachelor, difficult to remind sweetly. Tending to take offence. She couldn't help that. No boots was a firm house rule.

She heard his boots clumping in the hall, and her mouth tightened.

'Oh, Peter, do take your boots off.'

She smiled sweetly. He stood in the doorway, staring. He didn't seem to have heard her. His face was fixed and set, his body bulged with muscle. 'It's sausages for supper,' she smiled. 'Did you remember to take your . . .' Her voice faded. She had the dreadful feeling that something was wrong. *Oh my God. My boy's fallen down the steps. Broken his leg. Broken his neck*! 'Peter! Oh my God,' she whispered.

'I've sent the boy out to play,' he said.

She was so relieved that she felt tears prick the back of her eyes and the potato she was holding dropped back into the water. He was all right. That was the only important thing in the world. But for a moment she had thought that . . . She gave a sob, then fumbled for a tea towel as tears blurred her vision.

'I'll wipe your eyes, Edie,' he said in a soft voice. That was the old Peter: not the grouchy lodger of recent years, but the Peter who gave her a cuppa in that funny little cubbyhole he so proudly called an office, and a laugh to start the day.

'It's all right, really. I'm just being silly.'

'Silly? Not you, Edie.'

She didn't like to stand there in front of him, her eyes squeezed closed, showing tears on her face, she must look a sight. He started gently wiping her cheeks with the corner of the tea towel. She flinched, then let him. He smelled faintly of sweat. She felt him touch her cheek with his fingertip. She heard his breath in her ear, as though he was leaning close. She tried to clap her hands to her face because there was something on her skin – had something come off the tea towel, an insect perhaps? – but his body was in the way. If it was an insect it might be a spider and she hated spiders!

Edith's eyes popped open. At first she did not know what she saw: she was staring into Peter's enormous eyes, each eyelash as big as a blade of grass. He was trying to kiss her.

She tried to speak and his tongue licked her lips. She tried to twist her head from side to side but he held her with wooden strength. She felt some of his saliva enter her mouth. She tried to grunt 'No, no, Peter, please,' but no words came out. His tongue pressed through her parted lips and actually went inside, sliding to and fro over her clenched teeth, this physical tongue that meant love and possession, she felt it on her gums and on the inside of her cheeks, she tried to scream but didn't because she would have had to open her mouth. She couldn't breathe, her nose was crushed against his cheek. The muscles of his chest were like iron plates. Her hands felt helplessly soft clapping against them.

She clawed her fingernails down his chest and he gasped, not with pain she saw with horror, but with excitement. The strength fled from her legs, she swooned, but he caught her behind her waist and swung her round on the tabletop. Her legs kicked against air. Peter tried to climb on top of her. One of the chairs screeched on the tiles then fell over, rattling.

She saw Ben in the doorway. He was watching without alarm, his earnest expression curious and innocent. Witnessing this animal struggle, this hideous corruption. She was lying on the very table from which they ate.

'Ben's watching!' she gasped.

Peter's head twisted towards the doorway. It was empty. 'I learned the boy his orders,' he rasped. 'I sent him out. I love you, Edie. I need you more than him.' He fumbled at her with his great hands.

Edith groaned. She was frightened of shouting in case the neighbours heard. The walls were thin. 'No,' begged Edith softly. 'No, Peter, please, don't.' She tried to hold his head away from her chest. His eyes were staring and every muscle in his body stood out as he attempted to caress her body.

'No. No.' But the more she said *no*, the more it encouraged him. It was as if no meant yes. The more she hurt him, the more he loved it.

'Edie,' he said hoarsely. 'Edith. I love you.'

Love? Obviously he was lying, because this wasn't what she had for her baby.

The front door slammed, much louder than usual.

'*Oh my goodness gracious heavens, Ben's coming in!*' Edith gave a convulsive jerk. 'He'll see.'

'Edith, come upstairs with me,' Peter said urgently. He wrapped her wrist gently in his hand, his muscles feeling like iron. He did not use his great strength; he almost begged her. 'Come on Edie, be a sport.'

Edith clamped her knees tightly together and covered her chest with her arms.

Peter begged her: 'Come on Edie, be a sport.'

'Don't be silly, Peter.' She sat up, pulling the hem of her dress down to her ankles; it had ridden up almost as far as her knees. She did not understand the rigid, pathetic expression she saw on his face.

Confused, she said, 'Sport!'

'It's now or never,' he said in a shuddering voice.

She stared at him. Suddenly Peter interested her. Men had so few emotions that there was something fascinating in seeing a man ruled, for a moment or two at least, by feeling. Part of her wanted to be ruled by it too. *No*. But something fluttered in her stomach. She did not quite recognize it – a strange sensation of power. For a moment she felt what a deep ecstasy it would be for her to unlock him, to make him her own by giving him a little of herself, to transform him and control him not by saying *no* but by saying *yes*. Extraordinarily, for one moment she *could* imagine going upstairs with him . . . but the door had slammed.

'All right,' Peter said, letting go of her wrist, 'all right!'

They stood on opposite sides of the table, like strangers.

'Sport!' she scoffed faintly.

'Forget it,' Peter said. The life went out of his face. His body looked as though it was collapsing inwards as the strength left his muscles.

He could not even meet her eyes now. *Forgive me, Edie, I'm such a brute*. He didn't say it, but she was sure he was thinking it, and of course she did forgive him.

He looked down and about, anywhere that did not meet her eyes. 'Peter,' she said, clearing her throat. She wanted to tell him to do up his necktie before the boy came in and saw. It was essential to keep up appearances.

'Peter, I—'

'Yes, Edith?' Peter grinned. That grin again. It was as though he had made up his mind about something. He began to do up his tie. The way he did it made her shiver – a calm that was almost frightening. For the first time in her life she could sense that there was more to him than she saw, a force hidden within him, a coiled spring. And within every man? *Come upstairs.* She wondered how she could control it in him. And her.

So she said: 'Peter, we can still be friends, can't we?'

He looked at her and perhaps his mouth twitched. A grin. Yes.

'Look, we could have a day out, one day,' she said. He stared at her. 'The three of us,' she added.

He shrugged.

'I'm sure you'd enjoy it,' she said, then hesitated. Ben was standing in the doorway, just as he had before, with the same expression, definitely too innocent to have gone back and deliberately slammed the front door. She stood between them, putting Ben safe in her shadow. It was all right. 'We'll all have a day out!' she cried, relieved. 'We'll all go to Happy Hampstead!'

'Winter's coming,' Peter said.

'My hair must look a sight,' she said. She put her hand on Ben's shoulder and smiled. He did not move. She felt a brief electric stab of fear again that he knew, had seen, had witnessed their disgusting behaviour. For a moment she was so worried that she bent down and kissed him, which she rarely did, but thank God the boy showed no sign of emotion. That would have been something she would never have forgiven Peter and herself for. She wanted him to know only love.

'Come on, dear,' she said, 'Aunty needs to find another hairpin, let's have a look upstairs, shall we?'

From the hall she glanced back at Peter, but he kept his head down. She gave a flickering smile. He didn't cheer up. As she went upstairs she thought: I behaved properly. Why do I feel that I should be saying, *I'm sorry, Peter*?

I'm sorry, Peter.

Peter stood alone in her kitchen. Not even a French kiss. She would be back from upstairs in a minute or two. Nothing had happened. All put away and forgotten. He had obediently done up his necktie. He thought: I'm a husband, good as. Paint the kitchen, Peter, hang the clock, Peter. Have you done the wallpaper in the living room,

124

Peter? Have you beaten the carpets, Peter? I'm a husband, except where it's most important. If a man hasn't got it, that thing is everything. She wants it. She wants love. But she doesn't want me to love her. She's confused, but she's clever on the right side. Typical woman. I've got nothing but she's got me trapped. Face it. Where else would I get for four and six a week? She's beautiful, but she's been using me. How can anyone so attractive be so cold?

He put his hands to his head. He realized the truth. Where he had thought he was using her all these years, the truth was that she had been using him! Look at the work he'd done about the place! She'd been getting something for nothing all this time!

He raised his hands above his head. His heart thudded, the pressure hurting his throat, and little pains pulsed and stabbed around the inside of his skull. He thought: I don't need you, Edith. I can get a French kiss even if I have to pay for it. I can get anything I want if I pay for it. I need someone, Edith. I need someone to love.

But where else would you get for four and sixpence a week?
Nowhere.

He bunched his fist and crashed it down on the table.

The pain in his back twisted him round, but then the pressure in his throat and skull ceased. He let himself gently into a chair and dropped his head into his hands.

'Sorry,' he admitted in a muffled voice when Edith came in. 'Clumsy, just clumsy.'

5

That was the winter Mr Pungle grew his moustache.

Annie Saltings cried when she gave birth to yet another girl, her sixth to survive, and no heir yet for Jimmy's harness-making business. Edith told them of the Parrant family with nine hungry boys, and only a room and a flight of stairs to pack them in. Yet all Mr Parrant wanted out of life was a girl! Jimmy Saltings laughed, then told her a very sad story.

Mo, the blind girl, had died, run over by a motor-car on

the Mile End Road and the vicar at Guardian Angels would not allow her to be buried in a white coffin. Her mother En flew into a hysterical fit that her neighbours thought was drunken rage, and a few sharp words were thrown at her in the street. Then it turned out that she probably didn't have the money for any sort of coffin, white or not. The contemptible woman had drunk it years ago. Mo was buried in a pauper's grave and her mother hunted high and low for the place. A pauper's grave was dreadful, Edith knew. It was unmarked.

Eliza Baker married Sam Clizzard, the apprentice bootmaker who lived at number 81. His Mum couldn't find them a place in Lichfield Road so they had to move out to Trellis Street, wedged between the railway and the sawmills. Eliza, who was sickly, gave up her job at the Bryant and May match factory when she got pregnant, and became delightfully pink and fat. A few weeks before Easter Edith delivered her of a boy, eight pounds four ounces. This seemed an exceptionally heavy weight for a baby supposed to be premature. 'I've never known anything like it,' Edith said. Eliza said it was a well-known effect of the phosphorus from the lucifer matches. Sam said it was all the oysters she ate.

Peter came back from the Lord Tredegar, unwound the long woollen scarf from his neck, and sat at the table in Edith's kitchen drinking her brown sherry and stroking his moustache. He felt cosy and warm. It was his day off, and he didn't have many. Mrs Kent's visitors were an interesting phenomenon, he decided. They didn't enter through the street door. Edith was away doing a five-bob birth and the house was quiet. He sat for hours with his hands resting on the table and the sherry-glass between them, not drinking much, listening, watching, thinking. Occasionally a train rumbled slowly out of Coburn Road Station along the tracks that ran behind the houses. Each back yard ended in a ramshackle airey at the foot of the embankment. From time to time, he noticed, men sauntered across the railway lines and followed a path down to Mrs Kent's back gate, dropping out of sight behind the fence, unless they were very tall. You heard Mrs Kent's back door opening and voices through the kitchen wall. The voices mumbled, then faded away. Peter went out into the hall. He clearly heard footsteps going up the wall, the risers creaking. He slipped upstairs and went into his bedroom. Nothing. Of course; they must be in the front room. He crept into Edith's room and stood by her bed. He pressed his ear to the wall and heard it: very soft, a rhythmic creaking. His face broke into a smile. Now he understood.

Mr Savage, the auctioneer from Tredegar Square, got a motor-car. Mr Godbins's daughter got married at Holy Trinity. Mr Godbins was a tall man with a jolly red face and enormous white side-whiskers. He was a cabinet-maker with his own small shop and several employees in Bethnal Green. He liked organizing people and paid for a lovely white wedding with rice and confetti, and a flash-in-the-pan photographer, Mr Lancaster, and his apprentice to record the wedding party standing in a serious rank. Edith loved weddings and she had a grandstand view of them from her bedroom window. This time the newlyweds were driven away in a lovely old victoria.

Edith had mentioned her idea of a day out at Happy Hampstead on the Bank Holiday Monday in the green-grocer's, and the idea had caught on like wildfire with everyone else waiting in the shop. Annie Saltings said that she and her girls would love to go, except that Alice was sick, but Eliza Clizzard said that she'd look after her. Martha Parrant said that none of her poor boys had ever been to the Easter Fair. Miss Talbot, the secretary of the Metropolitan Association for Befriending Young Servants, said that some of the young serving girls in Tredegar Square and the vicarage would love a day out, if it was responsibly organized, and if their masters would let them. Mary Godbins, buying a pound of walnuts and some carrots, remembered that her husband had proposed to her on Hampstead Heath, on his knees. 'I'd love to go back! I think that there was a sort of pond nearby where the horses drank, and a wooden building.' Someone said they could make a party of it. 'My husband can organize a charabanc,'

Mary Godbins offered. The children started jumping up and down shouting with excitement, but Edith, smiling, kept her hand firmly on Ben's shoulder, and him obediently motionless. 'Come down to my house on Friday and I'll give you the tickets,' Mary said. 'It'll be a lovely day out for all the children, and it should only be a few pence.' *I've got that much in the biscuit tin above the range*, Edith thought.

'I'll come down on Friday afternoon,' she said.

On Friday afternoon, Peter followed his invariable rule and stopped off to buy a bar of honeycomb at Kemsley's. He ate it thoughtlessly as he walked home. Going in without knocking, he went through to the kitchen. No one was there. He sniffed at the stockpot brewing on the range as always, wrinkled his nose, hung his jacket over the back of the door, and boiled a pint of tea. 'Anyone home?'

Where were they? He put his boots on the table, leaned back and yawned. The pot warmed on the side of the range, *his* way. He leaned over and poured it into a fire-clay mug. This was best Assam, a lovely dark red. Edith always went on about adding the milk first. She chose Earl Grey nowadays, without sugar, another way of rejecting him. The idea of adding milk first was that you didn't crack the exquisite bone china. Nonsense.

'Now, don't tell me you didn't hear me, Mr Pungle.'

He sat up and jerked his boots off the table, putting his hand behind him to ward off the bolt of pain up his back. 'I didn't hear you, Mrs Kent, you were quiet as a mouse, and that's a fact.'

'The door was open.'

'Sorry, must have forgotten it.' Why was he apologizing to her? He scrambled to his feet. 'Come on in.'

She merely leaned in the doorway. He decided that Mrs Kent looked both older and younger. Her pale skin was webbed with fine lines, like the glaze of old china crazed by much use, although her cheeks bloomed attractively with health, or rouge, and her lips were glossy. She looked like a woman who took care of herself. Her large, slow eyes hadn't changed at all, or their grey-green stare taking in everything. She knew how beautiful she was, Peter knew. She wore a flounced lime-green dress and a lime-green hat fastened with a long black hatpin. Her hair fell beneath its brim to her shoulders in henna ringlets as large and round as peacocks' eyes.

She stood with one hand on her hip, an empty teacup dangling by its handle from her fingertip. He thought: She must be the only woman in Lichfield Road with long fingernails.

'I've come to borrow a cup of sugar.'

She dressed like this to borrow a cup of sugar! What a woman. Peter could hardly contain his mounting excitement. He wasn't born yesterday. She held out the cup.

'You're Head Porter, you say.' She had such a direct way of speaking that it made him feel clumsy.

'Well, yes, they do call it that.'

'It must be a most responsible position.'

Peter reached for the sugar bowl on the table. She said, 'No, I'll have fresh, if you don't mind.' He'd been thoughtless, taking her for granted that she was like other women. She hadn't let him get away with it for a moment. He revised his opinion of her upwards, and searched in a cupboard. He wondered if she liked his new moustache. It wasn't black and gleaming like Lord Kitchener's; it had turned out greyish. What was he thinking of? It didn't matter if she liked it or not.

Her eyes were roaming. 'You repainted this kitchen for Miss Rumney?' Then her eyes came back to his eyes.

Peter nodded. He stroked his moustache.

'I hope she paid you well.'

'Well, I only pay her four and sixpence a week rent.'

'With odd jobs thrown in.' She seemed amused. 'But you must be making a lot of money.'

'I don't do too badly, to be honest, Mrs Kent.'

'Head Porter,' she nodded. 'Miss Rumney is so fortunate to have a man around the place.' Was she saying more than her words said? His stomach burned with excitement and his fingers felt cold.

He found some sugar and filled her cup. He risked a snub, and met her eyes for a moment.

'I believe you used to be married, Mrs Kent?'

'Life's so hard for a widow,' she said smoothly. 'I find I'm all at sixes and sevens since my Harry went. It doesn't seem like a year, no, nearly two years since . . .'

'I'm sorry,' Peter said.

'I did my best for him, Peter, wonderful funeral it was. Tower Hamlets cemetery, no expense spared if I do say so myself. You know those lovely oak coffins they do, with the brass handles, and a real brass bell on top, and black horses with black plumes.' For a moment something genuine flickered in her eyes: real enthusiasm. Then she merely smiled again.

Peter grinned at her, nodding.

'It was my duty, Peter.'

'You couldn't do nothing less, Mrs Kent.' He wondered what her first name was.

'It's a fine thing to meet a man nowadays who understands duty, I must say.' He favoured his back as he closed the cupboard door, and as he turned he found her looking at him with a concerned expression. 'Does your back hurt?'

'It does, to be truthful.'

'My poor husband had the same trouble,' she said slowly.

Peter cleared his throat. He looked into her eyes. A false grin stretched his lips, then a real smile. He was dealing with a sophisticated woman. He understood her perfectly.

'I rubbed his back with oil,' she said.

'Lucky man,' he croaked. God what a hard woman she was. Any deal would be a fair exchange. He felt himself trembling with excitement. She saw. She knew that she had almost got him hooked. For a moment a smile twitched the corners of her lips, and her eyes dimmed, becoming only hopeful, making her look terribly old and weary. Then she regained her self-control, her indifference, her attraction.

'I don't have such a nice kitchen as this,' she said. 'But something could be made of mine, I'm sure.'

There it was: the offer. It couldn't have been put clearer if she'd written it down in black and white. And her figure:

not as lovely and plump as some, but well-moulded.

He tried to read the expression in Mrs Kent's eyes.

He said: 'But what about your children?'

'My dear Peter,' she said expressionlessly, 'they grew up long ago, thank God.' She flicked her fingers as though dislodging them from under her fingernails and gave a theatrical little shudder of relief.

He said suddenly: 'I don't think I want to hurt Edith.'

She looked at him. He realized that he could do anything he wanted. He said desperately: 'You'll have to let me think about it.' She actually laughed. She wasn't for him to accept or reject: she was herself, on her own terms. Take it or leave it. Peter realized he had met his match. He dropped his head. She gave him a voracious grin filled with yellow teeth. He said: 'But I don't think I want to hurt—'

She turned away instantly.

Peter followed her down the hall. 'Mrs Kent, please.'

But the front door opened before Mrs Kent reached it and a small figure darted in out of the light, colliding with Mrs Kent's skirts. As she recoiled, real, terrible feeling sounded in her voice for the first time: 'You clumsy little oaf, this is my best dress–' She struck out. 'If you've damaged it–' She had missed. Ben stepped back politely. In the backwash from the bright doorway his eyes were strikingly blue. He stared up at Mrs Kent. Incredibly, Peter noticed, he didn't seem frightened by her. His left hand was clenched into a fist and Peter suddenly understood that he knew about Mrs Kent. No, not *knew*, he was too young, too young to know anything, but he sensed. He sensed all about her. He hated her.

Amused, Peter said: 'I'm sorry Mrs Kent, he's too young to know better.'

Edith came up the steps. Her face stiffened as her eyes adjusted to the darkness in her hall and she saw who was there.

'Mrs Kent,' she said coldly.

The other woman glanced at Peter. 'Miss Rumney. Ta-ta, Peter.'

Edith watched her neighbour flounce down her

whitestoned steps then turned back to Peter, taking off her hat. 'What did that woman want?'

'Nothing, just a cup of sugar.'

'I don't like her in my house.'

Peter smiled tolerantly. 'I'll make you some Earl Grey.'

'I'll have whatever you're having,' Edith said, 'just as long as it's warm and wet.' She smiled.

'We got the tickets,' Ben said. 'We're going to have a day out at Happy Hampstead on Monday and we're going on a brake with two horses!'

'Yes,' Peter said, 'we'll have a lovely spree . . .'

Spree. For some reason, or no reason, Edith couldn't get that funny Cockney word Peter had used out of her mind. Spree, a day out. *Spree*. She was lying in her bed on Sunday night, staring at the chink between the curtains: it was bursting with stars. *Spree*. Lovely word. They were going to have a lovely spree tomorrow.

She lay in the dark listening to Ben snore in the smaller bed across the room. Annie Saltings and Martha Parrant both said none of their children snored. Ben did, Edith thought proudly. He was special. Ben had not come out of her body. He was pure and she would keep him that way. Poor Peter had acted the way he did, like an animal, simply because he didn't know any better. He had tried to seduce her not because he was evil, but because he was ignorant. He had no idea of the feminine virtues. She had tried to teach him friendship, and she felt he was coming round. His own words: *Yes! We'll have a lovely spree!*

The stars faded and she watched the dawn come, cloudlessly clear and bright.

Everyone turned up outside Fred's Eel & Pie Shop on the corner at the end of the road, standing in the sun, and she was pleased to see that they were all dressed to the nines for the spree. The ladies were done up in their Sunday bests, with dark velveteen dresses and broad-brimmed hats piled up with lovely flower arrangements smelling faintly of camphor, and long white gloves. They all admired each other's clothes and pretended that they themselves dressed like this every day. As each new arrival came in sight there were greetings of mutual congratulation. Edith was dressed in blue with red piping on her hat. She burst with pride. Her dress exactly matched the blue of Ben's sailor-suit that was so fashionable, a proper shop outfit purchased with the last of her capital account at the London & South Western and worth every penny.

The men wore stiff collars on their shirts, clubbing into their own group, apart and more serious. Men didn't talk to women. She watched Peter join them. She had insisted that he not wear his frightful uniform and he looked uncomfortable in a black suit and a tall white collar. However, she was pleased to observe that he was the most impressive-looking man in the group.

The children were running about getting over-excited and playing He. She kept a firm grip on Ben's hand so that he could not join them. In her other hand she held the large brown bag that contained their lunch. He begged her to let him look inside at the treats in store. She let go of him as something buzzed past her face. There was a bees' nest hidden somewhere in the eaves above the shop. The women *oohed* as Peter snatched one out of the air in his calloused fist, and one girl, she thought it was one of the Saltings girls, Henrietta, or Maria, in a straw hat, gave a little scream at the squashed yellow body. 'I hate bees,' said Edith, swishing nervously with her parasol, holding Ben close to her. He asked again if he could see the lunch, saying please, but she shook her head, knowing that this would keep him closer to her.

'I hope they send for a man to do that bee nest,' Edith called anxiously. The groups began to move together, united by the bees.

'Fred's too mean for that,' Peter said. 'He even keeps the salt and pepper shakers in a room out the back, so that if you want pepper on your eel you have to ask for it special.'

They heard the tootling of a horn. The girls clapped their hands and the women smiled. Everyone loved a tootling horn on the coach. It would pull them all together and get the party going. It wouldn't be a proper spree without a horn. The boys pointed. The brake swung across the Grove

Road tram-lines and pulled up with sparking wheels, the coachman hauling on the reins. The dray-horses stamped their great feathered hooves and shook their long manes, snorting. They wore lovely black leather harness with shining horse-brasses. Though they were enormously strong, they were called cold horses, Edith knew, because they lacked the fiery temperament of thoroughbreds. Their eyes were almost completely covered with black leather blinkers; behind them she could see the soft brown eyes moving, quietly watching the people.

'All aboard who's coming aboard!' shouted the jolly coachman. He had a face like a Toby Jug, very broad and smiling, but with watery eyes and rough skin full of broken red veins. He was known as quite a character along the Mile End Road. Edith remembered something about his son being an idiot. This must be the boy, scampering across the rows of wooden cross-benches with the battered brass horn dangling from his neck. He swung down and started trying to help the ladies up.

One of the mongol's shoulders was higher than the other and his face was unformed and uncalculating. He must be about eighteen years old, she guessed. The coachman must have loved him very much for him to have lived so long. Edith hesitated, not really wanting Ben to see him, but the little boy held up his arms to the mongol quite naturally, too young to understand. The mongol bent down with his face breaking into a smile at such trust and swung Ben up onto a cross-bench. Edith got up.

The coachman cracked his whip over the horses' heads and they were off with a jerk. Everyone shouted: 'We're off!' The demented boy went tootling *toot toot* on his horn, as agile as a monkey along the rails at the side of the vehicle. The boys shouted to know what the horses' names were. The coachman pointed with his whip. The one on the left, a darker red, the leader, was Jupiter. The other was Minstrel. 'She loves sugar. Not that brown unrefined stuff. Mr Tate's best white lump sugar.' He bent down and found a jug under his seat, took a swig.

A mile up the road they caught a glimpse of the lake in

Victoria Park. The coachman called back: 'I've seen twenty-five thousand people swimming in there all at the same time. All together in the altogether. You couldn't see the water for skin.'

For nearly all the passengers this was strange new territory. Everyone noticed how many of the names on the shop fronts were suddenly French: Michaud, Lafayette, Malivoire, refugees from some continental nastiness hundreds of years ago. Because of the Easter holiday the gaily painted barges were moored up along the banks of Regent's Canal and the bargees were swimming, their heads bobbing like white balloons on the chilly-looking water. The children shouted to them and one of the men waved and duck-dived, showing his bottom. The ladies opened their mouths in delicious shock and covered their blushing cheeks with their hands.

Now the brake rattled along Marylebone Road, still called by some older people the New Road, past Madame Tussaud's, and turned north up the long curving road that ran along the side of Regent's Park. The park railings were on their right; great cream-coloured houses on their left. Servants in uniforms polished the doors and windows.

The coachman took a swig from his jug and started cracking his whip at Jupiter and Minstrel: to avoid paying extra money to have more horses hitched up on Haverstock Hill, he'd chosen the gentler slope of Fitzjohn's Avenue. The mongol boy jumped on the seat and went *toot toot* on his horn as the brake dragged up the last, steepest part of the hill into Hampstead proper.

Tremendous open views stretched away to the smoky horizons. The coachman pulled up by White Stone Pond. 'This is the very place I remember them watering the horses!' cried Mary Godbins, looking around her, clapping her white-gloved hands excitedly. 'And there's the wooden building – Jack Straw's Castle.' The sun was hot, dust hung over the railway, and they could hear the raving of a steam calliope. Along the grassy slopes, the Easter Fair was in full swing.

'Back here five o'clock latest!' shouted the coachman, but

already the children were haring across the road between the vehicles, squealing with joy, then plunging out of sight. 'Give me your hand,' Edith told Ben. 'I shall look after lunch.' They stood watching the mongol boy leading the horses gently down the concrete ramp into the water to drink. He looked up and gave them a wonderfully happy smile.

'My throat's full of dust,' croaked Peter. He nodded towards the pub, Jack Straw's Castle. 'I need a Mackeson to wash it out. Find me there later.'

Edith led Ben carefully away across the road. She handed him some pennies that she had saved. Her heart swelled with joy to see the happiness on his face. 'You may go off by yourself, but be very careful not to get lost, because I may not be able to find you again. Do not speak to any strange men. Take off your cap politely if a lady speaks to you. Do you understand, Ben?'

'Yes.' He lifted one foot and dropped it.

'Answer me properly.'

'Yes, I do understand.'

Edith kissed him, then wiped his cheek with her handkerchief. 'I love you,' she said.

Clutching his pennies, he ran off, and she followed him down into the crowd. She didn't want him to be alone. She wanted to protect him, to see everything he saw, not to let him come to harm. Almost at once, near the calliope, she lost sight of him.

Ben watched. In the flames the sweat shone on the shovelling men, making them look bright orange, and the heat was so hot that he could feel it from here. The wonderful calliope was so loud that the ground shook under his feet and the shovels feeding the monster swung soundlessly. Against the sky rose the silver banks of organ pipes, just like church organ pipes, jetting deafening chords of steam. The song was 'Roll Me Over in the Clover'. He moved closer, until the heat was pushing at him and he couldn't hear the song, only the noise. Trembling brass pipes looped in every direction, squirting squealing white vapour from the joints. It was so alive, so glamorous.

He slipped on through the crowd. The sound of the calliope faded and he could hear voices again. A red-faced man in a bowler hat, with his white shirt sleeves rolled up and secured with shiny metal bands, shouted: '*Penny, penny a throw, come on ladies, who's going to knock my lovely nuts off, lovely coconuts?*'

A man in a flat cap and a check shirt shouted: '*Roll up gents, flex your muscles, show off to the ladies, pick up the hammer and make the bell ring. If you can make this bell ring you can make anyone's bell ring, just as long as you're married first.*'

Here was a crowd. He slipped to the front. A black man, tall and noble-looking. The board said he was a Zulu prince. He wore a grass skirt and brightly-beaded tribal bangles, and grass circlets swung from his knees. He was chained to a cage. The showman shouted that he had eaten a Christian missionary. The crowd gasped. The showman put his hat on the back of his head and his thumbs through his braces, nodding seriously.

The Zulu prince stamped up and down the stage on the end of his chain, yelling and kicking out at the terrified audience with his pink-soled black feet. The showman giving the talk at the front of the stage didn't realize that the black man behind him was working himself up savager and savager and out of control. Everyone in the crowd started shouting to warn him, but the showman couldn't seem to hear. The black prince bent down and broke his shackles with his bare fingers. Meanwhile the showman was showing off a short spear.

Everyone was shouting: 'Look out! Behind you! *Look out!*' The lucky children who had their mothers with them hid their faces in their mother's dresses or wrapped their arms around their father's necks and buried their faces against their chests, because the black man had come creeping up behind the chattering showman and now grabbed the spear from him. He ran up and down the stage leaping and stabbing at the air and hooting, rolling his eyes like a berserker.

The showman, who had jumped down into the crowd for his safety, now shook his fist and shouted up: 'You naughty

Prince Cetawatunga, it's back in the cage for you.' The black man gave a great gibbering scream until one woman at the front of the crowd passed the back of her hand across her brow and looked about to faint. 'Who will help me?' The showman turned and was appealing to the crowd for heroes. 'Who will help me, or else he'll get loose and kill us all!'

Two men in red uniforms with gold buttons and skin-coloured helmets ran forward through the crowd. No one had noticed them before, but there was an outburst of spontaneous applause. 'The Army's here!' The showman pointed and the soldiers jumped up onto the stage, and pushed the black man back with silver-painted bayonets fixed on wooden rifles. The black man dropped his assegai and cowered back into his cage. The showman bolted the door with a flourish, then held out his hand to the two soldiers.

'Thank God for the Thin Red Line and our British heroes! Give everything you can spare.' Pennies began raining down on the stage. 'God knows they deserve it, don't they, ladies and gentlemen, and girls and boys!' Ben, watching with his mouth open, unclenched his left fist and threw all the pennies he held there onto the stage. They rolled in circles, snatched up by the showman before they fell. The crowd must have been drifting away, because Ben suddenly realized that he was standing alone but for an older boy in fine clothes whose face still held the expression of wonderment and sadness.

Ben thought: *I know you.*

He had never had such a strange, strong feeling of affinity, it took his breath away, overwhelmed him so that he reached out automatically to touch him, although the other boy must have been twice his age and nearly twice his height, but a harsh voice broke in.

'Roland! Come here at once!'

The tall boy walked obediently over to an old woman in black, obviously his nanny, still looking back over his shoulder. He had long eyelashes and a sensitive mouth; he looked the sort of clever boy who would be bullied – except that his clothes were so good that he probably had a tutor, or went to a public school. Ben watched them until they disappeared in the crowd.

'That's all, lad,' the showman said casually, 'next show one o'clock.'

The stage was empty and they'd picked up all the pennies. The black man had gone from his cage.

There must be other things to see. Ben ran on. Here were two old people with wrinkled faces, the Pearly King and his Pearly Queen. They wore black clothes that were so covered with glowing pearls and sequins flashing in the sun that you couldn't hardly see the blackness beneath at all.

And there was Vulkan the Fireater who blew flames, even when bending over backwards until his head was between his ankles. He didn't have a single hair on his gleaming skull, not even an eyebrow.

You had to pay to see the Boy with Six Fingers and the Troupe of Dwarfs, but the Bearded Woman was a free attraction sitting in the entrance.

Then Ben saw the rides. Now he really missed his money; they wouldn't let him on without it. Gaudy cars whirled on the end of steam-powered cranes. He would have given anything to go aboard. There was a merry-go-round with shiny red horses with black eyes and gold manes, riding up and down on fluted poles. Little girls on them squealed with delight. One girl wouldn't get off when the ride ended. The girl's mother looked bright red with embarrassment as she dragged her off.

There was a terrific Ferris wheel from America, turning slowly against the sky. On the other side of the crowd, Ben saw a marquee that served teas. The black man, the Zulu prince, was sitting calmly at a table. He wore a tweed suit and was drinking a cup of tea with his little finger extended.

'Don't stare, it's rude.' Edith caught hold of Ben's hand. He wanted to tell her about all the things he had seen.

'Let's find Uncle,' she said, 'and we can have lunch.'

They climbed up the path to Jack Straw's Castle. Peter came weaving out wiping thick yellow beer foam off his moustache. 'Halloa,' he called, then tripped. 'Whoops!'

They bought a pitcher from the lemonade man and found a place amongst the picnickers on the side of the grassy hill. The sun in their eyes was hot but it was too early in the year for flies to bother. Edith opened the lunch bag and started pulling things out.

London town was spread out below them like the panorama of an atlas. They'd thought it would be all buildings – but it was green: the biggest city in the world was more trees than buildings. They could tell where the biggest streets were by the lines of treetops narrowing into the haze. Regent's Park was a big green circle, Hyde Park a green rectangle glittering with threads of water.

As they ate they squinted their eyes into the sun. The river Thames glared beneath them, growing broader as it twisted and turned away to their left towards the invisible sea. 'London's broadest street,' Peter said, starting on a whole pork pie in one hand and bagsing the last sausage roll by snatching it up in his other hand, using it to point at something glinting in the far distance. 'The Crystal Palace. Huge glass palace, got fully grown trees inside. I'll take more of that cheese, ta. See that black lump? The dome of St Paul's cathedral.' He stared at the sausage roll, then ate it in two bites.

Edith poured a glass of lemonade. 'Great spree,' Peter said. 'Enjoying it.'

'Let the boy have the last jam sandwich!' Edith said. 'Peter. Really.'

'If I'm hungry, why shouldn't I eat?' demanded Peter. 'Look, boy, Tower Bridge – got it? The twin towers? The bridge between them lifts up so that ships can go through. Water power. Always works, every time. Same system as does the lifts in the Savoy Hotel. Didn't know that, Edith? Can't know everything. Go on, twist my arm, I'll have some of that Dundee cake! I saw the first time that bridge ever lifted up. Didn't work.'

Drowsily they watched the sun sliding down the sky and the shadows lengthening. Edith began shivering and Ben crawled over and wrapped his arms around her.

'I'm going to put another Mackeson out of its misery,' Peter yawned, getting up.

Edith looked alarmed. 'But the brake leaves very soon.'

'I'll meet you there by the pond,' Peter said. 'He'll wait for me.'

The children pulled Peter aboard just barely as the brake was leaving. He stumbled across the seats against Edith and was snoring by the time they descended Haverstock Hill. Mr Godbins slept with his mouth open. The women talked quietly amongst themselves. Edith listened to the metal-to-metal brakes squealing ineffectually during the descent, watching the horses' hindquarters rolling from side to side as they strained back against the weight with stiff legs. The women stopped talking, yawning. Even the children slept, played out.

Edith sat wakefully. The bridge echoed: 'Hey Jupiter, hey Minstrel,' the coachman said softly. His mongol son smiled at the sleeping people.

No bargees were swimming in the canal now. Yellow lamps were glowing in their boats, ochre reflections glimmering beneath them from the pewter-coloured water, as if they were floating in air. The brake jolted across road works and Peter groaned in his sleep and held his hand into the small of his back. She held him up until Bethnal Green, when everyone started waking up and getting ready to get off, yawning and stretching.

Peter woke. He had a headache and his mouth tasted of beer dregs.

'Do you feel all right?' Edith asked.

'Of course I do, fresh air gives me an appetite,' Peter said. 'I could just do with a jellied eel in the paper.' They got down outside Fred's Eel & Pie Shop at the end of the road. Ben watched one of Fred's sons poking up under the eaves with a long pole. Peter glowered in through the lighted window at all the people inside the shop waiting to be served. The coachman pushed ahead of him to get his supper to take home, leaving his son in the driving seat, half-asleep. Peter gestured at the people. 'I can't wait all that time,' he said, favouring his back.

'Is it hurting?' Edith asked.

'It is a bit, love.'

'Listen,' she offered, 'you take the boy home, put him to bed and have a sit down. I'll bring you something.'

'All right,' he said. 'That's very friendly of you.'

This was a chance to get at the brown sherry. He steered Ben down the darkening street. The boy was very sleepy. He pulled him up the whitestoned steps into the hall, left him sitting on the stairs. He poured a glass of sherry, drank it, wiped the glass on his hankerchief, then replaced it in the dresser. 'Come on! Upstairs with you. Up the wooden hill. *Come on.*'

Edith's bedroom was dark. The only light came from the gaslamp outside in the street. Her alarm clock ticked, there was no other sound; nothing through the wall. He imagined Mrs Kent lying on the bed with her arms outstretched and her legs apart. He imagined himself being able to do no other than to obey her summons, not even taking his clothes off, lying on her and dominating her, clawing at each other in an ecstasy of lust. Then he glanced at Edith's empty bed again, with roses in pretty patterns across the coverlet.

The boy was standing by the window at the foot of his bed. He hadn't even got his clothes off. '*Come on!*' Peter said. He searched for the flannel. Edith always flannelled the boy's face for some female reason before putting him to bed.

Ben stood at the window watching Aunt Edith walking home along the road. She was carrying the parcel of newspaper that must contain the eel.

Peter couldn't find the flannel anywhere. 'Just get your shirt and trousers off or whatever you do.'

Ben, pulling at his buttons, watched Edith's face slowly brighten as she approached the gaslamp outside. A group of women who hadn't been on the outing called to her from the other pavement. Edith stopped. The brake turned the corner at the end of the road with the big rear wheels skidding outwards, one horse's head held low, the other tossing back, held high.

The women must have asked a question, because he

142

heard Edith call: 'Yes, the Easter Fair was wonderful. We had a lovely spree.'

He could hear the rumbling of the brake's iron wheels.

The women must have asked another question, because Edith called:

'Oh, the usual things, the Zulu warrior, the Fire Eater, all the sort of act that they usually have.'

Now the rumbling was loud; the brake must be coming very fast.

'Get your vest off,' Peter ordered. He heard the noise and looked impatiently over Ben's head out of the window. Under the gaslight Edith's eyes were black sockets, and her nose trailed a black spike of shadow that rippled over her lips, then curved down her chin. Peter thinned his eyes: beyond the glare of the gaslight, two sources of sparks were moving along the darkened street. The distance between them widened as they approached.

Now Peter heard a thin screeching above the deep rumble. He knew the sound: it was metal-to-metal brakes. If they were dragged full on, they screeched and sheeted sparks; you had only to look at a train. The gaslight glared in his eyes.

'Oh my God,' Peter said. Now he could see the galloping horses dragging the brake pell-mell along the road. Sparks shot from their hooves and flew in red sheets from the metal brakes behind. He saw the mongol boy standing on the driver's seat, leaning back like a pulled bow so that his head almost touched the backs of the seats behind, dragging on the reins. The reins were as straight as though they were made of steel, but the horses had the bits between their teeth. *Those bloody bees!* Peter thought. The road was too narrow, there was no room to pass between Edith and the group of women; the brake careered from kerb to kerb, then mounted the pavement, then skidded back down again. It was one or the other: the single woman or the group.

Let it be them, Peter thought, staring. *Oh Christ let it be them!*

The women were turning. Some were putting their hands to their heads. Others had bent over, as if they were trying to run.

The boy let one rein fly – the one that pointed towards the women. He was dragging back with all his strength on the other, his face full of terror and effort. The horses' heads pulled to that side.

Let it not be her – because who would look after the boy?

'What is it, Uncle?' Ben said. He was standing at the window too, naked as the day he was born.

Down in the street, beneath the glaring gaslight, Edith Rumney looked up, and Peter knew that she saw him, his pale face at the window in the backwash of light, and Ben's face, and her mouth turned into a black hole. He knew she was shouting: 'No! No! No!' and he thought: Christ, what does she mean? Don't let him see? She wasn't thinking about herself, only of Ben. He grabbed the boy's head and pulled it against him, burying the boy's face into his belly so that he should not see. He held his hands over his ears too, so that he should not hear. Her last wish. Blind him. Deafen him. Spare him.

Peter watched Edith disappear beneath the horses.

The horses stumbled.

Their harness seemed to fly apart. The breaking leather whiplashed.

The ash shafts cracked, the reins jerked loose, the horses ran free.

The front wheels, without steering, twisted into the cobbles, stuck, and somersaulted the heavy vehicle slowly into the air. It came down with a disintegrating crash, overturned, three wheels broken, the other still spinning, flashing light.

Hoofbeats died away into the distance.

The women were screaming, tiny breathless screams, very high.

The mongol boy lay in the road trying to crawl, paddling with his arms, his head rising and falling frantically, his legs dragging limply behind him.

The wheel kept spinning for a very long time.

Part III

THE WORKHOUSE

Chapter Five

1

London fog.

Everything had gone, everything had changed. The broad street had disappeared and no longer seemed dangerous, but she knew the fog only hid the danger. Hidden, the terrifying street was still there in front of her: the long dark buildings with black-painted windows, and doors and windows with curved tops. The fog didn't take anything away. It just hid it.

Ria Price crouched motionless in the safe, concealing mouth of an alleyway, the slimy walls protecting her. If anyone jumped out of the fog, even if they were as quick as her brothers Nigel or Vic, they would never catch her, because she would be gone. Within five paces – three at a run – was another low mouth that would take her to safety, with an arch to slow the pursuer, then steps down, then a court with three exits at ground level, hanging washing, uneven stones (she knew every one), and any number of ways out below ground or above it. Even Vic would not catch her here. She was safe.

But the street was out in the open, flat and dangerous. She could be caught out in that blank space with everywhere to run and yet nowhere to run to, because she would be in full view. She would be running in rings in the open with everyone chasing her. She didn't know why they would. Mum had said they would, years ago, when she was a very little girl, because she was pretty. Men would kick her and tear her clothes. 'Why, Mum?' Esther shouted that the pan needed to be filled and somehow Ria never knew *why* these nightmarish things would happen, she just knew they *would*.

Because I'm me, Ria thought, crouching in the mouth of the alleyway. Because I'm Ria Price. Because I'm different. I'm as old as I've got fingers on my hands. There's never been another Ria Price and no one's ever thought what I'm thinking now before, not ever. I'm me. I'm *me*.

Only hidden was she safe. Hidden by walls, or hidden by dark.

But the street was lit by gaslamps on poles, and was never dark.

She trembled with fear and want. The pile of rubbish in the centre of the street was still there, a darker lump in the fog. She could just see the doll's head sticking out of the top. No one had grabbed it yet.

To run out into the street . . . or not.

Ria wanted her more than she had ever wanted anything in her life. She never really had wanted anyone before, had let everything simply happen, because that was what things did, and nothing could be changed. But now there was the doll. A real doll. Ria had never felt so alive.·

But she would have to go out into the wide, empty, open street where nightmares happened.

Earlier, a man in a tall hat had come along and tossed the doll casually on the heap, and strolled on.

A waggon had rumbled past. The driver had hardly glanced at the rubbish; he could not have seen the doll.

Now two men stood talking by the rubbish, making a deal in low voices. One of them looked down and kept saying, 'No, no, mate. Can't do it.' He seemed to be looking straight at the doll. Ria crouched in an agony of suspense, yet her withdrawn, almost bored expression did not change.

The doll was too marvellous. She could never be Ria's.

Yet Ria wanted her, how she wanted a doll of her very own!

She held her chin clenched between her knees, her hands buried in her lap, compressed between her thighs and belly, her bottom almost touching the black stones within the circle of her dress. The tattered dress had once been yellow, the same colour as her hair.

In the fog her eyes were a mixture of blue and gold, neither the one nor the other, an opaque, unreadable tone in this sad light rather than a colour. The strange, pretty eyes would have been a beautiful feature had they not been so difficult to see into, not revealing the soul behind but hiding it behind their opal flecks. Her unwashed hair, which would have been gold, fell in flat, lank curls to her scrawny shoulders. Her face was wonderful, but her lips pouted like a sulky Cupid's, as though they had never smiled. Her smooth, pale skin was blackened with grease and dirt. She never did smile; she had nothing to smile about. Her eyes staring at the doll looked starving. Her bare feet stuck out grubbily beneath the hem of her dress, and her toes were flattened at the end into hard little hammers from the bare stones. There were thousands like her, all around her, within half a mile of her in the fog rolling off the West India dock. Yet she remained distinctive.

And still the men would not go.

At last they laughed and shook hands, going off in opposite directions.

Ria's tongue licked her upper lip, hesitating.

Then she heard the echoes of a trotting horse and clattering wheels, but it went by without her seeing anything of it in the fog.

She realized: the street's still there, yes, but the fog's hiding it. So, if *I* go out in the street the fog will hide *me*! She imagined herself scampering out, grabbing the doll, and scampering back before anyone saw her, before anyone could catch her.

Then she thought disdainfully: Why should I run? I'm Ria Price. I don't need to run for anybody. I'm not frightened. I'm me.

Go on. Slow as you like. Put your hand on your hip, like Mum does, and swagger. Put on a show! That's it . . .

Ria took hold of her doll between her palms and lifted her

out gently, standing holding her in a rapture, forgetting her surroundings. Dolly's wood was as white as skin, polished down the front by hugging. Her curly red mouth had been scratched by over-enthusiastic feeding. Ria hugged her and tried to cry. She held Dolly to her with a fierce, silent love.

From somewhere she heard laughter.

She ran, but tripped over the rubbish. The alleyway had gone. Somewhere a ship hooted mournfully, sounding all around her. She crouched on one knee in a smooth circle of fog with the doll against her neck. Stupid, stupid, stupid doll.

But it was pleasant laughter. It sounded neither drunk nor cruel. It was the laughter of people enjoying themselves. Ria crept through the fog, until a dark stain appeared, and then brilliant lights. A building. A playhouse. A hesitant smile flickered on Ria's lips. People were coming out from the bright doorways, laughing and chattering about what they had seen as they came down the wooden steps, then standing in groups, pulling up their collars against the fog, some of them coughing, but none of them noticing her. She wished they would; she, like them, was so happy. Her mouth widened into an eager smile and she looked radiant. She wished they'd ask her about her doll.

Now she could see inside the playhouse a little: some gaudy pictures of the players, laughing, or singing, or looking saucy or proud; another world. The people were going away but the doors remained open. She crept closer to the light. She could see bright red plush and the gleaming gold-painted frame of a mirror. She held Dolly to her cheek, her mouth open in wonder.

A man came out and slammed the doors. The world ended. He strode past her into the darkness and didn't even notice her.

She stood alone in the dark street with the fog swirling around her, a girl of about eight in a tattered yellow dress, clutching a pathetic doll. The ship hooted again. When the echoes died away she heard low voices coming out of the fog.

'It won't be for long,' the man's voice said.

Ria prepared to run. But which way?

'But where are we going?' the boy's voice said. A foreigner; perhaps the son of one of the foreign sailors off the ships, pronouncing all the sounds in a word clearly. 'Where are you taking me?' Why should he care? You went where you were told.

'Come on with you,' the man said. 'Not far.'

'But I want to know.' He sounded quite young, perhaps younger than her.

'You want to know too much.' Quite right; keep your mouth shut.

'Why won't you tell me?' the boy said in a high voice. That was cheeky, speaking to a grown-up like that. She waited for the sound of the blow.

Silence. Then the man said in a gruff voice, 'There are things you're too young to know.'

'What things?' Ria put her hand over her mouth, her eyes shining. She'd never heard anyone daring to answer back like this before.

Two dark shadows appeared out of the fog, walking slowly, the larger almost dragging the smaller. The man's form was very tall, even taller than Dad, but not as heavy, and he trod sort of delicately somehow, where Dad always walked as though he was still carrying a bale of wool wedged across his shoulders. 'Just things, that's all,' the tall man said.

'I want to go home.' The boy said this with a slight shake in his voice. He was going to cry. Ria stared, fascinated. He was no older than her; perhaps younger. But he looked very well fed and clean. His legs were straight and his lips were smooth. His fingernails were trimmed white and even. She'd never seen anything like him before. And standing up to the man like this. Each time the man spoke, she winced, as if expecting the lashing blow she sensed building up in him to strike her down too. Yet the boy simply repeated: 'I want to go home.' She stood watching, fascinated, forgetting to run away.

'The bank took it, you know that,' the man shouted, very

angrily, jerking. 'Come on, can't you? Do I have to drag you all the way?'

'I hope I'm hurting your back,' the boy said. Ria gasped. The man whipped round and gave the boy a good flat-handed clout around the head, then when he fell over dragged him up by his hand.

'You give me any more lip like that and I'll bloody use my fist on you, right? Right! And then we'll see you laugh on the other side of your face, won't we?'

But the boy said: 'There was some money left over.'

'Rubbish,' the man shouted, 'she'd spent it all on you! *Come on!*'

The boy held his face with his free hand, almost falling.

'I know she didn't go away,' he said. 'She wouldn't just leave me and go back to Norfolk, would she?'

The man turned.

'She's dead,' the boy said. He began to cry, genuinely, with long racking sobs.

The tall man looked down. He seemed unable to decide how to answer. He took out a white handkerchief and wiped the greasy droplets of fog from his own face, then handed it down to the boy. 'You're too young to understand,' he said quietly. 'It's grown-up business.'

'She's dead, isn't she?'

Again the man didn't seem to know how to answer. He started several different sentences. Ria knew what that meant: he was lying. He was a very bad liar. Perhaps he was trying to keep a secret. Everyone had secrets. The whole world was black with them.

Finally the man spoke to the boy, but in a very grinning voice. 'Listen,' he said, 'I only want what's best for you.' He wiped the boy's eyes, smiling with all his teeth. 'You do believe your old Uncle Peter, don't you? I wouldn't lie to you, would I?'

The boy looked up. 'No, Uncle,' he said dutifully. Ria giggled. He must have been born yesterday.

The boy heard her.

He looked at her – straight at her. She sensed that he knew her, all about her. He knew that she loved Dolly. He knew that her feet hurt on the cold stones. He knew that she had her own feelings, that she was a person, that she was hungry, that she was interesting, that she was only a frightened girl in a man's world but alive and unique and full of her own mysteries. He saw all this. His eyes were bluer than hers and his hair was darker. He didn't look away or make a face like most boys would have, putting his thumbs in his ears and waggling his tongue. He just looked at her. He didn't move his eyes from her. She knew he understood her. She knew that she could trust him. They already shared her greatest, deepest, most personal secret. She thought: *He knows that I am special.*

For a moment, for only a moment, she was not alone.

'*Come on!*' the grown-up roared, and dragged the boy away. The boy's shoes – he had real shoes – skidded on the slick stones. Ria watched helplessly. For a moment the boy's eyes looked at her, seeming piercingly blue in the colourless fog, the darkness around them, then he was tripping and stumbling after the man, jerked up every time he dropped to his knees.

Their shadows faded.

The fog took them.

Ria stood alone.

She looked back the way she had come: safety.

Then she turned around the other way and ran after them, the cobbles thudding against her feet, her toes feeling the line of the kerb. Sometimes she felt something soft beneath her feet. They were very close to the docks here. She was panting. The wide street, the circle of fog. A hissing street lamp. Her shadow swung around her like the hands of a great clock. There they were: she slowed down, keeping the shapes of the man and boy just in sight in the fog ahead.

Where were they going?

The fog darkened as a building began to appear. The man pulled the boy across the road towards it. They both looked small under the black walls and the narrow, pointed windows.

She watched them turn down the tiny side road where the entrance was.

She drew back, the doll dangling forgotten from her hand.

This was a building she knew well. It was the Workhouse.

2

Ben said: 'Are you taking me in here?'

Uncle Peter said nothing, just dragged him on with his enormous hand.

It looked like a prison. They had turned off Poplar High Street into a narrow lane. Bare black brick rose up on their left into the fog. It looked a hundred years old, frighteningly ancient and huge. On their right were some wretched old houses partly built of wood, with garrets jutting out of the crooked roofs.

Uncle Peter dragged him towards the left.

'I don't want to go in here,' Ben said. He looked up at the calloused hand dragging him on. Falling down hadn't worked. Crying hadn't moved him. Talking about Aunt Edith had only irritated him. Uncle Peter had shut up his feelings like an oyster. He couldn't get through to him. It was a strange, frightening discovery. He couldn't touch him at all. The suspicion of a tear had been enough to wind Aunt Edith around his little finger.

Ben said: 'Why are you doing this to me?'

'For God's sake shut up,' Peter said.

'What is this place?' They were close enough to smell it now.

'It's time you started learning things at school,' Peter said.

Does he think I'm that stupid? Ben thought. Why come here when there's the Grammar School just across the road at home! And there it smells of chalk, and wooden boards, and books. This place smells of stone.

'It isn't a school,' Ben said.

'Look, it's only temporary,' Peter said. 'Just until I can get things sorted out.'

'What things?'

'This and that.' Grown-up things. 'It's not my fault,' Peter said. He had kept saying that. That meant it was.

Peter pulled him to a black door set in the wall. In the stone arch above it was inscribed the word MEN. Obviously not a school. Perhaps somewhere nearby there was another stone arch inscribed WOMEN. Ben suddenly wondered if this was a place they put dead people. Peter tugged the bell. He looked down at Ben and Ben looked up, looking at Peter right in the eyes. He knew Peter wasn't a bad man. He tried to imagine if it was possible for a man who was as strong as Peter outside to be weak inside. Yes, he knew it was.

Peter looked away. The door opened and a voice said: 'Full up.'

Peter said: 'It's me. I've come to see Mr Madeley.'

'It's you. Come in, sir.' The Casual Porter, an old man who suffered terrible running sores on his lips, stood aside. Dragged by Peter's hand, Ben ducked beneath him into the vestibule. There was a smell of old people, and the sweetish stink of rotting pork and disinfectant. It was colder inside than out. A few old men stood around the walls, coughing because of the fog. The porter closed the door and they stood in the weak gaslight.

'I'll call the Master for you, sir,' the old porter said.

He went out through a side door.

Ben looked up at Peter. 'I'll do anything,' he said. He heard the desperate tremor in his own voice. 'I'll be good. I won't ask for anything. You won't have to bring me honeycomb, you'll hardly know I'm there. Please don't leave me here, Uncle Peter.'

Peter shook his head. They could hear footsteps approaching.

Ben said urgently, playing his last card, jerking at Peter: 'Why can't I live with Mrs Kent and you?' Guiltily he corrected himself, he never got anything if he asked for it wrongly. 'You and Mrs Kent,' he added, and knew that he had lost.

'She's a busy woman,' Peter said briskly, 'She doesn't like children around the place. She hadn't got time.' *For a little bastard.*

Ben felt himself going hot and cold inside and knew he was going to cry. He tried desperately not to, but the water in his mouth thickened. His lips began to stretch helplessly back into his cheeks. He couldn't make Peter do anything he wanted, but Mrs Kent could. It was all Mrs Kent this, and Mrs Kent that, and Mrs Kent's feeling poorly so I'm just popping round to see she's all right. Mrs Kent had replaced him, he hardly saw Peter at home any more. Mrs Kent wasn't even family, but she made Uncle Peter jump around like a little puppet on strings. Probably he gave the honeycomb to her. Ben pressed his fists to his mouth, determined not to cry now in front of Uncle Peter. When he grazed his knees, to get some peace Aunt Edith would say: *Only little boys cry. Men don't cry.* He choked back the tears in the same way now.

'That's better,' Peter said. 'It's not so bad. It's all for the best. You'll like it here. Make some friends. You've been very lonely up to now, haven't you?'

A big man turned through the doorway the porter had gone out of. He strode across to them, ignoring everyone else, not even giving them a polite hallo. 'Peter, you old bugger. This is the one? Come on.' Ben stared up at him. This must be the Mr Madeley that Peter had asked for. Obviously they knew one another. Madeley was an enormously fat man with a flat, pale face and very dark eyes and eyebrows, black sideburns, and black hair like matting down his forearms where the sleeves of his white shirt were rolled up. His belly overhung his trousers at the front but at the back his bottom looked shrunken, small and flat, with his brown serge trousers hanging over it in folds. 'Come on, let's go to the office and get this sorted out.' The corridor echoed with mysterious noises and Ben glimpsed big cold rooms lit by tiny jets of light, and people who always seemed to be motionless. It was as though Mr Madeley was the only one here with the gift of life.

Mr Madeley motioned them into his office. Ben gasped. It looked like a theatre, with a huge polished desk with carved legs and gold inlay, gilt mirrors, red plush chairs with gold backs, and three chandeliers glistening with electric light. 'Sit down, Peter. The usual?' He opened a thing like a wardrobe and there were casks of beer inside, with brass spigots. Ben sat, his legs swinging off the chair, watching Madeley draw two foaming silver tankards. 'Triple X. Best stuff north of the Thames. Down the hatch.' They drank and then Madeley walked past him and Ben found himself on the floor with his head ringing, and realized that Madeley had hit him. His ear burned. He hadn't done anything! 'Manners, boy. Sit when you're told, not until.'

Ben said: 'What manners?' He could see just by looking at him that Madeley was an oaf who didn't know what manners were; he probably didn't even know to put his knife and fork together after he'd finished his meal. Who was he to talk about manners? Ben almost said it. But then he decided not to. Obviously he had to win Mr Madeley round, not irritate him.

Peter said, 'He's very young at the moment, Bill.'

'If he cheeks me like that again I'll do him,' Madeley said.

'Understood, Bill.'

'Does he know that?'

'He doesn't know his arse from his face,' Peter said. 'Don't be too hard on him, Bill.'

'Well,' Madeley said, then drank his beer. 'This is quite a favour I'm doing you. I'll have to square it with the Guardians. Have you got the necessary?'

While he refilled the tankards Peter got a pouch out of his pocket and counted out ten gold coins. Before putting them down on the desk he said: 'I thought you said you could square them any time with a few beers and a dozen oysters.'

'Not Lansbury or Crook.'

'Crook!'

'Despite his name. Socialist extremist, pain in the arse.'

'I thought you said there was no risk.'

'There isn't, mate. We're supposed to draft them off to the Langley Receiving Home and the Forest Gate schools when the kids are three, but the Clerk to the Guardians is one of mine. Mr Lough, Mr Herbert Lough. He takes a

special interest in the training and education of the young.'
He handed Peter a fresh tankard in such a way that Peter
had to give the coins into his hand.

'That isn't his money!' Ben said. 'It's mine.'

'That's why he gave it to me,' Madeley said.

What would Aunt Edith have said? How would she have
coped? Once the grocer had given her the wrong change.
He copied her. He said: 'I'm sorry, Mr Madeley, but I'm
afraid there's been a mistake.'

'What's she like?' Madeley said, looking at Peter.

Ben thought: Does he mean Aunt Edith?

Madeley said: 'Does she shout when you give it to her?'

What were they talking about? Mrs Kent?

Peter leaned back, looking smug.

Madeley shook his head. 'You've really got it set up
right, I'll give you that.'

'So have you. You're in Matron's bed, aren't you?'

'Ssh,' Madeley said, and winked. 'Not just in bed.'

'You old rogue,' Peter said admiringly.

They were ignoring him! Adults had never ignored him
before.

Suddenly Ben understood. This was the sort of manly
gossip you heard going on in the pub through the wall of the
jug and bottle counter. Outside in the street the women
always talked about babies and knitting and what their
friend said. Inside, the men talked like this. It was a level of
talk that totally excluded him. He was not here. He felt a
terrible new emotion that made his throat ache, and he
didn't know what it was.

He was lonely for the first time in his life.

'Let's get him booked in,' Bill Madeley said. He burped
and went to the door. 'Moxon! Get your arse in here, sir.'

Ben didn't know who to turn to. He couldn't bear to look
at Peter. He could beg him to take him away, but he knew
he wouldn't. He didn't want to see Uncle Peter again. He
thought: *I'll never forgive him.* He felt the lips of this dreadful
place closing around him. Then the door began to open and
he did turn to Uncle Peter.

'Help me,' he said. He put everything he had into it.

I'm alive. I'm a living human being. You can't treat me like this. People care about each other. They don't do this to one another.

'It's not me doing it,' Peter said smoothly. 'It's Mrs Kent, you know. She insisted.'

'He'll do all right,' Bill Madeley said heartily. 'We'll make him into another Fat Boy like Moxon here, won't we, Moxon?'

'We'll do our best, Bill,' Moxon said. He was globular-shaped and no longer quite a boy, with hairs straggling his upper lip and chin. Ben stared up into his eyes: they looked sleepy and cunning, almost as dark as Bill Madeley's. He took Ben's hand between his big, soft fingers. 'Come on, littl'un,' he smiled.

'Don't be too hard on him,' Peter said anxiously, then the door was slammed.

'What's your name? How old are you?' Moxon asked out in the bare corridor as they walked. He had a soft, languid voice. He nodded at the telephone man in the box by the stairs. 'That's Willy Crosbie, and if you ever try to sneak in here or talk to him, he'll tell me, right? Where did you get those shoes? Lovely quality. You must have all sorts of things in your pockets. Did you have a life outside? Are you going to cry? No? I've lived in here all my life, and it's a good life, if you can eat and sleep all day, and if you don't have to pick oakum. Yes, if you can be a Fat Boy. But that's up to you, isn't it? Bill's a good sort. You've just got to get yourself set up right. Do you know what the first rule is?'

'No.'

'You've got to be friendly. You're going to love it here.' He sounded bored. He looked in one of the big bare rooms that Ben had noticed on the way in. It seemed that the men and boys in there had remained motionless since that time. 'Knuts!' he bellowed. One or two men looked round. They were dressed in grey cotton shirts. 'Get your shitty arse over here.'

The boy who had been sitting alone, with his eyes fixed apparently sightlessly on the one gas pendant that illumin-ated the room, jerked upright, then came shuffling over. 'Yes, Mr Moxon.' Ben thought that he was blind, but then

159

the watery pale-blue eyes found him for a moment. Knuts stood in a slightly stiff way in front of Moxon, as though that was the thing to do.

'Come with me,' Moxon ordered. 'Can you at least do that?'

'Yes, Mr Moxon.'

They returned to the vestibule. The outer doors had been locked. Moxon called the porter. 'Mr Haswell. Another one to book in.'

The porter rubbed his sore lips and grumbled, bored. He went behind a counter and got out a big ledger, opened it, found a stub of pencil and licked it. 'Come on then! Name? Where'd you sleep last night?'

Ben thought: *I will not cry*.

'At home,' he said.

'Where's that, matey?'

Ben shook his head. He couldn't say another word. In his misery he felt someone touch his hand. It was the other boy, the one Moxon had called Nuts. His watery eyes peered sympathetically at Ben. He gave a tiny nod of comfort. Ben gripped the friendly hand desperately.

The porter sighed and licked the pencil. 'London.'

Knuts said: 'His hair is light brown, Mr Haswell. Eyes blue.' So he could see; at least at close range.

'He's got to answer it himself,' the porter said grumpily. 'It's the rules. This is a Poor Law Institution, the spike, not a bleeding hotel. All right. Brown. Blue. Height?'

'Put down five foot,' Moxon said impatiently. 'We'll skip the rest, it can go in later.'

Haswell pointed irritably with the pencil. 'You got to have the bath. Through there.'

'Go on, Knuts,' Moxon said. They went into a room with stained brown walls and three big dirty baths. 'Clothes off, littl'un.' He watched. Ben had never taken his clothes off in front of anyone before. He started to fold them neatly but Moxon snatched them and went through the pockets at the far end of the room while Knuts filled the bath. The spouting water made a hollow metallic roar.

'Get in,' he whispered. 'Quick, before he gets back.'

Ben put his foot in. The swirling water was icy. 'It's cold,' he said. Knuts looked at him blankly.

'Of course it's cold,' he said. He turned it off.

'But where's the hot water?'

'You don't know much!' wheezed Knuts. 'There isn't any, for inmates.'

Ben got into the freezing water. He gasped. His heart raced. He drew up his legs and wrapped his arms around him. Beneath his skinny shanks the bottom of the bath felt slimy with human grease and dirt. He stuttered: 'Nuts? Is that really your name?'

'With a *K*. My father was a Scandinavian sailor, named Knut, I suppose. Knut's child. Who cares? Who knows?' He gave a quick, hurt smile. Ben stared at him. Should he trust Knuts? He had to trust someone. Knuts was clever, and he knew this place. There were bound to be all sorts of rules, like in a school. Raise your cap to the ladies. Call the masters Sir. Different ones, but lots of them. He came to a decision.

'Knuts, you're right, I don't know much,' Ben said with chattering teeth. He looked up into the older boy's eyes. 'Will you help me? Help me to learn?'

'I'm the last person to ask,' Knuts whispered in his high, almost womanish voice.

'I've got to ask someone the rules.'

'Not me.'

'Moxon?'

'The first rule is to stay clear of him!' Knuts handed down a stiff grey towel. 'Get out now. You're not allowed to wear your own clothes. I'll give you a cotton shift.'

Shivering as he dried himself on the smooth, sticky towel, Ben whispered eagerly: 'What's the second rule?'

Knuts said: 'When they hit you, scream. Don't try and hold it in, it just makes it worse. Let them know they're hurting you, or else.'

It sounded cowardly. 'Or else what?'

'Worse things can happen.' Knuts looked down. He didn't want to go on.

'What things?'

161

'They can damage you permanently. They don't mean to,' he added.

Ben held the shift in his hands. It stank. He pulled it quickly over his head.

He said, 'Who are they?'

Knuts said: 'Ordinary people.'

3

People wondered if it would go to his head: Mr Campbell-Bannerman was the first Prime Minister ever to hold the official title of Prime Minister. They said that his government's greatest achievement was to grant self-government to the defeated Boer states. Meanwhile, they noted, some twenty thousand children under sixteen were kept in Workhouses at the taxpayers' expense. It was a scandal. At the local level, allegations of extravagance were hurled across the council chambers. Every effort was made to reduce costs.

His supporters spoke of him as a future Prime Minister: George Lansbury said that society had a duty towards its weaker members which was not fulfilled by throwing them in the Workhouse. For a night's bed and a bowl of skilly to eat a man was made to break stones for a day. With this punishment only the most desperate paupers returned. A pauper had no money at all, not even enough for the doss-house or a lump of bread. Out of every thousand people in this parish, according to the official figures, not less than sixty human beings were paupers. The real figure was much higher. This year over eight thousand, starving and destitute, were charged to the rates in Poplar Workhouse during July.

The ratepayers were sick of paying for it.

Even Lansbury admitted that the Workhouse system of firm administration – in practice brutal administration – was necessary because of the large numbers of young men: some wards were in a state of continual rebellion. Mr Madeley sadly reported that he had no command over the inmates unless he gave them beer. The beer cellar was called 'The Madeley Arms', and that year, with beer at a penny a pint, and two hundred and forty pence to the pound, it somehow cost the ratepayers three hundred pounds. Madeley and his wife, on a salary of £100, were living at a rate of £1500 per year. Madeley was rigging the tenders for the supply of goods to the Workhouse: rival bidders were brought in for a friendly chat around his inlaid desk. Bad meat and impure milk was delivered to him – at ninepence a gallon, instead of a penny less from honest traders. Madeley's crony Henry Griffiths paid the Workhouse a couple of pounds a month to clean away rough fat and skimmings from the cooking coppers and drains to make into soap, candles and cough lozenges – in fact he also took away best meat dripping which he sold to butchers for threepence a pound, splitting the profits with Bill Madeley.

Lansbury was politically simple, but he was not corrupt. Nearly all the other Guardians went along with what was going on, so he got the blame, because that was the way of the world, because he had never attended Madeley's feasts of salmon, oysters, stewed eels, and paralysing xxx stout. He was so incorruptible that he was accused by the others of extravagance. After all, it was undeniable that it cost nearly two shillings a week to feed a child in the Workhouse, even though they got only half the portion of the adults.

The children called him Uncle George. Red-faced and kindly, dressed in old but well-cared-for clothes, and neatly polished shoes with paper-thin soles, he came into Block E, the Children's Ward. The children looked up indifferently. Lit by a single gas pendant, the long room was bare and unheated. In theory, he knew, exhaust steam from the laundry worked a Berryman heater that piped hot water past the women's rooms and into this block, but in practice the pipe was a dead leg, cold except when water was drawn off to waste. The children stared at him without any sign of interest or emotion.

Lansbury's heart thudded with rage. *What sort of people are we creating?* he wondered, and shivered from more than the touch of the icy air.

He held out his arms to the children.

Some of them, not understanding, lay back down again and turned away.

One shivering girl came across, hesitated, then took his hand. Others, watching, came over and looked at him.

'Good day to you!' he said, bending down. 'How are you all, my friends?' It was the lifelessness of the children that was so frightening. They were literally bored almost to death. When something happened to interrupt their indifferent world, a visitor, they seemed unable to react at first. Then slowly they gathered into a circle of ragged shifts around him. He tousled some heads. A little boy hung onto his hand. Then another girl reached out and put her fingers around his thumb. A boy at the back started jumping up and down, but shrank away cringing from Uncle George's hand when it was held out to him.

A girl held the side of his hand against her cheek for comfort while she coughed. A little boy held his knee. Dangling children, Uncle George shuffled slowly down the ward. The boy who had shrunk away touched his fingertip, then gave a shy smile. The children began to laugh and chatter. They wanted to show him a live mouse they had caught. They waved and laughed and called to catch his attention.

One boy lay still.

He was stretched out on a blanket with his friend – a spotty lad perhaps a little older, but stalky and ill-formed, with veins showing in his hands – sitting on the boards beside him. This boy's eyes were watery and he looked straight past Uncle George until the man bent right down, when he seemed to sense the movement, and his eyes fixed.

Lansbury said, 'Aren't you the one they call Knuts? I've seen you before.'

'Yes, sir.'

'You were in the infirmary.'

'I'm better now, sir.'

'Good lad. Well done.' Lansbury looked at the other boy. He appeared to be asleep. His face was bruised and one of his eyelids was puffed up black and blue. He looked as though he had been in a fight.

'What happened to your friend?'

'He fell downstairs, sir.'

'Downstairs? He was lucky not to break any bones.'

'Yes, sir. No broken bones, sir.'

'Which stairs were these?'

'I don't know, sir,' Knuts said, looking straight ahead.

'That's your story and you're sticking to it, eh?'

Knuts's eyes did not move.

Lansbury said: 'Was he in a fight?'

'No, sir, he wasn't fighting them.' *He didn't know how to. He'd never had to fight before. Not for anything. Now he has to fight for everything.*

Lansbury stood. 'Well, my boy, I hope you're looking after him.' The children jabbered around him for his attention.

Knuts confessed tearfully, 'He wouldn't cry out, sir. I warned him, I told him over and over, but he wouldn't cry! He just wouldn't!'

Lansbury frowned. He didn't understand. He said: 'Well, I think that not to cry was very manly of him.'

'Now we're too old to stay here in the mixed block,' Knuts said in a lost voice. 'They're moving us into the older boys' ward in a few weeks.'

The other children clamoured three deep around Lansbury. He couldn't give more than a few seconds of his time to each one. 'Very manly,' he called approvingly as he was tugged away. What else could he say? 'I hope he's better soon. Goodbye, Knuts.'

Knuts whispered: 'He just wouldn't cry. Oh, my friend, you fool.'

Ben thought: *I won't cry, and I won't die.*

Chapter Six

1

Ria Price crouched alone in the rain with Dolly huddled to her chest to keep her dry. She was watching the busy street. The night life both fascinated and repelled her. A cab splashed past the mouth of her alleyway, the horse gleaming with wet, and disappeared into the darkness. A motor-omnibus rattled by, crammed with the white shadows of people's faces behind the misty windows.

The danger; yet the appeal of the lights. She waited. The rain pouring between the protecting black walls pounded on the black cobbles around her.

She was a little older. Her face was paler, because she had not eaten today. The yellow dress had fallen to pieces long ago, put in the Monday bundle and sold to the ragman for a penny, and now she wore something dark grey that almost hid her. Across her shoulders she had draped a heavy shoulder-cape that Vic had got her, the oiled wool keeping the rain off, but of course she was soaked black below the waist. Deep inside the wet layers, her thin knees trembled with cold. Hearing footsteps, she looked up hopefully, but it wasn't Mum.

Mum wasn't frightened of walking along the street. She walked as though she still owned it. Ria sank her chin between her knees. After the first few gins Esther always lamented how far she had come down in the world. Her first husband, Dick, had owned a Dining Rooms next to a corner pub to draw in the trade, with another big pub on the side opposite, and she'd run the kitchen. Dick's Rooms had been a good business, nothing fancy, serving up meat pies with plenty of salt in them to make the customers pop back next door for another beer, then when they'd had more beer that would put the hunger on them for another pie. She still made a pie now, when Vic brought back the meat.

But like all the children, young Arthur, Nigel, and Vic, sitting in a circle with Mum tottering between them, Ria, the oldest, always looked forward to the end of Mum's story best. The publican next door had been Dick's friend, and one day he popped his head in and asked if Dick would help him lift a beer cask over the bar, and of course Dick did, and something inside him bust. Over the next day or two he started to swell up. They couldn't keep his trousers on him. Howling with pain, he split the buttons off his shirt. They covered him with a blanket upstairs but still he kept on swelling. They thought he was going to explode. Kids took bets on it in the streets. 'Peritonitis,' wept Esther. 'Nothing the doctor could do about it.' When he died they had to puncture him to deflate him enough to get him into his coffin.

Vic laughed, then Nigel would start to giggle, then he would laugh out loud too, and Arthur would start, and Ria felt so sorry for Mum, because she'd stand there with tears of inconsolable grief streaming down her cheeks. Once – Ria could imagine this – Mum had had her own bedroom with a mirror, and her own front room with a brass knocker, and proper glass in the windows, and carpets, and everything. With Dick gone, everything had gone. Now Esther had nothing but gin memories, and a second husband who she accused of being good-for-nothing, except copulating. Tom was a casual docker, in work when he could get it, in the pub when he couldn't, broad-shouldered, thick-headed and too kindly to control his sons, but he was a man of terrifying fertility. Every time they got into a bed together she had a baby. She'd had seven once; now there were just the four. Jane had been pulled from her, and lived for a gasping hour. The fever got Dicky as soon as he was old enough to run about, and Jim had drowned. It happened to every mother; that was the way it was. But Esther couldn't face it. She remembered them pulling Jim's little body from the river. The death of each of her children had been a little death for her. She had to stuff her knuckles against her mouth. But because the children were laughing so much, eventually she'd have to laugh too, giggling and weeping her heart out at the same time.

Only Ria did not laugh. She sat all together with them, yet withdrawn from them inside herself and alone.

I'm Ria Price and no one's ever thought what I'm thinking now before, not ever, not in the whole world.

She stared along the street. A plodding, motherly shape had passed under a light. Was that Mum? Esther always looked as though she should really be bigger than she was. She looked deflated, with heavy bones and big, flat, creased hands that should have been full and plump. Her cheeks were flat white slabs that would feel cold and hard if you were to touch them, instead of round and pink. If they carried two bright, hot circles of red, she had been drinking, just one or two little tots. More, and she would be smiling. But if she had been drinking all day, she would be sad. It was wonderful to be able to predict her mood in this way. There were all sorts of clues, and Vic was a genius at reading them. He could make Mum do whatever he wanted, if she could physically do it, by being kind to her or brutal to her at the right moment. They had the best Mum in the world, Ria knew. They were a lucky family.

Ria licked her upper lip. The figure was Mum, she was certain, plodding along the pavement as though she still owned it. She was holding a piece of tarpaulin over her head against the rain. Ria slipped out and joined her soundlessly. Esther said nothing, but then after a few moments widened her grip on the tarpaulin as much as she could so as to shelter Ria a little.

'How did you know?' Mum asked, flatly. That meant no drink. Her tots gave her life.

'Saw the runner,' Ria said. 'He was wearing the Workhouse clothes.'

'Yes,' Mum said distantly. 'That's clever of you to notice

that, girl.' Then she said: 'Cook's taken sick. I've been called in. That's why they sent the runner.'

Ria knew. It was the reason that she had nerved herself to take the short cut across the lock gates and lay in wait here. Mum wouldn't go anywhere near the lock gates with that long dark drop into the roaring water, and the smell of wet filling the air, since Jim went that way.

'They call me in sometimes,' Mum said. Ria knew that too. In the gap after the last Cook died she had often been to the Workhouse with Mum. She had been hoping it would start again. The present Cook had made more money than she'd ever dreamed of selling tobacco and sweets to the inmates, and turning a blind eye to various activities of suppliers and contractors, so now she could afford to go sick for a day or two.

'I'll come in and sit by the fire,' Ria said.

'You can't, dear, it's so against the rules.' She always said that.

'I'll be ever so quiet,' Ria promised as always, then lied for the first time: 'No one will see me.' Today, that was the opposite of her intention.

'Make sure you are, then, quiet as a bloody mouse,' Esther said, 'or I'll chuck you out myself. They're going to pay me for tonight.' Her eyes and teeth showed eagerly as she smiled. 'I'll slip you something to eat. You'll be warm and dry and full, Ria. Just like the good old days. Your old Mum will see you all right. What do you say?'

They turned in the staff gate and walked down the path beside the Administrative Block, the black bricks gleaming on their right, rising four storeys into the rain. Ria watched the wan beams of light from the windows illuminate Mum's pale cheeks. She was dressed in rags, literally in rags.

'And tea,' Mum said, elbowing her. 'Pints of tea, girl!'

'Yes.'

'You're a cold one, Ria,' grumbled Mum. 'I wish you had a bit more go, like my dear boys.'

'Let's get inside, Mum,' Ria said, hiding her impatience.

The heat and the stink of food hit them like a blow. Steam formed and eddied past them into the night. They felt sweat

169

condense on their faces immediately. The Workhouse boilers were said to burn more than three tons of coal a day and the laundry and the kitchen were always too hot; the Administrative and Executive Blocks where Bill Madeley and his officers and their families lived – most of them had their children in the Workhouse – were kept just right; and the wards, with stone floors, and stone walls, were kept as cold as stone, except in summer, when they were suffocatingly airless. Esther shook the water off the tarpaulin. 'Shut the bloody door!' someone shouted.

Esther drew herself up. Over her shoulders she wore a shawl torn from one end to the other. She must have been wearing several dresses, for where the black one on top was holed it revealed another of a different colour beneath, bottle-green. Her ankles – she suffered from swollen joints – were wound around with sacking, and her right shoe had peeled back to reveal her big flat toes. She put her hands on her hips, glaring around her. 'Who said that?'

'I did,' whined a boy in a grey shift. 'The door's open and it's freezing.'

All activity in the kitchen had stopped. Ria slipped past a steaming copper, noticing gobs of fat bobbing up in the bubbling scum across the top and sinking again. She pulled one out and rattled it in her loose fist to cool it as she walked down past the cutting tables. Behind her she heard Mum's voice: 'You lot obviously don't know who I am.' She glanced back: Esther was standing with her hands on her hips, a wooden spoon jutting out between her fingers, looking proud as you please. Ria held the piece of fat in her mouth to suck and walked on, licking the grease from her scalded hand. Mum was going to sort them out. 'Call yourselves cooks? Look at you. Hours behind. My name is Mrs Price. I am the Cook. Why haven't you opened that barrel of meat yet? Come on with it, oh for God's sake! Have you counted the pieces? *Can* you count? What does it say on the outside? Forty-eight pieces? Count them! If there aren't forty-eight pieces, tell me. Lord, that I, a professional person, should be brought to this. And you, yes, you boy! Shut that bloody door! It's freezing!' Mum's voice was

170

fading behind her. Distantly, Ria heard the door obediently slammed.

Ria stuck her head out of the doorway at the far end of the kitchen. An empty corridor. To her right, she knew, led back past the kitchen into the Executive Block. To her left, she heard the low murmuring sound that many people together make. She walked down, her clogs tapping on the flagstones, and stood by some shelves in the shadow of the doorway. Another cheerless corridor branched off towards the women's area, but this was the one she wanted: the low murmur of men's voices. She looked out.

The dining room was very large and dim, lit by a couple of incandescent electric arcs that burned the eye and cast little light. Hundreds of shivering men in the same grey shifts sat at the rows of tables. Many of them had white hair and appeared to be asleep, resting with their heads between their elbows, their scrawny bottoms sticking back uncomfortably off the wooden benches. Others stared at the ceiling. Some sat on their hands and rocked slowly from side to side. Someone shouted in a low, mad voice, then laughed, and giggles spread down one table. Ria's eyes brightened: younger men. They still had life in their faces, their eyes still held traces of suffering and shame and a determined cheerfulness. They hadn't been here long, recently put out of work; all the trades round here were casual, like the docks, or seasonal like the biscuit, jam or pickling trades, or ruined the health, like the sweated match-makers. Table-boys were nominated and called out to the kitchen to bring food. Ria stared over their heads as they ran past.

As the bowls of skilly were put down groans went up from a few tables, but most started eating listlessly. These would be the old lags. But there was a table of boys who ate just as indifferently, slowly spooning the watery lumps into their mouths, successful inmates: their spirit was broken.

There was a boy with a shaved head.

There was a boy who ate with his fingers.

There was a boy who stared at his plate with his head on one side.

171

There was a boy who chewed carefully.

There was a boy who had no teeth. He had white gums.

There was a boy whose teeth stuck out. They scraped indifferently on his spoon.

There was a boy who had watery eyes and blue veins criss-crossing the backs of his hands.

And she saw him.

2

His spirit was not yet broken. He did not see her, not that time, but there would be other times. She had stood in the doorway shivering, not with cold, but with longing for him to look up. He was different. No one was like him. He wore the same grey shift, but he ate furiously. She observed him, determined to miss no detail of him, to know him better than he knew himself, watching how he ate as though he hated every mouthful of gruel and every lump of fat. He ate it as though he was spitting it back down his throat, his hand clenched like a fist around the handle of his spoon, his eyes fixed on nowhere, as though they pierced the walls surrounding him. She stared eagerly, but he did not look at her. His hair was darker than she remembered. He was older of course, and thinner. He had learned anger. He had lost that smooth look, and his shoulders were broader. He sat bolt upright: he had not yet learnt to lie, to fade away. The others slowly sucked and chewed and nibbled their way through their food, but he ate it as though it was going to do him good. If he found a knob of gristle he held it between his white teeth and bit it through, then got it back in his mouth and chewed it angrily until he could swallow it somehow, spitting it down as though it revolted him.

Look at me, she thought, frightened by her need.

He didn't.

Had he noticed her, and was he just being obstinate? Had what he had seen of her that day in the fog revolted him? Just another girl in a yellow dress, with snot running from her nose?

No!

Or had he noticed her and just didn't care about her?

Her brothers were often cruel. It was the way boys were made. Yes, perhaps he was being cruel to her.

But he wasn't cruel. His mouth looked as though it could be taught to smile again. His fingers were long and sensitive. He looked like fun, like the sort of older brother she would have wanted. Perhaps not quite like that. A friend who wasn't a girl friend, but a real friend. She couldn't put it into words. Someone to share her greatest, deepest, most personal secret. He already did. She remembered: *He knows I'm special.*

I'm Ria Price and no one's ever thought what I'm thinking now before, not ever, not in the whole world. I'm me.

I'm me!

She stood in the shadows looking in to the dining room, watching every breath he took, taking in every movement he made.

But he didn't even notice her, that time.

The next time, she stood less in the shadows.

That day had been burning hot, it was high summer. Evening sun slanted down the wall of the Workhouse Chapel across the yard. Dust still hung in the air. At this time of the year there were fewer casual inmates and nearly all of them were old men. Most of the young men over sixteen had now been taken away to the Forest Gate Branch Workhouse which had opened a few years back. But the boys were still at the same table. Ria put Dolly down and hid back in the shadows beneath the shelves. She smoothed down the yellow ringlets of her hair with the palms of her hands, trying to press the curls neatly over her shoulders.

She stood in the doorway.

He saw her at once. He noticed everything.

It was the same as it had been. Time had not passed. She knew what he saw: a girl with eight fingers and two thumbs, ten years old, nearly more than that, standing in a scuffed blue dress with her little bare feet sticking out in hammertoes, untidy yellow hair, and a rather narrow mouth. She tried to smile. Her mouth wasn't narrow when she smiled. She never smiled for other boys because she knew they'd

173

put their thumbs in their ears and stick out their tongues She trusted him; she knew he wouldn't.

He looked at her, straight at her, and smiled. They shared the secret. She wasn't alone.

Her smile became radiant.

'Ria!' her Mum called behind her from the kitchen. 'Where the bloody hell are you, darling?'

Ria felt ashamed. That was Mum's loud, happy voice, with the bright red blotches spreading across her cheeks. Mum was on the bottle today, what with little Arthur being so poorly. Her yells would attract the attention of Bill Madeley. Ria ran back.

She missed the next time Mum went in. The snow had drifted deep and Mum must have gone a different way, because Ria waited and waited and she didn't come.

In the spring the officer came round and they made her go to school. Mum hated that because it meant she had to get up early in the mornings. Vic got her up and into school most times – he worked at Mr Blumenthall's stall down the market now, skiving out of school. Vic was so clever at things like that. The officer caught Nigel though, who everyone had thought was the clever one, and made him go. Nigel could read and write and add up long rows of numbers already. A fat lot of good it did them. Money was really short that spring what with the school expenses and Mum not getting a single call to go in as Cook. Esther was religious because Dick had been, and she made them all pray in his memory, because she hated the idea of anyone really dying. She knew they did, but she didn't want to believe it. Ria prayed that Mum would get a call to go to the Workhouse.

And she did.

It was autumn. The banana boats were in. Vic brought bunches back from the stall and everyone was sick of bananas. The summer had been so long and hot that the rats and cockroaches kept everyone awake, and the crawling lice nearly drove them crazy. Eventually, like everyone else, the family slept out on the pavement. That was lovely, watching the stars wheel between the crooked roofs, but sometimes the moon was so bright that no one could sleep, and she could hear a restless murmuring even from the other courts and alleyways down to the street. And then, quite early in the morning, the runner came from the Workhouse. Cook was sick.

Ria allowed Vic to see her to the Cheval Street school. Her younger brother was quite possessive about that, seeing she was all right, and she knew better than to argue, so she let him. He couldn't go quite to the school of course, in case he was seen, so he saw her off with a wave from Malabar Street, then stood watching her.

She looked back from the school gates. He was still there.

She ducked in and counted ten. When she peeped again he was gone. She dodged out before she was seen and hared barefoot down Maria Street past the Tooke Arms towards the river, flew across West Ferry Road between the lorries and omnibuses, and dropped down into the safety of the mass of warehouses and wharfs swarming along Limehouse Reach.

Panting, her hair hanging over her face, she began threading her way northward through the maze between the buildings and cranes. These dark corners and passages were her territory. She struck up through the cobbled network of slums into Poplar. Some of these courts were so deep and safe that they were chilly even now, never penetrated by direct sunlight. She crouched in an alley looking over Poplar High Street, clutching Dolly, waiting.

Mum was wearing a shabby black velveteen dress that made her look dumpy, and a silly broad-brimmed hat that Vic had found for her, with paper flowers on. She loved that hat, just because Vic had brought it, and she walked just as proudly as ever, but she looked silly. Ria loved Mum, but she didn't always like to be seen out with her now. Sometimes she wondered if Vic did it deliberately. When he brought *her* things, they were often really nice. Once there was a real gold bracelet which she didn't dare to wear because Mum would have killed her, because obviously it was stolen.

'Hallo, Mum.'

'Ria, you did give me a turn. I thought you were at school.' They walked together. Ria was as tall as Mum's shoulder now, and Mum's rolling walk made her feel very slender, very sensuous, taking only three little paces to cover Mum's plodding four.

'No school today, Mum, it's the public holiday.' She knew it would work.

'Yes of course, silly of me,' Mum agreed vaguely. 'You coming in?'

'I might as well,' Ria said. 'I suppose so.'

'Keep your old Mum company in the Workhouse,' smiled Mum. 'Oh, I've been so lucky with my children!' For a moment Ria thought she was going to kiss her in the street, and blushed with embarrassment in case. But then they turned in the staff gate.

Ria slipped swiftly through the kitchen into the corridor and went down to the dining room. She was wearing a faded lilac dress with three bands of deeper purple running just above the hem. The dress was a little small: it felt tight across her chest and she knew her ankles showed, but it showed off her waist beautifully.

There was the boy with watery eyes and thin, veined hands. He was coughing into a rag. He must have had a nose-bleed: the rag was speckled with bright spots of blood. The space beside him was empty.

Ria's heart jumped. She put her hand against her chest. He was gone.

'I wasn't sure that you would come,' a voice said behind her. She whirled. It was him. He was carrying a tray. He'd had himself elected table-boy. She held Dolly against her chest with both hands, embarrassed. 'Last time Cook was off sick, you didn't come,' he chided her. He'd noticed after all! She blurted the truth.

'I couldn't!'

He told his name, quite casually, then made a small bow. 'It's a pleasure to meet you, Miss Price.'

He knew everything. He really did. It was frightening. She turned away coolly.

'Shouldn't you get back to waiting table?'

'The table can wait.' Was that a joke? Was he being funny at her expense? No.

'No,' he said. 'I knew your name because it was my business to know.' He waited.

Finally she had to ask: 'Why was it your business?'

'Because I wanted to meet you.' It must be the Workhouse that had taught him such a slick, vital way of speaking, of getting a hold on someone so quickly. She felt how tough he was, how vulnerable.

'I don't want to meet you,' she said, 'I know plenty of boys who are more interesting than you.'

That was a lie, and she knew it, and so he knew it. She didn't quite like this feeling. It was all very well to be fascinated by the thought of someone who knew everything about you, but when it actually happened it was like meeting someone who could see through your clothes, and she didn't like it. Yet she did. She hung on to Dolly, confused.

He explained: 'There was a boy in the kitchen who told me that the replacement Cook who came in was Mrs Price.'

'So you didn't *know*.' She felt relieved. He saw, and smiled reassuringly.

'It was a reasonable guess that you were her daughter.' So he wasn't perfect. Good. Then he said abruptly: 'What's your first name?'

'I'm Ria. I'll be twelve soon.'

He touched Dolly. 'What's her name?'

How did he know that she was a girl? He knew too much. Ria took a step back. He must have thought he had lost her, because he said quickly:

'Why isn't she wearing proper clothes?'

She shook her head, coming back, stating the obvious disdainfully. 'Dolly doesn't need clothes. She never gets cold. She never gets hurt. She's perfect.' Yes, that was perfection: no pain.

He nodded, understanding. She watched him pick up the tray. He would have to go back to his table. Really wanting him to answer, she asked: 'How did you know that she was a girl?'

177

He looked back and spoke as though he too were stating the obvious: 'She has curly red lips like a girl. And if she had been a boy doll, you would have put proper clothes on him. Even rags.'

'Of course I would!'

'There you are,' he said. He paused in the doorway. 'Look, if you want, I'll get you some dress material for her. Sometimes I work in the tailoring ward. We made two hundred and ninety one coats last year. Miss Edins is the cutting-out dressmaker, and she always has bits and bobs left over, lying around. I could get you some. If you want me to.'

Her heart hammered. She would see him again. She shrugged: 'Don't go to any bother.'

He smiled with his eyes as well as his mouth. 'All right,' he said, 'I won't, then.'

That wasn't what she wanted at all! 'I didn't say that,' she said.

'I know you didn't.' He was obstinate!

'If you did find some lying around,' she stated, 'it would be very nice.' He nodded again. She was in his debt. Ria squeezed her lips.

'I've got to get back to table now.' He had turned his back to her. She could tell from the sadness filling his voice that he didn't want to go.

He took a pace into the dining room. Two paces. She called him back.

'Ben, listen. You could get yourself sent out as a runner . . .'

He had already decided about that, because he said immediately: 'Today's Friday. Cook's mother is sick and she'll certainly be away tomorrow, so they'll need to send a runner, and I can arrange for it to be me. But I don't know where your house is.'

Ria smiled.

'I'll show you,' she said.

Saturday was a bright, blowy day, the sort she didn't like. The wind eddying in the courts kept blowing her off-balance, her dress flapping, and the sunlight revealed every dark corner: that there was a way out by wriggling beneath those crooked stone steps, as well as running up them. The wind sent paper rubbish tumbling along the secret alleys, the wind-devils revealing their hidden entrances and exits by piling it in their mouths.

Looking withdrawn and distant, she leaned against a wall and stared with eager feelings down the street. She couldn't see him. A motor-omnibus clattered by, its shiny paint made dull by yellow dust. People said that this was a wind from Spain, or even out of Africa, from the great sandy deserts. Waiting – she was still early – she watched seagulls fight over a scrap of paper, shrieking. It must be a rough day at sea. She stared impatiently. A couple of dark-skinned sailors ambled by, talking foreign. One of them looked at her and clicked his tongue. It had happened one day last week, too – a man looking at her in that way. Was she drawing attention to herself somehow? She shrank away, and the men walked on. She crept back and crouched by the corner, staring along the street.

There he was. He looked so lost out in the street in his grey Workhouse shift, his face so pale, looking down as though he never saw the sun, stopping, startled, whenever a cart or bus went by. Of course; it must all be new to him by now. His feet on the dusty cobbles looked white and soft, and the wind blowing his hair and flapping at his shift seemed to bother him. He clutched his shift down the front and turned his face to the wind. Her heart went out to him, but at the same time she knew that she had secured an advantage over him. He was on territory strange to him.

'Hoi. Over her.' He looked startled again, then his eyes found her amongst the dark brick.

'Hallo!'

'Call yourself a runner?' she scoffed. 'You'd take all day.'

'I'm a slow runner.'

She thought about it. 'That's impossible.'

'I'm an ambler.'

She said: 'What's that?'

'A joke.' He entered the alleyway and stood looking around him into the shadows, already starting to shiver. She stepped back from him.

'Don't joke with me, all right?' she said. 'You behave properly.'

'I brought Dolly a present.' He said Dolly's name quite naturally. 'Here you are, Ria.' He held out his hand, slipped something over her wooden head, and there it was – Dolly in a green dress. Ria snatched her.

'Do you like it?'

Ria knelt, captivated, examining her. He'd guessed the size right. The material was coarse but it had been so expertly and carefully sewn that the inner side of the seams was as smooth as the outside.

'It's a bit big,' she said.

'That's for when she grows.' Yes, that was sensible. Ria was always growing out of her clothes. But of course Dolly was made of wood, she would never grow. Never felt cold or pain, so she didn't really need the dress. Dolly was just a child's toy. Ria stared at Ben uncertainly. He had deliberately turned and was staring back at the Workhouse with his hands wrapped around his shoulders.

'I never knew it looked like that,' he said wonderingly. He didn't need to explain to her; he knew that she had seen him, that day.

'Couldn't you see, through the fog?'

'No, I can't do that, Ria.' He sounded so lost.

She shivered. 'But you've been in there for years, and you never even knew what it looked like?' That was horrible. She told him, trying not to sound bossy: 'There are plenty of ways out, you know. It was all built at different times. You could even just walk out through the kitchen.'

'Not unless I wanted to be hauled up before the magistrate at the Thames Valley Police Court.' He pointed at the

Workhouse shift he wore. 'Theft of Workhouse property.' That was how they kept their hooks in you. You never escaped.

'You could always wear an overcoat.'

'I haven't got an overcoat!'

He had even less than her. She said: 'Haven't you got anything?'

'Only my brain.' Then he held out his hands towards her – she did not step back this time – and clenched them. 'And my fists.'

For a moment, for him, her face faded away into the red darkness and he only felt the pain in his muscles and fists and he wanted to cry, but he . . . *remembered* . . . Edith Rumney's determined face, how she had loved him like a son, though he had no mother, a bastard, remembered her kindness, her loss – and he had been thrown out. Peter Pungle's brutal features loomed out of the fog. Darkness, chaos, loss. But life, living. *If I am a bastard, I'll be a damned good one. If I'm damned, I'll be well damned. The way it is is the way I choose it to be. I can do something extraordinary. I can win.*

'*And my fists!*' he said.

'Don't!' she shuddered. She sounded so frightened that his heart softened. She was looking at him as though he had scalded her.

'When you talk like that,' she whispered, 'you sound like Vic.'

'Who's Vic?' he asked instantly.

'Oh, no one. One of my brothers.'

'I'm supposed to be running like fury to fetch your mother,' Ben reminded her gently. Then he added in a harder voice: 'I have to get back.' For a moment it was as though he didn't care about her at all.

'Do you *want* to get back?' she demanded. Make him face it; make him concentrate on her.

He looked at her with contempt. 'I hate it there. My friend is there. I live there.' His friend? He must mean the sick boy. He sounded so cold and cruel, but why? He was loyal to his friend, he was kind and thoughtful towards her. Ria wanted to cry with frustration. She stared at him,

181

wishing she was older. She wanted to understand everything about him, she was determined to. She wasn't going to let him get round her; he wasn't going to be able to hide anything from her.

'I know the short-cuts,' Ria bragged. 'Do you want me to show you?' She had hesitated over this beforehand, being quite prepared to make him walk the long way round by the street if she had disliked him, or if after all she had felt she distrusted him. He kept so much of himself hidden from her – or tried to – that she felt that she ought not to trust him. Yet there was a sort of a joy in giving – like Vic must have felt when he gave her the gold bracelet, or Mum the flower hat – and she trusted Ben to . . . keep faith.

'Yes,' he said.

She led him down, looking back over her shoulder. She went much faster than he, and had to keep waiting for him. All this must be new and strange to him. He was so clever with words that it was reassuring to find something that he was stupid at. He kept banging his head on the low arches and slipping in the stuff that had been thrown down, or not looking where he was going and splashing into the sewage channel. She went a little faster, then waited impatiently, withdrawn and smiling. He followed her obediently. Good.

They came to the open, the sunlight out there blazing so brightly that everything seemed colourless at first. Ben went out and opened his arms to the heat of the sun. She laughed at him. They had crossed the railway – waiting for a gap between the trains and scampering across – and now the choppy green waters of the West India Dock, swirling with gulls, stretched away beyond the bonded warehouses on their left. A ship was warping out on springs against the wind, water fountaining under the stern from the half-exposed propeller, the tugs seeming half-sunk with the strain, water wringing in sprays from the manilla ropes, black smoke streaming from their tall funnels. Grey-painted cranes trailing steam traversed the quays, and beneath them swarms of men manhandled bales, and bags, and slings, and crates from all over the world, from the ships into the vast warehouses. Ria wanted to say proudly,

That's where my Dad works, but she did not want to have to add, *Sometimes*, so she said nothing. She simply ran, and he followed.

She stopped at the lock gates. The wind jerked at her. This was the bit she didn't like. Panting, he came up. She ran out along the precarious angle. The lock gates were massive, of iron and oak. A freighter was locking out, and water roared in the sluices, making the gates tremble. She leapt across the gap in the middle and only when she got to the far side did she look back.

To her horror, he had stopped in the middle, like poor Jimmy.

He was standing with one foot on each side of the gap, his hands braced on the railings, the wind blowing in his face. He looked like a captain on the bridge of his ship. He knew that she was watching. He looked across at her and saluted. He was enjoying himself hugely. After three years in the Workhouse it must seem like heaven, like freedom. To him it was just a game. She beckoned to him desperately. He saluted away, laughing, but she couldn't hear him for the roar of the water, and when she started screaming at him she knew he couldn't hear her. He thought she was laughing too. She hated it. They were apart, she wanted to be with him, to make him understand, but she was too frightened to go back. Then he casually walked off the lock gates, not noticing them at this very moment starting to open behind him.

She shouted: 'Don't you ever do anything like that, ever again! Not ever, or you can go back in the Workhouse forever for all I care!'

He stared at her, shocked. She felt a slight, strange thrill of pleasure, of power.

'Ria, I'm sorry,' he said. He slipped his hand into hers as innocently as a little boy. 'Won't you tell me what I've done?'

Now she was deliberately unreasonable. 'If you don't know, I can't tell you!' Yet, though it added to her mystery and her stature in his eyes, it was true: she couldn't tell him about Jimmy, the horror, Jimmy just a lump floating in the river, Vic crying like a baby, the sailor with the gold ring on his finger passing the hook under Jimmy's belt-buckle, they thought he'd jammed it into his belly, winching him up, and she remembered how Vic had screamed as the river water came gushing out of Jimmy's gaping mouth where the fish had nibbled him, and from his eyes.

'It's a secret?' he said, nodding. 'Girls love secrets.'

'I hate them!' she said, determined to be different, for her mysteriousness to keep him off his balance; her withdrawal to keep him following her; otherwise she felt that she couldn't control him, and he was so clever and so strong that she needed to do that more than anything.

She jerked her hand out of his and ran across the busy West Ferry Road, then turned back and stared at him. He was standing on the far side, looking lost. She felt a bit guilty. She went back and took his hand. 'Come on,' she said, 'it's easy, I'll show you how.' She led him across, weaving professionally through the lumbering traffic, then smiled at him as they dropped down amongst the warehouses. He had looked so vulnerable that she felt quite endeared to him.

They walked along the river. The water lapped and jostled against the wharves. Big flat barges showing lips of foam tugged at rows of canted iron buoys – the tide was dropping. Out in the stream a steamship moved down with strange rapidity as the pilot maintained steerage way. Ria pointed: a wherry with a bulging rust-coloured sail was tacking almost straight towards them, now coming exactly at them as the tide carried her down, spray flying from the blunt bow, then the sailors let go the ropes and the long vessel turned almost close enough to touch, leaning into the dropped leeboard, and they could hear the rush of the wash and the creaking cordage, and saw the gold teeth glinting in the mouths of the sailors as they smiled. Ria looked to her side and saw that Ben was waving to them.

'What did you do that for?' she said.

'It's all new,' he said. She looked around the crumbling old buildings. He must be joking again. She tugged him on.

She noticed how he looked around him as they walked.

His eyes roved constantly, taking in everything, all the things she never even noticed because she took them for granted. He jumped when a rope squealed in a block, and stared at the groups of men working as though wondering what they were doing: had he never seen ropes spliced or fish gutted or hemp tarred, and what was so strange about a Turk's Head? He watched the old lighterman knot the rope as though he had never seen it done before.

But of course, she realized, he hadn't.

He'd been in the Workhouse nearly all his life. This *was* new – to him.

She stopped. 'Look, I'm sorry,' she said.

'What for?'

'Nothing,' she said. 'I'm just sorry, that's all. I like you really.'

Of course she liked him; that was obvious to him. He wanted her to, needed her to, otherwise he would not be here. And he did like her, even though she was subtle in ways that boys were not, sometimes even pretending – why? – that she didn't like him, which hurt him. She didn't understand that everything around here was so fascinating, the reality of it all, the real people, the vastness of the docks, the expanse of the river – he could see for miles – and, without the Workhouse walls, he could even feel the free wind on his face. It was impossible to give her all the attention that she demanded. She held out her hand insistently: they had to cross the road again.

They plunged into the slums.

There were no streets really, just crowded courtyards and crooked alleyways joined up in strings. The wind did not penetrate here, and it was sticky hot. And the people – thousands of people, covered with lifeless sweat. There were lanes where people moved in slow streams, pools, eddies, a human backwater where you couldn't even move your elbows, you needed a pilot to navigate you. Ria tugged him on. He said:

'Do you live here?'

She looked at him strangely, as if it was so obvious that he must already know. 'Yes, of course,' she said.

No wonder she wanted to escape, he thought. Yet after the dead boredom of the Workhouse, it seemed wonderfully interesting to him. The smells of the sweat and the garbage and the food cooking were intense. All the buildings, many of them made of wood boards, looked as though they had grown out of the ground, and had become part of the natural landscape of the Isle of Dogs, like mushrooms. Each side of the lane almost touched at the top, so that the sky was a jagged blue ribbon. Walls leaned together, holding one another up. He thought that if one fell, the others all around would collapse in on top of it. Children played hop, skip, jump, laughing, red-faced, brown-toothed, rags flying, happy. Broken windows had been stuffed with paper and rags. He looked around him, awed. There were brilliant colours: white doorsteps, red doorsteps, trellises with creepers climbing, clematis, and hanging baskets of flowers trailing red honeysuckle. Exotic scents mingled with the stink. Doves flew under the eaves into special cotes. He could hear pigeons, dogs fighting. A new wicker cage with a yellow canary inside hung in an open window, and he saw that the walls of the room behind were black with damp and mould. Flowers hung in the doorway, and a terrier slept on the step.

'It's like heaven,' Ben said. He meant it. He felt intoxicated, over-excited. 'Look at all the colours. There are so many things to see. It must be marvellous to live here! It's so full of life.'

Ria stared at him over her shoulder. A frown crossed her face, then a smile. 'You aren't joking?'

He shook his head.

'You are strange,' she said. 'I always thought this was hell. You know? Like the sermons.'

'But it's so full of people.'

'I just want to escape,' she said. 'I'm not a part of it. I'm not here.' He looked at her eyes. They had become flat, enamelled tones of blue and orange-brown and behind them, he realized, she really was far away. For a moment, he guessed, she was dreaming. What of? Then she said: 'Come on, Mum's turning isn't far. These are the back-doubles already.' He wondered what her dream had been. Had she escaped?

She shook her head, and led him on.

They pushed away from the busy thoroughfare. It was suddenly cooler as everything closed in around them like a tunnel. For a moment it seemed that only they moved, pushing beneath dirty washing, bending beneath walls. Poverty here was a big, black, motionless monster. Groups of men stood about. Babies crawled and toddlers staggered. One fell, and cried. Ria stepped over him, Ben picked him up. Ria said: 'Don't touch him! His Mum'll think you're making off with him.' The toddler ran into a smoky doorway. They walked on. Ahead, Ben saw a girl of Ria's age or a little older – she could have been her older sister – sitting on the kerb with her knees up and a baby in her lap, filing her nails on the sandpaper striker of a Swan Vestas packet. 'Wotcher, Ria!' she called.

'Hallo, Ann.' Ria walked past cockily. Ann's eyes followed Ben as he went by.

Ria waited for him at the corner. He knew that she had decided on something. She kept looking back at Ann.

'You came from a big house, before,' she told him. It wasn't a question.

'No, I didn't,' he said.

'Come on, don't be so tough.' She looked down.

'It was a little house, I can't remember.' Then, in a gush, there on the corner, Ria looking at him incuriously, not believing him, leaning back against the black wall, with her hands crossed behind her and one foot resting on top of the other, he *did* remember: Ria had unlocked feelings that he had buried deep to survive their pain, and now because of her they were like pictures coming back to life, struggling back up from deep down in his mind. He wanted to cry: his saliva thickened, his throat grew tight. 'The bedroom had wallpaper with roses on, Ria. The third stair creaked. The scullery was at the back, it had cream walls, and a scrubbed oak table in the middle which was always kept so clean that the grain stood out in grooves, like fingerprints.' He remembered them kissing.

Ria was unimpressed.

'Was your Mum beautiful?'

'. . . I don't know who my mother was.'

'But you must know your Mum.'

He shook his head violently. His eyes burned.

Excited, Ria said: 'I've got through to you, haven't I?'

'I'm all right.'

'I *have*. You're going to cry,' Ria said, peering up into his face, her hands clasped behind her back.

He shook his head.

'Go on,' Ria said proudly, glancing back at Ann, 'don't mind me.'

'Will you leave me alone for a minute?'

'Don't you ever speak to me like that again!' For a moment she looked fierce, as if he had kicked her instead of merely asking for a moment to regain his manly self-control, and he thought she would storm off. Then Ria's eyes went far away. 'I knew it. She was ever so beautiful, she was, your Mum, a real society lady with lovely dresses and furs and everything she wanted, and she fell in love with a handsome soldier and gave up everything for love, but he went off to the wars and was killed, and she was left with you. She pensioned you off with a nanny – well, they do do that sort of thing, it's not called the Wicked West End for nothing – and returned to her position in high society.'

'I don't know,' he said, 'I just don't know.' Ben didn't care how poor or ordinary his mother or his father was, he just wanted them.

'Then, on her deathbed, she's left you her fortune of diamonds in her will. And a stately home! But you don't know yet,' she added. 'The telegram could arrive any day. Next week. Tomorrow.'

He looked at her. Her face had become quite animated. He knew that for a moment, she was living the story she told. *I just want to escape. I'm not a part of it. I'm not here.*

Her eyes came back. She took his hand. 'You and me,' she said. 'Are we friends?'

'I'm from the Workhouse.'

She insisted: 'Friends for ever and ever?'

'Yes!' he laughed.

But she tightened her grip. She wasn't joking. 'Or you can go back to the Workhouse now. I mean it. I won't take you to my house and you'll go back.'

'All right.'

'Cross your heart and hope to die. Say it.'

'Cross my heart and hope to die! Now, where's your house?'

'This way.' He followed her, smiling. He had never met anyone like her before; and perhaps she had never met anyone like him, with a past that she could dream to be whatever in the world she wanted. She had found a boy she could create.

I just want to escape.

That made two of them.

This was a black, ugly turning, and seemed very poor even to Ben. They pushed past knots of narrow-eyed men. Ben had often spoken to casual dockers like these in the Workhouse. They broke the backs of their women. Otherwise they stole or received stolen goods, hawked, cadged, begged, or gambled, or drank and fought until they fell unconscious. When they gambled, they always lost. That was why there were so many of them in the Workhouse. The good ones had jobs, a union card, and were on the register. Fathers trained their sons, kicking them until they learned the ropes right. Often working gangs in calling were made up of whole families as far out as second cousins – you could trust family, one old lag had told Ben as they broke stone in the yard. The key to work, because no one knew when a ship would arrive, was to have relatives living down-river: there was one group of brothers and uncles called The Flying Eighteen; 'I reckon they used jungle drums to let them know a ship was coming up the Thames.' Ben regarded the men around him warily: they were the failures.

Someone called: 'Hallo, Ria.' She said nothing, but turned in under the flowers hanging in a dark doorway, and he ducked quickly down after her.

It was dark inside. It was a room like a cellar, but there

was a lovely perfumed smell. A canary twittered in a cane cage. Plaster had fallen off the walls, revealing the wooden lathes beneath, the fragments neatly piled into a corner of the stone floor. A row of blankets on the flagstones, a few wooden shutters, a scrap of curtain at one end, must be where they slept: a child lay there now, large head, small body. 'Ria, Arthur's poorly again,' Mrs Price said. Then she looked up from whatever she was doing on the table and saw Ben. She smiled and wiped her hands on her hips. 'Who's this?'

'He's an orphan,' Ria said dramatically. 'He's got no Mum nor a Daddy, or a home even, and he's my only friend in the world.'

'I'm Mum,' Esther said. Two spots of colour burned on her cheeks. 'Come on in. Did I hear that lazy Tom out there? Don't tread on the child. Look what Vic brought me, Ria, meat! Must be a couple of pounds, no offal, and fresh. So we'll have a pie. You'd like that, love, wouldn't you?'

'All right,' Ria said. She turned away. 'Mum always makes pies with too much salt but nothing I can say will make her change.' She picked moodily at Dolly's dress, then dropped her in the corner.

'It looks delicious!' Ben watched Esther wield the knife. The meat fell apart in lean chunks; it was the finest quality he had ever seen.

'My children always like to pretend I don't do them proud,' Esther said gratefully. 'He's a nice little boy,' she told Ria. Ria looked at him as if realizing that not everyone saw the same Ben she saw. Meanwhile Esther noticed his Workhouse clothes.

'Mr Madeley sent me,' Ben said. The perfumed smell was stronger over here and he wondered what it was. 'He's sorry, Cook's off sick, could you possibly come in?'

'I like you,' Esther said. She turned to Ria. 'Doesn't he put things nice and polite?'

'Thank you,' Ben said, eyeing the meat.

'Vic will be back shortly. I asked Vic would he get some veg from Blumenthall,' she told Ria.

'Vic, Mrs Price?' Ben wanted to keep her attention on

him, or this opportunity to get out of the Workhouse sometimes might come to nothing. She was the head of the family, not Ria. 'Is Vic your husband?' Ria had mentioned something about a brother called Vic, he thought, but names often ran in families.

'Vic? No, he's my eldest son, God bless him! He's everything to me, and a better bread-winner than his father is, God knows. Don't know what we'd do without Vic. Looks after his old Mum. He's your age. You'll like him, everyone does.' She put down her blood-spattered knife and ran her hands through her hair. The perfumed smell was not perfume, it was the gin on her breath. 'Without the money he brings in, we'd be in Queer Street, and no mistake.' She looked round, hearing boots on the cobbles outside. A shadow moved beyond the paper windows, and they heard joking laughter from the men outside. Suddenly Vic was inside.

He stopped, staring at Ben, who returned the stare.

'Now, boys,' Esther said nervously.

Ben stared at Vic. Big for his age. A round face, but with very flat cheeks, and very dark – the light from the doorway was behind him. Perhaps red. Even darker lips, very narrow. Black hair, black eyebrows, dark whites, black eyes. A trick of staring, the same as Ben's, but through different eyes.

Then both boys smiled at the same moment.

'Bill Madeley sent this nice boy to fetch me,' Esther said.

Vic's smile widened. Nothing gleamed inside his mouth. He dropped a cauliflower casually on the table and began to laugh. 'I told him your name,' Esther said, 'I told him how much we need you, Vic.' She turned to Ben. 'I'm sure you'll be the best of friends. My name's Esther, but you can call me Mum.'

Vic threw his arm around Ria's shoulder. 'This is Ria,' he said. 'She's my sister. I love her.'

Ben fought back tears. *My name's Esther, but you can call me Mum.*

You can call me Mum.

'Hallo, everyone,' he choked. 'Vic. Ria. Mum.'

'Just one big happy family,' Vic said, smiling with his mouth full of rotten teeth.

Chapter Seven

1

What everyone had expected didn't happen: the fuzzy blob like a hairy star in the dawn sky that year turned out not to be Halley's comet after all, although most people thought it was. In a few days the interloper was so bright that it cast a shadow, and everyone was pointing it out even in daylight. Ben looked up at the beautiful Daylight comet hanging above the snow in the Workhouse stoneyard, its white tail curled like a feather around Venus in the morning twilight above the black walls.

'The King's dead,' Ben said. It was the sort of news that usually interested Knuts. He had seen the black-bordered posters when Bill Madeley sent him running to fetch Esther from the Isle of Dogs this morning, and by the time he got back, still eating the slices from the tea that Esther had insisted on making for him, all the flags were flying at half mast — even the Workhouse flag. He was surprised that Knuts, busy cracking best Guernsey granite rocks into road-spalls almost below the mast, hadn't noticed. Knuts didn't even look up. 'The King is dead, long live the King,' he shrugged. 'Who is he?'

'George the Fifth.'

'Stop that noise there!' shouted the labour master. Ben squatted and started breaking stones into the rack. There was a knack to it some people never learned, an easy co-ordination between eye and the swinging arm, the angle of the hammerhead, and a natural sense of how the rock would split. They were supposed to break one and a half yards a day into fine chippings. Ben kept glancing at his friend, but Knuts said nothing more. A chipped spall flew up and Ben got an infection in his eye that pestered him throughout the autumn until the cold weather set in.

When the first snow fell, Knuts could no longer hide it: he had consumption. Dr Lamont in the Workhouse Infirmary called it an attack of influenza, as he had done last year and the year before. In the spring, it went away. In the summer, with all the outdoor work and the warm sun, Knuts felt as healthy as he ever did. But when the frosty weather returned, and then the bitter winter winds, this time the fever and the cough, and the little pains in his chest, did not go away. The spitting of brilliant red blood, so at odds with the blue veins covering his fourteen-year-old's hands, grew worse. People started shouting at him at night with his coughing, and someone stuffed a rag in his mouth. Knuts let them, too exhausted to resist. When Ben woke in the morning and saw the obscenity, he rolled over and pulled the rag out.

'What have those bastards done to you?'

'I'm dying,' Knuts said briefly. He never lied to Ben.

'No you aren't.' Knuts smiled at his friend's characteristic turn of phrase: no one else could say those words with such vigour. No you aren't! Knuts could almost believe him. He thought: *If I believed him, it would come true.* No you aren't. *No, I'm not dying!* In real life, Ben was saying anxiously: 'Why didn't you wake me?'

'You're such a sound sleeper,' Knuts murmured. 'You snore.'

'Aunt Edith used to say that,' Ben said. Since his visits to the Isle of Dogs began, and he could feel that he had another home, and a family that Esther insisted that he called his own, he could remember Aunt Edith without pain – a child's memories, like deep paintings.

Knuts saw. 'You aren't going to go, are you?' Each time Ben went to the Island, Knuts trembled that this time he would not return to the Workhouse. One day, he knew, he would not.

'Let's get you seen to, shall we?' Ben picked Knuts up

as if he were no heavier than a pillow, and carried him
to the Infirmary. Nurse Renahan made them wait in the
cold for hours. They sat peering into the long dark ward
full of old men, their white hair and white hands standing
out brightly against the shadows, unmoving. 'They're
even worse off than us,' Ben said. It was not allowed to
talk to them. A pauper nurse, he saw, sat beside one old
man who was as thin and grey as a skeleton, sewing his
shroud.

Knuts complained of pain in his joints. 'His joints hurt,'
Ben told the doctor when he came.

'Invariable symptom of influenza,' Dr Lamont said stiffly. He wore a faded black jacket and brown shoes.

'But it's been going on and on, sir, and he's been spitting
up blood.'

'Don't antagonize him,' said Knuts weakly. 'I'm all
right. I feel much better.'

'I'll put him on light duties,' Lamont said. That was all.

When they had gone out, he called Ben back. He had a
kindlier look in his eye as he leaned back in his over-stuffed
chair. 'It's tuberculosis. Do you understand? What lay
people call consumption,' he explained.

Ben got to the point. 'Is he going to die?'

'My dear boy, we are all going to die. The infection has
spread from his lungs to his bones. Yes, he will die. It isn't
infectious.'

'What, death?' Ben said cruelly. His eyes stung with
tears. He crushed them back. Knuts was going to die. *He
won't die.*

'Don't be stupid, boy.' The doctor's steepled fingertips
flattened whitely. 'I wouldn't let him cough in your face, if I
were you!'

'Thank you, sir.' *I won't cry.*

As he was carried back downstairs, Knuts raised his
head from Ben's shoulder and looked into his face.

'What did he say?'

Ben thought of all the answers he could give.

He said: 'He agrees with you.'

'I wanted to know,' Knuts said. 'If this is dying, it doesn't hurt. Thank you.' Then he said, as they turned down the next flight of stairs: 'Are you going to go?'

Ben knew what he meant. *Are you going to leave me?* He sighed. There was no future for him in the Workhouse. After he beat Moxon, that had become terribly clear to him. Yet here he had two meals a day and a roof over his head, reasonable conditions, and, now, no troubles. He had learned how to survive in here. Outside, he could rely on nothing but his wits. Out there, surviving was just as much of a knack as breaking stones and using your fists was in here – and if he stayed in here, he, like Moxon, would not be able to learn how to make the change. Like Moxon, he would soon become the Fat Boy, so well adapted to living in the Workhouse that he could not survive outside.

He would have to go.

But that would mean leaving Knuts to die here. Could he leave his friend? Should he?

As he carried Knuts along the corridor, he remembered the terrible fight. For years Moxon had been Bill Madeley's lackey and a bully, which was what life in the Workhouse demanded – as necessary as gills for a fish, or wings for a bird. There was no order without a hierarchy, and Ben assumed that every institution, every establishment, had its Fat Boy. As part of the price for being allowed to do the running to the Isle of Dogs, as well as his extra duties Ben was supposed to contact a bookie called Rixby under the steps in a courtyard off the High Street, to place bets, mostly on the gee-gees but also fights with badgers, cocks, dogs, dogs against a bear once, and whether it would snow on Christmas Day, and would Mr Asquith last out the year as Prime Minister. Moxon and his friends would bet on anything. Rixby rooked Ben of a few pence which he said was the new commission rate. Moxon was furious.

Ben stopped, remembering. It was exactly here, in the corridor, that they had grabbed him, and while they held him down Moxon rubbed his knuckles back and forth across Ben's infected eye.

'*Do it right next time.*'

'*Yes, Mr Moxon.*'

196

And he had.

Here, exactly here, in the stretch between these two sets of doors, where there was no escape. This was where he'd done it right. He'd set it up carefully. Gillman had been called away to the stoneyard. Roberts was delayed in the dining room. Moxon was alone but for Hodge as he walked down this corridor. Children from Block E came out of the doorways behind him, blocking the way back, and Knuts had turned the keys in the locks. Older boys blocked the way in front. Ben stepped out.

Moxon had blustered: '*What's all this about?*'

Ben said: '*We're going to fight!*'

'*I never fight.*'

'*We're the same height, but you're heavier than me, and stronger, and older. You have all the advantages.*'

Moxon said to Hodge: '*Get Gillman and Roberts, quick.*'

'*I don't know,*' Hodge eyed the crowd.

Ben said: '*This isn't your fight, Hodge. You can hold his jacket, that's all.*'

'*Get going, Hodge!*'

Hodge ran. Ben tripped him, held him down, all the while watching Moxon, until Knuts put his foot on Hodge's neck. Then Ben stood, still watching Moxon. '*Good old Knuts!*' the children shouted.

'*Don't hurt him,*' Ben said.

'*I won't,*' Knuts promised, '*I don't weigh hardly anything.*'

'*If you win,*' Ben told Moxon, '*you walk away free.*'

'*But the fists will mark our faces.*'

He had been sure that Moxon would say that. Ben gave away his last advantage. '*All right, Moxon, I'll give you an extra fair deal. Punches to go to the body only.*'

Moxon grinned. '*That's not fair, that's not fair,*' the children shouted. '*His blubber will soak it all up, you'll never hurt him through all that fat!*' It wasn't fat; much of it was muscle. Even Knuts looked worried when Ben said:

'*Fair deal, Moxon? Agreed?*'

'*Agreed.*'

'*Your word of honour?*'

'*Yes, yes,*' Moxon said impatiently.

'*Then put 'em up.*'

They circled. Ben remembered regarding Moxon between his clenched fists: the round face, cunning glittering
eyes, the long hairs growing on the cheeks and straggling
from the chin. Moxon hit him several times with great
weight as Ben danced away. Moxon was a bully, but not a
coward. He followed, flailing with his fists, panting, as Ben
backed away, head low, ducking and weaving from side to
side. Moxon came after him clumsily. The children
screamed. Ben's body thudded every time Moxon landed a
blow, his shift was torn, his pale skin showed through the
rents, covered with red blotches and the darker stains of
developing bruises. As Ben fell back, scraping along the
wall, Moxon came forward swinging wildly to finish the
fight. One of his flailing fists finally struck across Ben's
lip.

Ben jumped aside, shaking his head, then put the back of
his hand to his mouth. Everyone saw the hand come away
bloody. His eyes blazed fiercely blue.

'*Not punches to the face, Moxon. You gave your word.*'

Moxon's blood was up. He lumbered forward, swinging
and hooking with his great balled fists.

'*You broke your word, Moxon.*'

'*Moxon's broken his word!*' everyone was shouting.

Ben came forward, hitting Moxon's face. Moxon's face
was all he saw. Winning was all he felt. He didn't know
where he was, he just hated. He smashed at the face, not
f eling his own body, his own fists, his own face. Moxon
staggered back then began to weave from wall to wall. Ben
smashed into his nose and lips and teeth and tongue until
he went down.

He had won.

Ben shook his head, confused. Here; it had been just
here. The corridor was empty. The victory, so essential,
seemed so empty once the cheering died down.

Yes, he thought now, I am a hero in the Workhouse, and
nothing outside. And one day another Ben will come along
and they'll take me off to the Forest Gate Branch, blubber-
ing like Moxon.

198

Ben looked down at his dying friend. 'No, I won't leave you.'

'I want you to go,' Knuts said. His eyes brimmed with tears. 'There's no future in here for you, I know. Go on, go! I mean it! Don't worry about me, you have a place to go to. A family who will take you in. A home. You may never get another chance. Never mind me, take it!'

'No,' Ben said. He hugged Knuts to him with silent, fierce, ruthless loyalty.

'You're so obstinate,' Knuts said, half-laughing, half-crying.

'Why don't you move in with us?' Ria said.

'No.'

'Don't be so obstinate,' Ria sniffed. 'If Mum gets the Workhouse Cook's job, which she's bound to, look at her, all dressed up like a dog's dinner, we could look after you for a while until you found your feet and could pay your way.' She kicked little Arthur's foot where he was crimping the ends on bootlaces. Blumenthall paid only a few pence a gross, but every little helped. '*Not* like that, like *this* . . .'

'I look all right, don't I?' Esther said anxiously. She wore a rust-coloured coat and a hat covered with yellow feathers that looked to Ben as though they might have been plucked from Tom's canary. The garish hat had been a gift from Vic, of course – where did he buy these things? – and the posy of purple and white flowers was from Nigel. Ben wished that he had been able to buy her some little good-luck token for her interview with the new Master of the Workhouse, Mr William Walton.

Bill Madeley had been sacked, together with his wife, without compensation. His reign had lasted from 1894 to 1912, but George Lansbury had got rid of him at last, although at the cost of his own career in local government. Madeley's downfall was his obsession with Matron: Lansbury had spoken with Crosbie, the telephone man, who, from his post in the corridor, had seen much, and overheard more. This was the lever that enabled Lansbury to dislodge the Master: not his financial double-dealing, but his

199

immoral behaviour. There was a Poor Law Administration Enquiry, and accusations of extravagance were hurled at Lansbury, of all people, by his enemies. But Lansbury had always been ready to sacrifice his political career for his principles, which were unimpeachable, and he survived. Now he was a Member of Parliament, far away.

In the Workhouse, Ben saw everything appear to change. Mr Walton, the assistant master and storekeeper, became Master of the Workhouse. Mrs Elizabeth Usher, the assistant matron, replaced the Matron. He realized that nothing had really changed, only the names. The Cook was dismissed when one of her pantries was found stuffed with crates of Lazenby's pickles, Lea & Perrin's sauce, and Beluga caviar which she had not told the Master about; her position was advertised. The interview was being held today.

Vic put his arm around Esther's shoulder. 'You can't fail, if you've got any sense,' he said. He seemed quite eager for her to get the job. He was now definitely a young man, no longer a boy, shorter than Ben and stockier, but very strongly built, and he could look down into Esther's eyes now. He had an easy confidence that was very persuasive, almost compelling. His thick, heavy arm almost encircled his mother's shoulders.

'You'll be talking to the Board of Guardians, the Master, and probably a representative of the Local Government Board,' Ben said. 'All they want to know is that you're economical and Protestant.'

'Have some sense,' Vic said, hardly glancing at him.

Ria said: 'Oh, Vic,' and turned away. Tom, their father, sat hunched up in a bathtub in the corner with one foot on the rim, cleaning thoughtfully between his toes. Esther made him have a bath twice a year whether he needed it or not. The day was warm, so he was obliging.

'Listen, your friend here doesn't know what he's talking about,' Vic smiled. 'I'm sorry, Ria, Mum, but I've got to say it. Just let them know you'll grease a few palms.'

Esther started to draw herself up proudly, but Vic gave her a friendly hug. 'Come on, Mum, don't stand on your

200

dignity. It's not stealing. Don't you get the picture? They're stealing from you! They're offering fifty pounds a year, and that's just contemptible.'

'Contemptuous,' agreed Nigel, swinging thinly through the doorway out of the light, then leaning against the wall with one shoulder, the side of his long head against the plaster, unmoving, while his calculating eyes moved constantly between the standing people in the middle of the room, Esther and Vic, and Ria moving closer to Ben by the table.

'Treating you with contempt,' Vic said. 'Come on, Mum, you're doing me harm. Consider my reputation. What do you think people will say? Vic's Mum has lost her pride, she's letting the Guardians do her, when she ought to be doing them. Look at that last Cook, the crates of stuff she was flogging on the side.'

'How did you know about that?' Esther asked sharply. There was only one possible way.

'It was in the *Gazette*,' Nigel lied.

'He told me,' Vic lied, pointing at Ben.

'No I didn't,' Ben said. 'I knew about it, but I didn't tell you.'

'Will somebody scrub my back?' Tom asked.

'He did tell me, anyway,' Vic said. 'Someone isn't telling the truth around here. Right, Nige?'

'That's right, Vic,' Nigel said, looking at Ben.

'I'll scrub his back, then, if no one else will,' Ria said. She went over and started scouring Tom's big curved back with the brush.

'Aren't you going to walk with me, darling?' Esther asked her.

'You walk too slowly,' Ria said. 'I can't stand it.'

'You used to love walking with me. You used to wait for me then jump out and walk with me. It was nice.'

'She's a big girl now, aren't you, darling,' Tom said.

'She wants to moon over lovey-boy,' Vic said. 'Look, she's going red.'

'Ria's going red!' Nigel said. 'Re-ed!'

'No I'm not,' said Ria.

'Left a bit,' Tom grunted. 'Down a bit. Not so hard, darling.'

'It's nice that Ria does have someone to talk to,' Esther said. 'She's always been too quiet, if you ask me. It's nice that she has a friend.'

'She's got me,' Vic said.

'We never used to see you until our young friend Ben started coming here from time to time.' Tom had a very slow way of speaking that made Vic shift impatiently from one foot to the other and look away, sometimes catching Nigel's eye and yawning, but Tom never seemed to notice, and he always pushed on to finish his sentences to the very end. 'Since he's been coming here it has pulled us together, in my opinion. He has pulled our family together, Vic. I like to see more of you. I can't remember the last time I saw all of us in here together while I had my bath.'

'Is that all you were going to say?' Vic demanded. He turned from him shaking his head. 'If you don't get this job, Mum,' Vic said, 'I just won't believe it. I mean, do you really expect me to go on keeping us all?'

'I have my principles,' Esther said stiffly. 'I don't want to hear this talk about greasing palms again, Vic.'

Vic's face darkened. 'Then we can all go and live in the bloody Workhouse!' he shouted suddenly.

Esther recoiled. She was wearing shabby white gloves, patiently darned, which she now pressed fearfully to her lips. 'Sorry!' Vic laughed, putting his hands on her shoulders. 'It's just that you don't seem to realize what we're up against, Mum. They want to destroy us.'

Esther whispered: 'Who?'

'The world,' Vic said.

'Life,' Nigel said.

Esther whispered: 'Where are you boys working today?'

'They let us have the morning off,' Vic shrugged. 'We have to look after you.'

'But . . . they won't pay you.'

'This is more important.'

Esther's lips moved. 'What do you mean . . . Greasing a few palms?'

'If you got the job, you could put a lot of stuff our way,' Vic said.

'You mean . . . stealing? That I should be a common criminal?'

'They're common enough round here,' bantered Vic. 'Aren't they, Nige?'

Nigel started to say something, agreeing of course, and Ben stepped forward. 'I'll walk with you to the Workhouse, Esther. I've got to be getting back.'

'No, I want to understand this,' she said in a faint voice. 'I want to understand what Vic is saying.'

Vic glanced at Nigel.

'It's just harmless fun really,' Nigel said smoothly. 'Everyone does it.'

'Not my boys,' said Esther. 'Not me—'

Nigel said calmly: 'Where do you think the meat came from? Or the vegetables? Or your rent money? Or your pin-money? Or the money for all that gin you keep swigging, Mum?'

'Oh, my Lord,' wept Esther, dropping her head. 'My own boys.'

'Or that hat?' Nigel said.

'My boys, my God, my God, what have I done?' Yet Ben noticed that no tears flowed on her cheeks. She seemed tired more than anything. He guessed that a part of Esther had known for years. She looked at Tom. 'Did you know about it, you good-for-nothing?'

Tom said not a word. He stared down into his bathwater. Then he said: 'Of course I knew about it. Vic's right.'

'I want my drink,' Esther said. 'Just a tot or two.'

Vic said: 'Give her the gin we stole, Nigel.'

Esther's face screwed up with pain.

'We've kept the family together for years,' Vic said in a voice brutal with deep emotion. 'No, come on, Mum, it's harmless.' He hugged her. 'Don't get yourself in a state.'

'I've got to cross over the swing bridge and walk by police constable Jarvis, 162K, he's always there. However will I show my face? I'll go bright red and he's bound to wonder.'

'That's right, Mum,' Vic said encouragingly, 'put a brave smile on it, you'll be all right.'

'We know Jarvis,' Nigel bragged, 'he's one of Blumenthall's.'

'Shut it, Nige,' Vic ordered. 'You knew all along, didn't you, Mum. Of course you did. My Mum's not stupid.'

Esther said anxiously, 'You haven't ever hurt anyone, have you?'

Vic wrapped his arms around her. 'No, of course not. Just handled a little stuff, that's all. Nod and wink, a dodger for a little extra under the counter, you know.'

She sniffed with relief, then wiped her nose on her glove. 'That's all right, then. It's not as if you've done anything bad.'

'Just a matter of using your brain,' Nigel said.

'And knowing the right people.' Vic steered his mother to the door. 'Now, you know how to handle the interview, don't you? If they think you're too honest, they won't trust you, they won't think you're human, and you won't get the job.'

Nigel went out after them.

Ria turned to Ben. 'Off you go then! I know you can't wait to walk my mother back to Poplar.' She grabbed Arthur's hand and almost dragged the little boy to the door. In the doorway she spun on her heel. 'I hate Vic!' she hissed. 'I hate him!' The blanket hung over the doorway flapped and swung as she ran away.

Ben said: 'What did *I* do?'

'She's wrong,' Tom said. 'Pass me my towel, would you, son.' He stood and began to dry himself ineffectively on the scrap of material. He stepped out of the bath, stood dripping on the black flagstones. 'Yes, she's wrong. A son has no greater duty than to protect his mother, Ben. Vic's done it wonderfully, for years. For Esther. And for Ria. And for all of us.' He moistened his mouth and speckled seed from a small paper bag over his lower lip. Opening the cane door of the cage, he enfolded the yellow canary gently in his hand and took it out, murmuring, 'There, there, there's my beauty. Everyone round here speaks well of Vic,' he said.

'You won't hear anyone who doesn't like him. He's got that
. . . something.' He grunted with pleasure as the tiny
canary began to peck the seed from his giant lip.

2

Ben ran to the corner and paused by the Tooke Arms
watching the traffic stream along West Ferry Road. There
were hundreds of tiny shops, gracefully decorated, the
goods piled outside under rickety canopies of tin or tile,
displays of upturned buckets, churchwarden pipes, cages of
white mice, red poll finches, joints of meat, all lining this
side of the road – the other side was warehouses and the
river – and he wondered why the same names, selling the
same sort of stock, occurred so often on different shops. He
stopped looking for Esther's shape, the canary-yellow hat
that would be bobbing somewhere in the crowd, and stared
at the shop fronts. Henry Baggs sold fried fish both here and
twenty or thirty shops along. Okill the greengrocer had two
shops. Ben also saw three Stephens' Coffee Rooms.

The shops obviously had all the business they could
handle – though the slums were poor, they were vast, and
cash did not stay in pockets. Even if each customer only
spent twopence and you made a farthing profit, all you
needed was to pack in a lot of customers . . . Then why
didn't two or three shops join together, to make one big
one? A smile spread across Ben's face, making him look
open and innocent. Obviously, the shopkeepers did not
own their tiny shops, they had to lease them from the great
landowners, lords and dukes and such, and they could not
buy the shop next door when they wanted to expand – they
had to take up a lease when and where they could get it,
when it came available. He guessed that was not very often.
Houses, he knew, were often passed down through families
– most of those in Lichfield Street had been spoken for in
that way – and he guessed that the same must be true of
shops.

A blue cape caught his eye.

Ben stared, open-mouthed.

A wickerwork mannequin stood inside the bow window wearing a cream dress made of lovely soft-looking material, with a short blue cape draped off the shoulders. A big piece of card was propped against the hem: 22s 6d.

Ben memorized the name above the shop: Mrs Mary Walker, Dressmaker.

He ran to catch up with Esther, but he always took the short-cut over the lock gates, and she must have gone the other way. He had to hurry in case he was missed at lunch.

When he got back to the Workhouse it was nearly time for the meal. Knuts was not in the yard: he was lying on a blanket up in the ward. His flesh had become ice-pale and peculiarly transparent over the past weeks, even though the weather was warm. Ben knelt by him. He saw every purple vein in Knuts's hands, neck, and feet, like a map of the inside of a person. Knut's tongue moved, bright red between his teeth and his purple gums. 'Don't let them put me in the Infirmary,' he whispered. 'I don't want to die with the old people.'

'I can't leave you here.'

'You can do anything you want,' Knuts murmured. 'I can't move. It hurts.' Ben knew. Dr Lamont had explained how the muscles contracted around the diseased joints, so that the smallest motion could be agonizing. Knuts had not walked properly for months as the vertebrae in his back became infected; now it seemed that they had collapsed, and he could not walk at all. 'I'll take you to the dining room. Then we'll go out into the yard. It's still sunny outside.' Ben picked him up. He could sense the internal organs shifting as Knuts's body lost its life, the binding that held it together. The most dreadful thing was that Knuts gave no sign of pain, just lay curled against his chest with his face against the side of Ben's face, and his transparent hand tapping the back of Ben's neck as he walked.

Knuts was too far gone to sit at table: Ben settled him into a corner with some other sick youngsters and went to fetch a bowl of porridge.

Esther was standing in the shadows of the doorway where Ria used to wait. Ben said: 'Did you get the job?' He knew at once that she had not. Her cheerful face was misshapen, as though it had received a heavy blow. She gripped his shoulder.

'How am I going to tell Vic?'

Table-boys hurried past, disturbing them. He drew her in and they stood by the shelves. She hung on to his hand.

'Son, I didn't get the bloody job.'

'How? You were a racing certainty.' It was slang he'd picked up from Rixby; he had an ear for it: she knew what he meant, so probably she'd got it from Vic.

'There were six of us, they made us wait,' Esther said. Life started to come back into her face as she remembered. 'As soon as I saw that Edna Dakins woman who lives between the Picture Theatre and the Public Baths, I knew I was lost. Her husband who she says is gone away to sea was in calling – a casual docker – at the West India Dock. She got him in with a bad lot on her Dad's side and he was nabbed coming out dressed in heavy horse, pouches lashed to his legs stuffed with ginger, pimentoes, hashish, God knows how long he'd been doing it, and now he's inside.'

'Inside?'

'Prison.'

Ben pointed out: 'All you had to do was tell the Guardians.'

'Oh, no, son, I couldn't do that.' She looked horrified. 'That's not done.'

He nodded. 'It's the same in here. I didn't realize it was like that outside.'

'I keep forgetting how much you don't know about the real world.' Esther squeezed his hand sympathetically. 'Anyway, that was when I knew I wouldn't get the job. But I've got my pride, whatever Vic says, even if it's all I've got. I went in there and I said, "Gentlemen, I'll have you know I want this job. I'll say exactly what I mean, gentlemen, if you don't mind the compliment where none is due." '

'You spoke to them like that?'

'I did. I said, "Gentlemen, I'll lay my cards on the table. I know all the fiddles. I know about the greased palms. I know about the barrels of meat containing forty-eight pieces that suddenly only contain forty-six pieces. I know how to stir a tallow candle into the porridge to make it look richer. I know all these things, and I don't do any of them. So I know I won't get the job! Good day, gentlemen!" '

'I would have given you the job,' Ben said admiringly.

'Yes, but most wouldn't.' Esther held his arms, then hugged him impulsively. He felt an extraordinary warmth. She perked up whenever she saw him now. He was confused; it must be friendship. Was that possible, between a man and a woman? Even though she had four other children, could she love him, just a little bit, as Edith Rumney had? Was that true? Was that why she had more life in her when he looked at her than when he turned away? No, surely. Yes? She looked up at him. 'Come and stay with us,' she said.

He shook his head reluctantly. 'I can't.'

'Come on. I'll square it with Vic. Tom says he likes you, and he sees more than he says. We need you. You must. It's not charity, you'll more than pay your way. Our family needs you. Be a part of our family, Ben.'

'No,' Ben said. 'I can't. I can't.'

'Please,' Esther said.

He turned away.

'Offer's still open,' Esther said, in a more weary voice. Then he heard the unmistakable squeak-pop of a cork pulling out of a bottle. He looked back from the doorway. She took a sip, looking away from him. 'Medicinal,' she said. 'Mother's ruin.'

Ben crossed the dining room. Three great beams held up the ceiling, and he knew the lines inscribed on them as well as he knew the lines on the palm of his own hand.

On the first was written: GOD IS HOLY.

On the second was written: GOD IS GOOD.

On the third was written: GOD IS TRUTH.

Knuts was too weak to swallow. The skilly dribbled out of his mouth as though his flesh had become inert and apart from him. His unblinking eyes were filmy, like oil on water, but then they gained a little brightness. He looked from Ben's eyes to the window, then back again.

'Do you want to go outside?'

Knuts closed his eyes, then opened them.

Ben carried him out. The blue sky was about half full of hurrying white clouds, but the wind did not penetrate down here inside the walls. The men were breaking stones, the hammers sounding a light, uneven rattle, and the evil dust swirled slowly in the sunlight. He asked the labour master's permission, got Mr Barnes's grudging nod, and lay Knuts down against the yellowing sycamore in the centre of the yard. The top leaves were already gone, stripped by the wind up there.

Are you going to leave me?

'No,' Ben said. He sat with his arms around his knees. Barnes kept glancing at him, but said nothing. Ben's heart kept jolting as he looked at Knuts: he kept thinking that he had stopped breathing, but when he leaned down he saw that his chest still fell and rose in tiny, unco-ordinated breaths. He did not blink; he seemed to stare at the sun.

Ben thought: this is what dying is, like a clock running down, waiting for the last tick, the last tock. He held Knuts's hand. All he could do was wait.

Maybe Knuts would get better.

He heard a faint buzzing sound.

Coming from the direction of Woolwich, an aeroplane crawled above the wall. He stared, astonished. It was the first aeroplane that he had ever seen. It grew until the four wings looked enormous, until he could see the pilot and hear the engine popping and blaring. It moved impossibly slowly above the ground – no faster than a man walking. It seemed incredible it could stay up at such a slow speed. Then he realized that it was going against the strong wind, and it was probably flying into it at thirty or forty miles per hour. At that very moment another aeroplane appeared, swooping down on the wind from the other direction, the wings tilting, becoming almost vertical as it turned, diving on the first aeroplane. They saw the pilot look round, startled, shading his eyes against the sun, and his machine wobbled in the unstable air. The second machine dived again, like an ungainly insect, its engine clattering. 'He's forcing him down,' Knuts said. 'He must have flown over the Woolwich Arsenal prohibited area. It's illegal.' The second pilot pulled alongside, making jabbing motions downward with his hand; the sun glinted on his goggles. The pilot of the first machine waved in acknowledgement and turned away, losing height obediently, probably looking for a place to land, and disappeared slowly below the wall.

The rattle of hammers had ceased.

'Get on with it!' shouted Barnes. 'What have you stopped for? Do you think this is a hotel? If you haven't finished your work, how can you eat your supper?'

He must have flown over the Woolwich Arsenal. It's illegal.

How had Knuts known? How could he have known? That was the mystery.

Ben dragged his eyes from the sky. 'How did you know about a prohibited area? We don't get newspapers here, and I never told you, I didn't know myself.'

Knuts was dead. His eyes looked like glass and tears had trickled from them. A little saliva hung from his mouth, and his chin against his chest displaced his jaw slightly to the left. It looked completely unnatural. Was his chest moving? No. Was he breathing? Nothing. He really was dead. Ben couldn't believe it. He felt guilty at having watched the aeroplanes while his friend died. 'Come on,' he said, 'it's nearly time for supper.'

He heard Knuts's voice come out of the dark. He felt freezing cold, remembering the icy bathwater, and he felt so young. *'When they hit you, scream. Don't try and hold it in. It only makes it worse. Let them know they're hurting you, or else.'*

And his own voice: *'Who are they?'*

And Knuts saying: *'Ordinary people.'*

Ben thought: *I won't cry, and I won't die.*

But Knuts was dead. Ben's lips trembled. His eyes burned, but no tears came. He couldn't cry. *'I won't cry.'*

Except for love.

The tears began to course down Ben's cheeks. He opened his mouth and drew in an aching, gagging breath. Then he couldn't help himself: he bawled like a baby for his friend.

'Kicked it, has he?' Barnes said.

'Yes, sir,' snivelled Ben.

Barnes stuck his fingers in Knuts's eyes and pulled the eyelids down.

'Take him to the Dead House.'

Already.

Ben picked Knuts up. The body hung from his hands. He tried to get Knuts's head comfortable against his chest. Barnes pulled the arms around his neck. 'Mind he doesn't stiffen up, or you'll never get rid of him!' The men laughed.

Ben went inside. He walked along the stone corridor to the vestibule. His face was wet and cold with tears. He looked back for the last time. The porter was sitting at his counter, licking his pencil, filling in forms. The sores which had covered his lips were gone. He looked up incuriously. 'Got a dead'un?' He pulled his ring of keys off his belt and opened the black door. Both he and the door were smaller than Ben remembered. This time he was tall enough that he had to duck under the arch inscribed MEN.

He walked into the west roadway. He crossed towards the wretched houses opposite, the flat sun streaming above their crooked roofs and garrets throwing them into deep shadow. He turned down the alley by the Relieving Officer's quarters and came to the Dead House.

'Hell,' the Nurse said, 'I was just going off duty. My supper's on the table. Quick, bring him in, put him in there. Is someone playing a joke on you? Never wind a dead man's arms around your neck, the muscles tighten and they can throttle you, stupid boy, don't you know anything? Lay him on that. More work,' she fumed. 'Get out, get out!'

Ben ran.

The cobbles pounded against his feet. His sandal twisted, flew off. He hopped along, pulled the other off, threw it away, and ran on. The dock opened up, green and wide. The wind pushed back against his face, his body. His elbows banged his sides. A train hooted as he scampered across the gravel, jumping the metals, then over the fence, gasping, his heart hammering. Now the wind was behind him, pressing him forward as he ran, his grey shift flapping, hair flying. Here was the lock, the gap, the water roaring.

He pulled his shift over his head, threw it down, it fluttered, then the water caught it and it disappeared.

He ran on. The road; wharves, alleys, slipping and sliding, the road again, then running past the shut-up shops, 22s 6d, cream and blue, into the lanes and slums, balconies of creeping jenny and nasturtium, fading as darkness fell. A few people sitting out on their steps knew him by sight and raised their hands in greeting.

Now he was in the dark streets. The girl called Ann was walking her baby. She looked at him eagerly as he pushed past, and he ran on, not looking back. Here was the doorway; a blanket hanging over it.

'Come in,' Esther said. She had a knife in her hand. The family was just sitting down to eat. She didn't seem surprised to see him; almost he expected to see his place laid.

'Come in, son,' Tom said. 'Sit down. Plenty for all.'

'I've run away!'

Ria elbowed Vic and shifted up the bench. 'You can sit here,' she said, patting the space beside her.

There was a moment of silence.

Vic said: 'What was the name of that bird you were talking about, Nigel?'

'The cuckoo,' Nigel said. He had passed the Fourth Standard long ago and no longer bothered to go to school, but he had got into the habit of books.

'The one that moves into another bird's nest and chucks the other chicks in the family out to make room for himself,' Vic said. 'Is that the one, Nigel?'

'That's the one.' Vic looked at Ben. It was the same as it had been years ago, the dim light, the same trick of staring. This time neither looked down.

'Lads, that's enough!' Tom said. 'I don't want to hear any more talk like that. Is that quite clear? *Is that clear?*'

'Clear as mud,' Vic said. Then he smiled, standing, holding his hand out. 'Friends. All right? You've got a lot to learn. I'll look after you.'

They shook hands.

Ben sat, and ate. He had never tasted such delicious meat.

Part IV

THE FALL

Chapter Eight

1

They walked among the market stalls in the bright autumn sun.

'Listen, look, learn,' Vic said, putting his arm around Ben's shoulder. Nigel was growing thin and tall – taller than Ben – but unlike his brother Vic had grown heavier instead of taller. He was very strong, but quick, and his muscular legs could overtake Nigel in short bursts. His jutting nose and chin were sunburnt, and his flat slabs of cheeks were bright red, but he was highly coloured at any time of year. He smiled at Ben, then waved at someone he knew. His black eyes were never still.

'What sort of punishments did you have in there?' he asked.

'Flogging, caning, bread and water,' Ben said. He saw Ria look round for a moment. She walked about ten paces behind, her arms enclosing herself, her hands hugging her shoulders, secret and withdrawn, and Ben had not thought she heard anything he said. She heard everything. 'Solitary confinement—'

'We don't have any of that nonsense out here.' Vic saw another friend and gave him a thumb's-up in greeting. 'Unless you get caught. So, my old mate, what does that mean?'

Ben shrugged.

'Don't get caught,' Vic smiled. 'Here starteth the first lesson. Watch.'

He stuck his hands in his pockets and sauntered off.

Watching, Ben stuck his hands in his own pockets – real pockets! – and loafed back against a street lamp like Nigel, except that he didn't have a matchstick to chew. He looked at the clothes that Vic had found for him: a dusty black jacket, too short, with a shirt beneath three sizes too large; a cloth cap that felt perhaps one size too big, worn to one side, now trying to slip forward as he looked down at his torn trousers held up with rope, and his poor bare feet. He closed his eyes. They were hardened to cold stone, but not to this endless walking, and the raw soles felt as though they had been blistered on a stove. 'Watch,' said Nigel. Vic slouched past the greengrocer's stall, walked on. 'He really is the master,' Nigel said. 'You'll learn.'

'What's he doing?'

'He's done it.'

Vic returned. He pointed and they walked on to a safe corner. 'Here you are, have an orange.' He tossed the fruit over and Ben caught it clumsily. He had never played ball games.

'Thank you.' He thought: a real orange, all my own. He looked at it curiously.

'Well, go on then, share it round.'

Ben examined the orange. He remembered from years ago that it somehow split into segments, but this orange was a seamless variety. He turned it over and over, then pulled on the green bit of stalk on top. 'Would you believe this,' Vic said. 'He doesn't even know how to peel an orange.'

'Don't laugh,' Ria said. She hated it when they laughed at him. It wasn't his fault; it was so brutal. 'Here, give it me.' She dug her fingers into the skin and peeled it expertly, dropping the pieces on the kerb, then stuck her finger into the top to open the segments.

'You should have left him to it,' Vic laughed, popping a piece indifferently into his mouth. 'It would have been the funniest thing we've seen, wouldn't it, Ria?'

'Don't be nasty,' Ria said.

'It would have taken him hours,' giggled Nigel, rolling his eyes like an idiot.

'Right, mate,' Vic said angrily, prodding Ben's shoulder with his finger. 'Now you do it.'

'Don't let him do it alone,' Ria said. 'No, don't, you stick beside him, Vic, or I'm going home.'

'All right, don't worry.' Vic took Ben's elbow. 'This is how you do it. Relax. Walk in a slouch. Let those shoulders slump. Look bored. For Christ's sake don't look so interested in everything . . .'

It was hot under the bright canvas canopies. Stalls and barrows stretched as far as Ben could see. The air smelt musky and sweet, the smell of the crowd, all pushing and shoving, hats and elbows, and piercing cries.

'Rest your hands in your pockets, don't push 'em down,' Vic said. 'Sort of turn them so that they're just lightly resting in the mouth of the pocket and you can snatch out without anything appearing to move . . .'

Ben's heart was in his mouth.

'Easy does it,' Vic said. They were beside the pile of oranges now. 'Turn your back. Yawn. Ain't it so hot, I'm so sleepy. Man's not looking – now. Flick it in your pocket.

And saunter. Not bad – for a beginner.'

Ben winked at Ria, who was sulking. He took his hands out of his pockets. 'Two oranges!' Ria's eyes shone. 'He got *two*.' He tossed one over and she caught it expertly in the front of her dress. Vic gripped Ben's arm.

'You behave yourself,' he said.

'I thought you would approve. Two's twice as good as one, isn't it?'

Vic grinned.

Nigel mimicked viciously: 'I'm so terribly frightfully awfully sorry, I thought you would approve.'

'I don't approve,' Vic said. 'You do what you're told, and no more. Right?'

Ben shrugged obligingly. 'Lead on, Vic. You're the guvnor.'

Ria flounced: 'I want to eat my orange.'

He observed her so closely, ignoring Vic, that she was flattered. 'See,' she explained, 'you roll it round in your fingers for a minute to loosen it inside. Then you bite into the rind to get it started. Ugh. Not everyone likes to do this. Now you just peel it off. The bit I like is sticking my finger in the top and wiggling it down to open it up. There. Have a bit.'

'You're clever, Ria.'

'Look at your poor feet!' Ria cried. 'Vic, he has to have boots.'

Vic said: 'If I show him how to get one pair, will he take two again, just to show me up?'

Ria watched Ben curiously. Nowadays she stood like a lady. She no longer scampered through the alleyways; she no longer crouched fearfully, though there were people everywhere. For a moment she remembered Dolly, thrown away years ago. She thought: *Do I have a curly red mouth?* Had he noticed? Did he like the shape of her nose? She worried about her nose – perhaps it was too snub – and it had a tiny bump on it half-way down, and her nostrils were not perfectly regular in shape. She was sure he had noticed, as he noticed everything. *If only my face had more character, more femininity.* She wished her bust was bigger. It was growing, but not quickly enough. Her nails weren't growing either. Each night she prayed for a big bust and long nails. Mum had got her a part-time job in Brown's Laundry at number 81 – she knew Arabella Brown from the old days. The work was hard and the chemicals made Ria's nails crack, and she hated it. She played truant whenever she could – like now.

She watched him from the shade where a small tree grew, keeping her face out of the sun so that she would be properly pale and lady-like. People jostled around her, but she was motionless. A motor-van clattered past, but she did not to notice it, withdrawn and distant. All of her energy was concentrated on the figure over the road, sitting on the steps up to someone's front door.

He was wearing the same clothes as everyone else, but he was different, because he knew that *she* was different – he noticed her, didn't he? Nobody else did, not in the whole world, except Vic, and that didn't count. Ben wore a cloth cap and a black jacket and his trousers were held up with rope, but his boots were as good as Vic's, and better than Nigel's. He sat there peeling that orange with such concentration! She just knew that he was peeling that orange with all his heart. The way he was staring at it, she expected it to just fall apart.

He selected a segment, then frowned at it.

Go on! she thought.

He turned the segment over and over, staring at it. He frowned again. *Why?* she wondered. *What does he remember?* Did he remember when he was a baby, when he could have as many oranges as he wanted, all peeled for him by a footman? If he could care so much about the orange, why didn't he care for her? He never responded to her in that intense way. He smiled at her when she smiled at him, yes, held her hand sometimes, yes – but never *responded* to her in the way, whatever it was, she thought incoherently, that she felt he ought: never looked at *her* with that intense concentration on his face.

He ate the fruit then jumped down. As he walked off along the pavement she crossed the road in front of him. 'Hallo.' She slipped her arm through his and they walked together. He didn't pull close, but he didn't pull away from her either.

'I thought you were at the laundry today.' He patted her hand innocently. Not . . . *intensely*.

'It's my day off.' She felt disappointed.

'You're playing truant.'

That word – as though she was still at school! 'I'm not a little girl any more, you know!' He glanced at her. She changed the subject. 'Where are you going?'

'Meeting Vic. We're going to hold up a corner. Do you want to come?'

'I'll come with you,' she said. Then she said: 'You don't have to go.'

'He said he might be able to find me a job.'

Sucking him in. 'You like Vic, don't you?'

'I admire him.'

'All you men together. Yes, he's a man's man, isn't he.'

He pointed out: 'He lets you join in.'

'Yes, but suppose I don't want to join in!' He looked at her. She tried to explain, tugging at his arm. 'I want to be free. I'm me. I want to be me.'

'I know.' Everyone did, surely?

'You do know,' she said gratefully. She tried to communicate her innermost feelings to him, trusting him, masking them only with a smile. 'Is that so bad? I suppose growing up is this horrible for everyone!' She was almost crying. Her eyes were shining with tears as she looked up into his face. She would have cried, if he had wanted her to.

But perhaps her change of mood put him off balance (men's moods were so flat) because he defended Vic: 'Dad – Tom – told me that a son has no greater duty than to protect his mother. Even you must admit it, Ria, Vic does do that. Look at all the gifts he brings Esther.'

'Gin!'

'And all the other things. Why won't you wear that gold bracelet he gave you?'

She shook her head. 'But Vic doesn't *protect* Mum! He mocks her! I know that you must see that, it's so obvious that it makes me want to scream, but why won't you believe it? He *exploits* her – takes her love, and makes a fool of her in return!'

He said objectively: 'Maybe it's worth it, from her point of view.'

'Oh, don't pretend to be so cold. Why do you always play the innocent?'

'Things are so simple between men. Women see different things, and so they make everything between men and women very complicated.'

Complicated. 'Good!' How could she explain about the gold bracelet? Just that she didn't want to wear a thing like that given to her by her own brother. And so obviously stolen: it revealed too much. But how could she explain that to Ben, if he didn't know?

'There were no women in the Workhouse.' He shrugged. 'It's not innocence, Ria, it's ignorance. That's all.'

'There was me. I'm a girl. Or hadn't you noticed?'

'You're special, Ria.' Her heart flew. He was admitting that she was not like other girls. Her thoughts, feelings, were all new, unique – unthought, unfelt by other girls. All this was true. And he knew. Not too much, but she could teach him what she wanted. She wished that she could throw her arms around him, he made her so happy. Then she saw Nigel, standing on the corner ahead, and knew that Vic would be nearby. A bleakness settled over her heart.

'There's Vic!' Ben said. 'He's talking with those men.' He turned as Ria hung back. 'What is it?'

She tried to warn him what would happen. 'Vic doesn't do anything for love. He doesn't know what love is. He does it for hate.'

'Why?'

Why not? Because that was the way of the world. She tried to explain. 'Because he wants it for his.'

' "It?" '

'Whatever it is. He wants it for his own. To have, to hold.'

'Thank you for the warning.' But had he listened? He tried to walk on. For the last time, she tugged his elbow.

'Listen. Be careful. He'll suck you in. Believe me. He will suck you in until you can't get out. Ever.' And she would lose him. 'Don't go!' she begged.

She stopped, but he didn't look back. She followed twelve or fifteen paces behind him, then, when they came to the corner, she stood alone with her arms around her shoulders, sulking, watching the traffic. A motor-omnibus had broken down and the passengers were getting off. The sun had gone in and a chilly wind funnelled between the buildings. Ria shivered.

Vic was making a rough group of men dressed in rags and cast-offs laugh out loud: their harsh, grimy faces were lit up with animation. Ben waited, watching how he did it. They felt that Vic was one of them. There was no distance between them. He joked roughly, gossiped, mocked, shouted his opinions, held arms, roared with laughter, slapped his knees, punched the men, drew them close, listened, knuckled their jaws, kicked at their shoes, and they felt that they were the greatest bunch of fellows in the world.

It was a virtuoso performance.

Nigel saw Ben and hesitated. He came over and for the first time made a quiet but obvious effort to be friendly.

'Spion Kop holds the record for the fastest time in the Derby. Did you know that?'

'Shut it, Nigel,' Vic shouted.

'Vic's upset because he blew a topper on a nag at Hurst Park,' Nigel said in a low voice. 'Count Ross got left at the tapes, and he was supposed to have been figged.'

'Figged?'

'Gingered-up. Cost Vic a quid.'

Vic came over. 'All right, all right, what now? Do you know how to spit? Watch.' He demonstrated. 'There's all sorts of spits. Shut mouth and open mouth. Through top teeth, and through bottom teeth. Long distance, and short distance. Loud spits and soft spits. Don't know what you've been missing, eh? Cowboy taught me, Wild West Rodeo, long hair like a woman, but can Yanks spit, yes, sir. I'm getting bored to death, Nigel. Let's do something.'

'I don't know,' Nigel said, lighting a cigarette.

'Let's be drunk. That's always good for a bob or two. Gi' us one of y'r Woodbines.' He weaved along the street bumping into people and asking for a light. None of them obliged. One man jumped back before Vic touched him, and they could see that he was laughing and shaking his head. Vic came back smiling, flicked a match out of his pocket and lit the cigarette.

'Get a move on.'

Ben followed them down an alley. 'Why did that man laugh?'

'He knew the trick.' Vic fanned two or three pocket-wallets, a street map, a fountain pen and a diary in his hand. 'You see blotto kids all the time when they get sent out, sozzled on their parents' beer coming back from the jug and bottle, but if a drunk kid bumps you, he falls over. Rule of nature. They haven't been walking so long, so they forget how to quicker. I stayed on my feet, so I must be a bad'un. He knew. Let's have a drink.'

They went into a pub. Vic ordered three mild-and-bitters while Ria waited outside. 'All right,' he told Ben as they drank, 'I think I've got you a job for the winter. Blumenthall has got a grocer's shop and he needs a cashier who can count. You can count, can't you? So I can help two friends out at once. Strictly legitimate.'

'When do I start?'

'Strewth,' Vic said in disgust, 'you haven't even asked how much he pays.'

'How much does he pay?'

'Not much. Honest work, see? Go on, take it, my Mum could do with the extra. Anything, just so long as it gets you out of my hair. What do you say?'

'Thanks, Vic, that's very good of you.'

'That's what I like to hear,' Vic said. He finished his beer and wiped the froth off his lips. His breath smelled horrible. 'Listen. We've got all afternoon. Bit of harmless fun. We'll find someone who's got a bob or two on him, not just the little penny game like earlier, I mean a real bob or two, a shopkeeper going to the bank maybe, or a gent, or maybe a sailor who's just been paid off, who cares—'

'I don't like it.' Ben tried to turn his head away from Vic's.

'No danger, no risk! No noise, nice quiet street. Come up behind them, give them a quick bang in the back and take it off them, they don't make a sound, thank you very much, sir.'

Ben took a quick breath. 'What are you talking about?'

'Just come up behind them and fist them in the kidneys. The pain is so awful that they can't even scream.' Vic smiled.

2

Every day, shivering on his way to work at Blumenthall's Grocery, Ben passed the dressmaker's shop with the cream dress and the blue cape standing in the window. The price was still 22s 6d, but it hadn't sold and he reckoned that it would come down to 19s 11d in the January sale. That was too late. He wanted it before Christmas.

He blew a cloud of white breath over his hands and walked on. He could always pay Vic ten bob to lift it – Vic would think of a way, even if it was just getting Nigel or someone to put a half-brick through the window – but he didn't want to do that.

He wanted to buy the dress.

He wanted to pay for it with his own money, earned from his own work.

He enjoyed working at Blumenthall's. The old man was a shifty character with lank white hair and long knobbly fingers. His nose curved down and his chin curved up, like Mr Punch's; you couldn't have got more than a couple of fingers between the gap. He was said to be very wealthy, but he was a miser. 'Even a rich man, my boy, cannot eat more than one breakfast.'

Ben thought: *I could.* 'That's right, Mr Blumenthall.'

'Even a rich man, my boy,' sighed Blumenthall sadly, 'cannot sleep in more than one bed.'

It was all very well for him to talk like that; he was supposed to have a metal box with thousands in it stashed under his bed. In gold. Perhaps it was true: he lived above the shop and the ceiling did bulge downwards; sometimes Ben thought that it was only the goods stacked solidly on the shelves that held the walls up. He did not enquire too closely into the business that Blumentall did upstairs, where he spent most of the day, and where he was visited by the sort of people who preferred to come in the back way. Blumentall liked him, he knew – over the past few months he had come to trust Ben's discretion as well as value his honesty, realizing that Ben was not a Trojan Horse sent in by Vic to spy on him. Vic visited, often; but he was far too young and, possibly, vigorous, to be a member of Blumenthall's trusted inner circle. Blumenthall disliked exuberance and personal contact. He hated to be touched. He liked Ben and occasionally, when handing on his homilies and pearls of wisdom, went so far as to finger Ben's upper arm gently, as if testing the texture of a piece of meat.

Ben tied on his white apron – he had a clean one every week, courtesy of a certain employee of Brown's Laundry – shooed the cat out of the bed it made every night in the crate of Demerara sugar, and started sweeping the floor busily, looking forward to the first customer. He had broken with tradition by putting a Fray Bentos display on the counter to prompt the customer's mind. Let them look, let them touch. The airtight tins of biscuits hadn't moved at all until he took them down and let people actually handle them and see what nice tins they were – they bought the biscuits for the tins, and they were pricey.

He loved the business of using the till: it was a magnificent brass machine, very modern and ornately decorated, polished every morning by him after he swept the floor, with a glass window along the top where the prices shot up when you punched the keys, and a tinging bell, and when you pressed the TOT key the bell clanged and the drawer banged out, full of spoon-shaped mahogany compartments for coins: farthings, halfpennies, pennies, silver threepenny bits, sixpences, bobs, two-bob florins, tusheroons, dodgers, and even a rack for sovereigns which never needed to be used. His fingers learned to fly between the scoops, smaller denominations first, then he pushed the drawer closed with his stomach, the spring loading whirring as it wound up: 'Fivepence three-farthings. Thank you, ma'am, one shilling tendered, fivepence three-farthings and a farthing, that's sixpence, and another sixpence, a bob. Merry Christmas, ma'am.'

'Oh, and I'll have a tin of that Fray Bentos Argentinian beef.'

He pushed the keys, *ting*, then TOT, *clang*, the drawer banged out, *whirr*, 'Thank *you*, ma'am.'

The shop was a community meeting-place for the women, as the pub was for the men, and often it was packed solid, a babel of gossip. He quickly got to know their names, who was expecting, who had just produced, what Maisie Coburn said to Vera Kosky, the state of Lucy Cain's legs, who got knocked about, which families let their children run wild, who was friends with who and who was running a feud. As a shopkeeper his most difficult job was often walking the tightrope between the factions, retaining the business of each while supporting neither. Falling out with one customer often meant falling out with ten of their relatives. It was a subtle and complex task and he enjoyed it immensely, especially as Mr Blumenthall let him get on with it, and paid him on the nose at the end of the week.

After work that day he stopped on the ice outside Mary Walker's. The dressmaker was just shutting up shop so he went in. It was still gaslit, hissing and warm, and smelt mustily of cloth.

'Mrs Walker? I'll give you a guinea for it, as long as I can have it before Christmas.'

'It's still twenty-two and sixpence, love.'

'A guinea is all I have.' He showed it to her in his hand: a sovereign and a shilling. She was a big, kindly looking woman with shrewd eyes.

She looked amused a little bit, and compromised. 'If I don't sell it, you can have it for a guinea, after Christmas.'

'But I want it now, to wrap it up. And you'll probably drop it to nineteen and eleven in your sale. I see I might as well spend my one guinea in another shop. Good evening.' He touched the brim of his hat and turned. He walked to the door. He opened it.

'Come back,' she sighed. 'It's yours.'

Joyfully carrying the parcel, he walked past the Tooke Arms. A couple of men spilled out of the doorway and a crowd gathered, but it wasn't much of a fight, just fretful payday bickering at the end of a long week. The men just pushed one another back and forth on the ice until one of them fell over, then the other man helped him up, laughing, and they both went back inside. Ben went into Sam Poole's, the stationer, returned his daughter's smile, and purchased an embossed card with a gold border. Then he went next door into the newsagent's and bought the latest edition of the evening paper to read to Tom and Mum later. Going into the confectioner's, he bought a bar of honeycomb for himself and another for little Arthur, who was tending to be poorly again, as always in winter. Then he turned off into the dark streets and walked towards home.

The only light came translucently through paper windows, or diffusely through blankets or curtains, or in bright stars through rotting frames and brickwork. He had about eightpence left in his pocket, but he didn't bother to hide it in his sock. He could run faster than a man, and no youngster would stop him, because he was a friend of Vic's. Everyone knew their place. There were rules.

If someone stepped out in front of you, you knew that another had stepped out behind.

If you shouted, you knew they'd give you a whack on the head with a piece of wood or a fist in the kidneys, just hard enough that it made it agony to pee for the next few days, as a lesson.

All you had to do was take out your money and hold it out in your hand, preferably your right hand, and the man behind would take it. Both men would melt away, and that was the end of the transaction. If you went to the nearest pub ten minutes later, you'd find them drinking it. But you didn't. That wasn't the done thing. It was breaking the rules.

He had seen Vic and Nigel play it once or twice; it seemed harmless.

'Hallo there.'

She would be about fifteen now; Ann stood in the glow of light cast from a bare window, a heavy shawl draped around her shoulders. In the room behind the window he saw her eldest, who was by now toddling, curled up asleep under a blanket. The new baby was held in the corner by a pillow, and was also deeply asleep; she must have settled them down earlier so as to leave her evening free for relaxation.

She smiled, the oil-light glowing greasily down the side of her face, and held up a cigarette between her fingers. 'Give us a light?'

He nearly said *I'm sorry, I don't smoke*, but then he remembered that he did have a box of matches in his pocket, for re-lighting the gas fire in the shop, which was always going out, especially if someone slammed the door. Blumenthall didn't mind paying for the fire, since it got people into the shop, but typically he objected to buying the matches as well, spoiling the ship for a ha'porth of tar, so Ben had bought a box from the tobacconist next door with his own money.

'. . . aren't you?'

He shook his head. 'I'm sorry, I beg your pardon?'

She raised her eyebrows, as if surprised that he had not been paying attention to her. 'I said, you're living with the Price family, aren't you?'

'Yes.' He found the box. 'You're Ria's friend.'

'Hardly.' She looked down and to one side, very dismissively, then found his eyes again and put the cigarette lightly to her lips, pouting them forward to take the crimped end. 'Are you, Ben?' He struck the match without replying. '*are* you?' While it flared she looked into his eyes, holding his wrist, then dropped the tip of her cigarette into the pool of flame and exhaled an aromatic puff of smoke into his face. 'Got the time?'

'It must be about seven-thirty. Good night.'

She laughed harshly and bitterly. 'Remember me to Nigel,' she called. As he walked away he heard the baby start to cry.

Clogs rattled on the cobbles and a shape jumped up out of the darkness at Ben. 'Hallo, Uncle!' It was Arthur. He swung the little boy up with one hand; he weighed so little. Arthur put his arm around Ben's neck and buried his face shyly against his shoulder.

'What have I got for you?' Ben asked as he walked, playing the game.

'It's Friday,' came Arthur's voice, muffled.

Ben jumped as if he was surprised. 'What happens on a Friday?'

'I've got a present. Give Arthur honeycomb!'

Ben insisted: 'Give me my honeycomb, please.'

'Give honeycomb, please.'

'Here you are.' Ben spirited the sweet bar out of his pocket like a magician. 'Thanks!' Arthur grabbed it and

228

slid down his chest. He smiled all over his face, then ran off into the darkness.

Ben walked on alone.

Coming home – yet it was not a home for him personally, it was a home for him to be, not a home of his own, much as he loved Mum and Tom – Ben lifted the door on its broken hinge, pushed aside the blanket, and went in. 'It's me.' Tom was working on a pile of sacks at the table – when business was dependably slack at the docks he did outwork for Starkey & Room, the sack contractors. As usual, Vic and Nigel were out. Esther's cheeks were bright red and she looked very happy, wearing a yellow pinafore with big white spots so new that it still bore the creases.

'Merry Christmas!'

Ben pecked her hot cheek. 'Merry Christmas, Mum.' He always called her Mum. He didn't think of her deeply as his Mum, both of them knew that, but it would have been insulting to call her Esther. Mum was the respect due to her status as head of the family, and in the community. Christian names were widely held to be an American habit and a disrespectful one, leading to a breakdown in discipline. If Mum was called by her own informal name, whether it was Mary, or Peggy, or Esther, she could not carry out her formal home duties: she'd think, *I don't need to bother with duty, this is not a home, it's just a house.*

'Come and sit down.' Esther said, embracing him, looking up into his face. 'You look worn out.'

'Where's Ria?'

'I don't know, darling, I think Vic took her out somewhere. You know Vic. Always roaming.' She chuckled indulgently, with perfumed breath. 'Perhaps to Queen's? You know how Ria loves the music-hall.'

Ben sat at the table and wrote Ria's name on the embossed card in careful copperplate, the thin strokes curling beautifully into the thick strokes. Then he slipped it into the parcel, which he hid behind a pile of sacks in the corner that would not be sent back to Starkey's until after Christmas. He knew; but Queen's was too close to the Workhouse.

*

The family was together. The air stank of food. Ria sat with her head down, her hands on her knees. She had just cleaned the last smear of grease from her plate with a piece of bread. It tasted very dry and she was finding it difficult to swallow. She felt terribly unhappy and as alone as if she sat in total darkness – except for one, who sat at the far end of the table. He had ignored her.

'I reckon I got you the fattest goose in the Island, Mum,' Vic said, leaning back in his chair beside Ria and patting his belly. He burped like an Arab. She looked at Tom, sitting beside Ben at the far end. Ben had not even looked at her when everyone else gave presents. She had given him a tie-pin someone had left in their pocket in the laundry, with mother-of-pearl inlay. No one could call that stealing, the customer couldn't have liked it much if they just forgot it was in their pocket, deserved to lose it. Vic would have called it natural justice. In the end she washed the bread down with some water. Maybe he didn't like mother-of-pearl. Tom had given her a brooch that he had patiently carved out of bone. (Maybe Ben didn't like it because *she* had given it to him.) Vic had given her a necklace with an opal on it, very gaudy, speckled to match her eyes. *He* had given her nothing. Tears formed in her eyes for a moment, blurring her vision, then went away and nobody had noticed – not even him.

'In the old days my Dad used to take us to church on Christmas morning,' Tom said slowly. 'And on Christmas afternoon too. There was discipline in those days, not like you lads, spending all your time on the street. Now they've shortened the hours of work, but offered nothing in place of work except the street. That's my opinion. And people aren't grateful. Look at all these posters about strikes.'

'Don't pretend you can read,' Nigel said.

'You're not too big to be larruped,' Tom said in his gentle, level voice.

'When you've got a job, you can talk about striking,' Vic said. 'But you haven't got a job. You haven't worked for so long they've even taken you off the register, so you've lost your union card.'

'Let's sing a song,' Esther said, pouring herself another drop of medicine. Ria thought: *Oh no!* Mum sang hymns in a terrible maudlin voice, never remembering the words.

'At least I'm an honest man,' Tom said. 'I've never deliberately done a dirty thing, a dishonest thing, in my life. Can you say the same?'

'It's harmless,' Vic said casually. 'I've never hurt anyone.'

'You're young. You'll learn.'

'Stop it, you two,' Esther said. '*There Is a Green Hill Far Away.*'

'It is always harmless,' Tom said, 'until suddenly it isn't. One day it suddenly isn't harmless. You'll learn.'

'Our resident philosopher,' Nigel said.

'If he'd ever done a good day's work for a good day's pay, I'd respect him more,' Vic said. Tom opened his mouth to reply. 'Come on, Nige, let's go somewhere.' Vic looked at Ria. 'Coming?'

She looked at Ben. He merely glanced at her. Suddenly she was sure, she *knew*, as clearly as if he had said it out loud, that he didn't want her to go. It was woman's intuition: she was part of his mysterious plan. Her heart fluttered with excitement.

'Aren't you coming with us to church?' Tom said. 'I thought, the whole family together, we aren't together often, we could go—'

'Oh, you must be joking,' Vic said. 'Who'd want to be together with you? Go out and get a job, and pay your way.' As he went to the door, Tom called:

'I am your father.'

'What a *good* example you are to your family,' Vic shot back. He turned and rested his hand for a moment on Esther's shoulder. 'Mum. Ria. I'll take you some other time, all of us together – new hat – all done up – you'd like that, wouldn't you?'

'Yes, Vic,' Esther said. She patted his fingers. The curtain flapped down and the table seemed empty. The goose was a sad pile of bones.

'Sorry, love,' Tom admitted. 'I wish I could buy you things.'

'That's all right, dear.'

'But I am his father.'

'He's just jealous, dear.' Esther put the plates in the bucket, then said: 'Never mind these, I can do them later. Come on, Dad! Where's my coat? Let's get to the church on time!' She pulled back her hair and found her coat. Tom pulled on his black coat and combed his hair. Arthur was clapping his hands with excitement. They made him wash his hands and slick down his pale curls.

'Ria and I will follow on in a minute,' Ben said.

When they were alone, he looked straight at her and smiled. She smiled back eagerly, and it was at once the same as it always had been: she felt that they shared a secret, not a black secret like the secrets the rest of the world was full of, but a bright secret. She sensed all that he knew: he knew her feelings, the thrill inside her, her knowledge that she was part of a plan. She felt intensely alive and full of feeling and unique and full of mystery and wanted to share it all with him a little, and make him hers. She wanted him to feel her feelings. She wanted to give them to him. And he knew this – she was positive – woman's intuition.

He was holding out a parcel.

Her fingers trembled as she took it. A card fell out with her name on it in funny writing. She clasped it to her, thinking: *I will keep this card with his name on it next to mine forever.* Her fingers fumbled with the ribbons. She unfolded the paper – expertly folded in a shop, she realized, so that this was a bought present, a real present, not lifted or jumble or a hand-out, but real, meaning everything.

She pulled out the cream dress.

'Oh, it's lovely!' she gasped.

'And there's a cape too, that goes over your shoulders.'

She held the dress against her. It was perfect. It was a lady's dress.

'Do you like it?' he asked anxiously.

'It's just what I would have chosen!'

'If it needs any altering the shop will be pleased to do it.'

'It's mine, you gave it to me,' she said fiercely. 'I don't want anyone else to touch it.' She leaned forward and kissed his cheek. 'Thank you.' She wanted to give him a real hug and a bussing straight on the lips, but he obviously didn't expect it, he hadn't been brought up that way. For a moment she felt off-balance.

Ria thought: *He needs to show me he loves me.*

She thought: *How can I show him I love him?*

So she said: 'I'll put the dress on right now.'

She went behind the blanket hung in the corner and stripped off to her underwear, then stopped.

She could hear his voice saying: 'I wanted to give you something to thank you for all you've done for me.' She could hear him walking slowly up and down. She imagined him suddenly pulling the curtain aside and something happening. Her fingers caressed the material of the dress. That was what it meant, wasn't it?

'I mean,' he said, 'I wanted to thank you, Ria, because without you I should still be in the Workhouse.'

Yes, that was what he *said*. But . . . she imagined him pulling the curtain aside. She in her underclothes, flushed in the face. He'd say the sort of thing men say: *My God, you're beautiful.* And she'd back away with her arms crossed in front of her, but not too quickly.

His voice came from beyond the curtain. He was still walking casually up and down, waiting. 'You gave me my freedom,' he said. 'I wanted to show you my appreciation, in the only way I could think of. Does it fit all right, Ria? It isn't long until the service starts.'

Of course; he wanted to see her in her dress. She would come out from behind the curtain, looking radiantly beautiful, and walk towards him, and he would hold out his hands and take them inside his hands while his eyes stared into her eyes, piercingly blue, possessing them, knowing everything, needing everything, and she having everything to give. And he would say, in a trembling voice:

'*Will you marry me?*'

She pulled the dress on over her head, swung the short cape around her shoulders, and came out. He smiled. 'You look perfect. It fits perfectly.' That was all. He put his hand politely behind her waist and she found herself outside. She hooked her arm through his as they walked to St Luke's. She paused to admire her reflection in a shop window: she looked really smart. She patted her hair – she wanted everyone to see her in her new cream dress bought from a shop. Even if someone told Vic. She wouldn't be here much longer.

They'd move to the West End, where the money was. There must be records; they'd find his mother, his father, if they were still alive, and claim his inheritance. He'd buy a grand house and they'd have servants and she'd eat whole boxes of chocolates on a chaise-longue in his drawing-room, and all her dresses would be cream, it would be her *motif* in high society.

As they entered St Luke's and walked up the aisle to join Mum and Dad, she imagined getting married here, walking up the aisle here in a long white dress – that would be the only time she'd wear white – and a white veil over her face, and a white posy of flowers and half a dozen pink-cheeked bridesmaids carrying her white train, and she imagined Ann pouting enviously as she swept past, and the expression on Vic's face. She imagined the freedom.

Mum shifted over then stared at her, amazed, as she sat. 'My Lord!' she said. 'My little girl. Don't you look the cat's whiskers!'

'Your little girl?' Tom said gently. 'She's almost a woman.'

Ria's heart glowed.

Mum said: 'Isn't it lovely material? It really is. You feel that, Tom, that's not your ordinary stuff . . .' Ria hardly heard what her ears told her, so much of her was concentrated on the lightest possible touch of her right arm against Ben's side. She did not hear the service; all she could think of was being alone with him. She laid her plans. When they came out, the setting sun seemed very bright.

'Let's walk back along the river,' she suggested.

'I'm going to the pub,' Tom said, as she had known he would.

'I've got my chores,' Mum said, as Ria well knew. 'And so have you, my girl.'

'I won't be long,' Ria said. Mum looked from her to Ben.

'I don't mind walking with her along there,' he said.

Mum let the cat out of the bag. 'She wouldn't go, if you didn't!'

'What?'

'You don't know what you've started, my boy.'

'Mum, don't,' Ria said, embarrassed. Mum was treating it as if she was chasing him, whereas *he* was chasing *her*. He'd bought her the dress, hadn't he?

'You bring her back before dark,' Mum said. She'd never laid down the law like that before. *I hope not*, Ria thought.

'Yes, of course,' Ben said innocently.

'Come on,' Ria said, pulling his arm before Mum could think of anything else to say. They crossed West Ferry Road and stood by the Regent Dry Dock with the river lapping quietly below them, high tide. Over the river the sun was setting beyond Rotherhithe and the Surrey Commercial Docks, silhouetting the rigging like spiders' webs. They stood by a crane. Ben looked round as a door slammed. She saw that a man in a top hat was locking the door of Batson's office and wished that Ben would look at her, not at him.

'Must be one of the managers,' he said, 'working on the books. He's got ink on his fingers.'

'On Christmas Day?'

'He prefers the peace and quiet. He has no family to keep him at home. No ring: he's not married.'

Married. So that was what the romantic word sounded like from his lips. *Will you marry me?*

'You're the only person I've ever wanted to be with,' she said, turning her face up to him. The man in the top hat walked past them, his shiny shoes clacking expensively on the stones, and turned down an alley. It was dark in there but they could see him against the light at the far end. Ben was watching him, not her. This was not going the way that she had planned. She touched his chin. He paid no attention. Had he seen something? She looked.

For a moment they saw a second man slipping after the man in the top hat into the alley. A metal blade glittered for

235

an instant between his knuckles, very short, less than three inches, very sharp and sharply pointed. She'd seen men with them before, the handle concealed in the hand and the blade sticking out between the second and third fingers. She hung on to Ben's arm. The man in the top hat was going to get shivved in the kidneys or neck, either was fatal. Ben tugged at her. 'Shut it,' she hissed. 'Shut it, or he'll see us.' He didn't understand. They could be killed. The two shadows came together.

'Hey!' Ben shouted, running forward. 'Look out! Behind you!'

The man in the top hat shouted: 'Help! Police!' The shadows parted before they touched. The man with the shiv came running back towards them. Ben just stood there, looking at him. Didn't he understand? Or was he incredibly stupid or incredibly brave? Ria screamed. The man with the shiv hesitated, crouching, his eyes flicking between her and Ben. He was a brutal-looking type in his forties, with a very smooth, sinuous way of moving.

Ria screamed again.

The man jerked the shiv at Ben and his face contorted, then he ran away.

Ria almost collapsed. She threw her arms around Ben. 'My God. My God. My love. He nearly did for you.'

He sounded incredulous. 'He was carrying a knife.'

She examined his face.

'Don't you *know*?' she said. 'He nearly killed you.'

'Then you saved my life.'

'You need looking after,' she whispered. 'Let me look after you.'

'But Vic said it was just a quick bang in the back with a fist, at most, and then only if they made trouble.'

'That's what they all say, that's how it starts. Let's get away from here,' she begged. 'That's what will happen to Vic. Take me away. Look after me. Help me.' *Marry me, one day.*

'What?' he said.

She pulled away from him, looking withdrawn and distant, he thought, as if he had somehow rejected her. It was getting dark and she looked cold. He realized that he had been thoughtless.

'Come on,' he said, 'I expect you'd like to get home and have some good hot tea.'

If she had been a man, he mused as they walked, he would have thought her behaviour strange. She had that attractive aquiline bump on her nose – she put her hand towards it every time he looked at her, as if to draw attention to it.

3

It wasn't a public holiday, but it was for Mr Blumenthall's religion, so as Ben shut up shop that evening, bolting the door, undoing his apron, Blumenthall came downstairs and told him to take tomorrow off.

'Let's go out,' Ria suggested. By coincidence, as often happened, he had met her coming out of Brown's Laundry and they were walking home together arm in arm. People were hanging out baskets of early flowers – it had been a cloudless day, the first really warm one of the year, and bees were still droning through the narrow courts. 'The two of us could go out somewhere.' She stopped and looked at him, and he knew that the idea had taken hold on her mind. 'Well, why not?' she suggested. Her face glowed, making her look eager and happy, not withdrawn.

'And Tom and Mum could come,' he said. 'They never get out.'

She held his hand stubbornly. 'Just you and me.'

'Alone?'

'Why not? We could go to the West End.' Had she planned this? he wondered. She always said *West End* as though the words were magical. She saw his stare. 'It would be different, that's all! We wouldn't see anyone we knew. I get so bored.' She squeezed his hand. 'I'd wear my best dress.'

'Which is that?'

'My cream and blue, of course!' A magical dress for the magical West End.

'I was wondering why you haven't been wearing it.'

She said softly: 'Because it's special to me.' She held his upper arms and looked up into his face. 'Special, because you gave it to me,' she said.

A little boy running past shouted, '*Go on, darling, give him a kiss!*'

He didn't realize that they were almost brother and sister, Ben thought with a grin, but Ria had gone bright red.

'All right,' he said as they walked into the gathering darkness, 'we'll get up early and have a day out. I hope this weather has set in.'

It had. Early next morning, while Ria was dressing behind the blanket, the rest of the family still snoring, Ben stuck his head out: the ribbon of sky twisting amongst the roof-lines looked whitewashed, cloudless. 'Come on.' He wanted to run along the alleyway with her, enjoying the emptiness, the quiet, but she stood in her cream and blue dress looking very lady-like, waiting for him to come back. He returned obediently. She said: 'How do I look?'

'You look very beautiful.' He bowed and offered his arm.

Dawn came up behind them as they walked, stretching their shadows in front of them. She saw that he was wearing his black jacket and trousers, almost a suit, the holes neatly patched. It was a little tight across the chest, but she reckoned he looked not half bad. He seemed uncomfortable in the unfamiliar stiff white collar that she had insisted he wear, but she had wanted him to look smart, and he did. She stopped him and adjusted his dark red necktie critically. He lifted his eyes to the sky and sighed so amusingly that she laughed, then they were both laughing together.

'I'm so happy,' she said.

At this time of year full daylight lasted about twelve hours, with the sunrise and sunset twilights still quite long drawn-out, so traffic was already streaming along West Ferry Road, lorries, vans, carts, jam-packed omnibuses, hardly any motor-cars. They followed the river north – flat calm and dark blue under the brilliant blue sky – and then, as the river made its great blue swing left, turned into Limehouse and walked along Cable Street. Ben was interested: this must be the scene of the terrific workers' riots of a few years ago, but there was no sign of the barricades now.

Ria didn't like it when he wasn't looking at her, it made her feel unsafe. 'I'm hungry,' she said, rotating her hand on her stomach. 'I could do with a bacon sandwich.'

He had cash in his pocket. He pushed into a crowded eating rooms. 'Bread or toast, ducks?' He shrugged and bought one, halved it, and they ate as they walked along. The toast scratched the roofs of their mouths, the hot bacon burnt their tongues. Ria licked her fingers daintily. He punched her shoulder lightly at her show of lady-like sophistication. 'No, don't,' she said. She walked with her hand on his elbow. She thought: *All these people think we're already man and wife.* That was a delicious feeling.

They glimpsed the masts and funnels of St Katherine's Dock on their left now. Great cranes and derricks steamed and swung, unloading bales of wool from Australia and New Zealand, rubber from the Far East, wine and brandy from France – they could tell by the names of the importers. Everything was huge, and a swarm of activity. What they were seeing was not just a world centre. It was the centre of the world.

They walked past the walls of the Royal Mint, and more gloomy walls appeared ahead of them. Ria felt bored, but she pretended to look interested as Ben pointed out that they were looking at the Tower, Julius Caesar's imperial fortress, rebuilt by the Norman invaders a thousand years ago. The more you knew, the more you saw. 'Why have the towers got those funny-looking hats on?' she asked, complimenting him by asking him questions, making him pay attention to her.

'To keep the rain off, I suppose.'

They walked a few paces further. Now they could see down to the river. He pointed at two great black towers standing up out of the water in midstream, the span between them open to let a ship through. 'There's Tower Bridge. The first time they tried to use it, it didn't work, but it's worked every time since. Hydraulic power.'

'How do you know?'

He tried to remember; perhaps he had always known it. These strange fragments of excavated knowledge added to his life, but also gave him a nagging sense of loss, because often he didn't know where they came from. Ria hung on his arm, looking so eagerly into his face that he smiled, and felt less lonely.

'I think it must be because I've been here in Blumenthall's dray, collecting stock from the wholesalers in the Larder.' He told her that Blumenthall had an ancient dray with the name of the last owner, a dealer in horsemeat, still in faded letters on the side. The nag that pulled it was almost as old, and people were always calling out that the horse should be in the dray, and he should be pulling it. Ria laughed. She loved it when he was funny for her, it was so personal, for her alone, and he had such a vivid way of speaking.

He told her: 'Tower Bridge is the first place I can cross the river.' He pointed at the busy Bermondsey waterfront, called the Larder, facing them from the south side. Most of the capital's canned meat, cheese and bacon was stored there. A thousand tons of butter was carted along Tooley Street every day. When the drayman was too ill or too drunk to go, Blumenthall took over behind the counter and sent Ben to the Bermondsey provision merchants to fetch Peek Frean's biscuits, then on to Hay's Wharf for corned beef, to Peacock's for the imported eggs Blumenthall patiently relabelled Home Fresh, and back via Champion and Slee for Sarson's vinegar. 'It saves him about a penny a gross,' he shrugged.

Ria took the chance to show him that she was thrifty. 'Look after the pennies and the pounds will look after themselves.'

He laughed. His eyes lingered on hers for a moment.

'Take me away from here,' she murmured.

They sat holding hands in the little park behind the Tower. She did not take her eyes away from his eyes. He looked at her, and she drew him in. A bird sang, her heart pulsed. They were so close, yet her mouth did not go dry, in fact her lips felt moist, and the light seemed very bright, as if her eyes had adjusted to darkness, the pupils widening. He squeezed her hand. Did he feel what she felt?

Beyond the railings a man stopped and set up his cart on the roadside, selling pots of whelks.

'*Whelks, juicy whelks, lovely fresh pots o' whelks.*'

The moment had gone. Ben sensed the change in her mood instantly: 'What is it?'

He always knew how she felt. She said: 'It's nothing. Just that man.' She surveyed the whelk-seller almost with hatred as they passed. But the day was long; there were many hours left yet.

'Look at this,' Ben said. It was a memorial: they had been sitting on the site of public executions in olden times. He seemed more interested in that than in her. She determined to learn from her experience. When the moment came, nothing must be allowed to distract him from her. Meanwhile he was reading from a plaque, and he sounded so excited: ' "When Lord Lovat was beheaded here in 1747 – that's not long ago! – just before the fatal axe fell, a scaffolding holding a thousand people enjoying the spectacle collapsed, killing twelve" ' – He paused for dramatic effect – ' "a sight at which the old man, even at that terrible moment, chuckled merrily, enjoying, no doubt, the downfall of so many of his political opponents." '

'Interesting,' she yawned.

They walked down Tower Hill into muddy Thames Street. Ria thought to pick up the hem of her dress. It meant letting go of his arm, but in fact that made it better, because *he* now had to reach out to hold *her* arm.

She looked around her. They couldn't be in the West End yet; this wasn't at all what she had imagined it would be like. It was a street of tall brick warehouses, filthy and stinking of fish – they must be coming close to Billingsgate Market – overhung with threatening cranes, every alleyway blocked by heavy waggons, and great bales and packages being swayed up by rope to the top storeys. Porters in stiff leather hats rolled barrels of oysters, cockles and winkles through the crowd using language that made everyone jump out of the way. Fishwives screamed like gulls. Kippers hung by their tails in endless stinking rows. Surely it couldn't all be like this. The sun fell in bright shafts that made her eyes water. The black dome of St Paul's cathedral hung over it all. She cut it out of her mind, looking at him, enjoying the feel of his hand on her arm as he steered her through the turmoil. He had eyes only for the buildings and the life around them. She had eyes only for him. *Take me away from here.* When he looked at her, she had a smile ready.

'You look happy,' he said.

She said: 'Yes, with you.'

Now he smiled too. Her heart trembled.

Suddenly, the street became a tree-lined boulevard, the trees showing green shoots, and everything was strange and new. They were on the Embankment. A train rumbled over their heads. Even the horse troughs were ornate: METROPOLITAN DRINKING FOUNTAIN AND CATTLE TROUGH ASSOCIATION. Great houses, offices and ministries showed above the treetops. Motor-cars glided smoothly by. Big Ben tolled, bringing in the afternoon.

'It's real,' Ria said. 'I always saw the pictures but I never thought it was really real like this.' She looked at him.

'And they don't show colour,' he said. 'I never knew the numerals were coloured navy blue, I thought they were just black, like ordinary clocks.'

'None of it's ordinary,' Ria said eagerly. 'It's all extraordinary.'

The colours amazed them as they walked out of the government area into the shopping streets, past glaring windows stuffed with every sort of luxury, brightly coloured posters and sky-signs hanging from wires everywhere. 'Yes, yes,' she said, she wanted to buy it all. At Piccadilly Circus, the hub of the Empire, the signs advertising Bovril and Schweppes were brilliantly illuminated by electric light. They could have stayed, staring, for hours, but the air stank of exhaust fumes so much that they had both developed headaches. They threaded through the hooting traffic, were jostled by people swinging down off 'buses and pouring up out of the Underground station, then had to jump aside as a bicyclist in tweeds wobbled past ringing his bell. A gentleman's uniform, they worked out, was either tweeds, if he was at leisure or up from the country, or more usually top hat and tails.

'Working men wear cloth caps.' Ria had never thought about it before. Yes, she realized, he was right: you could tell about people just by looking at them.

'Clerks and businessmen wear bowler hats,' she said.

'Businessmen have shiny shoes, clerks have shiny behinds.' She gave him a fluttering glance under her eyelashes for saying the word. He didn't notice; he was so over-excited his fingers trembled. He looked up at Eros, then along Piccadilly.

When they tried to stop for a breather outside the Trocadero Restaurant, the doorman moved them on.

'People,' Vane yawned, 'everywhere,' and patted the back of her white-gloved hand at her lips. In her other immaculate white hand she held a parasol with a pink fringe. The two girls, Vanity and Marcelline, sat in the back of a shining black barouche pulled by two smart black horses. To the mild irritation of both, each was wearing blue. But the feather in Vane's hat was longer and whiter.

'Isn't this traffic too dreadful?' Marcelline said. She had strong, eager features with dark eyebrows and wide lips, the sort of face that men noticed, Vane thought, disgruntled.

'It isn't the traffic, it's the people,' Vane told her. *How adult that sounded*, she thought. *How adult we are – riding out by ourselves!* They had to be back at Mama's in time for tea, but until then she could make the coachman go wherever she wished in London. She could even make him drive in circles.

The barouche moved forward a few paces. She stared at the coachman's black back, irritated with him that he could not get around the traffic somehow. A bicyclist in tweeds rode past. He glanced at her face and wobbled. He had noticed her!

Vane knew that she was not beautiful in the same hearty way that Marcelline was. Vane knew that she was beautiful, simply because everyone said so, but she was perfectly pretty, too, like a doll. Her face was round, and her pale skin was as flawless as fine china, with a lovely rose glow on each cheek. Her eyes were large and brown, almost perfectly circular, and her mouth was as small and as perfectly charming as a doll's.

The bicyclist glanced at Marcelline. For her, he paused with one foot on the kerb and *smiled*. Vane looked at her friend. Marcelline was smiling back. Vane jogged her with her elbow.

'You mustn't smile at them.'

'Why not?'

Vane didn't know what to say. 'Because.'

The man rode away. Marcelline said acidly: 'Suppose you never catch a husband? You'll have to live on your own for ever and ever.'

'I wouldn't mind.'

'You wouldn't be able to have any children.'

'Oh!' Vane said. It was a woman's duty to have children, and you had to have a husband.

'Men are like moths,' Marcelline said smugly. 'It's no good just having them notice you. They've got to be attracted to you as if you were an electric light. You've got to sort of switch yourself on.'

'But I'm not ready to get married.' To tell the truth, Vane found men rather silly. She had never been attracted to the ones that she had met. They had spots and loud laughs and their conversation was boring. She had not the slightest intention of *switching herself on* and pandering to such types. She saw herself in the style of Jane Austen: she would do the choosing.

'You'll be too late,' Marcelline said. 'I'll get there first.' Vane stared: she had not suspected this competitive side to romance. Marcelline smiled sweetly.

'You can marry your bicyclist,' said Vane, twirling her parasol, 'I'll marry that one.' She pointed with her eyes.

'Oh, darling!' laughed Marcelline, 'if you're sure you're socially compatible!'

Actually, Vane thought, he's not half bad looking. She could see that he'd just come out of the Trocadero, which wasn't top-notch socially, but it wasn't too bad. He wore a black suit with a stiff collar, and he stood on the pavement as if he owned it. She liked that. She didn't like his maroon necktie, and she would have made him wear a handkerchief in his top pocket and a carnation in his lapel. But he had lovely eyes and a kind smile . . . She realized that Marcelline was looking at her with amusement.

'Love at first sight. Aaah,' grinned Marcelline. 'Poor Vane, he's already spoken for.' She nodded at a common-looking girl in a wrinkled cream dress that looked as though she had been wearing it all day. 'Competition, Vane?'

The barouche moved on with a jerk.

'When I see the man that I will marry,' Vane said, 'nothing will stop me. Nothing.'

Ben sat with Ria behind the flower girls and hawkers on the steps around the statue.

Ria wondered: 'Why do the men all carry umbrellas, when it isn't raining?'

He didn't answer, and she found his eyes fixed on her. 'That's what I like about you, Ria. You notice things. You're always watching. You do notice everything, don't you? You're always thinking.'

'I hope that's not all you like about me.'

'I do like you.' His cheeks had gone a bit red, either because of the sun or embarrassment. Boys, she knew, never liked talking about feelings the way girls did. He had no close friends. Neither did she, and that was another way she was unusual. All the other girls she knew had lots of friends and never walked around alone.

'I like you,' she said.

His cheeks were definitely red. Embarrassment! Boys were so much younger than girls of the same age. She realized that his emotions were much less developed than hers were. She smiled, sensing her advantage. This was how she could win. He tried to change the subject back again: 'And the ladies carry parasols, although the sun isn't strong.'

She lay back on her elbows. 'It's warm.'

'I suppose it's the fashion.'

'Lie back, you're blocking the sun. Doesn't it feel lovely?'

'I don't suppose Blumenthall's would sell many parasols. I don't know though, the fashion might catch on.'

'Do you really like me?' she asked, sounding casual.

She watched him carefully through her half-closed eyes. The way he answered was important. She knew how boys and girls behaved. If the boy felt nothing he'd say something like, *Of course I like you, except you've got a face like a plate of cats' meat*, or perhaps, *I dunno, give us a kiss and let's see*. But if he *really* liked her, he'd say something like: *Yes, you're all right*.

'You're all right,' Ben said.

She waited, but he didn't add any of the twists in the tail that she had often heard others endure, like, *For a girl*.

She dared to hold his hand. 'I like you,' she repeated. There was a world of difference this time, and he knew it. His cheeks were very bright red now. Hardly able to hide her elation, she said: 'My headache's gone. Can we walk?' He scrambled up gratefully. She waited until he came back, held out his hand and helped her to her feet. That meant he accepted her as lady-like. She had changed him.

Ben suddenly left her side and bought a rose from an old flower girl. He held it out to her. 'It's beautiful,' Ria said. 'You shouldn't've!' meaning he should. She sniffed it.

'Go on, sir, give her a kiss,' the old flower girl said. Her tone was almost bored. She'd seen this many times before, Ben had flushed to the tips of his ears. He gave Ria a peck on the lips. He'd been aiming for her cheek, but she turned her head at the last moment. The old flower girl, whose name was Susie, and who in her black dress, poke bonnet and with her osier basket full of crumpled blooms, was almost as well known a local landmark as Eros above them, gave a couple of claps. 'Well done, sir.' Ria's face had not flushed at all, but her body felt warm.

Ben said, 'Come on,' and grabbed her hand. She followed him. They got lost – not that he admitted it – and found themselves in St James's Park. 'Aren't there any pubs?' she asked. 'I could do with something to drink.' She looked around her. For the first time in her life, she couldn't see a pub anywhere. A herd of cows grazed in the long shadows amongst the trees, as if it was the country. Enormous wealth and power resided in the great houses around the borders of the park. The lords didn't need pubs, she realized with a sniff; they just sent the butler out to a wine merchant. Probably they even had their own cellars, with rows of bottles laid down by their grandfathers, and a servant who did nothing else but take them out and polish them all day, in case the lord came down.

Ben bought a couple of tumblers of fresh milk from the herdsman for a halfpenny. He pointed out what the old man had told him: 'You see that building over there, Ria? That's Buckingham Palace.' He swung round. In the opposite direction they could just see Big Ben through the trees. Then there were government buildings, the steps up to Downing Street, and a huge gravel expanse where soldiers with red uniforms and silver helmets were drilling in the evening sun. Ben sipped his milk. 'I shall live here,' he said flatly. 'There's always something to see.'

She stared at him. 'But you'd have to be incredibly rich.'

He said: 'I shall ask Mr Blumenthall for a raise.' He smiled at her, then his smile faded. 'What's the matter, Ria?'

She shivered. 'You have a peculiar way of saying things, you do.' *I shall live here*. There it was. She had believed him even to the reason: *There's always something to see*. Of course he would. Hook, line and sinker. There had been no doubt in her mind. It had seemed so obvious: you wouldn't want a house without a view, would you? But now he was smiling again. His eyes were the same piercing colour as the sapphire-blue of the twilight sky behind him, and the street lamps stood out like silver points.

'Are you cold?' he said. 'Let's walk.'

'No,' she said, 'I'm not cold.' She looked at him as they

crossed the grass and went up some steps towards a cream-painted mansion, now buff-coloured as the light faded, the lit windows standing out brilliantly. Where did he get his confidence from? she wondered. He was half adult, half child, a changeling, between the two. How much did he really know? How much did he remember? The park, these buildings? His inheritance?

He stuck his face between the railings. He looked at the house; as always, she looked at him.

Then an enormous gold coach with classical paintings on the doors, pulled by fine black horses, swept up the drive and halted beneath the porte-cochère. Postillions in red, gold-braided coats and red knee-breeches, wearing white periwigs like the pictures of George Washington, jumped down and opened the doors, lowered the steps. Ria gasped when she saw the lady. Her dress was of rich, imperial purple, gathered at the waist, and it shimmered under the light. Mum would have been horrified, Ria thought. It was almost indecent, West End fashion. You could actually see part of the lady's shoulders, the bare skin. You wouldn't show your face east of Aldgate Pump deliberately looking like that. It was all right here; it was fantastic here. 'It's the Duchess of Westminster,' someone said. 'No, it's Lady Astor,' someone else said, 'I'd know that smile anywhere.' She wore a diamond tiara that flashed and sparked in an unmistakable but understated way, muted signals of the power and wealth and status and pride – and love? – of her husband. The lady took his arm and ascended gracefully the steps beneath the portico towards the great doors, which were thrown open by footmen.

'I'm going to have a tiara with diamonds as big as eggs,' Ria said.

'I'm going to have this house.'

She realized that he hadn't even been looking at the dress or the jewellery. Typical man. His eyes were fixed on the magnificent entrance hall blazing with chandeliers.

She elbowed him. 'You wouldn't let me in.'

'Of course I would.' He hardly glanced at her. She wanted to get him away from here. She hated it when he was distant from her; when he treated her as she treated other people.

'It's a real Cinderella ball,' she said wistfully over her shoulder, as they left. 'Did you see that *dress*.'

'Don't you like what you've got?'

Her cream and blue. 'Oh, I *do!* Because you bought it for me.'

'I think you look all right as you are.' *All right.* He was complimenting her.

'Do you really think so?' She touched her nose.

He seemed to know that she was serious. He always did. 'Ria, you're pretty!' She wanted to say: *Do you love me? Will you marry me, one day?* But only the man could say that. She kicked at a stone lying on the grass. That was one thing about it being night. You could walk on the grass. She saw the shadow of a bench and went over but it turned out to be two people lying together doing the love business.

'Let's stay here,' she said, as they walked on.

'We'd better start walking back.'

'Haven't you got enough for a 'bus?'

'Not if I treat you to a port-and-lemon. Walk or drink? Which would you prefer?'

She didn't want to go back. She hadn't told him that she had a few pence in her bag, which would do for a few extra port-and-lemons and a sausage roll. The difficulty was finding a pub. They used Big Ben to guide them to the river and walked along the Embankment, then saw a place beyond the Hotel Metropole, up Northumberland Avenue, and went in there. After a couple of ports that cheered her up, Ria began to feel blackly depressed. She wanted to enjoy herself, anything but return home to the place she now realized was a bleak hovel. Mum would be drunk and Nigel would be fumbling with himself in the dark. Dad would be snoring, and Arthur would be whimpering as if he was in pain. If she woke him up he swore he wasn't, but it was an awful, quiet, desperate sound that would make getting to sleep almost impossible for her.

'That's the last of the money,' Ben smiled. It was the first time she had seen him drink much alcohol. It made the smile stay on his face. She pinched his cheek and he didn't recoil, just leaned forward and helped her carefully out of the snug. Outside they stood looking over the river while their eyes adjusted to the dark and the stars seemed to come out. He leaned against her and kissed her on the lips. They stood rubbing their lips together, panting through their noses.

By mutual consent they pulled apart and stood looking over the river again. 'Thousands of stars,' he said.

'Yes,' she said.

He turned and put his arms around her. She put her hands on his shoulders. He kissed her again. His tongue wiggled into her mouth. She pushed it back with her tongue, and gasped for breath, her eyes wide with shock and delight.

'Where did you learn that?' That was awfully naughty: she'd heard about that from Ann. He wasn't so innocent as he pretended!

'I don't know.'

'Have you ever done that with another girl?' He must have learned it somewhere.

'No,' he said doggedly, 'I've always known it, that's all.'

'Are you sure Ann —'

'No!' he said. She watched him. She was sure he was telling the truth.

'Well, I don't know,' she said.

'I rather liked it,' he said. So had she; the feeling of warmth and closeness had been extraordinary. This time she felt his slim hard body against her when he kissed her. Her own body felt soft and wide by comparison. She felt her breasts moving as she breathed, and his tongue inside her mouth melting until there was only her awareness of the warmth, the closeness, and her longing.

'More stars come out each time,' he said.

'You've got the same way with words that you have with your tongue,' she gasped.

'Did you enjoy it?' She could tell by his voice that he was pleased.

She said: 'It was all right.'

She slipped her arm round his waist and they walked. He put his arm around her shoulder; nothing more. The lights of the West End dropped behind them, the glow of them in the sky faded, and more stars came out remorselessly. Thames Street was silent and dark. They heard the rumbling boilers of a ship preparing to cast off from the steam-packet wharf just below London Bridge, and a few lamps still burned in the Customs House. He held her hand around his waist. She held his hand around her shoulder. Their footsteps tapped and echoed.

Then, to avoid the slope, they left the road as Tower Hill rose on their left, and walked the broad boulevard between the Tower and the river. The echoes stopped. The river was broad and motionless. Their hips touched. Ben's fingertips brushed the upper slope of her breast each time she breathed in, because of the way she held his hand. They crossed the Traitor's Gate, where traitors used to be rowed in to be tortured and have their heads cut off. Tower Bridge rose up, black and complicated against the stars. She held her breath.

They passed beneath a stone archway. For a moment the echoes returned. She looked back.

Tower Bridge was behind them now. They had re-entered the East End.

She breathed quickly, almost panting. The Bridge was so beautiful against the glow of the West End sky.

Ahead of them lay Wapping, mostly darkness. Cranes stood in ranks along the quays, like silent birds bowed over the water, until they disappeared in the dark. The lights of steamers showed in St Katherine's Dock, on their left as they walked with the river on their right. The gangways were lit and she felt the romance of the names: *Lapwing* for Amsterdam, *Mallard* for Antwerp and the Rhine, *Drake*, *Stork* and *Vesuvio* for Genoa, Naples and Monaco. It was high tide; the lock was open. There were great stone walls everywhere, all around them, and steps up and down.

'Stop,' she said, holding his elbow. He kissed her at once, with that same tremendous confidence, then pulled away from her. It was the end. She held him. 'No,' she said. She

251

held his hand to her breast, feeling the heat of his palm through the material. She enfolded him in her arms. 'Go on,' she said. There were some steps behind them. She took one step down, then two steps down, backwards, into the darkness. His hands were under her cloak. Three steps. His fingers found the clasp between her shoulder blades, flicked, and her dress loosened. She felt the cool night air on her naked shoulders, on her breasts. She looked down. The pale globes enclosed his dark head, the tips dark shoots. His hair brushed them like electric wires, making her twitch and tremble. His body felt hard and bony as she ran her hands over him, she was both out of her mind and yet keenly aware of every detail. She had no strength, was slipping down. She felt the stone on her back, the water lapping behind her head. He lay on her with his hips against her hips, not moving. This wasn't all.

'Now,' she said. 'Quickly.'

'What?'

This was all he knew. He remembered Peter Pungle kissing Aunt Edith, the fierce, desolate need in his eyes that he felt now in Ria's eyes, her body, her need; but nothing more had happened, all those years ago.

'I don't—'

He doesn't know everything, Ria thought victoriously. She felt it all. She moved her right leg to the right, as far inside her dress as it would go, opening the great emptiness inside her, and her left leg to the left as far as it would go, so that he slipped between her knees, and it was as she had planned, she felt his hard physical weight touch the centre of her emotions, together yet apart, making him hold himself up on his hands above her.

He said: 'Ria, I—'

She plunged her hands beneath his jacket. Her fingers found the buttons of his shirt, warm beneath, slipped down his hot body to the hard leather line of his belt. 'No, darling, hush,' she said. The tide was full. She saw the stars in his eyes. A green light slowly came up river, arriving. She felt the hot, hard muscles in his belly.

'Ria,' he said.

She looked up at him. He didn't know it, but she knew that he was too far gone to stop. She smiled. Now she had time for the difficult business, all with one hand, of pulling up her dress right up, getting her petticoat and slip out of the way, moving her knickers aside, all the while holding him with her other hand.

He said: 'Ria, please.'

She placed her heels behind his thighs and pulled. He slid into her. She jerked at him. He cried out with pain.

Got you, she thought. *I'm going to bind you to me with ties stronger than chains, stronger than a paper contract, stronger than marriage. I'm a woman, stronger than a man. I always have loved you and I will always love you. I'll always have you now. I'll bind you with a tie longer than my life. You're innocent, my love, but I'm desperate.* 'I love you, love you, love you!' she hissed as she raped him, but for a moment she felt a genuine sorrow in her heart.

The white wings of his collar framed his head above her. He was staring at the river. She looked. A red light was moving downstream, setting out on the sixty-mile journey to the open sea as the tide turned, ready to take advantage of the fall.

Chapter Nine

1

'I'll kill him!' screamed Vic.

The women cowered as he stormed up and down in the middle of the room. They looked like vultures in their black mourning clothes, Ria thought, staring at them from the corner. She sat on the stones with her knees out to one side and her head against the peeling plaster, where it was safer, holding her hand over the bruise spreading across her cheek. The hot summer sun struck in through the thinly curtained doorway.

Little Arthur was dead. They had found him inside this morning when they awoke, having slept in the street where it was cooler – this was the longest, hottest, most verminous summer anyone could remember.

While they slept, little Arthur had crept inside and sometime in the night he must have had one of his poorly fits and died, just died, and they hadn't woken. While they slept and dreamed, he had been dead, lying here, here, just here, in the corner where Ria now lay with the blood trickling down her chin.

He had not looked dead. He looked as if he was peacefully asleep. Ben, who got up earliest, must have come in and washed and used the bucket and obviously thought that Arthur *was* asleep, because he had gone off to work at Blumenthall's without saying anything. He was going to be upset. He had loved that little boy; had bought him honeycomb every Friday night when he came home from work.

Esther had come in next and Ria, waking up in the street,

yawning, had heard Mum saying, 'Wake up, Arthur lazy-bones, the sun's burning your eyeballs out, come and help me get breakfast—' And then her scream, her awful scream. Ria had jumped up and had stood in the doorway, clutching her stomach and feeling sick. A fly was crawling in Arthur's eye.

'He's dead!'

Vic had pushed inside. 'He can't be.' He flung himself down on his knees beside the body. Then he looked round at them with his great red face horribly distorted with grief. 'My brother's dead. He can't be. My brother's dead! Ria, he's dead!'

'I can see,' Ria said.

'Check his pulse,' said Nigel.

Vic brushed the blow-fly, already laying the eggs that would grow into maggots, gently out of Arthur's eye, then crushed the insect beneath his fist into the stones.

'Arthur?' Tom said. 'Arthur, wake up.'

'He's dead,' shouted Vic.

'I called him lazy-bones,' sobbed Mum. 'I said *Get up lazy-bones* and he was dead. I'll never forgive myself. God, forgive me. I'll never say it ever again, just bring him back, give him back to me, he's not dead.'

'Yes he is,' Nigel said. 'No pulse.'

Esther raised her fists towards the buckled ceiling. 'God, oh God, not Arthur!' Her voice rose to a shriek. 'Not Arthur . . .' She broke down into tears. That was when the women started to arrive, attracted by her screams or perhaps just sensing the tragedy and drawing in close, as they always did, like a big, warm family to comfort Esther in a grief that they all knew so well. Arabella Brown arrived first, then Mrs Gobel from across the way with Mrs Stark, whose son Alan was also weakly and had often played with the dead boy; and Mrs McCririck who had been comforted by Esther when Alastair had died last year, and Mrs Mabbs the widow she hardly knew, and Louisa Hiscott . . . to each of them Esther said: 'Thank you for coming.'

'I'll put a nice pot of tea on,' Mrs Mabbs said. 'Nothing like a nice cuppa at a time like this, I always say. Now don't go on so, dear, he'll be buried in white. You make the tea, Ria, you know where everything is, don't you? My, you are putting on weight nicely.'

Vic took his head out of his hands. 'Will you shut it, woman?' he demanded.

'I was only being friendly, at a time like this. I like my tea strong, darling. Extra spoonful, that's a pet. Whoops, I'm such a thoughtless one, aren't I, you'll want yours weak of course, Ria, what with the morning sickness.' She smiled maternally.

Vic stared at her.

He said: 'What are you talking about?'

'I don't suppose you would know,' sniffed Mrs Mabbs, 'but it's a pound to a penny that a woman gets morning sickness with her first baby.'

'What?' Vic said.

'It's women's talk, dear. You shouldn't listen.'

Vic stood.

'What baby?'

'It's true,' Ria said, staring at him defiantly. 'Don't you touch me, Vic.'

'You're going to have a baby?' he said slowly.

'Yes I am and there's nothing you can do about it.'

'Whose baby? *Whose baby?*'

'Her husband's, of course,' Mrs Mabbs said.

'Sit down, Harriet Mabbs,' Mrs Hiscott said. 'You've said enough.'

Esther said pathetically: 'But she isn't married.'

'I will be,' Ria sparked, 'and then I won't live here any more, I'll live far away on the other side of town away from you. I'm not frightened of you, Vic.'

'Have I put my foot in it?' asked Mrs Mabbs. 'I thought she was married to that lovely handsome boy who works at Blumenthall's. I always go there now, he gave me an extra slice of cheese last week, well it's nothing really but it makes a difference, doesn't it? Oh dear . . .'

Vic was speaking, his head down, as though he hadn't heard her, as though Ria was the only person in the room.

He repeated, very quietly: 'Was it against your will, Ria?'

Ria tossed her head. 'No,' she said.

He went on, in a very low voice: 'I will ask you one more time, Ria. Did the Workhouse Boy rape you?'

'No!'

He hit her. She cried out and slumped into the corner before he could hit her again, then sat with her head against the plaster. 'I just wanted to escape,' she told Esther.

'I'll kill him!' Vic screamed.

'Go on, that suits me just as well,' Ria yelled. 'We'll all tell on you and you'll go to prison and you'll rot, you'll rot away in prison forever, Vic!'

Nigel kicked her leg. 'You little bitch,' he said.

'Follow your master, Nigel. Go to prison,' she smiled. 'Look at all the witnesses here. We all heard the threats, and if anything happens—'

'He's going to wish he'd never been born,' Vic said simply. He screamed: '*He's going to wish he'd never been born!*' He tore the curtain off the doorway and flung it at her, then plunged outside. Nigel ran after him.

Everyone sat without moving in the shocked silence.

Then Esther said: 'Ria, what have you done?'

Ria's mouth opened. Tears poured down her face. She flung herself sobbing into Mum's arms.

'It isn't that I don't love him,' she wept. 'I do love him. But I hate Vic more.'

Still hugging her, Esther looked down into Ria's tear-stained face against her bosom. 'You've done it now, my love,' she said, 'so it's up to you to sort it out.'

'I can't,' sobbed Ria. 'You don't know Vic.'

'Vic's got into bad company, and Nigel too, I'll grant you that, but they're both good boys at heart—'

Ria said: 'But you don't *know*—'

'Look what they've done for us,' nodded Esther, as if she knew more than she said. She held Ria's head between her hands, staring into her eyes. 'You must warn Ben. You know what Vic's like when he gets in a state. You mustn't let him do anything that he would regret.'

'But Mum—'

'He wouldn't touch you, Ria.'

Ria said bitterly: 'He *would*.'

'Not my own dear boy.'

Ria said: 'He *has*.' She showed the bruise on her cheek. 'And other things,' she added in a low voice.

'I won't hear talk like that!' Esther said. 'You always were a dreamer. Always lying.' She pointed to the door. 'You started this – now you stop it!'

Ria ran.

Elijah Blumenthall liked making money but he disliked the huge till intensely. In the old days at the stall he just used to take the money in and out of his pocket and it felt so good. That way you were touching it all the time and you felt you were making real money. But the till was not so good. It was designed to keep you away from the money. It treated money contemptuously, as a classified thing, not a living thing. It kept itself locked until you pressed down on the keys, which took some little time, and unless you stepped back smartly the drawer banged you painfully in the stomach. The boy was perfect, he understood the machine. But today old George's wife had come round and said George the drayman was sick, which meant he was drunk, and so the boy had to be sent out to operate a machine that was even worse than the till: the dray. And that old horse cost a fortune. He would have to have it killed, beyond four years on the streets a horse was useless, and that old horse . . .

'Where is he?' Vic said.

'Vic, what a pleasure, my boy, I did not see you.' He called: 'Nigel, come in, come in.'

'He likes it by the door,' Vic said. 'Where is he?'

Vic was in a mood today. 'Ah, you mean the boy?'

'He's not a boy now, he's a man.' Then Vic screamed: '*Where is he?*'

'He's not here. I sent him to Bermondsey for custard powder, corned beef—'

Vic smashed the display of tins on the counter. They clattered across the floor.

'It's the truth, Vic,' Blumenthall said, frightened.

258

Nigel said: 'Shall I check at the back?'

'Don't bother. We'll catch him up.' Vic reached across and grabbed Blumenthall's lapels. 'Which way has he gone, you dry old stick?'

Blumenthall shook. 'Tower Bridge. Maybe by Cable Street, or Wapping High Street, but you find him by Tower Bridge.'

Vic let him go, clapped Nigel on the arm, and they ran out. Blumenthall went round the counter and started picking up tins with quivering fingers. There were some things it was better not to know.

Ria ran to West Ferry Road and stopped in the shadows, looking down towards Blumenthall's as Nigel and Vic came running out of the shop and swung aboard a passing 'bus. She heard the conductor ticking them off as the 'bus passed and knew that they would never have drawn attention to themselves like that if they'd done anything.

So they hadn't done anything.

Ben hadn't been there. She gave a tiny gasp of relief, pressing into an alleyway as the 'bus passed, then ran out. She had glimpsed the expression on Vic's face, the bunched set of his muscles, his curled fists. She shivered, sensing his terrifying fury like a weight passing over her.

The next 'bus appeared in the distance. She held up her hand, still shivering, although it was a hot day, and climbed aboard.

She followed.

There must be more to life than staring at a horse's backside all day long, thought Ben London, yawning, but he knew there wasn't. What he was doing now was all that most people did. All day, every day of their lives. Nowadays some of them stared through a windscreen at a radiator cap, like the driver of the van overtaking him, but the principle was the same. No escape; no way out of it. They probably wouldn't take it even if it was offered. He would. But he would probably do this for the rest of his life.

He didn't fight it today. The August sun was hot on his

259

head. Life was smooth and sensible, and everything had a reason.

The traffic along Wapping High Street had been light this morning, and he wondered why. The reason was not far to seek: as he entered St Katherine's Way he saw that they had known what he had not, that a big steamer was locking out of St Katherine's Dock, and the swing bridge was up. Everyone else had cut along Cable Street. The river on his left was grey-green and sparkling, the tide rushing out. The road twisted, and on the final turn before the swing bridge he saw Tower Bridge, the sun glinting darkly on the great medieval-looking bascules that dominated the seething landscape of quays and docks. Ria had ignored him since . . . Who knew the secrets in a woman's heart? She had not worn the dress either: but that meant she loved him more. He sat with his elbows on his knees while he waited for the swing bridge to come down. He suspected that her reason for ignoring him was to make him want her even more, and she had certainly succeeded. It was quite a game.

He saw two figures on Tower Bridge that looked familiar. They must have been on the 'bus that had pulled away a minute ago. He thought that they looked like Vic and Nigel – the shorter one, that would be Vic, standing braced with his legs apart and his hands thrust against his hips, and Nigel standing equally characteristically, close to Vic, with his spindly arms crossed, palely loitering. Ben waved, and they saw him, or recognized the dray. They came down and crossed the lock gates on the walkways, came towards him. 'Hallo Vic, Nigel. What are you two doing here?' Nigel went and stood by the horse's head, holding the bit, as if to stop the beast running away.

Ben said: 'Got any sugar for my horse?'

'No,' Vic said, 'but I've got this for you.' He showed a length of heavy wooden batten that he had been holding behind his back, and swung it. Ben got his elbow up; he felt the jar, then agony exploded in his arm. He held it with his other hand. 'Vic, what—' Vic swung the stick back, it bounced off the wooden seat-back then hit somewhere on

260

the side of Ben's head. The street disappeared in flashes of light, colour, and a sour taste in his mouth. Sprawled on the seat, he glimpsed the stick coming down again. He got his shoulder up and tensed the muscle, and then the muscle went numb and pain lanced into the other side of his body as the iron armrest jerked into him. He felt the top of the wheel against the side of his face as he slithered down across the footboard.

He thought he saw a girl running in the distance, her feet bare, her hair flying.

He thought she was Ria.

In a sickening flash, Ben understood. He groaned. She had betrayed him. For reasons of her own – guilt, fear – she had told Vic what had happened between them on the steps, so close by. Now she had come to witness her revenge. She did not love him; never had. Manipulated him, exploited him, and now betrayed him.

He thought she stopped, her arms around her, enclosing her. Then she was not there.

'Ria,' he whispered. 'Why did you betray me? I loved you.' That was the truth; he would never forgive her; never.

'Ria! For God's sake!' he cried out at the top of his voice. Now he had lost her too.

Vic grabbed his hair and pulled him down from the dray. 'Bastard,' he shouted into Ben's face. Ben felt his knees bang on the wheels then scrape across the stones. They were dragging him down an alley. Dimly he heard the clip-clop of the horse being led down after him, the rumble of the wheels. He thought: *They're going to run me over.* He reached forward and tried to grab one of Vic's ankles. Vic jerked his hair excruciatingly, then called back: 'Give me a hand.' Nigel grabbed Ben's arm and together they dragged him over the cobbles. Vic was crying, great sobs hiccuping in his chest as if he was drowning. 'He's dead, bastard,' he wept. 'Arthur's dead.'

'Oh Christ,' Ben said. He didn't understand. Some steps appeared beneath him. He tumbled down and sprawled on the platform beneath. It was the place, the very place he had been with Ria. The tide had fallen and there was a web of weed-covered platforms leading down. Vic and Nigel came down the steps. Ben dragged himself to the next flight and slipped down on his chest with a speed that increased horribly on the smooth weedy steps, but the green carpet cushioned his fall on the next platform.

He got to his knees, then slipped down. The weed squelched under him and he could hear water trickling. He tried to get up again but he couldn't. Vic and Nigel came down the steps. Nigel wrapped his long arms around him, behind him, and pulled him up to a kneeling position. A shiv glittered in Vic's fist. He held the blade against Ben's throat. His face worked.

'Remember,' Nigel said warningly.

'Remember?' Vic said. 'He's never going to forget what Vic Price did to him. Hold him! Hold him tight.' Then he smiled – and dropped the shiv. It disappeared into the weed.

Vic undid his belt.

Nigel's grip tightened.

Ben struggled for breath. His lungs strained, he felt his face flushing hot.

He thought he was going to pass out.

Vic had dropped his trousers and was crouching.

Ben writhed. He tried to bang his head against Nigel's chin but Nigel held him easily, laughing. He tried to dislodge Nigel's feet but he had no strength. Nigel was standing with his legs wide apart, and he couldn't find them. Vic was crouching, grunting, with his hands beneath him. Ben's heels drummed the weed. Vic stood, holding something in his cupped hands.

Ben closed his eyes. No. He gagged as Vic's palms pushed against his mouth, his nose, warm and stinking. He had to breathe, breathe or die. He gasped it into his mouth, choked. Vic held the heels of his hands against Ben's chin. Ben couldn't choke, couldn't breathe. His head spun.

Yet he understood clearly that he had to choose, life, or death. He writhed in an agony of revulsion.

'Eat it!' shouted Vic.

Ben's lips drew back from his teeth, and he gulped. He

couldn't vomit. He mashed the bitter mass against the roof of his mouth with his tongue, gagged, swallowed. Breathed. Swallowed. Breathed. Lived.

Nigel let him go.

Ben London sprawled on the weeds as though he had not a bone left in his body. His hands writhed at his mouth, trying to wipe the stink away.

The two brothers turned and looked back at him from the steps.

'I'm Vic Price,' Vic said. 'Remember me.'

Ria Price crouched in the mouth of an alleyway. Everything had gone, everything had changed. Except Vic. She heard her brother's voice still: *I'm Vic Price. Remember me.* He had not changed. She had nowhere to go; nowhere to run. *I'm in the same old cage, and no one's ever been here before, and no one's ever thought what I'm thinking now before, not ever, not in the whole world, and who cares anyway?*

Who cares?

She ran away, in case Vic saw her as he came pounding up the steps, so that she could be home before him, seeing nothing, knowing nothing. He had torn her beautiful cream dress from neck to hem months ago. She had hidden the shreds in a rubbish tip. She had tried to keep it a secret from Ben so as not to hurt him.

She wrapped her arms around herself. Everyone had secrets. The world was black with them. She dug her fists into her eyes.

She did not even have the courage of her love.

She did not even have the courage of her hate.

Ria ran away – ran away home.

I'm Vic Price. Remember me.

Part V

RAGE

Chapter Ten

1

Ben stared out over the stinking river. He knew the truth. *Ria betrayed me.*

He had lost Ria.

Lost everything – everything in the world that mattered to him, it seemed. The sun was falling in the sky, the water was rising. It sluiced shallowly across the flat weedy platform, it washed against his feet. He would not move.

What do you do, when you haven't got a single friend left in the world?

He did not care if the water covered his head.

Do you pity yourself? Or help yourself?

But the taste in his mouth was mortally foul. It stuck to his tongue, his teeth, it was in his throat, and it stank in his nostrils with every breath of air he took, an unbearable curse renewed with every beat of his heart. He couldn't wash it away, as long as he lived.

Do you want to die?

The water lapped around his knees. He clenched his fists above his head.

But you chose life.

The torment was unbearable. He felt his heart swelling as though it would burst up out of him or shake him to pieces so intense was his rage of grief, and loss, and hatred – for Ria, for Esther Price, Edith Rumney, Peter Pungle, and for his real mother, whoever she was, damned and ruthless, everyone who had betrayed him, or loved him, or died or left him to die.

The rising water tugged at his thighs.

What crime did I ever commit? he whispered aloud.

That I am a bastard? That my mother was probably a prostitute? Conceived from commerce, from hatred – is that my fault? Yes; all this is yours.

He could understand Vic protecting his sister's honour; it was outrageous, but it made sense. He could not understand why Ria had betrayed him.

The tide pulled at Ben's hips. The low sun glared in his eyes. They pricked and stung painfully, but he held back the tears that longed to flow. *I won't cry*, he raged. *I cried when Knuts died but I cried for love.*

Love does not exist, he wept.

The living weed swayed around his legs. The stinking water dragged at him: Father Thames.

I won't die!

I will never lose. Let them lose. I'll survive.

He felt his weight return as he pulled himself back up the steps. He looked down from the platform above.

I will win.

The evening sun struck in hot, flat lines amongst the platforms.

(I'm Vic Price. Remember me.)

As the light faded, the tide began to fall away.

Ben London waited, alone.

He waited while darkness fell.

Whatever I do, whatever I have to do, I will win.

Ben waited in the dark.

I will do whatever I have to do.

He held an iron capstan bar, a good weapon, in his hand. The church clocks had struck midnight, or perhaps that was hours ago. A drunk man, his breath reeking of lamp spirit, stumbled by him under the light. Ben drew back, and he was not seen.

Two sailors tottered along, their arms around each other's shoulders, arguing which of them had spent the last of their money. So he let them go too.

A woman, poorly dressed, hurried past looking fearfully

over her shoulder into the dark. Ben slipped behind the railings as two policemen came near, their torches flashing as they checked under tarpaulins and rattled the locked doors of dock offices.

This was no good.

He slipped under the Tower Bridge Road and loped down the broad lonely wharf on the far side. The stones of the Tower of London rose vast and dim on his right. 'Sam!' a distant voice was calling. 'Sam, dash it all! Where are you?'

Ben hefted the capstan bar, tightening his grip, then almost shouted aloud with startlement as something icy cold touched his hand.

It was the nose of a dog.

2

The lamps were going out all over London.

'Sam, dash it all, where are you?'

No one could appear more elegant than the Honourable Bertram Benton-Benson, no one more self-assured and in control of himself and his world than he. It was a lie.

He fought for what he hated – success in a world he cared nothing for, worshipping the cruel gods of his father. He knew his duty. Money, respectability, position – he had been born to them. They crushed him.

Tall and delicate, his finely chiselled features and long, slim hands gleamed in the darkness. Sometimes he dreamed of being free – as free as a bird.

Everyone was like him: wealthy, openly confident, secretly unhappy. Everyone dressed with casual assurance in conservatively tailored black evening suits and white Marcella waistcoats, which it was not done to unfasten, and ate gross dinners with Pater on demand, and smoked Hibiscus cigarettes with a languid air, and worked at the Bank – or the Bar – or did not work at all. They were the young gentlemen. Their lives were fixed. They did not admit they cared.

Bertie cared.

Like them, he was bored to death. He was highly educated, and he was angry: another duty dinner at the Guildhall for Pater. Icy gold platters and a frigid saddle of lamb, over-dressed horse-faced women and over-weight husbands with red faces, hard eyes, stupid conversation and tasteless laughter. And there was no escape.

And now his bloody dog had run off; no sign of the beast. He called again. Nothing from the darkness.

Bertie rebelled. He unfastened his tight Marcella and dragged the stiff collar off his shirt. If only his mother could have seen him now.

Bertie's Mater, a woman of great beauty and distinction, was one of the Prince of Wales's Set of the 1890s, whose intimate nickname she had taken for her son. She married Sir Ozwald Benton-Benson not for love but for money, quite happy to make the small sacrifice of religious conversion, and for her son to be taken from her and schooled in that one true religion. She captivated herself in the jewelled round of parties, galas, balls and events, and suffered no more children.

Sir Ozwald, now sexless, worshipped God and Mammon solely and brutally. He had a fine collection of German china and Italian paintings because he was wealthy: he cared nothing for them. He had his wife because of her beauty. He had his son for an heir. He had money because of its power. If he could have bought God, he would have. He worshipped Him remorselessly, browbeating God with prayers, deeply ashamed of Bertie's failure to marry: the aristocratic imperative. Sir Ozwald had even arranged a marriage – to the wonderful French girl everyone called Chouchou – but Bertie had got cold feet and backed out at the last minute. God forgave, but not Sir Ozwald.

Sir Ozwald, betrayed, despised his shy son, branding him a coward. 'Why?' he roared. 'Why did you do it to me? Don't you want her? Aren't you man enough, damn you?'

Bertie could not answer. Silent tears streamed down his cheeks. Sir Ozwald, seeing them, was ashamed of his son. He thought they were tears of weakness. They were tears of rage, hiding a truth that must remain hidden.

Truth and persecution, the Benton family knew those two old demons well: they had a long history of hiding the one and enduring the other.

Because they were Roman Catholics they had been fined and persecuted throughout medieval times. For his part in the Gunpowder Plot to blow up the Protestant House of Lords, Charles Benton was tortured to death in the Tower – this same Tower under whose massive walls his unhappy descendant now walked.

'You damned dog, where the hell are you?'

His dog was his best friend. Sam was extremely large, half Great Pyrenean, very rare now in this country, brought back by Tubby Bembridge in the dicky of his tourer from France, and half Gordon Setter. Sam was ginger, except for his ears, which curled with long black setterish strands. 'If you've gone swimming, my lad,' Bertie called, 'you won't be allowed on my bed, you'll be sleeping on the floor, do you hear?'

Sam always slept on his bed. Sam it was, no woman, who accompanied his master in the thundering Napier down to Brooklands race track, sat at his feet at the bar of the *Blue Anchor*, lay adoringly beside his hammock-chair in the sun on the Promenade des Anglais, stayed faithfully at his side staring into the firelight at home during the long, long, long evenings.

Further along the wharf, near Tower Bridge, a final street lamp shone.

Bertie began to walk towards it.

From Eton to Brasenose College, Oxford, and a First in Classics; the Newdigate prize for poetry won without effort. The futility of it. Born to lead, forced to, hating it. The present was dirty and the timeless world of The Lady of the Lake, the ancient romances, knights and dragons, or in a Mantegna nativity painting, was infinitely preferable. In real life there was no Holy Grail. There was no chivalry in commerce.

Bertie was without genius. He knew it – it confronted his slim face and his wide, dark eyes in the bathroom mirror every morning.

Nothing had the power to move him. Not even his beautiful collection of paintings; God was not there. Not in the face of his dreadful, private, unconfessed secret.

What is the darkest secret a man can have?

Bertie stopped at the lamp and stared into the darkness.

'Sam!' he cried. 'Where the bloody hell are you!'

Sam barked. Then the dog bounded under the light, staring at him, tail down. This was most unusual.

Now Bertie saw something else out in the shadows, perhaps just discarded rubbish, but it moved and it was not the wind moving it.

Bertie recoiled.

'Sam. Come here.' Perhaps some poor woman. A drunkard. Some diseased person. He felt sorry for them, but he didn't want to go near them. 'Sam—'

Sam ignored him. Tail wagging, he went over and stood by the person. Bertie followed him for a few steps and realized with incredulity that he and the boy – he could see it was a boy now – had already made friends. The boy stroked Sam's back, scratched Sam's ear. Sam loved that: his tail wagged as though it was going to come off. He nuzzled the boy's head where it was slumped on his chest.

Bertie thought: Well, if the boy likes my dog, and my dog likes the boy, he must be all right.

He said: 'Excuse me. I say, excuse me.'

The boy said nothing. He kept his head down, his face buried in the dog's coat, as if he was ashamed. Bertie almost turned away. It was bad manners to intrude. But he could see that the boy's nails, where he stroked the dog, were trimmed and well cared-for. How strange. And the left hand was clenched into a fist: the anger there. Bertie understood. The head bent in shame, Bertie understood that too.

Bertie said: 'Have you been in an accident?'

Terribly harshly: 'No accident!' Hardly the voice of a boy.

Bertie's sensitive mind explored the other possibilities that could account for the anger, the force, the terrifying fury. He had often railed with himself, questioning the

272

injustice of the world, but he had never felt this unreasonable power, had never seen that in the mirror.

The man raised his head and looked up at him. Bertie stared. It was a moment when everything is compelled to change: like falling in love, like falling from a tree, like a heart attack. The man was absolutely striking – not pretty – vivid eyes, blue, under the street lamp, strong features, open, and yet there was the sense of vulnerability, and rage. The grief, the strength, the love, the life. All revealed, all hidden. Something terrible had happened to him. Something unspeakable.

Help me!

Bertie decided instantly – not a moment of doubt. 'My poor chap, you must let me help you.'

'I don't need help.'

My God, thought Bertie hearing the accent, *he's one of us.*

'Of course you do!' He couldn't just leave him.

'I don't need anyone's help, thanks.'

Bertie hesitated. He held out his hand. 'I'm Bertram Benton-Benson.'

He dropped the aloof pose he affected to conceal his shyness, trusting the man. 'My friends call me Bertie.'

The man understood. 'Ben London,' he said. He gave the dog a last stroke. 'Go on, Sam, you'd better get back to your home in Bunhill Row.'

Bertie's throat caught. He thought: *How did he know my dog's name?* Of course, he'd been calling *Sam, Sam* loudly enough. Then he realized: *But how the devil did he know that Bunhill Row is where I live?*

He looked at Ben London wonderingly. Had they known one another before? Had they met? The blue eyes glanced at him innocently. The night was warm, but Ben's clothes were filthy and damp, so he was shaking with cold. Without shyness, Bertie came directly to the point: 'Look here, I don't mean to pry, but have you got anywhere to go to at the moment?'

Ben shivered. His voice darkened. 'Nowhere!' he said. 'London is my name . . . and my home. I'm happy.'

Bertie got down on his knees and took off his jacket. He

273

put it around the man's shoulders. In some invisible way, deep below the superficial injury, he sensed that Ben had been terribly hurt. He sought for words to reassure him.

'Trust me,' he said. 'Trust me.'

Ben amazed him: he needed no reassurance.

'What do you think I've done for the last five minutes?' For a shocking moment Ben London's eyes did not look innocent at all.

Survive.

Walking. The smooth feel of the rolled silk collar of Bertie's jacket against his neck. The cold, heavy flapping of his wet apron and trousers against his knees, the burning in his lips.

I'm Vic Price. Remember me.

Bertie hailed a cab. Ben climbed in the back, the first cab that he had ever been in, and settled onto the spacious leather seat as comfortably as though he was coming home. He struggled to relax the tendons standing out along the backs of his hands, not to show the tension betrayed by his white knuckles. One shilling for the first two miles, the same as horse-cabs. 'Bunhill Row,' Bertie ordered. The engine chugged and the cab pulled away along the deserted streets, Sam running behind. 'He gets his exercise that way,' Bertie explained. Ben nodded, watching, trying to miss nothing, to learn everything.

'Tell me what happened,' Bertie said.

Ben told him, instinctively leaving nothing out. When he finished, he found Bertie looking at him with respect, in fact with admiration. Amazingly, Bertie saw none of the humiliation that Ben felt. Ben realized that not everyone saw what he saw. People were different. They saw different things; and Bertie was very accustomed to his own very different sort of humiliation, he realized, as Bertie began to confess.

'God, you've led an interesting life! You've *done* things – you haven't stood around with your hands in your pockets. Me, I've done nothing. A bloody waste, but what else could I do? Eton, college, the friends I made, the business I'll go into, the girl I should marry, it was all mapped out for me.'

274

Ben thought that sounded wonderful. 'Wonderful, like living in a cage?' Bertie said. 'It would drive a person like you crazy. You're a foundling, you don't even know where you come from, you lucky devil.'

A cage, thought Ben longingly.

Bertie paid off the cab. Sam ran ahead of them into the building.

The flat was up several flights of stairs.

Ben thought: I've got a roof over my head for tonight, at least.

Perhaps he relaxed a little, because he felt instantly weak and had to hang back on the banisters. Bertie put his arm around his shoulder.

'Come on. Not much further, old chap,' he said kindly.

Ben said: 'Thanks.'

'Don't mention it.'

Survive.

I'm Vic Price. Remember me.

Ben felt his rage build up inside him until he thought he would burst. Pain screwed into his hand.

I'm Ben London. Remember me.

He looked at his left hand. Across the palm his fingernails had dug four fresh, perfect crescents, oozing blood.

Remember me.

He heard the sound of a key in a lock. They were on a top landing. Bertie twisted the handle and elbowed the door open. A room, dark and masculine, electric lights in brown shades, the walls hung with pictures, religious icons, trophies, a heavy table piled with books. Another door leading into a smaller room with a single bed, a mirror and a washbasin in the corner.

A real bed, good and hard.

'Sleep well,' Bertie said, closing the door.

It was warm in the room. Ben took off his filthy clothes and folded them neatly in the corner. He did not get into the bed. He filled the washbasin and washed himself. He washed his mouth over and over. Then he went to bed. His first real bed since . . . Edith. He turned over.

Morning light shone between the heavy drapes. Without yawning or rubbing his eyes, he got up and put on the dressing gown hanging behind the door. He went into the living room winding the cord around him. Sam, the enormous ginger dog, jumped up affectionately. Bertie was sitting at his sunny breakfast table by the window, also in a dressing gown, his hair tousled. He looked up, smiling, but before he could say anything there was a loud knock on the door.

'Come in, Mrs O'Keeffe.'

Ben observed the woman who wheeled in the trolley. He felt immediately that there were two sides to her. He saw that something had happened to her, not long ago – just now. She was in her sixties, a handsome, open-faced woman with happy lines radiating from the corners of her eyes and mouth. But now she looked like a person who had just received terrible news. He sensed that her cheerful flower-patterned housecoat suddenly didn't suit her mood. She should have been dressed in black.

Bertie said: 'Mrs O'Keeffe, Mr London will be staying for a few days.'

'Very good, sir.' She gave a distracted glance at Ben. She had lost none of her proud Irish accent, although he guessed that she could not have seen the Emerald Isle for a good many years. She wore a wedding ring, but on another finger he noticed a black circlet, so tightly rolled and treated that it looked like lacquer. A lock of her husband's hair, in the custom. She was a widow. Black hair, too; he had died young. He realized that she was now staring at him in the way women did. Perhaps he had been rude. No, there was no offence taken in her eyes, which were a beautiful Irish blue, flecked with charcoal. Eyes never changed, never lied; he realized that forty years ago she would have been her husband's very, very pretty young mavourneen. He smiled, and she actually smiled too, as though for the moment she had forgotten her anxiousness.

Bertie pushed the rolled newspaper aside and lifted the silver lid of the server. 'Kippers, good! Kidney, sausages, scrambled egg. And kedgeree, my favourite! My dear Mrs

O'Keeffe, you have excelled yourself.'

'Sir,' she said, dragging her eyes away.

Bertie waved his knife at Ben. 'Tuck in, don't be afraid to be a trencherman, there's nothing Mrs O'Keeffe likes better than someone who appreciates her home cooking.'

'Sir.'

Ben asked: 'What is it, Mrs O'Keeffe?'

She looked at him gratefully. Bertie unflapped his copy of *The Times*.

'Court announcements?' he said. He scanned the advertisements. 'I don't see anything.'

'I think you'll be finding it on the second page, sir.'

Bertie looked at her, then opened the paper, and everything changed.

'Oh, my God,' he said. 'It's war.'

Chapter Eleven

1

'Thank God,' Bertie said. 'It's war!'

'Thank God?' wondered Mrs O'Keeffe. Ben sensed her horror.

He asked: 'Who are we fighting?'

'Germany, of course!' laughed Bertie.

'Would they be the ones with spikes on their helmets?' asked Mrs O'Keeffe. Ben watched her clutching instinctively with her fist at something hung around her neck: a little gold crucifix.

'Yes,' Bertie said impatiently, 'and the French wear flat hats like little drums, coloured pale blue.'

'And the English boys will be wearing those lovely red uniforms with the brass buttons and the white helmets?' *She can't bear the thought of him going,* Ben realized. *She loves him like a mother, and she speaks so lightly because she knows already that she's lost him.*

'That's out of date. This will be a modern war. The uniforms are a sort of green now.'

'That's a disappointment to me, sure,' Mrs O'Keeffe said. 'Poor Sean was in the Army. Beautiful he looked in red with the brass buttons. My heart used to come into my throat to see them marching off, so glorious they looked, and the bugles, and everything shining in the sun.' She shook her head. 'He died in the Black Week, in the hospital at Cape Town, and the priest gave him the last rites, they said, and he's buried in the little Catholic church there.'

Ben asked: 'Why are we fighting the Germans?'

'To win!' Nothing could dampen Bertie's enthusiasm, or even slow it. He stabbed a paragraph with his fingertip. 'Because the fiends have invaded Belgium! Poor little Belgium. We're bound to them by treaty.'

Ben said: 'Where's Belgium?' Mrs O'Keeffe looked at him gratefully, sensing an ally in her hatred for the war; but Ben looked away.

Bertie pointed at a bookcase. 'Mrs O'Keeffe – would you be so kind – the Atlas. Ah, here it is. It's the country coloured yellow.' Spreading his fingers southward through the cities, he explained: 'The Germans have to go through Belgium to get to Paris, but the French Maginot line will stop them. If those fortresses are overcome, then look at all these rivers they'd have to get across in northern France – we'll stop them there. Then it'll be easy to throw them back. The war will be over by Christmas. We'll miss it if we aren't quick.' Zeal had transformed his sensitive features. 'They've been building up to this for years. We may be in for a few sharp battles,' he said seriously, then grinned: at last he had a proper enemy to fight. He had found a reason for living. Ben looked at him thoughtfully.

'Well, I don't like the sound of it,' Mrs O'Keeffe said. 'I think you should have a long talk with your Mater and Pater first.'

'Where's your patriotism?' said Bertie tersely. 'I'm sorry, Mrs O'Keeffe, but it's the duty of all us young men to go.'

'And it's a woman's duty to let you go.' Mrs O'Keeffe searched for a handkerchief, found one in her sleeve, and held it crumpled against her mouth. Ben saw how deep her affection for Bertie was, and how profoundly upset the thought of his going – worse, his desperate enthusiasm – was beginning to make her. She felt that he had discarded her.

'It's your duty to *encourage* us to go!' Bertie added in a lower voice: 'It's our chance to achieve something worthwhile in this worthless life.'

Worthless. Yet the riches that were stored in this room: Ben looked around him. The paintings caught his eye: ugly women and adult children, anguished faces transfixed by arrows, religious scenes painted on wooden tablets darkened and crazed by age. He sensed that they must be of value, but they decorated Bertie's life, they did not fill it. Ben studied him. A man stamps on his foot to take his mind off the pain in his head. Bertie had no lust for money or power. He remembered that extraordinary expression of admiration in Bertie's eyes last night. *You've done things! It's all been mapped out for me. It's like living in a cage.* This was Bertie's prison, Ben realized. The war was his escape.

And for me?

Ben shivered, and wondered how many other young men like Bertie there were, fenced in by Victorian parents and thickets of social convention, and the rigid rules of 'done' behaviour. If there were very many, the war would not be over by Christmas – they would never want it to end.

Ben smiled to himself. He understood that. Unending war.

'You poor darling, you're shivering with hunger!' cried Mrs O'Keeffe, mistaking the reason for Ben's tremor and taking the excuse to fling herself into her work. 'Enough of this talk, Master Bertram, and help him fill his plate. Here, I'll do it. You can eat two sausages, and here's the scrambled eggs . . .' Ben ate as though he was starving, making Mrs O'Keeffe know he needed her, making her want to feed him. The dark shadow of the Workhouse had taught him much; and he had learned much more since then. He had to grip them tight, or else they might chuck him out any moment, and he didn't know when he might get another meal then.

Bertie watched Ben eating. 'Things have changed more than a bit since your aunt's day,' he remarked. 'I can see I shall have to take you in hand. It's not been fashionable to hold your knife that way for ten years.'

Mrs O'Keeffe smiled. Watching Ben eat made her feel happy. Master Bertram ate like a sparrow. She poured the milk into the bone china cups, then with her red, lined hands and dainty fingers filled them up with tea from an elegant pot.

Ben observed how the teapot was the sort of pretty thing that a woman would choose, never a man. He knew that she would have agonized for days over whether to have the floral design or perhaps a country scene – she had chosen the flowers. He looked up and saw her smiling at him. They understood one another about the teapot. Bertie left his tea and strode up and down the room.

'It's time some country stood up to the Kaiser!' he was saying furiously. 'Do you know what those swelled-head Krauts call us? Swindlers! They've been sniping at us for years while we've bent over backwards to preserve peace. Well now they've gone too far.' He opened a cabinet, took out a Westley-Richards single-shot stalking rifle. 'It'll be skirmishes first, a test of skill. Full gallop, flying colours.' He looked at Ben. 'I'm a pretty fair horseman. How about you?'

Bertie had no idea how most of his countrymen lived. Ben had never been on a horse's back. 'Pretty fair,' he said.

'Were you in the Officers' Training Corps?'

Had he never seen a Workhouse? Did he think it provided the same leadership training as a fine public school? Ben almost said so, then pulled back from such a horrible mistake. It would be fatal to emphasize the social gulf between them. 'Actually, I missed out on that, Bertie.'

'Well, never mind. Are you with me?'

He meant, *Will you go to war with me?*

Ben knew he had no choice. The only way he could lose was by being killed. 'Why not?' he said. 'Yes, I'll join up with you.'

'Good chap!' Bertie said eagerly, shaking his hand. 'With any luck we'll fight the new war – the war in the air. Aeroplanes. That's where the real sport will be.' His eyes glittered eagerly. 'Knights of the air. Battles like jousts, just you and your enemy, skill matched against skill. There's honour and bravery up there in the clean air, Ben.'

Ben stared at him. 'Yes!'

Bertie looked at Mrs O'Keeffe with sparkling, victorious eyes. 'Aren't you going to wish us luck?'

'You're both fools,' she wept.

281

'Come on, Nursy, don't be sour grapes,' Bertie laughed, glossing over her grief. He didn't understand women, Ben knew; not anything, even when it was so blindingly obvious.

'I've looked after you since you were that high.' She held out her hand, low, shaking her head and holding the handkerchief to her eyes. 'I know you more than your own mother does. And now—'

Bertie looked embarrassed and Ben thought that he would hold her in his arms and comfort her, but he didn't. In the East End people hugged one another when they cried. They touched one another's faces. Bertie put out one hand in a gesture towards her elbow, but Ben noted that he couldn't actually bring himself to physically touch her. It wasn't the done thing apparently. Bertie studied the bolt on his rifle.

'It's war,' he explained.

Ben got up and put his arms around her shoulders for a moment.

'I'm sorry,' she said gratefully, dabbing her eyes.

'That's all right.' She sat in his chair.

Ben walked around the room. It was larger than rooms he was used to, and that the walls were not bare unsettled him. Even the corners were padded with little Christs in gold frames, their eyes upraised. They must be worth money, but there were so many of them, and so repetitive, then he saw that each one was slightly different. Like real people. He began to see into them. Slowly he began to sense that the paintings were very complex, very real. Here was a very dirty painting of St George killing the Dragon. St George looked rather girlish, yet he felt emotion in it. And the more he opened to the emotion, the greater his sensitivity became.

Who was Bertie's Dragon? Was it really the Germans?

There was a painting by a man called Lorenzetti. He stared at it, and it was absolutely real, and it was six hundred years old.

Here was another one, signed. He peered: Mantegna, Madonna and Child. But it could not be worth anything; it was almost black with dirt. Behind the two figures was a dim landscape of trees shaped like wineglasses, sudden cliffs, jagged outcrops of rock. It took his breath away. The girl was beautiful and young, the child she held seemed older than she, with eyes that looked directly out of the age-stained surface.

Bertie clicked the bolt on his rifle. 'Do you like it?'

'It's very old,' Ben said. 'Is it an original?'

'Does that matter?'

'Yes.'

Bertie avoided a direct answer. 'It's my favourite.' Of course it was original. Ben carefully made another mental note: anything that a gentleman possessed was exactly what it was supposed to be, so there was no need even to refer to it. To do so was to label yourself a common person as clearly as though you had hung it around your neck. Hearing a new sound in the street below, like the distant roar of the crowd at a football match, he went to the window and looked down.

Bertie said: 'The City Territorial Regiment has its headquarters in those buildings on the other side of the road. I thought we might pop over later and put our names down. You've got to join the Army to get into the Royal Flying Corps.'

Ben watched. The recruiting office was beseiged by men eager to serve their country. They were queued along the pavement, overflowing into the road, blocking the traffic, filling Bunhill Row from wall to wall. It looked very exciting. He picked out the bowler hats of city gents, undergraduates in straw boaters, and huge masses of cloth caps. Some nobs had their umbrellas up to ward off the hot sun. Other lads were singing. One young man in a bow tie was studying his fob-watch. Some of the boys looked hardly old enough to shave. An older man was wiping the dust off his shoes on the backs of his knees and spitting on his hand to slick down his hair, possibly to make it look less grey and himself younger, desperate to join up. Several much older men waited with very straight-backed military bearing, veterans of the Boer War probably.

Ben turned.

'The Boers were farmers, weren't they?'

'I believe so.' Yet those farmers had tied up the British Army for three years.

'And Germany has the most professional military machine in the world?'

'Planned down to the last minute on the railway, time-table and the final button on the last service tunic, so they say!'

Ben stared down at the crowd milling below. There was some jostling going on, then he heard good-natured laughter. They had started singing:

'*Why are we waiting, why-y are we waiting, why are we wai-ai-ting, why are we waiting . . .*'

Ben thought: *Madness*. Then he thought, *These are the men who will win the war*. Anything but winning was unthinkable.

'Do you know who always loses wars?' asked Mrs O'Keeffe quietly, at his elbow. 'Women.'

2

WOMEN, DO YOUR DUTY! SEND YOUR MEN TODAY TO JOIN OUR GLORIOUS ARMY.

Every twenty-four hours, they said, more men joined the Army than during the whole of last year. Still, compared to the size of the vast French and German armies, the British Expeditionary Force remained tiny – during the glorious retreat from Mons it was only eighty thousand men. Armed with rifles against machine-guns, and horses against trains, they stood no chance.

Back home, everyone read the stories in the newspapers from survivors who wore the Mons battle honours, who had seen heavenly angels fighting in the sky on their behalf. They could not lose. All they needed was more men.

They were going to win the war by Christmas.

WOMEN SAY: GO!

Lord Kitchener, whose glaring eyes, heavy moustache, and famous outstretched finger filled every giant advertisement staring across Piccadilly, said that the war would not be over in three weeks. The people cheered him.

He said that the war would not be over by Christmas. The people cheered him.

He said that the War might not be won in three years. The people cheered him.

He said that the only way the war *could* be won was with men, with very many men, with yet more men. It was the duty of every home to give up its man. The men cheered him.

It was the duty of every mother to tell her son that though she didn't want to lose him, she thought he ought to go. The mothers cheered him.

It was the duty of every wife not to selfishly hang on to her husband. The wives cheered him.

Lord Kitchener and the Prime Minister demanded one hundred thousand volunteers.

They stepped forward. Lord Kitchener and the Prime Minister demanded five hundred thousand volunteers.

They stepped forward. Lord Kitchener and the Prime Minister demanded a further half million volunteers. They stepped forward. The factories slowed down, so women volunteered to take the empty places at the workbench. The men who remained struck, fearing that because of the eager women they would be next to lose their jobs and be thrown into the bloodbath. They were right: Lord Kitchener and the Prime Minister planned a New Army of five million men. The Germans had stormed across Belgium, outflanked the mighty fortresses, lost their momentum in the face of a tenacious retreat, and got bogged down amongst the flatlands, swamps and rivers of northern France. Now the scene was set. It was to be a battle of dinosaurs. The size of the brain did not matter. The one with the biggest body would win.

But the generals who knew that it would be so brutally simple, didn't say.

And the soldiers who would have said, didn't know.

They were the ones who were dying.

And the wives were the ones who waited.

*

'How old are you?' asked the boy next to Ben. His name was Mayberry and he had a perky expression and grimy cheeks. He knew a lot about the Army. 'Just say you're eighteen. If you haven't got flat feet, that's all they care about. Freddie Briggs, the blacksmith's boy from down our street, got in, and he was only fifteen. I've heard some who got in were only thirteen years old. Fighting spirit, that's all they want.'

The men were cut off from the crowd and admitted to the Recruiting Office in batches of six or seven, then ushered into a large, square room smelling of Lysol disinfectant and equipped with a weighing machine, a scale for measuring height, a washbowl for the medical officer's hands and a dirty towel. There were two tables, one for the medical officer and the other for the clerk who sat busily filling up attestation forms.

The clerk called Ben over.

'Name?'

'Ben London.'

'Call me "sir". Address?'

Ben hesitated. He had no address. He glanced at Bertie, caught his eye. 'Give mine,' Bertie whispered.

'By Lamb's Buildings, Bunhill Row, sir.'

'Age?'

'Eighteen, sir.'

'Were you in the Officers' Training Corps at school?'

'No, sir.'

'Occupation?'

Grocer's boy didn't sound classy enough. 'Shopkeeper, sir.'

'Got any identifying marks or scars?'

'Birthmark under right ear, sir.'

'Who are your next of kin?'

He remembered Esther saying: *Be a part of our family.*

He frowned.

I'm Vic Price. Remember me.

Ben leaned forward across the desk. 'Why do you want to know?' he demanded.

The clerk looked up, startled. 'Steady on. Regulations, that's all.'

'I have nobody,' Ben said harshly.

The recruiting sergeant yawned: 'I wish I had a penny for every orphan we've had through here today, I'd be a rich man. I never knew we had so many in the whole blooming city. It's disgusting.'

'Bertram Benton-Benson,' Bertie said calmly, folding his hand over Ben's fist. 'Put that down as next of kin, would you, sergeant?'

'Cousins, would that be, sir?'

'That's right, sergeant.' The sergeant nodded to the clerk. Ben stared into Bertie's unconcerned-looking, relaxed-looking, aristocratic-looking face. That indefinable something; he had learned to look as though he was born to lead. For Bertie it was a lie; I *am*, Ben thought, *I must learn to show the truth*. While the others spoke he forced his fist to uncoil, to relax. He had learned long ago that wars were not won by fists.

'You were in the Officers' Training Corps at school, sir?'

'Naturally,' shrugged Bertie. 'I understand that the Royal Flying Corps has openings for pilots and observers. Put our names down, would you?'

'I'll do it, sir,' agreed the sergeant, 'but you haven't got a hope in Hades of getting in.'

'We'll see,' Bertie said. 'Both of us together, of course – my cousin and I.' Ben nodded encouragingly. He knew the way things were done.

Across the marbled foyer of the War Office stretched a long counter where the clerks dispensed orders and warrants. Bertie beckoned a commissionaire.

Ben watched, missing nothing.

The commissionaire listened politely while Bertie explained the position. The old soldier didn't think there was much chance but Bertie's manner, accent and easy self-assurance obviously convinced him that they were men it was unwise to refuse; he directed them to a busy staff-captain on the third floor. Pushing through the crowds waiting for an appointment they read the sign on the door: T.B. Bembridge, Captain GS03 Postings.

'Tubby Bembridge!' cried Bertie, breezing in. 'How are you now? Brought any more ginger dogs back from France?'

'How is that rogue Sam?' Tubby Bembridge asked, limping round his desk. His keen eyes flickered to Ben, who filled the doorway.

Ben knew that Bertie lived for his dog. As always, Bertie skirted what was closest to him, ready to laugh it off, or shrug carelessly. Ben said: 'The dog's fine. Same old Sam.' He held out his hand.

Bertie introduced them. 'Let's all take in a spot of lunch at the Piccadilly Grill. Look, Tubby, there's a small favour you can do us . . .'

After lunch Tubby told them about Room 613A. 'I'm afraid that's the best I can do. It's up to you now.'

They passed the afternoon in a long queue of applicants, many of them schoolboys. The Royal Flying Corps interviewing staff-captain was Lord Hugh Cecil. They shook hands.

'Hugh! How nice to see you.'

'Bertie, I'm dashed. How are you? You look on top of the world.' Ben noticed how Lord Cecil's world-weariness vanished. 'So, Bertie, you really want to fly an aeroplane.'

'Yes, absolutely.'

'You can ride a horse, can't you?'

'Born on one, old boy.'

'I remember you played rugger. School team?'

'House Colours. Wing.'

Lord Hugh glanced at their collar tabs. 'City of London Regiment?'

'We finish basic training by Christmas,' Bertie said nonchalantly.

'Excellent. I'll put you down for the course at Brooklands.'

Bertie introduced his cousin.

'Looks like he's got keen eyes,' Lord Cecil said. 'He's a bit long in the leg to be a pilot. I'll see what I can do. I'll put him down as an observer. School of Aeronautics at Reading.'

Ben blurted: 'Where's Reading?'

The two men stared at him, confused, then laughed heartily at Ben's joke: pretending he'd never even been out of London before! Not even as far as Reading!

I won't make that mistake again, thought Ben.

'By the way, Bertie,' Lord Cecil said, 'you really ought to be an officer.'

'I've always dreamed of being an Object of Respect,' murmured Bertie thoughtfully. 'We'll just have to hope the show isn't over by Christmas.'

3

'Ow,' cried Ria.

'Louder,' Mrs Hiscott said. 'Louder, dear.'

'Oh, oh,' Ria panted. '*Oww!*'

'That's better, dearie,' said Mrs Hiscott encouragingly, her lined face puckering into a smile. 'Let it out. Don't mind us.'

Ria tried to raise herself onto her elbows. She stared at the doorway framed between her knees, the safely closed door, the curtain hanging over it. She couldn't see the latch.

'Is the latch down?' she gasped. The bright, tawdry Christmas decorations brought by Vic flashed in the draught from the latch-hole.

'Never mind that, dearie, you concentrate on the job in hand,' smiled Mrs Hiscott.

'Mum,' wailed Ria.

Esther was standing behind her. She wiped the sweat from Ria's forehead. 'I'm here, darling.' Her breath was perfumed with gin.

'*Push,*' said Louisa Hiscott.

'I am pushing. How much longer?'

'Just a little longer.'

'I'm tired, I'm pushing and nothing's happening.'

'It's happening just as it should.' Mrs Hiscott told

Esther: 'Her hips are narrow. She's a very fashionable shape, you know. Thin hips, thin bust. Very much the coming shape.'

'We all know you're a seamstress,' hissed Ria. 'Is that door closed?'

'Lie back.'

'Check the latch.'

'No one is coming in,' smiled Mrs Hiscott.

'He's there,' Ria said. 'Mum, he's there, isn't he?'

'I won't let Vic in,' promised Esther.

Ria dropped back.

'The baby is lying perfectly normally,' whispered Mrs Hiscott to Esther. 'It's just that things take longer with the first one, and what with her being young and everything. And those narrow hips. I remember with my first, George, I thought it would never end. I could do with a sip, if you don't mind.'

'Here, I'll find another cup.'

'*Ow*,' Ria wept. 'Give me some. Give me some.'

'Don't swallow it, just rinse your mouth.'

'It helps. It helps the pain, Mum.'

'Now you're learning something, darling,' Esther said, gently wiping her forehead. 'Here – here we go again. *Push.*'

'I can hear Vic,' said Ria deliriously.

'Never mind Vic. One and a two and a *push . . .*'

'Mum, I can hear him walking up and down. I know he is. *Ow.* He's in there walking up and down, waiting. He's waiting, Mum.'

'They're all waiting, dear, and Nigel, and Dad didn't go in to work this morning because he was worried about you.'

'Tell him not to let Vic in.'

'Never mind that, darling. Push. And push. There. We're getting somewhere. Hold my hand. Now rest. Now a one and a two and a—'

Ria struggled up. 'Are you sure that the latch is down? The curtain moved. Mum. Help me. I can't stand it.'

'No girl ever believes how painful it is,' smiled Mrs Hiscott. 'Until it happens.'

'I believe,' gasped Ria.

'Men never do understand,' said Mrs Hiscott, her fingers working busily, invisibly. 'Men don't know what pain is.'

'He knows,' cried Ria. 'He's waiting. Mum, he's waiting for my baby.'

Mrs Hiscott looked up. 'Not long now.'

'It's coming,' panted Ria. 'Don't let him in.'

'No, darling, I won't let him in,' said Esther tolerantly. Every woman was beset by fears and phantoms before childbirth.

'Don't let him take my baby.'

'No, dear.'

'Promise me!' said Ria fiercely. Suddenly her thin fingers gripped Esther's arm so tightly that Esther's smile faded and the bright red spots left her cheeks. '*Ow*,' wept Ria, and her grip tightened desperately. Then: 'Promise me!'

The expression in Ria's eyes was awful, haunted. Esther asked hesitantly: 'Are you serious?'

'I've never been more serious in my life!' yelled Ria.

'But why would Vic—'

'Because my baby isn't *his*, Mum! To him – it's a monster! It isn't part of him, part of our family!'

Esther tottered.

Ria's smooth, withdrawn features changed. They contorted into lines of pain and commitment. 'My baby's mine, Mum. Even if it's the only thing in the world that I have that *is* mine. Mine!'

Esther's lips moved. She took a couple of mouthfuls from the bottle to help her get it sorted out in her mind. Yes, the baby was Ria's. She added fairly: 'And Ben's.' What was this about Vic? She didn't want to know. She had heard only the sketchiest details of the incident on the platforms below St Katherine's Dock from Ria, and nothing at all of the vile thing that Vic had done, and she still thought of Ben as someone who might one day return to them to see his child. She clung to the dream.

Ria confessed: 'Ben doesn't know anything about his baby!'

'Oh, Ria!'

Ria begged: 'I couldn't, I didn't tell him. Please, please

understand. I know it was so wrong, Mum. I was waiting until he would have no choice but to marry me. I didn't know Vic would find out first and . . . *Ow, ow*, oh Mum, I've been so wicked. Mum, I deserve everything that happens to me. But my baby's never done anything, Mum. Don't let Vic get my baby too —' She screamed.

'It's coming,' Mrs Hiscott said.

'Let me see,' gasped Ria. 'Get a mirror. I want to see!' Esther looked round the room, then took the mirror off the wall and held it up at what she thought was about the right angle. 'Down a bit,' groaned Ria. Then: 'I can see. I can see my baby! Oh, it's beautiful.' Her body tensed again. She laughed and cried. 'Oh, look, Ben, look how wonderful. Look. Your child. My child, my baby, look . . .'

'One more time,' said Mrs Hiscott. 'There.' She held up something as purple and shiny as a skinned rabbit. 'It's a boy.'

Ria fell back. 'A boy,' she whispered. 'Your son.'

Mrs Hiscott inverted the little fellow, holding him by the ankles, and gave him a sharp smack across the bottom. He began to cry.

'Isn't he noisy?' Ria said. 'And he's really ugly too.'

'All men are ugly,' Mrs Hiscott said.

'He's not ugly,' Esther said, putting her head proudly on one side. 'He reminds me a bit of your Uncle William, Ria, the one who wanted to be a painter. He ended up as a wharfinger.'

Ria cuddled her baby. She looked down at his funny little face. 'I shall call you Will,' she whispered. 'My Will. Ben's Will.' She felt that she ought to introduce herself. 'I'm your Mum,' she added. 'We'll get to know one another really well, won't we.' She jiggled him. He didn't respond. She tried to get him to clutch her finger.

'Newborn babes don't do that,' Mrs Hiscott said. 'It takes them a few days to learn it. He's normal enough.'

Ria looked around her, sad and helpless. 'When can I get up?'

'You need to rest for quite a while,' Esther said. 'Come on, smile.'

'I'm a mother too, now,' Ria said. 'You can't order me around any more.'

'I know a little more about babies than you do, my girl. Don't be sad.'

'Give us a bit of that gin. I'm so unhappy, I want to feel happy, beautifully happy.'

Esther gave a twitch of the eyebrows to Mrs Hiscott. She poured some into the cup. Ria sipped and made a face.

'Are those men still outside?'

Esther glanced at the door. 'I believe so.'

'Tell them to go away.'

'Oh, but they've been worried about you! They'll want to see the baby. It's not so much to ask. Go on, Ria, it's traditional.'

'It's my baby. We're breaking with tradition, everything's going to be new and modern from now on.'

'What did you say you're going to name the boy?' asked Mrs Hiscott, washing her hands in the bucket.

'My son's name is Will.'

'That's a nice name. That's what I call a nice manly name, don't you, Esther? It has such a *determined* sort of a ring to it.'

'Come off it,' Ria said.

'He's got such a pretty little face,' fluttered Esther.

'He's really ugly.' Part of Ria almost hated him. She felt utterly trapped by her new responsibility.

'I'll just let the men peep in from the door,' Esther said.

'I don't want them to see me. It's embarrassing.'

'But he's lovely, dear, really.'

'I don't want them to see me holding him. If you're so keen on him, you hold him. Go on. Here you are.'

Esther loved babies. The difficulty was affording them. It was much too easy to have far too many of them.

'You're not to let Vic near him, either,' said Ria defiantly. But she held out the child. Esther took him and settled him into the crook of her arm. 'Promise.'

'Yes, darling, I promise. But it's all a bit odd. I don't know what Vic will think. It is rather hurtful to his feelings, in my opinion.'

'If you let him breathe over him or touch him, or get up to anything funny, I'll scream, and I'll never let you hold him again. Is that clear?'

'Yes, dear.'

'*Is that clear?* Will is mine.'

'Yes, dear, you can have it whichever way you want it.'

Esther stood in the middle of the room, holding her grandchild as proudly as if he was her own, and Mrs Hiscott went to open the door.

Vic took his eye from the latch-hole. 'Still can't see anything.' He glanced around. Nigel was reading some old book still, Adam Smith, about a foot thick. All right, as long as it kept him happy. 'Take your thumb out of your mouth,' Vic said.

'Sorry, Vic.'

Tom was walking up and down. He'd taken the day off work. That was a nice touch, showed he cared about Ria. Did he really mean it? It'd be interesting to see if the old bastard worked on the Sunday to make it up.

Because of the war there was as much work on the docks as anyone could take now, and always ships waiting. Colossal quantities of stuff were crossing the Channel. The price of bread had doubled since August.

The war: what a golden opportunity, like a sort of revolution, best news ever for ordinary people. Bad for some, so sorry for them, honest men and women thrown out of work. Posh women felt it wasn't patriotic to buy new outfits, so in dressmaking and millinery unemployment was over half. That was why that interfering busybody Hiscott had time to come sticking her nose in here where it wasn't wanted. Poor Ria hadn't let him save her. He could have. He'd told her how. But she'd put her hands over her ears, shaking her head. He'd even offered to pay. She'd screamed no. All right, girl. You made your own bed, now lie on it. So be it. Scream with pain.

The war was the best news he'd ever had. He'd been frightened at first. He might get press-ganged, dragooned into fighting, but it didn't work like that. Incredibly, you didn't even have to join. It was even an excuse for a few booze-ups when your mates joined up, then you just waved them goodbye in the morning, thanked God for less competition, let the girls they left behind cry on your shoulder, and got on with earning the lovely grub.

The war caused shortages. Shortages caused black markets. Black markets lined pockets that had been empty before. This was a lovely war. Those who had contacts were minting it. Old Blumenthall was probably coining a hundred quid a week, nett profit, cash in hand. Or rather, in his case, cash under the bed.

'If you couldn't see anything through that latch-hole,' said Tom slowly, 'then why were you looking through it for so long?'

Vic felt anger like a hot burn. Who did the dumb duffer think he was talking to? Did he think Vic Price was still a kid in shorts?

'I asked you a—'

The door opened. 'Come in,' said Mrs Hiscott. Vic brushed by her, giving her eyes a stare for a moment. The whites were full of little broken veins and the pores of her nose were clustered with blackheads. He felt how she hated him, though it was in a very mild, spread-out sort of way, and he sensed that there was nothing personal in it. She hated all men. She was very hungry, and perhaps there was something he could use there. Her little husband, George, worked in the Millwall Docks office, and he was on the take. And always working late: obviously he had another woman. Somewhere inside her there was a little pool of corruption: she felt that life owed her more than it had given her. He sensed that hidden pool of jealousy and envy inside her. Evil existed in the world, Vic knew, and the only people who did not believe that did not have the eyes to see it, or the heart to sense it, or the emotion in their souls to feel it, touch it, know it. They were fools. He smiled.

Mrs Hiscott dropped her eyes. She was not a fool.

There was Ria. God, she was beautiful. He stood over her, and she was pretending to ignore him, her eyes closed, the back of her hand gracefully laid across her forehead, her lovely face framed in the pillow, a delicious little game that they played.

'Hallo, Ria,' he said hoarsely.

Her eyelashes fluttered open. 'Oh, it's you,' she said sleepily. 'Go away, Vic.'

'Are you all right, darling? Feeling better?'

She put her head on one side. Wonderful.

'Better out than in, eh?' Vic said. 'You're happy now.'

'Yes,' she said sleepily.

He turned to Esther, holding the baby wrapped in something white.

'I'll take him,' he said.

Esther said nervously. 'She doesn't want you to.'

'What does she think I'm going to do – throw it in the river?' laughed Vic, caressing the baby's cheek with his big blunt fingertip.

'Don't touch him!' shouted Ria. 'Mum, you promised you wouldn't let him.'

'Ria, for goodness' sake,' said Esther impatiently, 'he was just touching his face. The baby is Vic's own nephew, after all.'

My nephew, thought Vic, staring down at the pink face. *My own nephew, a bastard. Ben London's never going to let me forget him. He's going to rub my poor face in it every time I look at this child. Ria's child. His child. They even look the same, damn them. The Workhouse Boy, the seducer of my sister, rubbing my face in it day after day. In my mind he'll always be there on the steps by the river, seducing her, corrupting her, my sister, her lovely body squashed beneath his, the pervert, her struggles, her crying, her unavailing blows. And my guilt: she cried for me, I know she did, and I did not come. And there will never be a moment when that knowledge and that hatred will not be at the forefront of my mind and of my heart.*

4

What is the darkest secret a man can have?

After the preliminary officers' training course at Oxford Bertie bought a sword and became an Object of Respect to the private soldier, and was saluted wherever he went. He

wore a tailored uniform and reported to Regimental Headquarters, where he drilled twenty or thirty squads of men
every day on the dusty parade ground until his voice
squeaked, and inspected such things as entrenching tools
buffed to the highest degree of polish until his eyes watered.
He ordered stones to be painted white. Some of the men
asked him what it was like *over there*. He had faith in his
commanding officers, and no hesitation in repeating what
they told him: 'You are being given the best training and
preparation that can be given,' he said, as they saluted, and
drilled, and polished, and painted: their preparation for
trench warfare. Ben had written that the truth was very
different.

'Letter for you, sir.'

'Thank you,' Bertie said indifferently, but his heart beat
faster. *Why did he keep writing?* Bertie slipped the letter into
his top pocket and saved it up to read in bed that night,
recognizing Ben's old-fashioned copperplate writing.

Why won't he let me forget him?

Ben was enjoying the war. He had passed out of Reading
as an observer and been sent to France. He wrote vividly of
flights over the enemy lines to observe enemy troop movements, and how the officer pilot had to weave the aeroplane
between the shells bursting in the air over the Somme. The
thought that he might be killed did not seem to have
occurred to him. Such arrogance. Did he think he had so
much vitality that he could afford to sacrifice one or two of
his God-given lives, like a cat? Bertie bit his lips.

Does he need me? As much as I need him?

At last the posting to Brooklands came through.

The following Monday Bertie drove down in the Napier
with Sam standing beside him on the seat, his great ginger
paws braced on top of the dashboard and his head over the
windscreen, ears flapping. Aeroplanes rattled and whirred
above the old racetrack. These days, Bertie found, all the
talk at the bar of the Blue Anchor pub was about flying,
with technical terms like stalling speed and wing dihedral
growing louder as the beer dropped lower. Bertie listened
elegantly, content to let all this pass over his head. It was

not a gentleman's job to be concerned with details. They had riggers and fitters for that sort of thing. He was aware that they put oil in one end of the engine and petrol in the other, but he never concerned himself with why. It was his job to fly, not to be an expert. For a few hours a week, whenever the weather was windless enough to fly, he heaved an extraordinary-looking beast called a Maurice Shorthorn aloft and did circuits until finally he was allowed to go solo. He smashed up the suspension on landing, but everyone did that.

Every week he received that long copperplate letter from Ben. He must be frightfully busy; the trouble he took was amazing. Ben was a corporal now, but still an observer of course; pilots were nearly always officers, although – Bertie raised one eyebrow – that standard seemed to be relaxing now in the last months of 1915. The Royal Flying Corps was expanding rapidly, every Tom, Dick and Harry wanted to get in on the act; there weren't enough young men to replace the dying. Usually the aeroplanes burned.

In January, at the end of his training, Bertie was given the usual leave. He rode up to London on the smooth Great Western Railway. His sword was damnably difficult to manage in the crowded compartment, which seemed to be filled entirely with women wearing dresses half-way up their legs. How embarrassing these new fashions were. One silly girl with plucked eyebrows kept giggling at him. Bertie stared from the window.

The girls talked hysterically about the war, the barbaric German bombardment of defenceless towns, a woman had been killed; and Zeppelins were drifting at will over the streets of London – nets had been erected over important public buildings to deflect the bombs – and shops with German names, Bauer, Leibig's Emporium, Schmidt Carpets, had their windows broken and stock burned by mobs of patriotic women. 'Good thing too!' said a lady in a large hat.

Both Bertie's eyebrows went up.

The silly girl whispered that there were spies everywhere: it was the duty of every woman to be vigilant, and to report any suspicious behaviour to the police. They looked approvingly at Bertie in his uniform.

The lady said that it was common knowledge that some young men were shirking the war; it was the duty of every girl, every woman, every mother, to hand any young man in civilian clothes the white feather of cowardice.

Bertie was astonished when some of the women said they were ashamed that they were not allowed to fight at the Front, because they felt that if they didn't fight, how could they expect the Vote? Bertie was horrified.

Women, fighting?

How ever would a gentleman cope?

Bertie got off the train feeling absolutely staggered by these revolutionary ideas. But then, once down onto the busy platform into the safely male world of porters, smoke and guards, everything seemed normal again. He had a few minutes in hand before he had to report to the War Office to be told where his active duty posting would be. He waved down a cab – it was now against the law to whistle for one – and ordered it to take him to the busy Haymarket.

He went into Burberry's and bought one of their fashionable *Tielocken* flying coats – all the big stores, Dunhill, Harrods and so on, had displays of specialist flying outfits in their windows. He smoothed the palms of his hands down the soft leather. Now he looked the cat's whiskers. He ordered it to be sent round to his flat. Outside, a leopard-skin flying helmet caught his eye in Rowland Ward's window. He had a dashing reputation to keep up amongst his fellow trainee pilots, so he bought it.

On his way to the War Office, he was rather bothered by the number of girls who eyed the wings on his glamorous RFC uniform, and followed him along the street – at least with their eyes. One handed him a rose; another, a beautiful girl he had never seen before in his life, kissed his cheek.

Bertie wiped his cheek coldly. The war had changed the feminine race, and not for the better. He saw a woman bus conductor winding tickets out of her machine, joking merrily with the male passengers, and in Trafalgar Square a girl bill-poster passed him wearing rubber wellington boots.

carrying a ladder and a bucket of glue, a cigarette dangling from her lip. He was clearly able to see her hips and bust swaying beneath her overalls. He shook his head, surprised that the police allowed it. It wasn't lady-like, yet the government even encouraged it! The sooner the war ended, the better it would be, because then things could get back to normal. Women bus conductors indeed; women policemen next! And at that moment, he saw two police-women in wide-brimmed hats and long blue coats supervising the patrons leaving a cinema, bossily ensuring that they were not rowdy and didn't leave litter.

In the War Office the clerk handed him his posting order and his red rail warrant.

'Where to?' Bertie said.

'France. The aerodrome at La Houssoye.'

Bertie felt numb. La Houssoye was where Ben was.

Bertie walked blindly.

The Germans aren't the only enemy we fight! Some things never change. Ben had written that. How much did he know? Did Ben *know*?

Ben could not know about love, about men, about women. They did not teach love in the Workhouse any more than they did in a public school, and what could he have learned from a frightful girl like that Ria? Nothing about love, the best and purest thing in the world.

'God!' Bertie prayed aloud. Ben was too innocent to know the darkest secret, the most awful secret. Ben would kill him if he knew. Certainly he would not dare pursue their neat, copperplate friendship, even at a distance. Bertie writhed as he walked as though his love would destroy him – the love nobody knew of; that nobody dared speak of.

God knew. God knew everything. God had created his imperfect nature. The monster lived, lavished with money, born to sin, hiding behind a façade of well-bred elegance. Born to sin. *It's not my fault*, he whispered, but the teaching was quite clear, and there was not any secret in his heart that God did not know. No secret was too dark for God. 'I love him,' he hissed. 'God help me, I shall burn in hell. I love him. I helped him because I loved him.' Bertie buried his face in his hands. God knew that they were all, every one of them, all prisoners of their imperfect nature; but this time, no answer came out of the dark.

'Don't make me go,' he groaned against his palms. 'Don't lead me into temptation again. I shall burn . . . I shall burn . . .'

Someone said: 'All right, mate?'

'Yes, thank you, officer,' Bertie said. He wiped his hands calmly, gave a nonchalant smile. 'Just . . . a little tired, that's all.'

'It's a bastard, the war,' agreed the special constable, saluting. 'It's a real bastard.'

Chapter Twelve

1

'Let's have a look before Vic and Nigel arrive,' Ria said, 'then we can get it over and done with and get back home.'

But Esther had fallen in love with the little house immediately, and she wasn't going to give up so easily. 'It's an ideal place for a little child to grow up in,' she pointed out. The house was in about the middle of the long row of terrace houses that made up Havannah Street, half-way between St Luke's Church and the shops. It could not have been more convenient. Nearly opposite the narrow turning of Commons Street, it was close to the pub, but not too close, and the neighbours all looked respectable people. The only difference between the houses was the colour of the curtains and whether the doorsteps were red or white. One old man sat warming his face in the sun in a big old upright carved chair placed in the entrance to his scullery. Children played hopscotch in the road.

'Nice place to live, is this?' asked Esther of the old man.

'Not so bad. I've lived hereabouts thirty years. From near, are you?'

'Not very far,' said Esther. 'We're a respectable, quiet family, friends of poor Harriet Mabbs.' She brushed her fingertip along her lower eyelid.

'God rest her soul in peace,' said the old man. 'I'm Mr Osborne. Used to run the grocer's down on the corner.'

'Esther Price. This is my daughter, Ria. I was just

saying, doesn't this look a nice area, darling?'

'I suppose so,' Ria said. Will was tired of standing and she picked him up, splaying his legs around her thin waist and settling him.

'Lovely little house for the boy to grow up in,' Esther repeated, still without a response from Ria. She explained to Mr Osborne: 'When poor Mrs Mabbs died and her house was left empty, my dear friend Mrs McCririck spoke for me to the landlord's agent, and he is agreeable to us taking it over.'

'Mrs Osborne hearthstones our step every day, the windowsill every week,' nodded old Mr Osborne. 'White or red, it doesn't matter, long as it's done, and the pavement washed down every day too.'

'Bloody hell,' Ria said under her breath.

'Every day, she has, for the last thirty years, despite the trouble she has with her knees now. Proud woman.' He sounded proud of her too.

'Admirable,' said Esther, now certain that she was going to like living in this road – with Tom in full-time work, they could afford it, too. She turned, clasping her hands ecstatically. 'Oh, Ria, we'll be so happy here! If only you knew how it takes me back to the good old days with my first husband, my dear Dick.'

'I don't know if I want Will to grow up in a place like this,' Ria said. 'What's wrong with where we're living now?'

'But here's so much more convenient for your job at Brown's Laundry.'

'I don't know I want to go back to the laundry.'

Esther wrung her fingers. She had thought that they had already settled this point. She would look after Will in the mornings when Ria was out at the laundry. She had been looking forward to it so much – she adored young Wills, and she knew he loved her. Her heart had been flying, imagining the new house all sunny and bright and dry, and rooms enough for everyone, no rising damp, and glass in the windows, a proper place for a little boy to grow up in. But now Ria was sulking. Didn't she care? Esther's dreams threatened to collapse.

'You'll change your mind when you see inside. Come on, darling!' she said.

'I don't know,' Ria said. 'He's ever so heavy, Mum. You take him.'

Esther carried young Wills inside. She pointed out that there were two bedrooms upstairs. 'Isn't it big?' said Ria, then added: 'It seems ever so bare.'

'We can pick up some carpets down at the market,' Esther said. 'Vic will come up trumps, he always does. We're going to love it here, Ria – we'll be like a new family in our new house.' The ground floor contained a living room with a view over the street, a proper window with a windowsill, a fireplace made of shaped ochre-coloured tiles with a mantelshelf and a hook for a mirror above it. The walls were straight and prettily patterned with wallpaper in dark green and white. There was a kitchen with a stove, and a small scullery that opened on the yard.

'A back yard all of our own,' Esther said eagerly. There was a strip of earth down one side for vegetables and a privy at the end. 'Look, we won't have to keep the coal under the sink any more.' Esther pointed out a coal bin. There was a clothesline already hanging. 'You see, Ria, that's something we won't have to buy.' Ria shrugged. There was a knock on the door and Tom came through, having finished work. 'See, Tom,' called Esther, grateful for an ally – Tom had always wanted a nice house – 'you can keep pigeons here, there's a loft for pigeons – and look, there's a rabbit hutch!'

'I want to enjoy myself,' Ria said. 'I don't want to be stuck at home. I'm seventeen, for God's sake. I don't want to waste my life at home, changing nappies and cooking and getting old.'

'You're just going to have to face up to it, girl,' Esther said bitterly. 'Everyone else does. We all want a good time, but life isn't like that, and sooner or later you'll have to face up to it. A woman's place is at home, my girl, usually at the sink, and the sooner you realize that, the happier you'll be.'

'Just because it was good enough for you doesn't mean it's good enough for me.'

'She says she won't go back to the laundry,' fretted Esther to Tom.

'She's got to look after the baby,' Tom said.

'Mum says she'll do that,' Ria said eagerly. 'Look, Dad, if we move here we'll need money, won't we?'

'Every little helps,' Tom said. 'That's why your job at the laundry will come in so useful.'

Ria said: 'I was reading a newspaper the other day—'

'Since when do girls buy newspapers?' asked Esther, outraged.

'The *Daily Mail,*' Ria said. 'There was an advertisement in it which said that women who volunteer to make munitions get paid a minimum of twenty-four shillings a week. That's three times what I get now. And women are guaranteed the same piece-work rates as men.'

'That can't be true,' Esther said, looking at Tom.

'The men at the Front haven't got enough shells or enough bullets,' Ria said defiantly. 'The Ministry of Munitions says we can't win the war unless we girls go into the factories to help our boys.' She added off-handedly: 'I can get more than twenty-four bob a week down at the Woolwich Arsenal.'

'Have you been sneaking down there behind my back?' asked Esther furiously.

'I just enquired. All my girl friends are going. Ann's going.'

Tom said: 'It's not such a bad idea. It's a lot of money, and if we're to move here, Esther, we're going to need every penny we can get.'

'Oh, Tom!' said Esther, then she thought about it. They would need the money: the rent on this house was more than ten bob a week. And then there were all the things to buy. Even with Vic and Nigel putting in their bit, it would be tight. She hesitated.

Ria clinched it by saying: 'Mum, you wouldn't mind looking after Will, would you?'

Esther pretended to be unconvinced. 'Well,' she huffed, 'we'll see.'

Vic and Nigel arrived, their caps pulled down over their

eyes, their hands pushed down in their jacket pockets. It turned out that some girls had shouted at them off a 'bus for not being in uniform. Vic and Nigel had waved Reserved Occupation cards, but there were so many forgeries around now that the girls had just jeered. Nigel was in a towering, petulant rage about it.

Esther said: 'She wants to go and make shells in a high-explosive factory.'

Vic told Ria: 'Your place is at home.' He looked around him. 'We aren't going to move here,' he said. 'We'll stay at our proper home.'

'I like it here,' Ria said.

'They must be asking – what, Nige?'

'What with the way wages are going up, it must be ten bob a week,' Nigel said.

'We'll never get the capital to set up properly in business if we spend all our income on the roof over your heads,' Vic said.

'You see, to set up, you've got to have savings,' Nigel said. 'If we saved ten bob a week, instead of spending it, we'd have £25 in a year. Then we could invest that, and we'd really get going.'

'They're going to call up single men between the ages of eighteen and forty,' Ria said. 'You're going to have to go. You can forget all your schemes, Nigel, and you, Vic. They're going to put you in the Army and it doesn't matter how clever you are, you're going to have to go.'

On their first day in the new house, the 17th, Vic and Nigel received their call-up telegrams. Nigel held up the piece of blue paper, trembling. There was no leeway, no way out of it. Vic only smiled. They were to report forthwith.

2

Ben loved to fly. The height, and no parachutes, the thought of being enmeshed high above the earth in this frail incendiary tangle of struts and wires held up only by air terrified some men, but to him it was beautiful.

He had his friends around him. Behind him sat Bertie in the pilot's cockpit, his eyes hidden by goggles, the propeller like a whirling silver shield behind his head. Over to his left was Mackelroy the Australian who had come twelve thousand miles for this joy of fighting, and away on his right was Trewarren the Cornishman. Like Ben and the other observers he stood upright in the open, windswept nose of his machine, the scarf his mother had knitted him bannering like a tiny, proud flag. Even Ben had a scarf – the one Colleen O'Keeffe had knitted him.

Ben laughed. Life was an intoxicating joy. He was never frightened when he was with friends.

He looked down at the landscape of hell. How could it be so beautiful? The vast horizon encircled it in blue mist, white mist, then green mist, becoming greener the further down he looked, finally unrolling beneath him like a deep green map, very, very slowly. And there it was: the churned, pockmarked rift of the trenches far below, like a snake with its head on the English Channel, and its tail rattling somewhere in Italy.

They were fighting an enemy they did not hate.

The main roads were marked in bright red on the map, but in real life they were dusty scrawls scratched through a scribbled patchwork of French fields, almost impossible for a beginner to pick out. Ben had learned that the main roads were often straighter and lined with poplars which cast long, distinctive shadows. Railways inked boldly in black looked like threads of shining wire if the sun struck them, but often they were hardly visible at all – sometimes Bertie had to come down low enough to read the names on the stations. The woods that the map-makers drew in green looked black in winter, and lakes shown in blue often looked black.

Bertie would have to learn all this . . . but did he want to? Sometimes he didn't seem to care about anything, or anyone. The old laughter had gone. In the *estaminet*, where rank did not count, Ben had slapped his shoulder. 'Cheer up! What's the matter?' Bertie had flinched as though Ben had struck him.

Ben mentioned his worry about his friend in one of his letters to Colleen O'Keeffe, but in her next letter she was determinedly cheerful, as always. Vegetables were an extortionate price. London was a blaze of crimson and blue from all the recruiting posters everywhere. Regent's Park was full of soldiers on exercises. She had nearly been run over by an ambulance in Moorgate Street. Sam, the dog, was fine – missed them both. The kindness of her thought in writing the letter touched Ben's heart. But it was not a reply.

Was it jealousy he saw in Bertie's eyes, behind his aviator's goggles?

Ridiculous! That leopard-skin helmet alone must have cost him ten pounds. What did Bertie have to be jealous of, looking at Ben? Ben had scrimped to buy his flying kit second-hand; his cheap coat was stuffed with old newspapers to keep him warm. Bertie was swaddled in luxurious leather. He had everything – and because he was an officer he had been given a £25 allowance he didn't need to buy his clothes with!

To Ben, twenty-five pounds was a fortune.

Now he looked upward. The blue bowl above him was empty but for the deadly, blinding arc of the sun. If they were attacked, the first they would know of it would be the bullets whipping down out of that glare, where they could not see. A whole *Jagde* or squadron of German machines could hide themselves there. Ben lifted his goggles and held up his hand, scanning the sun.

He had learned to see.

There was a knack to focusing. Some men never learned it, just as some pilots never really learned to fly, they drove their aeroplanes like brutes. What an observer learned to see with his eyes was the difference between life and death. Ben looked carefully until he was as sure as he could be that there really was nothing up there, then gave the thumbs-up sign. Bertie's teeth showed white as he smiled.

Ben loved flying. Some men learned how to drive an aircraft, like Bertie, and could fly. Ben *felt* it. Aeroplanes were held up by feelings, because a natural pilot – and there were not many of them – *felt* how to fly. An aeroplane could be treated as a cold collection of wood and fabric that was forced through the air, but a natural pilot felt her, caressed her, flew *with* her, and she would do anything for him. Either you could feel this, or you couldn't. Each aeroplane was different; but there were very few of them who would not respond to love.

'You must be soft in the head,' Bertie had said.

Bertie hauled the FE2B into a long turn towards home, the wings canted over at forty-five degrees, the extra drag of rudder and flapping ailerons wearing the speed off her, and Ben felt the nose start to rise towards a stall. The big Beardmore engine behind Bertie, crafted out of the solid by a Clyde shipbuilder, lost its steady note and began to hammer. Ben looked back anxiously. Bertie pushed forward on the stick and the nose sagged down, picking up airspeed. He gave a polite wave: nothing to worry about.

There was a terrific crash, and they flew through a cloud of black smoke. Bertie dragged the machine to the right, then to the left. The explosions fell behind them.

Bertie cut the engine to a mutter and began the long routine glide towards the squadron aerodrome near La Houssoye, fifteen miles behind the lines. The Somme river wandered peacefully on their left and Ben could see wild duck flying across the tranquil surface. The airstream whined softly in the wires. Now he could see the aerodrome ahead, and hoped Bertie would give a burst on the engine to clear the plugs. The machine wobbled, then the engine gave an encouraging roar before Bertie cut it back again. The FE glided smoothly over the poplars lining the road, swayed, then bumped down onto the grass. Bertie taxied towards the canvas-covered Bessoneau hangars by the orchard, then stopped the motor. Ben jumped down as the mechanics ran out, stretching his stiff legs, watching them manhandle the machine back into the hangar to check it over. They were very possessive about their machines. For a moment Ben and Bertie stood together drinking in the silence, and the fresh smell of the grass.

Bertie said: 'Look here—' He stopped.

'Sorry, sir?'

Bertie shook his head. Nothing.

'See you tomorrow, sir,' Ben said. They would do the dawn patrol together. It wasn't the done thing for officers and sergeants to stand around chatting.

'Yes, fine,' Bertie said. The sergeants' mess was at the opposite end of the orchard from the officers' mess. Ben saluted and walked away. Something made him glance over his shoulder: for a split second, he could have sworn he saw a terrible expression on Bertie's face. He had not moved; he was staring after Ben, watching him. The smile that he had worn in the air had gone.

You are the only true friend I have in the world, Ben thought. *You saved me. I will not let you go.*

3

Nigel had a plan. It was an intricate plan, a beautiful, interlocking structure, like all Nigel's ideas. When he told Vic – he told Vic everything, always – Vic was enthusiastic. Vic always encouraged Nigel's ideas, so that Nigel loved to share them with him.

He wasn't sure that Vic always understood them; but Vic had a way of making Nigel's ideas work.

On completion of their basic training, before being sent out to France, Vic and Nigel were given twenty-four hours leave and issued with rail warrants for London. They travelled up together from Sussex and booked into a busy hotel near the railway station. The train had been late. Nigel looked at his wristwatch. They had already used six hours.

They rumpled the beds as though they had been slept in and screwed up the towels, then let them drop from the towel rails. They talked in loud voices and went out noisily: they were going to have an evening out on the town. The clerk noticed them. This was all according to the plan.

The strong summer sun still slanted hotly between the buildings. They went into several second-hand shops near the river and picked up two old jackets, trousers, and finally two pairs of shoes. They had to pay over the odds for those, and Vic would have lost patience with the wizened little man for holding out on them, but Nigel insisted. They must have shoes; it was all part of the plan. He packed them into his kitbag – no sight could be more common than a soldier carrying a kitbag – and they left.

Nigel looked at his watch. 'Eight o'clock.'

'Let's go straight there,' Vic said impatiently.

'We've got to stick to the schedule,' Nigel said. It was the Plan. 'We don't want to be too early, and be recognized by someone who knows us,' he muttered. 'It's light until almost ten.'

'We don't want to be too late, either.'

'Trust me. You agreed to my plan.'

'Let's get on with it.' Vic smiled, then squeezed Nigel's shoulder seriously. He never joked with Nigel, and he never lied to him about anything. 'I trust you.'

'Then we stick to the schedule,' Nigel said gratefully. He swung aboard a tram and Vic followed him. They got off at Piccadilly and walked into Soho. They went into a pub and bought some beers, the weak wartime brew, and picked up a couple of girls. The girls hung on their arms and drank gin, laughing loudly. There was a clock over the bar – pubs had to close early under the new licensing hours – so Nigel didn't have to keep looking at his watch. The pub filled up with girls and soldiers. Vic put his arms around his girl and started to dance. She put her head back and her knees against his knees – her dress was that short. At last Nigel looked at the clock and nodded. It was time.

Vic suggested, 'Let's go somewhere noisy, where they have champagne.'

The girl in the short skirt, who said her name was Pat, knew just the place. The other girl, Eth, put her arm through Nigel's and staggered a little as they walked over the cobbles. He had bought her seven gins: he had counted.

It was nearly dark. The electric lights were starting to look bright.

They went down into a cellar where a crush of people were dancing. Vic and Nigel reversed the usual practice and the girls had most of the champagne. 'I like you,' Eth said, embracing Nigel. He pinched her thigh. She rubbed the place: she would remember him. He poured her another glass of bubbly: he knew that she would not remember much more. He looked around for a couple of likely marks and saw them just coming down the steps, two young soldiers hardly old enough to shave, looking nervously around them at all the pushing and shoving and wanting to enjoy it but not sure how to. Country boys, they'd learn soon enough. He nodded and Vic pushed the girls over. 'Want you to meet some friends of mine. Say hallo. Shake hands. I know them, they'll buy you champagne, don't go away now.' The boys could hardly believe their luck. Behind the girls, Vic had already melted away, but they didn't even look round.

In an alleyway, Vic and Nigel pulled on the clothes they had bought over their uniforms, and hid their boots in the kitbag. They came out of the dark looking like different people and caught the 'bus at Piccadilly Circus.

Vic said: 'Is all this really necessary?'

'You promised that we'd do it my way.'

'Until we get there. Then it's my show.'

'As long as he doesn't see our faces.' They would hide them with kerchieves.

Vic said: 'It won't matter if he does see us.'

That wasn't part of the plan. Nigel said: 'What do you mean?'

Vic smiled, patted Nigel's shoulder. Don't worry.

Nigel said: 'If he recognizes us . . . Remember, Vic, he's got a lot of very nasty pals. And he knows you. He knows your voice and everything.'

'Don't worry,' smiled Vic. Nigel felt control slipping away from him. He could feel Vic taking over.

'I wish I'd never thought of this,' said Nigel, looking nervously through his reflection in the window into the dark.

Vic squeezed his arm. 'Keep calm, Nigel.'

'It's just that I tell you everything and you don't tell me a damned thing.'

'That's the way it should be, Nigel,' said Vic confidently.

Nigel shivered. He felt that he didn't really control Vic as much as he dreamed he did. Nigel developed beautiful plans in his head, but it always seemed to be Vic who made them work. It was Nigel who had said that what they needed was capital, and it was Vic who finally said: 'I know where to get it, and how.' It was Nigel who worked out the details of the plan; but it was Vic who put it into operation and was making it real, making it actually happen, and now Nigel was terrified.

'All change,' Vic said, and got down. They waited for another 'bus. The last of the light was fading from the western sky. A tug hooted on the river. The 'bus was late; there had been a breakdown. They walked on to another stop to catch the next tram along Cable Street. Nigel peered anxiously at the luminous fingers of his watch. If they missed the last 'bus back, they would be in real trouble.

'Take it easy,' smiled Vic. Yes take it easy. The tram came and they swung aboard, sitting downstairs. Nigel felt a warm relief steal over him. It would all be all right. It was impossible to doubt Vic when he radiated such a calm, tremendous confidence. It didn't matter if the plan ran twenty minutes late. Vic sat looking very relaxed, his fist lying in his lap. Nigel closed his eyes. Through the blurry gap between the lids, passing street lights made streaky patterns. The tram creaked and jolted. Nigel glimpsed a light flickering in Vic's lap where nothing should be, and his eyes started open.

A metal blade glittered in Vic's fist, reflecting the street lights passing outside the darkened interior of the tram. Vic was holding a shiv. Less than three inches long, the sharply pointed blade stuck out between the knuckles of his second and third fingers.

Nigel pressed the back of his hand against his mouth and stared out of the window. By the time he dared look at Vic's lap again, the shiv had disappeared.

But he had seen it; he had.

Vic wouldn't use it. No, not Vic. *It wasn't part of the plan*, Nigel thought. Vic was sitting quietly. If he asked Vic about the shiv, Vic would just say: 'What shiv?'

Nigel stared out of the window. They were near the Old Bull and Bush.

Vic stood up. 'Come on, this is where we get off.'

They walked down West Ferry Road. It was very dark; no traffic. Some of the shops still had lights on for customers returning late home from work, or starting shift-work. They kept their heads down, but saw no one they knew.

Nigel thought: *He won't use it. Only to frighten the old man. That's all. They have to respect you. Fear you. Vic often says that.*

People looked up to Vic. It was nothing to do with height – Vic was short – but they looked up to him, and somehow they never looked up to Nigel, who was taller.

'Slow down a bit,' Nigel said. Vic was forging ahead. Nigel hurried to catch up. Vic said nothing; didn't even acknowledge his brother beside him.

Nigel looked nervously up the side streets as they walked. Cuba Street, the Anchor and Hope pub, the smell of hot oil through the open door of Kosky's fried-fish shop; bringing memories flooding back of himself as a little boy. He must have run in there a thousand times and stood on tiptoe at the long steel counter for a ha'porth of fish. Here was Brown's Laundry, where Ria had worked before she started at the ammunition factory for five times the money, filling shells: and here was Havannah Street.

Vic crossed the road without even looking up.

Nigel thought: *Oh, Mum, you're so close.* He couldn't pick out their house in the dark, but his eyes looked where he knew it was.

Oh, Mum, I wish I was with you. I wish I wasn't walking on past. I wish I didn't have to follow Vic. The way I planned it was so clean and simple. Mum, he's going to kill a man.

Mum, he's going to.

That's all right. Yes, it's all right. Look at all the men who are killed in France. That's murder, isn't it, except that when governments commit murder, they're allowed to call it war. So what's wrong with it?

And Blumenthall's an old man. He's had his go. Everyone's got to die sometime.

And he's a Jew. All he ever cared about was money.

What person did he ever care for? Who did he ever like? What did he ever do for a living human being? No woman, no love, only money. And he gave a job to the Workhouse Bastard. *That's why Vic's got the shiv.*

Calm down. Vic's right. Always did have too much imagination.

He's an old man – just a weak old man, dry old stick. Vic won't need to use the shiv! It's just to frighten him. Good old Vic.

They were close now. There was the shop, with lights still on in the windows full of stock. The street was empty. Nigel pulled his kerchief over his face and plucked at Vic's sleeve for him to do the same. But Vic strode on through the darkness. Nigel ran after him. He could see Vic's silhouette at the lighted door. This was not the plan. They had been going to go in the back way, which was very private, but now Vic simply went in through the front door. Nigel saw Blumenthall standing by the till. Blumenthall's mouth opened and he heard him say: 'Vic! To what do I owe this pleasure? I thought you were fighting in our glorious Army.'

Vic walked towards him between the counters.

Nigel saw the shiv in his hand.

Blumenthall saw it too.

Vic walked as though the shiv was leading him on, his arm outstretched in front of him, the blade sticking forward between his knuckles like a silver tongue, the handle wedged in his palm. Nigel closed the door, pulled the blind. Now he saw Blumenthall backing away. Vic followed him sinuously behind the counter. Blumenthall turned and ran towards the stairs at the back of the shop. Vic jumped on him. He swung his fist into Blumenthall's back.

Blumenthall made no sound.

Nigel remembered Vic saying, once, long ago, *No danger, no risk, no noise. Come up behind him give him a quick bang in the back and take it off him, he doesn't make a sound, thank you very much, sir. Just come up behind him and fist him in the kidneys. The pain is so awful that he can't even scream*, Vic had smiled.

He remembered Ria saying, *That's how it starts, but we saw a man with a knife, and he was going to kill another man, and that's what will happen to Vic.* She had been hanging on Ben London's arm, saying that he had just saved a man's life.

Blumenthall staggered soundlessly against the counter. The display of Argentinian corned beef cans toppled and clattered across the floor. He pressed his hands into the arched small of his back. Blood trickled between his knuckles. Nigel said:

'God, Vic, you used the shiv.'

Blumenthall took a whooping breath, and he looked from Vic to Nigel, and from Nigel to Vic, then his eyes lost recognition and he simply fell over. It had only taken a moment. It seemed so incidental. Nigel waited for something more to happen. Blumenthall's body lay motionlessly amongst the scattered cans. His eyes were open and a gold filling gleamed steadily in one tooth. Nothing more happened. It was the end.

'My God, Vic,' Nigel said, 'you've killed him.'

'What did you expect?' said Vic simply.

'It wasn't in the plan,' Nigel said. Then he understood. Vic had had his own plan, too, all along. It was all part of Vic's plan.

Vic put his arm around Nigel's shoulder, and Nigel felt Vic's breath warm on his face. 'You're a very clever chap, Nige,' Vic smiled, 'but you wouldn't have had the guts, would you?'

Nigel found himself shaking his head in agreement. He wouldn't have had the guts. He would have thought he had, he would have made excuses, but Vic had known the truth. Nigel was a coward. Now Nigel nodded his head in agreement.

'It was too dangerous not to kill him,' Vic said.

'Yes,' Nigel said. He understood.

'I'll clear up these cans while you dump him in the river,' Vic said.

Nigel said: 'Do I have to?' But of course he already knew that he did have to.

It was all part of Vic's plan. 'It's Sunday tomorrow,' Vic explained patiently. 'No one will come to the shop until

316

Monday. By then the tides will have carried him up and down and around and by the time he's found, if he ever is found, no one will know when or where or how he fell in the river.' Of course; it was so obvious. He might have been killed anywhere, by any of his accomplices in the criminal fraternity. 'And we'll be far away,' added Vic. He smiled and hugged Nigel reassuringly with his arm. 'All right?'

Nigel nodded. He didn't like the idea of picking up the body.

But Vic made it easy, swinging it up without effort and hanging the arms over Nigel's shoulders. The old man didn't weigh much. 'Get your hands behind his knees,' Vic said. 'Piggy-back him.' Nigel obeyed. The old man's hands and face were still warm with life.

Vic looked out of the door, checking the dark, empty street. It was raining now. 'All right. Don't hang about.' Nigel heard the door close behind him. He crossed the road and dropped down amongst the warehouses on the far side, felt his way along the dark walls. He could smell the river now. In a few moments he could hear the rising tide sloshing against the pilings. He stopped, feeling forward with his foot. Further out, the river flickered with the reflections of the lights of Rotherhithe on the far side.

Nigel turned. He let go of Blumenthall's knees. The old man dangled by his arms over the edge. Nigel dragged at the hands around his neck, cold and stiffening, pulling him back. Then suddenly the locked fingers let go and a few moments later he heard the body splash into the water.

Nigel wiped the rain off his face in the dark.

He felt his way back to the road. No light showed through the blind over the door and Vic had shot the bolts. Nigel came in the private way at the back and went upstairs. His face glowing with orange candlelight, Vic was kneeling in front of a double-padlocked trunk he had opened with Blumenthall's own keys.

Ledgers; just ledgers. Vic tossed them out impatiently. Photographs – a woman with dark eyes, a little girl smiling, both in very old-fashioned clothes. Something like a Jewish

Bible, with an ornate candlestick gilded on the cover. Old papers. Vic started chucking them aside.

Nigel opened one of the ledgers. He gasped. Vic had not understood; but he did. Here was pure treasure. Columns of numbers and totals; names and addresses, some obviously coded, others identified by nicknames, many of which he knew, some he didn't. Details of all the pies that Blumenthall had his fingers in: some legitimate – a pawnshop in Poplar High Street, market stall pitches – others illegal: lists of bookie's runners – 'He's been tied in with Rixby for years!' Nigel hissed, realizing how cleverly the whole district had been fixed – organized theft, fencing stolen goods out to the markets. Nigel rocked back on his heels. 'He didn't tell us the whole truth about *anything*. He didn't pay us a tenth of what he owed us.' He clenched his fists, glad now that Vic had killed the old spider, wishing he'd made him suffer before he died. 'I would have made him suffer,' he whispered. 'I would have made him scream until he was sorry.'

'He was a fool to leave this stuff about,' Vic said. 'He was a fool to die for it.'

Vic was right. It was worth killing for. They held the keys to a whole network of crime in their hands. They were set up for life, now that it was too late – tomorrow, they would be in France, thought Nigel bitterly. The war might go on for months longer, perhaps even for years longer. Nigel began to curse. By the time they came back, the network would have disintegrated.

'We'll still have the names,' Vic said. 'We can rebuild it.' Vic had understood the importance of the ledgers after all, Nigel realized. Had understood, and taken the next step. Nigel looked at his brother with a respect so profound that it left him feeling drained. He realized that while he had been congratulating himself on how clever he was, Vic had already, intuitively, somehow, gone straight on to the crux of the matter, and never lost sight of what Nigel had known, then forgotten: what they would need to bring the people back to them. Nigel felt humiliated by his stupidity. Power: money.

'Look,' Vic said. 'Capital.'

He held out his hand, and Nigel looked. The bottom of the trunk was a mass of coins, gold coins, sovereigns, each one a week's pay for a working man, steadily gleaming, not in neat piles but just tossed in and spread about luxuriously between the steel walls of the trunk, beneath the heavy padlocks, as if once they were safe in there Blumenthall didn't care about the neat numbers or rows or racks, just weight.

'Capital,' Vic repeated. He smiled and put his arms around Nigel, dropping his great red face close, breathing warm gusts over Nigel's mouth and nose. 'Capital.' Nigel nodded. He was overwhelmed and he didn't feel humiliated any more.

He said: 'There must be three, four thousand pounds in there.'

Vic slammed the lid. 'Let's get on with it. It must weigh a ton.' They snapped on the padlocks, then bumped it downstairs. Nigel went to the stock room and wheeled the sack truck back. Vic tipped the trunk and Nigel got the sack truck underneath, and heaved backwards. The trunk swung into place at an angle of forty-five degrees. Nigel rolled it out the back way and Vic put out the lights and locked the door behind them. Together they pushed the sack truck along the alleyways until they came to the fence behind Louisa Hiscott's house. A single light glowed upstairs, the only one in the whole dark row.

Vic pushed open the gate. They had to lift the trunk off the sack truck to get it through. They carried it up the path to the scullery door by main strength. Vic tapped softly on the glass. A glow of candlelight appeared, and a shadow, then two bolts were clicked and the door opened.

'You're late,' Louisa Hiscott said in an over-wrought voice. 'My husband knocks off at midnight.' She held the candle up in one hand, clutching her dressing gown around her with the other. Vic kissed her on the lips.

'Don't worry.'

She wiped her lips, pretending distaste, then looked at the trunk. 'Is that all?'

'That's it,' Vic said. 'Household effects.'

'Pull the other one, it's got bells on.'

He dropped five gold sovereigns on her kitchen table as Nigel dragged the trunk through.

'All right,' she agreed tersely. 'Put it upstairs. Hurry, George will be back in a minute.' *Who are you kidding?* thought Vic with a smile. *He's still there with that girl he buys the flowers for from the florist on the High Street. And why else would your bedroom be the safest place on the Isle of Dogs for a stolen trunk? Because your husband never goes in there.* They carried the trunk upstairs, Nigel's breath whining with the effort, and settled the trunk neatly in the corner by the wardrobe. Louisa Hiscott threw an embroidered rug over it, then set a vase with flowers in and a vanity mirror on it.

'There,' Vic said. 'Part of the furniture already.'

'Aren't you going to leave the keys?'

'You're right, I may be young,' Vic smiled, 'but I wasn't born yesterday, Louisa.' She held up her face, pouting like a schoolgirl. He kissed her easily then pushed past her and went downstairs. He looked back at her from the scullery door. 'Give my love to Ria when you see her.' He pushed Nigel outside and closed the door after him.

'It's a hell of a risk,' Nigel said. 'I mean, leaving the trunk with that old cow.'

'Don't be so bleeding ignorant,' Vic said. 'She'd protect it with her life.' They went back to the road and dropped the sack truck off the edge of a wharf, then walked up West Ferry Road, all the time looking over their shoulders for a 'bus. No vehicles passed them and they began to think that they might have to walk all the way back to Waterloo. But then they caught the last tram along Cable Street, and it was two drunk soldiers who walked back over Waterloo Bridge, their arms around one another, singing and laughing amongst many others under the tolerant eyes of the police.

4

Ben worried that the war was getting to his friend, although they had flown fewer missions than many. The boys were all going into the *estaminet* in town for an evening out, a relaxation from the terrific stress of flying, scrambling up into the back of the Crossley tender, laughing and joking. And talking about flying, of course, as always. Hal Parrant was describing eagerly, swooping his hands to demonstrate what it had been like: the sudden appearance of the deadly enemy out of the sun. Ben listened, fascinated, seeing the aeroplanes weaving and soaring about the sky in his mind's eye. Someone pulled the rope up so that the last arrivals had to jump, then wriggle forward onto the high platform on their bellies. 'Sergeant!' shouted Bertie, staring up. 'What the hell do you think you're doing?'

'Sorry, sir,' Ben said. 'The lads were just joking.' He held his hand down to swing Bertie up.

Bertie said: 'Lower the rope, please.'

'Yes, sir.' Ben put the rope down and Bertie climbed up. He rapped on the back of the cab. 'Carry on, driver.' He sat on the wooden bench seat with his hands on his knees, reserved, but smiling and chatting with anyone who spoke to him, except Ben. His eyes avoided Ben's, and his manner became cold and distant when Ben looked at him. None of the other pilots noticed but to Ben this sudden change of attitude by his friend was like a slap in the face. He almost certainly owed Bertie his life; certainly he owed everything good that had happened to him to Bertie. Now he was being frozen out; Bertie was even pulling rank, which was most unlike him, as if to emphasize their separateness.

The tender jolted over the *pavé* through the night, leaving it almost unilluminated with its weak oil lamps. There was only the sound of the men's voices coming out of the darkness. Hal Parrant's voice: 'I put my stick forward, and hard right rudder, but when I pulled her out he was still on my tail as if he was glued there, and I could see the machine-gun flashing through the arc of the propeller . . .'

Bertie sat with his eyes shut. *If only I had not walked along by the river that night. I love him; I can't live without him; I don't want to live without him. I'd do anything to be with him. I'm crazy.*

When we talk about aircraft, all I think about is him.

When we fly, all I think about is him.

When a shell bursts ahead of us, I don't worry for myself, all I fear for is him. When I fight, it is to protect him.

Bertie's eyes popped open. *Does he know?*

Bertie imagined the shame if Ben did know: if he could read the misery and love in Bertie's heart. Bertie didn't know how to hide his sinful nature. Sometimes when Ben looked at him it felt to Bertie that he was naked. A tiny, wicked part of him longed for the revelation; his conscience and the thinking part of his brain dreaded it. If Ben knew, it would be the worst thing in the world.

Bertie thought: *Rather than reveal that horror to him, I'd kill myself. I'd spin my machine into the ground.* But of course, that was impossible, for Ben always flew in his machine too.

The other day, he thought that Ben was beginning to suspect. They had just landed. Bertie had been standing by the aircraft, watching Ben walk away, and Ben had turned. And Bertie had been unable to hide it: his struggling emotions, his need against his terror, pride against shame, loneliness against his fear of discovery, had shown in his face. He knew what Ben knew: *He knows that I am at war with myself. He knows that wherever I go, it is myself that I fight.*

How much longer before he knows the whole truth? wondered Bertie desperately. *I love him, I hate it, but it's the way I am, not naturally born but taken out of my mother in an unnatural way, before I killed her: what they call a Caesarian birth. A miracle of science: the both of us lived. They gave me the best of everything: not love, but the finest education, money, guilt, and I only wanted for one thing. Love.*

And now I have it. How much longer can I hide it from him?

But I shall hide it.

Not by a word or a gesture from me shall he ever know.

With a scream of brakes the Crossley tender pulled up outside La Houssoye's single *estaminet*. Ben dropped the rope and the men swung down. Bertie stumbled and Ben put out his hand to steady him. Bertie jerked back as though he had been attacked. 'I'm perfectly capable of getting down by myself, thank you.'

'After you, sir.'

He watched Bertie go into the bar, closing the door after him although the night was warm. He smiled. Bertie was obviously in love. He'd got a girl somewhere that he didn't want Ben to know about.

Ben jumped down and went inside. The brown-eyed girls waved to him and twirled their dresses provocatively. He went to the familiar zinc bar, then turned and looked at the fly-specked mirrors, and marble-topped tables so tiny and circular that they would only hold three or four glasses. Bertie was standing at the far end of the room, chatting to one of the girls. He stared at Ben and put his arm around her shoulder. Was that the one? She had a loud laugh; not Bertie's type.

Ben stayed at the bar and ordered a *fine*. The girls were very pretty, but he never went with them. Only once he had; but outside in the dark her face had turned into Ria's face.

Later, clouds moved in from the west and it began to rain.

5

Esther looked out of the window at the gleaming wet street. The rain had stopped. Perhaps she would take Will for a walk? She was lonely; Ria had skived off work to go to the Queen's Theatre, which was looking for acts to compete with the popularity of the new picture-houses (one had just opened not a quarter of a mile south along West Ferry Road). That Charlie Chaplin was a scream. She remembered seeing his parents play at the Queen's, long ago, even before poor Dicky had passed away, and she remembered that the boy had been brought up in the Workhouse, like . . . She put her knuckles to her temples: she had promised herself not to think about Ben.

But she did think about him. Ria had sworn that Vic had not laid a finger on him, and Esther had believed her, because not to believe your own daughter was unthinkable. Vic had warned him off, told him not to come back. That was all.

Esther turned from the window and looked at Will. Yes, Ben was gone, perhaps gone forever, perhaps come into that inheritance that Ria always had bragged about, or working in the City, or fighting in France, perhaps fighting in the trenches, perhaps dying, perhaps already dead and long forgotten – but half of Ben was still here, and always would be.

Because Will was his son. No doubt about it. Ria's Will; and Ben's Will. Esther's eyes filled with tears. She loved the little boy so much that it hurt her.

Will was a solemn baby, and looked at her seriously. She picked him up and cuddled him. He had Ria's eye colour and her blonde hair. He had something of her withdrawn manner. Yet, when he looked at Esther – as he was doing now – she felt that she was looking at Ben. Ben always understood. That had been what made him so very special to her, what made her want him for a son from that very first time Ria had brought him home from the Workhouse – a son who knew her, understood her, who knew what it was to be her, what she had been through, knew the girl she truly was. Vic was something the same, but he always brought her things – this pram, and this maroon hat with the white feathers that she was putting on her head. Ben had never brought her anything, but he gave her everything. Sometimes, as soon as she saw him, as soon as he spoke, he had made her want to laugh out loud. But Will, his son, was a serious baby.

'I love you, darling,' she said.

'Gran'ma,' Will said solemnly, trying to crawl in mid-air.

She tucked him into the pram, and put on her coat although the sun breaking through looked quite hot now. She always wore a coat because it was traditional and lady-like. She pushed the pram into the street, pulling her own real front door closed behind her. Then she remembered to turn around and lock it: what with the war, it seemed that there was more crime about, and it was no longer safe to leave your door open while you went out.

Ben was gone forever, and he would never be coming back.

Old Jack Osborne was sitting out on the pavement in his chair with the carved lions' heads snarling out of the ends of the armrests. He was almost crippled now, and no longer surveyed the street like a king. The newspaper lay in his lap.

'Good news about the Somme Offensive,' he told her in a rattling voice. His face split into a toothless smile. 'We're pushing Jerry back. One more push will do it.'

Esther was terrified at the thought of what Nigel must be going through in France. She didn't worry about Vic, nothing stuck to him, but Nigel was the delicate one, what with all his book-reading and cleverness. Poor Nigel. She hated the Jerries with a terrible hatred, everyone did: it seemed unspeakable that human mothers could have spawned such monsters. Yet they said that the British troops at the Front didn't even hate the Germans. Esther couldn't understand that. She had herself subscribed one pound that she couldn't really afford to the War Loan because of the horrible atrocities.

She nodded to Jack Osborne and he saluted her. She pushed Will down to West Ferry Road. The price of goods in the shops was going up every day, it seemed. Jerry submarines were sinking helpless British merchantmen bringing in food. Sugar and mutton had doubled in price, she noticed, and now was up by half as much again; fish and eggs had doubled, when you could get them. Shops had queues outside them from five o'clock in the morning, and by midday hundreds would be sent away with nothing. Carl-Otto Betz, the butcher on the corner of Tooke Street, whose father had been German, had his premises wrecked and stock appropriated by a crowd of angry housewives. He re-opened under the name of Charles Best, following the example of the Royal Family, who were also changing their German name patriotically from Saxe-Coburg to Windsor, and his customers came back happily. His beef always had been better than anyone's, with that lovely yellow fat.

Esther crossed the road. She wondered how Ria was getting on at her audition. It was silly, Ria wanting to be an actress, but she insisted that was what she had always wanted to be. 'Why did you keep it a secret from me, then, all these years?' Esther had demanded.

'You don't know how much I keep secret from you,' threatened Ria.

'Darling, don't be like that, you know I only want what's best for you.' Ria had nodded at that; it was so obviously true. There was nothing that Esther would not have done for any of her children.

'On stage, Mum, I can be happy. I was born to be an actress. Up there, you're a liar, and everyone in the audience knows you're lying, but you're an actress and you're allowed to, because it's your act. But somehow, when you're up there and all the people are looking at you, Mum, it *isn't* an act, and you find yourself telling the truth.' Esther found this difficult to believe, but she watched the light shining in Ria's eyes, and saw the life filling her gestures. Ria was not withdrawn any more: she was giving. 'Mum, it's wonderful. It's a lie, but it's telling the truth. All the girls at the factory say I'm a natural actress. When I'm singing "Ria", I'm out of myself. Mum, they all say how good I am, and how I make them laugh until they cry, and they love it. They love *me*.'

'That's as may be, but I don't want any daughter of mine on the stage,' Esther had grumbled. 'I know the sort of types you find there.'

'I can look after myself.'

Esther shot back cruelly: 'I'm sure you said that before you had Will.'

'That was different, I loved him,' Ria said, then burst into tears. 'I love him!' Esther stared at her. If she was acting, she was telling the truth.

And in truth, Esther welcomed the idea of a change of job for Ria. She was sure that working in the Arsenal was harming her health. Ria thought that anything was worth a pay packet of five pounds a week, but she was working with a group of girls making TNT explosive. They were called 'canaries' because of the yellow colour the chemicals stained their skin. Ria had developed a cough and a sore chest, and she suffered from giddy spells that made her sway as if she was drunk. The symptoms disappeared after a few days off work, but Esther was worried that if she worked there for very long they would not disappear at all.

It was fearfully dangerous work filling the shells or screwing down fuses; to lose a finger was commonplace, and several girls had been blown apart. A dozen had gone in one flash at Silvertown. The girls didn't care. For the first time in their lives, they had money to spare. They wore heavy leather aprons and strode out to the pubs at lunchtime with their arms linked, filling the pavement, knocking any pedestrians they met into the gutter. There were over a million of them now, a female army, singing in loud voices, drunk on gin. It was to try and keep them sober – and output up – that Mr Lloyd George had introduced the draconian licensing hours that reduced pub opening times from over twenty hours a day to a few at lunchtime and a few more in the evening.

Ria was not as strong as the other girls, but after a few drinks she came out of herself, and she could bring the house down. Her Charlie Chaplin walk made the whole department double up with laughter. She could blink through her curls as beguilingly as Mary Pickford. She memorized the poems of Rupert Brooke, and when she spoke them in a voice softer than her own the big tough girls, many of whom had sweethearts fighting somewhere in France, sat in a ring around her lost in their private thoughts, with tears streaming down their faces; and Ria was so affected by this well of real emotion that her skill had tapped, that she cried too.

'This has got to stop,' Mr Kirschbaum, the supervisor, told her in his office.

'Does that mean you're giving me the sack?' demanded Ria belligerently.

'You're affecting output,' Mr Kirschbaum said. 'There's a place for a talent like yours, and it isn't here.'

'So I'm out, then?'

'Calm down.' Mr Kirschbaum treated the women as though they were as dangerous and unstable as the nitroglycerine they worked with. The girls thought he was patronizing, but he was a quiet, kindly man with nine children and a genuine fear of hysterical explosions – emotions exhausted him, and all he wanted was a quiet life, which was a good ambition for the supervisor of an explosives department to have, Ria supposed. She glowered at him.

Mr Kirschbaum pushed a slip of paper across his desk. 'My brother Stanley is stage manager at the Queen's. Maybe he can get you in.'

Ria snatched the paper. She held it to her chest.

'You can thank me some other time,' Mr Kirschbaum said.

Ria folded her arms around her. She backed to the door. She imagined the limelights flaring in her face, and the roar of the audience safely back beyond the glare. She unwrapped her arms, dropped her hands onto her hips. She tossed her head, her hair flew out of her eyes, and she leaned down across Mr Kirschbaum's desk and gave him a bussing kiss on the cheek.

'Go on, get out of here,' Mr Kirschbaum said, flustered and fumbling for his handkerchief. After all, he was a married man.

'Thanks, Mr Kirschbaum,' Ria said from the door.

Anything is better for Ria than working in the munitions factory, Esther thought, *even the stage*. And she would still have plenty of time with Will, because actresses worked long hours, three performances every day.

Esther crossed the road to show Will the river. He loved the water and the wheeling gulls. She held him up. Her heart stopped. There was a body in the water. Two lightermen were down there, shoving a hook through his belt – if it was a he – to sway him up. Pc Jarvis stood on the dockside with his notebook out, staring down. Esther held Will against her, hiding his face. The body came swinging up out of the water, arms and legs splayed, muddy water spurting from his trouser-legs and the gaping mouth where the fish had nibbled him, and from his eyes.

It was Mr Blumenthall.

Esther remembered Jimmy's death, that same spurting of muddy water, and how she had screamed, and screamed, and screamed. It had no power to touch her now. It was nothing to do with her. She felt sorry for him, but she was grateful to be unconnected: she had known Mr Blumenthall only distantly. Vic and Nigel had known him better, and they'd be ever so upset that his poor, horrible corpse had been found floating in the river.

Carefully keeping his head turned away, she replaced Will in his pram and pushed him home. It was time for his feed; and she could do with a nice cup of tea.

6

Ben yawned and rolled out of the camp-bed. It was going to be brutally cold in the air: pilots and observers followed the example of London policemen, wearing ladies' silk stockings beneath their trousers. He paused, for a moment feeling bitterly homesick for his city.

Over long johns and leather jodhpurs, he dragged on the heavy sheepskin boots. Observers now had regulation-issue jackets: in tan leather, smooth-fronted and without visible buttons, it came down to his thighs and was secured by a flap down the side that provided no opening to the gale. Finally he pulled on the wrap-around helmet in soft leather which, together with the goggles, almost totally enclosed his head, and went outside, casually swinging his enormous sheepskin gloves, smiling and thinking: *Is this the day that I die?*

All the boys were walking over the grass, casually swinging their gloves and smiling. By the canvas hangar he saw a serious-faced Hal Parrant take a swig of Dutch courage from the miniature bottle of Teacher's, and button it back into his map pocket, then smile.

It was still dark on the ground, and the grass was too dull to show green yet, but the dawn sky was a tremendous arch of china blue above them.

Bertie was talking to Mackelroy the Australian, tapping

at a letter with his fingertip. Ben eavesdropped. 'Pater is not very happy with me . . . still says I joined up behind his back, etcetera.'

'Didn't you? Thought that was the idea!' Mackelroy said bluntly.

'What really irks him is that I didn't join his old regiment.'

'Tell him go jump in the lake!' came Mackelroy's voice. Living on a sheep station seventy-five miles from the nearest pub or telegraph office, he had seen the war coming long before the politicians had. He was the bravest man Ben had ever known – not a fool, but overcoming fear with courage. Ben understood that.

'Your life's your own, mate, isn't it?' Mackelroy asked Bertie challengingly.

Bertie shrugged. *That's not an answer*, Ben thought. Bertie simply said: 'That sort of attitude is hardly the best way to ensure Pater's continued goodwill.'

'Pappy's a big noise, is he?'

'Well, Sir Ozwald can tend to be noisy.'

'Hi, Ben,' Mackelroy said. Ben slapped his shoulder.

He tried to imagine – they all had, when Mackelroy told them – living seventy-five miles from the nearest pub. No fences, no trees, no churches, no villages, no stately homes. Mackelroy had to go as far as London to Birmingham for a drink – and nothing on the way! In London, everywhere you looked there was always something to see, and the more you looked the more you saw. The Thames was always churning up Roman coins and Viking swords for little boys to find. So much human life had happened that there wasn't room for it, and anywhere you stood it was stacked down in layer after layer beneath you, if only you knew about it. Not all the world was like that, Mackelroy said. In Waramgiri, if you dug down, you didn't even find water. It was vast and simple out there, but connected: the war had pulled Mackelroy twelve thousand miles. *Mackelroy's wrong*, Ben thought. *Even down there, his life was not his own.*

Ben said: 'Hallo, Bertie.'

'Good morning, sergeant,' Bertie said coldly.

'I'm away,' waved Mackelroy.

The despatch rider came from wing headquarters with orders, and as they walked out alone to the aeroplane Bertie, very spick and span in his Burberry and polished boots, instructed Ben tersely that it was to be a two-hour offensive patrol: they were going out looking for German machines. Who would doubtless be already waiting for them, higher, in the eye of the sun, Ben thought, but Bertie would just say that orders were orders. Major Trent-Maynard, the Commanding Officer, standing leaning on his stick, called over: 'Good hunting, chaps! Bring me back a Hun brush or two, would you?'

'Right-oh, sir,' Bertie said dutifully. The CO was mad keen on fox-hunting, and had bagged a large collection of their bushy tails as trophies. He loved war. *Play hard, fight hard,* was his motto, and Ben knew that a man under his command who did that could do no wrong; drink, womanize, stunt, smash up his machine, it didn't matter, as long as he brought back German tails when he flew up into the sky.

'Right-oh, sir!' Ben said, in the proper accent, pausing.

'That's the spirit,' the major glowed, blowing through his white moustaches. No pilot in the squadron was older than twenty-six, and he was old enough to be their father. Ben, looking into his eyes, realized that Major Trent-Maynard suffered hell each time he sent his boys blaring up into the air, because there was always one of them who would not come back; and tomorrow there would be another, while he stood here making poor jokes and sending them up. Ben nodded. The bright sun rose, scattering rays.

He followed Bertie to their machine. 'What height are we flying at?'

'As high as we can get, of course,' snapped Bertie.

Ben asked flatly: 'What's the matter with you?'

Bertie cast back over his shoulder, 'I beg your pardon?' as if that was not the way for sergeants to speak to officers. Ben stopped. He hated that cold upper-class condescension. He wasn't going to let Bertie get away with it.

'I thought we were friends,' he said in a dark voice. *I thought we weren't alone.*

Bertie hunched his shoulders. Dew speckled his boots. He turned back.

Different expressions struggled on his face.

'Ben, we are friends!' He hesitated. That was all.

Ben waited with ruthless silence. 'You're my best friend,' Bertie admitted at last. Ben watched his face. He loved Bertie like the father he had never had. 'My only friend,' Bertie said, 'the only man I trust.' It was true, Ben knew.

'But you have Colleen O'Keeffe,' he pointed out.

At that, Bertie's haunted expression changed. What did he see? His eyes widened. A smile – a quite different sort of smile – trembled on his lips. Almost a smile of relief.

'You don't know,' Bertie whispered. 'You don't know everything.'

Of course not; Ben had never pretended that he did. What was Bertie talking about? 'Know what?' he asked.

Bertie said: 'Everything. Secrets. Everyone has secrets.' He narrowed his eyes against the sun.

'Not friends.'

'Especially friends,' said Bertie. 'Yes. Yes!'

Ben said harshly: 'You've got everything. Father, mother, money, God, everything. Why do you want secrets too?'

'So that we can remain friends,' Bertie said. That was too neat, too clever. If it was the truth, it was not all the truth; the truth that hid a lie. When people lived lies, Ben knew, misery was born. He *knew*.

'Tell me!' he said, staring into Bertie's eyes. No more lies.

Bertie's face contorted, melted. He told the truth. 'I—'

'Airplane's fuelled and ready, sir,' the fitter interrupted, wiping his hands on a piece of oily waste.

Bertie recovered his poise. 'Very well.'

'Thank you, sir,' the fitter said, and saluted.

Bertie turned to Ben. 'We're the best of friends, that's all.' He touched Ben's elbow shyly, only with his fingertips, with an obvious effort. 'God, you're ambitious,' he said, 'like an iron wheel, that almost nothing could stop. Don't exploit me, Ben.'

Engines were starting up, racketing and blaring, the roaring slipstreams flapping the straps of Bertie's leopard-skin helmet out like wings.

'Wouldn't dream of it,' Ben said.

The Germans fell on them from out of the sun.

Ben fired the Lewis gun blindly into the glare, standing up in the cockpit. Bertie stood their machine almost over on the wingtips in a falling turn. Ben felt himself go quite light, and had to hang on to the Lewis gun mounting to pull himself down. A green vortex of fields revolved on his right, below him; and above him, to his left, was filled with blinding blue sky. Then the sun swung behind their upper wings, dropping him into shadow, and he had to stop firing in case he shot up his own machine – the gun-swivel was not fitted with stops.

He risked his sight and opened his eyes wide, glimpsed the German machine hanging vertically by its tail out the sun. It was a beautiful silhouette, one that he had never seen before, a new type of machine. And that terrific rate of fire: two machine-guns, actually firing forward through the propeller. A new machine! Which ace was flying it? New machines were only issued to the best pilots.

An ace in a brilliant new machine that could plummet out of the sun.

The German flashed past them, painted bright red, with black crosses on the wings. It swooped like a red insect across the map of fields below, then came up in a climbing turn behind them. Ben threw his empty drum of ammunition over the side and fitted a new one.

No Allied machine was so fast, so streamlined.

Is this the day that I die?

'God, help us!' Bertie cried.

He turned towards Hal Parrant's clumsy machine, trying to protect his tail from the German. Ben saw George Trewarren's scarf.

The grey-green FEs with their long wing-spans and slow, stately flight, majestic but lumbering turns, looked like giant butterflies cruising through the air, beset by stinging red insects buzzing and weaving around them.

One khaki-green butterfly slid below Ben pursued by a buzzing red gnat: he saw Mackelroy standing up in the cockpit, his legs stained with blood, firing back with the Lewis gun mounted on the top wing.

Above, a British machine gently heeled over then fell away from Ben's sight, dwindling until all he could see of it was a white flame revolving slowly down towards the French earth.

'Who was it?' he shouted. 'Who was it?'

He pulled the triggers. The German pilot pulled away from Mackelroy. The Australian looked up as he passed below Ben. 'I owe you one, mate!' he yelled over the swaying abyss. He had been hit in the knees, the war was over for him. He pointed at Bertie in some sort of warning for Ben, then his machine swooped for home. Ben turned.

Bertie had been hit: blood made red rivulets down one cheek, and the slipstream was pulling red lines around the side of his head. The German's first burst had caught them after all. But Bertie waved, the sun flashing on his goggles: *I'm all right.*

He pulled the FE back in a staggering turn towards Parrant's machine.

Ben felt a cold sweat break out on his face.

He isn't all right, he knew.

The observer's cockpit had no duplicate controls.

This was what no one ever talked about; the long fall, standing alone in the nose, waiting, helpless, and no parachute, and the instructors never mentioned it: bad for morale.

The German ace turned behind them.

The Lewis gun jammed. Ben cursed, banged the drum, tried again, nothing: he could hear the rising wail of the enemy's engine. They were wingtip to wingtip with Hal Parrant's machine. Bertie was lolling in his seat, senseless.

Ben, struggling to clear his gun, glanced across straight into George Trewarren's face: he was screaming with fear.

Ben saw the terrible moment of truth.

The machine crumpled, rolled sickeningly, swayed, skidded, then her wings lost touch with the gentle kiss of the slipstream, flapped, fluttered, dragged, her pilot was dead, shot to pieces, she fell slowly out of the air.

This time there was no one to hide Ben's face. He saw it all, hated it all.

The machine flew alone, steadily droning. Around them was clear air. Bertie lolled with his head on one shoulder, his arm hanging stiffly over the side of the pilot's cockpit: pressed backwards by the slipstream almost into the propeller behind.

The machine jarred briefly in some turbulence, and Bertie's head rolled from side to side. He was out cold.

No one was flying the machine. She was flying herself, and she would continue to drone steadily through the air until she ran out of fuel.

That would take about an hour, Ben thought. He thought about it like playing cards, allowing no trace of his feelings to show on his face.

Perhaps ninety minutes.

Then the engine would stop, the aeroplane would lose her balancing act, and she would probably start to spin, round and round, down and down, until . . .

He remembered George Trewarren's screaming face.

The FE rocked and swayed in turbulence again. A red shape rose up from beneath, so close that he could see the face of the German pilot. Ben froze, his hands clenched around the drum of the jammed Lewis gun, staring.

Both men raised their goggles. The other man wanted to be recognized.

Ben knew him from the photographs. Slicked blond hair, face smoothly clean-shaven, no sideburns at all, handsome features, thin-nosed, arrogant, a slightly pouting upper lip, cold blue eyes: Adolf Münchener. Each man stared into the face of his enemy, fascinated.

Then the German ace raised one gloved hand and pointed at the side of his machine. There was his name, proudly displayed in black. He tapped the stencilled letters. member me.

Münchener raised his hand in salute: not as one flier to another, because Ben could not fly, but as one man who flew in the face of death to another man. The chivalry of brothers in arms.

Münchener's machine swung agilely towards the sun, then turned away in a perfect curve, dwindled, disappeared.

And Ben flew onward, helplessly.

He looked down. Two miles below him crawled the Front.

He stared ahead. The Somme river was as blue as if it was drawn on an atlas.

Down river, Amiens glistened; he could pick out the great cathedral spire shining in the morning light.

Ninety minutes.

The fuselage sloped steeply back up to the pilot's windscreen. By lying on the slope maybe he could get his arms over the windscreen . . . and reach the control stick. But that would not help him reach the rudder pedals on the floor; and anyway that upright Triplex windscreen made it all impossible.

He didn't give up.

There had to be another way.

There was. Out there.

Ben swung his legs over the edge of the front cockpit and felt for the toehold. There it was – and only room for one foot. He clung on the side of the machine with his left leg dragged out into space, and the gale jerking at him.

His goggles tore off against a bracing wire and flew back, gonging into the propeller. The machine took on a faint but perceptible vibration. He could feel it where his body was pressed against the fabric, and in his fingertips. He reached back into the bracing wires between the wings.

A wire cut thinly into his cheek, pushing him out.

His foot skidded from the toehold.

He hung from the cockpit rim by one hand, the other around the wire.

He tried to swing around the wire at his cheek but it caught his collar. He was jammed. He couldn't go forward or back. The wire began to press into his throat.

He dangled, writhing, high above the earth. His left hand began to slip on the wire.

He was going to fall.

He jerked desperately and felt his collar tear free. A frantic lunge with his left hand brought Bertie's arm flopping over the pilot's cockpit rim above him in reach. He clamped his fingers around Bertie's wrist. It was slick with cold sweat and the flesh slithered through Ben's hand as he slipped down.

Ben let go with his right hand and punched through the fabric covering the side of the aeroplane. He found a strut and clung to it. It bent, but held.

He hung there for a moment, gasping. He could feel beads of sweat over his face, pressed upwards by the slipstream.

Then he jerked up again catching Bertie's elbow with his left hand, hammering with his feet through the fabric until he had a good enough hold to stand on with one leg, and pulled himself up. Done it!

He leaned over the side of the pilot's cockpit. No room for two. He stayed where he was.

Now for the difficult bit.

Ben searched for the airfield. The Somme river would make a curve that he would recognize . . .

Between the side of the machine and his dangling right foot, a field no bigger than his foot slowly disappeared and the river curved into view.

He could just reach the throttle with his fingertips, and the stick quite easily, but he could steer the machine only by pressing on one or the other of Bertie's knees to operate the foot-rudder. She was going down quite steeply; the slipstream seemed very strong.

Now he entered a layer of warmer air. He smelled growing things, and the odour of sun-warmed earth.

Now he could hear the cries of wild duck taking off in alarm from the river as he came wobbling in over the willow-tops.

Now the ground seemed to move fast. A herd of cows made a splayed pattern galloping away from him.

He could not see the airfield now; it was hidden by the trees. As the treetops raced beneath him, he heard the hiss of the slipstream following him in the leaves.

Between two tall poplars, an open space: the airfield, the Bessoneau hangars – he was coming from the wrong direction. They'd have to get out of the way. He tilted the wings between the two tall trees, a hedge flashed beneath, he hit the button that cut the motor. For a moment she floated, as if reluctant to leave the air, then he pulled back on the stick with his fingertips and she landed perfectly.

'My boy,' Trent-Maynard said, 'that is the most brilliant demonstration of flying that I have ever seen in my life.'

'My pilot's hit.'

Bertie was lifted down. He was murmuring, recovering consciousness. 'Only a head wound,' someone said. 'Bullet creased the side of his skull. Good thing old Bertie's got such a thick head.'

'Tell off the Crossley to take him to a casualty clearing station, get the Army Medical Officer to look him over,' Ben ordered.

Trent-Maynard took his elbow. 'I'm going to mention you in my despatch. A field commission. You're going to come out of this an officer, my boy, if I have anything to do with it!'

'Congratulations, Ben,' Bertie said from the stretcher. 'You always get what you want, don't you.'

Chapter Thirteen

1

'Break a leg,' said Stanley Kirschbaum cheerfully, which was his theatrical way, she knew, of wishing her good luck with her act.

'Thanks, Stan.' Ria, waiting in the wings, wound her string of false pearls nervously between her fingers. She was on next. On stage the ventriloquist was coming to the close of his act, making the voice of Kaiser Bill, the German marionette with a spiked helmet and outrageously up-turned moustache, rise to a gabble. Ria knew what was happening: Lord Tommy Atkins, the other dummy, dressed as a plucky British soldier, was going to punch the Kaiser smack on the kisser, and Kaiser Bill's head and legs would fly off on springs, with any luck.

She heard the audience roar with laughter. It had work-ed. She was on any moment now. Her tummy felt like it was trying to block her throat. The joints in her fingers ached and tickled frightfully, and her mouth was dry. She would have given anything for a glass of water. She couldn't go on without drinking a glass of water. Stage fright. She simply couldn't. Just one sip of water would give her strength. But there wasn't any. Perhaps there was just time to run back, there was a glass in the dressing room . . .

Stan peeked out around the edge of the curtain. 'Hoi, Ria!' he called.

She jumped nervously. 'What is it?'

He looked at her with eyes round with amazement. 'The

King's in the audience!' She forgot all about needing a sip of water.

'Oh, he *isn't!*' squeaked Ria, peering out in terror, 'is he?'

'And there's the Prime Minister,' Stan said. 'And look! There's Douglas Fairbanks, swinging down from the balcony!'

She pulled back, her face flushing, and tossed her long blonde curls angrily.

'Gotcha!' Stan laughed.

'I could give you a smack in the kisser, I really could,' Ria stormed.' 'See if your head flew off on a spring, what?'

Stan kissed her cheek. 'You're on, love.' She'd forgotten! He nodded to the boy on the curtain-ropes and stepped back. Ria was bathed in brilliant light. The audience began to roar. She walked into the glare.

Now she swaggered. She wasn't Ria Price. She was Ria the vegetable girl, out for a good night out. Her dress was electric-blue, and fell from her shoulders in layers of flounced, shimmering satin.

How they loved her! Ria's eyes glittered with tears; ecstasy.

The neckline was very décolleté. Such a low, saucy swoop would have been out of the question before the war. This, after all, was not the West End stage; but the East End audience had changed. The soldiers roared approval of her plunging cleavage – she was wearing a new invention called a brassière, and no corset. She crossed to the centre of the stage with a swinging, high-stepping freedom of movement unthinkable a few years ago.

And the dress showed her ankles; when she kicked her legs or swung round quickly, as the act required her to do several times, it even showed her knees. Mrs Hiscott had run it up to Ria's own design.

Ria paused at centre-stage, feeling through her dress, looking for something. Not there on her left side, not here on her right. It was silent mime because the noise was so terrific. Here it was! She pulled an apple from her pocket and polished it on her satin thigh, then stopped, looking across her shoulder at the audience as though she had just noticed them. The boys cheered her to the echo.

She swaggered to the front of the stage and held up the apple. 'Well, I *am* a girl what's doing very well in the vegetable line. No, I *am!*' She put one hand aggressively on her hip.

Most of the audience were soldiers. They jumped to their feet, waving their arms and cheering the vivid girl on the stage. They all wanted her. Some older people rose to their feet to walk out, offended by Ria's sauciness. Ria stood with both hands on her hips, as if she too was offended by the soldiers' rowdy response to her perfectly innocent remark. She shook her head. 'No, no.' The people sat down again. She repeated her catchphrase: 'Now, now, quieten down, boys.' That just made the boys noisier again, as she had known it would.

Ria pretended to take a honking bite out of the apple – she had to pretend, she couldn't eat and sing at the same time – then tossed it out to a soldier-boy who caught her eye. He grabbed it and held it to his lips. His mates elbowed him and tried to snatch it but he hung on.

Suddenly Ria threw out her arms, only a slim girl in electric-blue, golden curls tumbling over her shoulders, but an utterly commanding figure. Her tone of voice changed. 'Now, now, boys. Tons of hush. Let a girl sing her song, do.'

An expectant hush fell.

The orchestra down in the pit struck up the boisterous tune of 'Wotcher, Ria!' and Ria swaggered to the very front of the stage. She cocked her hands on her hips, and sang:

'I'm a girl what's doing very well in the vegetable line, And as I'd saved a bob or two, I thought I'd cut a shine. So I goes and buys some toggery, these here very clothes you see (it's called Electric Blue, don't you love it, boys?) – And with the money I had left, I thought I'd have a spree. So I goes into a music hall where I'd often been afore, I don't go in the gallery but on the bottom floor; I sits down by the Chairman and I calls: "A pot of Stout!" But my pals in the gallery spotted me, and they all commenced to shout –'

She held up her arms, gesturing upwards with her hands. 'Here you go boys, get it off your chests!' The soldiers, who knew the song as well as she did, stamped their feet and with deep male voices bellowed the chorus:

> 'Wotcher Ria? Ria's on the job!
> Wotcher Ria? Did you speculate a bob?
> Oh, Ria she's a toff!
> And she looks immensikoff!
> And we all shouted, "Wotcher, Ria?" '

They broke out cheering and applauding themselves. 'Now now, quieten down, boys.' They wouldn't. Ria, pretending offence, turned her back on them. She held her hands on her waist, standing with her hips slightly cocked to show off the lovely line of her bottom. The back of one of her knees showed through a slit in the dress, she knew, a shadowed, seductive curve. Whistles, then finally the noise began to die away. She felt for the right moment, then held up one finger. That was all. Silence fell.

She turned, very slowly. 'Oh, naughty boys,' she said, shaking her head, and before they had time to laugh, or the tension to break, the orchestra tore into the next verse, and Ria shouted:

'So I chaffed me old mates back again, but it weren't a bit of use, The poor old Chairman's baldy head they treated with abuse; They threw an orange down at me, it went bang inside a pot, The beer went up like a fountain, and a toff copped all the lot; It went slap in his chevy, and it made an awful mess, But what gave me the needle was, it spoilt me blooming dress. I thought it was getting rather warm, so I goes towards the door, When a man shoved out his gammy leg, and I fell smack on the floor!'

She stopped with a jerk, catching them out. Dead silence. She looked across her shoulder, blinking her long eyelashes through her golden curls.

I've got them, she thought. *They're mine. I can do anything with them.*

'Aren't you going to give it to me, boys?' Provocatively: 'I mean, give me the chorus?'

They did, cheering and roaring out the chorus, and she

sang along with them, and every time they shouted *Wotcher, Ria* she pointed at herself and marched like a soldier, elbows swinging, knees high.

She stopped.

The orchestra stopped. Not a sound. Only Ria's voice, holding them.

Ria said: 'So, this is what happened next. I turned around and spoke to this old gentleman with the wooden appendage very politely. I said' – she shouted – ' "*Wotcher want to go and shove your bloody old gammy leg out like that for?*" When my pals spot I'm having a row, and they see the old man has got a wooden leg, they shout—'

All together as she raised her arms the soldiers shouted '*Wotcher! Half a man and half a tree!*' They loved that line.

The orchestra struck up and Ria sang: 'Now the gent that keeps the Music Hall he patters to the bloke. Of course they blamed it all on me, but I couldn't see the joke. So I upped and told the guv'nor as how he'd shoved me down, And his jolly old wooden leg had tore the frilling off my gown. Me old Electric Blue, boys!' She lifted the hem high to show them the rip, actually an artfully contrived slit, one knee chastely bent against the other. The soldiers whistled and she innocently tried to show it to them better, then realized that they only cared about her long legs, put her hand to her mouth, and threw the hem down blushingly. 'Now now, boys . . . Lord bless you, it weren't a bit of use, the toff was on the job. They said: "*Outside!*" and out I went, and they stuck to my bob.' Fists on hips, she shouted indignantly: 'Yes, boys, they wouldn't even give me my bob back! Of course I left so wild, to think how I'd been taken down, Next time I'll go in the gallery with my pals, you bet a crown!'

She let them roar the chorus, *Wotcher, Ria!* by themselves. They didn't need her help: she held them, she knew, in the outstretched palms of her hands. She felt the power. A warm glow suffused her body and her eyes and lips were moist. They loved her. She felt it running through her.

She cupped her hands and drew them towards her,

enclosing herself in her arms, hugging them to her with the joy of giving and taking.

When the chorus was drowned in swelling applause, she curtseyed and pretended to go off, but when they wouldn't let her she gave them an encore, then stood there blowing kisses to them, walking away backwards into the shadows.

All through her song, she had hardly seen them: pale faces, waving arms in the glare. She had performed an intimate act with them, and she hadn't known them at all; yet no feeling could be cleaner, no emotion more pure.

She was happy.

Ria came out of the stage door into the dark. As always by the time the last show was ended, she felt drained, tired out of her mind. Will would be tucked up asleep. She would hardly have the strength to kiss him good night and put a smile on her face if he woke. She knew that she didn't have naturally motherly feelings like Esther, but she would never have done anything to hurt Will, and if she had thought that her career was affecting him badly, or that he wasn't getting the love that he needed, she would have given it up. She simply didn't know how to respond to him, or what his cries meant. Esther always said instantly: 'He's hungry,' or whatever it was, and it was always news to Ria. She even held him clumsily. She could *feel* an audience; she felt very little when she held Will, except a fear that she would drop him. She could show her love to an audience of strangers, but somehow to her own baby, her own flesh, she could not.

Yet she did love him.

A small crowd of soldiers waited for her under the light. Older players had told Ria that actors and actresses used to be cut dead in the street. It had changed. Onstage, Ria was not now a mere performer, she was an idol; and even in real life, she was a star. She, not the show, was *it*. People waited respectfully to meet her, usually men but not always, as if her star magic would rub off on them, and add to their life.

Ria said directly: 'Now now, boys, what's all this about?'

'It's her!' somebody said. 'It's Miss Price.' She prepared to sign a few autographs, and to smile her thanks for the shyly offered compliments about her act. Instead, a wicker-work bath-chair on three big black wheels was wheeled forward. Half-sitting in it was a crumpled, disjointed shape, a man in uniform, a cap crooked on his head, his knees covered by a rug. He looked around him blindly. He was awful. She had to say something.

What could she possibly say?

'Hallo, soldier,' she said. The head turned towards her eagerly. 'You know who I am, don't you?'

'Jim can't talk really,' one of the soldiers said. 'He got gassed at the battle of Loos, see.'

'Gas!' Ria said. 'You poor bloke. Those Hun bastards.'

The soldiers said: 'It was our gas.'

Someone added: 'The wind changed, see. Blew it back on us.'

Ria bent down. She had a horror of gas. She'd heard that it literally rotted the lungs away. She bent down and patted Jim's bony hand. 'Now listen here, soldier, you get better soon, you promise me?'

She watched his lips move. He was struggling to speak. Ria recoiled at the unspeakable stench of rotten breath as his mouth opened.

'Half a man,' he croaked, 'and half a tree.' He pushed at the blanket and it slipped aside. One of his legs was of shiny wood.

'He loves that line in your song, that's his favourite,' the other soldier said. 'You can see his eyes light up when he hears it.'

Ria squeezed the hand. 'You'll be singing along in a year or two, right as rain.' The fingers curled around hers. They both knew it was a lie.

Ria knew what she had to do. She bent down and kissed his lips.

'Thanks,' said one of the soldiers quietly. 'He adores you, and we didn't know how to ask.'

Ria said brightly: 'We're all fighting this war, aren't we. Men and women together, right? For the first time ever, together.'

'Miss Price,' said another soldier, 'we'd like you to know

that whatever anyone else ever says about you, you are a Star.'

<h1 style="text-align:center">2</h1>

Esther was wrong when she said that nothing stuck to Vic. He always felt injured whenever he heard that remark from his ungrateful mother. Vic knew that everything stuck to him for, like an elephant, he never forgot anything. He had a thick skin, but he felt wounds easily, and so he never forgave an insult. Neither did he ever forget a favour: someone who had done him good once might well be persuaded, or forced, to do so again. Either was a way into their heart.

But nothing could truly hurt him, he thought.

He was no good writing letters, so he sent Ria the printed Army postcards: *I am well/not well; I will be home soon/not soon.* They said all he needed to say.

If Esther had said that Vic was one of those people who always somehow manage to land on their feet, he thought, she would have been right. He had landed on his feet in France. What a lovely place, what a land of opportunity it was. Shame about Nigel: transferred straight to the Front where the Hun was breaking through. Poor old Nigel must be suffering, he thought, must be terrified of getting gassed or killed and losing all that learning his head was stuffed with.

But Nigel hadn't been quick enough spraining his ankle.

Besides, it would have looked suspicious if both of them sprained their ankles.

So Vic hobbled about on light duties in Supply. The supply officer was a weedy type with glasses and too high an opinion of himself to see that his accounting was sloppy. He spent a lot of time down at the village, too. It was a typical example of military waste: there was Nigel at the Front getting shot at when he would have been brilliant in the office, and here was Vic having the time of his life.

And there was such a lovely lot of waste. Vic had assumed that in a war, nearly everyone fought, except the generals. Not a bit of it. Nearly everyone was in Supply. Andy Blazey, the guileful clerk from Portsmouth, explained to Vic that for every one soldier actually fighting at the Front, ten were working on cushy jobs in Supply.

The quantities were so colossal. 'The Army deals in averages, see. They're clever. They know it takes a hundred shells on average to kill one enemy, so obviously they've got to have millions of shells. Every million shells, see, will kill ten thousand men, which must be useful.'

On average it took twenty thousand bullets to kill one man, and so tens of millions of bullets were stored and distributed by Supply. It was a huge task. Locomotives transported from England arrived every day dragging trainloads of the stuff – and paid the French railways twenty pounds a mile for the privilege, which kept thousands of clerks busy in administration. 'That's the lovely thing about a war – everyone has a job.'

There were half a million cans of corned beef, Vic knew, stored in this one depot.

The French were hungry, especially over in the town. You could see it in their faces. Vic wondered how much they would pay for corned beef.

He thought about that a lot.

The tents were all blown down in the autumn gales, so he was billeted with a French baker's family in the village. At first they were hostile; no doubt about it. Madame spoke a little English, and gradually he understood that it wasn't personal: they simply did not trust the British. They did not trust the British soldiers to leave when the war was won for *La France*.

Vic tried to eat the plate of foreign cassoulet that she put in front of him. It was years since this part of France had been ruled by the British Kings, but the peasants' blood remembered. Vic nodded; he could understand that. He sucked a piece of lard until it melted in his mouth. It was the only part of the meal which did not taste of garlic, which he loathed.

Later, as the French tried to win back control, there had been terrific battles. Knights and warhorses, bows and arrows. Gangs of English thugs and robbers had roamed the countryside, looting, burning and murdering. Nobody remembered back that far, Vic realized. But it was rooted in the blood: the fear that the British would not go.

'Don't worry,' Vic said, looking at the rain sheeting across the muddy courtyard, 'we can't wait to leave.'

'You are as bad as each other,' Madame Jacqueline said, 'you German peoples.'

But there was more to it than that. When Vic brought them a few cans of corned beef, which made the four young children dance for joy around the kitchen table, still the attitude of Monsieur Pierre and Madame Jacqueline did not unfreeze. Monsieur's van was abandoned in a corner of the yard for lack of what he called *essence*, and he had gone back to using his father's traditional cart, pulled by a large white and brown dog of great amiability and laziness. Vic lifted the bonnet of the van and looked at the engine: a petrol engine.

'Look, Pierre,' he offered, 'I can get you a few cans of *essence*, if you want.'

'*Combien?*' That meant how much.

Vic wrapped his arm around Pierre's shoulder. 'For you, cheapo,' he said. 'You are *mon ami*.'

They drank to it sitting by the fire. 'Your officer is a pig,' Pierre confided later, nodding seriously. Like all Frenchmen, he was capable of speaking English if he really wanted to. *Now I'm getting there*, Vic thought, *I've nearly got him.*

Vic refilled his glass. 'All officers are pigs,' he smiled encouragingly.

Pierre shook his head. 'This officer, Captain Schmidt—'

'Smythe.'

'Smythe. He is a true swine.' Vic waited while Pierre drank his glass. They had reached the stage of the confidences. 'The cousin of my wife is Jean-Claude, he is the patron of the *estaminet*.' Vic nodded; he could see the lights of the busy café across the road. 'His daughter is Alouette, a girl most charming and . . . with a hot nature.'

Pierre's English broke down. He patted his stomach.

Vic understood. He added lemon to his wine to take off

the horrible sharp taste, drank it, and leaned back with a
smile of pleasure. He knew how it would work. He would
use the pregnant girl to blackmail Captain Smythe, nothing
actually said, of course, but everything understood in the
smile: your wife back home; bad for the Anglo-French
relations the top brass are so very, very hot about. Alouette
crying, parents furious, French pride outraged. End of your
career in Supply, sir, no question of a court-martial, you'd
just find yourself posted to the Front. Hopeless. The end.

But I can help you, sir.

He would route goods to the village in Pierre's van and
even Army three-tonners. Thereafter it was up to Pierre's
brother Armand, a butcher in the town; Vic didn't even
want to know, as long as he was paid.

And not in French francs either. In gold, even if they had
to take out the fillings in their teeth to get it. Lovely.

On a wintry evening when the rain was turning to snow,
Vic walked out of the office and as he crossed the road
someone called his name. Vic stopped with a jolt and
turned. He didn't like people calling his name; his name
was his. It was personal.

Some soldiers were sheltering under bashas, tarpaulins
strung up against the side of a cart. A white hand waved.
'Hallo, Vic.'

He recognized Raymond Trott. Knock me down with a
feather, Vic said to himself. He went over. 'What are you
doing here, Ray?'

'Doing a turn in the support trenches, then a tour at the
Front, apparently.' Ray spat. So he'd learned that. Very
manly.

'Lucky bastard,' Vic said, 'I'm stuck back here in Supply.'

He looked at Raymond Trott indifferently. The War
hadn't changed the boy much. He didn't wear the gold
rings on his fingers now of course, and his ever-so handsome
black-stubbled face was dirty, and so was his blond hair,
but it was still neatly combed. What a poseur he was. His
dad owned the big Old Bull and Bush pub where West End
toffs sometimes came out for an evening slumming. Dad

was a tough, but Mrs Trott was a real lady, and nothing was too good for her little Raymond. He'd grown up into a real little nancy-boy. Vic thought that his eyes were too close together, which always seemed to make a man attractive to women.

Vic said: 'If you see my brother Nigel, give him my regards. Ask him if he's heard from Ria, that's my sister. I haven't had a word from her.'

'I didn't know that you had a brother or a sister.'

Vic clapped him chummily on the shoulder. 'And I didn't know you had a mother, Ray. Look after yourself, won't you, love?'

Raymond shouted an obscenity after him. *Dear me*, thought Vic as he walked away, *that's something real men have taught him*.

3

Temporary Second Lieutenant Ben London was enjoying life, as he always did. Since his name had been mentioned in despatches, several of the illustrated papers carried his picture, his expression serious, manly and military, standing beside the aeroplane he had landed single-handed. At first he played along with the reporters' questions.

'Gee, you were really hanging from the side?'

'Yes.' British understatement; expected of him.

'You really saved the life of the pilot officer?'

'I suppose so.'

Actually the aeroplane the newsmen used was a DH4, not an FE2B, but the War Office Liaison Officer said that most of their readers were women and would never know the difference.

But Ben did. The photograph was a lie. He hated lies. One reporter asked him: 'Were you frightened?'

Ben said honestly: 'Terrified.'

The Liaison Officer said hastily: 'That was off the record.'

At first Ben enjoyed the attention. It was wonderful to be wanted. Girls that he had never met came up to him in the railway station, clasped their hands in front of their bosoms, and affected not to notice him. They followed him silently to the W.H. Smith bookstall and pretended to examine the magazines while he bought his newspaper. He found it both amusing and exciting. If he turned round, they melted away, or became intensely absorbed in the cover of *Exchange & Mart*, or looked at him with a show of extreme indifference. When he walked away, he felt a dozen pairs of eyes follow him.

He realized that they didn't know anything about the war, only what they read in the newspapers. How could they? It was away on the dark side of the world. He thought: *If only you knew the truth*. He couldn't tell them, for today he was famous, a symbol of the light. It would have been dreadful to tell those young girls what their sweethearts were going through.

So, smiling, wearing the bright face of fame, he turned and waved them goodbye from the forecourt, hating himself because he had to live the lie.

On the 'bus, the conductress said: 'You're him!' He smiled politely at some passengers who stared at him. Very politely: as Edith Rumney had taught him.

Another girl was waiting for him on the pavement, her fur coat and fur hat framing the palest blur of a face, holding a newspaper. He'd had enough, and slipped past her with his smile painted on his pressed lips.

He ran up the stairs to Bertie's flat in a towering rage. Bertie had given him the key, but he didn't need to use it. He heard Sam barking, then Mrs O'Keefe opened the door. She spread her arms wide. 'Ben! Praise be to God, and it's such a wonderful thing to be seeing you again!' She was not crying, but her eyes gleamed with tears of joy. He still wore his smile, but it eased and became genuine as she clasped him to her and held him. He felt that she had lost weight; there was talk of rationing. He felt Sam slobbering over his hand, then Sam's paws on his shoulders. 'He recognized you as soon as you got off the 'bus!' Colleen wept.

'Sit! Good dog.' Ben looked up at her. 'It's wonderful to be here again, Colleen.'

'Master Bertram has never called me by my name in all the years he's known me!' she gasped, wiping her eyes.

'You always sign your letters Colleen O'Keefe, bracket Mrs, close brackets,' he laughed. 'May I call you by your name?'

She was flustered. 'I've got the water on, I'll make you a nice pot of tea. Yes, of course!'

'Come and drink it with me. I want to talk to you.'

'In Master Bertram's room? I'm only the housekeeper, sir.'

'Ben. I thought that you were a woman who was proud of saying what she meant, Colleen. I thought that we could talk. We agreed, didn't we?'

He knelt by Sam and rolled him over, scratching his ginger stomach. Mrs O'Keeffe had looked after him stalwartly, but she was not a dog person, and Bertie had missed his faithful retainer. Ben had promised to take Sam back with him when he could arrange it. Many officers had their dogs out there. He looked up as Mrs O'Keeffe wheeled the tea trolley in. 'Chocolate cake!' he said. He thanked her for the ones that she had sent him in France. 'Lovely and sticky and smooth.'

They sat by the window in the flat afternoon sun. Colleen sat enjoying its heat, and enjoying watching him tuck into her cake, looking at him across the glittering silver and the beautiful, delicate china cups. His features, always regular, had firmed out. She thought how good a moustache would look on him. He shook his head. She sipped her tea. His eyes had lost none of that openness it was difficult to describe. They were eyes that one wanted to look into. It could have been that piercing colour, or that the pupils were very large . . . or something else.

She put down her cup. 'What's the matter, Ben?'

'You always know.'

'I can see it in your—' she nearly said the conventional word, *face*, then told the truth. 'I can see it in your eyes, Ben.'

'Mirrors of the soul.' He closed them, smiled, then opened them again. She saw how angry he was. He said bitterly: 'The war's making us all mad, Colleen.'

'You're overwrought.'

He told her about the girls at the station. She smiled then said in a slightly fixed voice: 'Since when does a young man object to being followed around by girls?'

'It's hero worship! I'm just an object to them, not a person.'

'I'm sure you'll learn to like girls.'

'I don't like anyone very much at the moment,' he admitted.

She busied herself for a few seconds, putting fresh water in the pot, then poured him another cup. He said: 'Is there enough for you?'

'Yes!' she said. She poured it. 'I was just thinking.'

'I'm being used,' Ben explained. 'Why has all this attention been drawn to me? Plenty of men have done brave things in this war, God knows, what I did was nothing. Until now even the names of officers were hardly mentioned in the newspapers, and other ranks, like I was, never. Now I'm splashed all over the front page. Why, Colleen? What's the reason?'

'Does there have to be one, Ben?'

He said furiously: 'We've already dragged the Commonwealth countries in, Canada, Australia, New Zealand, South Africa. And the Indians. I've even seen squads of Chinese. You know what I think, Colleen? They're trying to drag the United States of America into the war and they're using me, and others like me, to influence the American people – to give them heroes to identify with, to make the war exciting. Half the newsmen the Liaison Officer set up were American.' He looked up at her and she saw how upset he was.

'Ben, you've got to relax.'

'When they're using me to drag America into the war.'

'Not only you.'

'I know. But why won't the governments running this war be happy until the whole world is dragged in? It's a world war. Why, Colleen? What are we fighting for?'

She cut him another slice of cake to go with the one that

353

he had forgotten and said practically: 'Whatever it is, we won't win it without America.' She put down the knife. 'It's not governments,' she said, 'it's people.'

'I never knew that people were so devious.'

She demanded: 'Why aren't you eating your cake?'

'Sorry,' he said, just like a little boy, and tucked into the two wedges on his plate. She told him about the last letter from Bertie in France. His head wound was completely healed. Ben wondered. As he read the flat words of the letter he thought that Bertie sounded very weary of fighting.

The new German aeroplane was called an Albatros and flown in large formations of experienced fliers called Circuses. It was what Bertie called 'rather bad news for us.' Ben read the strain between the lines. Losses must be very high. There was no chivalry in the air any more: neither side showed mercy to the other now. There had been a convention that aircraft with dead engines were left alone to glide home: now the defenceless machine was a fair target, and the helpless men were shot out of the air.

Bertie wrote that he had heard a British pilot who had done this to a German, bragging in the Mess: *And he roasted the whole way down.*

'That's all we're left with, isn't it?' Ben said, in a voice that laid his heart bare. 'Winning.'

He toyed with his cake.

Colleen cleared her throat and went to the escritoire. 'Talking of letters, I forgot, this came today.' She came back with an envelope. Ben wiped his fingers on the napkin and held it. The Bunhill Row address had been written in graceful script on lavender paper: the colour that a woman might choose. The 7 in the address was barred in the continental style, 7, and England was written *Angleterre*. On the back was printed: Hôtel Crillon, Paris.

Ben sniffed it. Perfumed.

'Bertie's keeping a woman in Paris, the old dog!' he laughed.

'I do not believe so . . .'

'Smell it. The ladies of La Houssoye are experts at

perfume – heliotrope, jasmine, roses – and this is like none of them. All perfumes are made out of flowers, and their scent doesn't last. This one does. It must be very expensive. Bertie's fallen in love with an aristocrat!'

Colleen explained: 'I believe it may be from his French relations. The Benton-Benson family has ancient connections with the Count of Coucy. His estates have been overrun by the Germans – he is now a Colonel in the French Army, although he must be in his sixties. This letter is obviously from Chouchou, his wife, the Countess. Everyone calls her Chouchou, she's a darling. I've met her.' Colleen's eyes shone, she had obviously fallen in love with the girl. Her Irish brogue made the gentle French name sound like the call of an exotic bird: *Shou-shou, Shou-shou.*

'She's young, I believe from an old but impoverished family. Before the war she completed her education in this country, you see . . . and fell in love with Master Bertram – an adolescent infatuation, to be sure, but Sir Ozwald had some hopes of a marriage.'

'The blood must live on.'

'To be sure. Also, Sir Ozwald has many business interests in France. But instead she married the Count, who is the last of his line. He loved his first wife dearly, but she was barren . . .'

Ben thought: *I don't even know where my blood comes from. These people have it stretching behind them for generation after generation. Rows of faces staring down from the wall. They must be driven by it.*

Colleen said: 'Master Bertram liked her very much, but he did not love her.'

'He doesn't love anybody. He's a cold fish.'

'But you like him.'

'I love him, Colleen. He's been like a father to me. He saved me when I was lying on the river bank, and he didn't have to! He could have left me – nearly everyone would have left me there, Colleen, stinking and helpless. He didn't.'

There it was. Her eyes burned and she felt her tears start. She felt for the tabletop with her knuckles, and thumped

355

down into the chair. Groping for her handkerchief, she tried not to let herself think what she would say. She must say what she felt was right. She choked her words back once, then twice. Then she gasped:

'He loves you.'

'I know,' Ben said casually.

'Oh, thank God!' She tried to look at him through her tears: he *understood*, he *knew*. 'I can't find my handkerchief, Ben, I'm sorry.'

'Have mine.' He handed it over. She unfolded it – it was huge, a man's handkerchief, it seemed to keep unfolding forever. She wiped her eyes, then blew her nose.

She said: 'I thought it was my secret. His secret.'

He said nothing. Then he said gently: 'Tell me all about it, Colleen.'

It was relief to unburden herself to someone who knew.

As he listened, Ben sat turning a gold sovereign over and over between his fingers. The flashes of light hurt his eyes as he stared at it, listening to her speak. *My God*, he thought, *I never had the faintest idea. He was ashamed to let me know. But I know that love is always valid. Between man and woman, between countries, between a man and his God, between man and man. There's little enough of it. If love is all it is, it needs no excuses.*

The sovereign turned and flashed.

She finished.

'Yes,' he said, 'I know.' He didn't hate Bertie. He admired him more; and pitied him more. In the eyes of society Bertie was a pervert. But always at the back of his mind Ben was thinking, *Truly, he did save me.*

Colleen was looking at him. 'You do understand,' she said.

People always expected so much. Ben kept his eyes on the sovereign. It was all that he had left out of his twenty-five pound allowance for officer's uniform, belt, sword. He pointed out the obvious. 'Love is not all it is. He believes it's a guilty love. For him, it's sin. Bertie believes that love is close to heaven, but you can't believe in heaven without knowing that hell exists too.'

Her fingers caressed the decoration at her neck. He could see that he shocked her by laughing.

'Do you know what the King said?' he asked. ' "I thought men like that shot themselves." And he wasn't joking. Shall I tell you what I think? That we shouldn't take ourselves so seriously. Catholic or Protestant. There's no need for Bertie to suffer, but he does, and there's still no need for it. There's no need for this war to go on, but it will. So let's make the best of our lives. Forward Chouchou's letter to him, it'll cheer him up. And give me another slice of your cake.'

She stared at him.

'Your chocolate cake!' he laughed, sticking out his elbows and rubbing his tummy. 'I'm still hungry!'

Vane waited. The sunlight became orange and fell away. The buildings grew dark. She stood staring up at the lighted window, waiting.

She was not cold. She was warm in her furs. Her hands, clasped together, were wrapped in a deep fur muff. She was no longer in mourning for Mama and she could wear what she liked at last, she could even put her hair up whenever she wanted.

Sometimes she felt the wind cold on her ankles, but there was always the street light to walk under, his face to stare at in the newspaper, looking out at her, the man of her dream.

She knew him.

He was so familiar.

She was sure that she had never met him before – certainly they had never been properly introduced, she had a first-class memory and she was positive that she would have remembered – yet there it was. The City address that the newspaper gave was certainly good enough, placing him at least on her social level and perhaps a little above. She knew him. Even from the grainy photograph she had been almost certain, instantly. On the pavement, when he paused as though he owned it, and when he smiled at her, she *knew*. It was him. That was the man she would marry. The feeling had been born in her as completely as though it had been planted long ago, as if it had been made in heaven. Perhaps it had! That would be lovely. And the rising moon was desperately romantic. Everything around her was invested with meaning.

Yet there was also her real feeling that she had always known him; there was a quality of memory about it.

Impossible.

And the impossible glamour of his name: *Ben London,* as if he owned the metropolis, London's streets, London's pavements, London's buildings, London's moon. It made her want to hug herself. Everything was his. Except her. She would make him come to her on her own terms, by being what she was. He would fall in love with her honesty, her face, her manners, and she would have him without surrendering anything of herself.

She stared up at the lighted window. They had been ordained in the stars. Her breath pulsed in the circle of her lips. This was what it was like to be in love at last. True love.

She saw his shadow at the lighted window once, twice. Then the fat servant pulled the drapes.

She waited. Perhaps he would come out.

What would she do? She would turn and walk away indifferently. Instantly, he would admire her. He would run after her. She would ignore him. And so it would go. He would give up everything for her. She would have a husband and then they would go and see a doctor and have children – wives always saw a doctor before they had children. The doctor sort of switched them on somehow, like lights, and they had babies. She hungered and thirsted for babies. It was an actual physical want in her that she could feel in her heart and tummy. Nothing satisfied it: not creams that she smeared on her face, or even putting her hair up, or anything she ate, nothing. If only Mama had been still alive, she could have asked her if all girls felt like this – if Mama had felt it as a girl. That would have been awfully impertinent to ask, but it might have helped. But babies were just something to be admired; it was unthinkable to discuss their origins.

But he did not come out.

She returned the next night. The window was dark. He was not there. Later the fat woman came out with an enormous horrible dog that barked at her, and barked and barked.

'You should keep your dog under proper control,' Vane said.

So he had gone away.

She stood there. Her round doll's face was perfectly composed. She felt coldly hysterical. Her immaculate thoughts were disordered, she could not think properly.

Her stubborn side wanted her to stand where she was and wait, and wait, until he came back. He would have to, one day. Her impulsive side wanted to run into the building now and find him, wherever he was.

She was used to getting what she demanded.

She thought: *What would Marcelline do?*

4

There were supposed to be German spies everywhere, but anyone who really wanted to know had only to pick up a copy of the *Gazette:*

GEORGE,
by the Grace of God, of the United Kingdom of Great Britain and Ireland, and of the British Dominions beyond the Seas, King, Defender of the Faith, Emperor of India, &c.:

To Our Trusty and well beloved *Ben London* Greeting.

We reposing especial Trust and Confidence in your Loyalty, Courage, and good Conduct, do by these Presents Constitute and Appoint you to be an Officer in Our Special Reserve of Officers . . .

Given at Our Court at Saint James's, the thirty-first day of December, nineteen hundred and sixteen, in the Seventh Year of Our Reign.

By His Majesty's Command.

Posted back to the School of Aeronautics at Reading University for a course, not on Observation this time, but as a pilot to learn the theory of flight, Ben was never able to remember much about it later; there was a lovely lot of drinking in the evenings and none of the lecturers could explain what they were talking about. Ben worked hard during the day and paid very close attention. None of these instructors had a real feeling for the air or flying. Many of them had been posted home under medical certificates of Flying Sickness D – the Royal Flying Corps's polite word for flying exhaustion. It was very bad now in France, Ben guessed. But all he read about in the papers was German casualties and Allied heroes.

At Castle Bromwich, on the aerodrome between the main railway line and the sewage farm, he flew for a couple of hours' dual instruction on a Maurice Longhorn. It was a fabulous, prehistoric beast that carried its tail ahead of it. Its wings were held together by a cat's cradle of piano wires and if there was any head wind at all it took off at walking speed. The engine made a sound like a sewing machine. If the pilot tilted the enormous wings by more than a gentle slope, the machine settled into a spin from which it did not recover.

'Let's go back now,' the instructor shouted.

'I'll buy you a gin in the mess if you'll let me loop the loop!'

'I heard what you did in France,' the instructor yelled. 'You're crazy!'

A few days later Ben was called before the CO to receive his transfer papers.

Upavon aerodrome was in the middle of nowhere on Salisbury Plain. Few days were windless enough to fly. Nearby on the undulating landscape was Death Valley, a wooded groove that caused turbulence that was the death of many pilots. Ben flew the Shorthorn, similar to the Longhorn but at least it carried its tail behind it.

There was no such thing as a natural pilot. The instructors said that there was, as though there was something mystical about it, a talent that one was born with. Ben did not believe that talent even existed; he had looked inside himself, and he saw no trace of it. No natural pilots; but there were pilots who naturally worked hard, and Ben was determined to be one of those.

If one could learn to *feel* it opened up so much more. To feel the trembling in the stick, the subtle flexing in the wings, to *feel* how she flew. The insubstantial air could feel like a solid wall. Some pilots never felt it, were too arrogant, too self-confident to be sensitive. They flew into the wall.

After an hour Ben went solo on the Shorthorn. He flew up into the blue bowl until he was half a mile high. Below him, the aerodrome was a postage stamp at the very bottom of the green bowl; the woods were still black patterns, Death Valley a jagged scrawl.

He made sure that his seat-belt was tightly done up across his lap. It was now or never. He was frightened – frightened of not doing it. He let the nose drop. The speed rose. The slipstream roared. The controls stiffened. Now they were heavy. He longed to pull the stick back, to reach up into the sky. She wasn't ready. The slipstream tugged the corners of his mouth into a smile, pressed his nostrils closed so that he could hardly breathe. Now she was there.

He pulled gently back on the stick. He looped the loop.

The green bowl dropped away and disappeared. Everything was sky. The engine chugged. He hung from the seat-belt across his lap. He was upside down. The green bowl rotated into view above him.

The slipstream was a gentle breeze. He looked up : there was the ground.

When he landed he wanted to jump out of her screaming and shouting and waving his arms, 'I did it! I've done it, I did it!' But that wasn't the done thing. He walked casually across the grass with his flying jacket slung over his shoulder. Someone in a group headed for the mess said: 'Oh, was it you stunting?'

'I'm afraid so.' The lie of modesty; expected of him.

'Don't suppose you'd care to join us in a gin?'

'Or two.' They broke out in male laughter and everyone

raced to the bar. 'Last man buys!' Ben called over his shoulder.

Later they sang to the out-of-tune piano.

Later still they played climbing round the walls without touching the floor.

Finally Ben climbed up on the roof with a cigarette tin full of paraffin and dropped it down the chimney onto the fire. It was a terrifically effective way of clearing a room.

As they came pouring outside he met them at the door, and they drove down through the dark to the pub in the village.

Next morning they were up at dawn, and flew with hangovers.

Life was like heaven . . .

But anyone who cared to do so had only to read the papers to find out that he had been posted to Gosport for advanced flying training on BE2Cs and Avros.

And after that anyone had only to look in the *Times* to learn that he had been awarded his wings; and that he was to go to Tern Hill, where the finest pilots received their final training.

And she had only to know that the award of wings was invariably followed by a few days' leave.

With his wings put up on his chest, which pleased Colleen O'Keeffe greatly since she now had two fliers in her family, Ben returned to Bunhill Row on leave, was welcomed by Sam, dragged the curtains closed, and slept the night through and long into the next morning. Waking, he found that it was the early afternoon already, and lay luxuriously in bed for a while with his hands behind his head, looking at the reflections of sunlight moving across the ceiling from the traffic below, wearing a pair of Bertie's pyjamas that were much too tight. Colleen had taken Sam for his walk. Ben got dressed, ate the cold ham and hard-boiled eggs that the dear woman had left, and went out for a breath of air. It was a lovely day. He looked up at the sky.

'Clumsy!'

A girl dressed in furs was standing behind him. She had

dropped all her shopping and was staring at him furiously. Had he knocked into her? He hoped he had; she was perfectly beautiful, with a face as pale and round as a doll's, and large brown eyes flashing with surface anger. An exquisite creature, an exquisite fury – which made her even prettier. He smiled, and played the game.

Vane stared at him. Marcelline had promised: *He'll say something like: 'Oh, I'm so awfully sorry,' and go red, because men always hate scenes in the street. Everyone will have stopped and be watching, and he'll feel at such a disadvantage that to stop your fuss he'll drop to his knees and start gathering all that shopping together – and you'll have made sure that you've got a terrific lot of it – awkward little things. He can't possibly cram it all back into your arms and still remain a gentleman, so he'll say, 'I couldn't possibly let you carry all this, allow me to carry it for you . . .' And you've got him hooked!* Vane had been impressed and delighted. 'Marcy, however did you learn all that?' Marcelline, who was now formally engaged to marry a wonderful man in the armaments trade, had given Vane an old-fashioned look with her hungry, sensual eyes, and Vane had felt a shiver run down her back. 'Behind me,' Marcelline nodded, 'lie a thousand generations of women who have been successful in catching their man.'

But this man just stood there, smiling, not to be caught so easily.

Vane was aware of the crowd watching them and felt her cheeks flushing hotly. It wasn't supposed to go like this at all.

'You knocked into me and made me drop my shopping!'

'You dropped your shopping. I didn't knock into you.' His eyes and smile were kind, but Vane didn't know how to rise to their challenge. She felt terribly out of her depth, and hated it.

If it gets out of hand, cry. Vane tried to cry. She was much too self-conscious to be an actress. She couldn't even make her eyes wet.

But she got him, because he bent down and picked up her shopping. He asked: 'I've seen you before, haven't I?'

'No,' Vane claimed, saving face. The crowd was dispersing. This was better. She prepared to smile into his eyes. *Eye contact,* Marcelline had advised, her arms on Vane's shoulders, her warm scented breath in Vane's face. *Get him to notice you – only you. You're the only girl in the world.*

He dumped the bags into her arms. And then he turned and walked away!

Vane stamped her foot. She flung her shopping down. He stopped.

She put her chin in the air, trembling with fury. She still had a bottle in her hand. She threw it down and it broke.

He came back.

'What did you do that for?' he demanded.

Vane stared up at him, adoring and terrified, seized with emotion: the mixture of brutality and caress in his eyes. She deserved both, and felt herself taking deep breaths. Then he smiled again, merely kind.

She's so perfect, he thought. Her complexion was flawless, her lips naturally ruby. Her cheeks burned with a lovely blood colour that compelled his attention. Her hair was wonderful – a rich dark brown, and though she was wearing it up at the moment he knew that when it was unpinned it would fall in gorgeous natural curls around his hands.

She said: 'I can do what I like.'

He picked up shards of glass. 'This would cut the paws of any dog that ran down here. Or suppose a little child came along . . . ?' She flinched; he was right. He sniffed his fingers. 'Eau de Cologne. An expensive brand. A man would have to work for three weeks to earn enough to pay for this.' God, all she'd done was break one little bottle, did they have to go into all this detail about it? And he was looking at her all the time! He didn't take his eyes off her!

His eyes were blue, clear but difficult to see into except when they flashed with emotion. She was pleased that he didn't wear a moustache, it wouldn't have suited him at all. She was five feet seven inches in her high heels; he must be nine inches more than that even in his socks (though that was a bedroom thought) and he was wearing officer's field boots, which added a couple of inches at least. If she threw her arms around his chest, she doubted if her hands would meet behind his back. She blushed to imagine herself doing that. Suppose he had hairs on his chest? The navvies who repaired the roads had hairy chests and she despised them. Really! He was looking at her bosom now as if she was something in her father's window he was considering purchasing! He was admiring her, it was true, but not in the way she wanted. She did not want to be admired for her body but for her mind, which was much more interesting. She had been taught to make conversation with a young man on any subject, even – in fact especially – topics that she knew nothing about, saying 'Gosh!' enchantingly, and 'Really?' in such a way that the young chap felt frightfully clever and simply adored her.

Vane was honest. She never joked, never lied, never played pranks: she was always absolutely serious. Desperation had driven her to this disaster. She drifted out of her depth.

Genuine tears filled her eyes.

He saw at once that they were genuine. 'I'm sorry. I didn't mean to upset you so badly.'

She clung on to that. 'It's my fault.' Her tears overflowed at last. She heard him drop the broken glass down a drain then scuffling sounds as he gathered up her shopping. That hateful shopping. She felt so angry and mortified and ashamed that her tears poured down her face.

'It's all right,' he said calmly. Then: 'Stop it!'

Vane wanted to scream at him: *You don't know about Marcelline, you don't know it all about this dreadful War. My Mama is dead, I have no one and everything is so ugly and shallow and hateful . . .*

She begged: 'Please, please don't be so brutal to me.' The sun had gone from the buildings, clouds were drawing over, and it was chilly. She began to shiver. The tears on her cheeks felt like ice. Thank goodness that her complexion was so perfect that she did not need to wear make-up; it would have run and she would have looked ridiculous. As it was, she would seem more beautiful than ever.

Ben was amazed by her.

How pretty she was: a doll's face that could have looked

365

as though it was painted on, but her tears gave her a feminine vulnerability that touched him. He wanted to protect her. He was sure – he recognized the white furs – that she was the girl he had seen outside on the pavement a few months ago, holding his picture in the newspaper. She only wanted to meet him because of his looks, his body, like the other poor girls made crazy by the war, looking for a uniform to give their love to, some way of Doing Their Bit – widows now, already, many of them. He felt terribly sorry for her: it wasn't only the men who were going through hell.

'I'm sorry,' he said.

Those were the words she longed to hear. She dabbed her cheeks with a tiny lace handkerchief.

He tucked her shopping under one arm. 'Come on.' She felt him take her wrist, laying his forearm over her own, and lead her effortlessly across the road.

'Where are you taking me?' she asked helplessly.

'You wanted to meet me.'

'I didn't!'

'To a place where you can have your wish.' She saw the lights of a Lyons Corner House. Surely he didn't mean in *there*.

He must have awfully broad tastes. The Corner Houses were for rather common people. There were simply hundreds of them all over the place. Oh, he *did!* He pushed open the door with his shoulder and they went inside. It was an awful bustle, with people queuing at the counters to choose between the silver boxes of mass-produced Maison Lyons chocolates, buying cakes, or selecting canapés to take home. Towing her after him, he breezed through them to the stairway that led up to the tea-room on the first floor. He waited only a moment at the brass rail. He did not look like a person who was used to waiting, she thought. It was lovely how the floorwalker came scurrying over and showed them to a table, pulling aside the hoop-backed wicker chair, waiting for her, bowing. Ben let go of her, and she sat. He dropped the shopping against the wall. A Nippy in a black dress and smart white apron, wearing a white starched band around her hair, came to take his order.

'Pot of tea for two, and mixed cakes,' he instructed.

Vane watched him across the red and white check tablecloth. Again he had taken her by surprise. Now that the time had come, she didn't know what to say. The charming small talk that she had dreamed she would make, having got him alone, had evaporated. Rudely, he was saying nothing, giving her no opportunity to enchant him by admiring his cleverness.

'You're very pretty,' he said finally.

Men always said that to her. It was a conventional compliment, but now she flushed and didn't know what to say, for he had said it as flatly as if it was a statement of fact. Which of course it was. But as a flat observation, the truth was difficult to deal with.

'Am I? Thank you.'

'You know you are.'

Of course she did. Did he think he was being profound? Poor man. He wasn't telling her anything she didn't know. Men were so strong and somehow so desirable, but so simple, and rather childish beside the emotional superiority of a woman. She knew that she could handle him. Her confidence came back and she surveyed him with amusement. He didn't know very much, obviously, about women. She would have to teach him how to be romantic.

At least he was admiring her.

He was attracted to her.

She had hooked him with the first hook. Now, as Marcelline would say, she had time to play him a little. This was against Vane's nature, but Marcelline knew about men and women, and she never failed.

'Excuse me,' Vane said. She went to the ladies' powder room and patted a little cold water on her cheeks to bring out their bloom. She put up a few strands of hair which had fallen down – she had not realized that she looked so wanton, what must he have thought! No, no, keep your confidence. Having straightened her hat, she decided that she had made him wait long enough, and returned to the table.

Balancing the silver tray over her shoulder, the Nippy ran down with their tea and cakes. 'Thank you.' Vane reached out to do the pouring: obviously, to get a man she must impress him with her awareness of feminine duty and her submission to the motherly virtues. Why else would he be interested in her, a weak woman? But Ben's hand was already there on the handle of the pot, feeling warm and rough under her fingertips. Imagine! she thought breathlessly, how awfully funny it must feel to have hairs coating the backs of your hands. She realized that her fingertips had lingered, and she snatched them away.

'I'll pour,' he said. She had never seen anyone put tea in the cups before the cream. It was rather coarse. Was he trying to shock her? He pushed across the sugar bowl and she used the tongs to choose two lumps.

He remembered: *Just like Aunt Edith.*

He pushed the tray of cakes towards her. Vane thought: *He's trying to possess me.* Perhaps I won't have a cake at all. Instead, she turned the tray round until the side that he had pushed towards her pointed away from her, and used the slice to put a fairy cake on her plate, a pink one, which was her favourite.

He stuck a couple of cream buns on his plate and started eating hungrily, using his fingers.

Perhaps she was being too precious for this tough man. He was a hero of the air. Those were the fingers that had pulled the triggers.

She hesitated, then picked up her fairy cake in her own fingers and commenced to eat it, patting the crumbs out of the corners of her lips with the tip of a napkin. She could not help glancing at him; there was something definitely satisfying about watching a man eat.

She held out the dish. 'Do.'

'Thank you,' he said. He made another display. Of course, it was all for her benefit. She felt warm and comfortable now: now that she knew she could control him. He was paying attention to her. *Get him to notice you – only you.* She waited until he had finished.

He leaned back, looking at her.

She tried another hook: 'Hasn't the weather been awful lately?'

'It hasn't been too bad, actually.'

'Of course, you're a pilot. You know all about these things,' she said politely.

He sipped his tea. So, he thought, she wants to talk. But I'm certain that she is the girl I saw. What she really wants to do is to go to bed with an airman, a hero, a dream.

He looked at her beautiful, precious little face: he wanted her. No two ways about it. There was something untouched, unbroken about her, a white purity that was intensely attractive, a sense that he could take her and shape her into a part of himself. She felt the same, obviously. Yes, he wanted to kiss her and hold her tiny, perfect body, and . . . and . . . and suddenly he shivered. When he put down his cup, it rattled in the saucer.

'Ria, I—' *He saw her face beneath him.*

The tide was full. A green light came slowly up river, arriving. He felt her hips beneath his hips. He saw her smile—

Yes, he saw her face.

He shook his head. The darkness disappeared. Vane regarded him seriously.

He smiled. This girl did not look like Ria; nothing like her at all. She had none of Ria's belligerent sexuality. He could not look at this girl and imagine Ria. He wanted her; he wanted her body of course; but more than that, he needed the love that Ria had never given him. Ria, who had rejected him and deserted him. Love was so close to hate. No one knew that better than he. He mashed his tongue against the roof of his mouth.

I'm Vic Price. Remember me.

Yes; best of all, she didn't look like Ria.

Vane said: 'Is anything wrong?'

She felt relieved when he laughed. He shook his head and leaned forward, putting his hands on the table close to hers, and they made conversation about the war. Conversation at last. Oooh, she was thinking, I never realized that it was nearly so horrible out there. Hospitals full of wounded men. Yet the horribleness was exciting too. Some of the things he said were not quite polite conversation for the drawing room and would have shocked many older ladies, she knew.

369

He was a bit of a rough diamond. He suggested that she ought to train to do something useful, as though she was not doing anything useful at the moment! Her usual compliments dried up. She certainly was not going to encourage him to criticize her.

She tried to steer her conversation with this fascinatingly unconventional man – he was utterly unlike the types that she had met before – to find out which school he had been educated at and whether his money was from commerce or property. She rather suspected the former, but of course there was nothing wrong with that nowadays, even her own father worked for his living. But he talked so interestingly and unconventionally about so many subjects that somehow she did not find out. A Buckingham was nothing to do with the Duke of Buckingham, apparently – it was an incendiary bullet used to shoot down the enemy's observation balloons. 'Gosh!' In case he was shot down the pilot carried a certificate to say that his ammunition was used for balloon strafing only, since it was illegal to use it against other aeroplanes. 'Really!' Because of the war, he said, in the last three years aeroplane design had advanced further than it would in thirty years of peace-time development, and soon aeroplanes would carry passengers. 'How wonderful!'

'You'll fly.'

'I can't believe it,' she said admiringly, looking at him, only him.

'You will.' That flat, factual tone devoid of emotion, that she liked so much. She believed him.

She said in Marcelline's earthy, laughing voice: 'I don't suppose you'd take me up . . .!'

Simply: 'Any time you like.'

She happened to put her hand on the table. He put his hand immediately on hers. This was awfully fast; it seemed, she thought disdainfully, that aeroplanes were not the only development the war had accelerated: touching hands in public, whatever next; but she didn't take her hand away. Marcelline would have smiled in that way that Marcelline had of smiling at men.

His hand felt warm and solid, dependably enclosing her dainty fingers.

Vane tried. She smiled.

He smiled warmly back at her.

He said: 'It must be late. Shall we go?'

'Go? Where?'

'Where would you like?'

'Do you often take strange girls out to tea?' she enquired in her steeliest tone.

He looked surprised. 'No. Why?'

'I just wondered, that's all.'

He sensed that she needed some sort of reassurance; perhaps she was getting cold feet. Like many girls of her class, she wore a protective veneer of hard innocence. He saw how she pretended to be ignorant about people and inexperienced about life, but he knew that was just the narrow arrogance of her upbringing. She's lovely, he thought, like a little exquisite bird peeping out through the bars of the cage that she's spent her life inside.

He knew that he could give her life, could bring her stiff, unbroken body and her steely sharp personality to bloom. She was cold; he would give her warmth. She was alone; he would give her himself.

She would fly.

You're starting to sound as though you're falling in love with her.

'You won't believe this,' he said, 'but this is the first time that I have ever been in a Lyons Corner House.'

He stood and pulled back her chair. She turned her precious, tiny doll's face up to his. Her ruby lips still wore the strange pouting smile that he could not decipher. He smiled with his eyes. Her brown eyes looked into his, but seemed to understand nothing.

'Yes, they are rather common, aren't they.'

That was very arch. The Lyons shops were a solid middle-class chain – she was trying to show herself off as being very upper class indeed. Perhaps it was true. He doubted it.

She'd set her sights on him, obviously: she wanted to tell her friends that she had seduced a pilot. In some circles, he knew, the social cachet of doing it was considerable. Perhaps she was from those circles. After all it seemed, perhaps, that all both of them wanted was to get the other into bed. He was wrong to think that there had been more to it than that. He picked up her shopping.

'Come on,' he said.

The Nippy counted the remaining cakes and made out their bill from the pad dangling from her waist. He paid at the till and they went down into the street. It was dark now and he felt rain falling softly. Keeping under the canopies, he walked her a few paces to the quiet, spacious doorway of Proudhon, the fine art dealers, and looked out. The shops were bright and busy still and the road was streaked with shiny wet reflections.

She said in a tiny voice: 'Thank you for the tea.'

He bent down and kissed her. She gave him a social peck with her hard little lips. It was like kissing a cold Meissen doll.

She said: 'When will I see you again?'

So she was pretending to think that he had kissed her goodbye. She wanted to be won.

But she said, 'Papa is having a small party, the first since Mama . . . passed on.'

'I'm sorry.'

'I am his only daughter, so of course I will be officiating. A very small affair. Tell me that you will come?'

'I cannot. I return to begin flight training on a new aircraft tomorrow. It's in Shropshire, miles away. I couldn't possibly.'

'Promise me that you will come!' she said wildly.

He frowned. 'It's impossible. I'm sorry.'

'Don't keep saying you're sorry!' she flashed. She looked up at him appealingly. He guessed that her appeals were rarely rejected. He put down her shopping and took her in his arms and kissed her gently.

'We have only tonight together,' he said. It was not a lie. It expressed what they both wanted. He told her the absolute truth: 'You're lovely.' He kissed her again. Vane jerked back.

372

She said: 'Don't do that!'

He stopped at once.

She said: 'I felt your tongue.'

'Haven't you ever been kissed before?'

'Stop it. How can you be so cruel.'

'What's the matter?'

She said in a hysterical voice: 'I want to go home.' He knew at once that she really meant it. He nodded.

'I'll call you a cab.'

'A cab's no use,' she said petulantly. She found a card. 'Telephone this number and they can pick me up here.'

He put down the shopping. 'Stay there. You're safe here.' He went to the post office nearby and gave the operator the number. In a few moments it rang. The card had no name on it but the address was somewhere in Primrose Hill; he asked for the motor-car to be sent to the corner of City Road and Old Street. He replaced the earpiece in the candle-stick telephone and went back to her outside. He was relieved to find her still there; he had honestly thought that she might run off.

'I've called the car.' He handed the card back. 'Are you all right?'

'Yes.'

'I'm sorry if I frightened you. Truly, I'm sorry.' He laughed: with her, he was always saying it.

She didn't see the joke. They waited for the car standing together, miles apart, as though the few inches between them were a great gulf. He could have reached out and touched her just by moving his little finger, but something about her was quite untouchable.

The motor-car drew up. It was an enormous laudalette Rolls-Royce, with the caped chauffeur sitting out in the open and the passenger compartment fully enclosed.

So she had not been lying; she was rich, possibly upper class, perhaps even aristocratic. His behaviour had been gross. But he could hardly say sorry again.

He opened the door for her. She stepped inside and settled back into the seat. Standing in the gutter with rainwater flowing over his field-boots, he pushed her shopping across the floor. She was so pretty and alluring now that he ached. For the first time in his life, he realized a little of the forces that could drive men to – if not to rape, at least to lust. To ache with desire. And women too? He stepped back. She was dangerous; fearfully dangerous. Suddenly she leaned forward.

'I'll see you again.'

'I don't know.'

'I do know.'

He said: 'I don't know anything about you. I don't even know your name.'

She leaned back again.

'Vanity, but everyone calls me Vane,' she said, as he closed the door. 'Vane Leibig.'

Chapter Fourteen

1

When winter had closed in on the breastworks at Croix Barbée, Nigel had never felt more lonely or deserted. Vic was gone. For the first time in his life, Vic was not there to tell Nigel what to do. Nigel missed his elder brother desperately – missed his confidence, his leadership. They had never been apart in their whole lives before.

But then the accident had happened.

Nigel cowered against the sandbags with his hands over his head. Living hand to mouth in the atrocious conditions, always cold, always wet, in constant fear of death, was awful: but the loneliness was worse.

He thought: *How will Vic live without me? He must be feeling what I do.*

Then he thought: *How will I live without him?*

Oh Mum, I'm so alone. Suppose I'm killed, and I never see you again?

I'm so sorry if I was ever cold towards you, but you never understood Vic, he thought. He cringed as something came dropping out of the night sky making a warbling swish-swish sound: a Minnie, a land-mine four feet long and heavier than a man, fired from behind the German lines and now tumbling down end over end out of the clouds – he could see the fuse sparking against the black. The earth shook, and then he heard the crump of the explosion . . . a Minnie blew a hole large enough to hide a house in. Nigel cringed.

Oh, Mum, how I wish I was home with you in Havannah Road in our lovely new house, I'd never do anything wrong again!

He pushed himself back into his tiny bivvy, a nest amongst the sandbags, and averted his eyes as a stretcher party hobbled clumsily by.

Oh Mum.

He still couldn't believe it – it had been such a silly accident. They had been on burial detail, and Vic had swung down out of the back of the lorry on the rope. The knot had come free and he had fallen heavily. Nigel and the sergeant had clearly heard the crunch of the cartilage tearing, and Vic had laid there writhing and screaming, clutching his ankle. The sergeant had looked at the rope suspiciously, but no man could have the courage to jump down deliberately holding his ankle askew to give himself an injury like that.

Vic had been sent back to endure the horror of a casualty clearing station. God knows what had happened to him since then.

For Nigel, life became unendurable. His imagination ran riot with horrors. He was trapped in the trenches. Whichever way his mind ran oh so nimbly along the maze, there was no way out. Many men endured life stoically until death took them or they received such a fearful wound that it took them back to Blighty to exist as cripples. They sat huddled in their bivvies on each side of Nigel now, silent shapes hunched under capes, only their tin helmets showing where their heads were, waiting.

Nigel thought: *I can't. I won't. I can't, I won't.*

They were brainless. He had intelligence, temperament. He had written a poem. It was called 'Waiting'.

The poem was one word, written over and over. The first line was: *Waiting, waiting, waiting,* and the second line was: *Waiting, waiting . . .*

Repeated, the words acquired the strength of great art. The poem summed up the war. *Waiting . . . waiting . . . wailing . . .*

The last word was different.

It was: *Alone.*

Then there was only The End.

The lonely breastworks stretched for miles across a swamp. Every shell hole was a pond, and the trenches wriggled through a landscape like an archipelago. Nigel had never looked across it – to do so meant death, for the German trenches were only a hundred or two hundred yards away, terribly close, and sound carried perfectly across the watery morass. Max Halder, who spoke German well enough to identify accents, listened then laughed and said that they were opposite a Saxon regiment.

'Ach, Nigel, that is very good news. We will have a quiet life. You see, the Saxons do not hate the English. They are the race which colonized England after the Romans left. We are of the same blood. They do not wish to fight us.' Smiling, he looked over the top of the sandbags, and was shot through the head. His body slithered into the mud and disappeared. It was an economical feature of the breastworks. Bodies buried themselves. Nigel stared into the mud.

Trenches could not be dug here: the water level lay only eighteen inches below the surface of the ground. So a shallow groove a foot deep was built up with sandbags on the German side to a height of seven or eight feet. It was like holding up an umbrella against a firestorm. Beyond the sandbags lay the wire, sinking into the slime.

Beyond that lay the Germans.

Waiting.

Then winter came, a cold snap very late that year, and the mud froze into cruel spikes. The soldiers had no proper clothes, but they knew better than to grouse to their officers. Nigel had groused in a trembling voice, but before he was more than a couple of sentences into it Captain Lockhart turned away and said, 'I think you've got a bit of a barrack-room lawyer here, Sergeant?'

And Sergeant Rhys-Davis said: 'I know how to deal with them, sir.'

Nigel found himself cleaning the latrines. He found himself first to be picked for night patrols amongst the wire in no-man's-land. Fortunately Rhys-Davis was killed and the punishment ceased.

He did not trust the officers after that. He no longer identified with them as being his leader, as Vic had been.

The companies on each side were Commonwealth troops, from Australia, South Africa, New Zealand and Canada. They were tough, boisterous men earning five times the pay he did, and Nigel noticed incredulously that they even called their officers by their christian names. There was no iron discipline, and yet they trusted their officers, and the officers looked after the men and trusted them. These officers actually trusted their men enough to show them maps before an attack – even scale models of the ground that they were expected to cover! They were actually shown what they had to do!

All the British officers said was: *Follow me.* If they were killed, which because of their bravery they usually were, their men had no idea what to do, except keep running forward towards the machine-guns, and die.

Nigel could see that the British discipline was by far the hardest on the Front. The soldiers were never asked to think for themselves. They were told to do everything, but never why to do it. Three hundred men had been shot officially for cowardice but Nigel knew that the real figure must be much higher. Everyone had heard of the British soldiers who got drunk in an *estaminet* and came out to find themselves facing a colonel and a machine-gun crew. At gunpoint they had been driven into the Lines, and during the next attack every last single one of them perished. That was the way it was done.

The ice melted.

The men lived in the mud again. They smeared stinking whale-oil over their feet to keep the water off. To come down with trench foot – almost inevitable after weeks and months of living with wet, cold feet – was a court-martial offence.

Nigel sat in the dark. He could hear the men joking and laughing quietly.

He thought: *I cannot stand it any more.*

He had received a letter from Mum, written by Ria. They were well. Vic was well. Was there anything he wanted?

Yes, I want to get out of here!

He closed his eyes. Vic was alive. Everything was going to be all right.

Now that spring was coming, the attack season would start soon. Already activity was hotting up. Bullets whined and cracked above the parapets, and Verey lights made an unearthly display; the ground shook from an artillery barrage, and the horizons glowed. A patrol had taken a prisoner: the Saxons had been pulled back and replaced with a crack Prussian unit. It was supposed to be a secret, but Nigel had himself seen him dragged over the parapet and had recognized the black-white-black cockade colours of Prussia, instead of the Saxon white-green-white that he had expected. The man's rifle tumbled down after him and he was dragged off for interrogation.

Prussian troops were always the best.

It meant that an attack was coming.

The rifle sank in the mud at Nigel's feet. As soon as no one was looking he lifted it out and concealed it in the earth at the back of his bivvy.

He had a plan.

The German rifle was quite different from the long British pattern. Nigel had recognized this one as the Kar 98 with a short barrel that the German shock troops often used. *Yes*, he realized, gleeful and trembling, *an attack is definitely coming.* The bullet was 7.9 millimetres, similar to the British but quite different in impact characteristics: British bullets tumbled, whereas the German bullet went straight through, leaving a clean wound.

In other words, a doctor could tell at once if a wound was genuine or self-inflicted.

Last year, that was how they caught out Jasper Clark. Jasper got a mate to shoot him in the knee, from far enough back that there were no powder-burns to give him away. But the type of wound the bullet left did give him away. That was what made this German rifle so valuable.

The doctor blew the whistle on him. When Jasper had recovered enough to walk, he was court-martialed and sentenced to death. Men from his own regiment were ordered to carry out the sentence. One of them happened to be the mate who shot him in the first place. In the final moments Nigel had seen recognition flare in Jasper's face. Guilty men often screamed the truth to earn their place in heaven: Nigel pulled the trigger first.

Now he crouched in his bivvy, waiting for the dawn.

The attack would come at dawn. They always did.

All night, the guns rumbled. The darkness flickered. With about an hour to go, Nigel dug out the Kar 98 and slung it from his shoulder with his own rifle, where it would not be noticed in the darkness and uncertain glare. He stepped over the legs of the sleeping men.

He scuttled down the communication trench to the latrines. This was an edge-on plank, supported at intervals, built over a sump. It stank like the devil.

There was no one there.

Nigel shivered. He flexed his fingers. They shook. He curled them into fists and forced himself to be calm.

Then he checked the communication trench. He could see along it for about twenty slimy paces – say five seconds' warning. He wedged the Kar 98 in the angle of one of the supports and sighted it on the top outer corner of the next one along, about eight feet away, which made a convenient target.

Still no one coming.

He checked that the rifle was firmly wedged. It was. In fact he could not move it.

Never mind. Better too tight than too loose; the last thing he wanted was to shift the aim. He released the safety catch and worked the bolt.

Now it was ready to fire.

Still no one.

He unslung his own long rifle – a Lee Enfield with a thirty-inch barrel, and the bayonet adding nearly another two feet to that – and held it out in his right hand at the point of balance, just behind the trigger guard.

He went to the target support and placed his left elbow in front of the top corner, then swung his right arm until the tip of his bayonet on the end of his rifle rattled against the barrel of the Kar 98.

He couldn't quite reach.

He swung his rifle away, his muscles twitching with the effort, then licked his lips and tried again, stretching further, straining his left elbow back against the top corner of the support, his legs spread wide.

Still no one.

The guns rumbled.

Now or never. The tip of the bayonet clinked against the trigger guard of the Kar 98, then touched the trigger. Nigel thought the gun did not go off. Then an awful tingling sensation, like the worst of pins and needles, spread up his left arm above the elbow until it reached his shoulder.

Then a dull ache spread up. Nigel stared at the rifle stupidly.

A numbing pain washed up his arm. He heard himself moaning. He couldn't do anything about it. He glanced at his elbow and closed his eyes, feeling sick. A Blighty one for sure. He would never fight again. He hung on to the support to remain upright. It had taken courage, real courage, to shoot himself like that . . . and the most private and brutal cowardice. It must be his secret to the grave. He could never tell anyone. Not even Vic.

A voice said: 'Nigel.'

Nigel turned slowly.

The voice out of the communication trench said: 'Who's been a naughty boy then, Nigel?'

In the trench stood a man from another company and for a moment Nigel did not recognize him without the gold rings on his fingers.

A handsome face, too handsome.

Eyes close together.

Blond hair.

'Oh my God,' Nigel said. He swung his rifle around, it had one up the spout, flicking off the safety catch with his thumb.

Raymond Trott's eyes opened wide with fear.

'Don't, Nigel. I won't say a word.' Raymond Trott backed away. 'God's my witness. Promise.' Then he turned and ran down the communication trench, slipping and slithering from side to side, hands out, banging from wall to wall. His pack wobbled and bounced.

Nigel held out his arm and aimed his rifle as best he could at the bobbing, dwindling figure, then pulled the trigger.

The recoil bruised his hand and the bullet went wild, somewhere into the sandbags.

Raymond Trott disappeared around the corner.

Nigel staggered after him but it was hopeless. He stopped.

What would Vic do?

Dimly Nigel sensed that Vic wouldn't have been so clever or so stupid as to get himself into this complicated mess in the first place. Vic didn't have plans; he just took advantage of opportunities.

Nigel thought: *I need you, Vic. I can't do anything without you.* He felt sick.

He went back and tried to tug the German rifle out of the wedge. It wouldn't budge. He kicked it and it jumped loose. He dropped it into the sump, then stuck his left hand between the buttons of his greatcoat in a makeshift sling. Any movement of his elbow was agony now, and his teeth chattered from shock.

He walked calmly back to his bivvy.

When the attack came, he screamed: 'I'm hit!' Brave men manhandled him back to the casualty clearing station.

'You're lucky,' the doctor said, 'you've got a Blighty one here.'

'I'm so sorry I was wounded,' Nigel said. 'I wanted to stay and see it through to the end.'

He thought he had gone too far; *don't be so bloody clever*, he thought, and could have bitten off his tongue.

But the doctor nodded, understanding. He often heard men apologize for being wounded. Nearly always they meant it. This one, with the guilty eyes and shifty gaze, twitching each time the tent flap was jerked open, didn't.

The doctor sighed. He didn't give a damn. War was hell and that was all there was to it.

'Next,' he called, and the pretty VAD nurse helped the next one to the butcher's block table.

The squadron's departure for France had been set for Wednesday, but it rained. Thursday dawned fine but very windy, and it was not until mid-morning that it had dropped enough for the tiny Camel aeroplanes to be wheeled from their sheds.

Ben stood holding Sam on a leash, watching the ground crews line the Camels up in three flights of four across the grass. The other pilots stood around joking nervously and pulling on their gear. Frank Laidlaw winked at Ben and loaded a wicker basket containing his bulldog puppy, Grit, into the compartment behind his seat. The squadron would fly in formation first to Dover, then across the channel to the central aircraft depot at St Omer, where they would be told their final destination.

His white silk scarf fluttering in the breeze, Ben walked Sam behind the sheds. A large RE8 two-seater reconnaissance plane of the Army co-operation squadron waited. The engine was running, but only the pilot sat in the two-man machine.

On the side of the rear cockpit the words were stencilled: DO NOT FLY WITH LESS THAN 160 LBS IN GUNNER'S COMPARTMENT.

Sam sat, wagging, the propeller slipstream blowing his ginger ears out like wings, and laid his head against Ben's hip. The pilot, James Laidlaw, Frank's brother, gave Ben the thumb's up.

'Come on, boy,' Ben said. 'Your master wants to see you. He's lonely at La Houssoye without you.'

James shouted back: 'How much does that beast weigh?'

'He's your ballast – more than a hundred and sixty pounds!'

'Christ, how are you going to lift him up?'

Ben beckoned and Wilson, the head fitter, and a couple of mechanics came over. They'd worked out the technique last night in the pub. Together they lifted Sam smoothly into the rear cockpit and put him in the seat, tying his leash to the gun mounting. Sam looked out of the aeroplane, quite unconcerned, with his pink tongue lolling casually out of his mouth, as though he did this every day. Ben stood on the wing and stroked his head reassuringly, then jumped down and gave a wave to James. The engine roared and the aeroplane took off across the grass, then turned in the air towards St Omer.

Ben ran clumsily back between the sheds in his heavy sheepskin knee-boots and joined the group around the major, polishing his goggles, checking that the haversack containing all his personal kit was firmly tied up. They consulted their maps and got final instructions about the weather from the major, then dispersed to their machines.

The Camels were all brand new. The red, white and blue roundels on the wings sparkled in the sun, and the machined aluminium cowlings shimmered. Ben's machine had the number B6235 painted in black letters on the red white and blue tailplane.

He climbed on to the lower wing, hung from the groove in the top wing, and dropped down into the tight cockpit. His knees only just fitted under the dashboard. All the controls were very close around him – he had got Wilson to move some of them so that they were all easy to hand. In front of him rose the Camel's hump over the guns.

He ran the engine up to test the magnetos. The noise was colossal and there was a tang of burnt oil in the slipstream. The rudder pedals rattled against Ben's feet and the stick quivered between his knees. He throttled down and held up his thumb. The mechanic kicked away the wheel-chocks and Ben taxied out with his flight. One by one they took off, circling the aerodrome until everyone had joined up, then turned towards Dover.

They landed in time for a late lunch. Ben looked around the aerodrome hoping not to see the RE8 – it had the range to make St Omer in one hop and would only have landed here if something had gone wrong. Obviously nothing had. Sam was all right. In the afternoon the Camel squadron took off for St Omer. It was a narrow airfield when the wind was from the south, as it was today, and two machines tipped up on their noses, but the pilots were unhurt.

In the mess Ben said: 'I hear the Germans have got a new sort of Albatros.' A mechanic had told him: a pale blue underside with a very small lower wing called a V-strut, the latest thing. The mechanic had whispered: *'They say it's as good as the Camel, sir.'*

Silence greeted Ben's words in the mess.

'Nonsense,' the major said.

'Of course!' Ben replied. 'That was what I said.' What he had really said was: *'Tell me more.'*

The mechanic had said: *'They're calling it bloody April already, sir. More than a third of our aeroplanes have been shot down. Begging your pardon, sir, you having been here before, but a new subaltern lasts about ten or twelve days on average, maybe three weeks if he's lucky.'*

'If anyone tells you about some new miracle Hun aeroplane, it's a lie,' the major said. He stared at Ben. 'Who told you this?'

'No one. Just a rumour in the air.'

'Anyone spreading a damned rumour like that ought to be shot. I don't want to hear any more talk of it, from any of you. Is that clear?'

So it's true, Ben thought.

The telephone rang and the major stormed off to wing headquarters to collect his orders.

Frank said: 'And I heard that there's a new Fokker Triplane – three wings, turns on a sixpence, climbs like an angel.'

'The Camel is better than any of them,' Ben said.

'We're one squadron,' Frank said. 'The Germans have thirty-seven Circuses of Albatroses and Fokkers. What chance do we have?'

The major returned waving a sheaf of papers. 'Good news, chaps. We've been posted where the fighting is hottest!'

Ben asked: 'Where's that?'

The Major consulted the papers.

'Place called La Houssoye,' he said.

Ben smiled as he flew. He would see Bertie after all. The pleasure at seeing his friend with his peculiar upper-class ways, the impulsive warmth of his personality desperately concealed behind a veneer of cold reserve, reminded him a little of that girl.

In his mind's eye, though he was still automatically sweeping the sky for any sign of enemy aircraft, he saw her perfect face. He wondered what she was doing now. Had she really been frightened when he kissed her? What had she really felt? She had wanted him to; he was sure of it. But then she had backed away, warmth concealed behind a cold veneer.

When he talked to Colleen O'Keeffe about it, she had laughed.

'It was as though she hated me.'

'Sure, and that means she's over her head in love with you!'

'With a picture.' He toyed with the cold collation.

'So she's in love with your baby blue eyes, and what's wrong with that?'

'I see.'

'Oh, no, you don't,' sighed Colleen O'Keeffe wisely. 'Men are a mystery.'

He shot back: 'You're on her side!'

She looked at him and shook her head. 'The best thing you can do is to forget about her.' She took pity on him. 'Was she so very pretty?'

'Beautiful.'

'Upper crust?'

'Obviously.'

'Forget about her.' Colleen put her hand over his. 'You're in love with a dream.'

'I'm not in love.'

'But she is.'

Ben's face broke into a smile. 'Is she? Do you really think she is?'

Colleen put her elbow on the table. She rested her chin on

her hand, grinning, looking along her nose at him through half-closed eyes. Her head moved as she spoke. 'Are you sure you aren't?'

'There is something about her,' he admitted.

'Yes,' Colleen O'Keeffe said, 'the oldest thing in the world.'

He was annoyed. 'It wasn't like ... that. I admit it, I wanted it to be, but it wasn't. She's a nice girl.'

'What makes you say that?' Colleen raised her eyebrows. 'She's pure poison. Everything you say about her proves it. I've been a woman for the last sixty years, and I know about women. Forget her, Ben.'

'You can't possibly know. How can she be poison when I—'

'Not poison in herself, mayhap. Nor you. But together. It would happen between you.'

He repeated, 'You can't possibly know.'

She repeated: 'Forget her.'

But he couldn't forget her.

Here, now, at ten thousand feet, he wanted her, that perfect body – and through her body her perfect heart. At any cost.

He remembered the line of her bosom under those soft white furs, her shapely ankles through the white silk stockings. Perhaps Colleen in her direct way was right: it was just sex.

But Vane was a lady, above all that sort of thing.

The formation of machines was losing height. Ben recognized the shape of the Somme winding below. Spring was well advanced here. The treetops were a gorgeous green, and the fields were quilted with growing colours. It was wonderful to be alive, he thought. Then he saw the hideous pocked muddy stain of the Front, wider than before, spreading out along the valley.

It had not moved from the last time he was here. It had merely grown. Meanwhile, he knew, half a million men had been consumed.

The Camel squadron landed and the machines taxied towards the familiar canvas Bessoneau hangars that he remembered so well. Hardly anything had changed, although it seemed as though he had been away for years: more huts had been put up, and the windsock was faded from bright orange to pale grey. The grass was rutted with muddy tracks and the place had an air of overworked, busy dereliction.

Ground crew and pilots clustered around them, eager to examine the new machines. Ben couldn't see Bertie. 'How fast does she climb?' 'What's the rate of roll?' 'I hear they're dangerous little beasts to fly.'

Ben said: 'Yes, they eat Albatros.' That got a laugh; too much laughter, too much strain. Ben walked out of the back of the crowd. He took off his helmet and goggles, rubbed his eyes.

Sam came bounding across the grass and made a fuss of him. 'Good dog! Sit. Shake hands! How do you like flying, Sam?'

'He knows you,' Bertie said. 'He knew your machine, I swear.'

'Bertie, how are you?' Ben walked forward. He held out his hand. Bertie waited on the path, not wanting to get the mud on his shoes, an elegant figure in his tailored uniform, one hand in his pocket. His other held a cigarette to his mouth.

'Not too bad, thank you.'

He looks so old, Ben thought sadly. Bertie's slimness had become thin. His skin had lost its tone and there were dark marks under his eyes.

This awful strained shyness between them. Ben put his arms around Bertie and slapped his back. 'Since when have you been smoking those awful French gaspers! What are you flying nowadays?'

They walked towards the Mess. 'I chain-smoke fifty a day. They're stronger. I've had three FEs shot from under me.' Bertie's voice shook. He lit another cigarette. 'The FE's bloody hopeless – outdated, outmatched, outclassed. It's a massacre. We've lost the war. Still they send us up.' He sat with his back to the window. 'Orderly! Two whiskies.'

'Yes, sir.'

Sam sat down beside them. Bertie stroked his massive head blindly as he talked. 'I fly a Spad now, French single-seater.'

Ben asked: 'Is it a good machine?' This was frightful; this stilted non-communication.

Bertie shrugged. 'Comfortable.' The whiskies came on a silver tray. 'Two more. Doubles.'

'Yes, sir.'

'It's good to see you, Ben!' A cry from the heart.

'It's not too bad to see you, chum.'

The whiskies came. Ben knew that it had been very bad. Then Bertie showed a flash of his old intuition. 'You sounded just like me then.'

'Imitation is the sincerest form of flattery.'

'I didn't know whether to be sad or happy when I heard that you were coming back to La Houssoye after all.' Ben knew what he meant. It was a kind thought. Then Bertie touched his hand and his face became animated.

'I say, I've got a couple of days leave due, I thought I'd pop down to Paris. Are you game?'

'Sure, if I can get leave.'

'That's no problem. We'll arrange for you to collect a new Spad from the French depot at Villacoublay to fly back here. Have a couple of days at the Hôtel Crillon in Paris on the way. I have a friend with a permanent suite there – la Comtesse de Coucy.'

Ben remembered. 'Chouchou! Who sent you the letter.'

'Since then we have been in communication regularly. We are very distantly related – curiously enough through both the Benton and the Benson side, a tiny offshoot from the *Almanach de Gotha*.'

'I've never met a real live countess.' Ben wasn't sure he wanted to; but Bertie was obviously looking forward so much to introducing them.

'Oh' – Bertie made a dismissive gesture – 'Chouchou's terrific fun, you'll adore her. I've mentioned you to her—'

'In the most favourable light, I hope.' But he still wasn't sure about it.

Vane was sitting in her favourite place, which was in front of the mirror in her bedroom. She admired her face – it was calm and unravaged, showing no sign of the chaos of feelings tossing within her. She wished some sign *would* show, some manifestation of the drama. She had hardly slept last night – the memory of that kiss. The revelation of it. The brutality. The attraction. Her dreams were a heavenly torment.

In her dreams, she threw her arms around his rough, tough chest.

He wrapped her in the safe, muscular solidity of his arms.

She turned her face up to his, and saw her beauty reflected in his eyes. Would she never see him again?

She heard a motor-car draw up at the pavement outside. She ran to the window and glanced through the lace netting. The yellow primroses were dying, and Primrose Hill was green again. The little houses shone prettily in the sunlight. At the kerb was the open tourer that Marcelline's fiancé Henry had given her, all for her own. The old chauffeur (impossible to get young men, they'd all been sent off to the war) was opening the rear door, and Marcelline stepped down, looking strong and extrovert, wearing a rather masculine tweed ulster to keep the dust off. Vane was disappointed; she preferred Marcelline to wear femininely-styled clothes in the dark, earth colours which suited her.

A moment later, she heard the little maidservant opening the front door.

Vane crossed back to her dresser. She wore a long pink satin dressing gown – it was only mid-morning, and she had not yet finished her *toilette*. Her hair looked too neatly combed. She flicked her fingers through it.

Lisbeth, the maid, knocked on the door and put her head round. 'Miss deWalters to see you, ma'am.'

'Vane! Darling.' Marcelline entered the room, smiling and pulling off her gloves, which she handed to the curt-

seying Lisbeth, then as the door was closed put her fingertips on Vane's shoulders and pecked her cheek with a kiss.
'How did it go? You must tell me absolutely everything.'

Vane kissed Marcelline's cheek and turned back to her
mirror. Marcelline's skin had a hot, musky scent today that
she did not like. 'Which is that perfume?' she asked. 'I don't
care for it.'

Marcelline smiled from the chaise-longue and crossed
her legs. 'Poor Vane. Tell me what's wrong.'

'I met him after all.'

'And you followed my advice?' Marcelline said. Her
smile broadened. 'He ignored you. Poor, poor Vane. For
once you didn't get what you wanted.'

Vane confessed: 'He kissed me.'

'The beast!'

'Don't. It isn't funny. You didn't tell me he would.'

Marcelline laid her arm languidly along the fluted pink
velvet backrest at the side of the chaise-longue. She rested
two elegant fingertips against her high, sun-browned
cheekbone, looking very modern. There was something
mocking about it. Sloe-eyed, she said: 'What did you
expect?'

'Not that a gentleman would be so forward.'

Marcelline shook her head minutely. Vane had been
nearly there! She loved talking with Vane; the little prig
made her feel so wise. She suggested: 'Perhaps he isn't a
gentleman.'

'He is!'

'Yet you let him go.' Marcelline laughed lightly. 'Vane,
darling, you live in a different world. It's a battle for
survival, didn't you know? There are too many girls chasing too few men out there. Only the fittest, and most
beautiful, and most forward survive nowadays.'

'Like you,' Vane said bitterly.

'If you won't set your sights on the man you want and go
out and get him, what does that say about you? That you
deserve what you get. Are you satisfied with second-rate?'

Vane sulked. 'He's gone away, anyway.'

'You went away, dearie. You didn't let him win you.'

'I'm not an object to be won.' Vane was determined.

'He kissed you, darling, and you ran a mile.'

That was the truth. 'Stop it,' Vane said.

Marcelline said: 'One is not born, one becomes a woman.'

And there was a hurtful truth in that. Vane felt unhappy, powerless to be a woman, something between a male and a eunuch – Marcelline had found the answer. Henry hadn't stood a chance, Vane guessed, excited. Marcelline was a man's woman. She gave away a little of herself, and got everything she wanted.

'I know you're right,' Vane said pathetically.

'You're bored. If you aren't interested in men, why don't you do something useful?' Marcelline stood up. 'I've joined a Voluntary Aid Detachment. They're training me as a nurse. They may even send me to France.'

Vane was horrified. 'Do they send women to France?'

'Lots. Come on, Vane, why don't you join up? They let you practise on schoolboys at first, and you don't have to go abroad if you don't want to.'

Another thought struck Vane. 'But doesn't Henry object frightfully to your working?'

'Henry merely loves me, he doesn't own me.' What a marvellous thought!

Vane imagined Ben being horribly wounded and her nursing him back to health, and him being dependent on her for everything. She imagined him trying to sit up while she pumped up the pillows in that no-nonsense way that nurses had. She imagined the grateful look in his eyes as she spoon-fed him. Men could be injured in battle in ways that kept them helplessly in bed for months, she knew. He would fall helplessly in love with her, she dreamed, and she would tell Marcelline, '*Ben loves me to death, poor darling, but he doesn't own me.*'

'I must dash,' Marcelline said, kissing her. 'Do give it some thought, won't you?'

Thoughtfully, Vane got dressed, which took several hours. She had given instructions for a very light lunch of smoked salmon and scrambled eggs, since they would be eating more heavily at the dinner tonight – the dinner Ben London had not seen fit to attend. She thought about nursing. It really was rather a good idea. Following the Duchess of Sutherland's example, all the best people did it now, and she was growing dreadfully weary of knitting mittens for the men at the Front.

She heard an engine chugging and knew that her father had arrived home for lunch. He no longer used the Rolls-Royce to go to and from work, and would have had it mothballed and put up in the garage on blocks but for her protests. Instead he drove himself to and fro in a common Model T Ford. She went to meet Papa Georgy at the door. He was pushing himself too hard, apparently actually serving behind a counter sometimes, and when she was not at home she suspected that he did not bother with lunch at all.

'Papa, did you have a good morning?'

He hung his driving coat on the hook himself – would not let the servant do it. His face, always red with pressure, was redder still. Balding, with a semicircle of curly silver hair, he had popping eyes. 'Look what they have done to me, Vanity.' He held up his hand: she clapped her fingers to her cheeks, seeing the bandage. 'A person threw a brick through the window, some glass cut me.' She followed him through to the sitting room. The maid was supposed to pour the first drink. He held the whisky bottle clumsily against his chest with the wrist of his injured hand, unable to grip it with his bandaged fingers, and pulled the cork out. He transferred the bottle to his good hand and poured a measure. 'Do they not understand?' he said as he put the cork back, 'I am as English as they are.'

That was true. Although Grandpapa Leibig had been German, Georgy – everyone called him Georgy, even the staff, behind his back – had never even been to Germany. Yet although his British accent was perfect, he phrased his sentences too clearly, saying *it is* instead of *it's*, and he said *frightfully* not *fraffly* like most others of his class – or at least, of Vane's class.

He sounded slightly foreign even to Vane, and she had had trouble filling the seats tonight.

Grandpapa had been a very powerful personality, as indeed Mama had been, and Georgy had never been able to rise above his upbringing. Everything that Grandpapa Leibig said and did was holy writ, and Georgy wouldn't change a thing, not even that slight taint of phrasing that had rubbed off on him. It was a stubbornness that she recognized in herself.

In some that might have been called strength, but Vane sensed that with Georgy it was weakness. It was awfully difficult to think clearly about one's own papa, but few of the things he did seemed to be for positive reasons: usually he did them because Grandpapa did them. He was afraid to change, it seemed to her. The last straw had been over the Rolls-Royce.

Vane had been furious. How could she show her face in a Model T?

He was weak and obsessive – about money, recently; but mothballing the Rolls-Royce! Even the thought! Grandpapa might have sold it, but never mothballed it! But Grandpapa had bought the car, so Gregory would rather have died than sell it, however bad times were down at the Emporium.

And with a name like Leibig, at the moment they were very bad.

But he worked so hard. He lived wholly and totally for Leibig's Emporium, as though it had been an absolute duty laid upon him in Grandpapa's deathbed command. Perhaps it had. Vane didn't know. Her father was all she had now, but he was not close to her. Sometimes she thought that he did not like her. She had been brought up strictly pampered, with the best of everything, so he told her, but that only contributed to the distance between them. It had only come up since Mama died. He wanted her to do something, but she didn't know what.

Vane rang for the maid and pointed to her father's empty glass. Lisbeth bobbed and brought the bottles on a silver tray. 'No, thank you,' he said. 'I must return soon. There is so much work to do after lunch.'

God, Vane thought, *he's going to talk about work again, and I'm going to die of boredom.*

'I'm joining a Voluntary Aid Detachment,' she said.

'Good!' he replied. 'It will keep you out of mischief.'

4

I'm so sorry I was wounded. I wanted to stay and see it through to the end.

Nigel was still frightened. He had been frightened when the conscientious objectors in the stretcher party dragged him back from the trenches to the casualty clearing station, frightened that he would see the truth in their eyes, his lie revealed.

But he hadn't.

Then he had been terrified that the doctor would say: *This is a self-inflicted injury! Call the military police. Get him out of my sight!* But he hadn't. Only: *You're lucky, you've got a Blighty one here.*

Later, at the base hospital in Rouen, he had been afraid that the nurses would somehow intuitively *know:* they would see the guilt, the cowardice, sticking plain as a birthmark on his face. Women were like that. They knew the darkest secrets.

But the little VADs treated him just as well as the other patients.

Because of the nerve damage to his elbow he was transferred to a specialist hospital in Folkestone. By now the flesh had healed to a clean, puckered scar; the injury was deeper, hidden. They put him on an agonizing physiotherapy machine with counterweights that flexed his arm back and forth and wriggled his fingers. He could move only his thumb and forefinger by himself, snapping them together like a little crab's claw. The nerves to the other fingers were permanently damaged.

The pain was bad, but the fear was worse. The mills of God, he knew, ground slow but fine; the Army Staff ground even slower, but if anything finer, and their punishment would come in this world. In his nightmares he stared down a rifle barrel, and Jasper Clark's screaming face turned into his own.

Or a little voice said: *Who's been a naughty boy then, Nigel?*

Nigel woke sweating. Raymond Trott. Raymond Trott *knew*.

Nigel prayed that Raymond Trott would be killed. Yes, it would probably happen. Everyone was killed.

Now Nigel was to be discharged from the hospital.

The military policemen stood around looking bored.

Smiling, trembling, he collected his rail warrant from the clerk.

No hand fell on his shoulder. He was not arrested.

From Charing Cross station he caught a tram along the Strand. People looked at him curiously, not because he was in a uniform – every man under forty wore a uniform, it seemed – but because he was wounded. He had his arm in a sling, he wore a glorious wound-stripe on his shoulder. To get some peace Nigel went up to the open-top deck, where fresh air blew in his face.

I'm still afraid, he thought. But at least I'm alive. Now I can do my duty to Vic. I'll prove how clever I am. There's bound to be a lot of confusion after the war, but when Vic comes back he's going to find everything organized and waiting for him to pick up the reins. There's four thousand pounds in that trunk, and if I can't double it by the end of the war, with all those lists and books, my name's not Nigel Price.

It was worth killing Blumenthall.

It was worth the agony in my elbow, the fear, the guilt. For money.

He imagined Vic coming home, and Vic's arm thrown warmly around his shoulder, Vic smiling into his face, and Nigel knew that he wouldn't be frightened any more. '*What have you done with our money, Nige?*'

And him saying eagerly: '*I've doubled your money, Vic. Eight thousand pounds.*' All of it, worth it – for Vic's approval.

The tram rattled and swayed down Cable Street. It was nice basking up here in the sun. The conductress smiled as she gave him his ticket. Even the driver was a woman, he had noticed, which surely could not be safe. He had had plenty of time for reading so he knew that they were paid the same as the men. Appalling.

There was no tramway down West Ferry Road, so he got off near the junction with Commercial Road. His feeling of dread increased. The Old Bull and Bush seemed to stand almost in the middle of the road where it curved around, looking like an island because of the side streets surrounding it. It looked strangely dark and empty, and the doors were closed. Nigel had never seen it looking like that before, it was always full of life and garish lights, toffs in toppers, and giggling girls. Then he understood. It was after three, and the Defence Of the Realm Act decreed that pubs must close. Nigel shivered. He wondered if Raymond Trott was peering out from those dark windows.

He almost turned round.

He could hardly face going home. Suppose they knew?

Suppose Raymond Trott had . . . for example . . . simply written a letter?

Dear Mrs Price, Your son Nigel is a coward. I saw him shoot himself.

And if Esther knew about it, the whole street would know about it by now. Mum couldn't keep a secret to save her life.

Nigel swung his kitbag over his shoulder with his right hand and walked slowly down West Ferry Road. He had looked forward so much to coming home. Now he dreaded it. He passed Kosky's fried fish shop. He turned the corner into Havannah Street. And the very worst thing happened.

It was full of people. They had been waiting for him.

They saw him, and cheered and clapped. Nigel gaped.

A banner was stretched across the street between the rooftops: WELCOME HOME NIGEL!

Someone slapped Nigel on the back. He walked up the middle of the road in a daze. Children ran around him, waving little union jack flags on sticks. Dogs barked. A man he didn't recognize toasted him with a glass and shouted: 'Well done, sir!' They started to sing 'Hail, the conq'ring hero comes.' Mothers held up their babies to see. The whole street was out.

Then the crowd parted. There were trestle tables set out

with sheets for tablecloths, and food, mostly pies and sausages. Mixing bowls had been filled up with punch – a glass was stuck in his hand. Nigel downed the rich liquor in one gulp and felt the glow spread through his stomach. He was so relieved that he felt sick. He was not a coward, he was a hero! 'What's all this?' he kept saying. 'What a turn-up! I was only wounded, I was so sorry, because I wanted to stay and see the business through to the end . . .'

Then he thought with a stab of fear: *Suppose Raymond Trott's here?* He looked anxiously around him.

Esther walked towards him with her hands held out, her eyes shining and her chin trembling with joy. She was wearing a yellow dress with purple circles on it, a dark red coat open down the front, and brown shoes. Nigel broke down as she embraced him. 'Oh Mum,' he said. 'Oh, Mum.'

'How's your poor arm?' she asked. 'Look everyone, he's got to wear his poor arm in a sling.' She began to cry. Someone gave her a glass of punch and she sobbed it down, then embraced him again. 'Welcome home,' she said, with cheeks glowing. 'We all love you, and we won't let you go back there again.'

Tom, dressed in a black suit with a tall white collar, scrambled up on to a chair. To calls of 'Speech, speech!' he stuck his thumbs under his lapels, shaking his head. 'All I need to say is this: it's grand to have you back home with us again, Nigel!'

Nigel said, 'Thanks, Dad.' They shook hands, man to man, Nigel limply, Tom bursting his chest with pride. 'My own son! God bless you!'

Nigel drank down another glass of punch. Behind him he heard excited voices saying, 'There she is! Here she comes! *Wotcher, Ria!*'

Ria elbowed through the men. 'Hallo, mate.' She stared into Nigel's eyes. 'Aren't you going to show us your dramatic elbow, then?'

He held it clamped defensively against him.

He hardly recognized her.

She was gorgeous.

Ria's shining blonde hair fell in curves from her head and lay in curls over her shoulders. She wore a lovely blue dress shaped to her body, trimmed with chaste white. That was a laugh: he wondered where the Workhouse Bastard's bastard was, her baby, Will. He must be two and a half years old by now.

But the most startling change was in her face.

Her features were so strikingly full of life that she was absolutely beautiful. Her eyes were still strange, vital, full of mystery, observing everything yet somehow reserved . . . something that drew men in, and made them stare. They flashed with sparks of different colours, depending how the angle of the sun struck them. And men *were* staring at them – Nigel had been eclipsed by his perfectly ordinary sister.

He held out his hand. 'Hallo, Ria.' That dress was indecently short. And he did not like his sister showing off to men like that. She was . . . *radiating*. He could feel the heat himself.

'Go on!' she said. 'Don't be so stiff and formal.' She hugged him and rocked him with a kiss. Openness, softness, warmth – she *gave*. He flushed to the tips of his ears. Disgusting. Immediately he felt something in her withdraw. She demanded: 'What's up with you? I've kissed more soldiers than I've had hot dinners. What's wrong with it? It's innocent.'

He sneered: 'Is it?' His own sister, dressed like a common tart.

'They're being sent off to the Front,' she said, as though that explained everything. 'Show 'em a bit of leg, give 'em a kiss, and off they go.' A moment of pain showed in her eyes. She veiled it by lighting a cigarette. 'And die happy, I hope, poor sods.'

Esther said nervously: 'Ria is an actress now, you see, Nigel.'

He said coldly: 'Does Vic know? Has she told Vic?'

Ria dragged on her cigarette and shrugged.

'What does that mean?'

'What are you, a quizmaster or something? I'm living my own life now!'

Esther tugged Nigel's elbow. She gabbled, 'Yes, Ria has her own life now, she plays the Queen's regularly. Well, I know it's not plush, it's all benches, and I know they're a rough crowd and they're supposed to have this tradition of cracking and eating peanuts during the performances, to put you off, but, Nigel, they don't, not when Ria's singing. She's got it, Nige. The gift. She's special. They love her. She's played the Paragon, too, and the People's Palace. She's got an agent, and he's trying to get her a booking at the Empire in the West End.'

'*Does Vic know?*' Nigel shouted.

'No,' Ria said.

'What are you up to?'

'Vic doesn't own me!' she screamed.

'She's under a strain,' Esther whispered apologetically. 'She gives it all she's got – all of those boys going out – so few of them come back.'

Ria overheard. 'Yes, only the lucky ones get it in the elbow, Nigel.'

He demanded: 'What's that supposed to mean?'

'They get their balls blown off. I don't suppose you'd notice any difference though.'

Nigel could have struck her down.

Esther stood between them. 'Now, that's enough. She didn't mean it, Nigel.'

'Of course she didn't,' smiled Nigel.

Clouds had covered the sun and the adults were drifting away. Children ran about scoffing the last wedges of carrot pie. The tables were packed way back in the church hall and the families said good-bye and returned to their own homes. Inside, Esther proudly displayed her shabby-looking sitting room carpet.

'Lovely,' Nigel said, dropping into a chair.

Esther called Will. The boy ran in, fell over, then looked at Nigel. Ria said indifferently: 'Meet your uncle.'

Will stared at Nigel as if struggling to understand why a grown man had his arm in a sling. He walked unsteadily over and examined it, looking from the sling to Nigel's face.

'Mr Osborne's died,' Esther said, pouring the tea. 'And

so did Mr Blumenthall.' Blumenthall! *It was Vic who killed him, Mum. Oh, Mum, it was nothing to do with me . . .* Nigel remembered the feel of the old man's hands sliding from his neck, the splash of his body into the river.

Esther eyed Nigel curiously. 'Don't you care? You and Vic were quite pals with him once.'

'Who's Mr Osborne?'

'He was our next-door neighbour. His widow's so arthritic that she can't look after herself. Her family have taken her in.'

Nigel pushed the child away. So there was an empty house. He would speak to the collector about taking the Osborne place on: he needed a place where he could be alone. He couldn't stand this.

Esther said: 'You do remember Mr Blumenthall?'

Ria said: 'You don't give a bloody damn about a bloody thing, do you, Nigel!'

Nigel said airily, 'That was before the war. It all seems so long ago. We were children then.'

After they had gone to bed, Nigel stayed up late. He wrote a letter to Vic.

Before turning in, he made a mental note to go to the ironmonger's tomorrow and buy a hacksaw. Vic had hidden the keys to the trunk, of course, and he didn't know where; he would need to hacksaw through the padlocks when he went to see Louisa Hiscott in the morning.

It was going to be a devil of a job cutting one-handed.

He clicked the forefinger and thumb of his left hand impotently together, like a little snapping claw, hating it.

It was a constant reminder of his cowardice, his guilt, his fear.

He closed his eyes. It was cold. He held the letter to his chest.

Vic, I need you. Come back.

5

Ben gasped when the fog lifted.

Paris was brilliant.

It had been a strange train journey from Amiens to the Gare du Nord. He saw a side to Bertie that he hardly recognized, laughing and joking with the French passengers and peasants, passing around a tin of fifty cigarettes: telling stories in fluent French with a perfect English accent, which alone creased up his audience with amusement. Ben, who knew few French words but had an ear for the accent, enjoyed it as much as they did. Bertie was on top form, gesturing with his long hands, Gallic expressions to illustrate his stories chasing themselves across his face, which lost its veneer of aristocratic aloofness: amazement, incredulity, the heel of the hand slapped to the forehead, the shoulders shrugged with splayed hands. He told the story of the airman who force-landed with a minor fault to his engine – a nothing – and by the time he had opened the cowling to look inside – *sacré bleu!* – the French peasants who had come to aid him had siphoned the petrol from his tank and filled up every motor-car in the village! That got a roar of laughter. They loved to hear guileful stories like that about themselves.

Ben noticed that Bertie did not talk about air battles, the reality, the dreadful stuttering moment of victory when the enemy machine turned to flame. Death was banished. In Bertie's world nobody burned, nobody died, nobody was lonely, or without love. Listening to him speak in a foreign language, Ben understood his friend. Bertie's dream world reminded him of a beautiful painting where the more you looked, the more you saw, until finally it was . . . it was whatever you saw hiding there.

A burly onion-seller asked: 'Why is it that you go to Paris?' He pronounced it *Paree*.

A woman wearing a white headscarf said: 'It is for *les girls!*'

'Oui,' Ben said. 'The Folies Bergère. Mistinguette. The can-can.'

The thin old man who wore the pince-nez of a schoolmaster held up his hand and said: 'We pretend to be so jolly, you understand, for France is bleeding to death.'

'I understand,' Ben said.

At the station the passengers shook hands like old friends, embraced, and departed. The schoolmaster saluted them. He had been called up despite his age and reserved occupation. Ben wondered if the situation could possibly be so desperate. Then he was astonished to see that the concourse was crowded, in fact jammed solid, with men in uniform: old men. With white hair, white moustaches, skin wrinkled with age, all dressed in horizon-blue, they waited wearily but proudly to be helped up into the cattle-trunks that would take them to the Front.

Ben's heart went out to them.

The battle for the fortress of Verdun – which had no military value – the mincing-machine that had torn the heart out of France, as it was meant to, had lasted for nearly a year. The German policy had been to bleed France to death and they had succeeded. Both sides were victorious: the French had kept Verdun and the Germans had killed most of their young men. Now the French sent out their old men. It was whispered that the Army trembled on the brink of mutiny. The young survivors said: 'We will defend the trenches, but we won't attack!' But still the old men came.

Ben followed Bertie into the brilliant Parisian sunlight. A few pigeons watched them warily – most had been eaten, cackled a toothless old flower-seller.

Ben looked at the people. They were not only determined to survive, they were determined to be gay. Smiling faces and bright colours were everywhere. The buildings shone with a pale light, not like London's vast gloomy masses of serious, imperial stone, and the people wore life lightly. A girl in a long striped dress and a white apron walked by them holding a croissant in one hand and a piece of chocolate in the other, looking straight into Ben's eyes and giving him a strikingly genuine smile. Very old men in shabby grey suits and caps, wearing colourful medals from the Sedan campaign off the 1870s – the last time the Germans nearly reached Paris – stretched proudly across their chests, seeing their RFC uniforms, came over and shook their hands with both hands.

There was little of the war hysteria one saw in London, Ben realized: only a desperate, garish gaiety. Let us be merry, for tomorrow we die.

The taxis had all been requisitioned, but the driver of a sky-blue *fiacre* with yellow wheels let them ride with him. 'No charge. For the war.' The horse's name was Charlemagne, he said. He had pulled fashionable tourists up and down the promenade of the Queen of Beaches at Deauville, but the war had changed all that. Now the tourists had left even Paris, they had all fled to Biarritz. He would have accompanied them, but the price of hay was an outrage: this drew their attention to the horse again, who was so thin that Ben said that instead of Charlemagne, he ought to be called Charlemange. This was apparently quite a good joke even in French, because the driver laughed. They felt so sorry for the poor beast that they thanked him and got down to walk the rest of the way. 'Shoot them down,' the driver called after them approvingly, 'make them burn.'

The lime trees shaded the boulevards with brilliant green. Patriotic tricolour flags hung from every building and the cafés all had their canopies open, red, green, blue, and seemed to be doing good business.

'Let's help them,' Ben suggested. They sat and ordered a few cognacs and fell in love with Paris, even Bertie. He wore a most strange expression on his face, Ben thought: he looked happy.

'I could live here,' Bertie said, stretching out his legs. 'They love life, don't they? I'll live here after the war.'

Ben was glad that he was talking about *after the war*. Bertie had been under too much strain for too long. Bertie glanced at him out of the corner of his eye and seemed to understand the way Ben's thoughts were going.

'No,' he said quietly, 'for me, the war will never end.'

That sounded like self-pity. 'Shut up, mate. *Garçon, deux fines!*'

'But it's true, isn't it?' Bertie said. 'No peace.'

'If that's the way you want it.'

'I'd give anything for peace.'

'Drink up.' Ben emptied his glass.

'Yes,' Bertie said, 'that's what I've been doing too much of.'

'If you don't cheer up,' Ben promised, 'I'm going to dunk you in that river.'

They walked along the Seine's equivalent of the Embankment. Between the log jams of rust-red and burgundy-coloured barges fishermen sat on the quayside with bamboo rods or shoots cut from the poplar trees.

At the Place de la Concorde, as they turned towards the Crillon, Ben saw a queue of young men, mostly very casually dressed, waiting outside the American Embassy. He knew why they were there.

Early in April, America had entered the war against Germany. Soon those eager young men would be wearing uniform. Girls would throw them flowers and blow them kisses as they jumped up into the cattle-trucks.

The doorman saluted them and the boy opened the door. They entered the vast gilded lobby of the Crillon. All of smart Paris was there, bellboys scurried to and fro, and Ben knew that the voice of the commoner was not heard here. 'Sorry, chum,' he told Bertie, who was chatting with the concierge, 'I can't afford it here.'

'You don't have to. I prefer the Hôtel de Paris myself. But Chouchou won't move from here.' Bertie nodded through the plate glass windows, and Ben followed his eyes across the river towards the huge building to the left of the Eiffel Tower, the hospital of the Hôtel des Invalides. 'From here, she can see his window,' Bertie explained. 'The Count was wounded in the chest at Verdun. Shrapnel, not serious, but troublesome, and he's been kept in the military hospital for some time. I think he's soon coming out to convalesce – they'll probably go to Deauville. The Royal has hospital facilities.'

Ben's room was huge and lushly carpeted. The chandelier glittered with electric lights. The four-poster bed, hung with drapes of white lace, was big enough for four, so high that there was a step up to it, and when he pressed down on it his hand almost disappeared, it was so softly sprung. The porter drew the velvet curtains, adjusted the set of the Louis

XIV chair by the writing desk, and opened the bathroom door with a flourish. Amidst plumbing exposed in the French style stood a massive white enamelled bath on four cast-iron feet in the shape of lions' paws, and taps with porcelain inserts in the handles marked CHAUD and FROID in black letters. There was a basin big enough to be a bath, a smaller basin for washing the feet, and a toilet with an open-fronted seat of gleaming mahogany.

Ben took out the money he had in his pocket and tipped him.

'*Merci*, m'sieu!'

Alone, Ben stood in the middle of the room. He started to laugh. He took off his shoes and wiggled his toes in the soft pile carpet. Then he threw himself on the bed and lay with his hands behind his head, staring up at the intricately carved woodwork and the drapes. This was a very long way from the Workhouse. He was going up in the world. He didn't mind. That chandelier was exactly the same design as the one which had hung in Bill Madeley's office. He had forgotten nothing.

He looked at his Ingersoll watch. He had arranged to meet Bertie down at the bar for an apéritif at seven. In the bathroom he doused his face and combed his hair, then went downstairs. He felt like a duke descending the grand staircase.

It was too early to be very busy. Bertie was not down yet. Ben was amazed to find something unheard-of: a woman standing at the magnificent bar. Not only that – unthinkable in England – her clothing was a practical, simple dark beige knitwear, like horse-jockeys wore.

She must be of the lower classes then; so he had a feeling of kinship with her and admired the way she leaned confidently at the bar. While he waited for the bartender to come back he tried to guess what her job was. Possibly a waitress. The tight little straw hat enclosing her hair looked neat and hygienic, and the straight shirtwaist styling of the beige dress, showing little of her breasts, not sculpted in at the waist, and ending a little below the knees, looked easy and comfortable to wear, enabling her to move around as her job required. Of course; she was the drinks waitress here – he had arrived early, before the bar was officially open. It was now well after seven, and he decided that it was time the bar *was* open.

He said: 'Would you fetch me a whisky, please.'

'M'sieu?'

'Whisky. Teacher's.'

She smiled, then went behind the bar and selected a bottle with a silver spout. He put her age at about thirty, although the clothes made her look much younger – almost an adolescent freedom of movement. She had not been in this job for long though: she could not find the glasses, which were on a rack above her head. He pointed.

'M'sieu is too kind,' she said.

Ben heard voices and turned. Bertie came in with a group of women all very casually dressed in loose, straight clothes. None wore a bodice. Showing the throat between the lapels – unheard-of – their waistcoats seemed almost masculine in cut. Their hats were close fitting, with broad brims. Beneath them, half a dozen pairs of eyes surveyed Ben with interest.

'There he is,' Bertie said. 'May I introduce the Marquise d'Aramon, the Princesse de Poix, the Comtesse d'Hinnisdal, the Princesse de . . . my God! Chouchou!' He was staring at the woman behind the bar. 'What ever are you doing there?'

She put down the bottle and gave Ben his glass. 'Ben London, I presume?' she asked, with a smile.

Bertie said stiffly: 'It seems that you have already made the acquaintance of the Comtesse de Coucy, Ben.'

'I do apologize for my mistake.' Ben smiled, and bowed to her. 'Forgive me. I thought countesses always wore tiaras.'

Chouchou gave a husky laugh, making him look at her. Her eyes were a rich golden colour, like a tiger's. She wore a chain of glowing pearls around her neck, casually allowed to be almost hidden by the dress. Her skin carried a suntan that surely would have been out of place in the *salons* before the war, and tiny crow's feet around the eyes: from laughter, or suffering. Her nose was fine and straight, with slim nostrils, and her mouth, though it smiled, carried a deep cleft in each corner: determination. It was easy to see both why Bertie had hoped to marry her, and why she had not: she would have eaten him alive. Sir Ozwald Benton-Benson must have been crushingly disappointed in his son.

'I lost my tiaras,' she said, coming round the bar, 'and my clothes, when the Germans came. I arrived at the sea in what I stood up in. These things were run up in Deauville by a little seamstress named Chanel. They have become quite the Paris fashion. Only the old folk go to Poiret now.'

'They are unconventional but beautiful.'

'Women have the right to be free,' one of the gay young princesses said, and Bertie nodded.

Ben turned on her. 'What does that mean?'

There was a moment of silence.

Bertie said: 'Steady on, old chap. We're all friends here, you know.' He began to apologize.

'No.' Chouchou help up her hand. 'I understand what Ben means. He is right,' she told them. 'None of us are really free.' Ben noticed the lines around her eyes deepen, then she grinned brilliantly. 'All of us here have lost our homes. All we have are our names. Our blood. We are the dispossessed.' She spoke so intensely and so gravely that he stared at her, impressed. *Our blood.* She had emphasized each word separately, with both an aristocratic and then a feminine intensity that stopped his whisky glass at his lips, and sent a shiver down his back. *Our blood.*

He nearly said, conventionally, *I'm sorry,* because Bertie was still staring at him, but he knew that Chouchou would only shrug impatiently at mere politeness. He said nothing.

Chouchou waited a moment, then flashed him a small smile. She knew. 'And you, Ben. You are too.'

Dispossessed? So Bertie had told her his history, or rather his lack of it: from foundling to Workhouse to officer in King George's Army, trusty and well beloved. And the secret void within him? Did Bertie have the sensitivity to feel that truth? Yes; beneath his veneer Bertie was all too dreadfully aware of it, longed to fill it, and never could.

'Yes and no,' Ben answered her lightly. 'I wasn't dispossessed from a château.'

'You came from nowhere. In my case it was a castle.' She shrugged, as if there was no difference; to her he was neither a peasant nor a bourgeois, he was simply from outside the structure, nothing and everything. He could be whatever she wanted him to be. He felt a touch of anger at her arrogance.

More people were coming in and the place was filling up. They took a table and Bertie ordered champagne. Chouchou took Ben's elbow. 'Sit by me. Let us all have too much to drink. Don't be angry with me.'

'Angry with you?'

'Yes you are.'

'Yes, I am. But only a little.'

'Why?'

'Because America has come into the war, and so the Germans will lose. You will get everything back.'

Her face filled with pain, so much that he was alarmed. Was it an illness? A heart attack? Surely she was too young. Then her eyes opened, her lips regained their gentle smile. The web around her eyes became faint again, and only the determined clefts at the corners of her mouth remained, making dark gashes in her soft skin. Not pain, he realized. Grief. Behind the easy manner, the calm amber eyes, he sensed a terrible weight riding on her shoulders.

'I have nothing,' she said.

'Somehow I've upset you. I'm sorry. I didn't mean to. May I get you a glass of water?'

'This will do.' She sipped her champagne indifferently. He noticed the pearls at her throat more closely: they were perfectly matched, as large as larks' eggs, with the deep internal glow that pearls gain from the touch of a woman's skin. Probably Cartier. Fifty thousand pounds' worth at least.

'Nothing?' he said.

'Nothing,' she said, 'because I do not have the one thing that would mean everything to me.'

He stared at her.

He did not understand. Then he realized that she was talking of her husband. 'But he will be leaving hospital in the next few days, I believe?'

'Yes,' she smiled. 'It will be wonderful to be reunited. I love him very much. The Count is everything to me.'

'Let's drink to his health,' Bertie said, raising his glass. 'To Charles Enguerrand, Count of Coucy.'

Chouchou raised her glass. 'To the long life and health of the Count of Coucy,' she said.

Everyone drank.

'I adore champagne,' confided the chinless princess, leaning across to Ben. 'Don't you love it when the bubbles go *Breeee* up your nose?'

It was very late.

Ben returned to his room. He turned on the light and clicked his door closed behind him, then leaned back against it, staring up at that chandelier.

It had been quite an evening. He had met a real countess. And he had been surprised to find that he liked her.

She hadn't been stuffy or stuck-up. She had been a woman with hopes and fears as human as any other woman's. Her smiles. That moment of grief. Her laughter. Her strong, husky voice.

To the long life and health of the Count of Coucy.

Ben yawned. It had been a long day. He pushed himself off the door. Maids had come in while he was dining and turned the coverlet on the four-poster, closed the heavy curtains across the window. He took off his uniform jacket. It was forbidden for officers to dance while in uniform, but he had danced with Chouchou. With more enthusiasm than skill. It had been something stately and rotating, not one of the more modern dances. He was subtly enveloped in her perfume, which was also Chanel, quite unlike any other scent. Instead of a simple flower essence, Chouchou said, it contained over eighty ingredients.

'Have you ever danced with a woman before?'

'Not a Countess.'

'Call me Chouchou.'

'Chouchou. Chouchou – what does the word mean?'

'It has no meaning. It is a term of endearment.'

'Chouchou.'

'We have danced enough. More would not be proper.'

'I was just getting the hang of it.'

'People are watching.'

'They are admiring my efforts at the dancing.'

'I am wearing soft shoes. I would require steel plates on my feet to go further.'

'Please.'

'No. We must not dance again tonight. I shall dance with Bertie.'

Ben had bowed to fate and danced with the Princess, who had fallen madly in love with Bertie. She asked him how many enemy aircraft Bertie had shot down . . . how many men he had killed . . .

Ben hung up his jacket, unlaced his shoes, and left them outside the door to be cleaned. He took off his trousers and put them in the press. When he was naked he threw the towel over his shoulder and went into the bathroom. The plumbing made a terrific noise. Clouds of steam arose as he filled the bath. He cleaned his teeth, then slid into the hot water and washed his hair, lay with his eyes closed. He remembered the little boy who had sat shivering in a bath of freezing water on his first night in the Workhouse. It was more than ten years ago, but it felt like yesterday. So quickly did boys become men. Tonight he had danced with a countess.

He got out of the bath and dried himself, then went back into the bedroom.

The chandelier was dark, the light was out, he could see nothing. The room was black. He stood naked in the bathroom doorway, staring. He could feel the carpet softly between his toes. The curtain had been pulled open, and the moonlight threw a pale rectangle on the carpet, casting a glow into the room. The outline of the stool at the foot of the bed had softened: a garment lay across it. He touched it. It was light as air, a woman's silken gown. He dropped it; it swirled and fell. He raised his hand and parted the drapes

411

of the four-poster. Silence. Neither of them moved. The subtle, intoxicating scent of Chanel Number 5, as dependent on the skin of a woman for its individuality as the chain of pearls whose nacreous glow he could just discern at her throat. He saw nothing else – all was mystery.

He lifted the single sheet covering her and slipped into the bed beside her. For a moment it felt strange that the bedclothes should be warm: he had always slept alone. He reached out and touched her with his fingertips.

She lay with the sheet over her body, the pearls shimmering, her throat a pale curve; her face turned half away from him. Released from the tight straw hat, her hair lay across the bolster as if windblown, in smooth curves. Leaning on his elbow, he kissed her cheek.

Her eyes opened, amber: pools of honey against the dark. Then they burned with an urgent fire as he lowered his head and touched his lips to her lips. She opened her mouth and raised her body in an ardent arch towards his. She seemed so small. The points of her breasts made soft brushes against the hard muscles of his chest, making him feel so strong that he caressed her with only the gentlest touches lest he hurt her instead of make her feel pleasure: the lightest movement of his fingers made her sigh with a desire he felt mirrored in his own body. He thought he would burst for joy as he felt her softness against his hardness, her smooth curves against his angled masculinity, her long nails and soft fingers guiding him. He lifted her and held her against him with all his strength, yet with all his muscles in opposition so that she was safe and unharmed in the centre. The sweat poured off him. He threw back his head and writhed in the exquisite torture. Then slowly he lowered his head on her shoulder. He lost his strength and his muscles relaxed, everything turned to softness, and they lay entwined in the dark.

She whispered: 'Darling, that was so wonderful. But what about me?'

'What?'

'A woman can feel pleasure too.'

He had never thought about it. A man naturally assumed

that the woman's pleasure came from doing the things women loved: wearing their jewellery and finest clothes, the dancing, and being bought drinks and supper. The bit in bed that followed was for the man. He said so.

'I shall show you more,' she said. 'Loving should be giving, by both. Yes? And a pleasure. To both.' This was a new idea for him. Surely it was a serious business, not one for lingering over. She cupped his hands in her hands and guided them over her body together. Soon his hands moved on their own, caressing her, and she began to sigh softly. He was amazed: she did feel pleasure and joy, and there was no shame in it. He still could hardly wait to get to the best bit, but he did make himself wait. She writhed gently. She ran the palms of her hands over his back with the lightest of touches, then harder, and finally he felt her nails fix on his muscles and she hissed 'Take me' and he did, with a gentleness that made her press her wrist to her mouth to hold back a scream: and then she cried a name.

'Charles. Charles . . .'

Coucy is in Picardy, where the Germans are now. In its day it was one of the keys to the kingdom, because the land was rich and the castle was impregnable. When was it built? Long ago, Ben, long ago. There were lords of Coucy for a hundred and fifty years before the first Count was even born.

Ben stood by the window. The stars were fading; mist dimmed the lights of the Eiffel Tower and crept across the city, obscuring the bulk of the Hôtel des Invalides, and finally he could not even see the river now. He could not fly today. But soon it would be dawn.

'Come back to bed,' she called softly.

'I wish dawn would never come.'

'It won't.'

He returned to her. 'Do you love me?'

'Give me your body. Take me. Quickly, this time.'

How long has there been a Count of Coucy? For nearly seven hundred years. That was the time when the English owned much of the west side of France below the Loire, down to the Pyrenees. And the Somme. And Calais. The first Count was a son-in-law to the King of England.

413

The maid brought breakfast on a silver tray. *'Merci bien. C'est tout.'* Ben looked under the napkin: croissants, apricot jam, bowls of milky coffee. Chouchou came out of the bathroom, wrapping her hair in a towel, her arms upraised. Her white skin showed three triangles of curly black hair, the two smallest under her arms. She smiled and sat herself on his naked lap as though that was the most natural place in the world. They ate the croissants. Later he kissed the flaky crumbs from her thighs, then took her back to bed. She wrapped her arms and legs around him. 'Such pleasure is intolerable,' she whispered at last, in French. It sounded the same in English. She did not mean it; he did not even bother to raise his head. They made love until noon; or midnight. He ordered beefsteaks from room service, with fresh vegetables, whatever was in season, and a bottle of chilled white wine, and a bottle of red wine, and a bottle of Badoît mineral water. And roses, red and white, in a silver épergne. As they ate in the window they watched afternoon settle over the city, and the blue river fade to purple in reflection of the sunset.

For seven hundred years Coucy castle stood, handed down the line of the Counts of Coucy, father to son, son to father to son. It survived earthquakes and the French revolution. And then the Germans came. For three years, they did nothing. Why should they? No reason. We lived in hope. But then on the orders of General Ludendorff, Chief of the German General Staff, the towers were packed with thirty tons of high explosive, and blasted to the ground.

'I love you.'

'No,' she said, smiling, touching his lips.

'Do you love me?'

'I adore you.'

'But do you love me?'

She held his head, saying nothing.

Then he said: 'Why?'

'Because.' He watched the lines deepen around her eyes. Then she tried to smile. 'Have mercy. I am the last Countess of Coucy.'

*

414

It was not far to walk: he in his RFC uniform and she in a dark brown knit dress that flowed with her every movement, loosely belted at the waist, and a broad-brimmed hat that shaded her face and allowed no one to see the expression in her eyes. They crossed the Pont de la Concorde and walked down the broad boulevard to the Hôtel des Invalides. The great dome behind the building shone gold in the hot sun and there was a smell of dust. They went into the shadows, cool stone corridors, then white, and the smell of antiseptics. Ben felt sick: the wards seemed endless. Her voice whispered: *'A million casualties so far. A whole generation of young men wiped out. How many years will the suffering last? How many girls full of life and hope will have to resign themselves to lives alone. Think of that. The men suffer and die. The women go on, they suffer, and live.'*

They came to a door where a *poilu* stood on guard. Since he wore no kepi he did not salute, but he stiffened to attention.

Chouchou turned to Ben and spoke in a low voice. 'What you will see in this room is secret and must never be referred to.'

'I understand.'

They went in. A fan rotated slowly in the ceiling. A man lay under the sheets, asleep. He looked very old, but it was not difficult to see the vital, commanding lines that had once dominated that withered face, or for Ben to imagine those loose-looking straggles of white hair once neatly swept back into strong silver waves. Ben whispered, 'He must have been very handsome.'

'Yes. My husband was most handsome.'

'I am sorry.' The man was dying; hanging on to life by a thread. If he had been wounded at Verdun, God knew what awesome will-power had kept his shrunken body hanging on this long. Yet Ben saw no sign of chest injuries.

'It was an . . . *Eierhandgranate*. Literally, an egg grenade, weighing only three hundred grams or so . . . It can be thrown like a cricket ball. Charles was leading a counter-attack, the objective had been won. It was the moment of victory. But one of the Germans was not dead.' She pressed her fingers to her mouth.

415

Ben said: 'I understand. You need not go on.'

She shook her head. She owed it to him. 'My husband . . . will not recover. He has lost his legs below the knee and he has severe injuries to the lower abdomen. You know what I am saying.'

'Yes.'

'Even were he to recover . . . but there is no hope. He may live a week, or a month, or six months. The doctors here can do no more. Tomorrow he will be moved by the Army from this hospital to a private clinic in Deauville, where we had such happy times before the war. I will try to join him there, if I can get a train out of Paris.'

There was a slight movement in the bed and Ben felt the old man's eyes on him. They were blue and fierce with the will to live. For long heartbeats he stared into Ben's eyes. Then the yellowed hand moved across the sheets and caught Ben's hand in a quivering grasp.

The old man nodded.

He knew.

Ben squeezed lightly with his fingers and the old man nodded again. Then he slipped back into sleep. Ben lay his hand back onto the bed-clothes.

'He knows,' Chouchou said in a low, heart-torn voice. 'He approves.'

They turned to the door and went outside. As they walked back to the hotel in the brilliant sunlight, Chouchou stopped on the bridge and looked directly at Ben.

'Have I done what is right?'

'You have done what any woman would have done.' *Driven by the blood.*

'I wonder,' she said.

'Chouchou, don't cry. Remember, you taught me pleasure though your heart was crying. People are watching us, I cannot kiss away your tears. I know life is serious, but we must wear it lightly. There is so much unhappiness in the world that we can cut ourselves off as much of it as we want. So let's be happy.' She took off her hat and shook her hair into its straight, almost Cleopatra lines, red-brown, shimmering in the sun. He said: 'Let's make love. It's what all of us want.' He didn't have to look back at the building behind him to feel that he spoke the truth. He said gently: 'We'll go back to our separate bedrooms, and you give your maids something to do to keep them busy, and my door will open even as you reach out for the handle.'

'Ben, I cannot, I have to attempt to arrange my train.'

'Don't worry about travelling. I will attend to it all.'

She stopped him with the lightest touch of her fingers, then stood looking at him with a quizzical expression flickering like yellow candle flames in her eyes.

'I feel a most strange emotion,' she confessed. 'I am proud of my family and I love my husband, and yet . . . and yet I wish that I had married you. Is that a terrible thing to think?'

'Smile,' Ben said.

They walked up the steps to the Crillon. 'Headquarters have been after you,' Bertie told him angrily. 'They want to know why the bloody hell you can't take off because of the fog when in fact it's brilliant sunlight.'

'I'll fly tomorrow,' Ben smiled.

It was simply arranged. The Spad was an easy machine to fly and had a large and comfortable cockpit. Instead of flying straight from the depot at Villacoublay to La Houssoye, Ben circled back as soon as he was out of sight and landed in a field near the main road. Chouchou ran across the grass holding her hat on against the airwash from the propeller. He could feel her giggling as he swung her up and then lowered her into his lap, although of course he could hear nothing. He put his mouth against her ear.

'Comfortable?'

She nodded, then gave a squeal as he opened the throttle. The machine bumped across the grass, rose, bumped again, then climbed between two trees and pulled up into the sky. She was not afraid: flying seemed so delightfully natural. With one arm around Ben's neck she held on her hat with the other.

Lying in bed in the Crillon with his head resting on her belly, she caressing his hair, he occasionally looking up for a

417

sip of champagne, the idea had seemed so impossible to her. Surely it was against the rules? He pointed out that it was so against the rules that there was no mention of it in flying regulations. Fighter pilots were not told that they could not keep bears; neither were they told that they could not carry passengers, so it was all right. Instead of waiting for days for a train out of Paris, he pointed out, she would be in Amiens within hours, and the trains from there were easy.

He kept well behind the Allied lines so as not to risk meeting a German machine. There was no danger of getting lost: all he had to do was follow the N16 main road, distinctive with its long straight stretches and lines of poplars, due north from Paris. Amiens was easy to recognize beneath its cathedral spire. He circled: the most promising field was by a wood conveniently near the road. He was sure that it was smooth, for he saw a dog, or perhaps a fox, running swiftly across it. He sideslipped the aeroplane to lose height and made a smooth landing. Taxiing close to the wood, he stopped the motor. In the sudden silence he could hear crashing noises in the trees. There was a sign: *Chasse privé*. The local hunt.

'Au revoir, Chouchou,' Ben said.

She touched his lips. 'Goodbye, Ben.'

As he lifted her down, horses came cantering out of the trees and milled around, startled by the appearance of the aeroplane. The riders wore red jackets. So it had definitely been a fox that he had seen: Ben frowned. He had not been aware that the French hunted the fox like the English.

Then he heard a roar of rage: 'By God, I know you! Lieutenant Ben London. And a passenger, by God!' Ben recognized the apoplectic complexion and white moustache of Major Trent-Maynard. He was riding a magnificent bay, and looked more at home there than he did on foot, where he needed a stick. Major *Bring-me-back-a-Hun-brush-or-two* Trent-Maynard. Ben closed his eyes for a moment then stood to attention.

He said: 'What are you doing here, sir?'

Trent-Maynard spluttered. 'This is the second time you've done this to me, isn't it?'

'Sorry, sir.'

'Last time got you a promotion. This time you are under arrest, sir. You will consider yourself under close . . .' His eyes widened as Chouchou, smiling her most beautiful smile, held out her hand to Ben and stepped down from the lower wing. Trent-Maynard said: 'Who is this damned woman?'

Ben said: 'Major Trent-Maynard – may I have the honour of presenting you to . . . Her Grace the Countess of Coucy.'

'*Enchanté*,' deigned Chouchou.

The major dismounted and hobbled over. 'Countess . . . Countess. What a pleasure.' He took off his cap and bowed, then kissed her hand.

Chouchou said: 'Where is my car?'

'My vehicle is nearby,' the major said, 'completely at your service.'

'How kind.' She smiled at Ben and allowed the major to tuck her hand under his arm. Ben called after them:

'Excuse me, sir, could I have one of your men to swing the propeller?'

'Wrighton, help him,' the Major told one of the riders. To Ben he said, 'And you, you get out of my sight, before I see you.'

'Thank you, sir,' Ben said.

He heard Chouchou call back from the trees:

'Goodbye. Goodbye. Goodbye.'

Chapter Fifteen

1

Nigel wrote: *My dear brother, Vic. The business is going according to plan and we are all well. Mum sends her love. Dad sends his love and he is working hard.*

He leaned back and stuck the pen in his mouth. He hated writing letters. He never knew what to say. It was like talking to someone who didn't talk back. He thought of writing something about Will, but what could you put about a child? It just ran all over the place making a noise. Thank God he had moved here next door into the Osborne place, but he could still hear the kid through the wall sometimes. What Mum had to put up with.

Nigel wrote a screed once a week, but Vic just sent back a standard battlefield postcard every couple of months, *I am well/not well,* and he seemed so distant and far away that Nigel almost felt homesick for him. He wanted Vic to notice him, to be interested in him; it was hard work, running the business alone, however well it was going.

Nigel bent forward over the page. He pushed the nib of the pen against the paper, forcing the words to come.

With the clawed forefinger and thumb of his left hand, he fretted at his lower lip.

The words came:

Vic, I am afraid that I have some rather bad news for you. It is about your sister. She has let you down. She begged me not to tell you. Mum has also begged me not to tell you, but Vic I know where my loyalty lies.

*I have to tell you that your sister has embarked on a stage career as
an actress against the wishes of everyone and despite everything I can
say or do to stop her. You know what actresses are like. She sings for
soldiers and kisses them and Vic it is a shameless act. She swears that
she is innocent and that is true. At least she does not bring any home,
but who knows where it will end? She flaunts her legs and body on the
stage showing them to any Tom Dick or Harry who cares to pay a
shilling.*

Vic, I am truly sorry to have to tell you this about your own sister.
Yours ever,
Nigel.

He leaned back, smiling. That would show the little
bitch.

2

'Orderly!' Bertie shouted. 'Two whiskies.'

'Yes, sir.'

Ben said: 'Bring a bottle of Badoît back for me.'

'Right away, sir.'

'Aren't you drinking?' Bertie asked. He yawned. 'God,
I'm tired. Tell me what you really got up to in Paris.' His
eyes flickered. *Who did you sleep with? Who are you exploiting
now? Why did you leave me alone?*

'I slept,' Ben said, with finality.

'Really?'

'Have you got any better ideas?' Ben said ruthlessly.

Bertie flinched, then covered the nervous reflex by deliberately opening his wafer-thin gold cigarette case and
carefully selecting a cigarette. He dipped the end into the
yellow flame of his gold lighter.

Then he looked at Ben. Neither man said anything for a
moment.

'You aren't even close to me any more,' Bertie said sadly.
'You've left me alone. I remember when you weren't strong
enough to stand on your own two feet. You needed me.' He
smiled painfully. *How little you know,* Ben thought, *I could
have killed you with the capstan bar just for your clothes.* 'You
terrify me,' Bertie said. 'You smile gently and kindly as

421

though you understand everything and it terrifies me. You're so ambitious. God help me if I stood in your way.' He was speaking as bitterly as a jilted lover.

Ben said: 'I'll never forget what I owe you. You know that.'

'Oh yes,' sighed Bertie, 'I know.' Ben watched Bertie's elegant profile turn against the light. Bertie put the cigarette against his lips and drew deeply into his lungs. Outside, it was raining and the grass looked the colour of khaki. The aeroplanes were all in the Bessoneau hangars lest the wings soften or the engines rust.

'Last week's new intake,' Bertie said, 'are all dead. Except one, I believe.'

'Alan Stark.'

'Stark, yes.' Bertie always called people by their last names, keeping them at a distance. Suddenly he turned to Ben, almost touching him.

'When I don't come back, it will be a mercy. Shut up, Ben! The statistics are all against me now, I've been here longer than anyone. I want you to have my paintings. You love them. Look after dear old Sam. Light a candle for me. That is my will.'

The drinks came. Ben picked up the bottle-opener for the mineral water and waved the orderly away. 'You don't want to go on like that, chum,' he advised Bertie quietly. 'When people fear things, they tend to happen.'

'It would be a mercy! Don't you understand?'

Guilt. So Bertie had turned back to religion again. That wouldn't help him; he needed practical help. 'Look, I'll ask the CO to put you down Flying Sickness D.' Ben tugged at the cap: it was jammed. 'You don't have to go up this afternoon,' he hissed.

Bertie stubbed out his cigarette and shook his head. 'Ben, I just want it to end.'

Ben wrestled with the cap. He glanced at Bertie; glimpsed an expression in Bertie's eyes through the veil of smoke: *There is your victory, Ben. You have all I have. You've got what you worked for.*

'No!' said Ben.

'I love you,' Bertie said.

The cap wouldn't budge. Ben flung away the bottle-opener. He tore agonizingly at the crimped metal top with his fingers.

'Those bloody Germans!' he said. The war was getting to him too.

The rain had stopped and Leutnant Adolf Münchener of Jagdegeschwader 1 sat in his quarters writing to his mother at home in Schlessheim. This was a duty which he performed once every week, without fail. His room was decorated with the serial numbers cut from the enemy machines he had shot down, twenty-two of them. In fact he had downed forty-nine, but most had burned. At first this had seemed a dreadful duty to perform – he had been gently brought up, his father was a pastor – but now it didn't seem to matter. He wrote careful, gentle letters to his mother describing the colours of autumn in the trees, and the beauty of the world so far below. He wrote thoughtfully of the honourable combat of man against man in the air: and of his whole-hearted love of combat that made the war, too, for him a thing of beauty. War gave his life a set of values, gave his life meaning: in war, men found their true home, because for men there would always be war. Men would always come to blows, tribes would fight, and races destroy one another. War was life.

Adolf had slim hands and long, sensitive fingers. His hair was blond and boyish, parted as if by a ruler from a point above his left temple almost all the way back to the crown of his head. His eyes were very pale blue under a broad forehead, and his high cheekbones sloped to a narrow chin – too narrow – so that his mouth puckered easily into petulance, which was weak. When he remembered to smile, he looked arrogant. That was good. The men respected arrogance, and expected it of their officers.

There was a knock on the door. He did not bother to look up.

'Enter.'

He glanced across, seeing the beautifully polished boots

423

of Sergeant Schlussler stamping to attention, then continued with his letter. He placed the blotting-paper carefully over his signature, pressed, and replaced it in the holder. He put down his pen.

'Well?' he smiled.

The cold blue eyes; the deadly smile. Schlussler fixed his eyes on the wall above the ace's head. He shouted: 'Sir, regarding the visit of inspection by His Excellency General von Bruck!'

Why was the idiot bothering him with this? 'So, is everything not arranged according to my instructions?' Manfred von Richthoven, the Geschwader-leader, was away on leave, as was very often the case. Until he returned, Adolf was responsible for orders of the day.

'Yes, sir, according to your instructions!' confirmed Schlussler.

'And the machines are drawn up in a perfectly straight line?'

'Yes, sir!'

'Then what is the problem?'

Schlussler said: 'Should we leave the propellers positioned at the vertical, sir, or horizontally?'

Yes, it was an important detail. 'What does it say in the regulations?'

'There – well, there seem to be no regulations dealing with this point, sir.' Schlussler waited silently to be told what to do.

Adolf lost his smile for a moment, then strapped on his leather coat and strode furiously outside. The aeroplanes were lined up across the drying grass.

'The blades should be vertical,' Bruno Lorzer said, 'because that is more erect and military-looking.'

'I favour horizontal propellers,' said Otto Brauneck. 'It looks neater, and does not break up the line of the wings.'

'You are both wrong,' Adolf snapped. 'We will put the propellers at exactly forty-five degrees. That will give the most daring, most rakish impression.'

General von Bruck turned out to be a kindly old cavalry gentleman who hardly glanced at the machines and made

Adolf very angry: an amateur. The infuriating old man would probably not have noticed if the machines had no propellers at all. And it was humiliating to be inspected by a base general anyway, Adolf thought proudly. Jagdgeschwader 1 was an elite unit, the only one of its type in the whole *Deutschen Luftstreitkrafte*, the German Air Force. He surveyed the old man with contempt.

The Circus had more than fifty of the latest aircraft, and the finest pilots. They didn't fly from any one airfield: they were moved up and down the lines, and the Allies never knew where they would strike next. When the Circus did strike, it was with all the advantages on their side. No formation was more feared than von Richthoven's Flying Circus.

In the best knightly tradition, they flew their own colours. Their machines were riots of scarlet, orange, green, gold. Adolf Münchener's red warpaint was streaked with gold and his name was blazoned in black Gothic across the top wing.

Ernst Udet's aeroplane was gold with a yellow spinner on the propeller, and Hermann Göring's machine was outfitted all in black, except for the tail, which was white. Horrible faces writhed across their engine cowlings, and the exhausts were painted like screaming mouths. The object was to create sheer terror, and they had succeeded. In one month the Royal Flying Corps had lost one thousand three hundred aircraft to the Flying Circus. The Flying Circus gave no mercy and expected none.

They were proud killers; and they had to waste time on this buffoon.

At last the General, full of schnapps, departed. The pilots stood around together. 'What a windbag,' the handsome Göring said, pushing his hands into his gloves.

'Full of hot air,' agreed Münchener, pulling down his flying helmet.

'He was a dear, sweet old man,' Udet said, hopping as he pulled on his sheepskin boots. 'We should be tolerant, we shall be like that one day.'

'We shall be long dead,' Münchener laughed over his shoulder. 'Rotten. Mouldering!'

'Good hunting, my brothers,' called Lorzer as they climbed into their machines.

'Our names shall never die,' Göring said.

Adolf Münchener gave the signal for the engines to be started, and the machines took off into the rain-washed afternoon air, and turned towards the sun in the west.

The roar of aircraft engines faded towards the east. Ben sprinted across the muddy grass with his uniform jacket half on and unbuttoned. Puddles dirtied his field-boots and splashed his trousers to the waist. He didn't care; he had slept for a moment, and Bertie was gone. Major Trent-Maynard, CO of the Spad squadron, stood leaning on his stick. Too late. The sound of the Spad engines which had woken Ben had gone. There was no sound now on the airfield.

Ben stopped.

Trent-Maynard turned. 'He insisted,' he said simply.

Ben closed his eyes. He blamed himself.

Trent-Maynard said: 'It's their duty to give high cover to an RE8 on reconnaissance patrol. You know how the enemy comes down out of the sun.'

Ben turned and sprinted towards his machine.

The sun glinted off the silver cowling of the Camel's hump. Sam ran after him with excited barks. 'Get down, boy. Sit!' Ben shouted for the mechanics as he swung down from the top wing into the cockpit.

Someone said: 'But what about your flying clothes – you'll freeze to death, sir.' The mechanic swung the propeller and kicked away the wheel-chocks. Ben took off without doing up his seat-belt.

Sam sat on the grass scratching his ear, then when the mechanics had gone away sat alone, staring motionlessly towards the east.

Bertram Benton-Benson was happy. War had burned away the lies. There was no glory in war's brief encounters, because war was nothing. There was nothing in war to be gained, only to be lost. It was a simplifying fire.

It no longer mattered to him that he was wealthy, or even that he existed, because that had no meaning without love. The only thing that mattered was love. He could not face it.

Love was sin. This evil love. His love. Yet it was what he was. That night by the Tower of London he had said: *Trust me.* And he had kept that trust. But all men were in the Devil's power because of their original sin. Their appetite. The teaching was quite clear.

Which is the worst sin – murder, robbery, or rape?

And the answer?

None of these. Sodomy is the worst sin.

Bertie sinned in his heart. He would burn in hell. Yet he could no more change his love than he could fly – well, he *was* flying – flying was easy . . .

On each side of him the Spads droned through clear air with the sun hanging over their tails. Far below, the RE8 crawled across the panorama of the battlefield, the gunner leaning over the side to change the plates in the camera from time to time. Bertie looked back to check that the inexperienced pilot Stark was keeping good formation, and waved at him to close up. Stark's machine wobbled then swayed closer, and Bertie smiled, remembering how he had flown like that at first in the insubstantial air.

The machines flew into the grey shadow below a small cloud.

A mile above, Adolf Münchener peered over the side of his Albatros. Behind the fluted red-gold trailing edge of the lower wing he glimpsed the tiny cross outlines of four British Spads, and far below them a few glints of sunlight from a reconnaissance machine, probably an RE8, almost too small to see. He had a moment to gauge the speed and course of the Spads. One of them flew unsteadily: that one was his, a certain victim who would bring his score up to fifty. Then they disappeared beneath the glaring white top of a cloud. He waved to his brothers in arms around him in the formation, then pointed down.

His machine rolled gracefully onto her wingtips, then fell away smoothly into a dive. The sun was exactly behind him: he was diving out of the sun. The shadows of the machines diving around him rippled across the white cloud-top and he knew that the Spads would appear beyond the far edge at any moment. He reached forward into the slipstream and armed his guns, then his thumb settled over the firing button set into the top of the stick.

None of them noticed the tiny shape of the Sopwith Camel three miles to the west of them and slightly below.

Ben lifted himself in his seat and stared over the top of the Camel's Triplex windscreen. He had no goggles and the icy slipstream cut into his eyes like a knife. Ahead, a white cloud hung against the haze. Four Spads twinkled as they came out of its shadow; above them a shoal of red, gold, blue, and green machines as bright as tropical fishes came diving down out of the sun. Ben dropped back into his seat. Look out, look out. There was nothing he could do. He pushed at the throttle but it was already full on. He loaded the Verey pistol and fired a warning flare, but the Spads were going almost directly away and could not see him.

Jolly good, Bertie thought, as Stark moved slowly into the proper position alongside him and a little behind. He looked around the sky just as the sun re-appeared, sending blinding shafts of light over the top edge of the cloud above them. Then the air was swarming with German machines.

One of the Germans seemed to have picked Stark out: Bertie turned back, firing his guns, and blocked the red-and-gold machine's attack.

The German came back and again Bertie blocked him, firing his guns.

Bertie saw Stark ahead of him, climbing towards the cloud. Good lad. Then the German swooped up from below. Red and gold: the colours of Adolf Münchener.

The brute was going for Stark again: Stark, poor lad, lost his nerve and started twisting from side to side, panicking, his machine losing speed.

Bertie turned in towards the German machine, causing it to break off its attack for the third time. Stark disappeared in the cloud. Now it was just the two of them.

Münchener stared through his gunsights in a state of rage: he had been cheated of his fiftieth score. This clumsy fool had cheated him time after time of the victory that should have been his. Very well. He would be punished. Münchener fired his guns.

Bertie had to turn away from the cloud. The German machine came at him first from one side, then the other. The Spad shuddered. Bullets punched holes along the fabric, splinters flew, the compass exploded.

Now fabric fluttered in long strips behind the Spad's wings, and Bertie could smell petrol: a fine spray blew back from the engine. The fuel line had been split. Bertie twisted and turned, but always the red and gold machine was there, and again the Spad shivered under the hail of bullets.

The grey underneath of the cloud raced by close above Ben's head. Away to one side, Stark's machine came spinning out of the cloud base and dropped away below. Ahead, he saw Bertie's Spad staggering defencelessly from side to side, the German machine coming at it again and again. The Spad was finished, rolling over into a vertical dive. Only when his guns were empty did the German turn for home. Ben read the name on his wings: Adolf Münchener.

This was the same man who had spared his life.

This animal.

Bertie's machine had disappeared. Ben wiped the mist of castor oil from his eyes. The cloud hung like ice-cream with him in the blue bowl of the sky. Far below him, he saw the green fields of France. Across them, slowly falling, moved a white spark, then a tongue of red flame.

Ben cried out aloud: 'No!'

The Spad flew onward, downward, burning. Bertie felt quite calm and very close to heaven. The broken petrol pipe had ignited like a blowtorch from one of the final bullets of the last, brutal attack, a ricochet sparking off the iron engine block . . . a single spark, then flame streaming back, roaring in the slipstream. The metal cowling ignited. The glass windscreen began to bend and melt.

Calmly, Bertie undid his seat-belt and lifted himself out of the cockpit. He climbed out on the left, as though he was getting out of the machine on the ground, and stood on the lower wing with a mile of empty air beneath his heels. He reached back into the cockpit and sideslipped the machine to the left, so that the flames were pulled away from him.

There was a dull *crump* as the oil in the motor began to burn. The heat became intense. The windscreen blew back in strings like melted sugar. Bertie swung himself back along the body towards the tail, clear of the fire. He heard the howl of a motor. He looked around, and waved calmly.

'No!' Ben screamed. 'No! Bertie! God help me! No!'

He watched as Bertie's weight on the tail pulled the Spad into a stall. The nose rose up, the Dassault propeller still rotating slowly, and for a few moments the flames boiled vertically upward from the engine like a bonfire. Bertie sat calmly in front of the tail, his legs wrapped around the burning body, looking out at Ben. They might as well have been a million miles away.

He saved me.

As the nose of the Spad dropped smoothly once more into a dive, Ben followed, circling helplessly. The flames poured back over the Spad's cockpit now, and even he could hear their greedy roar. Bertie wrapped his arms around his face, accepting his fate. The heat must be hellish.

Then the Spad's nose came up again, and she stalled. In the single motionless moment, free of flame, Bertie looked across to Ben and waved.

Ben thought: *He's going to be burned alive.*

They were still three-quarters of a mile above the earth. *And he knows it.*

Of a pilot's three choices, it was the most horrific. Bertie carried no pistol because his religion forbade suicide: it was the deadliest sin, worse than anything.

He could not jump, because that was also suicide.

Bertie had to burn.

Ben screamed.

The nose of the Spad dropped into a dive again. The flames blew back in the slipstream, covering the cockpit, reaching tongues towards the tail.

Bertie covered his face with his arms. The flames flashed

on the leather, blackening it. The sheepskin lining of his boots caught fire. Then Bertie showed one side of his face and waved for the last time, burning like a heretic. Ben could have sworn that he was smiling.

Why? Ben thought. *Why don't I understand?*

Bertie's coat began to burn. Ben couldn't stand it. With his right hand he reached forward and cocked the twin Vickers machine-guns.

Was there another way?

No.

Death was the only way he could save him.

Ben leaned forward. The Spad moved into the focus of the Aldis gunsight. Ben touched the rudder bar. The crosshairs of the sights stopped on Bertie's burning figure.

Ben pulled the triggers. He shot his friend – shot him out of the sky.

He wept.

3

Colleen knew. She knew at the moment she parted the lace over her window and saw the post office boy running along Bunhill Row.

She knew the telegram was for her.

Which one of them was dead?

Let him be at peace.

She heard the footsteps clattering on the stairs.

The knock rattled her door.

She could not bear to answer it. She stood by her window, the pretty lace still clasped in one hand, the other to her throat. She could not go.

She could not overwhelm the grief that kept her from the door; she could not overcome her fear.

She called: 'Who is it?'

'Telegram!' came the chirped reply.

'I can't. Can't you bring it back later.'

'Come on, missus, open up!'

He was a nice little boy, pink-cheeked, no taller than her waist.

'Look,' he said, seeing her face, 'it's all right, it's not the official War Office one.' *His Majesty's Secretary of State for War regrets to inform you . . .* 'Someone's done a clever wangle from France. There are ways,' the little boy added mysteriously. He held it out with an innocent smile.

BERTIE DEAD. I SHOT HIM. FORGIVE ME.

4

'Orderly! Whisky.' *I shot him, he's dead, forgive me.*

'And your usual Badoît, sir?'

'Just whisky.' *Yes, I'm a good one. Congratulations, bastard, you lived up to your name.*

'Another whisky, right away, sir.'

Ben sat alone in the corner of the mess. Nobody talked to him. He scratched open a tin of cigarettes and lit one with a match.

Bertie's personal belongings had gone, auctioned, as was customary. Ben could not bear even to attend. Nothing remained. He did not need mementoes to remember his friend by: he would never forget.

Ben tried to suck smoke deep into his lungs, as Bertie had, then coughed. He had not seen Sam since yesterday. Bertie's room had been taken over by Stark. Sam too had disappeared.

Ben had haunted the airfield for half last night, calling into the dark: 'Sam! Sam! Here boy!' as Bertie had. No reply.

No cold nose touched his hand; no gigantic ginger shape had come bounding up to him, the silver tag flashing on his collar:

My
name is
S A M
Bunhill
Row

Ben remembered saying: *'You'd better get back to your home in Bunhill Row, Sam.'* And he remembered the startled look of respect in Bertie's eyes, wondering how Ben knew about Sam and Bunhill Row. The simple explanation had never occurred to him, Ben was sure. Bertie always preferred a mystical explanation to simple reality. One by one, as they all had, he had lost his dreams in the war. But never that one about Ben. He died not knowing.

Ben wandered around the dark airfield wrangling over the past in his mind, as grieving people do. Calling, as Bertie had, for Sam. And Sam did not come.

'Here's your whisky, sir.'

Ben dragged the smoke deep into his lungs, and coughed. He drained his glass. He realized that Alan Stark had come in and was staring at him.

One of the new recruits asked: 'Who is he, Alan?'

Ben heard Stark's trembling, hate-filled voice say: 'That's Ben London – I saw him shoot down his best friend!'

Ben saw the disgust in their eyes.

'All he cares about is himself!' Stark cried. 'He's a bastard. Even his mother hated him, deserted him, left him in the snow. He kills his friends and loves his enemies – he didn't kill that German, did he! Shot his friend instead! I saw him! If he had any guts, he'd kill Münchener!'

Ben stood up.

Stark said eagerly: 'Going to hit me, Ben?'

Ben pushed past him.

What would you want me to do, Colleen? Shall I die? Shall I fly?

Adolf Münchener lay in bed waiting for his orderly to wake him; it was nearly first light, and soon there must be the dawn patrol. He would have to pretend to be calmly asleep. He would wait for the second knock, then he would call out in a sleepy voice: 'Enter.'

And the orderly would say in a pleased voice: 'It is a clear dawn, sir.' That meant they would fly.

And he would lie: 'Ah, that is good!'

All his life was lies now. The truth was that he did not want to go up. The joy of killing had left him. He feared it. There had been no glory in his combat with the Spad. He had been unable to write to his mother. Now that he was frightened of dying, he was frightened of living. His mother would know: she would see through to it in any words he wrote her, as mothers always knew their sons, and know that her son was so full of terror that he had become a killer, a mere killer. And must go on killing.

He had not even been able to claim that Spad as his fiftieth victory, for he had not seen it go down.

He was stuck on forty-nine.

So he lay there, waiting for the knock on the door.

It never came.

Instead, he heard the rattle of machine-guns and the approaching howl of an aeroplane's engine. The plane passed overhead close enough to shake the hut, the howl dropping instantly to a deep thunder as the machine pulled away.

Adolf jumped up and ran outside, naked. Others were already manning the heavy machine-gun or ducking behind sandbags. Stars still shone in the sky, only the eastern horizon showed shafts of blue light. The silhouette of a Sopwith Camel appeared briefly amongst them, then was gone.

A cigarette tin with a silk streamer attached lay in the grass.

Göring slapped at the machine-gunners. 'Open fire, you fools! You've got him cold!'

'It is too late,' Adolf said.

He opened the tin and pulled out a rectangle of paper.

'He challenges me to single combat,' he said in a voice as dry as dust. 'Three miles high above the trenches, every dawn, until I come.'

'Good!' Göring said.

Adolf fingered the *mensur*, the sword-slash scar of honour on his cheek. 'I shall go, of course.' He balled the paper between his fists, so that his brothers should not see his fingers tremble.

'This is only an Englishman,' Göring shrugged. 'We shall ambush him, of course.'

'Of course!' cried the others. 'We are your brothers in arms! He shall be your fiftieth victory.'

'My machine is unserviceable today,' Adolf lied. 'We shall go when our duties permit.'

He sat at his desk all day. The signature on the paper, Ben London, meant nothing to him, but he had recognized the number on the tail of the British machine: B6235. It was the same man who had caught him out the other day, maddened with the joy of killing.

He *knew*.

It would be a fight to the death. The ambush was an excellent idea.

But it was dishonourable.

But honour had no place in war.

They had to put all thoughts of human decency behind them. Only winning counted.

Adolf put down his pen. He could not even attempt to write to his mother. It was a stupid habit anyway.

Ben waited as dawn spread down through the upper air. He had written to Colleen, telling her in dreadful detail what he had seen, and what he had done. *Did I do right? Or did I do wrong?*

She wrote back in reply: *What do you believe, Ben?*

He watched dawn spreading across the ground. Here, in the rarefied air at twenty thousand feet, almost four miles high, he could not be ambushed. They would try, he knew. There was no honour in the air any more.

The sun rose blindingly.

The Germans had not come.

Almost out of fuel, he cut his engine and glided back to La Houssoye.

The second day dawned still and hazy. Even so high, there was a feel of thunder hanging in the air.

Still the Germans did not come.

Ben waited. *What do I believe?*

The strain of the war was showing now that rationing had come in. Esther made sure that Will got enough to eat, but she could do nothing for Ria, who came home looking exhausted. Esther scraped together enough coupons for a

435

meat pie every Sunday, but Ria ate like a sparrow. She was giving everything she had to her act, to the soldiers, to the Feed the Guns rallies. For herself, she hardly seemed to exist any more: it was always, 'I've got to rush, Mum, the boys are waiting for me.'

'The boys this, the boys that,' Esther said angrily. She'd had enough. 'Well, what about your own boy?'

Ria stopped at the door. 'What? You mean Will?'

'Yes, and I'm surprised you even remember his name,' Esther stormed furiously. She never had been able to hold herself back once she got going. 'Don't you even care about him? He's old enough to wonder why the other children have got dads, you know, and he's going to ask about his father, isn't he? Only natural. What are you going to tell him?' she demanded.

An expression of confusion and pain crossed Ria's face. 'I don't know, Mum.'

'You'd better think about it.'

'I've got so many things to think about—'

'Well this is the most important!' shouted Esther.

Ria stared at her. 'That's the first time you've ever really shouted at me since I was a little girl,' she whispered.

'I'm sorry, love!' Esther threw her arms impulsively around her daughter and was horrified to feel how thin she was. 'Ria, you've got to eat properly, you really have. You're skinny as a rake.'

'It's the fashion.'

'I'll do you a lovely meat pie come Sunday. Beef. I'll have a word with Charlie Best.'

'Mum,' begged Ria, 'I can't. I've got a personal appearance at Tilbury Docks on Sunday. Big troop-ship going out.'

Will ran in. He was dressed in dark grey shorts with white socks and a white shirt. His cheeks were chubby and red, and he had lovely blue eyes. He was playing with a wooden model of an aeroplane. Ria patted his head. 'Hallo, soldier.'

Will said eagerly: 'Rat-tat-tat-tat! Boom! Aaargh!'

'I wonder what his real Dad's doing,' Ria said weepily.

'It's all my fault. I deserve everything that happens to me.'

Esther put the comb under the tap and slicked down Will's hair. 'Let's see your hands. Clean hands? No. Come on. Wash them.' She lifted him up on the stool at the sink and handed him the new, transparent bar of Pears soap.

She said: 'He needs a man about the place.'

'He's got Nigel.'

'Nigel's next door, dear, and he's always busy anyway. Besides, he's not got what you would call a fatherly temperament. Of course, he'll settle down one day—'

Ria said forthrightly: 'You're saying I ought to get married, Mum?'

Esther explained carefully. 'It's rather embarrassing, Ria. All the other girls of your age are married or at least walking out seriously. And the child—' She shifted to her other foot. 'Everyone's always asking.'

'Gossiping!'

'You must want to.'

'I'm not like other girls,' Ria said defiantly.

Esther put it delicately. 'But most people *need* to be married.'

'I know what you're talking about.' Ria used the word the soldiers used. 'I've had that once before, thanks, and look what I got out of it.' She pointed at Will and burst into tears.

Esther got in a fuss and made a mess of drying Will's hands.

'Run outside and play with your aeroplane,' Esther said, then closed the door behind him. Ria sat at the table staring blindly.

'I'm so tired,' she admitted. 'I feel so lonely. I love him.' Esther knew she was not only talking about Will.

'I know,' Esther said. Neither was she. For a moment mother and daughter understood one another perfectly. Esther wanted to talk about her first husband, long lost. Ria wanted to talk about Ben, long gone.

Ria said: 'It wouldn't be the same. With anyone else.'

Esther shook her head. 'Nevertheless, my girl—'

'I give everything I've got on stage, anyway,' said Ria, with a flicker of a smile.

Esther said: 'Darling, what happens when the soldiers go?'

'When the soldiers go?' Ria shrugged. She couldn't imagine it. 'I don't know. Probably we all go back to living in The Warren, I s'pose!' As if she remembered her childhood in those dreadful conditions as a happy time, she began to laugh. Esther began to laugh too; they had been happy. Lightning flickered, then they heard a crash of thunder and the sound of rain starting. They ran to the door and called Will inside before he got soaked, and with him there, noting everything, they could talk no more.

Next door, Nigel heard laughter faintly through the wall. He looked up from his books. What did they have to laugh about? Were they laughing at him? But then there was thunder and the sound of rain, and he heard no more.

He sat back at his desk. He'd not heard from Vic – not even a battlefield postcard. The business was doing very well. In wartime you could hardly fail to make money; what with the shortages and the rationing the black market was enormous and there was a lovely racket going in registration cards and meat coupons, which were easy to forge and low risk, and the profits were immense, but he never had liked dealing with those sort of people. That was what Vic was so good at, not him. Vic was a people person. He thrived on them, whereas often the people he dealt with scared Nigel.

But even the money seemed meaningless without Vic. It wasn't fun.

And he couldn't spend it. That was the way to get the tax people and the police down on your neck.

It had to be his secret.

And there was that other secret.

The last ten days had been very bad for Nigel. He had met Jarvis, the policeman, by the swing bridge, and they had talked. At the very end, just as they were parting, Jarvis said: 'Bye the bye, Nige, your friend Raymond Trott is back on leave.'

438

Nigel's mouth went dry. 'Raymond Trott?'

'Just the usual ten days. He's at the Old Bull and Bush of course if you want to see him. He asked me to remember him to you.'

'Did he,' Nigel croaked.

'He said you two were pals together in France. What a coincidence. Small world, isn't it?'

Nigel had passed a ghastly ten days, waiting for the tramp of Army boots on the pavement, listening for Raymond Trott's knock on the door.

Who's been a naughty boy then, Nigel?

But he hadn't come.

Today his leave had ended and he had been posted abroad.

Please God, Nigel prayed, *let him receive a bullet in the brain.*

Rain washed down his sash window, and the wind shook the glass. Later the sun came out as the storm passed on towards France.

Ben took off his goggles and watched the German machines carefully, a brightly coloured shoal passing below him, weaving between the towers of cloud in the orderly formation he had expected. The leader was glorious in red and gold.

Ben reached forward into the hump and pulled back the cocking levers on the machine-guns. He checked that his seat-belt was tightly fastened, then rolled the Sopwith Camel over onto her back and let her fall away in a screaming dive.

Adolf looked behind him. He could not see his brothers in arms except in rare glimpses between these horrid cloud-tops. They had taken off at the earliest possible moment of first light, but the Albatros was clumsy in thin air. Did Ben London know that? He looked ahead, shielding his eyes with his black-gloved hand, staring into the rising sun.

He thought that he had heard the rattle of machine-guns behind him. But all he saw were the spires of billowing cloud.

He stared. And the sun.

Above him, the empty sky.

Around him, a landscape of clouds.

He jerked to his left. He thought he had seen something flash there – the sun glinting off an engine cowling.

Nothing.

He looked back. No sign of the formation. Now he regretted ordering them to come. It had been the act of a coward. Not that he feared death. He feared losing.

He jerked to the right, seeing a Sopwith Camel flying straight and level between the clouds. He turned right towards it, firing his guns, but the Camel turned to the right also. The tracers flashed harmlessly beneath it, never quite touching. Suddenly the Camel turned tighter still, and curved into a cloud.

Adolf straightened his machine and let it fly alongside the white wall. Flying into a cloud was crazy. The Englishman was mad. He was killing-crazy.

Adolf reached forward and changed the ammunition drums on his machine-guns. No man could afford mercy. There was not enough wealth in the world to pay for mercy. When he had Herr London in his sights, he would not stop firing until the drums were empty. A Sopwith was lightly built; it could not take much punishment before it broke up. He would follow London down, firing. When his drums were empty, he would change them and come in again . . . and again . . .

Adolf thought: *Yes, that is what I will do.*

And then he realized: *That is what he will do to me, if he can! He will not stop firing! His bullets will come battering through the fabric, splinters will fly from the airframe around me, and the engine in front of me will start to burn, and he will not stop!*

He looked up. Sky, no Englishman. Around him, clouds. No Englishman. Below him, a white canyon dwindling down until, in the purple haze at the bottom, he discerned the scribbled field-pattern of the land once known as France, now called Greater Germany.

The Englishman flew out of the cloud beside him, straight towards him, Adolf saw his face through the arc of the Sopwith's propeller. They were going to smash. Adolf shrieked and jerked away, one hand shielding his face. He pushed the stick right forward. He heard the deafening roar of an engine overhead – he even smelt the exhaust. The Albatros fell into a vertical dive down the wall of cloud.

Adolf looked over his shoulder.

London was behind him, closing vertically. Still he did not fire.

Adolf spun to the right. London followed, also spinning, appearing to Adolf's eyes to hang almost motionless while the cloudscape rotated wildly around them.

Adolf checked the spin. He felt giddy and sick.

He spun to the left.

London matched that spin too. There was no escape. He was very close behind now, the propeller a shimmering, widening circle behind the frail, fabric tailplane of the Albatros.

Adolf pushed the throttle wide open, over-speeding the engine. The radiator water boiled, blowing steam back into the slipstream.

He stared behind him. London was calmly changing the drums on his machine-guns. They were the new design, feeding disintegrating aluminium belts into the breeches, giving the Camel a phenomenal rate of fire.

Adolf cringed.

His bullets will come battering through the fabric here, splinters will fly from the airframe around me, the engine in front of me will burn, and still he will keep firing, he will not stop!

Adolf screamed.

They plunged into shadow. The grey world beneath the clouds opened up as they fell below the bottom layer. Sunlight made a bright circle off to one side, pouring through the hole that they had fallen from. Elsewhere, rain slanted across a dull green expanse of fields.

Still London did not fire.

Adolf stared over the side. His machine shuddered. The lower wing, braced by only one main spar, was always the weakest point. It started to bang up and down.

The fields expanded in front of his eyes. They were very low now.

He stared back over his shoulder at his killer.

Ben looked down through the propeller. His finger tightened on the trigger. He stared at the screaming face staring back at him.

That's all we're left with, isn't it? Winning.

He pulled back slightly on the stick. Mercifully, the gunsights lifted away from Münchener's face. Ben fired a long burst over his head, barely above the top wing.

He spared Adolf Münchener's life.

The Sopwith Camel pulled away in a long zoom above the trees.

Adolf heaved back on the stick. He thought he would pile into the earth. The airframe made loud cracking noises and there was a thud as part of the V-strut wing gave way, bending upwards but not tearing off. The Albatros would still fly, just. The furrows of a ploughed field flickered underneath, then he managed to gain a little height.

Ben circled back to the stricken machine. He kept his guns cocked but there was no fight left in Münchener. He just stared at Ben with the corners of his mouth turned down.

Ben looked at him without fascination. He had almost become that man. They had almost destroyed one another.

Did Münchener even remember sparing his life, once? He did not think so.

Ben raised his hand in salute. He touched the controls with his fingertips, and the Albatros dropped away below him as he turned west towards home . . .

Adolf endured London's arrogant stare. He watched London raise his hand in a mocking wave, making Adolf's humiliation complete. Then the Sopwith gained height, but instead of coming in to the final attack, turned contemptuously away. *So,* Adolf thought, enraged and crushed, *There is to be no coup de grâce. I am not even thought worthy of a death with honour.*

He flew on alone. The cockpit shuddered terrifyingly around him. He hardly knew what to do. His life was empty. The fear, the loss, was worse than death. He had been beaten, but not killed.

He was well behind the German lines: he looked for a field to put the crippled machine down. The meadow he chose was soft with the rain, and the heavy engine tipped the Albatros onto its nose. He jumped down and stared towards the west.

He clenched his fists, burning with injustice and resentment at the mercy shown him.

He would never forgive this humiliation.

He would never forget this hatred.

He struck a match and touched it to his aircraft. It burned in a glorious pyre. He would never fly again.

Chapter Sixteen

1

I want you to have my paintings.
  Look after Sam.
  Light a candle for me.
Ben sat alone in the mess drinking Badoît. There was a scratch on the door and his heart jumped. Someone let Sam in out of the dark. He was soaking wet and his ginger fur was covered with mud.

Sam looked at Ben. He barked. 'Come here, you mobile carpet,' Ben said affectionately. Sam shook all over him, then started wiping his mucky jowls on the rug between Ben's feet. Then he realized that this would be much more effective on Ben's trousers.

  Look after Sam.

'I'm your new master,' Ben said, 'if you'll have me.'

Sam rested his chops in Ben's lap, wagging his tail slowly from side to side.

Bertie had obviously allowed his dog on the camp-bed, and there was hardly room for two. That night Ben slept curled up into a ball with the dog sprawled across the bottom half of his bed, which creaked alarmingly.

Ben admitted defeat. He went to the quartermaster and drew a second camp-bed out of stores.

But when he set it up, Sam just stood there looking from it to him.

Ben went back to the stores, drew out a blanket, and put it on the bed.

444

Sam jumped up joyously and threw himself down on his new blanket with groans of delight.

Light a candle for me.

The cold hard rains and mists of winter were setting in. Ben took out the squadron's Phelon & Moore motor-cycle combination and squeezed Sam into the wickerwork side-car. Sam adored travelling in any vehicle, always sitting bolt upright like a ginger coffeepot, leaning into the corners, ears flying. The farmland that they passed through was even flatter than it appeared from the air. They crossed the market gardens watered by the Somme until they saw the towers of Amiens Cathedral sticking above the jumbled roof-lines of the old town.

Ben parked in the square and looked up at the great dark mass of stone of the Notre-Dame. Above the statues, a watery sun glinted across a vast, round window made up of complex arches of stone, and the spires seemed to spike the grey clouds.

'Come, Sam.'

There was a shop nearby with plaster madonnas and gilded crosses in the window. He went in and dug his hand into his pocket, put all his money on the counter. 'I would like to buy a candle.'

'*Une chandelle?*'

'*Oui, chandelle.*'

The old man counted the money and withdrew a candle from the rack.

Ben carried it into the cathedral and walked down the stone flags between the ornate oak choir stalls, his footsteps echoing in the great grey space.

At the far end of the cathedral he saw a raised platform where other candles burned.

'Monsieur!' A man in a black soutane confronted Ben. '*Regardez, le chien est interdit.*'

Ben pushed past the priest. He went to the platform and put his candle into a holder amongst the other candles.

I'm Ben London – the man who killed his best friend.

What should I say? *I'm sorry?* He was not sorry. He was sad.

He whispered the truth: *I'm sorry that I had to do it. But I did have to do it. I could not let you burn in hell.*

Everyone said he was wrong. *He's a bastard, and a good one!*

Below the lowest deep there was always a lower depth to sink to.

'Forgive me,' Ben whispered, 'I would do the same again.'

A second priest had joined the first. He tugged Ben's elbow and said politely, in halting English: 'Sir. The dog. It is forbidden. The cathedral, it is a place of worship.'

Ben pushed between them and walked away. The big circular window, from the inside, shone with a brilliant light of every colour. Ben paused, then walked on.

After Christmas Ben at last got ten days' leave. He left Sam in Frank Laidlaw's capable hands – Sam and Frank's bulldog Grit were firm friends – and caught the packet-boat to Dover. He had nowhere to stay now so he booked into the RFC Club, then took a bus to the City. He got off outside the Lyons Corner House and walked to Bunhill Row. Going up to the first landing, he knocked on the door of Colleen O'Keeffe's rooms.

The first thing she did was to embrace him. His sheer, terrifying niceness; that smile that pulled in everyone, and those striking, friendly, ruthless eyes. You had only to touch him to feel the truth: he was a man who had been born with nothing, who wanted everything.

She trusted him. 'You did the right thing, Ben.'

She pulled him inside. He followed. He had never seen her sitting room before: it was small and full of knick-knacks and momentoes. The old furniture was comfortable and the walls were decorated in warm, homely colours, mostly pinks, with plum-coloured fabric on the chairs and roses patterned on the carpet.

'Colleen – I wondered if you would ever forgive me. Should I even have told you? I could have kept it a secret.'

She put her fingers to his lips. 'Sir Ozwald is upstairs. I have not told him that you . . . and I do not think you should. He is a man full of pride and rather than lose face he would destroy you.'

Ben understood. 'It would break a father's heart.' *I killed your son.*

'No!' she cried. 'Sir Ozwald does not have a heart. He has everything, and feels nothing. He is successful. He is quite unlike Master Bertram!' She dabbed at her nose. Then she broke down. 'I cannot believe that he is—' She could not say the word.

'I know you loved him,' Ben said, 'and so did he.'

She added defiantly, 'More than his mother. She never cared for him.'

'I must go up,' Ben said, but he spent a further moment just standing there, gripping her hand to reassure her.

Ben went upstairs. The door was ajar and he pushed it open.

'I was wondering when you'd turn up!' Sir Ozwald said.

He was a big, flat-faced man in a bulging black suit. Sir Ozwald's stomach alone did not bulge. It was a smooth, hard curve; undoubtedly he wore a corset. Red veins showed in his cheeks, in the dark circles below his eyes, and on the sides of his nostrils. He looked prosperous, like a man who has done well out of the war, a victor who has earned his pound of flesh.

Ben studied him. Nothing about this man reminded him of Bertie.

He crossed the floor. The carpet was still down, but most of the pictures were gone from the walls. Sir Ozwald followed his eyes. 'Come to get your hands on the spoils? You're too late.'

'I don't understand,' Ben said, startled. He had not known what to expect, but it was not this talk of spoils.

'Your type always understand too bloody well,' said Sir Ozwald. He had already made up his mind about Ben. 'Well, you're out of luck this time.'

'What are you talking about?'

Sir Ozwald lowered himself heavily into one of the remaining armchairs, propping his elbows on the arms, steepling his short, strong fingers in front of his stubby red nose.

'Bertram's last will is null and void.'

Bertram. Was what Sir Ozwald called his son? Had he known him?

Ben looked out of the window. It looked bright and naked without the heavy curtains. The table where he had first eaten breakfast with Bertie, and taken tea with Colleen, was also gone. One of the chairs remained. The escritoire was gone. The bookcase where they had looked for the map of Belgium was gone. He felt something in his heart was breaking: it had nearly felt like his home. Perpetual loss. He wanted to be the richest man in London, to be safe, to be free, happy. Richer than people like Sir Ozwald. He let no sign of his pain show in his face in front of this hard, stupid man. He leaned calmly back against the windowsill.

Ben shrugged. He talked on Sir Ozwald's level. 'I didn't know he'd made a written testament.' This was obviously the subject on Sir Ozwald's mind.

'I gave him everything he had,' Sir Ozwald said. 'He never did a day's work in his life.' He paused. Ben waited. 'He nearly killed my wife when he was born, you know!' Sir Ozwald explained. He wanted Ben to understand. He was not an unreasonable man.

Was that why he hated his son?

'I understood that he was born by Caesarian section.'

'Doctor talk, boy!'

'Not *boy*.' Ben smiled. He always made a point of smiling when he was angry, so that his words should be clearly understood rather than give offence. The other man gaped up at him from the chair. Ben nodded encouragingly. 'Flight-Commander. I'll call you Sir Ozwald, you call me Flight-Commander,' he smiled.

Sir Ozwald realized that he was obediently nodding his head, so he stopped. 'Doctors! Yes, Caesarian section. Well, Flight-Commander, Macbeth put it better: untimely ripped. That's what he was, man. Don't you understand? Unnatural! Untimely ripped from his mother's womb!'

'That wasn't his fault.'

'Yes it was. Better that he had died, and saved us all the trouble.' Then Sir Ozwald softened, shrugged, sighed. His voice actually trembled with feeling. 'Ben, we gave him

448

everything. The finest education. He could have changed the world.'

He had loved his son. Ben stared. Sir Ozwald's flat, black eyes gleamed with wet – not tears, but moisture. Not of grief so much as anger, and of regret.

'He was my only son,' Sir Ozwald said in a strangled voice.

'I'm sorry,' Ben said. 'Truly.'

'I'm not interested in your damned condolences!' shouted Sir Ozwald. It was like a curtain swept aside: Ben saw the hate and failure and anger clashing together inside the common clay of this most successful man. And shame. Sir Ozwald knew what he had created.

Sir Ozwald said: 'He was mine.'

That was true. 'I know,' Ben said. Bertie had never escaped. Sir Ozwald had tried to make Bertie like himself, and he would have succeeded. The veneer would have thickened into a crust, the crust into an almost invulnerable armour of concealment and repression. But the war had come along. In thirty years' time Sir Bertram Benton-Benson might have – would have – sat here in his father's image, hardened and matured, public success and private failure, grief-stricken, angry, armoured, and without love.

I shall never allow myself to be like that, Ben thought.

Sir Ozwald said: 'He was mine . . .' Mine. Like property. Like an icon. Like a picture. 'He gave me nothing.' He was not the first father to accuse his son of ingratitude, Ben guessed. 'He lived a wasted life.'

'No,' Ben said. The spell broke, the curtain swept back, and Sir Ozwald ducked back into his familiar shell.

'Oh, I know what you're after.'

'No, Sir Ozwald,' Ben said truthfully, 'you don't know what I'm after.' He wasn't after anything. Sir Ozwald had nothing he wanted. 'You don't know anything, Sir Ozwald.'

Sir Ozwald laughed. He understood; a negotiating ploy to up the price. 'I'm a rich man,' he said. 'The war's been good to me, Ben. What do you want? A thousand pounds?' He waited for a heartbeat. 'Five thousand.'

'What are you talking about?'

'How much?'

Ben shook his head.

Sir Ozwald said: 'I'll fight you for them.' *I want you to have my pictures*. Were they worth five thousand pounds? 'I'll offer you ten thousand pounds!' Sir Ozwald said. 'Go on. Take it.'

'You make me sick,' Ben said.

Sir Ozwald stared at him. He dropped his hands into his lap. The man was a fool. 'You really were his friend,' he said.

'I believed so.'

'Some of the paintings are very valuable,' Sir Ozwald said. The ones that he had taken the precaution of removing, no doubt, Ben thought. Sir Ozwald stood up and walked to the wall, then turned by one of the remainder, the mother and child, with the trees like wine-glasses, the peculiar but compelling picture that Ben had been drawn to on his very first day here. Sir Ozwald said bluntly: 'I shall contest his will.'

'I thought you said it was null and void,' said Ben wearily.

Sir Ozwald said smoothly, 'That was before I knew you were his friend. I loved my son. My offer of ten thousand pounds still stands.'

That was an absolute fortune.

Oh, Bertie, thought Ben, *if only you could see us now*. 'I don't want your money,' he said.

Sir Ozwald shrugged. Very well. He said generously, although perhaps *gratefully* would have been nearer the mark: 'You may choose one painting.' He threw out his arm expansively. 'Any one.' He followed Ben's gaze. 'Very well. The Montagna.'

'Mantegna,' Ben said.

'It's yours. In full settlement.' Sir Ozwald lifted the picture off the wall, glanced at it with distaste, then handed it to Ben.

Ben stared at the strange, fascinating picture carefully. It was the only valuable possession he had ever owned that also had value in money terms – not much, but something. But Bertie had been his friend.

'In settlement,' repeated Sir Ozwald.

'*In memoriam*,' Ben said.

Sir Ozwald didn't believe a word of it. *In memoriam*. That was old stuff, soft stuff. The Flight-Commander could have had it all. This was a wicked, wicked world, and Sir Ozwald did not believe in the force of innocence. Evil existed. Sin existed. Men existed to be manipulated. Victory went to the hard, the brutal, the powerful. That was the fact of life. He did not believe in innocence at all.

Yet the Flight-Commander, richer by only a painting, repeated the words, and Sir Ozwald shivered, suddenly cold.

Suddenly, on the point of victory, morale in the German Army collapsed.

Ben flew above great streams of men falling chaotically back to the north and east towards their homeland. The slipstream hurt his eyes worse than usual, and his joints ached. He began to shake. When he landed back at the airfield, he had to be helped from his aircraft. The medical officer diagnosed influenza. 'The 'flu, old boy. Stay in bed for a week.'

'What, just for 'flu?' demanded Ben.

'You're young and fit, you'll live. It started out east a couple of years ago. Now it's spreading across the world. Millions have died.'

He was convalescing when Frank Laidlaw brought him the newspapers. 'They're finished. It's only a matter of time before the Kaiser goes.' He sat on the end of the bed, a rueful smile on his round face – his hair was already receding. 'What are you going to do after the war's over, Ben?'

'Never thought about it.'

'I've got a few ideas.' Frank reached into his pocket. 'Nearly forgot, letter came for you.' He handed it over then sat with his hands on his knees. 'You might like to think about this. My Pop's got a bit of money. We'll be able to pick up war surplus machines ten a penny, soon . . .'

' "Frank's Flying Circus"?'

'It's a way of keeping flying,' Frank said.

'I'll think about it.'

'Do that. Cheerio, mate.' He slapped the bed-clothes cheerfully, winked at the nurses, and left.

Ben looked at the letter. It had been forwarded, of course: the Bunhill Row address had been crossed out and the new one written in Colleen's large, round hand. But when he glanced more closely at the handwriting on the original address he felt an eerie flash of *déjà vu*: the 7 was barred in the continental style, 7, and England was written *Angleterre*.

There was no sender's address or other mark on the paper.

He sniffed it. Something . . . lingered.

Chanel No. 5. He knew who it was from.

He opened the envelope. It contained no letter, only a small printed announcement cut out of a newspaper with scissors. He held it up to the light. He could read French well enough to translate: 'BORN of the Dowager Countess of Coucy; a boy, weighing 3.73 kg: FRANÇOIS BENJAMIN CHARLES ENGUERRAND, Count of Coucy, at Deauville, 30.4.1918. Mother and baby are well.'

Ben thought: *I wonder . . .*

The end of April; it was late.

François Benjamin Charles Enguerrand, Count of Coucy.

I wonder . . . could it be . . .

He threw himself back into the pillows, laughing. The nurses looked alarmed. They did not approve of jollity, it disturbed recovery.

Ben did not fly again on active service during the war.

On 11 November 1918 Germany was starved into a humiliating surrender, and bankrupted to pay for the war that she had lost.

In London, the Armistice celebrations lasted for three days and nights.

Everyone wanted to forget the war.

They just wanted to enjoy themselves.

452

None of his family welcomed Vic home. None of the ungrateful souls were at the station to greet him. Too wrapped up in their own selfish pursuits, no doubt.

Why didn't they care about him?

He cared for them.

He'd heard all these stories about girls mobbing blokes at the stations when they came home from the war, throwing flowers and blowing kisses and all that. Not for him! The platform was almost empty apart from other demobbed, confused Tommies stepping down from the train, stuck into suits that were too tight or too long, or too loose, or too short. They walked awkwardly, some of them wearing thin civilian shoes for the first time in four years instead of heavy Army boots.

They were free.

Vic watched them mill around, waiting to be told what to do.

Yes, he thought, *as free as cattle*.

He swung his case off the train and surrendered his rail warrant at the gate, severing his last contact with the Army. The collector took it indifferently, almost contemptuously. Vic wanted to shout at him: *Where were you when we were fighting the war for you? Get out of my sight! You don't deserve to be allowed to live in this country!*

'Thanks, mate,' he smiled.

'You're holding up the queue,' the collector said.

It had been different before the war. People had manners then. Vic walked under the strings of garish electric light into the dark. He was cold and it was snowing: big, white, slow flakes swirling past the lights, soft underfoot. He turned up the collar of his jacket. Nearly two and a half years fighting for your country, and they wouldn't even give you an overcoat or gloves to keep your hands warm.

He caught a tram to the East End. He was pleased to see that the driver and conductor were both men: in those endless long letters about nothing at all, stupid Nigel had told him tales about conductresses – and ˈen women drivers. Out working, instead of doing their duty with their families in the home, cooking and cleaning, which was a woman's place. Peace had ended that nonsense now: all the other lighted vehicles crawling through the snowy dark were driven by men.

Vic swung down off the tram and went into the Old Bull and Bush for a half of mild. Ted Trott moved behind the bar, polishing glasses. There were very few tables. Ted preferred people to stand, he got more in. 'Hallo, Ted.'

'Back from the wars, then, Vic,' Ted rumbled. He was enormous now, with an overhanging beer belly. He'd got older, Vic noted carefully, the hairs on his chest were grey instead of black, his face was redder, and his greying hair was swept back. He moved slower too. 'Keeping out of trouble, then, Vic,' Ted said firmly.

Vic knew he was being warned off. He smiled. 'You know me,' he said, sipping his beer.

'I know you,' Ted said. He waited, then said casually: 'Want a job?'

'What, polishing glasses?'

Ted laughed. Very funny.

Vic shrugged: 'I'll think about it.'

'You do that, son. Think about it very carefully, won't you?' Ted must have built up a powerful organization during the war, and now he wanted to protect his investment. Vic drained his glass. The day he worked for this bag of lard would be the day hell froze over.

'Thanks for the beer.'

'On the house. That brother of yours has gone into the business, did you know?'

'It's nice in here, lovely red wallpaper. I like this place.'

'Get your eyes off it, or I'll bury you.'

Vic changed the subject. 'Has your boy Raymond come back yet?'

Ted looked sour. 'No. No word from Jerusalem yet.' He probably didn't care for his nancy-boy son any more than Vic did.

'Ta-ta.' Vic drained his glass and went outside. He stood

under a street lamp and turned his hot red face up to the
cool flakes of snow. Ted didn't know what he had started.
Nobody threatens Vic Price like that. He felt as though he had
been physically violated. Nobody buries Vic Price, nobody
forgets Vic Price. It made him feel sick: you fought for your
country, and when you came back, you had to fight for what
was your own. People thought that they didn't have to
respect you, they thought they could do without you.

They would learn different.

When he had his family around him, nobody would talk
to him like that. His family, his blood, and all his relations,
everyone he knew, needed him. Nigel's letters had made
that plain. They couldn't live without him. Look what
happened to them, without him to look after them. Gone
down. New house instead of a home, and Ria parading
herself openly on the stage.

He walked down West Ferry Road into familiar territory.
He no longer felt the snow or the cold. The Anchor and
Hope pub had been repainted and had the Christmas
decorations up, but Brown's Laundry looked just the same.

Vic strode on. Nigel's business had attracted the attention of Ted Trott. Couldn't Nigel do anything right? And
getting those letters of his, letter after letter without any
emotion or feeling or gossip, except about Ria, had been
torment. *The business is going according to plan.* What plan? He
wouldn't trust Nigel to cross the road by himself, let alone
run a racket. All he'd make was money. *Mum and Dad send
their love.* That was a lie. *Dad is working hard.* So he should be!
Ria has let you down.

Vic stopped. He closed his eyes.

*She sings for soldiers and kisses them and Vic it is a shameless act.
She flaunts her legs and body on the stage showing them to any Tom
Dick or Harry who cares to pay a shilling.*

My own sister. Vic gave a sob of anguish.

She was doing it deliberately – deliberately defying him.
Humiliating him. The Workhouse Bastard had ruined her,
possessed her like a devil.

Vic stood in the snow with his head bent, sobbing aloud.

Ben London had run a brilliant campaign. The intruder

had first turned Ria's love for her own brother into hate, then tried to wreck their family, and with his soft ways and iron will-power, he'd almost succeeded. He'd known what he wanted, all right: the family he'd never had and never deserved to have. And he'd got Esther on his side, and Tom, and finally all the women in the community, with his cunning, winning ways. All against him, Vic. Brilliant. Only Nigel had stood by him, loyal, clever, stupid Nigel.

Vic pressed the back of his hand against his teeth. Against me!

'I'm Vic Price. Remember me.

Vic smiled.

He remembered.

His confidence came back. He felt good again.

Poor Ria. Now she'd be all right. He'd look after her. And Nigel. Everyone would be all right.

He turned into Havannah Street and knocked on the door. Esther opened it. She had her hair in curlers and she looked awful. Vic wrapped his arms around her and kissed her. 'Mum, how do you do it, you're more beautiful than ever.'

She patted her hair. 'I wasn't expecting you until tomorrow.'

He closed the door behind him with his foot. The house had a warm, stewy smell, both familiar and strange. He didn't recognize the carpet or the curtains and there were new chairs. Christmas tinsel hung around the walls and there was a little green Christmas tree with presents in brightly coloured wrappings. Tom got up. He looked a little more hunched than Vic remembered – still massively strong, but carrying more weight.

'Hallo, Vic.'

'How's work, Dad?' Vic said casually.

'It's different from the war,' Tom said. 'The docks are easing off a bit, you know, and a lot of strong young men are coming back into the lump.'

A kid of about four ran in and stopped, seeing the stranger.

Vic said: 'Who is that?'

Esther said, 'Don't you recognize Will?'

Vic said: 'No.'

'Vic, please don't,' begged Esther. 'Let bygones be bygones.'

The past was never gone. Vic said: 'Get him out of here.'

'He'll be old enough to start school next year,' Esther said eagerly, picking him up and straddling his legs around her hip. She pecked his cheek, but Will stared at Vic, then wrapped his arms around Esther's neck, still staring. 'Let's be a happy family,' Esther begged in a jolly voice. 'Look, Will, that's your uncle Vic. Show him your aeroplane. Don't cry.'

Vic said: 'Where's Ria?'

Esther jogged Will on her hip. 'She's out – she's out, that's all.'

'She should be looking after that child!' Vic said emotionally. 'It's wrong to leave him with you. She had him. He's hers. She should be a good mother and look after him properly.'

'Would you like something to eat?' asked Esther guiltily. Every word that Vic had said was true. Esther shook to think what Vic would do if he found out that Ria had taken up a stage career instead of finding a nice husband.

Vic said: 'Where's Nigel?'

He went next door to the old Osborne place. Nigel had a mean little fire going in the front room, which was almost undecorated except for a desk and an expensive Persian rug. Nigel showed Vic into the captain's chair and fanned some papers out in front of him on the desk. Before Vic's eyes reached the bottom line, Nigel said:

'You're rich! Twenty-six thousand pounds.' He grinned eagerly.

Vic was unimpressed.

'Money only buys half as much nowadays,' he said.

Inflation; yes, that was true. As always Vic had put his finger straight on the weak point, even if he didn't use the proper word.

'I didn't waste my time,' Vic said indifferently. 'I've got stuff buried in a field in France. What a wonderful war.'

457

'The French currency is a bit rocky,' Nigel said dubiously. He looked for the newspaper article to back him up. It was around here somewhere.

'In gold. I'm not stupid.'

Nigel shook his head in admiration. Meanwhile Vic prodded at Nigel's balance sheet with his short, thick finger. 'How is this money held?'

Nigel tried to explain the complex arrangements in simple terms. Some of it was in cash. The rest was in various bank accounts.

'Stupid,' Vic said instantly. 'Money has to have reasons. Got to be seen, got to go into legitimate businesses. Blumenthall did. We got to.'

Nigel shuddered. He had not thought of poor Mr Blumenthall with the conscious part of his mind for years. He nodded helplessly.

'Look at him,' Vic said remorselessly, 'he always had legitimate fronts. What did he need that grocer's shop for? Or the market stalls? Or the pawnbroker's? Not for the money, Nigel. For the reason for the money.'

Nigel had never thought of it that way round: not hiding money away, but hiding it in the open. 'We've got to pay tax,' Vic said. 'We're successful people. It's our social duty.'

Yes, of course. 'That's brilliant, Vic.'

Vic sneered: 'It's obvious, Nigel. How did you get your heroic wound?'

Nigel licked his lips and lied to Vic. 'The breastworks at Croix Barbée – an attack by German shock-troops. I shot a couple, then—'

Vic was uninterested. 'Where's Ria?'

'You don't know how much it grieved me to write that letter,' Nigel said quickly. 'I'm sorry, Vic!'

'You did right to tell me. You can never go wrong by telling me everything, Nige. Remember that. I suppose she's playing at the Queen's theatre?'

Nigel nodded his head sadly. Vic's face flushed deep red with anger.

'Now?'

'Yes,' Nigel admitted.

'I'll kill her,' Vic said.

But of course he wouldn't, Nigel knew. Vic would never harm a hair on Ria's head. He thought: *You're for it when you get home, Ria.* She shouldn't have made that insulting remark at the street party: *Only the lucky ones get it in the elbow, Nigel. Some of them get their balls blown off. I don't suppose you'd notice any difference though.* In public, she'd said it; that was the unforgivable thing. In front of everyone. She'd pay.

'She'll be home in an hour,' Nigel grinned, 'her last performance ends at ten.'

'No it doesn't,' Vic said, 'it ends now.'

Nigel watched horrified as Vic simply stood up and walked out. A moment later the front door slammed. Nigel stopped to pull on an overcoat, then ran after him. He hurried to catch Vic up. Vic walked on, not even acknowledging Nigel's presence. He didn't dare say a word though. He had seen Vic in this mood before.

When they came to the theatre Vic brushed through the foyer, leaving Nigel to pay. Nigel cursed, paid dutifully and ran through.

Inside was stinking hot and smoky, roaring with noise. The benches were jammed solid and heads were silhouetted against the glitter of the lighted stage, At the back of the floor men walked along talking to the girls waiting there, and a few kissed and cuddled against the back walls. Nigel pushed into the crowd and stood on tiptoe. He couldn't see Vic.

Ria stood in the focus of the lights on stage, entering the last half of her Christmas act – a tiny, vivid figure dressed in a satin robe of Santa Claus red, trimmed with white fur. Her long, shapely legs, that on her high-steps seemed to take up more than half her body, were in sheer black dancing tights. No man in the audience could take his eyes off them, but even Nigel had to admit that though undeniably erotic, they were perfectly chaste; it was all in the mind.

Ria paraded up and down the stage tossing little brightly coloured gifts out, most' tiny bags of peanuts in their shells.

Where was Vic?

Nigel pushed forward through the crowd.

Vic's stocky, unmistakable silhouette appeared. He was pulling himself up onto the stage from the orchestra pit. Someone must have been tugging at his ankle from below: he kicked out and there was a crash of cymbals. The music broke up and faded away. Vic stood on stage.

Ria stopped.

She took one step backwards. She moved her head from side to side.

Her face began to work as Vic walked towards her, emotions chasing one after the other across her features with a range and speed that probably no actress could have mimicked: surprise, fear, guilt, desperation, resignation. The audience fell silent. Vic, with his suit stretched tight across his back between his shoulderblades, slowly reached out and took her hand.

The audience waited. Still they thought that it was part of the act.

Vic enclosed Ria's hand in his fist. She shook her head slowly, then only gazed at him, and her shoulders dropped. He turned and smiled at the audience with his red, angry face. A small man in white shirt-sleeves and pink braces ran out from the wings and Nigel recognized Stanley Kirschbaum, the stage manager. Vic didn't take his eyes off the audience. He backhanded Kirschbaum, knocking him down. He didn't look at the fallen man, he ignored him: he stared out at the audience, challenging them. Nobody said a word. Ria stood limply with her hand on her forehead, her fingers twined in her golden hair, which hung forward. Kirschbaum made a business of getting to his knees, but wisely no further. Vic stood there smiling his confident smile, his brown teeth gleaming, then turned and walked slowly from the stage with Ria tugging obediently along behind him.

And then the stage was empty.

Remember, Vic said, his mouth close to her ear.

She remembered Ben; how she had not had the courage of her love, how she had deserted him.

Remember what happened to Jimmy, Vic whispered.

She remembered his little body being pulled out of the lock on a hook.

'Better look after Will,' hissed Vic.

She pressed her fist to her temple, then wept.

'Come home with me,' Vic smiled.

3

Vane Leibig sat in front of the mirror in her bedroom. Rationing and shortages had not ended with the war, but of course Daddy – she called him Daddy now between themselves, being *fearfully* modern – Daddy employed buyers who purchased the very best of what was going. It was such an advantage. It was the one thing that really made Marcelline jealous of her; that and her slim figure. Marcy had rather lost her skin tone since she got married, and she was swelling up. A baby. And Marcy had sworn she wouldn't! Poor Marcy.

She heard the clatter of the engine as Daddy left for work. She had said goodbye to him earlier, over breakfast. She always ate breakfast downstairs nowadays, since her year in the Voluntary Aid Detachment as a nurse had got her rather in the habit of rising early. She still had the uniform, hanging proudly on the back of her door – it was hardly the sort of thing one would put in one's wardrobe.

She turned back to the mirror.

She was bored.

At any moment now, she would hear Peggy's little shoes tapping up the stairs. Lisbeth, the other maid, had been quite hopeless and had been Let Go as soon as the war ended. The ammunition factories had closed virtually overnight, and the situation regarding domestics had improved dramatically, thank God. Peggy, who had been with them before the war and ungratefully spurned them for a job in Silvertown filling shells for seven pounds a week, had simply begged to be allowed to come back. Even so, they had to pay her twice as much as that stupid Lisbeth since not as many girls were returning to domestic service as had left it.

Vane examined her face, touching her fingertips to her cheeks, moving her head from side to side. Despite her rapidly advancing age – she was nearly twenty-three years old – she was still perfect. In fact more perfect than ever. Not a single wrinkle or line. Round brown eyes with porcelain-clear whites, a lovely little nose, creamy skin, a small ruby mouth. She put her head on one side and closed her eyes. She ran her hands down her body. Her behind was a little too big and her feet were too small. Perhaps her ankles were too thick? She gave up and peered at her face again, now very close to the mirror. Blackheads on the sides of her nose were the bane of her life. On skin as pale as hers they showed up like beacons. Leibig's didn't sell cosmetics, but they did run a small pharmacy, and she had tried an astringent on her nose. It hadn't worked. Nor had alcohol spirit. Still the blackheads came.

No blackheads.

Good.

Then she sighed.

Since she came back from No. 5 Hospital at Rouen, life had seemed very flat. The days were very long. Daddy worked endless hours at the Emporium. Marcelline was busy with Henry's budding political career.

Vane hated Henry, for taking Marcelline from her. Marcelline was no better for going.

She started filing her nails.

Footsteps tapped on the stairs. Peggy with the newspapers at last. Would she knock on the door first or would she just come breezing straight in? Vane prepared to put Peggy in her place. Those years in the factory had been a very bad influence on the girl. She made it rather too obvious that she thought she was as good as her mistress, and sometimes she made too-familiar conversation. It had been different before the war. The knock came on the door.

Vane said: 'Come—' Peggy came in and laid the papers on the dresser.

'Here you are, miss!' She was a cheerful, bird-faced sort in a black pinafore and a frilly white apron.

Vane put down her nail file. She spoke severely. 'You

must wait to be told by me to come in, before you enter, Peggy. And address me properly.'

'All right, ma'am,' Peggy said cheerfully. She prodded the paper proudly. 'A woman's been elected to Parliament! Lady Astor. One in the eye for the stuffy old codgers, what?'

Vane felt a responsibility to put the girl's view of the world down in its place. She spoke as coldly, as humourlessly as Grandpapa would have done: 'You must not speak disrespectfully of your betters, Peggy.'

But Peggy shot nimbly back: 'They're not my betters, ma'am, begging your pardon. They're the ones what started the war and did jolly well out of it. Very nicely, thank you.'

It was quite incredible to hear a maid talking like this – like a Bolshevik, Vane thought. The girl thought that fifteen shillings a week and board entitled her to tirade her mistress! 'We are not interested in your ideas about the war, my girl,' Vane insisted, but tolerantly. She knew that there was no real harm in Peggy, and the girl was too quick with words and new ideas to tackle lightly.

'There's ever such a dramatic story here, ma'am.' Peggy had obviously been reading the newspapers herself – that was why there had been the delay. They were wrinkled. Vane decided not to say anything. 'Here it is,' Peggy said, folding back the page. ' "Real-life Tarzan Drama",' she glanced at Vane's face – 'you know, Tarzan of the Apes? Lord Greystoke.'

'I do not read that sort of book,' Vane said. She did. The novel had been a sensation a few years ago.

'From Our Own Correspondent – look, it's cabled all the way from Nairobi in Africa – the Dark Continent –'

'I do not care to look. Have you no duties to go to?'

Peggy's voice rose excitedly. ' "The aircraft carrying Lord Cleremont's son Roland crashed in nearly impenetrable jungle. When an expedition reached the burned-out wreck, three weeks later, they identified the pilot, Captain Henricks, by his diamond tiepin, but found no trace of the thirty-one year old heir to the Cleremont fortune. However" – there! you *are* interested, ma'am, I can see it in your

463

eyes – "However," ' continued Peggy in dramatic tones,
' "after a thorough search, in the muddy banks of a nearby
river they found the prints of *a human foot!*" ' she squeaked.

'Probably a native,' Vane said, trying to hide her excitement.

Breathlessly Peggy continued: ' "Like Lord Greystoke, is
there a survivor of the wreck? Will the young aristocrat,
who may have lost his memory, revert to nature? *Is there a
Real-Life Tarzan living somewhere in the jungles of Africa?*" ' Her
voice dropped. ' "Lord Cleremont says that he cannot
believe there is any hope." Oh, isn't that awful.'

But it was not the story which accounted for the excitement showing in Vane's eyes: it was the advertisement
below which had caught her attention. Deflating Peggy had
not worked: now she fidgeted in her eagerness to get rid of
the talkative girl.

'You may go now, Peggy!'

'Very well, ma'am.' Peggy bobbed, not without a touch
of insolence, and Vane watched her in the mirror as she
walked to the door, opened it, bobbed again, and closed it
behind her.

Vane grabbed the paper and unfolded it, flicked through
the pages. The advertisement which had caught her eye:

Grahame-White presents:

LONDON
&
LAIDLAW
Famous Royal Air Force Aces of the Great War
who will give
AN AERIAL DEMONSTRATION OF
SKILL & DARING
London Aerodrome, Hendon, N.W.
2.20 p.m.
30 April 1919

DEATH-DEFYING
STUNTS

TERRIFYING
SPINS

5/– at gate
inc. Tax

Vane pushed through the crowd. It was a bright, sunny day with fast-moving blobs of cloud, typical April weather. She wore her luxurious white furs and several people looked at her, wondering if she was a cinema film-star. The wind shivered the furs exquisitely around her but she felt warm and remote inside. Some rough types in billy-cocks, with their sleeves rolled up, were eating sausages dipped in mustard. She ignored them. A stall was selling barrelled scrumpy cider, and lots of little children were running about on the grass.

One little boy with a raspberry-flavoured lollipop stopped and stared at her. Then his eyes widened and rose above her head. A moment later a shadow flashed over them and there was a thunderous roar as an aeroplane raced above the crowd, then pulled away upward. Like everyone else, Vane clapped her hands to her cheeks as the aeroplane seemed to rise up vertically until its wings were outlines against the clouds. It lost speed. For an endless moment it hung motionless from the whirling propeller.

Then it began to slip backwards.

Everyone screamed. Vane screamed too.

The little boy with the lollipop said: 'He'll pull her out, you watch. I seen this before, over the beach at Scarborough. That's Ben London.'

The aeroplane slid backwards, then fell over onto its back into a dive that turned into a long swooping curve over the hangars.

Vane said, 'Was that the aeroplane called a Sopwith Camel?'

'Avro.' The boy sucked his lollipop dismissively. 'Not much cop. Not as good as the Camel.' Another aeroplane appeared and did jigs around the sky with the Avro. 'That's Fearless Frank Laidlaw,' the boy said. 'He's flying a captured Fokker DVII – triplane, got three sets of wings, see. Black. He's playing the Black Baron today.'

Vane wanted to see where the aeroplanes would land. She pushed through the crowd. The two machines twisted and turned overhead, round and round. The crowd grew denser and the people shoved back when she pushed at them. Unfortunately there was no royal enclosure or grandstand, it was all one price and the sweaty hoi poloi were simply everywhere. They craned back their heads as the aircraft thundered over close one after the other, and she slipped past. One particularly bulky person blocked her way until she took out her hatpin and jabbed him. She was determined. 'Excuse me!' she said. He shifted and at last she reached the railing. Beyond stretched the expanse of open grass covering the aerodrome. Not far away were the wheel-ruts where they would land. In her white furs, she would be unmistakable. He would remember her. He would remember the girl in white flinging down her shopping.

The aeroplanes climbed and rolled. It was very exciting. Vane pressed her knuckles to her teeth.

She remembered that special smile of his, and his kind, opaque, unreadable eyes; those powerful wrists and slim, sensitive fingers . . . her frightened sense of excitement and danger, but how gentle he had been. She remembered leaning forward towards him in the rain from the back of the Rolls-Royce, him standing there in the gutter with the water flowing over his field-boots, and what she had said:

'*I'll see you again.*'

'*I don't know.*'

'*I do know.*'

And she *had* known. It had been love at first sight. It did exist. He would remember her.

The aeroplanes fell out through a hole between the clouds in a terrific vertical dive, the Avro closing in behind the Black Baron's Fokker.

The Fokker spun to the right.

The Avro also spun to the right, matching perfectly.

Getting lower. Surely they were too low!

The Fokker spun to the left.

The Avro also spun to the left. The wind gusted and Vane's white fur hat, unpinned, blew off.

She did not move.

The engines screamed.

The Fokker pulled out and zoomed above the grass.

She stared up.

White streaks appeared at the Avro's wingtips, as though it was scratching white curving lines in the blue sky, pulling out of the dive. Mist vapour formed above the wings and streamed back.

Very low now. Almost on the horizon.

The crowd was suddenly silent.

The Avro's lower wing fluttered and started to bend, then suddenly banged upward, striking into the top wing.

There was a loud *crack* and all the wings folded upward like paper. The engine raced. The wingtips clapped together high above the pilot's head. Vane watched horrified. The machine plummeted fifty feet, then furrowed into the grass, bounced, skidded, bits flew off everywhere, then it slewed to a halt lying on one side.

Vane ducked under the railing. She ran. The wind flapped her furs behind her. She threw herself down on her knees in the ripped earth that the machine had ploughed up, careless of the dirt on her beautiful clothes or the wet slime seeping over her knees. Was he dead?

Flight-Commander London lay in a tangle of bracing wires and struts. His gorgeous hair had fallen over his face. She gently brushed it aside with her fingertips.

His eyes flickered open, piercingly blue.

'Ben!' she said. 'Oh, darling, your poor legs.'

He squinted at her against the sky. 'Snow Princess?' he murmured. He nodded. He recognized her. He remembered. Her heart fluttered.

Then he looked down. 'I've lost my legs,' he groaned helplessly.

No, he hadn't. But yes, he was helpless. 'I will make you better,' she whispered.

'Vane Leibig,' he muttered. She had rejected him before, after all. Perhaps she could hardly expect all his memories of her to be as good as her feelings about him. Even if he had played about by taking her to a lousy tea-house.

Some men came up and started pulling clumsily at the wreckage. 'Stand back!' she ordered them furiously. 'I am a trained nurse. This man is injured and in my care.'

He even sounded a little amused. 'I was so certain that you didn't like me.' What could she say? What would Marcelline have said?

Vane smiled radiantly.

'Darling!' she said. 'I'm so sorry!'

PART VI

THE RISE

Chapter Seventeen

1

I'm sorry. Vane, smart in her nurse's uniform with a starched white apron and black stockings pumped up Ben's pillows. She smiled down at him and smoothed his brow professionally, then took his pulse, timing it with the watch pinned on the upper slope of her left breast. *I'm sorry.* He would never know what it had cost her to say that, but it had been worth the lie. He had recognized her, all right, and remembered. But her radiant *I'm sorry!* had taken all the wind out of his sails, and she had been able to organize him easily. She had even paid for the doctor, because he didn't have a penny in the world. He was a foundling. She could make of him whatever she wanted.

He said: 'Vane, I—'

'Ssh,' she said peremptorily, without taking her eyes off her watch. For the first time in her life she had someone who was dependent on her who she could boss around, a handsome man all of her own. And she was totally safe: after all, what could a man with two broken legs *do?*

Ben closed his mouth and acquiesced mutely to her command. He knew that she always started all over again if he made her lose count. He needed her help for everything, even the bedpan, and she took her responsibilities very seriously. Peggy was not allowed to help. He hid a smile. Sometimes he felt that Vane was playing it like a sort of children's game, like Doctors and Nurses, or Nurse and

Patient. That was unfair. She mothered him beautifully – and she was very beautiful.

Who would have believed that life with both legs in plaster could be like heaven? Ben thought. But it was. With Vane.

Even Sam was happy. He slept in the scullery and Peggy assured Ben that Vane had ordered her to brush him regularly and take him for walks.

When he crashed, Ben had groaned with horror at the thought of what lay ahead of him – weeks, perhaps months, in hospital on a hard bed, with nurses like those he had endured in France when he had the 'flu. And this time there was no denying it, he *was* to blame. As soon as the Avro had lifted off, he had *felt* that the wires were badly strung, and he had *known* that he should not disregard what he felt, but he had been already in the air, and the crowd was waiting and expectant, and the show must go on . . . When she folded up and he crashed, he had no one to blame but himself.

Far from blaming him for his stupidity in breaking his legs, Vane seemed quite pleased about it. She had taken command of the situation and given orders to everybody, called the hospital ambulance, arranged for a doctor . . . while he slipped in and out of unconsciousness as they cut him out of the wreck.

His legs were set solid in plaster, and he would be bedridden for weeks. Protests were futile; she simply would not tolerate him returning to his flea-ridden digs to recuperate, and a convalescence in a nursing home was perfectly unnecessary. To be honest, he did not protest very much.

Because she lived in a mansion.

She called it a 'new little awful house' which she and her father, Georgy, had moved to only after her mother died. 'Our last house had rather more style, I suppose.' She pretended to hardly bother to describe the circular driveway, the fountain, the clipped topiary bushes in the shape of animals, as if that sort of thing was so taken for granted as not to need describing. Then for one of those very rare moments her face had slipped, and he had seen how much its loss had hurt her.

472

He did not often see through her.

Perhaps it was because the glamorous life she lived, and the wonderful house she lived in, were so different from anything he had ever experienced before. For the first time in his life since he was looked after by Nurse Edith Rumney in Lichfield Street he was living in a proper house. And there were servants. If you wanted a sandwich you didn't get a knife and cut it yourself, you simply rang the bell.

Not that Vane let him have sandwiches. He had to eat food that was good for him, like milk, and custard, and fish. And she watched him eat it, every last mouthful. Gradually her voice, which could be hard, softened.

'What was she like, your Nurse Rumney?'

'Not as beautiful as you.'

'Did you love her?'

'Yes.'

She took the tray, and their fingers touched.

Another time, she watched him eat with her eyes shining until he put down the spoon, then said: 'Tell me all about your adventures in the Workhouse!'

He told her about Bill Madeley, and the Fat Boy, and Knuts, and all the others, and the black walls.

'Gosh,' she said, resting her chin on the palm of her hand. Her eyes never left him. 'Really? How wonderful!' The fascinated way she said it made him feel as though he was being very clever and interesting, although it was only the story of his life. But of course, it was utterly different from anything that she had ever known. She listened raptly: she seemed to think it was so romantic. He smiled at her. She looked so alive with her round, sparkling eyes that he adored her.

'I'll bring you your tea,' she said.

When the pillows were up like this he could look out of his window, although it made his legs ache if he did so for too long, and see the June sunlight pouring down on Primrose Hill, and the nannies on the paths below pushing their old black prams with white parasols over them to protect the baby from the light, and girls in tight round hats and tall straight dresses strolling independently with their own children in the latest fashion, and the roofs of London stretching away beyond Regent's Park into the glittering haze. Life was perfect; Vane was perfect. She could not have been more perfect for him if she had tried to be.

She brought him his tea in a china cup with just one wrapped cube of sugar in the saucer. He stirred it in. 'Vane,' he said.

'Yes, Ben?' She turned by the window.

'I don't know how to thank you for all you've done for me,' he said. Some strands of her shining brown hair had accidentally escaped from beneath her trim white cap while she was out.

She smiled. 'Just you getting better will be all the thanks I need,' she gushed. She did this to him occasionally, saying something so overwhelmingly conventional and banal that he wondered if she was mocking herself. He really could not tell. Perhaps she simply did not want a personal involvement to disturb their professional relationship. But if that was so, why was he here and not in some rotten hospital? She reached over him to take the discarded sugar wrapping off the sheet. Her lips above him gleamed like dark, lustrous rubies. Her complexion was so flawless that he seemed to see deep inside her, as pale as cream, a pure femininity there, a coolness that made him feel flushed with warmth.

He touched her chin with his fingertips.

She stopped.

He kissed her lips lightly. She hesitated. 'Please don't,' she said. 'Girls aren't the same as men. You understand.' What can a man with two broken legs *do?* She waited a moment.

Understand? 'Yes, of course.' Of course he didn't.

The worst thing was, she looked into his eyes then gave him a grateful little smile as though he *did* understand. He wished he did. She made him feel inadequate.

He said: 'I love you.'

She did not move. The sunlight shone around her hair. One strand tickled his nose. He could see the line of her collarbone, he felt her breath on his face. She spoke in a very low voice.

'I loved you before I saw you.'

He touched her hand.

She said: 'Everything about you.' That was neither mocking nor banal; words were blunt instruments, but not this low, supple voice, or the clear brown intensity of her eyes peering, sparkling into his, then looking away. It was the truth.

'I need you,' he said. He stretched up to kiss her. His lips touched hers. Vane closed her eyes and gave away a little of herself.

He felt her hard little lips softening, warming. A thrill raced through him. He reached up.

She jerked back, smoothing her uniform. 'It wouldn't be right,' she said.

'It wouldn't be wrong.' He longed to caress her.

She stroked her hair back under her cap. 'You must respect me.'

Saying that, she sounded like any one of the girls hanging round the airfield pubs. Yet, he reasoned, it must be a legitimate fear for a girl to feel; it would be too easy for them to be exploited otherwise. He did not want to exploit Vane, or for her to feel that he was trying to. Perhaps she was saying that he must respect her social class, because he was a Workhouse boy, but in fairness to her he did not think that she looked down on him for that, in fact the opposite: she seemed to like it.

'I do respect you,' he said.

She smiled. He said: 'What is it?'

She laughed, half turning away and putting her knuckles to her lips: 'It makes me feel so happy, looking at you lying there all helpless in your bed.'

'I shall be up on crutches next week.'

'Only if I give my permission.'

'I'm bored with waiting.'

'Don't argue,' she said tersely.

'Darling.'

'Darling,' she agreed. 'Don't argue, darling.'

When he had the crutches he was able to hobble downstairs for his meals – except breakfast, which Vane insisted feeding him in bed – and check that Sam was happy. Vane would not let the dog into the living rooms, but Sam was obviously content with Peggy. She talked to him a lot and he wagged his tail from time to time. Mr Leibig came home for lunch every day, which seemed an inefficient practice, but apparently he had always done so: as had his father, the founder of the Emporium. 'The shop is closed from one o'clock until two o'clock.'

'Business must be much better now the war's over, Mr Leibig.'

'Please call me Georgy. Everyone else does.'

'Thank you, sir,' Ben said automatically.

'Georgy, please!' He had watery, popping eyes in a red face – even Georgy's bald dome was red above his half-circle of silver hair – and he looked to Ben as though he was perpetually angry. But Ben knew that his bark was far worse than his bite. With Vane, Georgy was always terribly strict, though. He criticized her table manners – though they were of course perfect – even in front of guests. He always called her Vanity, stiffly, as though keeping her at a distance, though he was relaxed and friendly with Ben. But he obviously loved her, doted on her, indulged her. Vane got absolutely everything she wanted.

Ben suspected that the shadow of Grandpapa was very long and that Georgy brought up his daughter as he himself had been brought up: and the way he indulged her was what he thought of as kindness, because it had never been shown to him. It was not kindness or generosity, it was indulgence. Vane was spoilt, that was all.

The other side of it was that excessive strictness and stiff teutonic way he called her Vanity, as if she was a cipher rather than a daughter. Duty, duty, duty; the shop, the shop, the shop. Responsibility. Living up to Grandpapa's name above the door. And she called her father *Daddy*, which sounded equally forced. Ben nodded. 'Georgy,' he agreed. Poor Georgy. Poor Vane. Unhappy people.

He needed them; he had nothing.

Vane smiled and rested her fingers lightly over Ben's hand on the table. 'I have to go to the jeweller's tomorrow –

some of Mama's old stuff simply had to be reset. Daddy, don't glower. Would you like me to allow Ben out? You can show him around your boring old shop.'

Georgy's eyes flicked to their hands. He nodded. 'It will be a pleasure.'

Ben rode sumptuously in the back of the Rolls-Royce with Vane. Outside, Bond Street was as busy as a hive. The high July sun poured light down between the glittering façades of the fabulous, exclusive shops that lined the road. Vane looked at Ben's eager face and smiled.

Near the corner of Piccadilly, the limousine pulled over and stopped alongside an immaculately scrubbed pavement.

Ben looked out at the imposing frontage of Leibig's Emporium.

He saw an enormous man with a white moustache, dressed in a uniform of imperial purple with plenty of gold braid and decorations, standing to attention in the mahogany, brass and glass-paned doorway. Customers filtered past him. Obviously he was the Doorman. Boys in uniforms of the same imperial colour, but without the long tails and imperious braid, waited in the shadows, and they were the ones who actually had to open the doors for the customers.

On each side of the central Doorman stretched gleaming display windows crammed with everything imaginable: wine, fruit, dried fruit, oatmeal military biscuits, coffee essence, tinned milk, vegetable extract, whisky, cheeses, a rack of coloured sausage meats that Ben did not recognize, rows of cured hams, and tubs of ice-cream, presumably empty.

'The whole display is removed, dusted, and replaced before opening time every morning,' Vane said. Just one of those little facts and figures about Leibig's Emporium.

'I see,' Ben said. The canopies over the windows had once been imperial purple too, no doubt, but the sun had faded them to a pale puce, and the gold gothic lettering spelling LEIBIG'S EMPORIUM had become blackened with traffic fumes.

Ben said: 'Who's the fellow in the purple regalia?'

'Oh, that's our Mr Hawkins. He's a terror. Everyone calls him Hawk.'

The chauffeur opened the door. Ben swung his crutches out and hobbled down. 'I'll pick you up later,' Vane called. The chauffeur closed the door, the Rolls-Royce swept away.

Ben swung himself across the immaculate pavement. He smiled at the Doorman. Hawk's eyes glittered beneath the visor of his cap.

Ben stopped.

He said: 'Good afternoon, Hawk.'

Hawk said: 'Good afternoon, sir.' He did not move an inch.

Ben said: 'Nice day.' He leaned comfortably on his crutches.

Hawk flexed himself slightly up on his toes. Then he said: 'Not too bad today, sir.' He had a voice as smooth and dark as melted chocolate.

'You're the doorman here, are you?'

Hawk said, very slowly: 'Head Doorman, sir.' He gazed steadily. People edged around them.

Ben said, in a very friendly tone of voice: 'Aren't you going to help me open the door, then, Hawk?'

Hawk stared into this man's eyes. He wasn't going to do it. Young men tried to show off their manhood with him a thousand times a year, usually to impress their simpering flapper girlfriends, but he hadn't been Head Doorman of Leibig's Emporium for thirty-three years for nothing, and he ate them. This chap with the bright blue eyes was going to learn a lesson that he wouldn't forget.

Then Hawk frowned. He shook his head like a man who hears a buzzing in his ear. He looked at the man again.

Those eyes. He almost—

Ben asked, 'Are you all right?'

'Sorry, sir,' Hawk said, and saluted him. One of his fingers was missing, Ben noticed, doubtless a war wound. Hawk reached round and opened the door with his other hand.

'Thank you,' Ben said, going in.

Hawk stared after him. He felt . . . something. Something had changed.

A devil with those hot blue eyes.

He shook his head again, then snapped his fingers for the boy to close the door, and straightened his back. It was damned hot weather.

Inside, Ben's eyes adjusted to the gloomy interior. Entering Leibig's Emporium was like stepping back into 1890. It was as though the Emporium had been set in aspic and forgotten, becoming browner and more impenetrable as the years passed. Dim light fell from lines of big pendant globes of frosted glass trimmed with brown iron. Gas lighting – in the 1920s, for God's sake. Ben manoeuvred his crutches clumsily down the steps of threadbare purple carpet to the main floor.

He stared, fascinated. The unaccountable excitement he had felt outside, pushing past the Head Doorman, was growing, and now it tingled through him.

He realized that his left hand hurt him. His fist was clenched.

He was where he wanted to be.

Like Aladdin's cave, the place was bigger inside than it had looked outside. It had a musty smell and somehow, perhaps because of all the dull shades and straight lines of brown wood, felt very masculine. He passed along rows of dark wooden counters, past tired-looking salesgirls in long black dresses. The male staff were dressed all in black, with stiff white Eton collars, except the floor-walkers, who wore morning suits with a flower in the buttonhole. Sales, he saw with the excitement of forgotten memories awakening to life, were rung up on big brass tills exactly like Mr Blumenthall's, and purchases were wrapped in brown paper neatly tied off with string, very quickly and professionally. Nearly all the customers were men, he noticed, mostly older men, straight-backed and military in bearing. Old men on pensions. In five minutes he saw no more than half a dozen ladies.

He paused by a long cheese counter. It was set out with every sort of cheese imaginable, with perfectly polished mirrors making up for the indifferent lighting. Nobody was waiting to be served.

He stopped at the lift. On one side there were stairs to the upper sales floor: clothing, pharmacy, account queries, materials, haberdashery, hats . . . On the other side stairs curved down to the basement level: wines, guns, sports clothing, uniforms, funeral department, household goods, carpets. Leibig's was not big enough to be a full department store, but it seemed that it sold a bit of everything, if you could find it.

Georgy stepped out of the lift, holding a letter which he was reading with a frown. He looked up. 'Ben. I am so glad that you were able to come. What do you think of our little shop? Quite a place, is it not so? he asked proudly.

'It's most impressive.'

Leibig introduced the man coming out of the lift behind him. 'This is Mr Clifford Ford, my financial director. He's a damned Scot,' he added fondly. That was the first time, Ben thought, that Georgy had ever sounded quite like an Englishman.

Ben shook hands. In the habit of tall, shy, bookish men Ford was rather stooped, and his kindly eyes peered out of his craggy features from beneath bushy rust-coloured eyebrows. Craggy, not lined; and his handshake was firm and warm. Ben summed him up: Ford was not much over forty, perhaps forty-three. What made him seem so old? This place? His hand was large and knobbly, and now as he stared back into Ben's eyes his touch became awkwardly light, as though he feared to intrude.

'Pleased to meet you,' Ben said firmly.

Georgy folded the letter with a shrug. 'I shall consider this matter, Ford, and give you my decision in due course.'

'I'll be needing your decision this week, though, Mr Leibig,' Clifford Ford said. His voice had a gentle Scots lilt, Ben noticed.

'Yes, yes . . .' Georgy looked around him like a man who wants to roll up his sleeves and get down to some proper work. Did he avoid decisions that needed to be taken?

'Look at those cheeses, Ben! From all over the world.'

'A wonderful selection.' But still no one was buying them.

'Perhaps I'll see you later.' Ford bowed to Ben and left.

Georgy walked slowly between the wooden counters. He came to the point. 'Ben – Vanity tells me that you have experience in the retail trade.'

'Yes, a general stores. I worked for Blumenthall's.'

'I do not know that I have heard of them.'

'I was *de facto* manager of their East End branch.' He did not say that it was the only branch, or that he had been fourteen years old.

'You must have been quite young?'

'I learned quickly. I doubled the turnover,' said Ben.

'Doubled! Doubled, you say.'

'More than doubled. The firm was expanding into wholesaling and' – Ben waved his hand knowledgeably – 'various allied activities.'

Georgy stopped and called for a cloth. He wiped busily some finger-marks on the glass top of a display counter. He turned.

'Then you will be familiar with stock control, inventories, cash flow?'

'And impulse buying and the techniques of salesmanship,' Ben said.

Georgy paused in the quiet area at the top of the steps by the door, surveying his domain. He touched the curved wooden banister with gentle caresses of his hand. 'My father set up a grocer's shop here in 1881. Open-fronted, one boy, deliveries by wheelbarrow. He was most determined, most successful. By the turn of the century, Leibig's Emporium had grown to what you see today.'

And no more, Ben thought.

'It's most impressive,' he repeated patiently.

'Tell me what you think,' Georgy said suddenly. 'There must be an improvement, however small, that you can suggest.'

Here was his opportunity. 'Georgy, one point does occur to me. Of course it's very minor really . . .' Ben led Georgy outside, pushed past Hawk, and waved his crutches at the row of faded canopies in the sunlight. They gave a bad impression even before a customer entered the shop.

'You are quite right!' said Georgy, staring upward, his face going redder than ever. 'They will be replaced. Coming in day after day,' he excused himself, 'one does not notice such a gradual decay.'

'Quite so.'

Hawk stepped in front of them, saluted, opened the door and they went back inside. 'I cannot offer you very much money,' Georgy said.

'I understand.'

'You would have to start at the bottom, or nearly so, initially. But of course, if you become . . .' He made a vague gesture with his hand and smiled.

Ben nodded.

'I know the way the wind blows.' Georgy looked down. 'Vanity is a very determined girl. She knows exactly what she wants.'

Ben said: 'Doesn't everybody?'

Georgy looked at his highly polished toecaps.

'I always wanted to be a carpenter,' he said. 'Working with wood gives me immense pleasure.'

He shrugged.

'Ben, I know you. I know what you are.'

Ben, his hand casually in his pocket, clenched his fist. No sign showed in his face. He did not take his eyes off Georgy's profile. Georgy did not look at him.

'Ben, you know what you want – like Vane. Born knowing, like her – or perhaps you have learned to know. You are a man who makes his own fate. You do not know where you have come from, but you know where you want to go and you are determined to get there. It chills my blood!' Georgy was not such a fool; he was cunning, and wise, and clever. Ben said nothing. Georgy said bitterly: 'Success isn't enough for you, is it. You've always wanted more.' He shook his head, then threw out his arm. All this. Then shrugged again. 'You have never been a prisoner, Ben. Even in the Workhouse, you were not a prisoner there.'

Ben stared at him.

'I am,' Georgy said simply. 'I know it. I know everything. I have been a prisoner all my life. Everything was plotted and planned for me long ago, and I have always done my duty, and I always will. I am all I will ever be and I know it. I will never escape. Do you deserve to marry my daughter?'

2

Nigel pulled the Vauxhall tourer in to the side of West Ferry-Road and stopped the engine. A circle of kids formed, admiring the glossy paintwork and the chromium-plated spokes on the wheels. Vic would have tossed a penny to the biggest and told him to keep the others in order, keep their hands off it, but Nigel didn't see why he should. If anyone mucked about they'd be sorry, that was all. 'Stand back,' he shouted, 'get out of my way.'

The newsagent's and the tobacconist's had been amalgamated into one single, larger shop since the war. He went in and bought his newspaper and a tin of fifty Woodbines – everyone had chain-smoked in the trenches and he'd never been able to kick the habit. When he came out, counting his change, the doorway was blocked.

Who's been a naughty boy, then, Nigel?

Nigel's heart leapt into his mouth.

'Christ,' he cried, 'Raymond Trott! The moment that he had feared for all these sleepless nights had finally come. He licked his lips for something to say. 'How are you, Ray?'

Raymond Trott smiled. He was just as handsome – and just as pretty. Nigel hated him. With that blond-coloured hair, arched eyebrows and a thin film-star moustache – wasn't he lovely. Wouldn't the girls just love him! Tanned facial skin, and lovely white hands with gold rings on his fingers, a slim body, and a small round bottom: Ray walked out. Types trying it on like this would have got beaten up on the street ten years ago, Nigel knew, but the films had changed all that. He followed quietly, and Ray turned lightly on one foot on the pavement.

'How am I, Nigel?' asked Ray theatrically, then nodded: 'All the better for seeing you, old son.'

'I thought you must be back.' Nigel tried to keep his tone calm, conversational. *Maybe I can get away with it. Maybe he didn't see as much as I thought. Maybe he's forgotten.* He stretched his lips into a friendly grin.

'I was in the desert,' Raymond said, 'Lawrence of Arabia, you know, all that?' He had a way of talking in questions that hinted at vast ranges of experience, of conquest. 'I ended the war in Jerusalem.'

Nigel tried to get away. 'Well, very nice to meet you, Ray, but—'

Ray said: 'How's your elbow?'

'Fine,' croaked Nigel.

'Quite the little local hero, I hear.'

Nigel confessed: 'You know what people are like—'

'Don't I just?' Raymond smiled. 'Give us a cigarette, Nige. I'm out.'

Raymond plucked the tin from Nigel's fingers. 'This'll do.' The whole tin! Ray tossed up the tin and caught it, then gave a broad, knowing smile full of white teeth. 'Bye-bye now, Nige. Look after yourself.' He winked and turned away.

That was all.

For now.

Nigel stood trembling. Creep, pervert, common little thief! He didn't dare say a word aloud. *Blackmailer.* He didn't even dare think about that. He bought another tin of cigarettes and lit up to calm his nerves. After all, what had happened? Nothing. No, and nothing would. Raymond didn't have the guts to tell anyone, filthy little scavenger. Everything was all right. He walked back to his car.

One of the kids was peering at his warped reflection in the paint on the Vauxhall, totally absorbed. Nigel gave the little brute a whack round the head with the rolled-up newspaper, then stared at the torn page. His mouth fell open. A genuine smile began to spread across his face.

'Oi, mister,' the boy said, rubbing his head, 'wotcher do that for? I wasn't doing nothing.'

Nigel flicked the lad a sixpence. Quickly, he started the motor and climbed in. He drove round the corner into Havannah Street. Climbing down, he slipped the newspaper into his pocket and pushed through the open door into Esther's house. It seemed dark after the sunny street.

'Mum? You in?'

He heard Ria's voice from upstairs and ran up.

Ria was in her front bedroom. She was sitting on the end of the unmade single bed and he realized that she'd only just got up. The window was closed and the room was suffocatingly airless. Her hair looked dull and hung down unwashed, that lovely golden glow only showing near the roots. She wore a pink flannel nightgown and a torn black shawl draped over her shoulders. Holding an unlit cigarette in her mouth, she was watching Will play with a wooden model of a motor-car by the cold fireplace. Nigel was disgusted. Mum always put flowers in the fireplaces in the summer, but Ria hadn't bothered even to rake out the grate from the last time she'd burned a fire, months ago probably. It was full of stale ashes.

'What, Nigel,' Ria said dully. She wasn't saucy now, she hardly looked at him.

Nigel smirked. He demanded: 'Where's Vic?'

'How should I know? Why do you want him?'

'I have my reasons,' said Nigel victoriously.

Will raced his motor-car to and fro across the tiles, spreading ash everywhere. 'Will, pet, don't do that,' sighed Ria. She looked at the end of her tether, defenceless.

Nigel said viciously: 'You always were a tramp, you know that? All those dresses, and paint on your face, and showing off those pretty legs of yours to all sorts of men. Proud of yourself now, are you? You look like the slut you are!'

For a moment her eyes flashed. Then she looked frightened. 'Come, Will, come to Mummy.'

Nigel drew himself up. '*Remember*,' he said. Ria clasped Will.

Nigel slammed the door and clattered back downstairs. Esther was just coming in, her arms laden with shopping, her cheeks flushed. She'd obviously stopped off at the pub on the way back.

Nigel said: 'Seen Vic, Mum?'

'He's at the pub,' she said, dropping the stuff on the kitchen table. 'Love, I am glad to see you, I'm awfully worried about Ria. She hasn't been out of the house for weeks. It's as if something went out of her when she left the stage. I'm ever so worried.'

'Ria's old enough and ugly enough to look after herself,' Nigel said.

'You don't understand women,' Esther said sadly. 'I know she pretends to be rough sometimes, but she's a soft and delicate creature inside herself, Nigel. Can't you understand? She'd never do anyone harm. You ought to tell Vic that.'

'There speaks a true mother. You won't admit that your little daughter could do wrong,' said Nigel over his shoulder from the doorway. Ria deserved everything she got. She'd dragged them all down. His own sister had been an unmarried mother by the time she was sixteen – God knows how many men she had slept with since. He'd heard all about actresses and what they did as soon as they got out of the stage door, so she probably had too. No doubt about it. It showed. And he was supposed to feel sympathy for her. Nigel gave a bitter laugh. 'Go and look at her, mother, see her for what she is!'

'But Vic says it's all for the best,' Esther called after him, but he was already gone.

But she was worried about Ria. She looked up at the ceiling towards Ria's bedroom. It was as if the life had gone out of her. Vic spoke good sense, she had no future on the stage, best to get her feet squarely on the ground and get her to take up her responsibilities, but men didn't understand how brutal they could be to women. Still, she consoled herself, that was life.

'Poor Ria,' she said. She'd make her a nice cup of tea, she decided.

Vic was in the bar of the Tooke Arms sitting on a bar stool with his feet on the brass rail. Vic spent a lot of time here. It was a convenient safe place and friends were always popping in, and there was a back room if he wanted to take them in there for a very private word.

'Hallo Nige,' yawned Vic. 'Half of mild?'

'Whisky,' Nigel said.

'Celebrating?'

Nigel showed him the paper. He waited in suspense while Vic read with agonizing slowness.

'Announcements, is that it?'

Nigel pointed. 'There. Engagements. London–Leibig.'

Vic read it out, haltingly, word by word. 'The engagement is announced between Ben London and Vanity Clarissa, only daughter of Mr G.R. Leibig of Primrose House, N.W., and the late Mrs C. Leibig. The marriage will take place at St James's Church at 2.30 p.m. on 20th September.' His face flushed and he flung the paper down. 'Bloody hell!'

'I thought you'd be interested,' Nigel said ingratiatingly.

'Have you told Ria this?'

Nigel shook his head. Had he done right?

Vic's lips parted in a wide smile. 'Lovely. How lovely. Good old Nigel. I love weddings, don't you? Yes. Oh yes. And so does Ria.'

3

Ben's heart thrilled when he saw her: she looked so perfect, so untouchable – a fairy-tale in her white silk wedding dress, Welsh lace, organdie bows, her eyes romantic shadows behind clouds of white veil, carrying a posy of white orchids, with two cherubic page-boys tending her flowing train as she entered the church.

But first, Vane had made them wait.

She did not get to the church on time.

She was very late.

'She's not coming,' said Frank Laidlaw nervously. They sat in the front pew. Frank kept bouncing up and looking back down the aisle at the empty, sunlit doorway. He was in a worse state than Ben.

'Of course she'll come,' Ben said calmly. He still walked with a stick and he sat with it against his knees, waiting. He loved her; she loved him. He needed her utterly. But first and foremost, Vane was always Vane. Of course she was late. He had known that she would be: she did not like to be taken for granted.

'I still don't know just how you managed to catch such a beautiful girl,' Frank said enviously. When Ben crashed, Frank Laidlaw lost his nerve, and now he worked as a clerk in his father's City firm. 'There must have been frightful competition. How on earth did a chap like you' – *without a father, without a mother* – 'manage it?'

Ben ignored the envy. He thought about Vane. Why did a girl marry?

'She trusts me. All her life, she's been afraid. She's never had anyone. Now she has someone.'

'How can you be so certain? You make her sound very innocent,' Frank said, glancing at his watch. 'She seems to me like a girl who's well able to look after herself.' It was often a mystery to him why people married the people they did. Ben could have had any woman he wanted.

'I can make her happy,' Ben said.

Frank bounced up. 'I'll have another look outside, see if she . . .'

But it was a girl's prerogative on this day of all days to be late, and Ben knew that Vane would make the most of it. She wouldn't arrive yet. The opportunity to keep fifty people waiting, including the vicar who was a Reverend Doctor, and Mr Barlowe, who was one of the finest organists in the country, was the sort of situation Vane dreamed of, he knew. She was the centre of attention, and she wasn't even there. Everyone would worry about her. Was she all right? Poor Vane! The low background mumble of relatives who had not seen one another for years, exchanging news, gradually died away to an expectant hush. Ben could not help grinning. Vane was going to make an Entrance.

The minutes ticked by. Frank kept reappearing between the pillars shaking his head, his grey topper tucked clumsily under his arm, wiping his face on his handkerchief. No sign of Vane. Ben looked behind and smiled encouragingly at Colleen O'Keeffe, one of the few people on his side of the church, an imposing figure dressed in emerald green. She threw him a determinedly cheerful smile back. She hated Vane; hated Ben marrying her, because she loved him.

Colleen's opinion meant much to Ben, but he knew that she was wrong about Vane. Sitting behind his great dark desk in Leibig's Orders Department he had rationalized their hatred as an instinctive woman-to-woman clash, no reason for it. She had never been prepared to like Vane, even when she had only heard of her as the interesting girl he described meeting that first time at the Lyons Corner House. *Forget her. You're in love with a dream.* Nevertheless, when he went to Bunhill Row to collect his Mantegna, he took the opportunity to bring Vane to meet Colleen personally.

They had loathed one another immediately: he had seen it in their eyes.

The two women had sat down opposite one another in Colleen's tiny flat, Colleen determined to try to like Vane for Ben's sake. Vane had been grotesquely patronizing: 'What a sweet little room you have, of its type. You must be so clever not to keep knocking things over.' Colleen had been bluntly rude, calling Vane a trophy-hunting strumpet. Vane turned to Ben, who was struggling not to laugh, wailing. To break the circle he got up and unwrapped the enigmatic Mantegna painting from its brown paper. Before he said anything, Colleen read his face.

'It is beautiful,' she agreed.

'It's so awfully dirty,' Vane sniffed. 'It doesn't even look real.'

Colleen's eyes gleamed with shame. 'Ben let Sir Ozwald cheat him out of an inheritance of thousands to get this picture!'

Vane had looked startled. 'Why on earth would you do something so stupid, Ben?'

Ben said: 'In memory of a friend.'

'Some friend,' said Vane, in a voice as enigmatic as the painting. 'Was he the same one you shot down?'

Ben closed his eyes. Inside his head, quite clearly, he heard Alan Stark's trembling, hate-filled voice: *'That's Ben London – the chap who shot down his best friend.'*

His terrible secret, the emptiness inside him, that dark guilt that lay with him during the nights when he could not sleep.

The two women, mistaking his guilt for love, both looked at Ben, and for a moment he brought them closer together. Colleen said in a low voice: 'Ben cares only about emotion, mavourneen. He knows no more than what he feels. You see, Vane, he truly doesn't care about money – yours or anybody else's.'

'Of course not,' Vane said. She clasped her hands, staring at Ben with loving eyes. She wanted to hug herself against him. She liked it that Ben had shot down his best friend – the sheer ruthlessness of it made him terribly attractive to her. *Those were the fingers that had pulled the triggers* . . . when they touched her, she would melt. They would make her more than herself.

But Colleen was asking, in a voice with a slight tremble to it: 'Ben, how is that dear dog Sam?'

And Vane interrupted furiously: 'That dear dog, as you put it, does nothing but lie in front of the boiler all day, and he has infested absolutely the whole scullery with fleas.'

'Sam didn't have fleas when I looked after him, mavourneen!' Colleen shot back.

Ben laughed. He gave up. The two women were oil and water, that was all.

Afterwards, down in the street, Vane had leaned on Ben's arm, wanting his sympathy. 'Oh my poor, poor darling, what a frightful woman. However did you stand her for all those years? Unforgivable,' she shuddered.

'Colleen speaks her mind.'

'That's what I meant, unforgivable,' Vane said. She turned up her face. 'I love you, darling.' She allowed him to kiss her lightly, then pulled her head away. She had noticed a wonderful pair of shoes in a shop window: she simply had to buy them . . .

'The car's arrived! Here she comes!' hissed Frank.

Vane made her Entrance. Ben's heart beat faster. His hand clenched the top of his stick as he turned on stiff legs.

Vane, her doll's figure in the flowing white silk chastely enhanced by white embroidered satin at the curves of hip and bust, walked slowly up the aisle, her white-gloved fingers resting lightly on Georgy's arm. His face was beetroot-red with pride. Marcelline Stoughton was the matron of honour, her young daughter being held rather awkwardly by her pig-faced, over-weight husband Henry in the congregation. One of the cherubic page-boys almost dropped his side of her train, and Vane turned and sulked at him – Ben could tell by the set of her shoulders. Then when she came up beside him, she lifted her veil and looked startled to see Ben smiling at her.

Her mouth changed. She reflected his smile radiantly. She looked so beautiful that he wanted to pick her up and hug her there and then. Her confidence grew: her eyes glowed. Her cheeks became flushed with joy. He took her hand in his, meshing his fingers through hers, in the way lovers do, comforting her. The church slipped away. She saw only him.

Ben glanced at the vicar.

Vane nodded, and the ceremony began. She did not take her beautiful brown eyes away from Ben during the hymn. He was her world. Georgy, even Marcelline, everything, was gone. Her heart trembled, her body melted with the romance and the meaning of it all, and she gave herself.

When he said *I do,* she knew that her brown eyes burned with the romantic fire that she felt inside her. She had him.

When she said *I will,* she gazed softly into his opaque blue eyes, meaning every word not just with her mouth but with her eyes and her heart, and every atom of her body.

When Ben put the ring on her finger, she gasped. They were joined. She swayed, as though she would swoon.

From far away, she heard the voice of the man of God intone: 'I pronounce you husband and wife.'

Vane was in heaven. Everything that she had dreamed of had come true. When the choir sang, it was with the voice of angels. She had entered the church, alone, leaning on the

491

arm of an old man; now she would leave it with a young man who needed her, who could not walk without her, who was nothing without her, who was hers forever. She gazed at Ben adoringly.

The organist played Widor's *Toccata*.

Ben turned.

He thought: *How happy Edith Rumney would have been if only she could have been here now.*

Vane made a show of helping him down the aisle, as though he was more of a cripple than he was. It was embarrassing because it was unnecessary, but she was obviously determined.

They paused outside the door for the photographer. The guests lined up below to throw rice and confetti.

'Careful, dear, mind the steps,' Vane said solicitously, holding Ben's wrist in one hand, his elbow in her other hand. He suppressed his irritation, thinking: *After all, it is her day.* He let her have her way. 'Careful!' Vane said, 'not too fast—'

He stopped.

They were only half-way down the steps. The crowd of faces looked up at them expectantly.

'What is it, Ben?' asked Vane. She tugged gently at his elbow. 'Is it your legs? Are you tired?' She looked up earnestly. 'Are you in pain?' Then she saw his face.

He had gone white.

Ben felt the blood draining out of his face. His lips and fingers felt stiff and icy cold. One face stood out from all the others down there in the crowd, as though a beacon was shining from within her features. He could not take his eyes off her. Everything about her had changed; and nothing. She looked fifteen years older and fifty years wiser and more defeated, as though the life within her only flickered where it had once blazed. She was shabbily dressed and she looked exhausted. Then she looked up at him, and he saw those strange, haunting opal eyes that he remembered so well, though he had forgotten so much, light up with life, a momentary flash, burning for him with hurt, and loss, and love.

Ria Price stepped forward. She towed a little boy of about five after her. He had plump red cheeks, neatly combed hair, and he was better dressed than she was. He looked around him questioningly with his thumb in his mouth.

Ria stood at the foot of the steps, staring up with one hand cocked on her hip, her other hand holding the boy.

'Ria!' said Ben.

'Didn't expect to see you here, mate,' Ria said.

Vane looked down her nose at Ria, then turned to her husband. 'Ben, who is this awful woman? Ben!'

'Oh my God, Ria,' Ben said, 'what are you doing here? Why have you come back now? Why now?'

Vane dug into his elbow with her nails. *Who is she!*

Ben licked his lips. *Someone I loved, who betrayed me long ago.* He shook his head. He answered truthfully: 'Someone I once knew, a long time ago.'

'This here's Will,' Ria said. 'You might say that you know him pretty well, though you've never met him.'

Father and son looked at one another curiously.

Ben felt his heart would burst.

He said: 'Why, Ria?'

Ria shook her head sadly. She stepped back a pace, then two, pulling Will after her. Ben had never seen such unhappiness. He felt it too, and tried to reach out. Grief ruled her face with terrible lines.

She backed away. 'I'm sorry,' she called. 'I didn't know. I wouldn't have come.'

'Ria!' he cried. A murmur ran through the guests. Ben hobbled down the steps, Vane dragging after him, trying to pull him back. Then there were people all around them, a jostling crowd, laughing and throwing confetti.

Ben pushed through them.

'Ria!' he shouted.

He stood on the pavement. Someone cheered. A flash-bulb popped.

Ria was crossing the road. Two men waited for her, conservatively dressed in black, by a white Vauxhall tourer. One of the men was tall and thin, very pale, with jagged brown eyes and his left arm hidden in the front of his jacket.

Nigel Price.

The other was stocky and very muscular, with oiled black hair and a wide red smile. Sitting on the running board, he held out his arms to the little boy, who tugged free of his mother, ran obediently over, and settled on his knee. Vic grinned with his smooth brown eyes, his mouth slightly open.

Remember me.

Ria climbed up into the back of the tourer and sat without looking at Ben. Then her face broke up and her mouth opened and she began to weep. Below, Vic dandled their little boy on his knee, smiling and clicking his tongue and making cooing noises as if to a baby. Ria held her wrists over her eyes. She dug her fingers into her hair. She wept her heart out at what he had made her do.

Vic got in beside her and threw his arm comfortingly around Ria's shoulders. He put his face close to hers. 'Darling,' he murmured, 'darling.'

Nigel swung the little boy up into the front seat and started the engine. Ben hobbled forward. Vic stared at him. He waited until Ben was close. Then he grinned and clicked his fingers at Nigel.

'Drive,' he sneered.

The Vauxhall pulled away.

Remember me.

'Ria!' Ben screamed.

'Ben!' Vane said. 'Ben?'

Chapter Eighteen

1

Ben and Vane sat together in the back of the Rolls-Royce going to the railway station. For some reason the grey velvet curtains had been romantically drawn. White orchids decorated the polished walnut woodwork. They sat with their elbows touching, and a gulf between them.

Vane said: 'Who were those awful people? Don't tell me that they could possibly be friends of yours?'

Ben pulled open the curtain on his side. Vane groaned at the flood of light and shaded her eyes.

Ben drew the curtain closed. They sat in the gloom.

He said, 'Vane, she—'

'I don't want to hear about her,' Vane said.

The Great Western Railway did them proud, a large private compartment, roses on the white-clothed table, and champagne. Vane sulked. The whistle blew and the train pulled out immediately. Soon they were passing smoothly between endless half-finished estates of red-roofed mock-Tudor villas . . . Ben realized that the middle classes always lived out of towns, leaving the centres to be prowled by the rich and the poor. 'What are you thinking of?' Vane demanded.

He told her.

'Why aren't you thinking of me?' she said. 'Don't you care about me?'

The train stopped in deep countryside, and the guard saluted. The hotel landau met them at the lonely halt and

495

the driver cracked his whip along a dusty track winding between the fields. Men in smocks working across the stubble in the rich evening light turned to stare at them. Ben waved. Scarlet poppies grew in sprays, as if in memory of the war.

Vane sat beside him, all in white.

He pointed out the hotel appearing against the blue backdrop of the winding river Thames amongst the willows. Marcelline and Henry Stoughton had honeymooned here and promised them that it was frightfully bucolic. Vane had been impressed. Ben, having met Henry, who had glazed, cunning and far from bucolic eyes, thought he probably meant alcoholic. The floors creaked and the food was French but, said Marcelline with an earthy laugh, looking at Ben, the beds were big.

The floors did creak and the bed was indeed big, in the Queen Anne style, with a view over the river through leaded windows. A heron flapped through the dusk. It was beautiful; like a fading dream as night gathered.

'Will sir and madam be taking supper in their room?'

'Yes,' Ben said.

'No, in the dining room,' Vane instructed. The man bowed and closed the door. Vane brushed past Ben. 'Why is there only one bed?'

Ben stared at her.

'What did you expect?' he said. 'This is our room.'

'This is supposed to be a high-class hotel,' Vane flounced. 'Do they expect you to sleep on the floor?'

'We're married,' Ben laughed. 'We sleep together in the same bed.'

'Certainly not,' Vane said. 'Mama and Papa had separate rooms.'

'That was probably later in life.'

'We can't possibly sleep in the same bed,' Vane said. She was serious, he realized. 'It's indecent.'

'Not between a man and his wife, Vane!'

'I'd never be able to sleep,' she said impetuously. 'Surely we'd keep waking one another up when we turn over. Besides, it's so unhygienic, surely.'

496

She really doesn't know, Ben thought. *She honestly does not know about love. To her it's a romance, not a reality. The middle classes only talk about making good marriages, never the poor marriage bed. Oh, Vane, what have they done to you?*

Seeing the sympathy in his eyes, Vane's lower lip began to tremble. 'Mama is dead,' she whispered. 'Who was left to instruct me in my wifely duties? No one. Except Marcelline. And she only talks about . . . fun!'

He took Vane in his arms and kissed her tenderly. Surely she needed no instructions; only love. She was so beautiful, he reasoned, that she must feel beauty. But he felt her stiffen away from him.

Vane tensed every muscle and closed her eyes, then threw her arms around him. He was huge – yes, she could not touch her fingertips behind his back – and he felt so different from her own soft body that she was terrified. Her delicate skin was rasped by his whiskers – she thought that he was clean-shaven, not hairy like a brute. But then she realized that he was really kissing her very gently, and electric feelings were running inside her body, and she felt something like hunger or thirst, yet different, she didn't know what, a feeling of melting away—

The dinner gong clanged down in the hall, once, twice, three times. Dinner was served in thirty minutes. She pulled back – almost falling, realizing that she had been both arched over backwards and leaning into him with her hips. She really could not meet his eye. She examined her hair in the mirror, embarrassed. Whatever had come over her? They absolutely must prepare to go down for dinner, and she looked a sight.

'I must change into my evening gown,' she said obliquely.

Ben sighed, understanding now. 'I'll meet you downstairs,' he said.

She came down, late, wearing a gown of such a delicate rose pink that it was almost white. Her hair was piled high. She looked so beautiful that every man in the room was aware of her. Yet none of their ladies were jealous: she radiated such an air of precious, doll-like innocence that she made them smile too, remembering.

The candles were lit.

The waiters brought the courses. The silver shone.

Vane made enchanting conversation.

After the meal, the band played. They danced. She was surprised that Ben, despite his stiff legs, danced quite well, and wondered where he could possibly have learned. There was so much about him that she did not know. She sensed that he had so many secrets, and shivered. He said he never lied, and she believed him. But she did not know what questions to ask.

Now the dance floor was empty.

'Let's go up,' Ben said.

'One more dance!'

'It's time we went up to bed, Vane.'

Bed. The menace in that single word. She trembled. Perhaps he would let her help him upstairs – but his legs seemed so much better. He did not need her any more.

He felt her shiver, and put his coat around her shoulders as they went up. He closed the door behind them. She turned by the foot of the bed, looking very cool, keeping him back.

'Who was she?'

That again. He couldn't blame her. But he knew that he would never be able to explain about Ria to her. Yet Vane never let anything go once she had got hold of it.

He took his jacket. She started to unpin her hair, but kept her eyes on him in the mirror.

'As I told you, someone I once knew, long ago.'

'She looked awfully common.'

Ben shrugged at the truth of this. The years had not been kind to Ria. Neither, perhaps, had he. Perhaps he should have gone back, at least once, and seen her. And found out the truth. If there was any.

'Who was the boy?' Vane demanded.

'I don't know.' She nodded, seeming satisfied. Her hair collapsed into gorgeous curls, and he took a pace towards her, wanting to bury his hands in them, to caress her, to make love with her. She said: 'May I turn the light out?'

He understood. Of course she was shy. He looked out of

498

the window as she undressed in the dark. There was no moon. He heard the springs squeak as she got into bed. He unclipped the studs holding on his collar and cuff-links, then put them in his trouser pocket because he could not see the dressing table. This had gone dreadfully wrong; he could not get Ria out of his mind. Truly a gulf separated him from Vane, in every way. He did not know how he could be kind to her. Poor Vane. Yes. He pulled off his shirt and trousers. The floor creaked as he went towards the bed.

He touched her.

Cold, smooth satin.

She was wearing a nightdress. With its cold surface between them he could feel everything that he had won slipping away from him. 'Darling,' he whispered, 'let's be happy.'

She didn't answer. Her body was a slab.

'Vane,' he told her patiently, 'unless we're happy, nothing means anything. Money. Health. Family. Nothing. Without happiness.'

He felt her turn her head away from him. He touched her chin with his fingertip.

'You don't understand,' Vane's voice came. 'You do not understand the different sorts of love a woman feels.'

Of course he understood. Wasn't he a human being?

'You're just a man,' she said, turning her chin away.

How could he persuade her otherwise – except by loving her?

He kissed her and caressed her, lips, cheeks, the lobes of her ears, the point of her chin, the tip of her nose, then his hands stroked her arms, between her fingers, down the curve of her throat. He touched the neckline of her nightdress: a harsh prickle of lace. She stiffened, perfectly rigid. He stopped at once. He went back to her throat. She did not respond. Her breath hissed under his lips. They could go on like this all night, he realized, transforming his loving caresses into refinements of cruelty. He broke the image. He opened her nightdress. He touched her. He entered her gently, and gave himself.

No response.

He waited.

Her voice came coldly out of the dark: 'Is there anything else you haven't told me?'

He did not sleep.

Later, as dawn broke, he heard her weeping at last.

He touched her shoulder and turned her over. In the grey light he saw that her tears had made ugly deltas of red powder across her cheeks: she must have been wearing rouge to heighten her beauty even further.

'Now I'm married,' Vane wept, 'just like all my friends.'

2

Every day, Ben arrived to start work long before dawn. Already his energy was legendary. *What drives him?* people wondered.

Like an iceberg, seven-eighths of Leibig's Emporium, that dark façade stretching almost to the corner of Old Bond Street and Piccadilly, was hidden from view.

A customer could shop for a lifetime on the three crowded sales floors of Leibig's Emporium – and some did – and never realize that extending far above them, and deep below them, were other levels swarming with life.

Ben loved it.

What drives him? they wondered. *Does he have to prove himself to his new wife? Does he work so hard to make her happy?*

They watched him go down.

Or is it simply that he loves Leibig's Emporium – all of it? All of us?

The sub-basement of Leibig's Emporium was deeper than Roman London. Neolithic spearheads and the bronze ornaments worn by womenfolk had been prised from the clay beneath the flagstones where the messenger-boys now scampered, and a small statue of a Roman goddess had been found, Ben knew, somewhere behind the walls of what was now a warren of damp, whitewashed brick.

He knew that people whispered about him behind his back. He knew that he was bound to attract attention. That was power. He had none; but they did not know that. True, he loved the Emporium, loved the people here, sensed that they could work together to make so much more of it all. But Georgy kept him at a distance: they did not work as closely as Ben made it appear.

Neither did he work to prove himself to Vane, because the more he loved her, the more she hated him. The more he gave her happiness, the unhappier she became.

Now he strode along passageways past subterranean store rooms stacked high with peeling cardboard boxes and mildewed packing crates, years old, their contents forgotten though doubtless still recorded on the endless stock-lists patiently audited by the clerks, who worked standing up at leather-bound ledgers mounted on tall wooden lecterns.

Surely that was not efficient?

'Good morning, Mr London.'

'Good morning, Mr Harrison.' P. Harrison, who wore pince-nez spectacles and affected mutton-chop whiskers like a Dickensian gentleman, was the Orders supervisor and Ben had worked under him for several months before his marriage. As always, Ben wondered what his initial *P* stood for. Peter? Patrick? To ask, he knew, would be considered an offensive familiarity. But perhaps it could be done.

Harrison looked shocked. 'Peter, sir.'

'You didn't mind my asking? I had to know.'

'Not at all, sir. But I beg of you sir, not in front of—'

A clerk came up with an order to be countersigned. Not in front of the working classes.

'I understand, Mr Harrison,' Ben smiled.

'Good morning, Mr London,' the clerk with the signed order sheets said, then coughed.

'How are you, Michael?' The air was so damp down here that everyone was prone to coughs and colds, and probably rheumatism too. Apart from it being unpleasant, it surely could not be efficient for the staff to work in such conditions?

However, it was company policy that if conditions were eased, discipline would suffer.

'Fine, thank you, sir.'

Ben noted Mike's pleasure at being noticed, and wondered, as he walked to the post room, whether the company policy was wrong.

'Good morning, Mr London, sir!'

'You're looking very cheerful today, Harriet.'

Another girl giggled. It was very dark in the post room. These girls lived in their own world, but they hated to be ignored. They needed to believe that they were not unimportant. Ben studied Harriet's thin, cheerful face.

'Are you walking out with a new boy, Harriet?'

Annie, the one with the giggle, squeezed her fingers over her nose to keep herself quiet, and Harriet blushed. She was indeed, Ben realized, then realized that he had also added to his reputation for seeing into people, though really it was not so clever – anyone could have seen that Harriet was full of life today and drawn the obvious conclusion.

Ben asked: 'Who—' Suddenly he guessed that it was David, the lad in the gentleman's department upstairs who had been off his work lately. Ben lost his smile. He would have to keep this secret. The staff were strictly segregated, and Harriet would be dismissed if she was found out. Annie was a silly girl to have given the game away.

'I'll take the post up now,' he said. They handed him the directors' letters and he signed for them – everything in Leibig's Emporium had to be signed for. There was no service lift from this level so he took the stairs to the upper basement. The morning deliveries were being assembled and sent out – trolleys of crates and parcels, milk churns, wine cases, everything imaginable from cheeses to coffins. Sweating men in leather aprons pushed them up the echoing ramp to be loaded into Leibig's purple drays across the courtyard above, with exits into both Piccadilly and Bond Street.

'Wotcher, Alf.'

'I got an order here for one pound of cheddar for South Kensington, Mr London.'

'So what?'

'Well, one bleeding pound, it's stupid, driver going all that way.'

That was the trouble with free delivery. 'What do you expect me to do about it?'

Alf looked at him. Of course; he had married the great man's daughter, so he must have the great man's ear. If only they knew. 'Just get on with it,' Ben said irritably. The lift doors squealed open and he flicked through the sheaf of envelopes going up. All the normal stuff.

'Wines, guns, sports clothing, uniforms, funeral department . . .' intoned the liftboy dutifully.

The last envelope was vellum, the address handwritten, but on the wax seal he made out the stamp of the London & South-Western Bank. Mr Phrane, the manager, was an old friend of Georgy's and indeed of Grandpapa Leibig and the Emporium since the early days. He was a stooped, almost bald man with dry, lined skin and white sideburns that curled backwards under his ears.

'Main floor,' said the liftboy, 'Cheeses, fruits, meats—'

'All right, Jimmy,' Ben said, 'let me out on the upper sales floor, would you.'

He walked out amongst the counters tapping the vellum envelope on his fingernail.

'Should we leave the umbrellas on the shelf, Mr London?'

'No,' Ben said, turning. 'Look over there, you're trying to sell an empty umbrella stand there, Harry, so why not put the umbrellas on that? It'll look more natural and people will be attracted to it.'

'Yes, sir.'

'There's nothing about an umbrella lying on a shelf that makes people want to buy it, is there?'

'No, sir!'

Ben found the person he was looking for and watched him lose a sale.

'David, try and look interested when you're selling something to a customer, even if it is only a tie. A salesman who is interested makes the tie interesting.'

'That old duffer's always coming in,' David yawned. 'He never buys anything.'

'Are you tired?'

'Sorry, sir.' David straightened. But Ben looked at him: willowy and with a naturally pasty complexion, the boy did look tired. 'How long have you been on duty?' Ben asked quietly.

'Since the bell at seven this morning, sir.' The junior staff lived-in above the administrative section on the next floor in the strictly separate attic dormitories. David would work from seven in the morning until seven at night. No wonder he was tired, especially if he was excited by dreams of the inaccessible Harriet. 'Take a breather of fresh air in the back courtyard for five minutes,' Ben said. 'I'll square it with Mr Courtenay the floor-walker.'

'Thank you, sir!' He scampered off. Mr Courtenay strode over, very tall, his head thrown back, his nostrils flared, the carnation that displayed his exalted rank shining in his buttonhole.

'Has the boy taken ill, Mr London?'

'I sent him out for five minutes to get some fresh air. He's dead on his feet, Mr Courtenay.'

Courtenay pursed his lips into a tight little grin. 'Really, sir, these boys will invent anything, won't they? You'll find it's best, sir, not to interfere with our arrangements. Another boy will have to take his place!' He clicked his fingers imperiously at the lad behind another counter.

'I'll look after David's station until he gets back,' Ben said.

'If you so wish, Mr London,' the floor-walker insisted, determined to have the last word.

'Yes, I do wish, Courtenay.'

Neither man would back down. 'You don't quite know our ways here in Leibig's Emporium,' Courtenay threatened.

'I don't like your ways.'

'I know who your father-in-law is, sir. But you'll learn that Mr Leibig won't help you. The Emporium is an institution greater than any of us. Leibig's Emporium comes first, last, and always.'

Ben said: 'Courtenay, what is your job, exactly?'

Courtenay didn't answer. He turned on his heel and

strode haughtily away, but then twice Ben caught him looking back over his shoulder with a new, uncertain expression flickering on his face. Uncertainty was something, Ben guessed, that had never entered the Emporium before. He smiled. Courtenay seemed to find even his smile threatening.

Ben sold a tie to a young man almost immediately, then his eye fell on a handkerchief of a similar shade of green. 'Oh, and we have handkerchiefs to match, sir.'

'Matching colours? Is that the done thing?' asked the young man nervously.

'Very much the coming fashion this season, sir,' Ben said confidentially, 'amongst people in the know.'

'Yes, of course,' said the young man eagerly. 'I'll take one. I say, you haven't got anything to go with this blue I'm wearing now, have you?'

'The very thing, sir!' Ben smiled.

When he took the vellum envelope up to Georgy's office, it crossed his mind that Mr Phrane must be close to retirement age.

3

Vic was bored to death. Life was too easy. Success in the things in life that didn't matter had come too easily to satisfy him. He hadn't even worked for success, the war had accomplished it for him. And one little murder. It had all been too easy, too nice. Money – just ask Nigel, there it was, neatly totalled, gross total, nett total, Nigel knew it all. Respect – easy, from people who didn't matter. Vic was respected all right, he'd killed Blumenthall, hadn't he?

People looked up to him.

Vic Price was a real man.

It was a lie.

Vic was crying out inside. The only things he really wanted, he didn't have.

Yet.

Remember me.

How could he forget him?

The hatred woke up with Vic in the morning and went to bed with him at night and slept with him. He could never forget him. Him. The one who showed Vic up. The one who did what Vic did, but better every time: if Vic had stolen one orange, he stole two. If Vic had stolen a pair of shoes, he stole a better pair. When Vic gave Ria a beautiful bracelet she wouldn't even wear, *he* gave Ria a cheap bought dress she wore with joy.

Leaning over the desk, Nigel was murmuring with the accountant.

'Shut up!' Vic shouted. They stared at him dumbly.

A picture of them together on the steps by the river never left him, day or night.

She had shouted *No!* – hadn't she?

Vic went to the place often, sometimes waiting for hours for the tide to fall, for the weedy platform slowly to reveal itself. He would crouch on it, on the weed, thinking, imagining. She *had* shouted *No!* – hadn't she?

Not . . . something else?

Not . . . *Yes, yes, yes!*

Forget him? Never. Never out of his mind. Sometimes Vic went up to Ria's room, just stood there watching her while she said *Get out*, waiting.

'You do hate him, don't you, Ria?'

'Who?' Ria would say dully, finally.

'The Workhouse Bastard!' shouted Vic.

'Get out!'

'He raped you – didn't he?'

'Vic, go away,' wept Ria.

The debate went on endlessly in him, tipping one way, then the other.

She had said no, he decided. It must be so. Ria was true. Yes, she had said no. And the expression of loss on Ben London's face outside the church when he saw Ria, that was true. And Vic had wrapped his arms around his sister, protecting her, saving her. And won. He had his sister. The Workhouse Bastard had lost. Lost.

And I killed a man, Vic thought proudly.

The Workhouse Bastard had killed his best friend.

Always, always, always better.

Married a rich bitch. Going up in the world.

Someone had to stop him. Someone had to show the truth. Sub-total, gross total, nett total. Buy Consols. 'Shut up!' Vic shouted again.

'Sorry, Vic,' Nigel said.

'Get him out of here,' said Vic, pointing at the pen-pusher. He said furiously: 'You asked for it, Nigel. I'm going to show you what real money looks like.'

Nigel ushered the adviser out and came back.

'We're going to France,' Vic said, putting his arm around Nigel's shoulders, breathing into his face. 'Real money. Gold. I'll show you! We'll bring it back under Ria's dress. That's a suitable place. Customs. Go and tell her.'

Nigel didn't dare refuse. But when he came back, he had to tell Vic: 'I'm sorry, Vic, she won't come. She just won't leave her room.'

'Leave her,' Vic said. There was something about Ria, he decided, that he still didn't quite trust.

Yet.

Warm rain fell in France. Nigel hated it. It seemed so unnatural; back home, winter was coming. Holding the wheel between his knees, he wriggled out of his overcoat as he drove. It was so warm that the windscreen had misted up, and condensation dripped from the canvas roof. He was tired out of his mind, but Vic wouldn't stop.

Vic sat huddled in an overcoat, his hat pulled low over his forehead, thick leather gloves on his hands.

'I'm sorry Ria wouldn't come,' Nigel apologized. He always felt guilty. The cemeteries seemed endless, not smooth and green but like huge building sites of red, raw earth where workmen dug amongst the fields of white crosses. The ochre puddles reminded him of Croix Barbée and the dreadful secret he dared not reveal to Vic. He had paid fifty pounds to Raymond Trott to keep quiet. Trott had not even needed to ask, the look in his eyes had been enough, the knowing smirk on his face . . .

507

'She'll come round,' Vic said later, waking up as they came to a village.

'You can lead a horse to water,' Nigel joked, trembling, 'but you can't make it drink.'

'You can do anything with a woman,' Vic said. 'That's what they want.'

Nigel had to say: 'Yes.'

'I can,' Vic said. He settled deeper in his seat and tipped his hat down to his eyes. 'Nearly there.' Lights passed them in the rain. Here was Jean-Claude's *estaminet*, and there was the bakery of Monsieur Pierre and Madame Jacqueline with a smart automobile in the yard – and the *pâtisserie* had been much enlarged, and gleamed now with electric light.

'Keep going!' Vic said.

The road turned uphill out of the village and they drove along a boulevard of poplars shedding their leaves in the rain. Vic counted a dozen trees past a water-tower.

'Stop here.'

'Is it here?'

Vic didn't bother to answer. He took the shovel they had bought in Calais off the back seat and handed it wordlessly to Nigel. Pulling on his overcoat, Nigel got out and turned up his collar against the rain.

'Real money,' Vic promised. He stamped his heel into the grass half-way between the milestone and the tree. 'Start digging.'

He got back in the car and closed his eyes.

Nigel dug.

'There's nothing here,' Nigel called.

That was possible. The Germans had swept over this area in 1918. But they hadn't stayed long – not even long enough to blow up the water-tower, obviously. That had been the big worry in Vic's mind – that the water-tower would be gone, because he had forgotten the number on the milestone.

'Keep digging,' he yawned.

He was woken by a cry of disgust. The dark green .303 ammunition box that he remembered was rusted and slimy

508

with red earth now. Nigel, opening the lid, was stepping back with a horrified face.

Vic scrambled out of the car. Had some bastard found his box, emptied it, and replaced it in the earth to torment him?

It was all right. Vic pushed his hands into the mould-filled box and pulled out a variety of coins, one or two Napoleons, dull nuggets of filling, small gold ornaments such as women wear, rings worn thin, their inner surfaces inscribed with some French gibberish . . . real gold.

'What is it, it's horrible,' Nigel shuddered, staring at Vic's hands.

Vic was surprised. 'It's only mould,' he shrugged. 'The tooth fillings probably had bugs on them or something. What do you call them?'

'Bacteria,' Nigel said obediently, then burst out: 'It's revolting!'

Vic dug his hands down, held them up. 'Real money,' he said. 'What did you expect?'

'Thanks, Jimmy.'

Early in winter Ben came out of the lift and knocked on the door to Georgy's office. 'Have you got a moment? There are some points I'd like to cover,' he said politely and inflexibly.

'Come in, please,' Georgy said stiffly. His father-in-law did not like informal visits, Ben knew, but there was never time to arrange formal meetings: there was so much to be done. Besides, if he gave Georgy the slightest chance, he just got fobbed off.

Ben knew how the Emporium worked now.

He wasn't going to be fobbed off again.

Georgy looked at the sheaf of papers Ben carried with disfavour. 'Sit down,' he said wearily. His head thudded. Papers. Ideas. Changes. His son-in-law always wanted to make changes; too many changes. He worked eighteen hour days, yet he never seemed to look tired. Ben's face radiated enthusiasm – high-handed enthusiasm, arrogance, in Georgy's view. Ben's arrogance frightened him. Georgy pressed his fingers to his temples. Only the most rigorous attention to the details of a formula which was known to work – and Papa Leibig had proved that formula – would ensure the success of the Emporium. It was a hard and brutal world, and risks were too dangerous. There was an economic recession. Look at the price of money. Things were bad enough already. Only the meek survived.

At least Ben loved it, the Emporium, however misguided and arrogant his ideas for it were. Vanity hated it. Soon, hopefully, there would be grandchildren . . . Georgy's heart softened. He adored children. The great sadness of his life had been that Clarissa had only been able to have one baby. They had poured all their love into Vanity, but it had not been enough. Or perhaps it had been too much.

Ben cleared his throat.

Georgy jerked himself back to the present.

'Yes, Ben. I have a minute or two. Please sit down.'

'I'd prefer to stand.' Ben liked to walk up and down while he talked.

'If you really must.'

Ben thought that Georgy looked worried and ill. If only he could encourage him to face up to facts and look to the future of a changing world, instead of clinging to the past. Georgy retreated into his shell at the slightest mention of change. They often argued, and Ben had to give way. *Ben, Mr Courtenay tells me that you have had the umbrellas taken off the shelves and put into stands. One cannot have the clients touching the merchandise, Ben. Fingerprints! They have to be wiped off. Have you not considered the extra work?* Yes, but a customer who picked up an umbrella very often bought it. Georgy wouldn't believe it. Papa hadn't done it that way. The umbrellas went back on the shelves.

When Ben, trying a different tactic, in the mildest terms mentioned the lack of sales at the cheese counter, which was the same size as it had been in the last century but was only doing half the business, Georgy simply said that cheese had been the foundation of the Emporium's success in the 1880s, and that was the end of the matter.

Yet Ben felt how successful the Emporium could be. He spent hours doing something that Georgy had never done: he learned. He went walking meekly around the other department stores, Selfridges, Harrods, Army & Navy, with a notebook in his hand, writing down how Leibig's competition had achieved their success. He spent long hours talking with Clifford Ford, who knew the business inside-out, but was too shy to speak his mind. He had a wife who he adored, who had been an invalid for many years, and he could not afford to stick his neck out . . .

So Ben formed his own ideas. When he had worked out the details on paper, he went to see Georgy.

'Sir,' Ben started with disarming mildness, 'may I make a suggestion?'

'What is it now?' Georgy said wearily, toying with a pencil.

Ben exploded his bomb: 'I think we should change the name of Leibig's Emporium.'

It worked. Georgy gasped, then surveyed him with horror, giving Ben his one hundred per cent attention.

'Change the name of Leibig's Emporium! To what?'

'To anything else, it doesn't matter what. The military clientèle Leibig's used to rely on wouldn't come in during the war because of Leibig's German name: they all joined the purchasing clubs run by the Army & Navy Stores and the others, and they haven't come back – and they won't.'

'They will.'

'They won't, Georgy. They haven't yet, and why should they? It's the name, plus the fact that most of them live over in Kensington, as do the retired colonial administrators. Why should they bother to come back all the way here to Piccadilly?'

'We deliver free,' Georgy said.

'That's my second point. Cliff and I have done a long survey of accounts and deliveries.'

'But I authorized no such thing.'

'We found that they fall into three main groups,' Ben continued remorselessly. 'Firstly, we have account customers who never come to the shop, order by letter and pay promptly.'

Georgy nodded.

'Secondly,' Ben said, 'we have account customers who order by letter and *do not* pay promptly. But still we supply them. We shouldn't.'

'But then those clients would not come back!'

'We don't want those ones to come back!'

Georgy gaped at him. 'But the client is always right.'

Ben said impatiently: 'Thirdly, we have customers who order a lot and pay well. These, obviously, we want to keep and encourage in every way we can, including free delivery. But Georgy, now we come to the fourth group, who buy one packet of biscuits, or one pound of cheese, and expect free delivery. We deliver free within a radius of four miles, twice a day. We should deliver once a day and charge for orders under, say, £1.'

Georgy's eyes popped with horror. Business had been falling off and Georgy knew with absolute certainty that any change must make it fall off faster. Any change was change for the worse.

'Georgy, we must expand our range of customers!' Ben said angrily. 'At the moment the store layout is so muddled and confusing it puts people off. It's one reason why so few young people come in. And we have so few women! Why should they come in when we do nothing to attract them? We don't carry bright, new lines—'

'Women are unreliable customers. Their tastes are unpredictable.'

'But Georgy, the future is in women! They have more money now, and more freedom! They want to spend, so why won't you sell them the things they want to buy? We need a cosmetics department, up-to-date fashions. The Emporium is *boring* for them. We'll make money with change, not lose it. And we should man a switchboard to take telephone orders – including during the evenings, when people get home from work.'

'People who have to work cannot afford Leibig's Emporium.'

'That's changing.'

'Have you quite finished?'

Ben hadn't. 'Hawk keeps people out of the shop, Georgy. He's supposed to help them in, make them feel welcome, not intimidate them. If he doesn't mend his ways, he'll have to go. We're not running a club where only people Hawk approves of get in.'

'But Hawk has been here since—'

'I know, since 1886. This is today. That silly purple uniform is out of fashion too.'

'Imperial purple is Leibig's house colour.'

'It's out of style. We want something newer, fresher. What about yellow? Make people feel refreshed when they come into our shop. It's all too gloomy and musty at the moment, all those cramped rows of wooden counters, the gas lights . . . we really ought to have electric lights, you know.'

'The extra expense!'

'The extra profits.'

'No,' Georgy said. 'No, no, no. You work too hard. You give me a headache.'

'At least consider a cosmetics counter.'

'No. I will not allow painted ladies in my Emporium.'

'But most girls wear make-up nowadays. It's the fashion.'

'No.'

Ben scratched his head. 'Won't you change *anything?*'

'No,' Georgy repeated.

Ben went to the door, then turned. 'These big Transatlantic liners – a lot of tourists are coming over since the war. Americans don't know London – we ought to get on the tour companies' list of places to visit. We must make ourselves more accessible, Georgy – we've got to make them want to come into the shop.'

'We don't want that sort of person.' This was a view Ben was getting very fed up with.

'You want their money, don't you?' he shouted. He

nearly came out and said what he knew: Leibig's Emporium was up to its neck in debt.

Mr Phrane, Georgy's friend of many years, had died during the summer. Ben had handed the letter to him personally, and Georgy had gone white at the news. He did not know the new man, Smythe, a mere cashier before the war who had made quite a reputation for himself in the Army, apparently. Smythe launched a reappraisal of Leibig's standing with the London & South-West Bank. He had not liked what he found any more than Ben did. But Ben did not like Smythe either. Smythe, who still called himself Captain, was prim and white, with glittering spectacles. Tiny and erect, every crease fastidious, Ben classed him as a person who would order one packet of biscuits to be delivered.

Clifford told Ben – though loyally in more discreet and diplomatic language – that the only major capital resource that Georgy had left, apart from the Rolls-Royce and a lot of old stock, was that the premises were owned outright. He had borrowed against them to the limit. Leibig's Emporium was haemorrhaging money like blood. Now Smythe would probably bring that borrowing limit down from Phrane's generous level. Georgy was facing the unthinkable: losing what his father had built. Georgy couldn't face up to that, or even think about it.

Now Ben tried to badger Georgy out of his shell.

'We have to hold a sale.'

'No,' Georgy said. His stubby fingers gently followed the whorled walnut grain of his beautiful desk.

'Our windows should be lit all night,' Ben said, 'like Gordon Selfridge does. And if we're going to go to the bother of wrapping customers' purchases, we shouldn't use plain brown paper, it should at least be distinctive and have our name on it.'

'*No!*' Georgy banged his fist on the table. His face was a deep red and his lips were twisted as if in pain. Ben wished he hadn't pushed him so hard.

'Are you all right?' he asked, concerned.

'Yes,' Georgy said.

Anyway, that was enough to start off with. Ben asked him again if he felt all right, then pulled open the door. Georgy, recovering, said calmly: 'I will think about everything you have said and give you my decision in due course.'

I've heard that one before, Ben thought. But he smiled to himself. He had given Georgy plenty to think about, and perhaps some of it would bear fruit. He yawned as he walked down the corridor to the lift. He felt very tired; he must have been more keyed up than he knew. Instead of working late as usual, he fetched his British Warm from his office and caught the bus home to Primrose Hill, where he and Vane still lived, having taken over one wing of the house. Vane would be happy to see him, he knew: she thought his hard work was not a virtue but a vice. 'Why?' Ben had asked. 'Because you aren't with me,' she said.

Peggy took his coat.

'Is my wife in?'

'No, sir. She must be still out shopping.'

Ben frowned. 'But I saw the car when I came in.'

'She was collected by a friend of hers, sir,' said Peggy happily. She loved to talk. 'A red tourer – the very latest model.'

Marcelline Stoughton then. Ben took the opportunity to call Sam up. The great ginger dog came galumphing across the tiled hallway, skidded, then sat and thrust his head into Ben's hands, wagging his tail, staring up adoringly with mahogany eyes. Ben bent down and sniffed.

'Flea powder, sir,' Peggy said apologetically.

'But Sam hasn't got fleas.'

'Mrs London says he has, sir. She insists.' *Mrs London.* Even after these months, it still sounded strange. He asked Peggy to bring him tea then went into the living room and sat on the rug in front of the fire with Sam, scratching him behind the ears, taking advantage of Vane's absence to have him together with him. Vane hated Sam unreasonably, he mused, just as she had instantly hated Colleen O'Keeffe. It was as if she couldn't bear the thought of any competitor in her love for Ben. He stared into the flames . . .

Sometimes it seemed to him as though her love for him was almost jealousy.

5

'Thank you, Mrs London,' grinned the little receptionist girl, opening the street door for her. Vane, glorious in the furs and the fabulously expensive white mink hat she had simply *had* to buy this morning, walked outside in a mute daze. Hardly knowing what she was doing she walked along the pavement of Harley Street and crossed the road without looking. The brakes of a white tourer squealed. The traffic stopped.

'Oranges!' cried some filthy street-beggar. 'Oranges, oranges, who'll buy my oranges? Come on, lady!' he called after her.

A few years ago no one would have dared talk to a lady of quality like that. Vane would have quelled the street-beggar or whatever he was with a single glance. Now she did not know. She did not care.

She could have wept.

I'll look dreadful. My complexion will come out in spots. Because I'm so beautiful everyone will notice how ugly I am. Even the common people will look at me and laugh coarsely as I swell up, knowing what I have done. They'll know that beneath these wonderful furs, behind the elegant façade with which I hold the world away, I am an animal. Rutting and grunting and clasping the same as them, merely human, grossly human.

There was Marcelline, at a snow-white table on the far side of the restaurant. 'Vane – darling!' she mouthed, waving. Treacherous Marcelline, who had rejected Vane to marry Henry. Now Marcelline was desperate to be friends again. Vane permitted the bowing *maître d'* to sweep her imperiously through the bustling waiters.

Marcelline wore an earth-coloured red-brown dress that brought out the glow of her smooth brown hair. She had now recovered after the birth of her daughter, Ambrosia – no, not quite recovered everything. As Vane sat, surveying her friend critically, she decided that Marcelline had definitely lost ... that certain something. She no longer looked quite so ravishing, so feminine, so mysterious. She looked ... very slightly motherly.

Poor Marcy!

Marcelline looked concerned. 'Vane, darling, is something wrong?'

'Wrong? How could there possibly be?' Vane had hidden her appointment with the doctor.

'I'm sorry, darling, I obviously shouldn't have asked.' The young waiter brought two White Lady cocktails. It was perfectly fashionable to drink gin now. Vane tossed hers back. Marcelline smiled up at the waiter with her white, even teeth. It did not look coy or coquettish, it looked earthily sexual. With a waiter. This was awful. This was what it did to you. Vane waved her fingers at her glass for another drink.

'Nothing's wrong.'

Marcelline changed the subject. 'You haven't asked me how Ambrosia is.' Her face lit up expectantly.

'How is your little bundle of love?'

'Oh, she's *adorable*.'

Vane wanted to scream. She drank.

Marcelline put her elbows on the table and leaned forward adventurously. 'Vane, what has got into you!'

What has got into me! That made Vane want to laugh.

'Marriage is certainly good for you,' Marcelline observed, with a single bat of her long eyelashes.

Vane giggled.

'Where shall we go shopping this afternoon? Your father's place?' asked Marcelline casually. She got a discount there and they could hardly make her pay on the nail, considering who they were. Because of the time Henry's burgeoning political career took, she was down to her last ten thousand.

'I simply will not go to the Emporium,' Vane said.

'Why not?'

Vane said: 'I might meet my husband.'

Marcelline was startled. This was the first hint of trouble, though of course she had expected it. Her interest was

517

aroused. 'Darling – something's not wrong between you and Ben, is it?'

'Everything's wrong,' Vane claimed. She did not feel at all tearful now. She looked at Marcelline, wanting her to feel sorry for her.

'Poor darling!' Marcelline said eagerly. She feared Ben: when he looked at her he saw too much into her and she knew, because she was wise and knew herself and men, that she could not handle him. He had a lovely manly smell about him though that was terribly attractive, very masculine, dark and earthy, like truffles, almost irresistible. Those eyes . . . A good friend, terrifying lover. Marcelline shivered. 'Men are beasts!' she lied sympathetically.

To Marcelline's experienced eye Vane did not have the glow about her that going with a man gave. In fact, poor Vane looked frightful – more in shock than in love. Poor Ben; what a challenge. Marcelline wiped the corner of her lip with the napkin. She wondered what he was like in bed.

'Ben doesn't love me,' Vane cried. 'He loves the Emporium! He married me for the Emporium.' That O'Keeffe woman had said otherwise. *You see, Vane, he doesn't care about money – yours or anyone else's.* It was certainly true that he had renounced a fortune's worth of horrible-looking paintings – but he'd kept one, hadn't he? He had everything all planned out. They were all victims of his appetite, just toys to his magnificent ambition. Of course he was ambitious, he had no breeding. She was so glad Daddy understood. He wouldn't get anywhere while Daddy was alive.

If Ben truly loved me, Vane thought, *why did he make me ugly?*

'He does love you,' Marcelline shrugged. 'You're so lucky.'

'He's a monster,' Vane wept. 'You don't know what he's done to me.'

'What?' Marcelline asked, interested. Vane said nothing.

'Vane, grow up, darling,' Marcelline said suddenly. Vane was astonished to see that the corners of Marcelline's mouth had turned down – almost in disgust. 'You've got everything, Vane, don't throw it all away.'

Vane regarded her suspiciously.

'I am speaking to you as an envious friend, and that is all,' insisted Marcelline. She took the menu. 'Now, let's eat.'

'I'm not hungry,' Vane said.

'Shall I order for you?'

'I'm not ugly. Look at the people looking at me.'

'Yes, yes,' Marcelline said. *'Poulet* or *poisson?'*

'You don't love Henry, do you,' Vane said flatly.

Marcelline ordered.

'Do you,' Vane said.

Marcelline put her elbows on the table and braced her hands in front of her mouth. 'Henry and I suit each other very well,' she said.

Vane said: 'That's not good enough for me.'

'No man could give you what you want,' Marcelline said. She turned over her fish with distaste. 'You're right about one thing. Ben was too ambitious.' Suddenly she burst out bitterly: 'Vane, he gave you love and all the things people dream of to make you into something good. You got more than most women get, believe me. But you just want to throw it away.'

Vane's eyes sparkled. 'Marcy, you *are* envious!' she laughed.

'Yes, I am.' Marcelline put her knife and fork together. 'I hate this fish. It isn't even Friday.'

Vane ate hungrily.

Marcelline watched her.

Over coffee Vane said: 'Let's go to Fortnum and Mason's, then.'

'I don't know . . . I ought to get back to Ambrosia.'

'Haven't you even got a nanny?'

'All right,' sighed Marcelline. 'Just an hour or two.'

Vane signed the bill and Marcelline drove down to Piccadilly. She parked near the Ritz to get some air during the short walk. Vane hated walking. As they went along the pavement, she sulked, and kept looking back over her shoulder. Finally Marcelline looked back at the white tourer too.

'Do you know them?'

'No,' Vane said.

An omnibus turned out; but a minute later, the white tourer was kerb-crawling behind them again.

Marcelline said: 'Do you think they're following us?' She could see the outlines of two men behind the windscreen.

'I don't know,' Vane said. 'Isn't it exciting!'

Marcelline stumbled, becoming acutely aware of the way she walked.

She stopped.

The tourer stopped.

'Vane, they know *you*.' She looked at her friend: *Own up*.

'I've seen that car several times,' Vane admitted.

'Have you told the police?'

'I thought I'd see what happened.'

'Vane, don't be silly,' Marcelline said.

Vane took a couple of steps back towards the car.

Marcelline said: 'Vane!'

The tourer turned away out into the traffic, then parked on the far side of the broad road.

Now Vane recognized it: that same angle, parked on the far side of the road, and it came together in her mind.

She . . . *remembered*. The white tourer. It was the same. She had to go. She had to know.

The same two men got out of the car. They stood watching her.

Marcelline also watched Vane. 'Don't,' she said.

Vane looked at the muscular man, the one with the smile. There was no sign of the common girl this time. Good.

'Why shouldn't I go over?' Vane said. 'Just to see can't do any harm.'

'You don't know that. I'm frightened.'

'*You*, Marcy?' laughed Vane.

'Don't play games. He frightens me.'

Vane felt no fear. She was interested in the man. He was a change. She liked his smile, wide and grim, drawing her in. He was interesting, that was all. And he knew everything she wanted to know.

'You're jealous,' Vane scoffed. Marcelline made such a

thing of being a great man-eater, but as soon as she saw a real one she backed away, apparently. Frightened of being treated like a lady. Vane glanced at her with contempt.

'There's no . . . sex about him.' Marcelline tried to explain what she felt. 'He doesn't smell right. He . . . smells. He stinks! Oh, Vane, don't.'

Smiling, Vane stepped off the kerb.

'I won't come with you,' Marcelline said. But she felt foolish.

Vane crossed the road alone.

6

Ben was woken by the front door of Primrose House slamming. The silver teapot and tea service on the occasional table which had appeared beside him while he slept felt cold to his fingertips. Peggy must have tiptoed around so as not to wake him. That was kind. She had drawn the curtains too, so it must be dark outside. He heard Vane's footsteps tapping across the hall tiles.

'In here, darling,' he called, and sat up on the sofa, yawning. Sam was sprawled in front of the fire like a vast, lumpy ginger rug. 'I came home early,' Ben yawned, 'but you were out. Did you have a good day?' he asked.

Vane crossed the room taking off her furs. Beneath, he saw, she was wearing a fashionable small-busted pale green dress with pleats that swung enticingly from her hips as she walked. He bit his tongue rather than ask her how much it had cost. Pulling off a white fur hat, she tossed it in the corner – thank God, it could not be new or expensive then, he thought – and he watched her stand patting her hair in the gilded Louis mirror.

'What's that dog doing in here?' she demanded in the glass. Obviously they were going to argue.

'Leave him,' Ben sighed, 'he's happy. Tell me about everything you've bought today.' He did not really want to know, it was a kindness: telling him would please her. She loved talking about her purchases more than wearing them.

Vane turned. 'I haven't bought anything,' she hissed.

It didn't matter whether that was true. Ben knew by now that nothing less than a blazing row would satisfy her; sometimes frustration and hatred and loss fuelled a fire in Vane that love did not.

It was a waste of time, he thought bitterly. She had everything she wanted, but she always wanted something she did not have. He wished he could have been the man she dreamed of, but that was not possible for any man. Vane's unhappiness fed on itself and grew hungrier, creating more unhappiness. In Vane's mind everything she touched turned against her, and she blamed their inability to start a family on him. To Vane love was social, not sexual – he was the only person she did not peck on the cheek and call darling. She had wanted babies desperately, he knew, but in a possessive, antiseptic, modern way – nothing would have made her happier than going down to Boots the chemist and buying a blue tablet to have a boy, pink for a girl. The more she fought against her nature, the more she lost. Vane hated real love, real life.

'Come and sit down beside me,' Ben smiled, very friendly, trying to help her, patting the cushion beside him. If only she would calm down; give in to him a little; if only she would trust him and stop trying to prove her superiority all the time. 'Where did Marcelline take you?' he asked.

'Oh, your little spy told you did she, Mr Know-all?'

Accusing Peggy was ridiculous, but Ben shrugged. He hated it when Vane was in this mood; it got neither of them anywhere. He knew that it was just her unhappiness talking, but he did not know any more how to make her happy. They were married, they *had* to be together, they *had* to make a success of it. He took the initiative.

'Vane,' he said, 'I've got so many ideas. We can make a real go of the Emporium together. Something amazing! Something—'

Vane ignored the cushion, ignored him, and turned back to observe herself in the mirror.

'Vane, I can make the Emporium' – he clenched his fist – 'into the best, the richest, the most glamorous shop the

522

world has ever known. We can do it together. It can bring us together.'

Vane stared down at his reflection. There it was. Naked ambition.

She swung. 'But you're *nobody*,' she spat.

'I can do it.'

'Over our dead bodies!'

'Together we—'

'Leibig's Emporium is *ours!* It's mine! Daddy would never let you!'

'Do you know you've really got some very good people working for you? But they're hidden away – their abilities are buried. All they need is the chance—'

'I don't care!'

Ben promised: 'The most glamorous shop in the world, Vane. All you have to do is say *I will*.'

'I said *I will* when I married you and – and—' Her face cracked and she turned back to the mirror. 'You destroyed everything. You broke everything I had.'

But he had given her more. 'Vane, I'm sorry but—'

'You're not sorry, damn you, you're glad,' she snarled. 'It's not the first time you've done it. Taken over. The most glamorous shop in the world – do it together – rubbish! Oh you bastard.' That was a word she had never used before. Who had taught it to her? 'Bastard!' Vane repeated. 'It's us you want. You've done it before! I know it all!'

Ben said: 'What has happened to us?'

Vane shook her head, then he was surprised to see her image smile. She ran her hands down the sides of her body.

'Actually, darling, if you really want to know,' she said in a lilting voice, 'a rather nice man took me to tea at the Ritz.'

'Good!' Ben said. What was he supposed to say? Was he supposed to be jealous? The Ritz did wonderful cucumber sandwiches, very thin yet crisp. He had been wondering if he could persuade Georgy to open a small restaurant in the Emporium. He suspected the secret was a slick of mayonnaise on the top layer. 'Did you try the cucumber sandwiches?' he enquired, interested.

'You always have a funny little joke to make, don't you?'

523

'No.' He waited patiently. There was no arguing with her in this mood.

Vane twisted. 'I'll make you laugh on the other side of your face,' she said viciously. 'I'll make you pay attention to me. I know you for what you are. *He* told me. *He* knew all about you. The truth. You raped that girl,' Vane spat.

'What girl?' Ben asked, aghast.

That got him, Vane realized, thrilled.

'You raped her just as you rape me every night,' Vane shouted. She didn't care if the servants heard.

Ben struggled to understand her dreadful accusation.

'What the hell are you talking about?' he demanded.

'Don't swear at me,' Vane screamed, 'don't come the innocent with me! I know you now, you bastard. God help me, I must have been mad to marry you!'

Ben got up and closed the door. He crossed back to Vane. 'Calm down,' he said. He did not feel calm himself. He tried to understand her, but she backed away, as if he had threatened her, almost tripping over Sam. She kicked out at the dog with her pointed shoes.

Sam yelped, then bared his teeth for the first time that Ben had ever seen. 'Sam! Come here,' he said. Growling, Sam came to heel.

'He tried to bite me,' Vane panted, staring at Ben. 'You set him on me.'

'Calm down.'

'I won't!'

This had gone too far. Ben unstopped the whisky decanter and poured a tot, held it out. Vane took it and threw it at him. The glass rang on his elbow, then rolled unbroken across the rug: the Emporium's leaded Waterford Crystal, as tough as nails. He picked it up, then sat on the sofa.

'Come and sit down, talk to me,' he said, trying to wipe the smell off his sleeve.

Vane bunched her little fists. 'You raped his sister.'

He understood.

'Oh my God,' Ben said. 'You mean Ria – not Ria!'

Now he knew who had found Vane.

'He told me everything!' Vane shrieked, raising her fists.

Remember me.

'Vic Price,' Ben said.

Vane's eyes glinted victoriously. 'So you do remember. He said you would.'

'I remember.' Ben pushed his fingers against his lips, not tasting the whisky there. He shuddered. Vengeance. The past never died. 'I'll tell you the truth.' Vane covered her ears and stamped her foot. She didn't want to hear it.

She squeezed her eyes shut. 'He told me everything.'

'Everything but the truth. Did you believe him?' Of course she did.

'After what you did to me, I could believe anything,' Vane sobbed. She seemed unaware of the small bubble of saliva trickling from the corner of her mouth. 'He was a nice man,' Vane added wistfully. She opened her eyes. They gleamed with tears. She held out her hands, but not to Ben. 'He put his arm around my shoulder, Ben. He knew how unhappy I was. He understood. He had been there, because of what you did to his sister.'

'He was manipulating you.'

The glow went out of Vane. 'Did you rape her against her will?'

'No, of course I didn't.'

'Promise?'

'Promise.'

'I don't believe you. I hate you,' Vane said dully. She put her hands on her stomach as if in pain and sat on the far end of the sofa with her knees together. She shook her head. 'Not as much as he hates you. He hates you, Ben. He was such a kind man but when he said your name' – she shivered – 'I was frightened. He called you the Workhouse Bastard.'

'Did he threaten you?'

'Oh no, he was smiling and kind, you see. He said to call him if ever I was in trouble. He knew how vulnerable I was. He showed me how everything was different from what I thought it was. Poor Ria can never love another man because of what you did to her. You took her and broke her like you broke me. You're a bastard. You gunned down your best friend in cold blood.'

'He was burning alive.'

'That's not what Vic says.' She shut her eyes; the horror. Vic Price had made her feel what it was really like.

'My only friend,' Ben said. 'The only thing he needed, I could not give him.'

'So you shot him. Are you going to kill us too?'

This was crazy.

Ben cried: 'Vane, can't we love one another?'

'You already have a son,' she howled. 'You don't need me.'

He cried out: 'But I don't know about him, Vane! Help me!'

Her face crumpled up. She hugged herself, bowing her head down almost as far as her knees. Her hair swung in limp, open curls, showing the crimp marks of the tongs. 'You must have known. I know it. I feel it inside me.' She looked up. 'I lied to Marcelline. I went to the doctor this morning. I'm pregnant. I'm going to have a baby, God forgive you.'

He put his arm around her. 'Darling, that's marvellous news.'

She pulled away. 'Don't touch me! Now you've exploited me just like you exploited her. Congratulations. You got what you wanted. Now I'm going to be ugly like Marcelline – or poor Ria!'

'You're beautiful.'

'I was beautiful, you bastard. Who have you got your sights on now? God help them!'

'Vane, we can be happy.'

She wouldn't believe him.

'I don't want to sleep with you any more,' she said. 'I want to move back into my own bedroom. I'm going to sleep with myself. Get out.'

7

Esther hesitated on the third step of her stairs, looking up anxiously at the door of Ria's bedroom. It was almost noon, and she had still not come down. Esther had fed Will and packed him off to school. All morning, that door had stayed closed. Ria was getting worse. It was worrying.

Esther dropped back to the second step and put her hand to her lips, looking around as if for help. But Tom was working or down at the pub, and there was no one else in the house to turn to.

She didn't want to go up.

She wanted a drink. Just a little one. She felt empty inside. She longed for the hateful hard feel of the round neck of the bottle against her teeth, the moist sucking feeling as air bubbled into the bottle and the hot liquid spilled down her throat, spreading life through her limbs, giving her the courage to face another hour of another day, bring her moments of joy amongst the indifference. But the price of gin was going up horribly: government policy. Beer was to be the drink of poor women now that West End folk had discovered gin and tippled it in cocktails. Esther detested beer. She did not care for port much. But there was still that door.

She clasped her trembling hands over her bosom and went up. She knocked softly on the peeling paint. 'Ria? Are you awake, love?'

'I'm all right,' came Ria's flat voice. 'Leave me alone, Mum.'

Esther turned the handle and peered in. Ria was lying in bed on her right side, her head in a dark yellow mass of greasy hair on the dirty pillow, the shape of the blankets showing that she had her legs drawn up. The skin on her face looked like uncooked pastry, Esther thought, and her eyes stared blankly at the window withdrawn, colourless, a tone rather than a colour. 'Brr!' Esther rubbed her shoulders. Ria made no response. It was freezing in the room, ice coated the inside of the glass, and the fire was out. Will's little bed had not been made or his toys cleared up. Esther picked one or two things up and put them away, watching Ria all the time.

'Come on, love, why don't you come down?' she begged. 'Do you good. I've got some lunch on – you look like you could do with a bite to eat.'

'I don't want anything to eat,' Ria said.

'You've got to eat,' Esther said desperately.

'I don't want anything.'

'Are you ill, love? Is there anything I can do?'

'Go away,' Ria said. 'Leave me alone.'

Esther backed to the door. She held out her hands, then closed it and walked slowly downstairs. Ria had given up, she was pining away. Esther stopped. She couldn't leave Ria like that. Maybe she should take her a tray up with a steaming pie on it and mashed potato and a good hot mug of sweet tea, and see the life come back into her daughter. It was horrible seeing Ria in bed like that. Esther could hardly recognize her daughter in this grown woman who was too sad even to get out of bed to see her son off to school. Ria had been so beautiful; now, unloved, she was ugly. She was wasting away, deliberately ruining herself.

Esther knew who she ruined herself for.

Him. Love.

Impossible love. Forbidden love.

A broken heart was a deeper malaise than pie and mash could cure.

Esther stooped by the kitchen table and rummaged through the cupboard under the sink. Finally, her fingers felt the smooth neck of another bottle right at the back. She pulled it out carefully, still in its brown paper bag.

Still on her knees, she uncorked the bottle and put its round mouth against her teeth. The hot liquid pulsed down her throat.

Dutch courage.

She would go and see Vic about Ria. That was the only thing to do.

Vic would know what must be done.

Vic was a man. He had the strength. He would make Ria see sense.

Esther pressed the back of her hand to her mouth. She forced the cork back into the gin bottle and replaced it behind the bleach, then raised herself to her feet, grunting with the strain on her knees, and slammed the cupboard door. She would put on her hat. Vic always liked her to look nice, he hated her to let him down. As if she would. Hat it was.

She went next door and knocked. Nigel answered. 'Can I come in, love?'

'We're busy,' Nigel said. The boys were worked off their feet nowadays.

Vic came into the hall. 'Never too busy for my mum,' he said, embracing her. He looked ever so the gentleman, in a sort of plaid jacket and plus-fours. Nigel was dressed in a black suit that set his tall, slim figure off very nicely. He closed the door behind her and Esther walked nervously down the hall into the sitting room. The fire was roaring and the heat brought a flush to her cheeks. There was a thick rug on the floor with lovely blues and greens and rose pinks. Nigel had told her it was Chinese.

Vic helped her into a soft chair. He sat on the arm of the chair opposite, looking down on her, smiling. 'Like your hat, Esther,' he said. Nigel stood behind her.

Esther's hands wrestled in her lap. 'Vic, I'm ever so worried about Ria, darling! I think she may kill herself or do something stupid. You see she's given up, darling. I'm so afraid, and there's knives in the kitchen and bleach under the sink, I shouldn't have left her there alone . . .'

Vic could smell the gin on Esther's breath and she looked stupid in that hat. Vic listened to her gabbling on about his own sister committing suicide with mounting hatred for Esther's ignorance: committing suicide was the last thing that Ria would do, she was never the type. Ria wouldn't break: she'd bend. And she had. Esther didn't have the sense to see that Ria had finally come to heel. Vic had won. Still Mum gabbled.

'All right now, Esther!' Vic shouted.

Esther stopped. Her mouth moved, but she couldn't say anything.

Vic put his face close to hers. He said softly: 'Would you like me to have a word with her, then?'

Esther nodded.

'I'll go and see her for you,' Vic said. 'You sit here quietly with Nigel, all right?'

He stopped by the door, looking back.

'Thank you, Vic, ever so,' Esther said. 'I owe you ever so much.'

Vic nodded his head slowly and went out. Nigel unbuttoned his jacket with the nimble fingers of his right hand. 'Want a cup of tea, Mum?' Esther shivered, relaxing.

'That would be lovely, dear,' she said automatically.

Slowly, Vic went upstairs.

Ria listened to his footsteps coming. She could tell it was Vic. The pillow felt greasy, she realized. Her body itched, and the bed was hard. She made herself stare indifferently at the window.

She heard his knock on the door. She could tell him to go away, but she knew he wouldn't. She could delay him by saying that she wasn't decent, or asking him to wait a minute, but it wasn't worth the bother any more.

She heard her voice say: 'Come in, Vic.'

He came in and looked at her silently, then crossed to the window and opened it.

'Nothing like a breath of fresh air,' he smiled. 'I love the smell of the river, don't you? Better than the smell of bodies.'

The air did smell good. She could hear the gulls mewling over tidbits in the water.

'We're going down to the pub,' Vic said. 'You come. Make a change for you.'

Ria licked her lips. She could hardly bear her loneliness any more. It would be lovely to see people again. Hear laughter. People would say: 'Here's Ria Price back again,' and she'd call back: 'Hallo, mates!' That had been one of her catch-phrases.

She'd have to have a bath first. Do her hair. Everyone would look at her in her electric blue silk dress, the one she used to wear, the shape was a bit out of date now but they'd remember and say: 'Ho ho, there's Ria Price in her electric blue again,' and nudge and wink, and she'd hold up her hand and say:

'Now now, boys, quieten down, do!' That would bring

the house down, even if it was only the Tooke Arms.

'What are you going to wear?' Vic opened the wardrobe, flicked through her old dresses. 'Green? No, don't fancy that.' He held out a brown sleeve. 'What about this? Not impressed? Back it goes.' She watched him eagerly. The next one was the electric blue. His hand paused.

He smiled into her face. She pushed her hair out of her eyes, sitting up holding the blankets tight around her.

'This?' Vic said. He pulled the lovely shot-blue dress out. He held it against him, looking down at it. It shimmered gorgeously. One of the arms wafted silkily in that faintest breeze from the open window. It was as though it was alive. She felt her eyes soften, and held out her hands. 'Yes, Vic!'

Vic smiled into her eyes.

He bunched his muscles and tore her electric blue apart from neck to hem.

Ria gasped. Dragging the blankets after her across the bare boards, she crawled across the floor. She gathered up the remnants of the beautiful dress in her arms. The light shimmered on the ruined folds. She was too badly hurt even to want to kill him.

She looked up at Vic. He held out an old dark navy serge dress from the end of the cupboard.

'I like this one.'

She buried her face in the ruined electric blue, then stared at him again. She bit her lower lip. Her back slumped. She knew that she was beaten. 'But that's such a boring dress,' she said in a breaking voice.

'That's right,' said Vic easily. 'No one will look at you in it.'

8

'So you have come at last,' Georgy said coldly.

It was a very posh nursing home, Ben saw, the sort where they brought you biscuits on a plate to go with your cup of tea while your wife had her baby, and there was a soft carpet and armchairs in the waiting room. He was amazed to see Georgy sitting bolt upright in the corner, as though he had an iron rod for a spine, still wearing his hat. Ben glanced at his watch: it was already after midnight. He had been lost in his work when Peggy found him, he had not been back to Primrose House yet: the house where he slept alone, unhappy. The Emporium was his home. His life was there. Then Peggy had arrived with the news.

'Have you seen Vane? Have you made sure she's getting the best treatment?' asked Ben, sipping his tea, scalding his lips. He was terribly thirsty. The nurse had already assured him that there was nothing he could do. If he must stay at all, he must wait. He thought that obviously poor Vane, friendless in some white room, so near, so far, must be terrified; but perhaps for him to see her revealed in the condition she was in would be a worse humiliation for her than the birth itself – he knew Vane. Anyway, the nurse was very strict: fathers must wait in the waiting room provided and not cause any bother. A wife's first labour was usually prolonged, the nurse added mysteriously.

'Vanity has been in labour since a little after seven.' Georgy's tone was accusing, yet to Ben's mind he did not seem concerned for Vane's sake. 'It is a husband's duty to be with his wife at this time,' Georgy said. That was what mattered most to him, as it had to his father before him: duty. Keeping up appearances.

He stared at Ben with a censor's eyes. Ben knew as well as Vane did that Georgy did not love his daughter. It had been obvious from the start. Georgy had wanted a son to be the dutiful heir that he himself had been. Vane was a girl and she had never stood a chance. Ben had dreamed of earning that right, of becoming that son, of belonging. Georgy blinked and looked away.

But now that I am a man I am a free man, Ben thought. *I will do what I will. I have no father or mother and I am free, and that freedom of mine is my curse that they pity, and fear, and envy, and covet, and hate, and love, for all that it gives me, for all that it takes away.*

He closed his eyes. *Will I have to spend my whole life searching for a real home? Will I always have to be a nomad in my town, surrounded by people, and terrifyingly alone?* He did not even know his own son, only his name: *'This here's Will,'* Ria had said. *'You might say you know him pretty well, though you've never met him.'*

Like father, like son. *Oh, Ria,* he thought, *I'm so sorry.*

'Where were you?'

'I came as soon as I got your message,' Ben said impatiently. There was thunder in the air outside and there had been a long string of summer storms today. Apparently the telephones were not working so Peggy had gallantly put on her mackintosh and galoshes and walked down Primrose Hill, across Regent's Park, then down Marylebone High Street and Bond Street to the Emporium in the dark. She said she had not been frightened: she had Sam with her to protect her.

'I suppose you were working late as usual.' Georgy always left promptly at closing time, and he still drove home for lunch. Perhaps he felt guilty about the hours Ben worked. More likely he did not like the feeling that control was slipping away from him: there was nothing worse in business than to be pushed about by a subordinate who was full of energy and ideas when those were not required.

Georgy did not know what Ben felt. Ben had told Vane his secret, only Vane, trying to bring her round, to bring them together, to bind their marriage with a dream, a seed that he had hoped might blossom into true love: they could make the Emporium the greatest and most glamorous store in the world.

There they could be together.

Together they could be safe.

Together they could achieve it.

But Vane had rejected him. *'The most glamorous shop in the world – do it together – rubbish! Oh you bastard. It's us you want . . .'*

'I had a lot to do,' Ben explained to Georgy. The tourist season was at its height and light casual clothes had sold unexpectedly well – the cheaper and more brightly coloured the better. Some lines had to be re-ordered, but Georgy had refused to allow it. He considered the garish colours to be in bad taste and he always refused to stock clothes he himself would not have worn.

Ben had changed the numbers and ordered them anyway.

Then he studied the architect's plans he had commissioned for the conversion of the staff dormitories on the top floor, which he hated as the worst sort of Victorian relic, to store rooms and a good manager's flat. Georgy had not sanctioned those changes either, but Ben had learned that the only way to get Georgy to do anything was to present him with a *fait accompli*, something planned so completely that it was impossible to pick holes in it.

'It is not necessary to work so hard!' Georgy said, refusing the plate of biscuits that Ben offered him. 'The business will look after itself. I am quite capable. Your new child is more important.'

'Yes of course,' Ben said, munching. He couldn't explain Peggy's epic journey again.

'I think I heard a cry,' Georgy said. They listened. Nothing.

Ben said: 'David told me today that he's asked Harriet to marry him.'

'Who are David and Harriet?' He didn't even ask if the girl had said yes.

'David's in haberdashery and Harriet works down in the post room.'

'I do wish you would refer to them correctly.' By their last names. 'They have not told me,' Georgy added.

'Well, she might say no.' Ben knew she wouldn't. They were hopelessly in love, he could feel it between the two like a warm aura whenever they were together. Ben had personally allowed David the fullest discount on the engagement ring from the jewellery department. 'But strictly not sale or return, get it?'

'Yes, sir!' David had laughed. 'Thank you, Mr London, sir!'

'Get back to your work now. I expect extra sales from you today.'

Now Georgy said: 'How can you eat those biscuits at a time like this? Since we are talking about haberdashery, I must tell you that I have noticed that we are selling umbrellas coloured a dark navy blue. There is only one proper colour for an umbrella, just as there is only one proper colour for a hat or a car, and that is black.'

Ben sighed. 'I'll tell Peter – I mean I'll tell Mr Harrison to see to it.' He sat back and closed his eyes for a moment.

Suddenly the young nurse came in.

Ben jumped to his feet.

She smiled: 'Congratulations. You're a father. You have a boy.'

'A boy!' cried Ben.

'A son!' Georgy said. He clenched his hands in prayer and bowed his head over them.

Ben asked eagerly: 'When can I see him?'

'Oh—' There was a call from down the corridor and the nurse said, 'Just a minute.' She went away.

She did not come back.

Ben walked up and down. From time to time he looked at the empty plate and realized he had eaten all the biscuits. He remembered to put the plate down. Vane, who hated him and lived with him in the same house only for the sake of appearances, and who refused point-blank to sleep with him, had produced a child that might be a bridge across the gulf between them that the Emporium was not.

It was still not too late between them, Ben realized.

'A son,' murmured Georgy. Of course he was even more over the moon than Ben, if that was possible. Georgy had no son of his own, but now, through his daughter, he did. Leibig's Emporium had an inheritor, Leibig's Emporium would live on. Ben touched Georgy's hand, trying to show the older man that he understood what this meant to him. Georgy stared at his son-in-law blankly, rejecting Ben's attempt to make contact. A son-in-law was a pale shadow of a grandson of one's own blood.

Ben walked up and down. He looked at his watch.

It was three in the morning.

Still no word from the nurse.

Was something wrong with Vane?

Had something happened to his son? Anything could happen to a baby. Something wrong inside. A failure to breathe. Too hot, too cold. A hole in the heart, a fault in the brain.

He waited. Nothing he could do.

He walked up and down again, then yawned and stretched.

He sat on the edge of the armchair.

Then he sat back in the chair. It was only four a.m., but it seemed like hours. The early birds were singing. He closed his eyes a moment.

'Mr London!'

A nurse's voice startled him. Dawn filled the window. He rubbed his eyes, then looked up. 'What? Is—'

'Congratulations, Mr London,' smiled the pretty young nurse. 'You have *another* boy!'

Vane came home.

Georgy adored the twins. Vane named them after him: George was the eldest by three hours, Ralph his identical brother. *Mine*, she thought victoriously, *truly mine. At last I have something that no one can ever take away from me.*

She felt it tragically that she was never able to tell them apart, when Ben knew one from the other at a glance. He humiliated her, showing her up, and then he pretended not to understand her anger.

'I know my own children!' she wailed. 'I'm not ignorant!' He looked at her as if he didn't understand why she should need to say it. He was such a patronizing bastard. He didn't understand the depth of her humiliation.

She hated him to see her breast-feeding anyway, it was embarrassing, especially as her breasts had swollen up like a cow's. Her nipples had lost their delicate pale brown and become extended teats, a gross dark red in colour, and she couldn't get back into her old dresses. Her nose was speckled with blackheads. He pretended – surely he was pretending – that her humiliatingly obvious failure as a mother meant nothing to him.

'George is a touch chubbier,' he explained, 'and Ralph has got a mole on the side of his leg.' He played it as a joke between them, pretending that George was the more determined one, and Ralph more active and clever. It was easy to tell them apart! They were so different!

They weren't. They were identical. Vane tried to muffle her tears of humiliation and rage, because when she cried, that set the babes off too, and for the first time in her life she had to learn to hold herself back. It made her feel inadequate. She prowled around their cots. Why couldn't they have had brown eyes, like hers? They had their damned father's colour, although a much deeper, gentler blue, as babies always did. Their hair was dark though, and would be the same shade as hers.

She was so proud of their hair that she struck on the idea of parting George's curls to the right in the conventional way, and Ralph's to the left, so as to tell them apart. They looked awfully neat when she walked their pram in the park, all wrapped up in white lace swaddling under a white fringed parasol. She compared them ruthlessly. None of the other mothers had babies that were half as sweet as hers, she noticed.

Fortunately Ben was working most of the day, but Daddy still came home for lunch and she loved to see him sitting in the back garden with them, rocking them to sleep in the drowsy afternoon sun, the leaves falling around them, his lined red face relaxing from the cares of business, the years dropping away, and looking young again as she remembered from when she was a child herself and Mama was alive.

Her sons were special to Georgy in a way, she sensed, that she had never been. Suddenly she hated watching him, and backed away from the glass. Mama had such wonderful plans for her; but Mama was dead. Vane felt as though she was surrounded by enemies. She had given birth to her children, she had been bypassed by them; she was merely mortal, she would grow old. Now her father could turn her children against her. Take them from her. Love them as he had never loved her. Give them everything that was hers. Take them to Leibig's Emporium, every morning, at nine a.m. precisely, and Hawk would play the game with them that once he had played with her on the spotless pavement: 'Hallo, Vane!'

'*Me not Vane!*'

'*Yes you are!*' Hawk had always adored her.

So long ago. Now she had no one to help her, no one to turn to.

Everything, everything had gone wrong.

She was so unhappy. Through tears of unhappiness, Vane discerned what she believed to be the truth. Her husband hated her, used her, abused her, exploited her for her money and her body, and now that he had married her he had got her, so he didn't need her any more, and she could not control him.

Her only friend, poor, dear Marcelline, had coldly deserted her for that boon-dock northern constituency of Haworth and Clere that Henry would be fighting for in the next general election.

Her maids spied on her, Vane knew.

That great dog preyed around her house, terrifying her.

Vane put her fists to her temples.

Georgy yawned. The autumn sun was not as warm as it had been, and it was time he got back to Leibig's Emporium. His lunch hour was turning into two hours nowadays. He bent stiffly and kissed the twins, first George, then Ralph, and called Peggy to keep an eye on them: the pram would need moving soon as the sun swung behind the sycamore tree. Sam was sleeping outside the french windows and opened an eye when Georgy scratched his ear, gave a friendly slap of his tail on the paving stones, then went back to sleep. But only lightly, Georgy knew. He was doing his duty, guarding the twins. When Sam was deeply asleep, he snored.

'Good dog,' Georgy said.

He went inside. Vane was standing by the window and he realized that she had been watching him through the glass. Her expression was haunted and petulant. 'I am going back to work now,' he called. She turned away. The doctor said that she was suffering from post-natal depression. That was silly. Girls spent their lives longing for babies, then pretended to be unhappy when they had them.

What Vane needed was a good smack on the bottom, which she should have had years ago. Vane had always had what she wanted; she should have had a little more nothing. It would have given her some iron in her soul. She had never come up to his expectations. It was very difficult to think of her as a woman; a spoilt girl in woman's clothes. He had done nothing to deserve her.

'I will see you later,' he called. 'The usual time.' That would make him just in time for the twins' tea, which was always fun.

'Goodbye, Daddy,' Vane said without moving.

He parked his car in Leibig Emporium's rear courtyard and went up to his reassuringly dark, wood-panelled office. Clifford was waiting for him and he recognized at once the too-familiar shape of the letter-heading he was holding, and even the grade of the bond paper – a letter from the bank. Georgy pulled off his coat and hung his hat on the hook. He sat down behind his desk. Clifford waited respectfully, then slid the letter diffidently in front of him. Georgy didn't look at it. 'What does it say?'

'Mr Smythe regrets . . . they won't extend us any more.'

'Why is he so damned unreasonable? Doesn't he know how long Leibig's has been here?' Georgy laid his wrinkled hands flat on the smooth wood. 'How much are we in?'

Clifford balled his fist in front of his mouth and gave a low cough. 'Fifteen thousand.' Once nothing to them; now a fortune.

'Foreclosure?' Georgy's heart thumped. 'We cannot find— It is an insignificant sum.'

'Not if you haven't got it it isn't.'

Just at that moment from upstairs came a loud banging noise, and the sound of workmen's voices. Georgy looked up. 'It is this sort of unnecessary expense which has broken me,' he said. 'I know whose fault this is.'

Clifford said: 'It is the only development you would agree to, sir.'

'Change for the sake of change,' Georgy complained. 'We should not throw the past away, Clifford. Old Mr Phrane would never have treated us this way. He was a gentleman.'

'Mr Phrane is no longer the manager of the bank, and times are not what they were.'

'It is almost as though this fellow Smythe hates us.'

'There are good business reasons for his decision. Unless we—'

'Leibig's Emporium is not a pack of cards,' Georgy said urgently, 'I cannot lose it. I will not.'

Clifford confessed: 'That is exactly the situation I fear you are facing, Mr Leibig.'

'No, you do not understand. We are an institution. A London institution. Our customers depend on us.'

Clifford knew what Ben would have said now: *What customers?*

Clifford could not bring himself to utter something so cruelly truthful. Waiting respectfully for Georgy's decision, he said nothing.

Georgy put his elbows on the desk. 'I am so tired,' he explained.

Clifford tapped the letter with his nail. 'But what do you want me to do about this, sir?'

Georgy took his head out of his hands and again laid his palms flat on the beautiful wood top of his desk, and stared at the grain between his spread fingers. 'A lifetime of responsibility. I am worn out.'

Clifford gave that low cough into his fist again.

Georgy said: 'I will think about it and give you my decision in due course.'

'I'm sorry, sir,' Clifford said dutifully, and respectfully, but for the first time with a firmness that Georgy was not accustomed to hearing from him, 'But I am afraid that an answer, now, is imperative or—'

There was a knock on the door. 'Come in,' called Georgy quickly.

'But—'

'Enter!' Georgy called. Ben came in. Had he overheard what they were shouting about? The door was thick wood; no, surely not.

Ben's eyes flicked to Clifford and he smiled, then he asked Georgy:

'I'm not interrupting anything?'

'No, no,' Georgy said. 'What can I do for you, my boy?'

He watched Ben move soundlessly across the room. It was easy to see why Vane found him so attractive, if women liked men who moved with confidence and grace, as Ben did, and probably he was handsome to women's eyes too. Certainly his features were regular, and he was very well-built. In Georgy's presence he adopted a rather military bearing that suited him very well, but with other people he was more relaxed, even to the extent of having his jacket buttons undone, and when he wore a hat it was often rather rakishly on one side.

Georgy's first impressions had been of a well brought-up boy, and Vane had assured him that he was rich. By the time the truth came out – and to be honest it was Vane who had deceived him, blinded by romance, not Ben – it was too late. And Georgy had by then liked him immensely, seeing him, hoping to see him, as the son he had never had.

But Ben, it seemed, had his own ideas.

Georgy's enquiries had revealed the existence of no such firm as Blumenthall's, although a single shop of that name was listed in street directories before 1917 in one of the poorest, and probably shadiest, parts of the East End. Ben was an upstart. A street urchin.

A leopard couldn't change its spots.

He should be down there in the road, unloading the stock from the vans. Hawk had been right about him: he was the sort of person who should be kept outside Leibig's Emporium. Georgy's head was thumping away behind his eyes. He felt he had a cold coming on. He picked up the letter in his left hand and dropped it. His whole arm hurt. Had Ben spoken?

'What?' Georgy said.

'I wanted a word about the cheese counter. I thought we should change the display.'

Never! But this time Georgy was glad of the distraction. 'I'll come down with you and have a look,' he said. He heard Clifford cough discreetly for attention and felt a burst of anger. 'I have told you that I shall give you my decision in the fullness of time!'

'Yes, sir,' said Clifford obediently.

'The cheese counter,' said Georgy. 'Yes.'

He put his knuckles on his desk and pushed himself up. Ben opened the door for him. He wondered what had happened between the two men – he had never seen Georgy look so angry, although Clifford was his usual dutifully diffident presence in the background, folding up a letter.

No customers were at the counter. Cheeses were piled high on the dark wood as usual, a terrific selection of them – not only English cheddar but Canadian and Australian, Bavarian and Swiss cheeses, red roundels of Dutch Edam, a castle made of pungent Stilton, slivers of gooey Brie, a rather gummy-looking Rocquefort. The serving-girl pretended to be busy.

'We should cool this,' Ben said. 'The store temperature is too high—'

'No,' Georgy said.

Ben said: 'I do think we would sell a lot more if we cooled it slightly. The cheese could be better displayed—'

'More money!' Georgy said in a raised voice. 'No!'

The girl behind the counter looked at them nervously.

Ben said encouragingly: 'Think how clean and smart it would look if it was all under glass, Georgy. And the hygiene—'

'From the very first day you have hated this cheese counter,' Georgy shouted, 'from the very first day!'

'Let's talk about this reasonably,' Ben said. He smiled, trying to make Georgy understand. 'I am on your side you know, Georgy – I just want to increase sales.'

'No!' panted Georgy. 'Again, no!'

'Well what the hell do you want?' shouted Ben. He'd finally had enough. 'Do you want to make something of this place or don't you?'

The girl stared at them, then started paring nervously at her nails with the cheeseknife.

Georgy's eyes bulged.

'Don't –' he gasped, 'don't –' He grabbed at his arm,

groaning. Then he staggered and seemed to lose his balance, and before Ben could catch him he crashed suddenly forward into the counter. The wood splintered, the glass shattered and starred. As Georgy went down cheeses wobbled and collapsed inward across him. A red wheel of Edam bounded away across the floor. One of the white-coated staff ran out and held it down with his foot.

Ben knelt by Georgy, knocking the cheeses off his back with his forearms. Georgy lay with his head on one side. His eyes and skin looked almost transparent, as though all the blood had drained away from his face. His popping eyes found Ben's. His mouth moved.

Ben couldn't hear. He put his ear almost against Georgy's lips.

'Never throw the past away,' Georgy grunted, and Ben realized that he was chuckling.

Ben looked at him, not understanding. Georgy drew in three quick breaths, then nothing. Ben stroked away the spittle bubbling out of the corner of his mouth, then after a moment felt delicately for the carotid artery.

Somebody shouted: 'Call a doctor!'

Ben said: 'He's dead.'

Chapter Nineteen

1

The cause of death was certified as cardiac arrest.

'No,' Vane cried. 'I don't believe it.'

Although a doctor who had been in the Emporium had arrived at the moment of Georgy's death, Ben requested a full post-mortem.

'I'm sorry,' he told Vane.

Georgy's heart had rotted away inside him, it was as soft as sponge: the findings showed that he had been chronically diseased for many years, perhaps for much of his life; never knowing, every moment of every day, with every beat of his heart, how close he was to death.

Vane refilled her glass from the leaded crystal decanter.

'No, I know you're lying. You killed him.'

Ben said: 'Vane, I would never lie to you,' but he knew she would never believe him. He stood by the doorway of the lounge, his hands by his sides. He wanted to reach out to her, to touch her, to show her he did care, but Vane was untouchable: there was a wall of glass between them through which they observed one another in every detail, but they could not feel each other, they could not understand one another. Ben shut his eyes for a moment.

He had ordered the Leibig flags on the roof to be flown at half-mast. Then he had given orders for the female staff to wear black, and for the men to wear black ties. Leibig's Emporium would go into mourning for its dead owner. Still, for an hour, confusion had reigned. No one knew where they stood. Hawk kept customers out by locking the doors. Ben had to act quickly. 'Should we shut for the day?' Clifford had asked.

Ben said: 'Can we afford to lose our customers?'

'No, of course not.'

'Then the Emporium stays open.'

Ben opened his eyes.

Vane turned on her toes by the fire. 'Are you going to kill me next? After all, I am next in line.'

'Don't be stupid.'

'You did kill him.'

Ben said truthfully: 'He was medically ill. But more, something inside him wanted to die, feared living. And that was always the situation.'

'Such ruthlessness,' Vane slurred. 'You drove him to his death. Such audacity. You take my breath away.'

'You've had enough to drink.'

'I'll never have enough. I'll destroy you.'

Ben made a last effort. 'Vane, I've always told you the truth, what more can I do for you?'

She twirled her glass. 'Thank you, Ben.' She opened her fingertips, let it drop. This time it struck the fireplace, and smashed to pieces.

Vane smiled: 'Leibig's Emporium is mine now.'

The reading of a will was a sad and serious business. To Mr Bookkeeper it was routine and he tried to put people at their ease.

'My name, Bookkeeper, is the only word in the English language containing three sets of double letters in a row.' He waited for the polite laughter that made everyone so much more comfortable.

These three people, the two men in black, the woman in an extravagantly-styled black mourning dress, just stared at him. He could have cut the tension with a knife.

'How much? That's all,' Vane said. 'Why are *they* here, Mr Bookkeeper? I'm the only one who matters.' She ignored her husband totally and looked at Clifford with disdain. 'He cannot be a beneficiary.'

Bookkeeper looked up. He cleared his throat.

'None of you are beneficiaries,' he said.

Vane looked stunned.

Charles Bookkeeper smoothed the papers in front of him. 'Mr Leibig made a new will on the birth of your twins . . .' The look in her eyes through the black veil, the hatred shining there, made him flounder.

Ben said gently: 'I have to get back to work, Mr Bookkeeper. I wonder if you could just cover the main details for us.'

Vane threw her veil back and showed her grief-twisted face. Her eyes were dark holes and her nose and chin were shiny.

'I only want to be happy,' she sobbed.

Ben looked at her sympathetically. Even now, he would have forgiven her everything in a moment, given her everything he had: love, tenderness, time. She didn't want it. Because Vane had not spoken the truth. She did not want to be happy. She was not content with the greatest gifts. She just wanted . . . Wanted. He turned away from her.

'The provisions are complex and technical,' the solicitor said. 'To summarize: under the revised terms none of you are beneficiaries of Mr Leibig's estate. You are executors and trustees.'

Ben said: 'Of the Emporium?'

'Leibig's Emporium is to be held in trust.'

Vane gasped.

Ben sat back. He hardly dared hope.

'No!' shrieked Vane. 'It's mine! It's been there all my life! Leibig's Emporium has always been there in my life!' she lied hysterically. 'You men can't take it away from me—'

'Your father—' Bookkeeper insisted.

She turned venomously on Ben. 'You planned this all along. The only reason you married me was to get your grubby working-class hands on Leibig's Emporium!'

That was beneath contempt.

'Admit it!' Vane screamed.

Ben was silent.

'Condemned,' sobbed Vane passively. 'Condemned out of his own mouth.'

'You aren't the only one the Emporium means a lot to,' Ben said. 'It's more than just an institution. It's more than a job of work for a hundred people. It's a way of life. Not one you've taken the slightest interest in, until now.'

She said: 'You love the Emporium more than you love me.' Her eyes glittered. 'I'll take it from you. I'll make you weep out loud. I'll make you crawl, Ben, darling. Get out!'

'This is my office,' Charles Bookkeeper said firmly, catching Ben's eye. 'In summation, Mrs London, Leibig's Emporium is held in trust, in equal parts, until the coming of age of your two sons, George and Ralph.'

Vane frowned: 'You mean my little George and Ralph own Leibig's Emporium?'

'In a trust administered for them by the trustees until they come of age and are able to take their own decisions in twenty-one years' time.'

Vane's face broke open into a grin. She pointed at Ben. 'So he hasn't got his hands on it after all! It passes straight to my children!' She laughed: 'You're out of it, darling!'

'Please,' Bookkeeper said, 'let me finisn—'

Ben came to the nub of the matter. 'Who are the trustees?'

'With myself in an advisory capacity,' said the solicitor, 'each of you here is a trustee: Mr London, Mrs London, and Mr Ford.'

Never throw the past away. Ben shook his head ruefully. No wonder Georgy had been chuckling at the moment of his death: he had done his duty to Grandpapa Leibig and ensured even from the grave that his policy of no change would live on.

Ben, Vane, Clifford. A tripod.

Georgy had been very clever.

Ben would have modernized the Emporium in ways Georgy did not approve of, and Vane knew little about business and cared less. Clifford Ford, shy, diffident and dutiful, would balance them. He knew the business inside out – and he was Georgy's man.

The duty laid upon Clifford was to preserve the Emporium for George and Ralph, and Ben knew he would discharge that duty faithfully. Clifford's responsibility had always been to a Leibig, so, Ben knew, he would defer to Vane.

Clifford wouldn't risk change. He wouldn't gamble with the twins' inheritance. He wouldn't play roulette with well over a hundred jobs. Georgy had locked them in beautifully. Leibig's would go on just as it had done, faithfully preserved in Victorian aspic.

And in Ben's opinion, preserved straight on a course for disaster.

Never throw the past away. That was wise for a man, but bad for a business.

The Emporium was dying.

Ben shut his eyes. He couldn't bear the picture of the future he saw. For Georgy, whatever his intentions, had ensured that the Emporium would die too.

Did Clifford know that? Perhaps, inside himself.

Would he have the guts to do anything about it?

Because Vane would oppose whatever Ben suggested.

Charles Bookkeeper completed the details. 'Lastly, Mrs London, we come to the life insurance policy held in your benefit – a modest but useful sum, about two thousand pounds.'

'I'm ill,' Vane said.

'We need you here,' Ben said, very firmly. 'There are decisions we must take at once.'

'I'll go to Frinton, darling. I think the sea breezes, for my health . . .'

'But you can't possibly,' Ben said. 'I forbid it.'

'I can do what I like now!' snarled Vane.

'Who will look after the twins?'

'Don't worry about *them*, darling,' she smirked, 'I shall take them with me. I am their mother, I know what's best for them.'

She dropped her veil, stood, and walked to the door. Clifford got up and opened it for her. She turned and surveyed them.

'Incidentally, Primrose House is in my name. The property of the wife is no longer automatically the property of the husband, I understand, so you *will* be completely out of my house by the time I return.'

Her footsteps tapped downstairs, then they heard the door at the bottom slam. Clifford looked embarrassed.

'We'll have lunch at Simpson's,' Ben said.

'There's something about the Emporium that you and Mrs London ought to know,' Clifford said as they were shown to a table by the first-floor window.

The less Vane knew the better. 'I'll tell her later,' Ben promised.

Clifford downed his sherry in one. 'A letter that you should see. It would not have been proper to show it to you before, but now . . .'

'Now everything's changed.'

Clifford stirred pepper into his brown Windsor soup, then drank the second glass of sherry Ben had ordered. Finally he handed the letter over. Ben unfolded the stiff bond paper and glanced at the text. He was surprised but not shocked. 'Fifteen thousand pounds!' The Emporium's wage-bill for a whole year.

Clifford leaned back for the waiter to take his soup-plate; he couldn't face it. 'Yes.'

'Have we got it?'

'In a word, no.'

'Can we get it?'

This time Clifford did not mince his words at all. 'No!'

'Have you tried?'

'Everything.'

'Absolutely everything?'

'Ben, we've borrowed to the limit against everything we have. We are simply not generating enough business.'

'Then our backs are to the wall?' Ben had forgotten his soup.

'You're smiling.' Clifford stared. 'You're enjoying this!' he accused.

'Yes. Oh yes. Because now I know we can win.'

Ben leaned forward across the table. 'We'll win! We'll do it somehow. We'll find a way. Because now we have to. Now we will make the Emporium the greatest, most glamorous store in the world!'

Clifford said incredulously: 'We're struggling to keep our heads above water!'

Ben said: 'I promise you.'

Looking doubtful, Clifford considered any alternative. There wasn't one.

'I believe you,' he said. He had no choice.

Ben smiled and supped his Windsor soup quickly, then tapped the letter with his fingernail. 'Now, does Vane know anything about this?' Clifford shook his head. He rubbed at his brow with the back of his hand. He looked tired, but hopeful, Ben thought. That was a good sign. Ben tasted the wine and nodded to the wine waiter. 'Yes, that'll do.'

'I'll tell her this afternoon,' Clifford said.

Ben said: 'No! You can't. Impossible, my wife is away on holiday. You heard her.' He looked at Clifford steadily, then held up his glass. 'Cheers,' he grinned.

Clifford drank. 'I don't know how you can take it so calmly,' he said. The roast beef arrived, was served covered with thick gravy by a trembling hand. Simpson's waiters always seemed to be about ninety years old.

'Let's decide what to do,' Ben said.

You've already decided, Clifford realized. He was too terrified to eat. This wasn't a meal, it was a council of war, and it frightened him.

'We can't sell the premises and lease back?' asked Ben, while they waited for the vegetables, leading Clifford towards the conclusion he had already decided on.

Clifford's agreement was vital.

'Premises? Not ours to sell, they belong to the trust,' Clifford said. 'Besides, they're secured against loans. I'm afraid that the situation is hopeless.'

'Not hopeless,' Ben said. The waiter asked: 'Duchess potatoes, sir?'

'Pile them on,' Ben ordered. He did not take his eyes off Clifford.

The old waiter cheered up. 'And the roast potatoes too for sir?'

'Yes. And I'll have peas and another Yorkshire pudding, please.' He disliked eating at lunchtime but it was necessary to give Clifford confidence.

'Yorkshire pudding, sir!' said the waiter happily. It was enjoyable to serve people who enjoyed their food.

Ben made Clifford wait, then took a mouthful of beef. 'Listen,' he told Clifford around the hot mustard, 'I'll tell you what we're going to do.'

He made Clifford wait while he chewed, then swallowed. Clifford waited with his fork frozen half-way to his mouth.

'What we're going to do, Clifford,' Ben said, rinsing his mouth with wine, 'is hold a sale.'

Clifford stared.

'And not just a *sale*, Clifford, but the biggest sale in the history of the Emporium. The biggest sale in the history of London. We've got enough old stock, God knows. We'll change all that old stock into money. We'll get customers into the place who never even knew we existed!'

2

Because Frinton was on the east coast, the sun glared off the sea each morning, making Vane worry about the twins' eyes. She had arrived on the train with a nanny, a woman of impeccable credentials, but you obviously couldn't trust anyone nowadays. In Vane's opinion this large, comfortable woman didn't worry nearly enough about her children, their poor eyes, the dangers of nappy-rash; she was a poor disciplinarian who let George cry and tantrum for as long as he wanted; and she appeared quite unconcerned when Ralph sicked up his dinner, saying that he'd be better in the morning.

Vane dismissed her.

In the morning, when Ralph was better, Vane lay her two darlings into their big double pram as she did every day, pulled its white parasol right down over them to protect their eyes, and pushed them proudly down the esplanade and along the immaculately mown greensward above the crumbling cliffs. Frinton was isolated from the world; itinerants were not allowed. There were no hurdy-gurdy men, no tinkers, no Italian ice-cream sellers. The only other people were old men walking their dogs and plump young mothers pushing babies who were not nearly as pretty as hers. The twins attracted attention, which was nice, but these motherly types had no conversation at all. They didn't talk about clothes and dancing and having fun, with them it was all about feeding times and things like wind and croup, which simply bored one to death.

Vane avoided these people.

But there was no picture-house in Frinton.

There wasn't anything to do.

Frinton, Vane decided, wasn't fun.

There was a rather interesting man with the sallow complexion that she knew goes with long years of service in the tropics. He always wore a dark overcoat whatever the weather, as though he was cold, and he always raised his top hat to her politely whenever they passed on the sward. She was dying for him to start a conversation; she even smiled at him. But he only raised his hat politely, and passed on. The next time, Vane ignored him. He stopped with his hat raised. His hair was lovely silver wings at his temples, and tiny lines around his eyes hinted at a great experience of life. Vane's hands tightened on the handle of the pram. His eyes were the colour of tropical nights. 'May I?' he said, lifting the fringe of the parasol. 'Ah. Twins. Every time I see you, I wonder whether you have one or two babies hidden under there.' So that was all he had been wondering; not a thought about her. He touched his hat again, and walked on.

The next time Vane saw him, she ignored him. He raised his hat politely and walked by. She turned and stared after him, but he did not look back.

That night the man took her to the picture-house and the hurdy-gurdy man played as they danced under the stars, around and around on the greensward, a whole orchestra playing on the edge of the clifftop, then he raised his top hat and took her into one of the shelters from the wind, quiet and secret inside, where a table had been laid for two, with a candle, and a bottle of champagne. As she gulped the bubbles he nibbled her ear, his silver wings glinting in the candlelight. He touched her down the sides of her body and she wanted him so badly that she couldn't wait, but he couldn't get his buttons undone, and as he fumbled with them she thought of Ben and her guilt grew and grew until it woke her.

It was a dream; just a dream.

Vane dragged the pillow over her face. If only Ben understood how much she *needed* him. The only thing that would make him happy was a divorce. But she needed him – yet he was so insensitive that she could not make him understand her. He was so wrapped up in his damned work that he had no time for her: he loved the Emporium more than he loved her. But she had the Emporium, so she had Ben London, wrapped up and guaranteed, for as long as she wanted. He needed her. But he never brought her presents any more, she grumbled, no candlelight dinners, no dancing or champagne. Of course she was cold towards him. Any woman would be. He didn't treat her as she deserved.

She instinctively knew that the man in the top hat would. She was not married to him, he had no hold on her body, she could deny him when she wished. He would never really get his buttons undone, that was what the dream meant. She was safe. Everything would be perfect, and she would be happy.

She did not see the man in the top hat the next day, nor the next. One of the mothers she met on the cliff-top told her that he had ended his holiday and gone home.

Vane sat in a shelter and sulked. Life had singled her out as a person to be unfair to. She was alone in this awful, lonely place. She had only the twins, and they weren't real people. But, she thought, there was one man who she could still control.

Ben would come running whenever she called him. He had to. He had nowhere else to go. A foundling had no home, no family, no place, and longed for those things above all else. Sensing his weakness, she felt the hatred and the power well up inside her.

Walking back to the hotel, she remembered all the terrible things he had done to her, yet that just made it more delicious, because she could make him do whatever she wanted, in revenge.

While the twins napped, she lay on the bed. Staring into the pillow, she saw it all. She could control him like a puppet on a string: she had all the power. She could not make him happy, but she could make him dance. She could make him weep. A big, strong man. Because he was tied to her by marriage. He was tied to her by Leibig's Emporium. And by the trust. And by the twins. And by now he must surely hate her even more than she hated him.

She pulled the pillow off her face and took a deep breath of air.

Delicious.

She couldn't wait to get back to him. She would end her holiday early.

Vane stared at the canopies, faint with shock. They should be purple. Imperial purple.

There was writing on the canopies. It was not in gold, and it was not in that difficult gothic script. The name was printed in a striking navy blue against the yellow in simple, elegant-looking Roman letters.

She gave a gasp of horror.

She read the words printed on each canopy: London Emporium.

London Emporium?

Above the main doorway, which had been extensively widened, stretched an enormous sign that repeated the name in huge gold letters piped around the edges with navy blue: LONDON EMPORIUM.

Vane stormed across the road. A van driver shouted and she shook her fist at him. Poor Hawk! He had been relegated to a sort of hutch like a sentry-box where he would have to actually foray out to prevent undesirable elements from entering the Emporium – and his uniform had been changed! He was wearing a tailored uniform jacket in pale yellow with navy blue piping, and his trousers were a practical navy blue with a thin yellow stripe down the outside leg. People were pouring in and out of the shop, and they were actually going up to him and speaking to him. Vane heard one. 'Say, which way is it to Eros, feller?'

Vane closed her eyes. Hawk hated colonials.

To her amazement poor Hawk merely pointed and replied politely: 'Piccadilly Circus, you'll find it just along that way, sir.' What had happened to him?

What had happened to Leibig's?

Vane got caught up in the flood of people going into London Emporium. She pushed to the side and clung on to the banister, gaping. The sales floor was crowded with people, yet it looked much bigger. Half the counters at least had gone and the floor area was brilliant with electric light. The stock was piled high. Banners hung everywhere: Sale SALE, Sale – first day – last day – half-price – prices reduced – prices slashed – finest quality – everything must go.

Everything must go!

Such awful people, and so many of them! Shoals of them, more heads than she could count, in patterns and swirls, moving this way and that between the bargains. *Oh my God,* thought Vane, *bargain-hunters.* Bargain-hunters in the Emporium!

People went out carrying whole tea-sets between them: Ma, Pa and two kids in cloth caps. Vane stood aside fastidiously. People like that couldn't possibly appreciate such fine china.

There was a woman over by the potted meats who was actually allowing her child to eat a chocolate sweet inside the shop!

There was a woman in a shabby coat, smiling all over her ugly face, carrying one baby and walking a toddler, buying sheets and pillow-cases as if there was no tomorrow.

There were people from all over the world, she saw, of every colour and race, white, pink, black, yellow, brown. And if God made people coloured green, they would have been there in London Emporium that day.

Like bees around a pot of honey.

Her honey.

Ben came up the steps. He said: 'I'm sorry, Vane. You're back early. I had planned to break it more gently.'

Clifford Ford was with him. Vane stared haughtily. 'Is this your doing, too?' she asked, and the bony Scot drew his red brows together and looked ashamed.

'I'm sorry, Mrs Leibig – Mrs London,' he corrected himself. Then: 'We had to do it.'

Vane turned to her real enemy and hissed: 'I am never never never going to forgive you for this, Ben . . .' Her voice rose.

Ben took her elbow and opened a door behind her. They went inside and talked in the window. She jerked her elbow away and turned on him furiously, accusing him of changing everything.

He had the gall to agree.

She stamped her foot. He had changed the name of Leibig's.

He explained that people wouldn't come into a shop they thought was run by Germans; feelings about the war still ran high. So many women had lost their fathers, brothers, their lovers, their husbands, their sons, every male member of their family, perhaps all their children. Vane saw the hurt and sympathy in those striking eyes of his. *Lying,* she thought, *lying to me as always*. Ben stated flatly that every single woman in the country knew someone who had been killed, and most of them would not come into a shop called Leibig's.

'How dare you change our name!' she cried. The blinding electric spotlights made tears run down her cheeks. 'What did you do to Hawk?' she demanded.

'I read him the Riot Act,' Ben said gently. 'He was keeping people out of the shop. We want them to come in.'

'He only let the best people in,' she wept.

'I'm sorry you feel that way,' he said sadly.

'I can take it all away from you,' she hissed venomously.

'It's our duty to our children to be successful,' Ben said.

Vane shouted: 'London Emporium belongs to my sons!'

'Ours, yes,' Ben said.

'It isn't yours!'

'No,' Ben agreed, infuriatingly, 'it isn't mine.'

'You've made yourself very happy here,' she sneered. 'Thank *you* Vane, I've got what I wanted from *you*. You never loved me. It was the Emporium. That's what you've wanted. Now you think you've got it. Well I'll make sure that you don't enjoy it. Your little home from home. I'll take it from you and you won't like it one little bit.'

'You're living in another world,' Ben said coldly. 'Face facts, Vane.'

Clifford reached into his pocket and unfolded a letter. He held it out to her.

'Fifteen thousand pounds,' gasped Vane.

Clifford pointed at the people passing the window, coming into the shop, and other people streaming out with their purchases. 'Money.'

'The only capital we had was in the form of unsold stock,' Ben said. 'If we can get people to come in once, we can get them to come in twice. We took out advertisements in the Cunard and White Star Lines' ships' newspapers, even in the *New York Times* and *Boston Globe*. We financed raffles on all the major incoming liners from all over the world: the prizes were reduced price vouchers to spend at London Emporium.' He added: 'I don't have to tell you that everyone won.'

Vane folded up the letter and slipped it into her handbag. 'I want to study this,' she said.

'That's your right.' Then Ben reached out towards her: 'It'll be tough, and I know you don't like it, but we are keeping our heads above water, Vane. For George and Ralph, our sons.'

She stared at his hands fastidiously. Those thick, brutal wrists, the masculine hair, those slim fingers that lied about their sensitivity. One of them was blistered; another had a nail cracked, and his palms were calloused. He had been shifting the stock about himself, like a common navvy. He must have worked like a Trojan to get everything ready in time. Sickening.

Those were the fingers that pulled the triggers.

She looked at him – straight into those blank eyes of his.

She wanted to scratch her nails down his face just for the pleasure of seeing the agony flare in them, of making him react to her.

By an effort she kept her hands motionless, coiled around the handle of her bag.

'I'll destroy you,' she said. 'I'll bring you down, Ben. I'll make you understand me. I'll make you weep on your knees in front of me. I know your Achilles heel, I'll make you scream, I'll break you. I'll destroy you, Ben.'

Clifford said in a high voice: 'You can't stand in the way of progress, Mrs London—'

'There's one enemy he can't stand up to,' Vane spat. 'There's one man Ben can't fight because of what he did to him' – she shivered deliciously – 'an awful thing, the worst thing in the world. There's one man who hates him enough to do that . . . one man who can shatter all these glorious dreams, one man who understands the truth, and loves me, and I can use him, and he can use me, and we'll destroy you, Ben. You took everything from us. We will take everything away from you and you will have nothing, and no one. Which is what you were born with and what you deserve! And I can do it!'

And she knew how.

3

'Vane! Is that you?'

'Sorry, sir,' Peggy said brightly, wheeling in the tea, 'it's only me. Shall I draw the curtains?'

'Thank you,' grunted Ben. Poor man, Peggy thought, I feel so sorry for him and I wish I could do something to help him – but a wise parlourmaid keeps her thoughts to herself and her nose clean, she decided wisely. Then she pursed her lips and threw good sense to the winds for him.

'Sir,' she bobbed, 'I'd just like you to know, sir—'

He looked up, surprised. 'What is it?'

'It's that we do wish you well, sir, all of us, but—'

'Thank you very much, Peggy.'

'It's just that, well, we've got to worry about our jobs, see.'

The grapevine works fast, Ben thought, *and it seems that they've decided that I've lost.*

'I understand,' he said. 'Thanks anyway for your good wishes. And for saying so.'

Peggy bobbed again, and closed the door silently behind her.

Ben did not see Vane at all over the weekend, which made him sad and unhappy, sitting with Sam by the fire in the lounge, because he had needed to at least try to explain to her why he had made the changes he had to the Emporium, to try and help her understand why they were so necessary. Had Vane been well-intentioned, she would have understood his reasons. But she, standing romance on its head, thought of him as an ogre consumed with hatred for her, and took his sound business decisions as a personal attack on her, her family, her whole disappearing class. She couldn't believe that he did not hate her; so he couldn't help her.

He sat waiting to tell her the truth, and she did not come.

Despite her command in Charlie Bookkeeper's office for him to quit her property Primrose House forthwith, he had been caught out by her early return from Frinton, and the staff flat being prepared for him in one of the dormer-windowed attics high above the Emporium, with a small bedroom and bathroom but a large well-lit lounge with a pleasant view across the rooftops towards Piccadilly Circus, was not yet ready. She knew that he was here, but she was determined to stay away.

Still Ben waited.

Still she did not come, until finally he knew that she never would.

On Monday morning Ben climbed into the Model T and drove around the Outer Circle past the gracious fronts of the homes overlooking Regent's Park, then down Bond Street. It was early and the traffic was light. Outside London Emporium, the cleaning ladies on their kneepads were already scrubbing the pavement with brushes. He parked behind a white Vauxhall.

'Good morning, ladies! How are you this morning?' They often told him what they had done over the weekend, or cracked rough jokes, or grumbled about the weather, but this morning they were uncharacteristically subdued. Daisy, with the biggest mouth, was pushed to the front by the others.

'What's happening, Mr London?' She sounded very worried. Their jobs were precarious and not well paid.

'I've made all the changes I'm going to make for the moment, Daisy. No need to be concerned. I'll keep you all busy, don't worry.'

She jerked her thumb at the white Vauxhall. 'That's not what *they* said, begging your pardon, sir.'

Ben began to understand.

He felt a cold hand closing slowly around his heart. He stared at the white tourer out of the corner of his eye. *Remember*.

He said: 'Them?'

Before she spoke he knew the answer. Yes.

Daisy saw his face. 'Yes, and your wife with them, sir! She arrived with two men, one tall and thin, and the other shorter but all covered with muscle and with a way about him of walking, sir, and a smile so that you didn't really notice the other one at all . . .' She stopped gabbling. 'Are you all right, sir?'

Ben's briefcase dropped from his unclenched fingers. All the strength drained from his hands, and he felt the muscles slacken on his face, his mouth losing its confident smile, his shoulders losing their straightness, so that his smart jacket did not fit. He licked his lips, remembering, and his face twisted and the muscles cramped up until they stood out like bars under his flesh with the strain. Defeat, and it was crushing.

He felt that his face might collapse any moment.

He walked slowly across the pavement.

Hawk moved over and stood up in front of him.

'I wouldn't go in there, sir. Wait until you feel better.'

'Hawk?' Ben articulated with his mouth. 'Is it true?'

'Chop-chop, you lazy women, get on with it!' Hawk called over Ben's shoulder. 'Better move on, sir.'

Ben didn't move. Neither did Hawk.

Ben forced himself to smile.

Hawk's gaze flickered. He spoke to Ben in a low voice, not daring to look at his face. 'I'm sorry sir, but – I've had orders not to let you in.'

It had happened, Ben realized. He was ruined. There was nothing that was not lost. Again.

He was nobody.

And no one would sense that more clearly than Hawk.

Ben looked up. 'Hawk . . .' he said.

Hawk planted his feet and crossed his arms, standing like a statue.

Ben summoned all his personality and stared directly into Hawk's eyes.

'Get out of my bloody way, Hawk!'

Hawk looked strangely startled, then confused.

He fell back a step.

'I've done my duty, sir,' he said – and stepped aside. *Blimey*, he thought, *I'm glad I'm not in the shoes of them upstairs.*

Wiping his mouth on his wrist, trying to hide his trembling hands, Ben went in.

He paused on the steps. The main hall, seeming much larger in its new livery of pale yellow and navy blue, was empty but for women cleaners and male porters bringing out stock to be displayed. None of them met his eye.

Who is my mother? Who is my father? he wondered desperately. *You, or you, or you? Any of you? Would any of you leave a little baby on the steps of London Hospital? None of you? You? Or you?*

He walked down the steps. The cleaners and porters watched him . . .

He remembered Peter, for no reason, no possible reason except sheer random brutality, dragging him through the fog, snarling *'Come on!'*, saw the glaring street lamps rotating their shadows around them, and the black walls of the Workhouse looming up. *Why?*

He started walking quietly up the stairs. His shoes made no sound on the navy blue-patterned carpet.

He remembered Vic saying: 'What's the name of that bird that moves into another nest, and chucks the other chicks in the family out to make room for himself?' Looking at Ben. Ben had never belonged, and Vic had never forgiven him.

Ben turned up the last flight of stairs below his office.

He remembered sparing the life of his enemy, Adolf Münchener.

He remembered shooting his own best friend. He remembered . . .

Ben walked slowly down the corridor. He dragged his feet on, one pace at a time, towards the half-open door of his office.

He heard laughter.

Remember me.

Vic Price was sitting behind Ben's own desk, turning one of his pens in his fingers.

Nigel was holding a piece of paper in Clifford's hands. Clifford looked stunned. It was Smythe's vellum letter.

Vane was standing beside the desk, smiling.

They had raised the money.

Vic laughed again.

Ben's hands trembled. He remembered . . . he *remembered*. He couldn't face Vic. He mashed the bitter taste against the roof of his mouth. He stumbled along to the washroom and held his fingertips across his lips, feeling sick. He had to face him.

He couldn't.

He simply couldn't.

The washroom was very small, not much bigger than a wardrobe.

Ben leaned against the dark, unhygienic wood.

Vic Price controlled London Emporium. He shuddered.

Ben crept out the back way. He would not give Vic the satisfaction of seeing him beaten.

Colleen O'Keeffe was sitting in her tiny lounge doing the clever sewing that brought her in a few shillings a week. As soon as a lady bought a dress she invariably wanted it altered, and Colleen's stitches never showed. She was working on a dress of lovely *crêpe Georgette* when the knock came on the door.

She put the material down on the table and stretched her stiff back, stuck her feet into the open-heeled slippers that she habitually wore nowadays, and turned the handle.

There was a joyous bark and the door flew wide. Sam galumphed inside and jumped up, barking and whining, putting his paws on her shoulders and licking her ears, his tail going so happily that it wagged out of control as it always did when he was overjoyed, she remembered, up and down and round and round as well as from side to side.

'Sam,' said Colleen fondly, wiping her ears. 'What are you doing here, you rogue?'

She looked out of her doorway onto the landing.

Ben stood leaning on the wall. His collar was undone and she had never seen him look so tired, or so utterly defeated. He had dropped his kitbag, all he carried was a slim package wrapped in brown paper, and she noticed that his shoes were covered with dust as though he had walked for many miles. There was no life in him. That hot blue fire that understood everything had given out; he had given in, given up, was merely a man. He needed her.

'Come in!' she said at once. 'You'll be wanting a cup of tea.' He smiled gratefully, but the smile was dead, just stretched lips.

He didn't move.

She picked up his kitbag and helped him inside.

'My poor Ben,' said Colleen. 'So she got you at last.'

4

METROPOLITAN DRINKING FOUNTAIN AND CATTLE TROUGH
ASSOCIATION
THE EMBANKMENT

Ben was thirsty. He walked slowly past the workmen with sledgehammers who were breaking up the stone trough. He saw no horses along the Embankment; this constant stream of motor traffic needed petrol garages, not water troughs.

Against the low grey sky the plane trees sprouted vivid spring-green leaves and the river stank. He stood by the retaining wall staring down at the brown water lapping the stones. It smelled of ammonia.

Where do you go, when no one can help you, and you have nowhere to go to?

You keep walking.

It was coming on to rain.

What do you do when the world ends?

He turned up the collar of his coat.

You give up.

The rain beat down on his rounded shoulders. Ben London walked aimlessly through London.

When Ria heard what Vic had done, she screamed. But silently, to herself. She wrapped her arms around herself, enclosing herself, and kept it all hidden and secret inside her, lest Vic see the truth.

Ben, don't give up, she begged silently. *Don't let him beat Ben London down like he has all the others.*

Then she thought: But *you* did, didn't you?

No! I'm Ria Price! I'm all right!

Lies, Ria thought bleakly, everything around us is all lies. Now I'm even lying to myself.

Secrets. I have secrets all right. Each of us is secret inside, and no one knows us, and we live alone, and we give up alone, and we die alone.

Once I dreamed I was so special. I was unique. I was . . . Ria.

Sitting alone on the side of her single bed with a shabby brown shawl hugged around her shoulders over her dull brown dress, her garish lipstick smudged, her hair in lank tails, her adult heart softened as she remembered a little girl in a tattered yellow dress, trembling with fear and want . . . yet whose eyes of blue and gold felt so full of hope.

Herself. Long ago.

Long gone.

I'm Ria Price and I'm special and no one's ever thought what I'm thinking now!

But it wasn't true, was it? Now that she was a grown woman even her hopes for herself were lies. She knew she wasn't special, she wasn't different, no one loved her, she gave herself to no one, she wasted away.

You lost the dream. You threw it away.

You're an animal, Ria Price.

Once she had dreamed of walking up the aisle at St Luke's, of leaning on the arm of a gorgeous man, of having a fortune and a vast house and servants and now it meant nothing. She had put girlish things behind her. She would have settled for a man who was kind.

Like Mum had.

Ria went to the mirror by the washstand and cleaned up her lipstick, then pulled the comb through her hair. Vic demanded to feel proud of his sister when he showed her to people. She didn't dare shame him, because she was frightened what he would do to her if she didn't behave properly, so she lied to him by plastering a smile on her face, although she felt as sad as though she was dying. A woman was so easy to hurt, and he would hurt her without mercy if she deserved it. He demanded that she keep up standards and she knew he was right. They said Vic had killed a man. No one could stand up to Vic's sort of rightness.

Lies. That was how she survived. By not letting anything touch her, by giving up. By smiling when she wanted to groan aloud with grief.

And secrets. *Yes! Yes! Yes!*

Especially by secrets. Living in her secret memories, destroying herself to keep herself alive, because they hurt her, how they hurt.

Because she still did not have the courage of her love.

Soon Vic would come upstairs for her.

And still she did not have the courage of her hate.

Where was he?

Here was Aldwych, lined with great buildings, with the broad expanse of Kingsway striking north between them.

Ben wandered through the rain. In Fleet Street the paper-boys shouted out the late morning editions, and a train rumbled over his head on the iron railway bridge. The dome of St Paul's loomed out of the smoke and steam.

In the City the wind from the west gusted, flapping Ben's collar like a wing against his cheek.

He held his collar down with his scalded hand and looked around him: he was standing in the road by the Bank of England. Traffic swirled around him. He stared uncompre-hendingly. A couple of minutes ago this same wind must have been blowing across the bright glass and flapping the yellow window canopies of London Emporium.

London Emporium. He squeezed his eyes shut, but could not shut powerful visions out of his mind.

Hawk would be standing immovably in the doorway while the wind eddied around him.

Clients would be filtering meekly past him into the shop.

Mr Courtenay, a hothouse flower erect in his button-hole, would be padding along the floors checking up on the staff.

Never throw the past away, Georgy had chuckled.

You never could, Ben realized.

Vic Price would never love the Emporium, Ben knew. He had assumed the debts, he had taken control with his fifteen thousand pounds, but what cost had he paid for that money? Not love. Vic would be proud of the Emporium for a day or a month, but all Vic truly loved was himself. For Vic the money would be well spent when the Emporium withered, decayed and died, a monstrous symbol of his hatred and revenge.

And poor Vane?

Lost.

And their children?

Ben put his hands over his head. Hers. There was nothing he could do, nothing he could give them. He could not even save his own children. He was no one.

He stood alone in the London rain.

'Are you just going to sit there and let them beat you?' Colleen had shouted at him this morning, driving him out of her tiny, comfortable sitting room. 'Are you just going to give up?'

He cried: 'What else can I do!' He tried to make her understand the truth, but she refused, her great arms folded, her face set like iron. What had got into her? 'I have nothing of my own,' he whispered in a shattered voice, 'I don't even know where I come from – out of the dark, that's all. Can't you understand? My mother betrayed me – left me to die—'

'Or left you to live!'

'How can I?' he yelled. 'Vane betrayed me and has my children, Ria betrayed me—' His voice broke. He was ashamed.

'Don't give up,' Colleen said. Tears poured down her cheeks. 'Please, Ben, you can't give up. You look so beaten. You can't be.'

'I worked so hard,' he murmured. 'Do I have to be a monster to win?'

She found a tiny lace-bordered handkerchief in her sleeve and plumped down into her favourite old armchair by the window. She blew her nose.

'I'm sorry if I upset you,' he said. She shook her head. It was a woman's duty not to show how upset she was. She must be strong and steady and understanding of a man, and as hard as a rock.

He looked for the kettle and boiled the water to make her tea.

She said: 'Ben. You know – there is one way.'

He knew it; she could tell by the set of his back. He was pouring out the boiling water. He said nothing.

She struggled up out of the chair. 'You have your picture,' she said in a gentle, desperate voice.

He spoke without looking round. 'That's Bertie's picture, Colleen.'

She whispered: 'Sell it.'

'No!' He sprayed scalding water over his hand. 'I can't! It's all I have!'

Colleen held his hand under the cold tap, her tearstained face close to his. She must be so strong, she must be so hard.

'Ben, think about it.'

He stared into her Irish eyes. She did not let him go.

He had never thought of Bertie's picture having a money value.

Only an emotional value – to him.

Selling it was too high a price for success.

'I can't,' he groaned.

He pulled away from her and dragged on his overcoat with wet hands, then backed to the door.

She wanted to say: *'Stay here, Ben! It looks like rain later. Don't go out in the rain!'* She wanted to hold out her hands to him but she made herself flatten them against her hips.

'He saved me,' Ben said.

Her voice pleaded – trembling, though she tried so hard to keep it strong – following him down the stairwell: 'At least think about selling it, Ben.'

'I can't,' he begged, looking up. 'Do you see why? It would be a' – he nerved himself to say the word that haunted him – 'betrayal.'

She set her face. Her tears had made lines like rust down her cheeks. 'Then betray him!' she shouted brutally.

She turned back alone into her tiny room. *Don't you understand?* she whispered secretly to herself, *he loved you, so he would have wanted you to. Love knows everything and forgives everything. Only hate never forgets, never forgives. I'm so sorry, Ben,* she whispered.

Ben stared up with a face of pure anguish. He knew.

Ria listened to Vic's foosteps thudding upstairs. She opened her door before he knocked on it.

'I was just coming down.' She hated him to come into her bedroom.

'Come on!' Vic said, looking over her shoulder. 'I'm dying for a beer.' He glanced at her. 'You look all right. I'm going to pay for you to have your hair done. Don't want people saying my sister doesn't get the best.'

'But my hair's all right.'

'It's too short, girl.'

She pulled her bedroom door shut behind her. Vic's eyes,

which were a smooth, persuasive brown in natural light, looked black indoors. His lips, which were red in daylight, turned very dark inside, and so did his flat red cheeks. He was flushed with victory, so excited that he hadn't slept for days. She could feel the door against her shoulderblades.

'I'll get someone really expensive who will make it look just like it used to,' Vic said. 'Put some life back in it.'

'You can't—'

'There's nothing money can't buy,' Vic said.

'I don't want to go down to the Tooke Arms,' she begged suddenly.

He took her hand. She could feel the violence there. Vic wasn't a loser like everyone else. The strength went out of Ria's back. She gave in; let him suck her in. He led her downstairs and held out her coat for her. As they went outside he stopped her with his hand on her shoulder.

'He's disappeared,' Vic smiled. 'Gone to ground. I reckon he'll kill himself, don't you?'

She didn't ask *who* because she knew he'd call Ben the Workhouse Bastard, and she couldn't bear it. She knew it was silly to care about something like that, only words, only hate, but she did. It hurt her.

'The Workhouse Bastard,' Vic said.

'Don't – please,' Ria said.

'You must hate him.'

Ria clenched her nails into her hands. 'Of course I do, Vic.'

'Yes!' Vic said remorselessly. 'I've got him. What else can he do?'

Get away, Ben, Ria thought. *Run away again, don't give up!*

Yes, no one could stand up to Vic's sort of rightness. No man, certainly no woman.

Ria plastered a smile on her face.

She held out her arm obediently for Vic to take.

As they walked down Havannah Street it began to rain.

Ben walked out of the City with the wind pushing on his back. He couldn't sell the picture; never. It was all he had of

569

a friend who had never betrayed him. To sell his picture for money would be . . . a betrayal of him.

An obscenity. He bunched his fist. The nails of his left hand dug into his palm.

Edith Rumney had died and left him alone. Betrayal.

Peter Pungle sold him into the Workhouse; he remembered the flash of the gold. Betrayal.

Ria Price told her brothers where to find him. Betrayal.

Bertie, in agony, was faithful to the end. Selling Bertie's beautiful Mantegna for gold was too high a price.

He walked on. Bands of rain swept ahead of him up the Whitechapel Road. He was returning to the past. Here it was: he came to the London Hospital.

The two glass collecting boxes by the steps had a few copper pennies scattered inside, some foreign coins. He recognized a lot of worthless French francs and looted pfennigs from the war, used bus and tram tickets, cigarette cards of Footballers of the World, and an enamelled badge with KISS ME printed in raised red letters. It must always have been like this.

But he remembered that sweet shops and tobacconists and newsagents had usually been three different shops, but now most of them sold sweets, newspapers and smokes together, and tuppenny-ha'penny fast French novels with lurid bedroom covers and sexy titles too. As he walked on, Ben saw no temperance meetings, and there were as many pubs as ever, although they looked more comfortable and not as full as he remembered. It seemed that official disapproval had shifted from drink to sex.

The Mile End Road was much busier than he recalled, full of cars and vans and clanging trams. And it all seemed smaller, and meaner. In fact he missed the turning to Tredegar Square completely and had to turn back to find Lichfield Street. It was raining heavily now. Rain trickled inside his collar. He felt cold and empty.

Everything had changed.

He hardly recognized where he was. Fred's Eel and Pie shop had gone. In its place was a bicycle shop. Even the name of the road had been changed.

Ben stared at the sign. All these years, his memory had been wrong. It wasn't called Lichfield Street after all.

Lichfield *Road*. It was called Lichfield Road! How could he have forgotten? And the houses seemed so much smaller than he remembered. The water standpipe where the kids had such fun and the housewives all got together for a chat, had gone; the focus of the street had been removed, and now it was just a long featureless row of little houses, indistinguishable from one another except by their brightly painted doors. He walked along to number 35 and looked at the dark windows. Strange curtains hung in them; it was just someone's house. Shivering, he pulled his collar tight against his neck and walked down to the Lord Tredegar.

And he was there, a face from the past.

'It was so easy!' Vic bragged. 'His wife was lovely. She called me. She came to me. She told me everything.'

The poor girl, Ria thought as they walked down towards the Tooke Arms. A thin drizzle blew into her face on the wind and she lowered her head.

'Dead easy,' Vic said. 'And of course Smythe's an old friend of mine from the war. Eats out of my hand.'

'Nice,' Ria said automatically. She couldn't fight Vic, not even by a single word. She didn't flinch when he threw his arm around her shoulder.

'Real money. Real power,' Vic said. 'Selfridge would have bought the dump up for the pleasure of closing it down. But I like to look at it. I like to think about him. You know who—'

'I know!'

'I'll kill him for you for sure,' Vic grinned. 'He'll do it for me, you'll see. He isn't a real man. He can't fight me. What with? Nothing.'

They walked in silence for a way.

Then Ria asked: 'What's his wife's name?'

'Vane. Why?'

'I feel so sorry for her,' Ria murmured.

'Don't. She's one of us.'

'One of you.'

571

Vic laughed and rattled the doors of the Tooke Arms. 'Open up!'

Ben closed the door of the Lord Tredegar softly behind him. Peter Pungle had not changed at all. Ben recognized him immediately.

Old Peter Pungle was sitting crouched motionless on a stool by the fire, his head down, nursing a half-pint of mild beer between his knees in his enormous, withered hands.

Ben stared at him. Peter Pungle was still alive. What a poor pathetic wreck of a man he was. His great face had lost its flesh and hung between his shoulders like emaciated planes of uncovered bone, as cruel as a modern painting. The years spent in Spitalfields Market proudly carrying crates of vegetables on his head had set his neck, fusing the bones, storing up this dreadful immobility for his old age. The scars and bruises of his boxing days, so long past, showed clearly now, and Ben never remembered seeing them so clearly before. The lives that they had lived broke through onto the faces of old people, and Ben saw revealed on Peter's face everything that Peter was.

There was no evil there.

Of course. He should have realized this truth before: Edith Rumney would never have lived with an evil man. Self-interest, pride, cunning, lust, greed, frustration, an aching vulnerability, were stamped on the features of this punch-drunk old man, but never evil, surely. Ben knew that Peter must have had reasons, motives for that vile thing he had done, but he could see he was just a failure, and always had been.

For a moment Ben felt there was something solid he could depend on, a rock in an uncertain world: Edith Rumney's goodness.

Yet he sold me to the Workhouse, Ben thought bleakly.

He knew he had to speak to Peter Pungle.

He searched back into his memory, remembering that marvellous, appalling day at Hampstead, and Peter getting drunk on stout. Ben went to the bar. 'A bottle of Mackeson, please.' He paid for it with almost the last of his money.

Then he sat down quietly on the stool opposite Peter. Without a word he held out the distinctive black bottle.

Peter's face didn't move, but his eye shone with a cunning light.

'Why me, sir?' he said. His voice was almost exactly the same; a little higher, a little drier.

Ben said: 'Don't you remember me?'

'No.'

'You should, Peter.'

'I don't drink Mackeson nowadays anyway,' Peter said, jerking back his glass. 'My belly's gone. No, guv'nor,' he added indifferently, 'I don't remember you. Should I? Who are you?'

Ben said: 'I am the little boy you sold into the Workhouse.'

Peter stared into the fire. He showed no other reaction. Ben was sure that his brain was wrecked, that his life was just a punch-drunk haze. Then he saw tears trickling out of the corner of Peter's right eye.

Peter whispered: 'Don't hit me, guv'nor.'

'I won't,' Ben said.

'I thought you were dead,' Peter quavered. 'You died at the Fever Hospital. I never got away from you.'

Ben said gently: 'You're thinking of someone else.' He couldn't hate this senile old man.

'It was you all right,' Peter said. 'Benjamin.'

Ben stared. 'Yes, that is my name.'

'Doctor Benjamin, damn you.'

Ben felt a lump rise in his throat. He wanted to know everything. *Is this where my name comes from?* he wondered. He said: 'Can you tell me about him?'

'Him? Just a photograph. He died long before you were born. Edith loved him. I'll have that drink now.'

Ben had to know, had to see back into the dark he came out of, perhaps a little of himself would be revealed there. 'Do you know where this photograph is?'

Peter wiped his eye. 'Photograph? No. What's it to you?'

Ben said: 'I am Ben London, who you sold into the Workhouse. You dragged me screaming through the fog. London fog. Don't you remember?'

No reaction. Ben waited. Then he said: 'Why did you do it, Peter! *How* could you do it?'

Peter said simply: 'For love.'

That was the last answer that Ben had expected. He had not thought that there could be any justification at all for such a bestial act to a child; certainly not love.

Peter's cold, bony hand closed slowly round the Mackeson bottle and lifted it from Ben's fingers.

'For love, of course,' repeated Peter. 'She was lovely. I'd do anything for her.' He crouched forward towards Ben a little, his good eye flickering eagerly. 'You knew her. Mrs Kent. Theodora Kent. What a woman,' he cackled.

Ben shook his head. 'She lived near us in the road, didn't she?'

Peter roared with laughter. 'She ran the brothel next door, boy!'

And I never knew, Ben thought. *We were so innocent, Edith and I. We never knew.* He remembered Mrs Kent vaguely; her commanding looks, the crazed lines breaking through her skin, her slow, experienced eyes.

He demanded: 'You loved that woman?'

'I loved her all right, my young sir,' said Peter, swigging from the mouth of the bottle. 'There was no satisfying her. But she couldn't have a little boy running around the place, could she?'

Ben closed his eyes. So there it was, the reason for it all.

'But I didn't sell you, believe me!' said Peter righteously. 'Wouldn't have got anything for you anyway,' he added.

'Go on.'

'Well,' confided Peter, 'the God's truth is, I had to *pay* Bill Madeley to take you. I had to give up my last ten sovereigns from what Edith left, you ungrateful little bastard. All of it. The stupid cow had sold her house to the bank to get money to feed you, so when she died, I got evicted. You owe me,' he accused. Then he stretched the right side of his mouth into a grin and reached across, felt the sleeve of Ben's overcoat between finger and thumb. 'Looks like you done pretty well in life. I knew you would, sir. The bastards always do best in this world.' His eye flashed with vindictiveness.

'Did you marry Mrs Kent?'

Peter looked down. He swung his head stiffly from side to side: Ben could hear the vertebra clicking in his spine.

'She took everything I had,' Peter confessed. His eye filled with tears again and the corner of his mouth twitched up and down. 'When she'd had everything, and I'd lost my job, and she'd had her fill of me and sucked me dry, she threw me out. Threw me out, sir!'

His lips wriggled and he gave a quivering sob.

Ben looked at him sadly. No love, only lust, and poor Peter had never even realized the difference, never known love. Half of him felt sorry for Peter, the other half could have killed him mercilessly for what he had done.

'I felt guilty about you, guv'nor, course I did,' said Peter, eyeing Ben's overcoat.

'You didn't do anything about it.'

'Only because I had my own life to live,' Peter said. 'You never did understand, did you? No, you never cared about old Peter Pungle. You always hated me, you never called me Dad. I've got my needs, you know. Oh, I've managed, but it's not been easy.' He patted his pocket. 'Spare us a few bob, would you?' he said, holding out his hand.

'I wouldn't spare you the time of day,' Ben said.

'What?'

Ben said: 'You're contemptible.'

Peter didn't understand. 'Go on, just a bob or two. You won't miss it.'

Ben stood up and walked away. He opened the door, then stood there, staring out at the sheeting rain.

He went back to Peter Pungle, dug his hand into his pocket and took out all the money he had. He dropped it into Peter's outstretched palm.

'I never want to see you again,' he said.

As he went back to the door turning up his collar, he heard the chink as Peter examined the denomination of the coins, then his low voice:

'Ungrateful bastard.'

575

Peter stared at the bottle of Mackeson in his hand, wondering where it had come from. Edith's boy, that was right, he remembered. Old Peter Pungle, only worth a few coppers and sprowsie sixpences! He remembered the heavy trunk stored under his bed with those old things in, useless old things, hadn't looked at them for years, worthless. But the ungrateful bastard would love to get his hands on them, no doubt. There was Edith's old rubbish. He remembered a navy blue cape. And there was an old teddy-bear with only one eye and the stuffing leaking out of his ears, and around his neck a red felt collar with his name sewn around it: Mr Benjamin.

Ben walked. The rain pelted him from his right: he was walking south. A road cut across ahead of him and he could go no further: this was Poplar High Street. On the far side rose black walls, streaming with wet, and he saw a few bent-backed old men trying to shelter from the rain beneath them.

Ben was looking at the Workhouse.

Somewhere not far from here was an alleyway where a girl called Ria Price had seen him, followed him, freed him, loved him, betrayed him.

Near here was a family who had taken him in.

He remembered Esther's warmth; her love.

He went down the cobbles between the Workhouse and the Dead House.

The dock opened up ahead of him, the waters grey and rainswept.

He walked down across the railway and crossed the lock, jumping across the gap between the gates, the wind pushing at him, the water roaring below.

He turned down West Ferry Road and walked as far as Mary Walker's shop. All changed – slim, short, latest styles in the window now.

He entered the Warren.

The flowers were gone. No children played in the cold shadows.

No canaries twittered from cages in the dark doorways.

The decaying walls leaned together close above his head, held up with rotting wooden beams across the dripping, deserted lanes. The whole area must be under a condemned order, but as he walked he realized that there were still a few people living in these hovels.

Ben looked around him. It was such a labyrinth of alleys and courts that he could no longer identify the way to Esther's house. As he stood, uncertain of his direction, a horrid-looking woman stared at him and then waddled towards him, followed by several crouching, barefoot children; as he had been once. He felt moved by a terrible sympathy. The woman had broad hips and a diseased face.

She held out a trembling hand. Three of her fingers were missing.

'Ben?' she said. 'Ben London?'

She knew him.

He realized that he was looking at the girl called Ann. She pushed back the hair out of her eyes and proudly showed him her mutilated hand. 'Lost 'em in the ammunition factory. Mercury fulminate. Flash. Gone. Don't suppose you're staying here? Why don't you come in with me?' One of her smaller children tried to push forward and she clouted him round the head, then smiled desperately again.

Ben asked: 'Where's Esther?'

Ben walked along Havannah Street. The rain had eased off and the pale overcast glowed with a clear early afternoon light. Water gurgled cheerfully in the gutters and down-pipes, and doors slammed as the children came out to play, swarming around him joyously.

There was no white tourer anywhere in the street.

Ben found the number that Ann had given him and knocked.

The door opened and Esther stood there.

'Hallo, Mum,' Ben said, as he always had called her, as if the years had not passed.

She had hardly changed. There was a little more on the bust and hips, white in the hair, red on the cheeks, but the new clothes more than made up for that. Ben smiled. 'Hallo, Mum.' He didn't need to say anything more. Neither did she. She was examining him too: the good quality overcoat, his muddy but beautifully made Larsen shoes, his diamond tiepin, his bright, sad eyes.

Esther took his hand. She looked at him, smiling and crying.

'I always dreamed you'd come back one day! I knew you would!'

Then she embraced him. She spoke in a muffled voice, her face squeezed against his lapel.

'Oh Ben, Ben. Ria said you were married. Come in. It's lovely to see you. Lovely.'

She let him go for a moment, then took his hand and tugged him down the hall towards the living room, showed him in with a gesture that displayed the carpet and curtains, and the nice chintzy furniture. 'Home sweet home, be it ever so humble.'

'It's lovely,' he said. It was; it was obviously a home.

'Ria said you were doing ever so well. She was very happy for you.'

Ben shrugged. 'I don't have two pennies to rub together now.'

'Money isn't everything,' said Esther quickly. 'I'm sorry Vic and Nigel aren't here, they're usually down in the bar of the Tooke Arms at lunchtime and evenings with Ria. Well, it gets her out of the house. And little Will's at school of course. Tom's fine. Dear, you've missed everybody. I'll get you a nice hot cup of tea. Sit down here, do.'

Instead, Ben followed her bustling form into the kitchen and eased himself down onto one of the hoop-backed wooden chairs at the table. Esther put the kettle on. Thank God she'd cleaned the place this morning, she thought.

'Ria said that you had married such a beautiful girl?'

'Beautiful outside,' Ben said.

'I am so sorry.' Esther spooned tea into the pot. 'Truly, Ria did hope that you would be happy.'

'She didn't help at my wedding,' said Ben mildly.

'She didn't know!' Esther turned tragic eyes on him. 'It

was Vic's doing. He must have thought it would be a nice treat for her. Ria was dreadfully upset.'

Ben hadn't thought of it that way. Yes; she had cried.

'She's been so sad,' said Esther pathetically. 'She loved you.' She wrung her hands. 'She loves you!'

'She betrayed me,' Ben said.

So that was it. 'No, it wasn't Ria!' said Esther. 'Oh Lord, have you thought that all these years? No – it was old Mr Blumenthall who told Vic where to find you!'

The kettle began to whistle. Esther shouted over the noise: 'Ria tried to stop him! She ran and ran! She was in an awful state!'

Ben thought about the truth of what Esther had said.

He said: 'Does Ria love me? I loved Ria. Always. But . . .' His voice trailed off.

'She's always loved you,' Esther said quietly. 'Oh, Ben, Ria's all girl. She can't live without a man, but she has a deep and tender heart, and she is so easy to hurt that she must live hiding it deeply inside herself, or she would scream. And you know it, don't you, Ben?'

That was the truth.

'I know.'

'And Ria knows. A woman's heart is full of secrets. She's never looked at another man, Ben.'

'I thought she betrayed me,' Ben said numbly. 'She tried to save me.'

'She was not strong enough alone. Who is? Well, no use crying over spilt milk!' Esther stirred the tea. 'Vic does look after her, I must admit, he's so kind, but he doesn't always seem to know what she wants in my opinion, and he is a touch jealous sometimes,' she smiled confidingly.

Ben saw it.

Esther would not see: she was blind, wilfully blind, hanging on to her proud, cheery smile. Her children and her home were everything in the world to her. She would endure blindness, humiliation, exploitation, ingratitude, whatever she had to, to keep her family. Whatever happened, she would keep her proud, cheerful smile. Esther knew her duty. She would endure.

But Ben remembered the very first words Vic Price had ever spoken to him. He had taken them lightly; now he took them literally.

This is Ria. She's my sister. I love her.

Ben understood.

'I've been so worried about her lately,' Esther prattled. 'I don't think that Vic knows her as well as he thinks he does. She's been awfully meek and it's not like her. I do hope he hasn't hurt her. He can be — but I'm not saying anything against him, mind — he *can* be just a touch violent on occasions. Not that he would be!' She found some cups and saucers, poured out the tea, added the milk. 'Some people say horrible things about him. He does treat Ria well, though. I mean, while she's got no young man interested in walking out with her, he does look after her. Buys her drinks. They're down at the Tooke Arms every evening,' she said proudly. Then her back slumped. 'But she's so meek, Ben, and so sad.'

This is Ria. She's my sister. I love her.

Ben drank his tea.

'Love?' he said.

I'm Vic Price. Remember me.

He did not intend to forget Vic Price.

He borrowed the money for his bus fare off Esther, because he did not have time now to walk back to Bunhill Row. Colleen was putting the finishing touches to the *crêpe Georgette* dress when she heard his footsteps tapping rapidly up the stairs.

'You're going to do it,' she said as soon as she opened the door. And she sensed more than that. The spring had returned to Ben's walk, and the life had grown back into his eyes.

'I am,' Ben said.

'Praise be to heaven. I knew you were a fighter.' Colleen stood aside. She loved it when a man stood up for himself against the world, even if he lost. Win or lose, it didn't matter, in her opinion. It was the fighting that was the thing.

'In more ways than you think,' Ben told her.

'The fight is back in your eyes,' she said eagerly. Then she saw that there was more.

He laughed and picked up the slim brown package from the corner.

He said: 'Ria did not betray me.'

Colleen felt fear close around her heart.

'Ben,' she said, following him around the room, 'it's only money. Fight him only with money. The picture will give that to you. Go no further, I beg you. It's not a fight to the death.'

She watched his face as he slipped Sir Ozwald's signed receipt into his pocket.

'There is only one thing worse than winning,' Ben said.

She saw at once it was not losing he meant. The muscles stood out along his jaw, but his movements were very gentle. She saw ruthless lines in his face, but now felt no fear. She sensed the tension rising within him, but her heart warmed to him. She had to know. Her hands fluttered on his shoulders. 'What is worse than losing?'

Ben said: 'Never to have loved at all.'

Chapter Twenty

1

Saturday had been a perfect spring day.

All day, the sky was a peerless, perfect china blue above the dark rooftops of London.

All day, the phone that he had installed in Colleen's sitting room rang unanswered.

Sparrows and thrushes trilled their song invisibly down there amongst the unfolding leaves of the trees that lined the busy street.

Ben sat silently in the window.

He stared out.

Above the shining roofs of the traffic, dark buildings rose, trailing shadows that were so deep the people who walked into them seemed to disappear.

Colleen worked on her sewing, glancing at him nervously. He was dressed in black trousers and a pure white shirt of finest Egyptian cotton. His back against one side of the window, his gold watch glowing on his wrist, resting one gleaming black shoe on the ledge. How elegant he looked against the light, she thought.

She wished he would answer that telephone . . . How could a man have the strength not to answer a telephone that jangled and rang all the day long, hour after hour?

At midday he saw the first cheerful summer dresses and the first young, laughing girls, but it was for only an hour.

Colleen cut corned beef sandwiches for lunch. The phone rang again.

'But it might be important!' Colleen said at last.

He shook his head.

The sun swung round, the shadows shifted.

'You've been on that telephone all week,' Colleen begged, 'you've virtually run the Emporium from here. Why won't you answer it now?'

'Don't worry,' he smiled.

His smile did not reassure her nowadays. 'I'm terrified!' she confessed, looking at the leather attaché case beneath his knee.

'Trust me,' Ben said at last. 'When you're most frightened what I might do, trust me.'

'But I'm frightened for *you*.'

'Then trust me most.'

'I do,' she said.

He turned from her and watched from the window.

Slowly, the traffic cleared.

Towards evening the football crowds came out.

The traffic began to build up again.

Ben got down from the window. 'I'll have a bath,' he said, undoing his gold cuff-links.

She heard the geyser running the hot water; she went to lay Ben's clothes out on his bed but Sam was sleeping there, his great ginger head curled round on his paws, watching her, so she hung them over the dresser.

'Look after him tonight, Sam,' she said.

When Ben came down the uniformed chauffeur held open the car door and saluted.

'Sorry I'm late, sir. The traffic was terrible.'

'All right, Simmonds,' Ben said. 'You know where to go, don't you?'

'I know my orders, sir.'

Ben sat alone in the back of the Rolls-Royce with his mirror-polished Larsen shoes sunk into the deep grey pile of the rug which covered the floor.

He leaned back into the gentle support of the soft leather seat, one hand resting lightly on his thigh over the finely worked grey pinstripe of the elegant dark business suit he wore. His other hand lay across the pigskin Vuitton attaché case which bulged on the seat beside him.

In front, beyond the glass, with Sam sitting up next to him, the chauffeur sat out in the open air, threading the long car through the evening traffic. Ben noticed that he often turned off the main thoroughfares and detoured smoothly through the back streets, predicting some traffic jam ahead and expertly avoiding it.

This was how it was to be rich.

The engine sighed more deeply and the Rolls-Royce ascended Tower Hill without Ben feeling any movement or effort, passing in a flashing moment the little green square where he had sat with Ria. He remembered it as clearly as if it was yesterday, still tragic and joyous: too intense in him for gentle nostalgia.

The Tower passed by on his right, silhouetted darkly against the blue glare of the river in the setting sun.

He glimpsed the intricate web of St Katherine's Dock outlined in shining water.

It had been so dark then.

Now his Rolls-Royce entered the East End, the big tyres rumbling softly over the cobbles down Cable Street. Somewhere along here, he knew, were the eating rooms where he had bought a bacon sandwich and broken it in half to share it with Ria, and they had walked along here eating it together. He remembered how they had burnt their tongues, how they had laughed.

Now there was the Old Bull and Bush pub ahead, standing like a malevolent island of dark red terracotta and sooty stone almost in the middle of the road, its frosted windows like blind white eyes gazing back towards the West End.

The Rolls-Royce swung down West Ferry Road.

Ben leaned forward. On his right was Batson's Wharf, where he had shouted at the man with the silver shiv sticking out between his fingers, and Ria had screamed, thinking that Ben would be killed too.

Kosky's fish and chip shop passed outside, people already queueing at the stainless steel counters for their supper. Their grimy faces swung, hearing the murmur of the engine, their eyes following the black limousine down the road.

Ben said: 'Slow down, please.'

The car whispered past the end of Havannah Street.

There was the Tooke Arms.

'Stop here.'

The Rolls-Royce pulled into the kerb.

Ben waited.

The chauffeur walked around the back of the car and opened the door for him.

Ben stepped down. He paused for a further moment, the Vuitton hanging heavily from his left hand.

The Tooke Arms was just as he remembered, typical of East End pubs, cracked beige tiling below the windows, dark red wooden pillars beside them, a few florid decorations carved above them. The glass was too dirty to see through.

'Stay here.'

'Yes, sir.'

Ben crossed the pavement and pushed through the swing doors into the pub.

Ria had spent the worst week of her life. When Esther told her of Ben's visit, Ria honestly hadn't believed her, then she *had* believed her and cried because she had missed him; then she had laughed with relief that she had missed him, because she had behaved so dreadfully that she couldn't bear the thought of enduring the look in his eyes she knew she deserved; then she cried again, because she dreamed of seeing him.

Could she ever explain to him?

She ran over her excuses and explanations in her mind, getting so tangled up that she hardly knew what to feel more: elation or guilt, joy or remorse, happiness or fear.

Esther said he would come back.

He had promised.

Ria jumped up at each and every knock on Esther's door. She rehearsed endlessly what she would say. She would put her hands together, she would stand by the fireplace, keep well away from him, not look at him directly. 'I know you must hate me,' she would say, then: 'I'm sorry, that's all! I'm sorry! Go away! Go away!'

But he did not come.

Well, all right, Ria sighed. She hadn't really expected it. It was a good thing, really.

And there was the terrible danger that Ben might have met Vic.

But he could have crept in the back way, she reasoned.

No, it was good that he had stayed away, she wept.

It saved her the problem of what to say! Saved her the humiliation of a long, stuttering, useless explanation . . .

Sometimes, lying in bed with her hands under her head, staring up at the dark ceiling, she dreamed that there was a simple way, that he would simply know everything without words, that she could somehow communicate herself to him without a word of speech. He would feel her emotions, everything she felt.

That was the stuff of beautiful dreams, not real life: real life would be Vic's footsteps thudding upstairs to take her down to the Tooke Arms this evening, as usual.

But Ben had *promised* he would come.

She trusted Ben's promise. She lived in hope and fear. What would she say? she wondered. *How?* she dreamed.

That night, as always, Ria sat at the bar wearing the dull old dress Vic had chosen for her, with a smile plastered on her face, as always. Hope and fear had gone. Secretly, she had gambled everything. Inside herself all was ecstasy and terror.

Ben stood with the immaculate Vuitton case clenched in his left hand, brushing against his left thigh. His right arm also hung by his side. He heard the door closing itself behind him, and then the click of the latch.

It was too hot in the Tooke Arms, and too much cigarette smoke drifted in a blue haze down the deep but narrow room. There were perhaps a dozen people in all, he noticed, quietly drinking and smoking.

He saw a lot of cheap red plush, dark wood, nicotine-yellowed wallpaper, and an open fire on his left. Ahead of him was the bar, all shining brass and polished wood, racks of glasses, and a row of tall stools spaced along the counter.

Three were occupied.

Vic Price was sitting with his back to the fire, one elbow resting casually on the bar counter, his foot hooked over the brass rail that joined the legs of Ria's stool beside him. His outstretched hand was laid on Ria's shoulder and his mouth was open, laughing some joke into Ria's face.

Ria had her back to Ben and he could only see the back of her head, her hanging yellow hair. She wore an ugly blue-black dress, such as a much older woman might have worn ten years ago, with brown shoes. Then Ben saw her face reflected in the mirror above the bar: Esther had been right about Ria's expression, too. There was a meekness there that suited her as little as the clothes she wore. Vic had broken her spirit.

There was no doubt about it.

Her gorgeous eyes were dull above her garish, painted smile.

Ben saw Nigel standing tall and relaxed against the bar on the other side of Ria, also leaning on his elbow, his right hand curled protectively around his left, his jagged features hollowed by the dull interior light. His head was thrown back. He too was laughing at Vic's joke.

None of them had seen him.

Then Ben saw the mask of Ria's face turn up to the mirror behind the bar. It was such an indifferent, routine glance that he knew she looked in the mirror so often that she had given up hope, because she never saw anything there, only herself. She almost looked away again.

Then he knew that she saw him, because her gaze fixed, but for a moment her eyes were blank. She no longer believed in herself, he saw. She had hidden herself deep; it was how she coped. She survived by living her life inside her head.

Ben smiled at her in the mirror. Now Ria's body went rigid with shock as she recognized him.

He saw her eyes light up with life – and fear.

'Ben!' she cried.

Nigel stopped laughing.

Vic leaned forward into Ria's shoulder, still laughing into her face, only hearing his own laughter.

'Vic!' Nigel said in a high voice.

Vic stopped laughing. He looked out of the corners of his eyes. Slowly, he swung round on the stool.

Old Turner, the landlord, was polishing glasses behind the bar. He kept polishing automatically. The cloth made tiny squeaking sounds on the damp glass.

Vic did not move. He stared at Ben. The fire flickered.

'Workhouse Bastard,' Vic bragged suddenly. 'What have you come crawling to me for?'

'Ben, don't,' Ria said.

Nigel said in a terrified voice: 'Oh God, Vic, he's got a gun.'

Vic showed no fear, no doubt, no loss. He slid down from the bar stool. 'He can't touch me.'

Ria begged: 'Ben – don't do anything.'

Ben walked three paces forward. Nigel took a nervous step, but Ben held up his finger.

'He hasn't got a gun!' Vic said. 'He hasn't got the guts for one. Get on with it.'

But Nigel, incredibly, stopped, staring at Ben's upraised finger. Did he *know?* Nigel cradled his hurt elbow indecisively, snapping his thumb and forefinger impotently like a crab's claw.

'Ria,' he said, backing to the bar, 'tell him to go away.'

'Tell him yourself,' Ria sparked. She could feel her eyes shine. She no longer felt how awful she looked in this dumpy blue-black dress.

Vic glanced at her, then pushed past her. She put her hand on his elbow. He peeled back her fingers viciously.

'Ow, Vic!'

'I've got you!' Vic swore at Ben, ignoring her. 'I made you eat my shit. Your wife loves me, I take her out for tea at the Ritz. I've got your shop. I'm living in your head all the time. You hate me, you can't forget me. Can't get me out of your mind.' With his black eyes glittering, grinning, he held up his great red hands and squeezed them shut. 'I am your life.'

Ria creased up her face with humiliation. She felt every barb of Vic's cruelty embedded in her own flesh.

She looked at Ben with infinite sympathy in her eyes. *Why? Why come here to punish yourself in front of me?*

Ben walked forward.

Vic grinned at him confidently. He laughed, exhaling a stinking gust into Ben's face.

Ben walked straight past him.

Vic stared at his back, his hands flexing.

Ben stood at the bar. He opened the locks with a flick of his thumbs and emptied the Vuitton case across the counter. Money spilled out in a stream of paper bundles, sprayed across the shining wood, knocked the glasses aside, piled up, and kept on coming.

A few bundles tumbled off the edge, fell to the floor. Vic caught one automatically. He flicked his thumb down the edges.

'Christ!' he said.

Ben closed the empty case.

'Count it,' he said. He felt Ria's knee against his hip, warning: Nigel was creeping round the side.

But Vic ordered: 'You heard him. Count them, Nigel.'

Vic stared at Ben while Nigel counted, his hand squeezing and flexing possessively on Ria's shoulder.

Ria pulled her shoulder away. 'I'm not your property!'

Vic snarled, but Ben was between them. Ria rubbed her shoulder, trying to hide the fact that she was shaking like a leaf. She could feel Ben's amiability, how ruthless it was; his politeness, how intimidating it must be; yet none of it was against her, it was for her. She stood feeling the violence all around her and hating it. She wanted to lay her hands against his chest, to melt into him – and it could not happen. She knew that it could not. Ben's eyes neither wavered nor blinked. Ria cringed. Something dreadful had to happen. Vic and Ben were so close. Vic looked from side to side. The violence in the air made her skin tighten with fear.

Nigel's voice droned on, counting.

Ria imagined murder. Vic shifted from one foot to the other.

Blood and death: it was almost close enough to touch. She could feel it. Her teeth began to chatter.

Still Nigel counted.

Vic tried to grin. 'All right, I believe you, old mate, it's fifteen thousand quid. Where did a Workhouse Bastard like you get his hands on that?'

Ben watched him, obviously still waiting for Nigel to finish counting, and the seconds stretched out longer and longer until Vic looked away.

Nigel finished.

'That's it exactly. I'm afraid it's all there, every last penny,' he said, then gave an embarrassed cough between his thumb and forefinger.

Then Vic gave a jolly smile and slapped his hands together. He grinned at Ben over Ria's head. 'No hard feelings, chum?'

Ria forced her knuckles between her teeth.

'You can have your damned Emporium,' Vic said. 'We'll call it a draw this time.'

Yes, Ria tried to say, *yes, yes, that's a fair offer, get out of here, get out of here, Ben, get out of here quick!*

He did not move.

'Ben!' she whispered.

Then she understood.

A draw was not enough for him, she realized, as her excitement rose.

Vic promised in a grinning, deadly voice: 'I won't forget this, bastard.'

Ria screamed.

Ben raised his clenched fist and punched Vic. Vic's cheeks puffed out and the teeth came splattering out of his mouth like brown pegs. He tumbled backwards and fell on his knees by the fire.

'I'm Ben London,' Ben told Vic quietly. 'Remember me.'

Ria gave a clap of excitement and jumped up on her toes.

Vic groaned.

590

Ben enclosed Ria's hand in his own, as if knowing what she would do.

Ria drew back her foot to give Vic another good wallop while he was down. Ben lifted her up easily, then backed to the door and put her down, holding on to her with a gentle grip.

'Let me!' she cried.

He said: 'Not now.'

Nigel threw himself on his knees beside Vic. 'Ria,' he called over his shoulder, 'where are you going? Vic needs you.'

'Well he's not going to have me!' shouted Ria. 'I'm not his. I'm me!' She looked up. 'He doesn't own me, does he, Ben?'

'You're free,' Ben said.

Ria shouted defiantly: 'Then I'm mine!'

Vic crawled towards her. His face was a mask of fear.

Ben reached back and opened the door behind him, then pulled Ria outside.

It was dark; street lights glittered.

Ria asked: 'What's happened?'

Ben replied: 'The best possible thing in the world.'

He took her arm and they crossed the pavement towards the Rolls-Royce. The car door was already open. The chauffeur saluted. Ria looked back. 'But what's happened to Vic?'

Ben said: 'The worst.'

She stared up at him. The street lamp threw a harsh light down Ben's face and for a moment his nose trailed a black spike of shadow that rippled over his lips, then curved down his chin, and his eyes were dark sockets – then he smiled, and the mask of shadow disappeared as if it had never been.

Ria gave him her hand. He enclosed it gently and helped her inside the back of the Rolls-Royce, then turned.

The pub doors rattled open.

Vic dragged himself down the step and rolled outside. He stared at Ben, then past him into the car, seeing Ria's slim figure gracefully outlined by the interior lights. His face contorted.

'Ria!'

She ignored him.

He raised himself on his knuckles. 'Ria! No! No! No!'

'Get into the car, Ben,' Ria begged.

Vic dragged himself across the pavement on his fists. His mouth uttered shapeless cries: No . . . No . . . Ria . . . You can't . . . He gave a great howling scream of pure hatred: *'You can't!'*

Ben turned to Ria. 'It's up to you.'

'You can't!' shrieked Vic.

'I can!' she shouted through the car window, 'I will!'

Ben climbed after her into the Rolls-Royce, let Simmonds close the door with a muffled thump behind him, and tapped on the partition when he was in his place.

'You may drive on when you are ready, Simmonds,' he said calmly down the speaking-tube, then replaced the cover.

The car drew away. The street lights rotated their shadows around them.

'How can you be so calm?' wondered Ria.

He began to laugh.

'Because I am happy,' he said. 'This time, love wins.'

She gasped: 'Do you truly love me?'

'I always have,' he told her, 'ever since I knew the truth.'

Now, in the peace and calm, they looked at one another.

How did you survive?

They felt the Rolls-Royce swinging smoothly through the dark London streets. Thick grey drapes cloaked the limousine's windows and the glass partition. A yellow light glowed steadily between them in the ceiling.

They told each other everything.

Ben leaned forward and opened the walnut cabinet, withdrew a bottle of champagne from the ice-bucket.

Ria said: 'Where?'

'Have you ever seen the sea?' He opened the champagne with an expert flick of his thumbs.

'Brighton? We'll have a spree!' chuckled Ria. 'Bit more comfortable than last time!'

She began to weep. He handed her his handkerchief. 'Sorry,' she said.

'That's all right, just wring it out before you give it back.'

She roared with laughter. He filled her glass and she drained it with a theatrical flourish. She leaned back luxuriously into the seat. 'It's good to feel good,' she said, holding out her glass between her finger and thumb on the stem. 'I've always dreamed of seeing the sea.'

'With us dreams come true, Ria.'

'For tonight, anyway. You make me feel like a proper Cinderella!'

He shook his head seriously. 'This car doesn't turn into a pumpkin at midnight. I'll never let you down, Ria.'

'Promise?'

'Yes.'

'Do you forgive me?'

'Yes.'

She began to cry again. 'I don't know whether I'm coming or going tonight. You know I was on the stage, plain old Ria Price? Wotcher, Ria! I was a queen, Ben, I gave them everything I had, and they loved me. What girl could ask for more? Now I must look a sight,' she sobbed.

'You're a very pretty sight.'

'No, don't, I know I'm ugly.' This time he did not hand over his handkerchief, but leaned across and gently wiped the tears from her eyes with his fingertips.

'Anyone would look ugly in that dress,' he said. 'You look like Queen Victoria.'

'She had lots of children.'

'I do blame you for not telling me about my son,' he said. She put her hand on his.

He said: 'Tell me what he's like. Everything about him.'

Ria scratched thoughtfully at that tiny bump on her nose. 'I don't know,' she said. 'Who knows children?'

'But I *want* to know. Stop scratching your nose. Have you taught him to do that?'

'He gobbles his mashed potato just like you used to.'

'I hope he hasn't met any girls like you.'

'No, he's like his father, he doesn't like nice girls, he goes for the upper-class sort. Like your wife.' She held out her glass defiantly for more. 'Vane, isn't it?' Her voice broke up.

'I don't love her, Ria.'

'I feel so sorry for her. She never stood a chance. Some girls are born unlucky.'

'She got everything she worked for, everything she deserved.'

'I'd better keep this soaking handkerchief, hadn't I? Souvenir of Brighton.'

He said simply: 'She'll never let me go, Ria. She hates me. We're married and there will never be a divorce. Ever.'

'I understand that,' Ria said fiercely.

He felt momentarily lighter as the Rolls-Royce swooped smoothly downwards. They must be entering the Blackwall tunnel beneath the Thames. The car jerked from side to side: the tunnel changed direction sharply several times, designed by the Victorians for the sedate speed of horse-drawn vehicles. The first few times Ria kept her balance on her side of the seat, but the last corner threw her into his arms.

'Girls have dreams too,' Ria whispered. She felt the leather slipping softly against the back of her head as she slid down the seat-back. His arms took her between them, enclosing her, and as they slithered together to the floor she knew that her blonde hair was a shining fan slipping down the seat above her, and that her opal eyes, half-open, were sparkling and coming up full of life as it rose in her. He caressed her gently, sending hot shivers running through her, until she hardly felt the surfaces of her body at all; it was all feelings inside herself, all of her love for him. His caresses set her alight as if she was on fire; her throat, her knees, her toes, to the very top of her head, into her heart: she wanted to give herself to him as though she was life itself, and for him to know everything. His hands stroked: the vile blue-black dress the colour of a bruise slipped off her shoulders. She strained upwards towards him, dying to get rid of its heavy artificial folds, to slip into her natural skin. She felt it fall away . . . and heard his startled intake of breath. She saw the electric shimmer in his amazed eyes.

How did you survive?

'Only you will ever know,' she whispered, holding his head between her hands, staring up into his eyes. 'All the time he thought he had me for his own, I defied him. Beneath, I was myself, I wore my Electric Blue. I was his prisoner, but my heart was free.'

His voice trembled. 'I love you.'

'It took me ages to restitch it. Every stitch a dream. My secret life. My secret—'

'What?'

'Love.'

She arched herself into his body and pulled his lips down onto hers, crushing his hard chest against her soft bosom as the electric blue silky folds slid down. Her naked arms curled above her head like swans' wings, pale curves brushing the velvety panelling on the doors, the smooth walnut, feeling the deep rug vibrating sensually under her shoulders. Her need burned her, her hands twined in his hair behind his head as he caressed her, splaying his fingers down her body to reach her melting groin. She upthrust to meet him, took him inside her and moved with him, crying out with ecstasy, and took his love, finally, with all her love.

The Rolls-Royce swept smoothly out of London into the curves and crests of the North Downs' range of chalk hills, then down across the flat Weald while they lay loving in the moving dark. His tongue explored the inner sides of her arms, beneath her breasts, the tingling nipples above, the inner slopes of her thighs, and the very centre of pleasure itself until she could bear it no longer, and took him again, twining her legs around him, her body writhing with ecstatic joy to the melting release.

'Pleasure,' she whispered in a voice that trembled like his, holding herself close to him, enfolding him. 'I thought it was just pain and duty.'

'Now you sound like Queen Victoria again.'

Then they were rising up into the South Downs, winding between the hills, the last barrier before the sea. He cuddled her sensually, rocking her with the movement of the limousine until her eyes flashed wildly, and her back arched.

'Ben, I love you! I'll always love you! As long as I live!'

Who was the lady?

Nice for them to draw the curtains and have a nap; all right for some, Bert Simmonds grumbled to the big ginger dog beside him. Personally Bert preferred small dogs, they were more controllable, a couple of kicks with the boot brought them into line, but this one looked like it might take your head off with one bite. 'Sit, boy,' Bert said nervously.

It was long before dawn. Bert Simmonds was chilly, but one thing was bloody marvellous: there was no other traffic around at this early hour to disturb him. He reckoned that more than half his life had been spent sitting in traffic jams. Since the partition curtains were drawn and he could not be seen Bert took one hand from the steering-wheel, took off his peaked cap, let the slipstream blow his hair.

He saw his reflection in the windscreen: a small white-haired man in the proud uniform that signified his trade, the buttons tight over his pot belly. Nowadays vehicles had foot pedals instead of the old hand brakes, which played merry hell with the varicose veins in his legs.

'Sit, boy!' he said.

Mr London was a born aristocrat. Bert could sniff out the New Rich – the bastards who had done well out of the Great War – from a mile off, but that Mr London had obviously been born to it: he had that natural way with him.

Bert liked working for the Emporium. He'd driven for the Great Central Railway for a few years, then, what with all the Undergrounds opening up and arrival of big motor-lorries, the Railway didn't need cart drivers any more. Hawk, his cousin, had got him in at the Emporium, and he'd driven deliveries until the war. When Mr Leibig took the Roller out of mothballs on Armistice Day, Bert had been the natural choice for promotion. No one knew London better than Bert.

'Sit, boy!'

Bert quickly slipped his hat back on as Mr London drew the curtains. They were descending the last hill, and beyond the Royal Pavilion the sea stretched out as flat and grey as lead towards France.

Bert turned the car left past the tram terminus at the Aquarium and let the Rolls-Royce idle very slowly along Madeira Walk. He hadn't day-tripped Albert and William here since twenty years ago or more and he was disappointed to see that the Daddy Long-legs sea-going railway had been shut up. The Great War had done more than kill a lot of young men: it had broken something in the nation's heart. Bert remembered the old, glorious days before motor-cars and aeroplanes. There was no romance nowadays; young people didn't know what they were missing.

He turned the car round and stopped. Mr London got out and that huge horrible dog jumped out over the door and bounded off down the beach, barking. Bert watched with interest to see if the lady would get out.

My God, she did, and she was no lady.

This was disgusting.

'Let's walk for a while, Ria,' Mr London said.

Bert was outraged. She had golden hair that she didn't even wear up properly – it fell in a loose, brilliant cloud around her shoulders. Her dress was a sheath of shimmering blue that left no curve to the imagination, and he could even see the gorgeous patterns her legs made as she walked.

He put his hand on top of his head as a gust of wind from the sea nearly blew off his cap.

Ben and Ria walked hand in hand along the promenade with the low murmur of the Rolls-Royce's engine pacing slowly along the road behind them.

Past the Palace Pier they went down onto the beach and threw pebbles into the wavelets breaking there. Sam tried to catch them, galloping barking into the water and swimming bravely out after the skipping stones.

'We'll stay and have breakfast in the Grand Hotel,' Ben said.

He took her elbow, called Sam and they walked along the promenade again with Sam shaking the water off his fur and the Rolls-Royce murmuring behind them. Ria stopped. Her stomach was starving, but her heart ached terribly.

'No!' she said. 'No, Ben, it wouldn't work, would it?'

'Us?'

'Everything,' Ria said. She was determined not to cry. She smiled up at him.

He started to say something but she put her finger on his lips. 'You've got your wife, Ben. I won't be your mistress, you know. I mean, you know Ria – all or nothing!'

'But—'

'I'm Ria Price, Ben. I'm me. I'm a grown woman and I love you, I love you. I won't be number two to another woman.'

'Ria, I love you.'

'And you've got London Emporium back.'

'That doesn't stand between us,' he said desperately. 'I can't make anything of it without love. Without—'

'Don't say it!'

'You.'

'Don't kid yourself, you'll do it.' She forced herself to laugh. 'You terrify me and I love you. You make me go cold and hot at the same time. You've got it. I love you and I won't come between you—'

'Vane doesn't—'

'You and the Emporium, Ben! I won't risk getting crushed. Poor Ria from the East End with her cheap Cockney accent.'

'Where do you think I come from? Don't you ever talk about yourself like that!' he said furiously.

Her heart glowed, and she loved him so much. She straightened his collar. 'I've got my self-respect,' she said. 'I'm proud of who I am.'

'I'll show you,' he begged. He waved the Rolls-Royce alongside them.

'Ben, don't you understand? I don't want to see.'

'Take us to London Emporium, Simmonds,' Ben said.

They sat cuddling one another as the sun rose. The car flew, seventy, eighty miles per hour, trailing a long cloud of dust along the A23, and out in front they could see Sam's ears flapping and his tongue lolling out as he peered eagerly around the windscreen at the road unwinding ahead. Ria held on to Ben desperately.

He said: 'What's the matter?'

'The future.'

He laughed. She laughed too, with tears trickling from her eyes.

Piccadilly was deserted. The Rolls-Royce drew up outside the yellow canopies of London Emporium, and the engine stopped. Now they could hear the silence. Ben crossed the pavement jangling his keys and opened the doors.

Ria followed him inside.

He went to the lighting bank and pulled down the rows of brass switches. Ria stood on the top step watching light spread along the sales floor, illuminating the counters and the goods piled high, waiting for Monday. She knew what she was being offered: all this. But she didn't want all that, only him.

He said: 'I'm having the counters stripped back and the dark stain removed – they'll look fresh and new. All purchases will be wrapped in gold paper with London Emporium printed over in blue, I've got the orders out now. We'll have refrigerated displays in the food section, a restaurant and cloakrooms on the second floor . . .' He walked eagerly along the main aisle, then turned. Ria had not followed.

'You're going to make a big success of it,' she called from the top step. 'I can see that, plain as day. You're going to be richer than I can imagine, and everyone will adore you, Ben. You'll have a big house with servants, maybe even that mansion on St James's Park, remember? I'm sure you will.'

He held out his arms. 'Us,' he said.

'What's it going to do to you, Ben?'

He stood with his arms out below her, not understanding.

'This is it,' Ria said. 'This is victory. Winning. Everything. You've got it now, here, this moment. This is all you'll ever have. You can't have more than this, Ben. You're successful now. Success costs. Will it ruin you? Money has its price. Will you keep on paying it? Will I have to pay it for you, one day?'

'But I don't own the Emporium. It's in trust.'

'All,' Ria said, 'and nothing.'

'But I love you.'

'One bed, one breakfast, Ben. Not two beds. I won't be the second woman.'

'Ria, please, please, believe me—'

'I do!' She tried to explain: 'Here, inside here, when you aren't looking at me, sometimes I don't like the look in your eyes now. You haven't even asked about Will's future!' she sobbed.

'What do I have to say to you about our son?' he cried wildly. 'I think about him, I love him, I'll pay all bills—' He dropped his arms and turned away.

Ria said quietly: 'It's time I got back to Will. Suppose he woke up and found I wasn't there?'

Ben ran up the steps to her. Ria put four fingers across his lips.

'I'm not asking you to give up, Ben. But I know what a woman knows.'

'You're wrong.'

Smiling, she wiped her tears away with her wrists.

'About me,' he said, 'you're wrong.'

She embraced him tenderly.

'Please,' he said. 'At least let me go with you. Let me see him.'

'I usually let him sleep late on a Sunday . . . the poor little lad needs his sleep. He gets so tired at school.'

'Please.' He promised: 'I'll be as quiet as a mouse.'

He turned off the lights. The Emporium disappeared into the shadows.

'All right,' Ria said.

They sat in the back of the car with their arms around each other. Each mile took them closer to the moment when they would part. Now they entered the East End, another world.

The Rolls-Royce turned silently into Havannah Street.

'Stop here,' Ben ordered. He helped Ria out. 'Stay, Sam.' The air was fresh and clear. The church bells were chiming and no children were playing in the street on a Sunday.

'I'm going in,' Ben said. 'I promise I won't wake him.'

Ria opened the door and they went inside. Ben smelt bacon frying in the kitchen. Esther bustled around the table. She saw them in the hall, and her face turned into a picture of joy.

Ria winked, whispered *Sssh*, and tiptoed silently upstairs. She held open the door.

Ben crossed the bedroom through a mess of scattered toys and comics. He knelt soundlessly.

His son Will lay deeply asleep, flat on his back in bed with the sheets rucked around him. His hands were clasped thoughtfully over his chest. He had lovely red cheeks and long, dark eyelashes. He was bigger than Ben had thought: he touched his boy's face with the side of his finger. His skin felt very soft and warm, vital with coming life.

Ria watched them. *The chains of blood,* she thought. *We never escape them. I am my own prisoner.*

Ben turned to Ria. She put a bright smile on her face. 'Thank you,' he said.

Will murmured and turned over. He did not wake, and his breathing slowed as he slipped back into deep sleep.

Ria waited. *Will he stay, or will he go?*

Ben swung on his heel and walked from her small, warm bedroom.

Ria followed him downstairs. Esther had tactfully closed the kitchen door but they could still hear the tempting sizzle of bacon. He turned away and went out into the street.

Standing on the whitestoned step of her little house, a cheap shawl hauled around her shoulders, Ria called after him: 'Good luck, Ben.'

'Good luck?'

'With the Emporium.'

She watched him walk a few paces, then he stopped. He looked over his shoulder.

'Come with me, Ria.'

'No,' she said.

'Because—'

'No,' she said. '*Because* I love you. And I always will.'

Epilogue

It was winter. Ben had been to a very fine house on Prince Albert Road, between Primrose Hill and Regent's Park, to see a wine cellar he was considering purchasing on behalf of London Emporium. He walked a little way along the pavement, then decided to cut back through Regent's Park. As he crossed the road he could see that, despite the cold weather, to his left a lady was sitting on one of the park benches, dressed in navy blue. He noticed her because she sat motionless staring at the impressive houses beyond the railings, and her face was so striking. Her eyes glanced at him as he crossed between her and the houses, then followed him. The gate needed oiling and squeaked as he opened it and came into the park. He touched the brim of his hat in salutation of her attention, and walked on.

She didn't see where he came from. Suddenly he was there, a shadow crossing the road. She saw a well-dressed man with the sort of powerful build and rugged, sensitive features that would make any woman look at him twice. He wore no gloves and she could see that he had strong, fine hands. The gate squeaked as he opened it.

For a moment his eyes seemed to stare directly into her own, piercingly blue.

He touched the fingers of his left hand to the brim of his hat, and walked on.

She stared after him.

She put her hand to her mouth.

He walked swiftly down past the boating lake.

She gathered up her handbag and umbrella and followed him. People came between them. She pushed past them and started to run.

She saw him again as he crossed the south side of the Outer Circle, leaving the park by York Gate. She ran after him, the breath gasping in her throat, her handbag jolting against her hip.

He walked ahead of her down Marylebone High Street, crossed between the shops, then disappeared. She looked around her.

She had been here before. These streets were familiar to her. Men swarmed around her.

She turned down Marylebone Lane and ran.

There he was, waiting with a group of other people to cross busy Oxford Street. She could see the left side of his face as he waited. She tried to push through to him. Elbows jostled her. A gap came in the traffic and he crossed ahead of her, and she saw him turn down New Bond Street. She tried to run after him, but a black-whiskered man with a barrow got in her way, she nearly fell over it.

'*Nice 'n' hot, piping hot, who'll buy my nice hot chestnuts?*'

She dodged around him and ran between the traffic down New Bond Street. It was hardly moving; some delay. There he was. She glimpsed the left side of his face as he crossed Grafton Street into Old Bond Street. She had nearly caught up with him now, he was walking on her right. She couldn't *see*. She pressed the side of her left fist against her mouth.

She swerved around a street cleaner, pushed past a fat woman window-shopping beneath the yellow canopies of London Emporium, and came up behind him. He turned to the right to go into the shop.

The Head Doorman stood to attention and saluted. 'Good morning, Mr London, sir!'

He backed to the door and opened it proudly.

The tall man paused for a moment. She thought: *Turn your head to the right, go on, please! Please!*

He turned his head slightly. 'Thank you, Hawk.'

Beneath his right ear, almost hidden in his hair, was a tiny red birthmark in the shape of a four-leafed clover.

Lisa gasped.

She had seen her son.

THE FIVE FAMILIES
Ben London's Family Tree

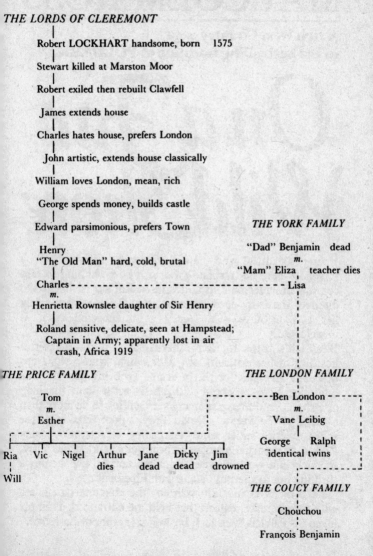

THE LORDS OF CLEREMONT

Robert LOCKHART handsome, born   1575
|
Stewart killed at Marston Moor
|
Robert exiled then rebuilt Clawfell
|
James extends house
|
Charles hates house, prefers London
|
John artistic, extends house classically
|
William loves London, mean, rich
|
George spends money, builds castle
|
Edward parsimonious, prefers Town
|
Henry
"The Old Man" hard, cold, brutal
|
Charles - Lisa
m.
Henrietta Rownslee daughter of Sir Henry
|
Roland sensitive, delicate, seen at Hampstead;
Captain in Army; apparently lost in air
crash, Africa 1919

THE YORK FAMILY

"Dad" Benjamin   dead
m.
"Mam" Eliza   teacher dies

THE PRICE FAMILY

Tom
m.
Esther

Ria   Vic   Nigel   Arthur   Jane   Dicky   Jim
                       dies   dead   dead   drowned
Will

THE LONDON FAMILY

Ben London
m.
Vane Leibig

George   Ralph
identical twins

THE COUCY FAMILY

Chouchou

François Benjamin

More compulsive fiction from Headline:

MALCOLM ROSS

**A rich West Country saga
in the bestselling tradition of POLDARK**

*On a Far
Wild Shore*

Young, beautiful and newly widowed, Elizabeth Troy travels to her late husband's Cornish home hoping to find comfort in its fertile hills and valleys. But she is shocked to discover the vast, decaying acreage of Pallas is now solely her responsibility – a legacy as unexpected as it is unwelcome.

Elizabeth's plans for her inheritance provoke the bitter hostility of her sister-in-law, Morwenna, whose word has been law at Pallas for thirty years. To bring the troubled estate back to prosperity Elizabeth must look for help elsewhere. And there are many very willing to be more than a friend to the widow – David Troy, a poor relation whose sober exterior hides some disturbing secrets; Courtenay Rodda, the sensual newspaper proprietor; and James Troy, the rich and worldly wise American cousin who begins a thrilling but dangerous liaison with Elizabeth . . .

'The book is beautifully written, the characters depicted with a passionate realism that held me entranced. I simply loved it!' Patricia Wendorf, bestselling author of *Larksleve*.

FICTION   0-7472-3001-3

More compulsive fiction from Headline:

HARRY BOWLING

Conner Street's War

Behind the grimy wharves of London's docklands lies Conner Street, where women stand gossiping in doorways, small boys play marbles on the cobbles and the dockers pop down the 'Eagle' for a quick pint. Corner shops nestle beside tiny terraced houses and two minutes away is the Tower Road market where, it's said, if you can't buy something then it's not made.

Children swap cigarette cards while the wardens hand out gas masks. And when the wail of the air raid siren splits the night all of Conner Street rushes out to the shelter . . . silly Bobbie – a bit slow since his father beat him round the head once too often; Patrick Flannagan, the genial Irishman who likes a drop and Stanley Nathan the grocer who falls for pretty Julie Brett, little guessing her dark past. Meanwhile, down the 'Eagle', Florrie the landlady tempts innocent Albert Conlin behind the blackout curtains with disastrous consequences . . .

FICTION/GENERAL   0 7472 3063 3

JOSEPHINE COX

JESSICA'S GIRL

In the grand tradition of Catherine Cookson

'Don't let him break you, child'

Despite her beloved mother's deathbed warning, Phoebe Mulligan has no choice but to throw herself on the mercy of her uncle, Edward. Wrenched from all she holds dear, the tragic young girl is delivered to Blackburn town, where she must live in a household terrorised by the cold, forbidding presence of her mother's brother.

Phoebe cannot understand why she is treated so harshly by Edward Dickens. She is not to know the guilty secret that lies in his past, a secret that casts its sinister shadow over his feelings for his lovely niece.

But Phoebe's spirit will not be broken. Her natural warmth and cheerfulness win her many friends and although she must endure horror and heartbreak, all the riches a woman can have come within her reach.

'Cox's driven and passionate book...stirs a pot spiced with incest, wife beating...and murder.'
The Sunday Times

More Compelling Fiction from Headline:

E V THOMPSON

His exotic new saga

Blue Dress Girl

A stirring tale of adventure and a moving and tender love story played out against the exotic background of China at one of the most turbulent periods in its history.

Fleeing from the busy port of Canton to avoid scandal and danger, blue dress girl She-she is caught in crossfire and rescued by Second Lieutenant Kernow Keats of the Royal Marines. Instantly moved by her fragile beauty, the young man takes She-she to Hong Kong, to the home of missionaries Hugh and Hannah Jefferies, where she can regain her strength. As she comes to know the handsome hero, the girl's gratitude becomes love – and her feelings are returned.

But a love affair between a Chinese peasant girl and an English officer seems unthinkable in 1857. And as the Taiping rebellion gets underway, Kernow is torn from She-she's side to do his patriotic duty. Can their great love cross the chasm of race, class and background that divides them?

'Thompson enjoys working his backdrop – lots of chaps fighting on boats, warlords, pirate raids, skirmishes and bloodshed...' *The Sunday Times*

'It will keep you turning the pages and certainly appeal to the vast readership who enjoy top quality historical novels.' *Sunday Independent*

Don't miss E.V. Thompson's poignant saga *Wychwood*, also available from Headline.

FICTION/SAGA   0 7472 4136 8

VICTOR PEMBERTON

OURSTREET

From the bestselling Cockney author of
OUR FAMILY

The war is five years old and, in bomb-torn North London, fifteen-year-old Frankie Lewis sometimes thinks it will go on for ever. But one foggy night his life takes an extraordinary turn. Inveigled by his mates, 'the Merton Street gang', into playing yet another vindictive prank on the old German-Jewish widow who lives just off the Seven Sisters Road, Frankie finds himself hauled unceremoniously across her doorstep and pulled into a world of books and culture he never knew existed.

Fascinated by Elsa's tales of life before the war, and with her now-dead British officer husband, young Frankie, who, although close to his elder sister Helen, has an unhappy relationship with his own apparently uncaring parents, soon becomes good friends with Elsa, helping out in her chaotic *bric-à-brac* shop and confiding his troubles to her – from his own crush on the pretty Highbury schoolgirl Margaret to his sister's unwanted pregnancy.

But Elsa, determined to give Frankie a start in the world, has plans for his future which he would never have dreamt of, plans that her scheming brother-in-law, local property owner Jack Barclay, is equally determined to thwart...

Don't miss Victor Pemberton's first Cockney saga, OUR FAMILY, 'A wonderful story' Nerys Hughes

FICTION/SAGA   0 7472 4144 9

—— HARRIET SMART ——

The magnificent Scottish saga from the author of *A Garland of Vows*

GREEN GROW THE RUSHES

In the long hot summer of 1900, a group of people is brought together in the decaying splendour of the Quarro, a Scottish country house owned by the down-at-heel Lennox family.

Jessie Macpherson, newly appointed cook, dazzles the Lennoxes and their guests with her skill – but even in her triumph, she realises there has to be more to life. Sholto Hamilton, a poor, ambitious lawyer, offers her a glimpse of other delights, and Jessie is quickly trapped in the sensual web he has woven. But what future can there be for a gentleman and a servant?

For Celia Lennox, daughter of the house, there can be no more eligible a suitor than Ralph Erskine, heir to an Edinburgh steel magnate. He certainly admires her, but it is another man who catches her eye – and perhaps her heart.

Ralph's sister Alix overcomes parental opposition and society's disapproval to win herself an education and against all expectations finds a man who shares her view of life – until a shocking stroke of fate robs her of happiness.

As their lives touch, new alliances are formed – some doomed to failure and bitter despair, others that will endure against the odds to bring lasting happiness.

A sweeping, panoramic saga that moves from country house to industrial slums, from bohemian free-thinking to High Tory politics, *Green Grow the Rushes* is an outstanding successor to Harriet Smart's first novel, *A Garland of Vows* ('precisely and lovingly observed… excellent' *The Sunday Times*), which is also available from Headline.

FICTION/SAGA   0 7472 4050 7

AN IMPOSSIBLE WOMAN

JAMES MITCHELL

CREATOR OF *WHEN THE BOAT COMES IN*

1929. A New Year and the champagne is still flowing, the music still playing for Jane Whitcomb. Wealthy, attractive and adored, she has no right to feel dissatisfied, but ever since her heroism in World War I, she has been uncomfortably aware that there are more important things to do than dance the night away.

Helping Felston, for instance, the North East town that was the home of her dead fiancé and is now in the grip of the worst depression in history – the Kingdom of Rags to Jane's Kingdom of Riches.

When the Wall Street crash plunges Felston into yet deeper poverty, Jane pulls out all the stops to raise more money, even agreeing to a Hollywood film of her adventures in wartime France. But money alone is not the answer. She organises a Hunger March from Felston to London – three hundred weary miles by ex-soldiers, herself among them, to show the world how a town is dying of neglect. It is a magnificent gesture, focusing all eyes on the tragedy. But it is barely over when Jane goes to Spain and there sees the gathering clouds of an even greater disaster – the Spanish Civil War.

Many men love Jane, rich and powerful ones among them, but she remains elusive – too intelligent to settle for less than the best. Courageous, determined, unconventional, by the standards of her time she is simply... *an impossible woman.*

'A clever chronicle, sharply, confidently, elegantly done, with panache and skill'
Sunday Times

James Mitchell's *A Woman to be Loved* is also available from Headline
'Terrific story, a guaranteed page-turner...should be his biggest best seller' *Daily Mail*
'A novel of stature and honesty and immensely enjoyable' *Sunday Telegraph*

FICTION/SAGA   0 7472 3919 3

JOY CHAMBERS

who plays the popular Rosemary Daniels in 'Neighbours'

MAYFIELD

An epic saga of nineteenth-century Australia

Eve Herman and her sister Clare find themselves orphans in Sydney town, 7000 miles from the land of their birth. Clare – beautiful, impressionable, addicted to pleasure – soon takes the easy way to earn a living, and Eve – strong and reliable – is left alone.

Naval sea captain Alan Fletcher intends to take up his rightful position as Squire of Long Moss. But his ruthless cousin's plotting means he is instead transported on a convict ship bound for New South Wales.

Revered and respected throughout the colony, John Stuart Wakeman is the owner of Mayfield, the largest, richest and most renowned property in New South Wales. The first moment he sees Eve he is captivated.

On their wedding day, Eve's life is forever altered by a fateful meeting in the bush, and the realisation that there is a secret she must keep from her husband. When she is brutally attacked, her secret comes back to haunt her and cause bitter estrangement between her and her husband. Heartbroken, Eve is all too vulnerable to the magnetism of Alan Fletcher – the man her husband has sworn to destroy...

MAYFIELD is a story of the overwhelming and consuming love of two men for the same indomitable woman, and of the valour, losses and sacrifices that each must make in the fight for her love.

FICTION/SAGA   0 7472 3863 4

A selection of bestsellers from Headline

THE LADYKILLER	Martina Cole	£5.99 ☐
JESSICA'S GIRL	Josephine Cox	£5.99 ☐
NICE GIRLS	Claudia Crawford	£4.99 ☐
HER HUNGRY HEART	Roberta Latow	£5.99 ☐
FLOOD WATER	Peter Ling	£4.99 ☐
THE OTHER MOTHER	Seth Margolis	£4.99 ☐
ACT OF PASSION	Rosalind Miles	£4.99 ☐
A NEST OF SINGING BIRDS	Elizabeth Murphy	£5.99 ☐
THE COCKNEY GIRL	Gilda O'Neill	£4.99 ☐
FORBIDDEN FEELINGS	Una-Mary Parker	£5.99 ☐
OUR STREET	Victor Pemberton	£5.99 ☐
GREEN GROW THE RUSHES	Harriet Smart	£5.99 ☐
BLUE DRESS GIRL	E V Thompson	£5.99 ☐
DAYDREAMS	Elizabeth Walker	£5.99 ☐

All Headline books are available at your local bookshop or newsagent, or can be ordered direct from the publisher. Just tick the titles you want and fill in the form below. Prices and availability subject to change without notice.

Headline Book Publishing PLC, Cash Sales Department, Bookpoint, 39 Milton Park, Abingdon, OXON, OX14 4TD, UK. If you have a credit card you may order by telephone – 0235 831700.

Please enclose a cheque or postal order made payable to Bookpoint Ltd to the value of the cover price and allow the following for postage and packing:
UK & BFPO: £1.00 for the first book, 50p for the second book and 30p for each additional book ordered up to a maximum charge of £3.00.
OVERSEAS & EIRE: £2.00 for the first book, £1.00 for the second book and 50p for each additional book.

Name ....

Address ....

....

....

If you would prefer to pay by credit card, please complete:
Please debit my Visa/Access/Diner's Card/American Express (delete as applicable) card no:

Signature .... Expiry Date ....